MORE BY THE AUTHOR

SPECIAL AGENT KIM KUPAR

Jade Eyes
They
The Why Files

THE TSCHAAA INFESTATION

Book 1: The Gathering Storm
Book 2: The Tsunami
Book 3: Typhoon of Steel
Free Range Protocol: Tales of the Tschaaa
Beyond the Great Compromise: Tales of the Tschaaa
Survivors: Escaping the Tschaaa

ANTHOLOGIES

Monstrosity (Unnerving Anthology)
Descent (Unnerving Anthology)
Wicked (Unnerving Anthology)
Nightfall (Unnerving Anthology)
The Mighty Pen
Unconditional
Cascadia
Tales of the Slug
Super: Unexpected Heroes Arise

COLLECTED WORKS & MORE

Inhumanity: A Year of Stories
The Island (The Haunting of Orchard House)
Shane (Angels of Anarchy)

THE TSCHAAA INFESTATION
VOLUME 3

MARSHALL MILLER

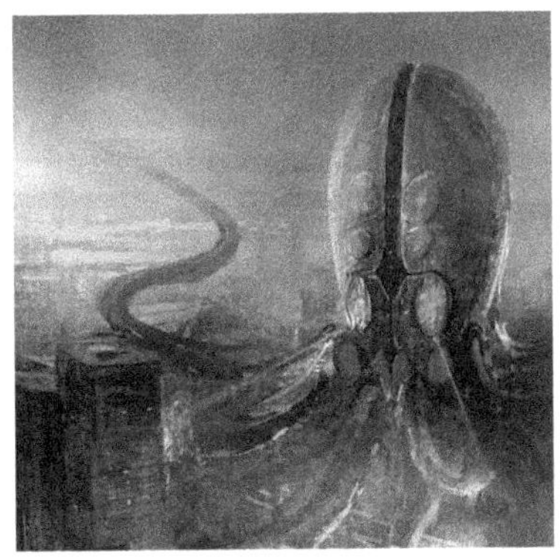

BLUE FORGE PRESS
Port Orchard, Washington

Blue Forge Press is the print division of the volunteer-run, federal 501(c)3 nonprofit company, Blue Forge Group, founded in 1989 and dedicated to bringing light to the shadows and voice to the silence. We strive to empower storytellers across all walks of life with our four divisions: Blue Forge Press, Blue Forge Films, Blue Forge Gaming, and Blue Forge Records. Find out more at www.BlueForgeGroup.org

Blue Forge Press
7419 Ebbert Drive Southeast
Port Orchard, Washington 98367
blueforgepress@gmail.com
360-550-2071 ph.txt

*To my wife, who puts up with my ramblings and ranting,
and serves as the two-legged mother to our four dogs.*

ACKNOWLEDGEMENTS

This is the Second and Revised Edition of *The Tschaaa Infestation*, a three-volume chronicle of what was once referred to as "the War and Peace of alien squid invasion novels." Thanks to the hard work of my publisher, Blue Forge Press, I now can present a new and improved version of a long labor of love and creativity. I have had many people help me in learning my craft of being a 'Wordsmith.' This is a career and an endeavor of beating words and phrases into a finely tempered work which, like a blacksmith does with steel fresh from the forge, cuts with a clean blade, but ideas rather than wood or flesh. At the same time, like a samurai's katana mentioned in the series, it can also bend to new concepts and opinions without breaking due to its flexibility.

Of course my wife, Sheri, has often times been a Writer's Widow as I disappear for hours on end, especially late at night, to hone my craft. Thus, without her understanding and support, this would have been a stillborne offspring.

Author and Esquire Thomas Mengert helped me with the first editing of this work of speculative fiction as well as suggested a companion volume of short stories. Thanks for all the hours spent with me on this futuristic War and Peace.

My good friend Gregory Brashear, an accomplished local teacher, was a sounding board for many of my ideas. Truth be told, a main character of the series is based on his life and adventures. I'll let the readers figure out which character fits this mold.

All the members of Kitsap Literary Artists and Writers helped provide ideas on designs, marketing, and publishing. The Bremerton Kitsap Access Television interview show I do on a monthly basis is an outgrowth of this group. The KLAW show was the reason I met Jennifer and Brianne DiMarco and became affiliated with Blue Forge Press, which is leading to bigger and better things. Sometimes it takes a while for "good things and people" to come into one's life.

I hope all "wannabe" Authors read my artistic endeavors and think "Hey, I can do that!" For writers must write. We all hope that what we write will find a group of readers who will appreciate our ideas, concepts, and the worlds we create as we spin our web of ideas. Especially when those ideas involve humans being cattle for invading alien squids.

In closing, I also must thank all the people I have met and worked with over the years as yes, you all provided models and fodder for my characters and stories. Hopefully, those who knew me will read my books and say "Hey! Cool!"

As a final thought, remember:

Watch the skies! The *Tschaaa Cometh*!

THE TSCHAAA INFESTATION
VOLUME 3

MARSHALL MILLER

CHAPTER 1

New life often distracts humans from noticing signs of impending danger. Then, like an ocean typhoon, the danger strikes.

-Excerpts from the *Works of Princess Akiko*, Free Japan Royal Family

GREAT FALLS, MONTANA

The "European Café and American Eats" was packed. The attendees of the Russian Orthodox christening and baptism for Gage and Tristan had taken over the entire restaurant, overflowing from the large back meeting room that the owner Fedir Pavlenko had reserved for Aleks and her party. She had become adopted family, he being full Ukrainian and outnumbered by all the Russians in the area. So half-Ukrainian was good enough for him and his wife, Anastasiya. Most of celebrators were Russian, ninety-nine percent military personnel. Aleks was one of their own, and everyone had better remember that, or else. Of course, Torbin was now an honorary Russian, as was "My Lady of Cold Steel," Abigail. Everyone else was basically tolerated.

General Reed had been correct when he said the base chaplain corps could provide a traditional Russian Orthodox Service. Actually, truth be told, Aleks had wished it had not been quite so traditional, as Russian services tend to run long. But then again, it was also just what was needed. Now, Aleks sat beaming next to the brand new bassinets containing her sons. Stalin and a contingent of Russian Spetsnaz had shown up at the end of the service with the two bassinets in tow. They would not take "no" for an answer when Aleks tried to refuse such a generous gift from her fellow soldiers. An argument began until Abigail, in her perfect Russian, stepped in.

"Please, my sister. Just accept the fact that Gage and Tristan have the largest group of 'uncles' in the history of Montana. They are family. You cannot criticize family for giving or spending too much, can you? There are no strings attached with true family."

With that, Aleks had acquiesced, thanked them all, kissing them all on their cheeks. Even Stalin. Then she had hugged Abigail.

"Thank you, little sister. You always know just what to say."

"Not always," Abigail replied. "I still get tongue tied around Ichiro."

"Which you shouldn't be. Nothing you can say will ever chase him away. He is yours."

Abigail blushed and changed the subject. That had been a while ago. Torbin had been lured away to match the Russians drink for drink in vodka shots, with Abigail being cornered to watch. She left Fuzz behind to guard the trolls—the nickname Aleks had given to her sons—which he had decided were definitely his. Anyone who came near them, he watched them like a hawk. Every man and women came up to the back area of the meeting room to pay respects to the newborns, the first of a potential new breed of humans. Small envelopes and packages containing cash, jewelry, traditional small painted Orthodox icons were presented to a reluctant Aleks. The new mother finally just took it all in stride, realizing that everyone wanted to be connected to these very special little Russians. They all, thanks in a large part to stories from Stalin, respected her for her service to the motherland.

There was food, of course. Fedir had provided a spread of cheeses, meats, traditional pastries, potato dishes and borscht. At Torbin's request, he also served spicy buffalo wings and fresh local potato chips. All he would take in payment was a gratuity for his staff and—of course—a cash bar. He was not stupid. He knew that if he provided free alcohol to this particular crowd, he would soon be bankrupt.

Fedir and his wife Anastasiya had also come to the table where Aleks was sitting to hand her an envelope. "*No!* You have given enough already. I am not some spoiled American princess who needs to more things to be happy."

"It is not money," Fedir's wife Anastasiya said. "Please look inside. It is not much."

Inside were two small stainless steel crosses. "For your sons. Steel to remind them what may be needed in days to come. The cross to remind them that God is on their side, and will watch over them."

Aleks had teared up, hugged and kissed her.

"I do not deserve these riches. I am just a former farm girl shaped by fate. Nothing more."

"Not so. You and your sons are symbols of hope for a new beginning. Never forget that."

Torbin had returned to his wife, managing to take a short leave of absence from his new found Russian drinking buddies to check on his wife and kids, and to visit the little soldier's room. Aleks regarded him with her eyebrow cocked. "Is that a Russian Special Forces beret I see on your head, husband?"

Torbin smiled. "Yes, my love. They made me an honorary Spetsnaz team member. Said that killing a Squid with a knife met minimum standards. Go figure."

Aleks laughed. "Perhaps. Or perhaps since they have not yet drunk you under the table, they felt they had to make you an honorary member."

Torbin leaned close. "A secret, my wife. I coated my stomach with some cooking oil and milk. Slows down the alcohol absorption. Otherwise, even though I'm a Marine, I'd be staggering around right now, even more incoherent than normal."

Aleks smiled at her love. "Your secret is safe with me. I had to do as much at my Commissioning Party. I do not have a hollow leg." For the party, Aleks had brought along some bottles of breast milk with her, so she could sip vodka and join the festivities too.

"Now, my dear, I must go drain the lizard."

"Ever the witty conversationalist with women. I can't imagine why you stayed single so long." Aleks grabbed him and pulled him in for a kiss. "Now, don't go into the ladies room by mistake, and accidentally pick up some bimbo. You're mine. Da?"

Torbin for the umpteenth time realized how lucky he was. "No worries, my love. You alone own my heart and soul. Forever."

Aleks sighed with contentment as he left for the men's room. Next week, she would start going to Stalin's training sessions and work out with the trainees. She knew it was a rather extreme way to get back into shape, but she felt a need to really push herself since the birth. She wondered if her metabolism which had increased during the pregnancy would remain at a heightened state due to the Tschaaa interference. They had received intelligence info concerning a rise in aggressiveness and competition for sexual favors among many of the young women in Key West. One source had stated that some areas were turning into "catfight cities", where were an excessive number of altercations between women.

Ancient tribal groups had often raided others for their gravid females; violence for sex partners usually being between the male of the species. After all, the human male body was designed with greater muscle mass, size, and overall strength. It was designed for violence during hunting of prey. They did not have to worry about injury to an unborn being carried in their bodies. Would pregnancy or menopause reduce this alleged Tschaaa caused aggressiveness?

Aleks knew that she may have been moody, but she had felt no desire to start yanking some other women's hair out over Torbin. If she caught him with another woman, she'd take it out on him, not her. He was the one responsible for keeping his "lizard" under control.

She noticed a tall, blond woman, clad in a winter coat, long winter dress, and boots walking across the restaurant toward her. She immediately recognized her. Brynhildr had decided to brave the mass of drunken Russians, apparently to pay her respects. Then Aleks noticed through the din that she had Big Rolf Knudson and Ichiro in tow, along with two other smaller females. As the group neared the corner of the back room, Aleks recognized dark haired Hannah Weitz, dressed in the same manner as Brynhildr. She realized the fourth figure was the news reporter Sally Reid, broken right hand in a cast and all. The reporter had on a sensible winter coat, sweater and pants. She seemed to have a wrapped package in her good hand.

Brynhildr broke into a wide smile when she saw the bassinets and the two boys. Aleks stood as the group approached, greeting them.

"Hello. I see you have brought some more visitors, Brynhildr."

"Good evening and congratulations, Aleks. Your sons look healthy and handsome. They take after their parents, that's for sure."

Aleks then looked at Sally Reid. "I see we have gimps bearing gifts. Hello, Ms. Reid. Where are the cameras?"

Sally gave a shy smile. "Home, where they should have been that day in the hospital. Here. This is a peace offering." Aleks took the bulky package as she nodded to the rest of the group.

"Hello, everybody. I am honored you came out on this could night to see my new sons."

"Well, there is food and drink, ja?" This was from Rolf, which resulted in a shot to the ribs from Brynhildr. Aleks laughed.

"Just like my husband. Food, drink, then sex. In that order."

"Here." Hannah also stepped forward with a small wrapped item. "I made something in the forge for your sons. And a little something for you too."

Ichiro then stepped forward and set a small group of intricate origami figures on the table, clearly representing Aleks and her family.

"Once again, Ichiro, you outdo yourself." Aleks hugged him, then all the rest. Including, to her surprise, Sally Reid. Ichiro gave a short bow.

"I go to find Abigail, and rescue her from the Russians. I will return shortly." With that he was gone to the other side of the restaurant.

"Here, let me open this peace offering before my husband gets back." She quickly had package the opened. Inside were a substantial amount of disposable diapers, not something easily obtained post-Strike. Aleks smiled in approval. "How did you find these?"

"I have a friend who has a warehouse full of stuff he's scavenged over the years. Before I decided to try and be a reporter, before the Squids, I actually was a homemaker with kids. I know what modern conveniences mean when you have newborns." Suddenly, her eyes became a bit cloudy. Bad memories. Just about everyone had them.

Aleks looked at her arm in the cast. "My peace offering is an apology that my husband had to go so far as to break your arm. But, well, you made us both extremely angry. How is your friend the cameraman?"

"His jaw is wired shut. He had one hell of a concussion. I can see how your husband was able to kill a Squid with a knife. He has a unique skill set for destruction and violence."

Aleks gave her a bit of a hard look. "Which we need right now, don't you think?"

"Sorry. That came out a bit wrong, didn't it?" Sally sighed. "I think I have a unique skill set to piss off people I'm trying to apologize to. Alesha Taylor called me, said that I need to reach out to you and your husband. Madam President had called her, General Reed, and my boss at the local station and newspaper. Said we're all on the same side. She's right."

Sally put out her left hand. "Please accept my heartfelt apology. I know I would have beaned someone with a bedpan if someone had stuck a camera in my face after giving birth to my kids."

Aleks took her hand. "You have children?"

"Had." The one word said it all.

Aleks looked in her eyes, saw the pain. She stepped forward and hugged Sally.

"Peace offering accepted. Do you still want an interview, story?"

Sally suddenly had a surprised look on her face. "Why, yes. That would be great."

"Here comes my husband. Torbin, come here. More guests."

Torbin's expression turned a bit dark when he saw the reporter. "Sorry, you cannot interview my sons."

Aleks smoothly stepped in to diffuse the situation. "She just made a peace offering and I accepted. We are on the same side. And Madam President wants us to play nice. I know that is hard for you, but do it for me. Okay?"

Torbin paused for a minute. Then he stuck his hand right hand out, realized his error, switched switched to his left. "Okay. Peace. Sorry I broke your arm. I really just meant to throw you out."

"I understand. I just got carried away. I'd like an interview, now that I understand the situation better. I also have a slightly different slant than what I originally thought was the story."

"Oh? And what would that be?" asked Aleks.

"That women have had to step up more than any other time in

our recent history. The number of men has been steadily decreasing worldwide, partly due to military action. But now we have good information that not only are men harvested first, but that the Tschaaa may be manipulating us women to give birth to substantially more girl babies. This is in addition to everything else they did to us. So, no matter what happens, the role of women is probably forever changed."

Sally paused, then added, "Not to mention reports of increased aggression by women on each other, specifically in competition for men. Still trying to work that one out."

Aleks, ever the intelligence agent, surveyed her. Sometimes, reporters were like spies, able to get just the right dirt. "How did you come up with this information?"

Sally smiled. "Just like spies, we never give up our sources on pain of death. Or so I've heard."

Aleks laughed. After her initial reaction, she could learn to like this medium-sized brunette, right now with her hair tied up in a bun. She looked to be in her thirties, in decent physical condition. Then again, the herd had been culled out over the last six plus years.

"Well, what you say has an interesting slant to it. How about grabbing us some vodka and we'll have a little talk now, sans tape recorders. Then we can decide if we are photogenic enough for television."

"Deal. I'll be right back." Sally made a beeline through the small horde of Russians packing the restaurant, definitely not dissuaded by a bunch of drunk soldiers.

"So Hannah, while Sally is gone, let me take a look at what you brought us." Aleks opened the package, found a small box under the padded wrapping paper. She opened it, and gave a little gasp. In the box were two small pure silver Russian Orthodox Crosses, each overlaid on a small sword.

"I figured a symbol of your faith and the steel to back it up would be a good symbol for your sons. The chain is silver metal also."

Behind it was a small set of crossed flags, Russian and U.S., made to suspend from a gold chain, also included. Aleks looked at Hannah.

"These are much too fine. Please, I can't accept these for my trolls, or for me."

"Keep them until they get older. Then let them decide. I made them for your sons as I know they'll have a special place in our future. And you already have."

Torbin looked at the pieces. "You are wasting your talents on private presents for us, Hannah. As much as we appreciate it, you could be making a small fortune on the open market."

Hannah shrugged. "I'm already rich. Thanks to you and others, like Uncle Johann and the Commissioner, I have a second chance at life. And a second family who loves me. What type of riches could be better than those?"

Torbin carefully examined her. Here was a young lady who had survived unimaginable horrors in the Pits, by all rights should be ate up with bitterness. Yet, all she seemed to want to do was create things of beauty for her friends, in addition to the occasional bladed weapon. Her soul shined through like no one else's, other than maybe Abigail's. Torbin stepped closer and slowly hugged her, kissed her on her forehead.

"I consider it an honor that you say I and my wife are part of your friends and family. We met due to a selfish desire on my part for revenge, nothing noble."

Hannah hugged back. "Does not matter the reason. Only the result matters."

"Now, I have a big lump in my throat," Torbin said.

"And I have another little sister." Aleks was trying not to tear up. Time to start toughening up again, and not wear her emotions on her sleeve. She needed to be tough as the steel Hannah alluded to.

With that, Hannah hugged Aleks. "I'll take as many new extended family members as I can. The bigger the family, the better." Hannah's statement expressed the reality of the current human family structure, post-Strike, post -Invasion. Unrelated people, having lost most, sometimes all of their blood related family members, banding together in new family units. These new units were based on love and affection between people who came together due to the horrible results of the Squids Infestation, and harvesting. Everyone adopted everyone else, whether you had any common bloodlines or not. Basically tribal in nature, they allowed for those completely alone to be alone no longer. Now, everyone could have a support system, no matter what had happened to your parents, siblings. If you said you were now sisters, then you were.

Brynhildr moved a bit closer. "May I hold one of your sons?"

"Why, of course. And Rolf can hold one also. I'd like them to get used to the presence of friendly people from both genders."

Brynhildr picked up Tristan, and Aleks handed Gage to Rolf. The tall blonde woman broke into a large grin, her eyes twinkling. "Such a fine son. He must have Viking in him from somewhere. Some of my ancestors made it to Moscow. Maybe we are distantly related."

"Keep acting like that and I may ask you to babysit them, Brynhildr."

"Job permitting, you won't have to twist my arm. This brings out a maternal feeling I had forgotten about." She looked at Rolf, who was also grinning. He held Gage as if he were holding his own son.

"You seem a lot more comfortable holding babies than I do," Torbin interjected. "I keep thinking I'm going to squeeze something too hard, or drop them."

Rolf smiled at Torbin. "Before the Squids arrived, Gunnar and I used to babysit our young cousins. Young ones like these are not as fragile as you think. And these sons... they have strength already. They would be fine Thor's sons, fine young warriors."

"Well, they're American on my side. I'll let you discuss the rest of their family back ground with Aleks."

Rolf suddenly looked up at Brynhildr, and said something in Norwegian. This elicited a short barking laugh and some comment in return that sounded a lot like, 'Do not be foolish.' Rolf repeated what he had said, adding more words. Brynhildr fixed Rolf with a firm look.

"Aleks, would you mind if I gave you your son back? I must be rude and discuss something in private with Rolf."

Aleks cocked an eyebrow. "Of course. Here, husband, take Tristan. Rolf, please hand me Gage... Thank you." With that, Brynhildr grabbed Rolf's massive arm and pulled him to the opposite corner of the room. They were soon involved in a serious and animated conversation.

Torbin glanced over and saw Young Hannah beaming.

"All right, smartypants. You've been learning Norskie. What's up?"

"Aleks probably has some of it figured out," Hannah answered with a twinkle in her eye. "But Rolf suddenly started talking about wanting and having children. He alluded to Brynhildr and him both being of good... how you say, breeding stock."

"My, isn't that a romantic way of putting it," stated Aleks. She looked at Torbin. "You men have no concept of timing, of patience. It's all hey, let's throw it out, see if it sticks to the wall."

"Hey, wife, you forget who came to whose room the first time. And the second. And how I began to…"

"Hush. That is not important. What else exactly did they say, Hannah, dear? My Norwegian isn't all that good."

Hannah kept grinning. "Brynhildr told him not to be foolish or joke about that, she was not in the mood. Rolf said he was *not* joking, he was serious. And now they are over there, being serious.

The three looked over to the serious conversation between the two tall American Vikings. Brynhildr, despite her height, had to look up a bit to stare directly into Rolf's eyes. Which is what she was doing as they talked back and forth. Rolf gently took both of Brynhildr's hands in his larger hands and began to gently rub them with his thumbs and fingers as he spoke. Brynhildr was reduced to one and two word answers as Rolf demonstrated serious speaking skills no one had realized he had. Rolf was known to be a joker, good with a weapon, and a bull in battle. The Great Communicator? Hardly. Until tonight.

Brynhildr blinked her eyes a bit, a sign that emotional tears were forming. A statuesque Wagnerian Shield Maiden she might appear to be, but she was still a human with feelings. She began to nod her head up and down. Then she threw her arms around Rolf's rather massive neck, and proceeded to kiss and hug him as if she was about to ravish him on the spot. He returned the favor, the two large people wrapped in a very loving embrace.

Aleks began to cry a bit. "Oh hell. Sorry, Hannah. I'm just still trying to get over all these emotions from being pregnant. I didn't use to blubber as much." Torbin produced a handkerchief for Aleks to dab her eyes with.

"You are definitely learning, my husband. I do so love you." She crushed Torbin in an embrace.

"Oof. Being pregnant did not make you weak, Aleks." He tilted up her head and kissed her. "You, my dear, are one special woman. And I am one lucky man." Aleks kissed him back, a big wet eyed smile on her face.

"Yes, you are lucky. Never forget that. Now if you could go and round up Sally Reid, Ichiro, and Abigail. I think they were all hijacked by the Russians."

As Torbin went to the other side of the restaurant, Rolf and Brynhildr walked back to Hannah, Aleks, and her sons. The two Vikings were holding hands, smiling.

Aleks grinned at them. "I know that look, my friends."

"Yes, Aleks, you do," Brynhildr answered. "I just never guessed it would happen to me so soon, just starting a career, killing Krakens…"

"Love waits for no one," Rolf said. The large warrior, having a reputation of a one track mind, was unexpectedly showing a side few had noticed. Maybe it was Brynhildr's influence. Or maybe he had put on a bit of an act at times.

With that, Brynhildr began to act like a little school girl, giggling, holding his arm. "As you have probably figured out, Rolf and I are basically betrothed now. He gets to

come up with a ring, I get to come up with a dowry."

"No you don't. I have a lot of money saved from my military service. We need no dowry."

"Please, it's tradition. I know you wish to take care of me completely, get me barefoot and pregnant. But just remember who I am."

Rolf displayed a well-used sheepish look, then answered. "Yes, Shield Maiden, slayer of many. Arrester of many others. Special Assistant to the Commissioner. Driver in rickshaw races. Mistress of all that she surveys." With a quick motion, he grabbed Brynhildr and swept her off her feet, cradling her in his massive arms as if she was as weightless as a feather. She began to scold him in Norwegian, demanding to be let down. Then, the large female warrior began to giggle again, kissing him, and literally trying to snuggle up next to him. With someone a lot smaller than Rolf, given Brynhildr's size, it would have looked ridiculous. But with him and her, it looked like two young high school students snuggling after the Friday night football game.

"Alright you two. As Torbin would say, get a room."

With that, Rolf flashed a large smile and deftly set Brynhildr down. He kissed her forehead, she grabbed his ears and forced him to kiss her mouth. Rolf let loose with one of the happiest laughs Aleks had heard in a long time. Something very special was happening.

Hannah went up and hugged them both, talking to them in

Norwegian. Rolf picked up Hannah and swung her around, then set her back down. She giggled and blushed.

"Rolf, please go and find us some cheese and meats," Aleks asked. "And some cider to drink until Sally Reid returns with the vodka for some toasts. I wonder where she has gone?"

In fact, at the far side of the main room in the restaurant, Sally was surrounded at the bar by a group of boisterous and horny Russians. Just as she pushed one set of hands away, another set tried to glomm on. She had been around the proverbial block, and had dealt with aggressive men before. But here, there were so damned many of them.

She had talked the bartender into a literal carafe of vodka. It might be cheap bar vodka, but it was vodka. As she laid some cash down, the Roman hands and Russian fingers began vying for her attention. She smiled, said excuse me, pushed hands away, tried to make an escape. But she was blocked in.

Then she heard a firm but definitely female voice sound off in Russian. She looked toward the source and say a beautiful blonde young woman with shoulder length hair in a nice evening skirt with a matching jacket. She did a double take as she had only seen her on TV or photos in uniform. But even in feminine attire, Sally could see the physical power and presence of Abigail Young.

"Captain Young. I did not recognize you."

Abigail gave a small smile as she pushed in to join Sally near the bar. "Yes, Aleks Smirnov demanded I dress up for her children's christening. Getting used to high heels has been…interesting. Though a four inch heel on the instep seems to get a man's attention."

Abigail looked at Sally and the cast on her arm. "You're the reporter that Torbin injured."

"Yes. I'm trying to get back to his wife's table."

"Follow me." Abigail began to push physically and verbally, trying to form a path out for Sally.

Unfortunately, several Russians were either so drunk or so stupid they did not recognize My Lady of Cold Steel. They tried to push back.

"Please. Gentlemen. Let my Comrade and I through. We need to return to Major Smirnov's table." Despite her native sounding Russian, Abigail's request did not sink in. One soldier made the mistake of grabbing her butt cheek. He collapsed to the floor holding his family jewels in a silent scream.

A large figure suddenly began to push his way through to the two women.

"Move aside. Captain Young wishes to leave," Rolf's voice loudly proclaimed in English as he shoved his way through by shear strength. Russians began to loudly protest in both their native language and in accented English.

"Hey, don't push."

"Who do you think you are, you big oaf?"

"Stop pushing me or I'll…" A large fight was about to ensue.

"Comrades! *Stop!*" A well-recognized voice boomed out. People froze in place as they recognized Senior Training Instructor Stalin."This evening is for the celebration of the christening of two new children of Mother Russia. The sons of Major Aleksandra Smirnov, a daughter of Russia. Who dares to disrupt this sacred affair?"

Noise suddenly stopped, other than the clinking of glasses from behind the bar. One Russian soldier staggered up to Stalin, fell in to him. In a blink of the eye, the offending person was flat on his back, only semi-conscious.

"And this young lady in the beautiful vestments is My Lady of Cold Steel. You dare to offend her? In *my presence?*"

The next thing that happened was everyone was trying to apologize all at once. The group of inebriated Russians began to part as if they were the Red Sea and Abigail was a female Moses.

A somewhat disheveled Ichiro then appeared next to Abigail. "You disappeared while they were teaching me the Cossack dance. Tell me next time."

"Sorry. I saw that Ms. Reid needed help getting out from the clutches of a bunch of drunk men. I just acted."

The Japanese Officer recognized once again that this was a characteristic he would have to get used to if he stayed around Abigail. Which he was bound to do.

With Stalin in the lead, the small group made its way back to Aleks' table in the back room.

Sally had managed to hang onto the vodka and some glasses.

"Ah, they return," Aleks greeted them. "Well, vodka for toasts. But no food."

"Sorry, I go." Rolf started to leave.

"Please, you stay here, my very large friend," Stalin said. "I will go fetch some cheese, meats and pastries. It is easier."

"I'll go with you." Sally spoke before she knew what she was doing.

Stalin looked at her, a small lopsided grin displayed. 'You wish for what Americans would call Round Two?"

Sally shrugged. "I've had my boobs and butt squeezed before. It didn't kill me."

"Come then. Even with that cast on, you can carry some snacks." He left, with Sally in tow.

Everyone made a deferred path for Stalin as he and Sally made a path to the refreshment tables. With efficient ease the Russian soon had plates of meat cutlets, cheeses, some buffalo wings, chips and breads. Sally balanced some of them even with her arm in a cast.

"You came with me for a reason, Comrade Reid," Stalin said in passing.

"Well, you saw right through that. You're that Crazy Ivan people have been talking about, aren't you? No military rank, but everyone defers to you."

Stalin displayed a small grin. "Why do Americans always seem to like the name "Ivan" when referring to a Russian man? I have one name I go by. Stalin. I know who I am, I need no other names."

"Sorry," Sally apologized, "I did not mean to offend you."

He shrugged. "No offense. I was just stating an observation of mine. But I guess you, being a reporter, the one Major Bender injured, you have some information, a 'story' you wish to obtain. Da?"

Sally blushed a bit. "So, I guess my broken wrist, arm in a cast is a badge of dishonor. News does get around on Malmstrom even without an official news report."

"There is no dishonor in t trying to do your job, if being a bit too aggressive in getting the story you wished. I have been known to charge in, like the proverbial bull in the china shop. I'm just the one who usually does the bone breaking, not the other way around."

He fixed Sally with a steady gaze. "So, what do you want to know? What is the story you are seeking?"

Sally looked into his eyes and saw blue steel looking back. That was what she was looking for. "How did you become you? An enigma, according to everyone I have talked to. Hated, feared yet greatly respected by all who are trained by you. A person who takes a Christmas dinner to a prisoner you helped put in confinement."

Stalin saw her locking eyes with him, saw an inner strength that many did not. Decades of experience made him a good judge of characters. This woman had suffered much, but had bounced back. Much like himself. A small smile formed on his mouth.

"You have already found out much about me. Are you an intelligence agent?"

"No. Just a nosey reporter in the same mold as old U.S. print reporters were before television. Read a lot about them while trying not to freeze and starve to death. Decided if given the chance, I'd try to resurrect the breed."

Stalin gave her a quick once over. Not a model, but a well-built woman. "Come, let us get this food back to Aleks and company. And after you are done talking with her, I'll give you a private interview."

The sun had been up for a while when Sally was awoken by the smells of someone cooking breakfast in the kitchen. The person was also humming a tune she did not recognize.

"Jim, are the kids up…" Her brain went back to memories of long gone mornings when she had awoken to the sound and smells of breakfast being made. Then reality came crashing in. A small sob passed her lips as the dream made her feel that love and contentment from years past. Now it was gone, with her Jim and the kids. Forever. With a final mental wrench, her mind came back to the present. And she remembered who she had brought home with her. The first time in years anyone had been invited to stay over.

Sally exited her now messy bed, found her old robe and threw it on to cover her nudity, her approaching middle age body. She then made a beeline to her apartment kitchen.

Stalin was at the stove, working on three separate pans of food at once. "You are up. Good. Breakfast is almost ready and I hate to eat alone. There is plenty for two."

Sally blushed, a bit from anger, a bit from embarrassment. "Glad you made yourself at home after fucking me." She regretted saying that as soon as it came out of her mouth. Her memory was that she had suggested he come home with her, not the other way around.

But the words seemed to slip from Stalin as water off a duck's back.

Stalin turned, a wry smile on his face. It now dawned on Sally he was wearing a large bath towel of hers, nothing else. She saw in the light of day that his chiseled granite upper torso body was crisscrossed with scars of every type imaginable, and then some. Sally vaguely remembered feeling some of the scars during their passionate love making.

"I think, dear lady, that you fucked me also. At least that is what I remember happened in your bed."

Sally looked away, ashamed of her nasty remark. "Sorry. Just... sorry."

Stalin set a large plate on the kitchen table. "Here. What you Americans call 'Wrecked Eggs', a little bit of everything I could find in your larder. I have made some strong Russian version of coffee here also." He locked his eyes on her. "Sit. Please. Eating will make you feel better."

Sally sat, took the knife and fork Stalin had set out, and began eating. Despite her emotional upset, the food was excellent.

Stalin set down a plate for himself, in addition to a stack of toast. He then placed a cup of hot coffee next to Sally, and sat down with another in his hand. He slurped the rich dark coffee.

"Hmmm. Not bad for weak American coffee. I was told some farmers are growing coffee beans in hot houses around here. This seems fresh so it must be true."

"Toast?" he offered.

Sally sat her fork down, and was finally able to meet his eyes. "Sorry about the 'fucked' crack. I can be a real bitch sometimes. Just ask Torbin Bender."

In between bites, Stalin began to talk. "You Americans apologize too much for expressing your feelings. So you are bit angry with yourself for bringing a strange man home. For the first time in a long time. No, don't protest. I am not insulting you. I'm stating a fact. And now you are worried that this will all blow up in your face, as if I'm some type of unstable explosive."

He barked out a laugh. "We fucked each other last night, early this morning. Like rabbits, you Americans say. Russians often mention minks. But the idea is the same."

He looked into her eyes. "And we both enjoyed it. A lot. Now I cook you breakfast. A good breakfast, if I may say so. Which we will also enjoy. We may screw again. Which we will again enjoy. No bombs in your face. Just some lovemaking."

Sally tried to stutter something out, then stopped. Stalin took ahold of one of her hands.

"I would like us to be friends. I have few friends outside the military. Many who I call as friends are probably closer to Comrades in Arms. So, a friend outside my work would be a gift. What do you say, Sally Reid? I mean, you did get an interview out of me. Even if some was horizontal rather than vertical."

Sally's mouth dropped open a bit. Then she began to giggle. Then laughed, followed by a few tears.

"Sorry. Keep getting these flashbacks. Kids and family."

Stalin stood up. He moved over and hugged her. Sally stood up so she could return the hug. They held on to each other for a while.

"We all have memories of 'before', Sally Reid. Cherish them, but do not live through them. Today is today, not yesterday."

Sally caught herself caressing the Russians body, his scars. She yanked off his towel.

"Minks, huh? Minks are classier than rabbits. Your breakfast was great. Can I have some dessert?"

CHAPTER 2

MALMSTROM ARMED FORCES BASE
GREAT FALLS, MONTANA
GROUNDHOG DAY

Pappy Gunn arrived at his base office before sunrise. He had trouble sleeping since he had a whole bunch of irons in the proverbial fire. Everyone who had ever gotten to know him said that he must have two or three separate brains in the skull of his as it seemed like he was dealing with numerous chains of thought and projects all at once, all the time. And, doing them all efficiently. Because of his abilities, Pappy had become *the* Logistics, Munitions Production, and Weapons Development Chief Executive Officer all in one. Historically, the closest person to doing what he was doing was Albert Speer, Hitler's War Production Manager during the last half of World War II. Luckily for him, Pappy Gunn did not have to deal with a psychotic wallpaper hanger like Speer.

Spread out on a large table in his office were the reports and results of several projects that had reached fruition. As he examined them all for the umpteenth time, he smiled. He just loved it when things came together the way he wanted them to, even if at times they had been major pains in the ass. So far, the Tschaaa and their minions, the Krakens, had held off on attempting any major reprisal for the attack on Key West. Some of that may be due to the Cattle Revolt in the three walled off states that had created a distraction. But with all the fire power the Squids had demonstrated during the Invasion, Pappy was still a bit mystified. Had he their resources, he would have smashed the upstart Unoccupied States back into the Stone Age, nuke threat or no.

The U.S. government had just over fifty thousand people under arms (not counting the state militias), with thousands more finally working their way through the training system. The Russians had provided just over another twenty-five hundred personnel, most the crème of the crop. The Japanese had provided another thousand, mostly new trainees. More Canadians were coming forward, and some Finns and Romanians had somehow showed up. Whatever was about to happen, Pappy knew he had to provide the weapons of war for almost all the military forces in the North American area. Japan had provided some salvaged equipment from former U.S. Bases in Japan, sunken naval vessels and a few items provided by trading with now existing Chinese warlords. They also had provided the F-15J Kai aircraft, pilots, and air to air munitions, plus some artillery and tank gun rounds they had shared with allied forces before the Tschaaa showed up. But they kept their limited F-35s and other advanced munitions in Japan, to defend the home islands.

The Canadians found some eight Leopard II Main Battle Tanks that someone had hidden in a large warehouse complex. Now, they and Pappy were trying to get them sent down to Malmstrom Allied Armed Forces Base for retrofitting and reconditioning. Pappy himself had found an M-1 Abrams MBT from an active unit that had been stashed during the long retreat, as well as an M-60. He had also found an old M-48 from an Armed Forces museum that was still operational. A military equipment collector had come forward with an M-4 Sherman that Pappy had rearmed with a Russian provided 76mm cannon.

Pappy gazed out his office window. Sitting in the parking lot was a monster of an armored vehicle, looking like something that came from a Japanese anime sci-fi movie. Cobbled together by the Russians from various armored fighting vehicles, it was a large block of a steel beast self-propelled gun. Twelve inches of steel, with another bolted on plate of depleted uranium on the sloped front surfaces. Even a M-1

'Silver Bullet' would have trouble penetrating it. No turret, just a gun mount with a Russian 125mm gun, salvaged from many wrecked T-80 tanks. With the barrel shortened, it could still fire the same shells and anti-tank missiles as the Russian tanks, but with shorter maximum ranges and velocities. Using special adapted sleeves for the ammunition, it could also fire older 122mm shells, as well as some western 120mm ammunition—one just had to watch the chamber pressures. A couple of fixed 23mm cannon and some turret mounted 60mm mortars to throw smoke and anti-personnel shells rounded out the metal breast. Some armchair historian had said it looked like the German World War II Grizzly Assault Gun on steroids. This, plus homage to a certain she-bear they all knew and loved, led to them being called Kodiaks. They may lumber along, and not be incredibly fast and maneuverable, but you did *not* want a Kodiak to get its claws into you. It was a testament to the Russian 'don't ever throw anything away' mentality, make it work one way or the other. Little comfort, but very functional.

A couple of museum piece armored cars, two Bradley Fighting Vehicles and two dozen "technicals" (heavy machine guns and cannon armed four-wheel drive SUVs and pickup trucks) rounded out his basic maneuver and armor element. The Squids had been pretty efficient at gathering and literally piling up armored vehicles left behind when the fractured units had fled to the interior states. Large piles of equipment were to be found up and down the east and west coasts of America, left to rust and deteriorate under the watchful eye in the sky. Similar actions had been taken with the surviving large military aircraft.

Being short of artillery was another problem. The former U.S. Armed Forces had lost almost all of its artillery in the retreat to the center. Pappy had a single operational single self-propelled 155mm artillery piece with a limited amount of ammunition. Free Japan was sending them some ammunition now, as they used similar weapons, but they were afraid to send too much as their ability to produce more was limited. Pappy had also had a single Multiple-Launch Rocket System (MLRS) vehicle with a dozen missiles. Once again, Free Japan was trying to supply some compatible munitions.

In addition, the Canadians had appeared with a battery of four ancient 25 Pounder guns with a quantity of ammunition. The guns had been part of a battery used for ceremonies, but once again were being placed in combat. The Russians were shipping over an eclectic type and quantity of various guns and artillery pieces, both more modern and museum examples. Some 152mm self-propelled guns were being sent, modified to make use of a bunch of mothballed Shillelagh Anti-Tank missiles from the Sheridan Light Tank found stashed in a warehouse. Thousands built, few used, and now they had another lease on life.

The Russians also were sending a complete crap load of mortars of all sizes and types. The poor man's artillery, they had pieces all the way up to 240mm in size. Add to that anti-aircraft guns, some from museums, with ammunition scrounged from all over, including former European and Asian countries with former Soviet connections. Add hundreds of anti-aircraft missiles, and Russian equipment was soon ringing major population areas, most often manned by newly trained American personnel. Thus, U.S. Forces became more dependent on foreign supplied equipment, a danger when the Tschaaa could easily shut down the supply route through the Bering Straits. Pappy needed a lot of basic equipment. Small arms were in a rapidly shortening supply. A thousand each brand new M-16 clones and Browning pistols from Deseret had appeared days after Abigail Young had arrived. Since then, they were getting a few dozen weapons and some ammunition each week at the Wyoming/Deseret border entry point, some new, some not. In return, the U.S.A supplied refined oil and petroleum products. Russia sent each of their soldiers with a rifle, plus some machine guns and grenade launchers. Ammunition, not so much. Free Japan sent soldiers and swords, few guns for them. Though in fairness they were supplying major airpower assets.

Pappy Gunn had dealt with the ammunition problem first. He reached out, obtained contact with every surviving ammunition re-loader that had survived. These men and women, some older children, were soon organized as Re-Loaders R Us. Using some powders, shell casings and bullets from sport stores and private homes, they began to load military calibers, including some 50 caliber SLAP rounds. They also broke down ammunition from odd calibers that were not used. All of this activity added up to a million rounds so far. But those numbers would be used up in one battle.

Then a Finnish Colonel showed up, after being escorted with a large sealed shipping container by the Free Russians. In it were thirty Valmet rifles, and a million rounds of ammunition, primarily 7.62 Russian. He said they had more stashed, it was a matter of getting it through the Arctic or Siberia to the Alaska without drawing attention from the Squids. This was what Pappy worked on now. The Squids left them alone now due to the cold climate, and the light skins of the survivors. The Finns would just as soon that did not change. However, if someone else wanted to use their weapons to kill the Squids, have at it.

The issue of slow transport still presented a problem. Pappy looked to what else he could produce in the Unoccupied States. Two former fireworks companies enabled Pappy to make what he called Chinese Artillery Rockets. Five foot long,and five inch in diameter black powder and Pyrodex powder rockets were produced, some twelve hundred of them. They were loaded six to a box-shaped disposable launcher and had just a shade over a three mile range under favorable wind conditions. The warheads were primarily black powder, with some nails and ball bearings thrown in for shrapnel. Even though unguided, they generally would all still land in the area of a football field at the worse, within a couple of dozen yard at the best. Throw them in the back of a pickup truck, run them out, set them down, light them off, then skedaddle. Six hitting a grounded harvester ark should do some damage.

Using some lengths of eight inch pipe from the North Dakota oil fields and some of the fireworks powder, Pappy soon had over one hundred shoulder fired rocket launchers. Only at almost a hundred pounds, you had to have big shoulders. These weapons were soon called Benders, after a certain Marine with a reputation. The expression was that the rocket may not break you, but it sure would bend you. He replaced an initial black powder warhead with a shaped charge modern explosive one, using some mining explosives he had scrounged. Not good enough to take out a modern tank, it could still damage tracks, and blow the crap out of fortified positions. You just had to have someone light the three second fuse in the back, then get out of the way. Pappy was trying to keep things as simple as possible.

Finally, his pièce de résistance. Using spare and scavenged Minuteman Missile parts, he developed the She-Bear Missile. Capable of laser guidance, these 12 foot missiles hurled a thousand pounds of explosives some nine miles. He only built a dozen of them, with towed launchers. They were as much psychological as they were practical. Pappy had a dozen nuclear Armed Minuteman Missiles with a ninety-nine percent chance of functioning, and another dozen with various chances of launching and detonating where they were aimed. They just needed spare parts and upkeep. The twelve She-Bears were all the extra equipment he could spare for large weaponry.

Pappy had then turned his supplying weapons of war to locally produced small arms. First it was a conventional stamped metal AR-18, what had been envisioned in the 1970s as a poor nan's M-16. The Japanese had found some of the original production tools and gigs for the assault rifle stashed away. They had at one time produced the AR-18 for possible export until pacifistic sections of the government had stopped the export of weapons of war during Vietnam. Pappy located a couple of small gun manufacturers in Montana and South Dakota that he was able to get up and running again. They were now producing the AR-18 at a fairly decent rate that was limited by the supply of usable sheet metal. Re-opening metal ore mines and recycling scrap metal thru two smelters up and operating would enable him to provide some thirty thousand weapons by year's end, in addition to some spare magazines. But that was not enough to supply the continuing needs of a large allied military force.

Another former M-16 rifle high end clone manufacturer had been located. It had specialized in larger caliber, highly accurate rifles that had demanded a premium price and were a favorite of SWAT teams. Using their expertise along with his team, they had used their large frame rifles in developing a squad automatic weapon in .308 caliber. Either belt or magazine fed, with a special quick change barrel, it was a model of modern workmanship and design. The Armed Forces were short on squad level machine guns. This helped to address that weakness. After a thousand had been delivered, he had then used the same design and heavy barrels, sans the quick change adaptation, to make a designated marksman/sniper rifle. Just shy of five hundred had been delivered so far.

Pappy found a pistol manufacturer that had made 1911-style .45 caliber pistols before the Squids had shown up. He got the owners up and running, completed a production run of a thousand match grade weapons with spare magazines for Special Operations. He then had them make two hundred 9mm versions, then two .40 Caliber and two 10mm pistols. He gave the Forties and the Tens to Commissioner Miller for use by law enforcement. The Nines were supplied to the Military. They were now looking for spare parts to make some more.

Another manufacturer had been making replicas of the large Sharps Western Rifle prior to the first rock strike. Pappy now had them making a small batch in modern large rifle calibers, including .338 Lapua. With good optics, they would make adequate sniping rifles. The two pit raids had netted some three thousand weapons of all types. A thousand were ceded to the military, most going to training units. The rest were given to the militias and law enforcement. Some twenty thousand rounds of ammunition were also distributed.

Pappy smiled to himself as he looked at an example of what he considered his crowning achievement in creative weaponry. On his desk tip was a slightly boxy looking assault rifle. It looked a lot like an M-16 but with a thicker looking receiver group and rather square front grip furniture and sight frame. The plastic/polymer magazine next to it was an identifiable M-16 .223 thirty round magazine. Thanks to 3D printer technology, examples of this military weapon were being produced like Twinkies in a former Hostess factory. Pappy Gunn had scrounged every single 3D printer he could find, no matter what the size. Then he had gone about producing the media that was fed into the printers to produce the equipment he needed. Petroleum-based strong plastics, metal-based media, even his own take on the Tschaaa organic ocean crustacean-based material the aliens used to shape the Delta aircraft and connected equipment. The United States had been working on armor based on the shell material produced by crustaceans when the Squids had hit. The aliens had used this technology for centuries prior to their voyage to Earth.

He had started with the simple single shot rifles he was supplying to the Occupied Areas, along with the small disposable automatic pistols with integral silencers. Six to twelve rounds and the disposable guns would begin to self-destruct under the high pressures generated by modern ammunition. So, Pappy began working on a more permanent solution.

First, he printed and spun copies of the military rifles that were copies of the standard M-4 .223 Carbine. They began to self- destruct after about twenty rounds. He modified the design to make it more like the stamped metal and gas piston system AR-18. He tweaked the printer medium a bit and began to obtain some examples that lasted one hundred rounds. Those may be of use for throwaway training or guerilla weapons, but not for an organized military force.

The magazines he was producing using polymers and plastics were working just fine, as good as any aluminum pre-strike examples. He even went so far as to produce 45, 75 and 100 round drum magazines for the .223 and .308 rifles he was producing from his supply of conventional metal. But this was of limited use if he had an inadequate supply of rifles.

Finally, two weeks ago, Pappy had assembled all the parts for the rifle on his desk. He called it an AR-18DP, for 3D Printer. He had tweaked and modified the parts using the available 3D media material, now turning into a hybrid weapon. Pappy found that if he used a metal-based media material for the bolt, chamber, and first two inches of the barrel, those parts would last at least a couple of thousand rounds before showing any real wear and tear. He had gotten one rifle through three thousand rounds before the bolt face and chamber began to show pressure and stress cracks. The weapon still functioned but jammed a lot. He stopped the test before he had a catastrophic failure. A tough combination of ceramics, polymers and Tschaaa developed crustacean based mantle material was used for the rest of the rifle, including a butt stock sufficiently strong to be used for a butt smash to any enemy. Further testing showed he could replace the barrel and bolt at the first signs of stress and run the rifle through another couple of thousand rounds with no problems. Thus, he started making a spare bolt assembly and barrel for each weapon produced.

Even then, Pappy had managed to produce and deliver one thousand of the final design assault rifles just last week. Another two thousand should be ready for delivery later this day. All of his 3D printer magazine and drums were already numbering in the tens of thousands. As long as he could keep up the supply of printer media, Pappy Gunn should have no problems meeting the production demands. He was also producing spare aircraft and vehicle parts, though this was taking a bit of tweaking to get the necessary quality control down.

In the back room sat another little experiment. Using spare 3D printer plastic and polymer material, he had made all the parts for a Colt black powder cap and ball revolver. He had managed to fit them together and found out the less sharp explosion that black powder produced (being a low order explosive) was easily handled by the polymers he had developed for his modern weapons. So far, the commensurate scrounger had produced a single black powder revolver each week in his spare time. They could become emergency back-up weapons or guerilla weapons he could drop behind the lines in Cattle Country. They lasted a lot longer than the throw away designs he had made for smokeless powder. One just had to come up with the percussion caps, powder and lead.

Pappy Gunn smiled. Things seemed to be coming together. Now, if he had just a few more weeks to work on all this he would feel a lot more secure.

The hotline to Security Control lit up and the phone range.

"Pappy here." He listened for a few moments.

"Thanks for the call, Captain. I'll start my recall." He hung up the telephone. Damn. Tanks entering Kansas City, Kansas. And they weren't friendly.

The proverbial balloon had just gone up.

CHAPTER 3

That which does not kill you, makes you stronger.

-Friedrich Nietzsche

The Free Russians, Free Japanese, Free Americans proved him correct. As they say in America, proved him right in spades.

-Excerpt from the Collected Works of Princess Akiko, Free Japan Royal Family.

KANSAS CITY, KANSAS

Sergeant "Whitey" Brown was sitting on the roof of the high rise overlooking the I-70 bridge   that crossed the Kansas River from Kansas City, Missouri. The first rays of sunlight were just beginning to show over the horizon, not yet sunrise. The early stages of daylight caused the human eye to begin the switch between rods and cones eye cells, and made a person's vision less distinct, objects a bit hazier. But Whitey's ears were unaffected by any lighting changes.

Sgt. Brown had gotten the nickname Whitey as he was claimed to be the lightest-skinned African American in the U.S., with the except a possible albino. His mother had been rather dark-skinned, his father had been a light-skinned Englishman. He had the broad nose, thicker lips some tribes in Africa seemed to primarily exhibit, but his skin color belied his mother's ancestry. Thus, the nickname.

He suddenly turned to look at the 1-70 overpass, as Kansas Militia Sergeant Jim James spit a wad of chew over the edge of the building for the umpteenth time. Whitey stood up in a low crouch and tried to pierce the pre-sunrise gloom with his eyes.

"What's up, Whitey?" Both men were retreads, having prior service in the days before the Squid Invasion, or Infestation. More and more people were wont to reenlist since a speech by Madam President. Sgt. James had joined the local militia some five years ago in order to help protect his community from the ravages of roving bands of Ferals. Whitey Brown had stayed off the radar until after the attack on Key West, when he saw there just might be a chance to get some payback against the Squids. A lot of so called "late bloomers" were sent out to work with the militias after going through Major Bender and company's retread training. The thought was that the experienced militias would not put up with any crap or hidden malcontents when it came to protecting their homesteads. It also served to help improve communications between regular forces and the militias.

Whitey grabbed the high-powered binoculars they had for use at this lookout post.

"I was a tanker in my previous life. I could swear I hear the unique sound of an M-1 turbine engine. No other sound quite like it."

Just then, a large shape came out of the indistinct lighting. It was an M-1 main battle tank moving at speed across the bridge toward the barricade of wrecked cars. If you wanted access to Kansas City, Kansas, you had to climb over the cars, or swim the river below. The M-1 was not going to do either.

"Crap!" Whitey exclaimed as the M-1, large dozer blade attached, slammed into the wrecked cars. It seemed to slow a bit, and then it was through, an M-1 sized path pushed through the makeshift barricade. "I did not want to be right." He scrambled for the Bender rocket launcher that had been provided, more for noise and signaling than as anti-tank defense. It was an early black powder warhead type, would just scrape a MBT's armor. Jim James grabbed a signal flare gun and let it rip. The bright red flare arched over toward the center of what was left of the city. Then he yelled over their field telephone. "Tanks in the wire. I say again, Tanks in the wire."

Behind the tank was another, then two more. Then a Bradley Fighting Vehicle, followed by a couple of pickup trucks with figures in the beds. Whitey man handled the oversized eight inch Bender up to his shoulder, almost a hundred pounds of it.

"Got a light, Sergeant?"

"Sure do," replied Jim James as he produced a well-used Zippo lighter. "Want her lit?"

"Go for it." Whitey tried to aim at a slowing pick-up truck. Sgt. Brown lit the three second fuse in the back of the launcher, jumped back. "Fire." he yelled as he made sure he was well away from the rocket backblast area.

A small explosion, a loud whooshing sound, then a cloud of black powder smoke engulfed them as the rocket left the tube. The projectile arched toward the now stopped pickup, some three hundred yards away. Surprisingly accurate at a hundred, at this range it was all Kentucky windage and by guess and by golly. But luck seemed to be on their side, as the large rocket arched right into the passenger side open window.

The armed Kraken male had just enough time to look toward the projectile as it smashed his face in. The warhead failed to detonate, the pocket engine flaring out into the vehicle cab, setting the ceiling liner on fire and splashing the driver with flames. The driver screamed, as did a couple of the occupants in the bed. The hair and clothes of the driver and smashed in face passenger were aflame, the driver screaming as he tried to free himself from his seat belt. The truck steering wheel turned and the vehicle went down an incline to a lower side street. The armed Krakens in the bed started to bail out of the moving pickup now in flames, screaming and cursing. One tripped on the side of the bed as she leapt out, her left arm being run over as she fell partially under the rear wheel. The noise of everything else drowned out the snap of her forearm bone. At the bottom of the incline, the pickup turned onto its side. The driver's screaming stopped as his badly seared lungs and throat stopped functioning. He was soon dead, as was his cabmate.

50 Caliber rounds fired from one of the M-1s, as well as small arms rounds from various assault rifles that began to pepper the top floors of the high-rise building. Whitey grabbed the binoculars, and Jim James yanked the wires loose from the field phone. They made it to the roof exit door with their rifles and equipment as chunks of cement began to fly around their former fire position. As they clambered down the stairs, Whitey yelled out a question.

"Hey, how'd you get named James James?"

"Drunk dad, and mom was out of it from the drugs they used for the pain. Dad thought it was hilarious. Doesn't matter now."

"You got that right." Just then, a Bradley 25mm chain gun opened up, and pieces from the upper stair well began falling on top of the fleeing soldiers.

"Fuck!" Whitey exclaimed. "Hell of a way to start Groundhog Day."

MALMSTROM ALLIED FORCES BASE
GREAT FALLS, MONTANA

General Reed sat in the Headquarters conference room, looking at the computer images displayed on the wall screen. The other attendees were Pappy Gun, Head of Intelligence Major Aleks Smirnov who had just returned to work, and Colonel Anton Popov, Free Russian Forces and uncle to Inna Popov (Russian intelligence, spy and one of the original Russian three sisters with Aleks).

"So," John Reed started. "Based on our limited drone surveillance and HUMINT sources on the ground fighting, we have some four MBTs, eight Bradleys, and an a sundry of other support vehicles, both military and civilian that have just smashed through Kansas City, Kansas. How many troops estimated total, and how many fighters are there, Major?"

"Some two thousand in the initial tip of the spear, General. But coming up from some ten miles away are an estimated thirty-eight thousand more."

"We missed such a massing of forces near borders how?"

It was Pappy's turn. "We are short on surveillance drones and other aircraft. I've got some more in the pipeline but have been concentrating on munitions production. Guess I was wrong."

General Reed looked at Aleks. "Knowing you just came back from maternity leave, any idea how our hacking into still existing surveillance and global mapping satellites and HUMINT sources gave us no clue?"

"General, there was some movement noticed. But it looked like a response to the revolts in Cattle Country. People thought any additional forces were being massed to use against the rebels resisting being harvested."

The General paused for a moment, staring at the screen. Then he spoke. "Like they used to say, hindsight always seems to be twenty-twenty. So, now we need to have a very timely response."

He addressed Colonel Popov. "Think you can get a blocking force down there in forty-eight hours?"

Colonel Popov, senior Allied Field Commander, was a stereotypical looking Russian. A bit broad, stocky, no taller than General Reed, with a Slavic face. He gave a textbook sly Russian smile. "I already have a few people en route to aid the militia, General. Including one of your snipers, with a reputation from Key West, who magically appeared and volunteered. I hope you don't mind that I accepted."

The General snorted. "Why not? I have a small core of soldiers who have a tendency to charge toward the sound of gunfire without going through the chain of command. I know who you speak of and we can spare him. But the main force, please coordinate that with my commanders. I need to keep track of who is where. This may not be the only attack and I have a limited number of bodies I can submit. About fifty-five thousand trained soldiers this minute, with thousands more in the pipeline."

"General, you have twenty-five hundred Free Russians, ninety-nine percent are Special Forces Trained. Another thousand are a few days away. I have already contacted our Japanese friends. They will give us who we ask for, but their primary support are the F-15J-Kai aircraft, as well as some other trained pilots for American air assets you are bringing on line."

At the mention of air assets, General Reed glanced at Pappy.

"The Fairchild assets we found are ready to go?"

"Ninety percent are, General. I have a few Russian supplied armor assets ready also. Artillery, still limited."

"Alright, people. Marching orders. Colonel, two thousand troops in Kansas tomorrow. Americans and Russians primarily. I'll get the Japanese air assets ready to go, though I do not want to draw too much attention yet. I still have visions of lined up Squid Falcons, frying everything moving."

"Not worried about the deltas, General?" Pappy interjected.

"Not really, thanks to all the SAMs and air to air high speed missiles the Russians and Japanese have supplied. Plus all the Russian anti-aircraft guns that were scrounged up. They may be able to outspeed and outmaneuver our jets above five thousand feet, but they can't dodge those missiles all day. Their air to air stuff is not really better than ours, if we use the right tactics. They won't have surprise this time."

"Pappy, get everything that can fight up and ready."

Pappy grinned. "Aye aye, Sir."

"Major, coordinate with Pappy here, get some surveillance and intelligence going. I need real time info on what these Kraken assholes are up to." He paused for a moment, then continued.

"This is strictly a punishment raid. They'll pound through poor Bloody Kansas, maybe into Colorado. If they wanted an all-out war, robocops and Falcons would be kicking our asses right now. We need to protect the civilians from the cannibalistic and murderous Krakens, then kick their balls back to Squid town. Any questions? Good. Give me a SITREP every two hours, or if something drastic happens. Dismissed."

Colonel Popov and Aleks stood and saluted. As they began to leave with Pappy, the General motioned to Aleks. "A quick word, Major."

General Reed waited until the other two had left, then spoke.

"A certain Marine we both know and love has been ringing my telephone to death. I know what he wants. But he can't go. Not yet. I still need him as a heroic symbol. In one piece. He and Abigail, and you to a lesser extent, have been a huge boost to civilian morale. I can't have your, his invincibility questioned, not yet. I just thought I'd warn you that he will not be happy when I finally talk to him. Understand, Aleks?"

She looked at the man who was the godfather to her sons, and was becoming a father figure to Abigail Young. She knew why he was making this decision.

"General, I understand. I do not want Torbin to be wounded, killed either. But..."

"I can tell that "but" means something large. Please, spell it out."

Aleks sighed. "My husband is a warrior, through and through. That is what he does, that is what he is good at. Keep him from that, eventually he will become so bitter as to be useless to everyone. Or he will disobey orders, and go to the sound of gunfire. Then you will have to court martial him. Then you will lose your hero, anyways."

John Reed looked at the Russian-Ukrainian woman, who was becoming more like a daughter-in-law every day, because Torbin was like a son to him. He knew she was right, knew that it took a lot to let him go and get shot at. But she also wanted him happy, contented. If he was not allowed to fight again, he had get that desire out of his system himself, and what she said was true.

"Okay, Aleks. I understand. But this operation right now is not how I need him. I'll know when the time comes when and how to use him and his special talents. Okay?

"Of course, General. You are in command." She started to salute him again but the General did something completely out of character. He reached over and hugged Aleks.

"Not military decorum, but you and Torbin are family to me. And those godsons of mine. Pass this hug on to them."

Aleks hung on for a few moments more. Yes, he was family. Then, she stepped back and smiled. "I will give my sons a big hug, and tell them it is from their godfather. Now, I go to fight the war."

On the way out of the command building, Colonel Popov approached her.

"Pardon me, Major, but I have to ask. What is the significance of Bloody Kansas?"

"American Civil War. All about slavery, trying to decide who was on what side. A lot of civilians were massacred."

"Was it as bloody as our Civil War? Battles in the Revolution?"

"Colonel, to them it was. And that is what matters to the General."

CHAPTER 5

KANSAS CITY, KANSAS

John Talbot, former President of the Kraken Motorcycle Gang and now Commander of the Kraken Invasion Force, watched the transport vehicles drive by. He was standing up through the sunroof of a high end dark SUV, his command vehicle. He watched as an eclectic assemblage of vehicles went by, jammed to the gills with as many people as they could hold.

Greyhound buses, school buses, former armored bank cars, cattle tucks, horse trailers pulled by heavy pick-up trucks, semis, and even an ex-military deuce and a half, all slowly motored by. Talbot figured that they may be averaging twenty miles an hour through the area surrounding Kansas City, Kansas.

The former biker chuckled to himself. Somehow, this rag tag force completely surprised the U.S. Forces. The two thousand somewhat well trained point personnel, supported by the tanks and AFVs, had quickly cut through the militia forces that supplied border security. Which was good, because he had no real forces in depth.

The forty thousand troops looked good on paper. But in reality, they were more a mob than an organized military unit. Most had barely a month of basic training, had been shown basic combat tactics, then been pushed into some semblance of minimum physical conditioning. Talbot had placed people with former military or law enforcement experience in charge of groups of people whenever he could. That, or used hardcore former prison convicts who he knew would follow his orders and keep them in line by fear. Many of these people in "authority", as well as their closest followers, were fanatical Krakens, followers of the Church of Kraken. Quite a number had filed their teeth to sharp points and ignored Tschaaa prohibitions against eating the flesh of their own kind. Cannibalistic behavior seemed to bring them—in a fervor and religious state—closer to their Kraken God, which every day began to appear more and more like Cthulhu, the Ancient and Dark One.

Talbot swore under his breath. He was the one who first appropriated the name Kraken for his motorcycle gang, his flying squad of primary enforcers for the Director in the early days. Now the symbol and name had been taken over by a bunch of religious fanatics—churchers—who did shit even he found objectionable. The Director had turned into a wimp, allowing the Reverend Kray to take the lead on dealing with the Rebels.

Talbot still had a limp, thanks to a certain Torbin Bender. Plus his stock had dropped drastically after that Deseret slut and Bender had decimated his band of men when they tried to capture the two en route from Deseret. But Kray knew a hard worker when he saw one. He also recognized a man eaten up with the desire for revenge for his humiliation at the hands of a young female reenager and a single Marine. So, the promise of Tschaaa medical science to start healing his shotgun mangled foot and the mission to punish the Rebels for attacking Key West, killing Tschaaa young, were given as incentive.

Talbot shook his head at the thought of the Squids going apeshit over a few thousand dead young. Hell, that many human young died each day in various countries before the Squids were even in near orbit. Humankind didn't go nuts or catatonic. Seeing that happened had been the final decision maker. The Squid successful invasion had been a fluke, done on the backs of a Fifth Column of people like Talbot and a bunch of weak and incompetent world leaders.

If he, Talbot, had been in charge, he would have nuked the fuck out of the Squids, and made them come to the bargaining table. Too bad for collateral damage. Enough humans would have survived, the

Squids would have left earlier with plenty of provided dark meat and breeding stock. And those of a darker complexion would be gone, or enslaved, with the white race triumphant. Hitler was a piker compared to Reverend Kray and Talbot. And in Talbot's mind, especially in comparison to him.

He glanced over to the area of the nearby roadside embankment. The pickup truck that had been struck by the homemade bazooka rocket was still burning. The warhead had never really exploded. Instead, the warhead had leaked black powder and gone up more like a roman candle than a large firecracker. The bodies of the two dead were being burned to ashes, and Talbot had to beat off a few of the hardcore Krakens that wanted to retrieve the barbecued flesh for a quick snack. If he started allowing that to happen, he would quickly have a sizable revolt on his hands.

Probably a good ten percent of his forty thousand personnel were the fanatical cannibal or near cannibal type. Almost half of the army were of the fawning, tell me what to do oh great god Squid type, looking for some Higher Being to give their lives meaning and purpose. The rest were a mixture of opportunists, Ferals, ex-convicts, and people forced into participation by having nowhere to go, nothing to live off of other than the Squid largess. And Squids never gave away anything for free. He had even seen a small number of Mexicans who came from family groups press-ganged into working in the huge industrial complex that covered Baja California, sea and all. That same complex and workers produced the rebuilt firearms they were using. The Tschaaa had rounded up the Mexicans and Indios they knew were hiding in the jungles and countryside and given them a choice: work and survive, your families fed, housed. Hell, the workers were even paid, given some time off as the recent Homo sapiens genome robocops, the ones created since the Invasion, had convinced Lord Neptune and company that a happy serf was more productive than an unhappy slave, looking for a chance to flee. They had been right, as not only did the laborers work hard on taking piles of weapons that had been sitting rusting away and making them functioning equipment again, but none tried to escape. Plus, the small numbers with military or drug cartel enforcer experience had volunteered to come along on this operation.

Those that refused to work were butchered in front of the others as an example of the stick over the carrot. Talbot had found out later that His Lordship purposefully allowed groups of Feral dark meat to exist as a supply of free range genetic material should his Cattle become too inbred. His Lordship knew his genetic science.

From the some forty thousand soldiers, Talbot had handpicked a dozen to be his Praetorian Guard, beholden to him. Should things fall completely apart, they would help him bug out, away from the wrath of His Lordship or Kray. They would make a quick trip to some area he knew in the Feral areas, and voila—he'd set himself up a satrap with him as the Lord of the Manor, get ahold of a few of his old motorcycle gang members who were floating around. He had tried to get his old Lieutenant Ray Sparks reassigned to him, but he had become the primary goto guy in the Siege of Atlanta. The last word was he was doing a pretty good job of starving the surviving rebellious Cattle in Atlanta, the rest of the cities having surrendered after a quick and brutal beat down.

So, Talbot had made the best of the situation. He had identified those with some military or gang experience and made them the squad and platoon leaders. Any with AFV experience were put in the four Abrams and eight Bradleys. The rest of the experienced and trustworthy were put in the point of the spear. Some twenty former armored bank cars were turned into poor man armored personnel carriers, with SUVs and four wheel pickup trucks (some armored up) rounding out the transport. The rest of the force made do with cattle trucks, horse trailers, buses, a few semis, and a bunch of pick-ups, and even some U-Hauls. By jamming everyone together, he had just about enough mobile transport for nearly everyone. Small groups may have to hoof it at the rear, but eventually would get a ride.

Despite the mobility, weapon wise he had a bunch of light infantry. Everyone had an assault rifle and around four thirty round magazines of ammunition. He had only about a thousand machine guns and Squad automatic weapons for support. Add a few grenade launchers, small numbers of hand grenades and improvised explosives, and this was his military force.

The four tanks and the Bradleys were his assault's heaviest weapons. He had exactly two 81mm and one 60mm mortar for fire support. Artillery? One old museum piece of a five inch British howitzer with remanufactured shells. He had tried to get more, but was told this was to be a hit-and-run punishment campaign, not a siege. Air support was a half dozen small private aircraft and a single former traffic copter. He was told the B-25 used to bomb Atlanta may be available in a day or two, as well as some Deltas if some U.S. Aircraft showed up.

Talbot snorted. Bottom line, he was on his own. He knew this was more of a psychological terror and revenge mission than it was a physical invasion. Thus, everyone was up for sacrifice. It did not matter how many Krakens were killed as long as the Fear of God (or Squids, Cthulhu, whatever) was put into the civilian populace of the Unoccupied States. This fear would result in them telling the officials behind the Key West nuke to "knock their shit off." Then they would go back to enjoying their new internet access, bootleg Tschaaa medical supplies and equipment, and the knowledge they would be left alone, not eaten. Most importantly, their children would not be harvested. And everything would go back to the pre-Key West attack "normal".

Whatever. Time to get back to the present. The MBTs and AFVs were exiting the built up area of the city, just a mile or two to the beginning of Kansas flat. He had a couple of the bank armored cars running recon, and had used the small cessnas and like type aircraft to drop a dozen skirmishers miles out front. They were making contact with militia Forces that had been heading to fight in the city streets, delaying them. That and a few motorbike delivered soldiers were distracting them from attacking the tanks with any anti-tank weapons.

He got on his handheld radio that had a direct contact to all the small unit commanders.

"Keep those doggies moving. The sooner we can get everyone out of the city, the faster we can move across Kansas. No slackers. If you can't keep up, you get left behind."

Near the town of Salina on I-70, two Free Russians and an American sniper were making contact with the militia units. They had been brought to the area by two small civilian aviation aircraft, which had also dropped off some specialized equipment, including some RPGs. Free Russian military personnel Capt. Mikhail Vasiliev and Senior Sergeant Vlad Popkov flew in on a small formerly private plane, the pilot landing on a straight stretch of highway. They had taken up the limited cargo space with a couple of RPG launchers and several reloads, plus a couple of suitcases with two dozen pounds of high grade plastic explosive. A separate single engine Cessna brought in a third soldier with some special skills. Benjamin Black, commensurate sniper, late of the Key West Attack, arrived with his Barrett 50 Caliber. He had been helping train new snipers, but had convinced the powers-that-be that his skills were needed in Kansas.

The three regular army soldiers met the combination militia and army forces in Salina, Kansas. I-70 ran directly into the city, some one hundred seventy miles from Kansas City. The Kraken primary force seemed to be driving directly toward Salina as their destination, not having wavered off of I-70. Using the main guns of the main battle tanks and the automatic cannon on the Bradleys, they had hit the taller buildings along their route of travel, preventing any attacks from above on their vehicles. A shortage of anti-tank weapons also hurt a meaningful response. Thus, the pointy end of the spear, the armored vehicles, were soon through Kansas City. Dismounted infantry engaged those defenders trying to fire from nearby buildings. Soon, some two thousand Krakens were through and motoring toward Topeka.

The armored units up front paused for a quarter hour, waiting for some of the cattle trucks, horse trailers and other unconventional transports to catch up before entering Topeka. Then, Topeka was a repeat of Kansas City. A few well-placed 120mm main gun rounds and about a hundred automatic cannon rounds soon made the defenders go to ground until the front of the Kraken force were through the built up areas. Once again, there was a pause to allow some of the infantry in the unconventional transport vehicles to catch up. Then, they pushed forward again.

A problem was becoming evident. The rear units and vehicles were becoming more spread out as the day progressed. But Talbot as the Commander was willing to accept casualties in the rear personnel in order to keep the momentum up front.

In Salina, Captain Vasiliev and Senior Sergeant Chekov were reviewing maps with the local commanders as Sergeant Black sat at a separate table cleaning his Barrett 50 caliber. He did not need to be in on the planning. All he needed to know was where and when they wanted him to use his special skill. The Captain pointed to a spot the map a short distance west of Abilene, Kansas.

"There, my good Colonel Mills. Is that a substantial overpass on the Solomon River?"

"Yes, Captain. Two parallel overpasses on I-70, one in each direction."

"Good. If you could get Sergeant Chekov and I there as soon as possible, I think our plastic explosive we brought can be put to good use. And my understanding is you have some sweaty dynamite you'd like to get rid of?"

"That's right, Captain. But I hope you know what you're doing. That old dynamite is looking for an excuse to explode."

Captain Vasiliev smiled. "Trust me, Sir. We are quite experienced at transporting questionable explosives. If you can get us a decent vehicle whose suspension is not too worn out, we should have no problems." He looked over at Sgt. Black.

"Sergeant Black, would you care to accompany us?"

Sgt. Black looked up. "Is there a good chance I'll get to shoot something?"

"Very good, Sergeant. Very good odds."

The sniper gave his signature smile, just enough of one to show he was pleased and interested.

"Well, Sir. That would be just dandy."

Talbot had sent one of the converted bank armored cars out front of the column to act a scout and to draw fire. He was more than willing to sacrifice lesser vehicles in order to protect his Abrams and Bradleys from any ambushes. Behind the armored car was a pick-up truck filled with armed men and women. Their job was to dismount and engage at the first sign of a possible attack.

The armored car did not slow from its thirty mile an hour speed as it began to travel the westbound I-70 overpass that crossed the Solomon River. As it reached the point on the overpass that was directly over the rain and snow swollen river below, a large explosion took out the section of bridge roadway just in front of the moving vehicle. Unable to even brake, the armored car was soon plummeting to the river below. The river waters themselves were near eight feet deep, just enough to swallow the vehicle. Shocked and thrown about by the fall at speed, especially the non-seated belted personnel in the back of the armored car, the vehicle was flooded before anyone could react. Not even the driver and his assistant in the cab could get out before the vehicle settled on its side. As people have been known to drown in a bathtub, drowning in eight feet of cold water was not all that difficult. The pickup following it was able to brake to a stop just before plummeting down to join the armored car. The driver quickly screamed over his radio what had happened.

Talbot began to curse. He stopped only when someone said the eastbound lanes overpass were still in one piece. He began to snap orders about.

"Get someone with some engineering experience to check out the eastbound overpass, make sure it's clear to use. Get somebody up here with some EOD experience. I find it hard to believe that the other span wouldn't be wired for explosives also. Move. I don't want us to be caught all bunched up here."

Just over a half hour later, Captain Vasiliev was using a high powered spotting scope to watch two figures make their way down and under the eastbound overpass. He turned to Sgt. Black who was prone next to him.

"Think you can hit those charges from here? I don't know what happened, but they did not go off. I think a 50 caliber round should do the trick."

Sgt. Black gave him his signature slight smile. "Piece of cake, Captain. Want it now?"

"No. Wait until they are within a few yards, as they try to figure out what to do with the explosives attached to the supports. Take a couple more of shit eating whore Krakens out when you do it."

"With pleasure, Captain."

The EOD-experienced Kraken was on the radio with Talbot and in mid-sentence when the charges blew. Only a few feet of roadway and bridge were soon joining the other span in the river. Nothing was found of the two Krakens bodies. Someone must have noticed what had set off the charges as the call of "sniper" reverberated up and down the spread out column. Talbot began swearing again.

"You! Get on the horn! There is an exit just this side of Abilene that leads to a parallel county road. At least the map says it does. Start routing people to it. If we take it easy, that road's bridge should get us over. And get me a machine gunner up here."

Talbot spat. "I want some plunging fire over where that sniper is probably located, southwest of here."

One of his Lieutenants spoke up. "Sir, we're short on gunners and ammunition."

"I don't give a fuck. I'll be damned if I let some asshole pick us off one by one as we drive past. Now, move!"

Captain Vasiliev and Sergeant Black had already left the spot from where the shot had been fired. Low-crawling for some ten minutes, the two then got to their feet, crouching, and moved out.

"Sure you don't want me to stay back, pick a few off?" Sergeant Black asked.

"No, my good Sergeant. For General Winter will be here within the hour."

Sgt. Black gave the Russian spetsnaz a quizzical look. "General Winter?"

"Why yes. I was notified a large storm front is moving in before we came out here. It should produce a nice ice storm, if your American weather people are correct."

The Captain clapped his hands together. "Just what we need. A good old Siberian ice storm. Oh, I guess no one informed you, Sergeant. General Winter follows us Siberian Russians no matter where we are. We'll soon see just how prepared the Kraken scum are for severe winter weather. From what I can tell, they are not."

The Captain looked up at the sky. "Yes, a definite feel of snow and ice is in the air. Come. Let us hurry. A hot cup of coffee will feel good about now."

It took Talbot about an hour to get his forces re-routed to the parallel county road. During that time, he had also started a single line of troops slowly making their way across the remains of the overpass, consisting of a single person sized walkway on the right side of the span. This section must have been made of a better quality of concrete and asphalt than the rest to remain standing. By spacing themselves at least two yards apart, the passage of the infantry did not seem to overburden the damaged remains.

Then the temperature plunged. It must have been some twenty degrees in as many minutes as an ominous bank of clouds and mist swept toward them. Wind driven frozen rain suddenly hit the stretched out column, the front encompassing everything from Topeka, Kansas west. The Krakens were now the recipients of a good old East Kansas ice storm. Some five hundred foot soldiers had made it across the span when the full force of the storm hit. Others were in queue to begin the crossing when they were pelted with freezing rain and ice crystals. None of them had anything past the basic heavy coat and boots as no one had planned for a bad storm. And the powers-that-be really did not care. The average Kraken was expendable.

A few dozen more made it across on foot when strong winds blew two people off the overpass remains and into the freezing water below. Hours later, as the river actually froze over, the two bodies bobbed to the surface and were frozen in the rivers surface, a grim reminder to others. The rest, over five hundred, quickly looked for shelter in some abandoned and stripped farm houses along the freeway and connecting roads. As Talbot tried to yell orders over the hand held radios to head south from the freeway and connect with the units beginning to travel up the parallel roadway, only some two dozen attempted to follow his orders. Half of these Krakens would become lost in the near white out conditions and would freeze to death.

A former bank armored car and a Bradley made it across the smaller bridge first. Then, the freezing rain and icy snow began to hit in earnest. Within minutes, the roadway was a sheet of ice. Transport vehicles such as buses and pick-up trucks began to slip and slide, skidding off the road and into ditches. Finally, Talbot had enough, and used his radio again.

"Everyone, stay where you are. Pull to the side of the road and wait until you hear from me. Wait this storm out."

What he did not realize was that would take some thirty-six hours. A day and a half where he would lose numbers to frostbite, hypothermia. At least one SUV full of armed personnel would be found with the engine running, the occupants dead from carbon monoxide poisoning. The dozen who had crossed on foot then followed his directions, finally hooked up with the units on the west side of the river, half-frozen. A burned out gas station was used as shelter, several discarded oil drums used as makeshift stoves by filling them with whatever would burn.

All along I-70 up to the outskirts of Topeka, groups of Krakens huddled around their vehicles and makeshift bonfires. At some if those bonfires, the smell of barbequed pork soon wafted into the freezing rain swept air. Only it wasn't pork.

The units at the tail end of the extremely stretched out column were stuck around Topeka. The problem for them was a shortage of vehicles. Even with people crammed in the busses, RVs. cattle trucks and semis, at the start of the attack there were some two thousand Krakens who had to be moved in waves in order to keep them in sight of the rear vehicles. Now, with small unit attacks by the defenders, snipers, and vehicle accidents, it was worse. Thus, several thousand moved back into the edges of Topeka, looking for shelter. Just as they were starting to get comfortable, the hardy local Kansas defenders began attacking. They were used to the bad winters, and they knew the area. The Krakens, many from the southwest and California, neither knew nor were prepared. A rot began to set in among the rear personnel.

In Salina proper, Captain Vasiliev was talking through a secure email connection with Malmstrom Armed Forces Base. Finally, he smiled, and broke the connection.

"Well, Colonel Mills, the weather is so bad we cannot even get a decent picture from a hacked satellite, or a drone. Which tells me that General Winter is doing a fine job of destroying the Krakens' plans, and probably freezing some of them to death. Just like in the great patriotic war with the fascists."

"Yes," answered the American Colonel. "My Kansas militia members have already found some frozen Krakens with no other signs of violence. They definitely do not understand blizzards and snowstorms."

Captain Vasiliev chuckled. "Yes Sir. And Colonel Popov sends his regards. He will be down here soonest with some two thousand regular army, including a thousand of my countrymen. General Reed will have a full division to hit the Kraken mess of a column in the northern flank in seventy-two hours. Your militia and Colonel Popov's forces are to, as your General Patton once said, hold them by the nose while the others kick them in the ass."

That brought a satisfied grunt from the Colonel. "I'd just as soon poke them in the ass with a sharp bayonet. Then gut them with a dull spoon." Colonel Mills knew personally some of the civilian casualties. Rumors of what was being cooked around the Kraken campfires was beginning to reach him. He wanted to tear into them so bad that he could taste it. Captain Vasiliev looked at the tightened jaws of the Colonel.

"Have you ever heard the stories of what out women soldiers used to do with captured Nazis? Perhaps that will help us pass the time while many more Krakens freeze to death. Here, Colonel, please join me a drink of vodka. A toast to frozen and dead Krakens. And to a few live prisoners for the women to play with."

CHAPTER 6

MALMSTROM ARMED FORCES BASE
GREAT FALLS, MONTANA

Torbin Bender was at his home in the Base housing area holding his sleeping twin sons, one in each arm. He had just feed them again some of Aleks' expressed breast milk they kept in bottles in the refrigerator. A short time in the bottle warmer and voila, instant nourishment. Almost as good as fresh from Aleks' herself. All of the time he had spent rubbing Aleks' pregnant tummy, talking to them in the womb with a calming, male voice had paid off. Now, if he talked to them in the same manner, maybe reciting a nursery rhyme from his childhood, they did not fuss. Once they had a full stomach and Dad's calming voice, and bam, out like a couple of lights. They seemed to know that when Dad was around, they were protected, and all was right with their world.

The whole concept of having sons was all still pretty new to him. About a year ago, the idea of having children was completely foreign. Now, it seemed like the most natural thing in his world, and he wondered why he had never thought of it before. He glanced at the wall clock. The witching hour approached, and Aleks was still working. Training had been suspended as the training staff was put on alert for possible deployment. All of the staff, that is, except for Abigail and Torbin. Even Ichiro was down with the Japanese air unit, getting checked out again in fighters, his original job in Japan.

Since o-dark-thirty that morning, Aleks had been with the General's Command Staff, trying to ascertain why this attack had happened so fast, so unexpectedly. And now, to determine a correct response. As head of the Intelligence Unit assigned to the General, Aleks was one of the go-to people the General would use.

Torbin was left out, marking time. He had come home when the balloon went up and their babysitter, Sue Brown, had to go home and say goodbye to her husband, Lt. Brown. But with training suspended, the General refusing to answer his telephone calls, staying at home with his sons was the most constructive thing he could do. It just that there was a gnawing in his gut that he should once again be charging to the sound of the guns. He heard a familiar vehicle engine pull up near the duplex. Aleks was home. Torbin carefully put his twin sons into their bassinets, quietly went to the front door. He slipped through it and met Aleks.

"Glad to see you home, babe." Aleks looked worn, yet she still managed to smile.

"Glad to be here, if only for a short while."

Torbin frowned as he opened the door for his wife. "You can't stay home, and get some sleep?"

Aleks sighed. "I have to go back, to help get Fanny up to speed on all the information. Then I can get some sleep. I need a shower, and to use the breast pump. This chest of mine keep filling up quickly. My metabolism must still be in overdrive."

"Do you want your back washed?"

Aleks smiled at her love. "Yes, that would be nice. As long as it is just my back you wash. I'm too tired for anything else."

"Here, you go get in the shower. I'll get you some clean underwear. The kids are sleeping soundly. I just fed them."

Aleks reached over and kissed him. "Someone up above must like me to have found you. A woman could not ask for a nicer husband."

"Hey, we're in this together. Besides. I have to do something to help the war effort, being as the General wants to keep me on base." Aleks knew his inability to go to the sounds of gunfire was grating on him. And anything that hurt him hurt her.

"Come, meet me in the shower. Bring the baby monitor with you. I'll talk to you in the shower, bring you up to speed on what's going on."

"Deal. Be there in sixty."

Aleks shucked her uniform with practiced ease. There was a fresh one hanging in her closet, as this one was getting a little ripe. Stress had a tendency to make one sweat more, despite the cold weather.

True to his word, Torbin was back in sixty seconds, baby monitor, extra towels and clean underwear for Aleks in hand. He was already naked. She looked at his body, and felt a bit of a stirring in her lower regions. But she was too pressed for time, and too tired to do much about it. At least she could read the menu.

Torbin smiled. "See something you like?"

"I see something I love. Come here." They embraced, kissed deeply, Aleks quickly feeling the response of Torbin's body. But she could not enjoy it right now, there was too much to do.

"Darling husband, could I have what you Americans call a rain check? I really want to spend time with you, alone. But duty calls."

Torbin smiled again. "Rain check duly noted. Now, hop in the shower, start washing up. Then, I'll do your back."

Ten minutes later and Torbin was giving a combination back rub and wash in the shower. Aleks moaned with appreciation. "You have always given the best back rub, my love. It helps take the tension out of my neck and shoulders."

"I give great front rubs, too. Just ask around." Normally, that smartass remark would have prompted a shot to the ribs. But Aleks was too tired. She turned around, hugged him, enjoying the feel of her body against his.

"Darling husband, you do most things well. That is why I know it is extremely frustrating that you are not allowed to go to the fighting in Kansas. But I will have to admit, I have a selfish glee that you are here safe, with me. I think you and I have earned a rest from violence and killing. They can use our skills next time, maybe when the trolls are older.

Torbin sighed. "The General won't even return my calls. I know he knows what I want to bug him about. I also know his reasoning. But that doesn't mean it makes me happy."

He moved back a bit from the hug, tilted his wife's head back so he could look down into her eyes. "I don't want to leave you and the kids. But I feel a responsibility to fight. I'm incredibly conflicted."

"I know, husband. I want to get into the mix of things also. But to be separated from you and the boys would be horrible right now. So, I do what I can here."

Just then, the baby monitor beeped a bit, signaling activity in one of the cribs. Torbin and Aleks looked at it, then at each other.

"Another duty calls, husband. How about two rain checks?"

"Took the words right out of my mouth. Come on, I'll dry you and you can go to the kids. I'll be there in a minute."

"Have I told you lately how much I love you, Torbin?"

"No need to, babe. I can see it in your eyes."

CHAPTER 7

BLOODY KANSAS
UNOCCUPIED STATES OF AMERICA

Twenty-four hours after the storm had hit, and Colonel Anton Popov was in place with the first part of his blocking force. His Siberian Russians had moved the quickest, being long used to quick movement in bad weather. The Americans were not far behind. About twenty-four hours behind this movement, there would be the full First Division coming down from the center of Nebraska, ready to hit the Krakens on the northern flank. That attack would occur after the worst of the storm was past. Otherwise, there was too much chance of blue force fratricide under horrible visibility conditions.

His Russians were digging in around the outskirts of Salina, in direct opposition to the Kraken force coming down the state and county roads that were parallel to I-70. After the overpass destruction, the Kraken Commander, apparently recognizing his forces' limited ability to maneuver, had not bothered to try moving back to the Interstate. Besides, the elevated roadway was an ice skating rink. And the wind and ice were only now beginning to let up.

Colonel Popov had a primary Infantry Force, with some twenty technicals coming down with the Americans. The local militia had provided an old Sherman Tank that some collector had kept in his backyard, its main gun replaced with an operational Russian T-34 76mm gun from WWII. Almost the same size as the original, 75mm, it fit just fine. He had a four gun Canadian battery of former ceremonial twenty-five pounders with some ammunition, as well as some Russian 82mm mortars. That was the extent of his artillery, mechanized and armor equipment. Some half dozen Russian-made Kodiak Assault Guns were slowly making their way down to his location on the back of heavy semi-truck flat beds. Due to their slow speed but heavy armor, they could be of use as mobile pillboxes, not as an armor maneuver element. The maneuver element, some U.S. and Canadian main battle tanks, would be coming with the flanking division.

It was the Colonel's mission to hold onto the nose of the attack, to keep them occupied while the full division kicked them in the ass. So, he was to be defensive in nature only. Which, recognizing his limited forces, was fine with him. About twenty-five hundred regular plus militia forces concentrated under his command in Salina was not a force to try and attack many thousands more of the enemy slowly advancing toward them. They were to set up a 'killing field', and let the Krakens come to them. The bad weather had not only frozen the attackers in place, but it had also extremely limited the U.S. forces from gaining any information from air surveillance. One hardy soul had taken up his private plane, and somehow had kept the winds and ice from crashing him. He had done one fly over of the I-70 area back some five miles from the furthest point the Kraken forces had moved from the destroyed overpasses. He had obtained a picture of people huddled around fires and vehicles, trying to get or stay warm. Colonel Popov had been correct in his suspicions. The Krakens were *not* prepared for bad weather past a few snow flurries.

He was looking over the local maps for the tenth time with Colonel Mills, the Militia Commander. He also looked at the handful of photos the small aircraft pilot had obtained.

"This pilot needs a hero's medal. How he was able to fly without the weather killing him, take pictures, and not get shot down is beyond me."

Colonel Mills grunted. "Transplanted Alaskan bush pilot. They have a reputation for being nuts, and flying in all sorts of weather."

The Russian Colonel smiled. "We are all a bit nuts to be here, trying to fight the Tschaaa, rather than just hiding, not drawing attention. But I never liked the idea of some slimy sea creature telling me what to do while eating other humans." He pointed at the map. "There is the point of the spear. When the storm stops, they will continue down this road, East Old Highway 40. They can still connect with I-135 once thru Salina. If they do that, they can decide to go north or south, or get back onto I-70 and head west. I think after the problems General Winter is causing, there may be pressure to head back south after ravaging Salina."

"Can't fault your logic there, Colonel Popov. But as spread out as the forty thousand Krakens are, I think the possibility of all of them being able to follow in some semblance of order as remote. I think we Kansans will be trying to track stragglers down for weeks."

"Unfortunately," said Colonel Popov. "You are right. Thus, we stop them here at Salina, the First Division slams into their north flank, and we try to kill as many confused Krakens as possible. Then we help you track them down. Madam President and General Reed want prisoners to interrogate, as well as parade before the cameras, along with any proof of cannibalism."

Colonel Mill's jaws tightened so much that Popov thought he was about to chip teeth. "I already have proof. Remains of humans taken from a large campfire. These fuckers are eating children, pure and simple. Trying to outsquid the Squids."

Colonel Popov produced a flask and two small cups, poured vodka in each.

"Here, my fellow Colonel. A drink to the Gods of War, beseeching them to help us wipe out these two-legged monsters passing as humans. If it is possible, they make the Nazis' and Stalin's purges look like trips to the park." They touched cups, threw the shots back.

"Ah, nothing like Russian vodka to take the edge off. Now, Colonel Mills, you were telling me about a surprise your militia has come up with for a tank or two…"

Talbot stood outside the former rock star tour bus that functioned as a command post. He looked at the overcast sky, feeling the wind. Things were finally beginning to clear up. He went back inside the bus.

"All right people. Get the armored cars, tanks and personnel characters on the horn. Start them moving slowly down this Highway

40. There is still a lot of sheet ice out here, and heavy tank treads can act like ice skate blades. So, give lots of space between vehicles for braking. Got it? Just get people moving."

As the word was passed, information on weather caused casualties and injuries began to filter in. Some one thousand personnel had signs of frostbite or hypothermia. At least a hundred were found dead, frozen. But the worst was some five thousand just flat out were not reporting in, who had disappeared. Some may have been picked off by militia members. But many seemed to have just gone completely "off the grid", never to be seen again. Talbot knew many of these were Krakens who decided that raping, plundering, and finding fresh meat and a warm place to cook it were more important than the organized invasion.

Slowly the "point of the spear" armor units began moving. Talbot had a couple of the converted bank armored cars start out first, followed by an Abrams Tank, then a couple of Bradleys. He then began spacing the other main battle tanks, Bradleys, armored and unarmored transport vehicles, and started yelling for vehicles miles back to start moving. A few vehicles slid into ditches on sheets of ice. Luckily, none were the ones with military type firepower. But then delays were caused by either pulling the vehicles out or transferring the people in them to other transports. Still, the Kraken forces slowly chugged along, entering the outskirts of Salina from the northeast on East Old Highway 40. As the weather slowly cleared, the flatness of the surrounding area could readily be seen. This part of Kansas, like much of the midwest, was definitely flat earth.

The two former armored cars, two person cab crews with six personnel in the back, were a half mile in front of the Abrams MBT. Some mist and ice in the air helped to obscure the old military weapon collector's Sherman Tank poking its nose from behind an abandoned gas station. The former Soviet 76mm tank gun fitted into its turret spoke, sending an armor piercing high explosive round through the half inch side armor. Bank armored cars had been armored to protect from small arms fire, not tank guns. The shell penetrated, the high explosive filler detonating in the cramped confines of the back. Within seconds, six dead and dying Krakens were the result, the driver sending the vehicle into the roadside ditch. The Sherman's gun spoke again, and the second armored car met the same fate as the first.

"Enemy fire, two o'clock!" The Abrams commander yelled over the intercom as he tried to locate the threat in his commander station periscopes. Due to the extreme cold, he had been running buttoned up, hatch closed, using his turret vision slits and periscopes rather than having his head outside the turret hatch. Both he and the tank gunner, using his periscope system, quickly located the Sherman, just as an AP round bounced off the front turret armor like a ping pong ball. Although the Abrams crew was not exactly the most experienced tankers around, they managed to load and fire a sabot "silver bullet" at the threat. The depleted uranium round and its pyrophoric effects completely destroyed the turret and its crew. Only the tank driver in the hull was able to escape the now aflame armored vehicle. Later, Talbot would scream about the use of such an expensive and scarce round. "Hell, a practice round probably would have penetrated that old turret. Think next time, goddamnit!"

The armored vehicles shifted themselves around, and prepared to move again. As a Bradley Fighting Vehicle moved up toward the lead Abrams, two militia men with a Bender Anti-Tank Rocket popped out of a spider hole. The assistant lit the three inch fuse with a butane barbecue lighter and jumped back out of the way, alerting the shooter with a slap on the helmet. Three seconds later, there was a loud whooshing sound with a lot of dark powder smoke as the eight inch in diameter rocket sped toward the side of the Bradley. Pappy Gun had made all but the first few rocket heads with modern explosives and a cone shaped design to make them more like HEAT rounds than just plain explosive shells. The large diameter of the warhead, though making it heavier and shorter ranged, made it more effective against modern armor. It hit the lower side of the Bradley as it passed by some hundred yards distant. The track broke, a road wheel was destroyed, and a dime-sized hole appeared in the hull side. One Kraken sitting in line with the penetration absorbed it and was killed instantly. The Bradley ground to a halt, the back hatch was thrown open and the rest of the personnel bailed out. The next Bradley in line opened up with its chain-gun cannon, as the militia men dove back down the spider hole. Luckily, it had been dug before the ground had been frozen solid, so a tunnel some ten yards long led to a small culvert near then highway. There the two militiamen, actually a man and a woman, huddled, hoping no one found the tunnel anytime soon. The chain gun collapsed the spider hole completely.

"Get some flankers out, you ignorant fucks!" Talbot screamed over the radio. "They have RPG teams out there. *Move!*"

As confusion among the lesser trained reigned, a four wheel pickup appeared out from behind a pile of rubble. Mounted in its bed was an old 105mm Recoilless, once used on anti- avalanche control at some ski resort in the Rocky Mountains. A failed weapon, replaced by the superior 106mm Recoilless, it and its brothers had done yeoman duties for years, helping the wealthy to ski safely. Now, it was being used as it was originally intended.

The HEAT round that was fired slammed into the turret front of the lead Abrams tank, which shrugged it off. Now hit twice, the crew was pissed. The driver accelerated, giving chase in a multi-ton vehicle that could still go over forty miles an hour on a flat surface. The tank commander popped out of the commander's hatch and tried to bring the 50 Caliber machine gun to bear as the gunner tried to get the 30 Caliber coaxial on target. The pickup raced down the highway, slipping and sliding, the tank behind. So intent on shooting the crap out of the pickup, no one noticed that a twenty-five yard stretch of highway was actually just a colored tarp stretched over a ten yard deep hole, a couple of feet wider than the tank. Perfectly lined up, the Abrams went straight into the hole, its main gun barrel slamming into the end wall as it sank into six feet of icy and near frozen water. Actually, it was more like slush than water in the bottom of the oversized tiger pit.

The more experienced tank commander of the group, who had been hanging back, saw the whole disaster and notified Talbot. The commander began to curse up a storm. "That's what I get for agreeing to lead some half-trained assholes."

He managed to get his second in command, Dukes, on his cellphone. "Dukes. Find those tow trucks we brought along. They're probably miles back. We need to try and pull that stupid fucker's tank out of the tiger pit. And find some spare parts to fix that track on the Bradley."

"We have limited spare parts, Boss," Dukes replied. "But the main problem is getting someone really experienced on fixing AFV tracks."

"Well, we have some heavy equipment operators, mechanics

floating around. Find them. They should be able to get that track repaired somehow."

"Will do, Boss."

Talbot then rang up the experienced tank commander, Jenson."Since you're the one with common sense, set up a three sixty perimeter around the tank in the pit. Put some infantry way out front, have them keep an eye on all the abandoned homesteads, buildings around here. And watch those damned tree lines and high brush around the lines and areas of irrigation. Next we'll be getting snipers and RPG teams hiding among them."

Talbot paused. "Kansas may be pretty flat around here, but the closer to towns and cities, the more they planted trees and brush. Tried to turn the areas into something it wasn't. That and all the abandoned storefronts and homes make for good hidey holes. Okay, get a move on."

The Kraken Commander managed to get ahold of the damaged Bradley Commander on the radio. "You stay with your vehicle, use its chain gun to help cover the perimeter until we can get you moving again."

"Sir, we have a man dead in back, and…"

"Goddamnit, this is war, you simple asshole! Get used to lots more dead bodies. Now, get the body out of there, and set up over watch from you turret. *Move!*"

Talbot put his head in his hands. Why hadn't they given him another month to prepare, maybe longer to dodge the winter weather? Why did they have to attack the USA now? Talk about a Mongolian goat rope. He knew most of these people were considered expendable, but this was ridiculous. If his position hadn't been so tenuous since losing that asshole Bender, he would have turned this assignment down, tried to do something for that wussy Director Lloyd instead. At least with him, he could usually pick his own men.

He shook his head. No rest for the wicked.

At the reconstituted National Guard Range and supporting air strip on the west side of Salina, Colonel Popov watched as some batteries of Pappy Gun's Chinese rockets were being offloaded from a twin engine C-23 Caribou and a Northrup Air Commando. He would soon have seventeen, six rocket boxed batteries of the five foot long, five inch in diameter black powder munition. They might not be very good against armor, but against these half trained foot soldiers, their psychological effect would be devastating.

The Russian Colonel smiled. The militia's ambush had gone perfectly. Now the idiot Krakens were trying to recover the Abrams Tank from the tiger pit and set up a full perimeter, rather than just leaving it and pushing ahead. Even down a tank and a Bradley, they still had more armor than anyone for hundreds of miles. They could have smashed right into Salina, stopped the Russians and their allies from digging in. Now, their near complete inexperience was showing. With the rear units catching up, they were beginning to get crowded and disorganized. This army had never fought together before.

Popov listened to his Russian Troops as they expertly offloaded the Chinese rockets and listened while some American troops gave them the quick and dirty on how to use them. True, the Russians and U.S.A. troops had not fought together yet. But his were spetsnaz and many of the Americans had combat experience during the last six years. Plus, many of the new ones had gone through Comrade Stalin's training regimen during the last couple of months. If anyone could shake out the chaff, it was him.

He shook his head at the thought. How in the hell did that old counter revolutionary bastard stay alive all these years? Well, it may be a mystery. But Popov for one was glad he had survived. He looked at the final stages of offloading, rubbed his hands together. Time to have some fun.

CHAPTER 8

General Reed looked at the most recent intelligence and surveillance reports from the Kansas front. It was just over three days since the Krakens had busted through Kansas City, Kansas and the bad weather had pretty much broken. It was still below freezing in most areas, but the ice storm was gone. So the Krakens were trying to move into Salina, Kansas. But Colonel Popov and Colonel Mills, using militia and regular army forces, had created some nasty surprises for the invaders. Now, the Krakens were stalled again, as they tried to recover an Abrams from a tiger pit and become better concentrated and organized. Night would approach early this time of year, so the time for movement this date was limited.

The reconstituted First Division was nearing the north flank of the Kraken Forces, traveling through the remains of Fort Riley, Kansas. Fort Riley had been hard hit during the Invasion, so it had basically been abandoned after many survivors fled the area due to harvester ark operations. The arks had left, leaving a desolate area behind into which people were just now returning.

However, the First Division had met a disorganized yet still armed force of Krakens in the area who had apparently left the main column. Probably they were simply looking to rape, pillage, and slaughter some fresh long pig (human) flesh to cook. It tipped off the Krakens what was in store, and resulted in a delay in the flanking movement. Still slick roads were causing problems with speed. The better trained, concentrated First Division should hit the Kraken Column out of range of their armor.

Now he had another new and puzzling problem. On his desk was fax from Commissioner Miller that a new port of entry on the Wyoming/Idaho Border had been over run in the past couple of hours by an unknown combined force of Krakens and Ferals. Cameras mounted at the POE (just north of Cokeville, Wyoming, and some fifty miles from Evanston, aka Eaterville) broadcasted a few images of at least one or two transport trucks presenting themselves for inspection just before someone shot and destroyed the cameras. All contact with the dozen Federal Law Enforcement personnel in the area was lost. Someone had hit the panic button that connected with Paul Miller's main Communications Center in Bismarck, North Dakota. Next they received panicked calls from civilians from Cokeville to Evanston that Krakens were attacking.

General Reed had gotten units of the Wyoming mounted militia, now almost a thousand strong, to start moving back to that border area. They had been en route to Colorado in case the Krakens continued westward. Now he needed someone there who knew the area, as well as had the capability of coordinating with Deseret, as this was close to the independent state's border. Any force of Feral along their border definitely made them nervous, though so far they had declined to help with the Kraken forces. The President/Prophet Smith said he was studying the situation and asked for Divine guidance. Yeah, right.

Despite his initial hard decision to *not* use Tobin Bender, General Reed had a situation that he was made for. His fame would help him with the locals, and his knowledge of the area would make it easy for him to ascertain the threat.

Sending Abigail Young and Sgt. Fuzz, war dog, would also help with the locals, as both had become celebrities thanks to the television coverage and the President's PR efforts. Plus, she might be able to convince her fellow Mormons to come to the aid of a favorite daughter. And, she just might help keep Torbin out of trouble.

As a result, Torbin and Abigail were en route to his office at that moment. He sighed. He knew he would have to sit on the Marine's head a bit, as well as placate his wife Aleks. Although she said she recognized her husband's abilities and desires to use them, deep down she wanted him to remain safe. Then, the intercom buzzed from MSgt. Johansson's desk in the outer office.

"General Reed, Major Torbin and Captain Young here to see you, Sir."

"Send them in, Master Sergeant, then shut my door and take a break."

"Sir, I could stick around…"

"Did I stutter?"

"No Sir. Sorry Sir. Going for a walk, Sir."

John Reed chuckled. MSgt. Johansson acted like an old mother hen around him, protecting her final chick. The General did not know what he would do without him. With that, Torbin and Abigail marched in, stopped in front of his desk, and snapped to parade ground salutes in unison. Straight backs, tucked chins, he swore they were peas from the same pod.

"Sir, Major Torbin and Captain Young reporting as ordered, Sir."

General Reed paused for a moment. Would that he had an army of them, but not need them, not have to expose them to the grim reaper. He snapped a salute back.

"At ease, then rest, and have a seat."

Both sat ramrod straight in the chairs. General Reed snorted. "I swear to God, you two are long lost twins. Would you just relax, loosen your spines?"

"Yes Sir, sorry Sir." The two warriors relaxed a smidgen. The General sighed. Oh well, I guess that's the best I'm going to get today. He tossed a file folder to each of them.

"Well. Major, you got your wish. You now have a mission in the field."

The two comrades in arms eagerly surveyed the files. A smile came to the Marine's face.

"So the bastards are trying to sneak in the back door, General, through Evanston."

"Seems to be so, Major. Though a lot of people who busted

through may just be opportunistic Ferals. Whatever the case, civilians are taking casualties. There are initial reports some of the miscreants are killing adults, and keeping the kids. I don't want to think why that is."

General Reed noticed that with that comment, Abigail's jaw tightened to the point where he thought she would break teeth.

"We will go, General," she spat out. "We will save the innocent, punish the wicked. You have my word before God."

"Captain, all I want is for you two—no, three, counting Sgt. Fuzz—to get in there, scout it out, rescue any civilians you find, then get out. I've got some Wyoming mounted militia en route to help, with some regular army to follow later. Commissioner Miller is putting together a SRT to head there also. He lost a bunch of people at the POE."

"He's sending people Abigail and I trained, General?'

"Of course. Only the best. And I'll have some Medevac standing by for casualties."

Torbin turned to look at Abigail as she turned to look at him.

"One hour?" asked Torbin.

"Yes Sir, one hour," answered the Avenging Angel. They both looked at the General.

"Good," said the General. "Be at the airfield in an hour. We'll insert you by chopper. Take what you may need now, as I don't know when I'll be able to resupply anybody in that area."

He gazed directly at Abigail. "Captain, I'll give you a satphone to contact your friends in Salt Lake City, to see if you can convince them to send you some help along the border. Right now, Prophet and President Smith seems to want to sit this one out."

"I will try, General. He does have a mind of his own."

"Well, if anyone can get him to change his mind, I think a daughter of Deseret will have the best shot."

The General stood up. "One other thing. You two protect each other's behinds, no hero stuff. I don't want to have to explain to a crazy Russian spy or a Japanese samurai how I managed to get their loves shot all to hell." At this statement, Torbin grinned and Abigail blushed. She still had trouble acknowledging that everyone knew that she and Ichiro were a couple.

"And Torbin, one last thing."

"Yes. General."

"Were you always such a stubborn, hard-headed pain in the ass, or did you have to work at it? Do you know how many times you called here, trying to get me to send you to Kansas?"

"I count twenty-four, Sir."

"At least, Major." General Reed stuck his hand out and Torbin took it. "Godspeed, son."

John Reed turned to Abigail. She started to salute, and the General interrupted it with a hug. "Screw military decorum, Captain. You're our daughter now, just as much as Deseret's."

Abigail controlled the lump in her throat. The General felt like her father had—warm, strong, loving. She knew now she had another one.

"Now, both of you, hit the road. Torbin, Aleks already knows, and she will meet you at home with your gear. Good luck."

Fuzz was standing by the office door as Abigail and Torbin came out. Suddenly, the General stepped out.

"Sgt. Fuzz. Your mission is to get Captain Young back in one piece. Understood?"

Years later, General Reed would swear Fuzz, War Dog, nodded his head once as if to acknowledge him, and then winked his left eye. Fuzz gave a big doggie grin and fell in next to his mistress and human, Abigail. After the three had left, General Reed stood quietly for a few minutes. Over six years ago, he never thought he would be sending out what were basically adopted sons and daughters to fight beings from another world. The universe was cruel sometimes.

"Well, Big Guy or Gal upstairs, it's in your hands now. Though I would really appreciate some help with this. Thanks. Amen.

CHAPTER 9

While Torbin and Abigail had been meeting with General Reed, John Talbot, Kraken Invasion Force Commander, was cursing up a storm. Ever since the Abrams had hit the tiger pit, things had gotten worse.

Somehow, they had found a ladder to help get the bruised and shaken (but still alive) tank crew out of the pit. The Abrams sat at the bottom of the pit, the engine compartment flooded with icy water. When it had slammed into the far wall of the pit, the 120mm gun barrel had become jammed with semi-frozen dirt and muck. Even if it were removed from the pit, it would take a long time to bring the tank back to operational status. But Talbot had located the heavy duty tow vehicles needed to pull it from the pit, once they knocked down the near end to form a ramp.

Then the sniping began.

It appeared that it might be the same sniper who had set off the charges on the overpass, or at least the same caliber of weapon. One Kraken with some military experience said it sounded like a Barrett 50 caliber. Whoever was behind it, he (or she) was deadly. The first casualty was a Kraken with engine maintenance experience who was climbing back up the ladder after examining the tank's turbine for any serious damage past the water immersion. Just as the man reached the top of the ladder and began to climb onto the side of the pit, he was blasted in half. Due to the size and velocity of the 50 Caliber round, a body hit with it was often blown into pieces. Death was instantaneous.

Talbot had again tried prophylactic fire with a machine gun, using plunging fire in the direction from which the shot seemed to come. The sniper must have been set up well out of range of the 30 Caliber as ten minutes later, as one of the tow trucks drove up to stand by the tiger pit, a round through the driver's side window redistributed the driver's upper torso and its contained blood all over the exterior of the cab. It took an hour for Talbot to get someone to clean the mess out of the truck so they could move it.

Talbot called for a Bradley to move up near the tiger pit. He had the vehicle commander fire a burst of 25mm toward the area the shot had apparently came from. Nothing. Maybe the sniper was scared away. No such luck. A SLAP depleted uranium round slammed into the barrel of the Bradley's chain gun. During World War II, both the Germans and the Russians had quickly learned that if you were fighting a tank with a lot more armor than your tank gun can handle, you shoot and wreck the tank's main armament barrel. Then they have to ram you to do any real damage until they get their gun fixed. This concept and the SLAP round worked perfectly, smashing and piercing the barrel a foot out from the turret mantle.

Talbot screamed in anger. He called for patrols to swing out wide a mile or so out from the flanks of the lager and protective circle he had set up around the tiger pit. Then he called for his limited mortars to be brought up, and had them start throwing random rounds out beyond the perimeter. The patrols soon started taking fire from forward ,ilitia skirmishers, and ran into booby traps.

The Chinese rockets began next.

An odd screaming sound, and then large black powder rockets began exploding in and around his perimeter. Many of the five inch rockets' warheads had been wrapped in nails and ball bearings thanks to strips of ubiquitous duct tape. Everyone went to ground, jumped into or behind armored vehicles. Then the barrage of some two dozen rockets stopped, and the screams of the wounded and dying began.

A more rational man would have moved on, abandoning the tank in the pit. However, Talbot was now in a rage. He screamed for and received several cattle trucks brought up and used their metal sided trailers to encircle the pit. He ordered men and women to start knocking down the rear of the tiger pit, to form a ramp in order to tow the tank up and out of the pit. Everyone around the tiger pit and up and down the invasion column were then pelted by a front of ice rain for a quarter of an hour, bringing almost everything to a halt.

This just was not Talbot's day.

CHAPTER 10

WYOMING/IDAHO BORDER
NORTH OF EVANSTON, WYOMING

At Malmstrom, Aleks had made sure all his gear was ready to go. All Torbin had to do was pick up a Designated Marksman/Sniper .308 rifle that Pappy Gun had set up for him. Built on the AR-15 design, Torbin had just sighted it in the day before. For once, the Gods of Combat were smiling on him. Aleks kissed him and gave him a big hug.

"If you get hurt, I'll kick your ass, husband."

"Perish the thought, dearest. Pass this hug to our sons, tell him their father has gone a-soldiering."

She looked at him with moist eyes. "You had goddamn better come back to me. That's an order."

He kissed her one last time. "Yes, Ma'am." He then grabbed his gear and left for the chopper pad.

Abigail had been able to leave a voicemail for Ichiro as he was on alert in a Japanese F-15. At the end of it, she'd used the "love" word, something that still made her blush. She knew that what she was about to do was far from safe, and the thought of not being able to see Ichiro again was not exactly something she wanted to consider.

At the chopper pad, both Torbin and Abigail put on personalized Ghillie suits. There was a lot of snow on the ground so the suits were a montage of white and some pine green patches to fit in with the twisted and lodgepole pines, as well as other shorter bushes of the high plains and foothills to the Rockies. In a lot of areas, because man had moved out, forests and brush were making a big comeback. As they were loading their equipment, doing a quick function check, a figure approached.

"Excuse me, my good friends," Senior Instructor Stalin called out.

Torbin laughed. "Come to stow away on the chopper with us?"

"No, Major. I have something for each if you." The granite bodied Russian walked up and handed each a fairly large bladed weapon.

"Here. A *Spetsnaz* survival knife, or machete. It's been called and used as both. Not to replace your Ka-Bar, Major. Just to supplement it."

Torbin hefted it. "Yeah, I've played with one before. Built like the proverbial brick craphouse."

Abigail took the one Stalin had handled her, and hefted it as well. She smiled. "I like this. Looks like it could chop through anything. Thank you, Comrade Stalin."

"Only the best for My Lady of Cold Steel."

Abigail looked at him, a fondness in her eyes. He had become like a crotchety uncle to her during training, always grumping at people, telling them how they screwed up. But his toughness helped to make others tough, and he was just as quick to acknowledge a job well done.

"May I give you a hug, uncle?" she asked in Russian.

A small smile formed on his lips. "Just this once, Captain. I cannot be accused of favoritism, or of being soft."

She hugged him firmly, resulting in a small grunt from him. She let him go.

"You must tell me the secret of your iron strength, Captain. You always surprise me, being so strong."

Abigail grinned. "You mean strong for a woman. Just let this be a lesson to you that looks can be deceiving, Comrade Stalin."

With this, Stalin snapped to attention and saluted the two. "Godspeed, comrades. And return safe. Breaking in two more American trainers would be rough." As usual, Stalin acted like he was the originator of everything. Torbin saluted back, grinning.

"I will be sure to make it back so as not to burden you, Senior Training Instructor Stalin. Now, it's time to go. Vaya con Dios. See you when we get back."

Some two hours later, and they were set down outside of Evanston. A former Customs and Border Protection Blackhawk helicopter inserted Torbin, Abigail and Fuzz onto the same flat field that Torbin had used for the Medevac copter months ago. The area around Evanston had just began to be repopulated last month. Eaterville still made all but the toughest locals nervous. And now this. By using the field, they did not have to fast rope down with Fuzz, though he had seen Abigail do it. How she handled a dog that actually outweighed her and fast roped down with him was a mystery. Dynamite apparently came in medium sized packages also. They were down and moving north in sixty seconds. Abigail had been issued one of Pappy Gun's 3D printer assault rifles just the other day as part of an ongoing test as to its stamina and toughness. She had sighted it in, practiced a bit with it. She would always prefer her lever action Marlin .44 Magnum rifle, but in the combat zone she was going into, she needed the added firepower of an automatic weapon.

They had been moving for about five minutes when they heard faraway shots and what sounded like screams in the direction they were traveling. Almost immediately, they heard more shots and some screams one hundred and twenty degrees from the first sounds.

"Fuck!" Torbin exclaimed in a low voice. "Of course we have to have two things at once. Well, we'll hit this one first…"

"No, Torbin we can't."

"What? We can't be in two places at once. It's called triage. We do what we can."

"There are civilians, probably children in both places, being attacked, hurt. We have to hit both."

"Yeah, like I'm going to let you go by yourself, split up. Aleks will kill me…"

"I am not alone. Sergeant Fuzz is with me. You're the one who will be alone. And with him in the lead, scouting, I can move faster."

Torbin paused for a moment, seeing the determination in her eyes. She had a point. The thought of allowing some children to suffer the depravations that Krakens would visit on them made his blood boil. Plus he was used to working, doing by himself. Push comes to shove, he could snipe at any enemy until the promised militia showed up. Fuzz was also good at protecting people in his own right.

"Okay, no time to argue. I'll head back this way, you continue on. Stay frosty, little sister. Aleks will not like it if you get hurt."

Abigail smiled. "And you the same, big brother. Don't get carried away. You may be a Marine, but you are still just one Marine."

Tobin looked at Fuzz. "You stay frosty also, Sergeant."

Fuzz looked back at Torbin as if to say, "Is there another way?"

With that, they each headed in their own direction, toward their separate near futures.

CHAPTER II

SALINA, KANSAS

Benjamin Black used his Barrett's powerful scope to survey the activity around the tiger pit. He had hunkered down under the shelter half he carried, keeping his weapon and Ghillie suit as dry as possible from the short freezing rain. With that past, he was out again, looking for targets. To say he was in a 'target rich environment' was an understatement, especially when you had a Barrett 50 Caliber. In the hands of a shooter like Sergeant Black, one could blow people apart at a mile away with little difficulty.

Sergeant Black scanned the area, then saw a clump of people standing by a tow truck in a gap between the covering cattle trucks near the edge of the pit. There was one larger Kraken talking with what appeared to be authority. Good. An Officer, NCO, or a head mofo who's in charge. Time to get back in the game. "Eenie meenie miney mo," Sgt. Black said softly to himself. "Shoot a Kraken in the… toe."

The Barrett spoke with authority, the Kraken exploding into pieces in front of the people he was talking to, the sound of the weapons report catching up to the down range effect. Spattered with pieces of now just meat and flesh, the Krakens that had been standing together opened their mouths in screams and cries, and jumped back. One female fell backward into the tiger pit.

"Nice. Time to move, Ben," the sniper said to himself. They had tried to hit him with chain gun and mortar fire so far, but had missed. He was not going to give them an easy shot.

NORTH OF EVANSTON, WYOMING

The woman huddled with her two children, as the two Krakens finished stripping the bodies of the other man and woman with whom she had been fleeing.

"Mommy, they hurt Daddy," her little girl cried.

"Shut that little shit up, bitch," growled the smaller of the two Kraken males. "Can't stand my food whining." That set off a spate of laughter between the two hardcore Krakens, their faces covered by an entire tattoo of a Kraken octopus, marking them as the truest of True Believers.

"Yeah, maybe we can cut off a small snack before we leave here." The larger Kraken opined.

The woman cast around with wild eyes for a weapon, some help. She would fight to the death for her two children. And death was near.

"Yeah, they do look like sweet meat. Especially that little gir..." The Kraken never finished his thought as a brown colored blur slammed into him, steel jaws on his throat stopping further speech. Another part of the nearby foliage came to life as the second Kraken had his throat slashed out by a *Spetsnaz* survival machete. Blood spurted as the poor excuse for a human being toppled over. Both Squid-lovers died choking on their own blood.

Abigail spat on the body of the one she had killed. "The wages of sin are death." She turned to the woman and her two children, pulled back her head and face covering.

"Are you hurt?"

"Not yet. Not physically," the mother answered.

The little boy, the older of the two by a year but still only six years of age, looked at Fuzz in wide-eyed amazement.

"Look, Mommy. It's Sergeant Fuzz, from the television."

Recognition suddenly flooded his mother's face. "My God. That means under all that stuff, you're Abigail Young. You really do exist!"

Abigail gave a little smile. "Guilty as charged. But we need to get moving. There are bound to be others…" Just as she said the words, someone whistled in the distance, as if looking for an answering sound.

"Quick, we have to get moving." Abigail retrieved the assault rifle from one of the dead Krakens. "Do you know how to use this?"

"Yes, Ma'am."

"Good. Start moving that way…"

Another whistle sounded, from a different angle.

"Mommy, I'm scared," the five year old girl said.

Abigail removed her Ghillie head and face covering completely, handing it to her.

"Here. This will help you hide, and give you good luck. But you can't be afraid, can't cry. Okay?"

The little girl nodded, and took the offered head covering.

"Okay. I'm going to stay here, to try to intercept, and draw the two groups to me. You follow Sergeant Fuzz out. There are some militia members headed this way, hopefully you'll run into them. Got it?"

"Got it," the mother said.

"Fuzz," Abigail said in Romanian. "Lead, scout, protect." She pointed to what looked like an animal trail to follow.

Fuzz began to whine, as if to say, "Not without you."

"Fuzz, now. Lead, scout, protect." With a final small whine, he began to go up the trail.

"Go, Ma'am. Now."

The mother looked at Abigail as she moved. "You be careful."

"That's my middle name."

As the three humans followed Fuzz, Abigail moved a few yards toward the location of the first whistle, then slipped back into the brush and shadows. She figured out a quick bug out route from her location, took a deep calming breath, and then crouched a bit. The wait began.

Torbin, on his own, had not made as good as time as Abigail. However, he traveled a shorter distance when he heard voices. One of them sounded as if the person was in pain. Torbin slipped in behind the two people he saw in a small clearing in the brush and trees. Two militia members by their uniforms, a woman and a wounded man. He carefully approached them, removed his Ghillie face and head covering.

"Friendly, don't shoot," Torbin said in a calm, low voice. The woman, a Sergeant, jerked around, grabbing for her rifle.

"Whoa. Sergeant. Major Torbin Bender. Supposed to meet you militia, get civilians out."

The man lying injured on the ground spoke. "Helen, it's okay. The Hero of Key West."

The female Sergeant lowered her weapon, still visibly upset. She started rapidly spilling her story. "Sergeant Troy, Sir. Everything is fucked. We had a group of civvies, got ambushed. Only Sergeant Puller and I made it out. They killed the rest of my team, grabbed the civvies. We're fucked. Can't do anything, need to fix up Chaz here, need to get the civvies away from…" Her chin began to quiver so much she could no longer talk. Torbin walked up to her, put his face a few inches from hers.

"Sergeant. Are you with me?"

"S-S-Sir?"

"I said, are you with me? 'Cause I need you. Now. You can breakdown later. It is not an option right now. Do you understand, Sergeant?" He locked her eyes with his, his voice low, firm, unwavering.

Sergeant Troy suddenly stopped quivering. She straightened up, looked back.

"Yes Sir. Sorry Sir."

"Good. Cover my butt while I examine the good Sergeant Puller here."

The man called Chaz coughed out "That's Gunny. Not some ex-army puke. Semper Fi."

Torbin smiled. "Semper Fi right back. Let me look at you."

He did not look good. He was leaking a lot of red stuff that his body needed. Torbin grabbed his first aid bandages, plugged the leaks as best he could. Then he heard the scream. Loud, chilling, several hundred yards away in the trees.

Chaz coughed, spoke. "Fucking forget me. Get the women and kids. That's who they have. Just get me my rifle."

Torbin looked into the eyes of the seriously wounded man. He saw what was once called old corp steel. Seeing that, he made a quick decision. He reached over, retrieved the man's rifle, did a function check.

"Locked and loaded, fresh magazine. Ready to rock."

The former Marine grinned through the pain. "This is my rifle…"

"There are many like it, but this one is mine." Torbin answered back.

"I'll cover the rear, Major. No problem."

"I learned a long time ago not to argue with a Gunny Sergeant when he has his mind made up. Want some morphine?"

"No Sir. Need to stay sharp."

Torbin stood up. "Don't go anywhere. We'll be back."

He looked at Sergeant Troy. "Show me how you got here. We need to sneak back to where you last saw all the civilians"

"Yes Sir. This way." She began to move out, back the way they had come.

"Major," Gunny Chaz Puller rasped out.

"Yes, Gunny?"

"Did you really kill that Squid with a Ka-Bar?"

Torbin chuckled. "After a fashion."

"That must have been a sight to see."

"I'll tell you the whole story when I get back."

"Do that. I'll be waiting."

"Semper Fi."

"Semper Fi, Major."

With that, Torbin and Helen Troy moved out.

The screaming and loud voices continued as they approached. Torbin and Sgt. Troy moved as fast as they could and still maintain some silence, even though the loud screams seem to drown out most other sounds. Finally, after travelling a bit less than half a mile, they came within sight of the clearing where a bunch of people could be seen moving around. Torbin motioned the Sergeant to stay back as he snuck closer, his Ghillie suit providing extra camouflage.

He moved to a clump of lodgepole and twisted pine trees, with some other low brush around. He was some twenty-five yards from the clearing, which could have been either natural or man-made. From his vantage point, he watched some thirty women and children huddled together off to one side, while some Krakens took turns beating and abusing two women. A couple of other Krakens seemed to be trying to build a bonfire on the partially snow-covered ground. Toward the opposite side of the clearing, four partially stripped figures were hung upside down from a tree. By the remaining pieces of clothing still on the bodies, they were dead militia members. It appeared that they were being drained of their blood. Torbin moved back to where he had left Sergeant Troy.

In a very low whisper, Torbin told Sergeant the situation.

"The Krakens look like they are preparing a meal of Long Pig. Follow me up to the point I was just at, stay low. I'll swing off to the southeast corner. I will hit them from there. Do not fire unless I go down. I will try to send the civilians your way. Got it?"

"Yes. Sir. I won't let you down."

"I know you won't. Stay frosty."

With that, he moved out with Sergeant Troy in file behind. They arrived at his original surveillance point and Torbin split off. Years of training and experience made this all automatic to him, with no hesitation in his actions.

From the southeast corner of the clearing, he counted some dozen Krakens or Ferals milling around. A couple of them stayed close to the huddled civilians, covering them with their assault rifles as they jeered at them. For the first time Torbin noticed a female Kraken with the hard-corps face tattoo trying to aid what appeared to be a badly wounded comrade.

"Bonin!" She yelled out with authority. "See if those dead assholes have any first aid kits on them. I need some bandages to stop this bleeding on Melissa here."

"Hey, I need to go take a dump in the woods," the male called Bonin answered. "I'll do it after that."

"You'll do it *now*! I'm in command. You'll do it or be singing soprano."

Bonin glared at the apparent Kraken female commander. He stomped over to the four hung bodies, dug around in the pile of equipment and uniform pieces, and came up with a couple of packets. He then stomped over to the commander.

"Here, Evans. Now can I take a shit?"

The commander named Evans grabbed the bandages from him. "Go now. Maybe you won't be so full of it after."

Kraken Bonin walked away grumbling. He walked by the prisoners, reached over and grabbed a scarf off the neck of one of the children. "Need some ass-wipe you little bitch."

He continued on, past the two women the Krakens had beat the crap out of, both lying on the snow with swollen faces. He walked into the brush, found a log, pulled his pants down, grumbled. He was halfway through his business when a silenced .32 pistol bullet hit him behind his right ear. Bonin toppled back into the last pile of crap he would ever produce.

Torbin kept the 3D printer polymer pistol with the fitted silencer in his left hand, his .308 rifle pistol grip in his right as he moved up past the body. Someone started calling Bonin's name, apparently noticed he had been gone awhile. A female with only minor tattooing began to walk toward where Bonin had entered the brush.

"Hey, Bonin. Come here. We need help getting the fire going…" A .32 full metal jacketed bullet entered the woman's right eye, penetrating into her brain. She collapsed where she stood.

Torbin let the pistol loose, a bungee cord lanyard keeping it from disappearing into the brush. He brought his rifle up to his shoulder, proceeding forward in his "Groucho" close quarter battle crouch.

"I have become Shiva, death, the destroyer of worlds," Torbin mumbled to himself as he began to exit the shadows. His first round in the rifle was a subsonic velocity one, the attached sound suppressor on the barrel reducing the noise to a light snapping. The bullet blew the top of the head off of the nearest Kraken guarding the civilians, the body falling forward onto the seated prisoners. The next rounds were all supersonic, so even with the suppressor, there would be the supersonic crack as the bullet broke the sound barrier. But it did not matter, as the screaming began.

Torbin had flicked on his laser sight, a green dot appearing wherever he pointed his rifle. Each time it illuminated on a human head, he pulled the trigger. Thousands of mission hours over the years had led to an automatic muscle memory few others possessed. He already had a pattern of targets figured out based on near and far, left and right parameters. He had three threats down, nine to go as he had counted an even dozen scum, minus the wounded one. The remaining prisoner guard on the left of him received a bullet between her eyes. Four Krakens who were bunched around the attempt to start a bonfire all went down before the death of any one Kraken registered. One male who had been standing by the hung bodies took a bullet to his frontal lobe as he reached for his rifle. Two Krakens who turned to run at the same time received a bullet each at the base of the skull.

The last effective, the female commander called Evans, managed to get a pistol shot off as Torbin took the right side of her face off. The bullet hit his body armor low on his left side, leaving him a bruise but failing to penetrate. The wounded Kraken female, Melissa, held her shaking hands up in surrender. Torbin continued up until his rifle barrel was inches from her face. The Kraken closed her eyes and began to whimper.

"Move, you die. Got it?"

Eyes still closed, the woman nodded yes.

"Gettin' slow. One got a shot into me." Torbin said to himself. Ten rounds, ten seconds, all with his rifle. He turned to the huddled civilians.

"You have thirty seconds to move thataway," he pointed toward where Sergeant Troy waited.

"A militia member awaits to get you out of here. I am Major Bender, U.S.A. Not a bigfoot like this Ghillie suit makes me look like. Got it? *Move*." The spell was broken. They moved.

One of the two badly beaten women, right eye swollen shut, refused help, and got up on her own. She picked up a Kraken rifle. She walked over to the wounded female, Melissa, whose eyes went wide. The battered woman smashed the butt of the weapon into the

Kraken's face as she tried to mouth the word "No". Then again. Then again. Then again. The former captive dropped the bloody, cracked stock rifle, picked up the pistol the Kraken called Evans had dropped. She limped over and grabbed a different rifle, fell into the rear of the departing women and children.

She fixed Torbin with her one good eye.

"We good?" She managed to croak out.

"We're fine," answered Torbin.

He waited until she was disappearing into the woods before he swung around, took a quick couple of pictures with his cell phone of the four bodies hanging and a wide photo of the Kraken dead. He would send someone back to cut the militia personnel down. He did not have the time right now. He knew they would understand. Then, he took up rear security for the women and children. A few minutes later, as they escaped through the trees and brush, a mummer began.

"Ten Krakens, ten seconds." It became a mantra. Then someone pointed out he must have taken the other two out prior to stepping from the shadows. But "Ten Krakens, ten seconds" had a nice ring to it, and who was counting, really? Another legend was born.

Abigail had been waiting for about five minutes in the shadows when she heard a loud scream come from the direction where Torbin was headed. The extreme volume of it pointed to a high level of pain and abuse, pointed as well to just the right environmental conditions in the area around Evanston to enhance the travel of sound. She thought that Torbin was headed to a point about two miles distant from her, at least as the crow flies. Abigail knew that Torbin would not allow the abuse and violence that caused the scream to continue.

She heard the short whistles, apparent attempts to make contact with the two she and Fuzz had killed. Neither had a radio on them, so for whatever reason they had departed a main group without long range communication. Abigail thought she heard some voices about two hundred yards away, possibly parallel to her position. But nobody seemed to be moving toward the small trail on which the woman and her two children they had been captured. She stood still for a minute more, heard nothing, saw nothing coming her way. Time to move, catch up with Fuzz and the three civilians. She stepped out from the shadows, started in the direction Fuzz and the three civilians had traveled.

One moment she was walking, the next it felt like she had grabbed ahold of a live electrical wire. She fell onto her back, stunned, paralyzed. For the first few moments, even her lungs would not work. Then she was able to draw a breath, and her hearing returned. But she could not move her limbs. She heard odd clicking noises, interspaced with clucking similar to a chickens. She tried to turn her head but could only move her eyes. Anger and frustration began to course through her body, which led to some tingling in her extremities. She concentrated on that by force of will, mentally praying to God to give her strength. Then she saw them.

She had seen photos of grays before, even a couple blurry films, but never in the proverbial flesh. And now there were two, standing over her, conversing in that clicking and clicking language. They had stunned her with some type of weapon, probably their version of a taser. In that moment Abigail knew they wanted her alive for some reason. They bent over and began to fondle her Ghillie suit, taking a minute before they realized it was just some odd human covering. Upon that realization, one of them produced a scalpel-looking instrument which it used to slice open her suit. With what seemed to be practiced ease, they moved her limbs and body enough to remove the Ghillie. They ignored her rifle that lay just inches from her grasp. But it just as soon be miles away for all the ability she had to grasp it. One gray then produced what Abigail would later say looked like Mr. Spock's tricorder device, which seemed to have the same purpose. All this time, her body became less numb, as she silently screamed at it to wake up, damnit.

Possibly the device they were showing reflected the changes in her body as the two grays quickly stood up, conversing more rapidly. Then she got her right arm and hand to move. Seeing this, rapid talk, and one gray reached into a satchel it was carrying and removed an object that looked dangerously like a gun. Abigail tried to scream in protest and anger, but produced a croaking sound, nothing more.

A large brown shape slammed into the gray with the supposed pistol, propelling it into its fellow. Then everyone crashed to the ground.

Fuzz. He had come to her rescue.

Sergeant Fuzz snarled, growled and bayed a type of war cry as he took the measure of the aliens with his teeth and jaws. Eerie screams and shrieks came from the grays as they tried to fight back. As Abigail fought to move her body, she heard a yelp from Fuzz, then a huge growl, followed by a snapping and crunching sound. An alien cry was cut off in mid shriek.

Then it was like a dam broke or a switch had been turned on, for suddenly she could move again. She rolled over, grabbed her rifle and was on her feet before she knew it. She heard a crunching sound and looked to see Fuzz literally crush the somewhat bulbous head of a gray, bluish tinted blood squirting from it.

"Fuzz. Out." The War Dog dropped the dead alien. Looked at her and wagged his tail. He started to come to her, then seemed to stumble. Abigail quickly knelt down, grabbing him.

"Fuzz, are you hurt, big fella?" She automatically started a physical pat down of her canine partner. Fuzz looked at her, gave a doggie smile, licked her face, and then started to fall over.

Abigail quickly laid him down, began pulling his Kevlar vest off of him. Her hands came back soaked with blood.

"Hold still, fella. You're just cut somewhere. I'll bandage you up, carry you out, my turn to save you…"

Fuzz extended the paw of friendship, laid it on her arm, with his claws gently grasping her. He managed to steal a slurp kiss on her face, gave a half of a doggie laugh as if to say "I love you." Then, with one last sigh, his eyes went dull. He was gone.

"No!" Abigail cried out. "Don't go. I need you. I want you. You're my big fella."

But Fuzz had moved on, someday to meet her on the other side, over the rainbow bridge.

Abigail cradled him as her heart and soul shattered. She held him, sobbing, began to wail. It felt like her insides were being ripped out with grief and pain, and in a way they were. For he had been her family. Now he was gone. Abigail had no idea how long she cradled Fuzz, sobbing. She did not hear the screams and gunfire from Torbin's location. She neither heard, nor reacted to anything until a rough voice called out.

"Hey, fucker. Hands up. Show me your hands, damnit."

Abigail stopped rocking Fuzz, still crying.

"Hey Joe. We've got some bitch with a dog here."

"That's no bitch," his comrade told him. "That's the Deseret piece of ass, the one on TV. And that's her dog. Shit." The Kraken jumped back as he noticed for the first time the dead grays.

"They're deader than dog shit. They must have come out to get her. Nobody ever would tell us why they were here."

"Well," the first one began. "They must have wanted her alive to get close enough to get killed by her and her mutt. So, I bet you she's worth something to them."

"Yeah," said Joe. "Maybe worth a lot to them. If not, then we at least have a nice piece of ass."

The one called Joe stepped up, grabbed her fatigue collar. "Get up, bitch. Or we'll…"

As Abigail turned her head, Joe's last sight was the face of Death, personified.

Torbin caught up with tail end of the column of civilians just as he heard a loud, almost unearthly scream from the direction where Abigail had gone. Then gunshots, then more screams. He would not have believed a human voice could scream like that, that loud, if he hadn't heard the screams of the two women being abused with his group of civilians as he had approached. But, this scream, soon followed by others after a short pause, sounded like someone's soul was being ripped from their body. It was not Abigail's voice, he was sure. But it came from her area.

Then more shots. Muffled cries, screams. Then silence.

He did not like this. Something in him told him to run, get Abigail. But he had a responsibility to the thirty women and children he had in tow. And it was just him and Sergeant Troy. When they had gotten to Chaz, he had passed away. Another Marine to guard heaven's gates, just like the hymn said. He grabbed his dog tags, and took a quick position check so he could find this place, then moved on. The Gunny would get a decent Marine Corps burial if he had to do it himself.

The woman with the one good eye and the Kraken rifle was doing rear security when he caught up. She nodded at him, wincing a bit when she did.

"Want a little bit of morphine, take the edge off?"

She nodded again, whispering "Yes" from her swollen lips. Torbin pulled out a miniature syringe from his first aid kit, and administered it. The women sighed.

"Thanks."

"You're welcome. Here's a small plastic baby bottle of water. You can squirt it into the back of your mouth, past you lips. I always carry a couple just in case."

The woman looked at him. "Connie."

"Good to meet you. Hang in there, I need to get up front, to talk to Sergeant Troy."

Torbin beat feet up to the front of the group, found Sgt. Troy speaking low into her radio phone. She turned toward Torbin when she saw them coming.

"There's a mounted team nearby. They made contact with Fuzz the War Dog and three civilians. One man is going back to check on Captain Young."

Torbin thought about trying to get Abigail on the radio after hearing that, but figured the Wyoming Mounted Militia would soon be there. And just talking on the radio does nothing but cause a distraction. He would wait.

"Thanks, Sergeant. I'll head back, watch the rear."

"Major."

"Yes?"

"Thanks. Just thanks. I was losing it. You took out twelve enemy soldiers by yourself."

Torbin spat. "Those weren't soldiers. They were scum who got the drop on you. It happens."

"Well, thanks anyways, Major."

"Just doing my job. See you in a few."

As Torbin made his way back to the rear, a mother and her child came up to Sergeant Troy.

"He's for real. Isn't he?" The woman asked.

"Yes, he is," answered Sergeant Troy. "And thank God he is."

Jacob Dark Wolf, cousin to the Mounted Militia Member of the same name, saw the women and two children first as they hurried through the bush. Then he saw the big assed dog, and recognized him. Sergeant Fuzz, the War Dog. Even though Jacob's family name was Dark Wolf, he has been known since he could crawl as Talks With Dogs. As a baby, he was always crawling off whenever he saw a dog, trying to get to it. On more than one occasion a nursing female had accepted him as one of her own, which caused some consternation on the part of his mother and grandmother. As he became older, dogs naturally came to him. And woe to anyone caught abusing a dog when he was around. No matter how big the person was, he or she soon found that there was a Tasmanian Devil in their midst. As he grew, people knew not to hurt any dogs, ever. Today he was tall, slender without the bulk and size of his cousin. His body was more a runner's physique.

Jacob had wanted to train to be a vet. Then the Squids came. He swung his leg over and slid down off his horse, calmly greeting Fuzz.

"Hello, Sergeant Fuzz. You're even bigger than I realized."

Fuzz came cautiously up to him, sniffed his extended hand, gave it a quick lick, He wagged his tail twice, gave a doggie grin, a woof, then was off back the way he had come.

"Where is he going?" Jacob asked.

"Back to Captain Young. She was going to stop some Krakens who were following us. She and Fuzz killed two already."

"How far back is she?"

"One, two miles. Hard to say. I was concentrating on moving here."

In a flash, Jacob made a decision.

"Corporal."

"Yes Sergeant?"

"I'm heading down to help the good Captain until more of us arrive."

To the woman, he asked, "You can ride, right?"

"Yes Sir. Kids too."

Within moments Jacob had both children and their mother on his horse.

"What's your name, Ma'am?"

"Susanne."

"Well. Susanne, just follow the good Corporal here. We have some more militia moving in behind us, so you should be able to hook up. Corporal."

"Yes, Sergeant."

"Hit up the other Squads. See who's around. I'm going after Captain Young and Sergeant Fuzz. Hit me on my cell phone if you need me." He turned to Susanne.

"You'll be okay."

"Bring them back. Bring back Sergeant Fuzz and the Captain. We owe them."

"Will do." And then Jacob Dark Wolf was gone down the trail where Fuzz had disappeared.

He made good time in a jogging lope, much like his four-legged namesakes did when following prey. It was said that only humans could outlast wolves in this type of long distance running, although wolves had the edge in short bursts of speed. He did not want to rush in too fast, not knowing what he was getting himself into so no sprints, burst of speed. He had been moving for several ten minutes or so when he heard the gut wrenching scream. Then the shots. Then more screams, shots, wails. Then silence.

Jacob Dark Wolf flicked the safety off his assault rifle, then slid off of the trail he had been traveling on. He took a slight detour, found an area where the trees and brush were thinner, then headed parallel to the actual trail. He was close, he could sense it. Finally, through an opening in the brush and trees, he saw a figure, kneeling, rocking back and forth. At first, he thought the person wore a new reddish brown form of camouflage, a bit out of sync with the local flora and fauna. As he moved closer, he saw the figure was actually covered in blood, from head to toe. It was Abigail Young. She held Sergeant Fuzz in her lap and arms, rocking, sobbing.

Jacob slowly walked up to her. In a soft low voice, he called out.

"Captain Young. Sergeant Dark Wolf ... "

Something that was no longer in a human state glared and growled at him, her blonde hair soaked in blood. Too much blood to be Fuzz's. He slowly backed off. She stopped growling, went back to holding and rocking her dead friend. Jacob got on his cellphone, obtained a signal. He quickly texted "Dustoff Medevac *now*. Captain Young, Sergeant Fuzz down. Need help ASAP." Then he put in the coordinates he could get off of his GPS feature, as well the approximate distance from Evanston. He had red smoke he could pop when they got close. He then circled around Abigail, checking for possible threats. What he found he never forgot.

The grays were surprise enough. But the bodies... He crossed himself, being a Christian. As he pulled a small digital camera he always carried from his ditty bag, he began to recite the Psalm 23.

"The Lord is my Shepherd. I shall not want; he maketh me lie down in green pastures. He leadeth me besides still waters…"

"Yea, though I walk through the Valley of the Shadow of Death, I shall feel no evil, for thou art with me…"

Though Christian, Jacob also recited a couple of short Cheyenne chants to ward off Evil Spirits. Death had come to live in this place. It would take years for this area to be with life again.

Jacob counted twelve bodies besides the grays. These did not include two more he found about twenty five yards away, which apparently were the ones that had tried to abuse Susanne and her children. Those two had died quickly, simply, their throats ripped out, slashed. The other twelve humans…Jacob shivered. He had never seen the type and level of destruction done on human bodies. How could one person do this? He shivered again. The Wyoming Mounted Militiaman did a wider circle around where Abigail Young stayed with her K-9 friend. A radio on of the dead Krakens crackled for a moment. He heard someone approaching from the approximate direction that the other dead had been coming from. Two voices, not exactly quiet or subdued. Jacob did not what to use his rifle, as he did not have any sound suppressor system on it. So he removed his fighting tomahawk he had stuck in his ditty bag, his fighting Bowie with the knuckled hand guard from his belt. Then, he stepped in the shadows, waited.

The two men, Krakens, walked up, talking about finding the missing squad. Then they came upon the bodies farthest from Abigail.

"What the fuck!" The larger of the two hard corps Krakens, face tattoo and all, exclaimed.

"Look at these bodies. It looks like they ran into a meat grinder."

"I don't like this, Bud," the smaller one said. "Let's call for backup." He began to reach for his radio. Jacob stepped out from the shadows behind them. He swung the tomahawk in his left hand into the throat of the larger Kraken, slashing the smaller Kraken with his Bowie, the neck severed and spurting blood. They were dead before they realized it.

Jacob said a small prayer for forgiveness, then wiped his weapons on the dead Kraken to clean the blood from them. He went back to check on Abigail. She was in the same location, cradling Fuzz. The scene tore at his guts, knew what it was like to lose a beloved and loyal dog. To Jacob Dark Wolf, dogs were better than most people, were honest, innocent. They would die for you, just as Sergeant Fuzz had done for Abigail. Which is why he knew it hurt her so much. She would just as soon have it be the other way, in which she died for Sergeant Fuzz. He watched her in silence, listened for any more approaching Krakens. Then he heard the chopper.

Jacob moved closer to where the first two bodies were, into a small clearing. He popped the red smoke, then texted on his cell phone to Security Control that the chopper was in sight, watch for the smoke. The Squids had never tried to hack into their communication systems, and the Krakens demonstrated no proclivity for such action, so he did not worry about it at this late date. Besides, they needed to get the Captain out of here.

He watched as two figures fast roped in, then the helicopter circled away. No need get shot at by staying and hovering. The two Pararescue troops were down in a flash and Jacob stepped from the shadows.

"She. Bear." Simple default challenge words for the day to prevent accidents.

The nearest of the two Paras was a bear of a man, with subdued Chief Master Sergeant's stripes on his fatigues. Well over six feet with a handlebar mustache, he had used some camo stick to cover the light gray in his hair.

"Chief Leroy Thompson," he said in a low tone." You Sergeant Dark Wolf?"

"Yes Chief."

"Good. This is Staff Sergeant Sean Mason." This second man was of good size, but nowhere near the size of the Chief. He had dark hair, would later say he was from the black Irish.

"Please come with me. I have a unique situation here." They followed Jacob the some twenty-five yards through the brush, then saw Abigail.

"My God. What happened?" Chief Thompson was not easily surprised. But *this.*

"She and Sergeant Fuzz killed some Krakens. Rescued a woman and her two children. Captain Young apparently sent Fuzz to lead out the civilians to us, which he did. He then took off, back here. Captain Young had apparently stayed back to intercept some approaching Krakens, and draw them off the scent."

Jacob took a breath let it out. "As near as I can tell, she was hit by two grays. What the hell they were doing out here, God only knows. But it looked like Fuzz saved her. Then, I think the grays killed Fuzz in the struggle, or some of the next ten Krakens did. I don't know for sure. All I know is there is a charnel house over there in there bush and trees." Jacob pointed out the area.

"Only Captain Young and Fuzz are around."

"Her condition?" asked Sergeant Mason.

"Some type of major psychic disconnect. She snarled and growled at me when I approached. It's like she is a K-9 protecting her pup. Like she took on a War Dog's personality."

They were all quiet for a few moments. Then the Chief spoke.

"Well, the chopper comes back in ten, unless I wave it off. So, I need all the extra morphine you two have. We'll try to sedate her, a little at a time, get her controlled to be put in the rescue basket."

"Sergeant Fuzz, he goes also," Jacob interjected.

"Sergeant Dark Wolf. He's dead."

"He is a soldier. No one gets left behind. Or I'll carry him out."

The Chief fixed him with a cold stare. "You'd do that, wouldn't you?"

"Yes, Chief. I would."

The Chief looked at Abigail, who had been ignoring their low-toned conversation, still holding onto Fuzz.

"Well, I guess she won't let go of him anyways. We'll try to take them on the same basket. The cable will hold several hundred pounds in a pinch. I'll have them drop a spare rope just in case."

He looked at Jacob. "You look like you weigh the least. You go up first with them. Been in a chopper before?"

"Yes, Chief."

"Okay. Let's get this ball rolling. Morphine out."

The three men slowly approached Abigail, Jacob doing the talking.

"Captain Young, it's Dark Wolf again. The Sergeants and I here are going to help you and Fuzz, Medivac you out of here. We just need to…" Jacob lightly put his hand on her arm.

All hell broke loose.

Later the three NCO's would testify that it was like a whirling dervish, Tasmanian Devil and demon all wrapped into one. She began to scream, kick, punch, bite, scratch, and do other things the human body should not have been able to do. Sergeant Mason was thrown yards away, Jacob held on despite having the wind knocked out of him with a kick to the stomach, and the Chief tried to use his many pounds of extra weight to hold Abigail down, She literally stood up with the two men hanging onto her, started to pry their hands off .

Sean Mason threw himself on her, began pumping morphine via injectors into her. Abigail sunk her teeth into his forearm.

"Goddamnit!" he cursed. "We're trying to help."

The Chief grabbed her hair, tried to pull her loose from Sean. She let go, then head butted the Chief in his nose, breaking it. But this was not the first time that had happened, so the Chief hung on. Jacob, some of his wind back, tried to a punch to the gut to knock the wind out of her. It was like hitting a sheet of iron. Suddenly, Abigail grabbed Jacob by the throat with her left hand, lifted him off the ground as if he were a doll. Sean slammed another morphine injector into her,

"Much more and it will kill her." Sean cried out.

"Do it!" The Chief yelled. "She's killing *us!*"

Abigail began to wobble a bit. The Chief took this slight imbalance to trip and push her to the ground. For his efforts, Abigail broke his left pinky finger.

Then the three men pig piled on top of her, trying to hold her down. Sean Mason readied another injector, but was afraid it would kill her. Finally, Abigail began to go limp, groaning and whining. Then, she was down for the count. As Mason monitored her vitals, the Chief reset his nose, then taped his left little finger to its brother.

"I have not had a fight like that since… ever."

Jacob looked at Abigail. "She is affected by… something else. In the Old Ways it would be said she had been touched by a spirit of some sort. Her mind, her soul is… elsewhere."

"Well. She is breathing steady, thank God," Sean Mason interjected.

Then they heard the approaching chopper.

"All right, Gentlemen. I'm calling them to drop the basket as soon as they get here. I'm popping smoke so they drop it right here. I don't want to move her any more than we have to. Dark Wolf, get ready to go up with the basket."

"Yes, Chief."

"All right, here goes." The Chief popped the smoke flare.

The chopper was a former Customs and Border Protection Blackhawk that had been found hidden at a small remote field. Now it was set up for combat zone dust off. No sooner had it began to hoover that the basket stretcher was dropped on a quick line. With practiced ease, the Chief and Mason quickly steadied the basket on the ground, undid the straps. The Chief and Jacob picked up Abigail, laid her in the basket, and adjusted the straps. Jacob then lifted up Sgt. Fuzz, and they strapped the dog on top of his mistress. They knew she should would not mind.

"Alright, Sergeant. You're up."

They hooked a safety line onto Jacob as he balanced himself on the basket. The Chief signaled and the Crew Chief activated the hoist, and up the basket went, Jacob balancing as best he could.

Within moments, the Crew Chief was steading and swinging the basket in by the movable hoist arm. Jacob unhooked his safety strap from the basket, hooked it to a d-ring in the chopper, then helped unhook the basket from the hoist and secure it.The Crew Chief quickly swung the hoist back out with body straps and sent the line back down. Jacob removed Sergeant Fuzz's body from the basket, laid him long ways on some seats and strapped him in. He then turned back to Abigail. He checked her breathing. It seemed normal for someone that had just been jacked up by morphine. He turned toward the open access door and watched the Crew Chief steady the line as he activated the hoist.

Hell chose that moment to reappear.

Abigail's eyes popped open and she let out a howl.

The chopper pilot, a Captain Blue yelled out, "What the hell is going on back there?"

Abigail began to strain at the straps as Jacob moved toward her.

"Captain Young. It's okay. You're being Medevaced…"

Straps began to break as Abigail howled, twisted and kicked. This was not supposed to be possible, but it was happening. Jacob tried to hold her down, received a nasty hit to the testicles as the Crew Chief tried not to be thrown out the door. Despite the Blackhawk's size, Abigail's thrashing while the hoist was swung out and lifted two bodies caused the chopper to yaw, vibrate.

"Goddamnit. Secure her or shoot her. I will not lose my chopper to a crazy bitch!"

"No!" A new voice screamed out. Lt. Shannon Bell, co-pilot, unhooked and scrambled back to the passenger seats. The Crew Chief was hanging half out of the bird while trying get the hoist up, the Chief and Mason dangling helplessly just below the side door. Jacob was trying to get up, holding his painful family jewels. Shannon saw Abigail's wild eyes, and her heart sank, her stomach knotted. It appeared as if no one was home behind those eyes. Abigail screamed *"Fuzz!"* and Shannon knew what she had to do.

She grabbed Abigail's face in her hands, screaming at the same time. *"Abigail!* Look at me. It's Shannon." Abigail paused in her thrashing about for a moment and Shannon pointed over to Fuzz's strapped down body.

"There is Fuzz. See? We have him too. Okay?"

Shannon finally saw a bit of recognition in Abigail's eyes.

"Shannon… Fuzz hurt."

"I know. We're going to the hospital. But you have to calm down. Okay?"

Abigail looked at her. "Shannon… Fuzz hurt bad." Then she closed her eyes and fell back into the basket. She was out again. Shannon tried not to sob, but failed.

"It's okay, Lieutenant." It was Jacob, up again. "I'll strap her in again, sit with her."

She looked at him. "Okay. She's my sister." With that she made her way back to her co-pilot's seat.

"Lieutenant, you ever leave your seat again like that and I'll… "

"You'll fucking shoot me, right Captain Blue?" she spat at the pilot.

"Fine. Do your worst. That's my sister back there. And she's dying inside."

The Captain had a puzzled look. "Your sister? How… "

"You wouldn't understand. You can court martial me when we get back. I don't care."

Other than the minimum communication to help fly the aircraft, Shannon Bell was silent all the way back to Malmstrom.

The Crew Chief finally got Chief Thompson and Sgt. Mason off the hoist, into the chopper.

"That was not a pleasant experience," said Mason.

"That was very screwed up," added the Chief. "Thanks, Crew Chief, for not dropping us on our heads."

"De nada. Is that Captain Young, the Avenging Angel?"

"The one and only."

The Crew Chief looked at her and Fuzz.

"You know, she doesn't look ten feet tall, like she does on the boob tube. But goddamn she is strong."

Chief Thompson snorted. "You don't know the half of it. Sergeant Mason, get another morphine injector ready. Next time she may break loose. It would be very embarrassing if we lost her over the side after all this shit."

News often travels fast in military units. Especially bad news and rumors. Torbin heard through Sergeant Troy that Abigail and Fuzz were being medevaced, with both near death. Then the word that Fuzz was dead.

Shit, shit, *shit!*" Torbin exclaimed. "I should not have let her go alone. I should have made her stay with me."

Sgt. Troy looked at him, as a Mounted Corporal with a woman and two children on horseback approached where they had stopped the column of civilians.

"Major, beggin' your pardon, but then those three civilians on horseback there would be dead. Or I and some others of this group here would be dead. You did what you had to do, just like she did."

He looked at Sgt. Troy. "Fuzz saved my wife, my then unborn sons. Now they will never have the chance to grow up with him around. And I may lose Abigail. She's my little sister."

Sgt. Troy paused, then spoke again. "Sgt. Fuzz died like the trooper he was. He died for his partner. Just like Gunny Puller did. And a lot more will die before this is all over. You made me do my job, not cut and run."

"You wouldn't have done that, Sergeant."

"Yes, I might have. See, you saved me from not just dying today. You saved me from dying many times over, by being a coward." Sgt. Troy snapped to attention, saluted Torbin.

"Thank you, Major Bender. It is an honor to serve with you."

And with that, Torbin realized how easy he had it in some ways. He was always ready to go, almost on a form if automatic pilot, no time for real fear. This young lady was not a professional soldier. She was a volunteer militia member, had been through hell in a very short time. She was right. It could have been worst had he stayed with Abigail. Or her with him. Sgt. Troy may be dead now, or dying slowly as a coward. One thing led to another. Torbin stood straight, returned the salute.

"The honor is all mine, Sergeant. The honor is all mine to have served with you and the rest." He looked around at the group of civilians who were all looking at Torbin. They depended on him to get them to safety.

"Okay. Sergeant Troy. Let's get this show on the road. Where did you say the other mounted militia was coming from?"

CHAPTER 13

Pain is inevitable. Suffering is optional.

-Kathleen Casey, Canadian Parliament

SALINA, KANSAS

The news and rumors traveled fast to the two thousand plus Free Russians and U.S.A. troops in and around Salina, Kansas. As the sun began to set on the short winter day, word came back that a Medevac had been sent for Abigail Young and Fuzz. Next, that the Avenging Angel was dead. Then that both were dead. Finally came the truth. That Abigail was badly injured, and Fuzz was dead. It was like the Americans had been kicked in the gut. One problem with heroes is that when they die after being larger than life, it often hits people hard. Then, those who had invested the most in their heroes are hit the hardest, as heroes (like in the movies) are supposed to be indestructible.

A line of defensive positions had been dug and constructed in preparation for the coming attack. Everyone knew that the Krakens would try to break through somewhere around Salina, to hit the roads and Interstate going north or south. The theory was that trying to head west would take too long, the weather and the forces around Salina had delayed the Krakens to such an extent as to cause the enemy to loop back around toward Kansas City. In preparation for an attack, militia members had scrounged some plywood, poster board and sawhorses to set up some crude dining tables, with whatever could pass as a chair set around them. Some field kitchen equipment as well as scrounged bbq grills provided at least one more hot meal for everyone.

Sometime in the early morning, they would have to hold the Krakens by their noses so that the mechanized division coming down through the former Fort Riley area could hit them, turn west and start rolling up and kicking their asses. The only problem with this scenario were the reports of the First Division being less than quick or aggressive in closing with the main column. Now it looked like Combined Force Kansas, the name someone had created, would have to hold on the enemy nose a lot longer than planned. The negative information about Abigail and Fuzz added stress to this new problem, and had definitely caused a pall to settle over the area.

One average-sized female Staff Sergeant walked over to one of the makeshift tables and set down her tray of hot food. She bowed her head as if in prayer. Then, in one quick motion, she straightened up, her right hand pulling a long non-standard issue two-edged blade weapon. Some would say it looked like an Arkansas Toothpick Bowie. Whatever the official category, in a flash she had slammed the ten and a half inch dagger knife into and through the quarter inch plywood makeshift table. Items on the table jumped from the impact, as did the surprised troops sitting around the table. "Cold. Steel." The Sergeant said it firmly, a bit loud but not a yell.

About seven yards away another female soldier suddenly turned and began walking toward the sound. "Cold steel," was all she said.

Then another female, and another, and another approached the area near the table. They all pulled a small almost cross looking object suspended on a chain next to their dog tags, rubbing it between thumb and forefinger. Soon a dozen female soldiers, from Privates to Staff Sergeants formed a low tone talking group a few yards from the eating table, which now had an extra hole in it. Next from some twenty five yards away, a voice sang out as if it were performing an aria during an operatic production in a theater.

"Cold... steel...," the song rang out. The dozen women walked toward the origin of the beautiful sound. At the mess table, the men and women still there murmured in confusion.

"What the hell was that all about?" A large farm boy private asked his chow mate.

"I don't know," answered his much smaller comrade. "But dibs on her food. It's getting cold."

Sergeants Dagan McDowell and Lupe Peña were checking over their respective Technicals and their two person crews when they heard the aria.

"That was right pretty, don't you think?" asked Dagan.

"That it was," answered Lupe. "Let's go check it out." The two NCO's told their people to make sure that the their 'Technicals', a pair of four-wheeled pickup trucks, with a little armor plate and Russian 14.5 heavy machine guns mounted in the truck beds, were ready to go. The Sergeants said they would be back in a few. The two women had been attending some Mechanized Infantry Training at Fort Bliss, El Paso, Texas when the first rock hit. They were both from El Paso, had enlisted in the army together under the Buddy Program, and had been friends for years. Covering each other's behinds had enabled them to make it to Malmstrom and offer their services.

Now, they were each in charge of a "Technical", a poor man's fighting vehicle, each with two other people on board. Their respective vehicles were part of a twenty vehicle force that made up the closest thing to a mechanized maneuver unit in Salina, Kansas. When the Kraken attacked, they were expected to go Road Warrior on their asses, harassing the flanks, trying to piss off the Bradleys and Abrams. Their heavy machine gun armament was overmatched by the Kraken's armor, unless they could hit a Bradley in one spot with a crap load of rounds. Then they might knock off a track, damage the chain gun, and maybe even penetrate the hull if the Gods of War were smiling on them. Not likely, but they were both crazy enough to try. No family other than each other, what else was there to do?

They were the study of opposites. McDowell was a tall, slender, almost lanky woman but still with some curves. Peña was shorter, stockier, about 5'5", and more curves up top and down below. She was a dark faced Mexican-American, McDowell a lighter skinned Irish-Scottish mix. Both had black hair they helped each other braid to keep it under a helmet. They walked up together to check out what was going on. As they approached the group of some two dozen women in a small clearing behind some bushes, they were met with suspicious stares from some. The grouped women seemed to know each other already, or at least know "of" each other.

"Evening, ladies," greeted McDowell. She was met with stares.

"Can I help you?" the Staff Sergeant with the "table knife" asked.

"I don't know. Can you?" Peña asked back.

"Are you being a smartass?" one of the other women sneered.

"Mira, puta, no deme problemas…," Peña began to square off at the sneering woman.

"Whoa, whoa, let's backup, start over," Dagan jumped in before things went from bad to worse.

"My friend here can be a bit hot-blooded at times. What say I just ask a simple question?"

"Which is?" the Staff Sergeant asked.

"Well, Sergeants McDowell and Peña here, Mobile Technical Unit. We were just wondering if this is a private chingadera, or can anyone join in?"

The Staff Sergeant sized up the two newcomers. She was the closest thing to a ranking member they had in their definitely non-standard group. She knew that others, both known and unknown, noticed something happening, and were beginning to approach. They would soon start to draw the attention of command staff, something she did not want to happen. In a second, she made her decision.

"Staff Sergeant Kira Samson, here with First Platoon, Regular Infantry." She stuck her hand out and Dagan took it.

"To answer your question, you may not want to join after I tell you what we are planning. But you have to keep your mouths shut when I do."

Dagan smiled. "My lips are sealed. Yours too, right, Lupe?"

"You got it."

"You heard the news about Captain Young, Sergeant Fuzz?"

"I heard rumors they were being Medevaced out."

"No rumors. Fact. War Dog Fuzz is dead. Captain Young is bad off."

Both of the newcomers' faces went dark. "Fucking Krakens,"

Lupe blurted.

"So this, chingadera, as you put it, has to do with payback. You in?"

"How?" Dagan asked. "I thought we were supposed to wait until they attacked us, just hold on while the First Division kicks tail."

Sergeant Samson looked at Dagan with steely eyes.

"That may not happen. And this is for Fuzz and Abigail."

The rest of the group murmured assent.

Dagan looked at Lupe. "Shall we dance?"

"Hell, why not. I'm getting tired of other people having all the fun."

"You two ladies have blades—Cold Steel?"

With that question, both Dagan and Lupe grinned. "Do we have steel? Lupe, want to go get them?"

"Hell, yeah." She took off, jogging to their Technicals.

Dagan looked at the rest of the group and saw they all had the same unique dagger in a sheath on their belt.

"I'm a Texas Girl, but those all look like Arkansas Toothpicks, pig stickers."

"Close enough. Double-edged ten and a half to eleven inch blades."

"So, you must have a name for your little set to."

One of the younger women stepped forward, barely eighteen.

"Sisters of Steel." She had the chain suspended object that looked like a cross from a distance but was actually a stylized blade. Dagan looked at it.

"That's really nice. So, how does one obtain such a fine piece of jewelry?"

"Only sisters are given them," the young troop answered.

Dagan smiled. "So, you have an application form?" This caused a few laughs among the assembled soldiers.

"I think that tonight will be considered an interview and an audition," Sergeant Samson answered.

About then, Lupe arrived with two sheathed weapons.

"This is mine, " Dagan said with a grin. "An old artilleryman's sword, nineteen inch two edged blade, circa 1832. Used by a great-, great-, great-granddad during the War of 1848, when my ancestors killed Lupe's ancestors."

"Yeah," said Lupe. "We were taking Texas back when the Squids showed up."

Lupe pulled a much longer machete out of her sheath. "Used by my grandfather in the fields."

"You two used those for something other than cutting brush?" asked Sergeant Samson.

"Well," answered Lupe Peña. "We ran short of ammunition on our way up to Malmstrom. Had to cut a few 'gentlemen' who tried to take liberties with our bodies. So yeah, the blades, they've been christened."

Sergeant Samson watched Lupe as she spoke, figured she wasn't bullshitting her.

"Okay, Sergeants. Say your goodbyes, meet us over by that old abandoned farmhouse across that field over there. Short meeting, we head out."

"How do you plan to get past our and the Kraken sentries?" asked the Mexican-American.

"We have an understanding militiaman on our side, and most of the Krakens on their side are fatigued, half-frozen and poorly trained. Plus, we know one foxhole where the two Squid lovers are smoking dope. We can smell it."

Dagan chuckled. "Definitely my kind of party."

A half hour later, after making sure their crews were standing by, Dagan and Lupe met a growing group of women in the remains of a barn. There looked to be just at a hundred female soldiers, pretty evenly divided between current Sisters of Steel and newcomers looking for some payback. Abigail Young and Fuzz were on their lips. They formed a circle around Sergeant Samson, who spoke in low tones.

"Follow us. A couple of experienced Sisters will take out the two pickets we have identified. Then, a single file, seven yards apart we cross. No one does anything until you hear Marianne with the Voice sing her aria, unless you're about to get shot. We need the maximum infiltration before the Krakens realize what's going on. Then we hit, hit hard. Thirty minutes after the first alarm, you'd better be crossing back. Got it?" Murmurs of ascent, heads nodding affirmative.

A short whistle of warning was made.

"Shit. Someone is snooping."

A man's voice was heard, and as many women as possible slid into the shadows of the barn's interior. Sergeant Samson started toward the main door but Dagan beat her to it.

"Why Lieutenant Barton. I thought I recognized your voice." Dagan's West Texan drawl took on honey tones aimed at convincing any young man that he was the center of attention.

"Sergeant McDowell. What are you and all those women doing here?" The Lieutenant was a nineteen year old butterbar, fresh out of training, still trying to get a handle on his position and authority. He had come by and inspected the Technicals earlier in the day. Dagan had flirted with him then, the attention of an "older woman" leaving him a bit flushed and flattered. Dagan had learned a long time ago that her slightly sultry voice and her West Texan drawl soothed the most agitated young man, like honey did to a sore throat. Dagan noticed behind him a stern Russian female, with Senior Sergeant Stripes. She had most likely been sent with the young officer to insure some feminine wiles did not dissuade him from his duties. Dagan saluted the Lieutenant, then nodded to the Russian.

"Senior Sergeant. I have not had the pleasure of meeting you before."

"Never mind that, Sergeant," Barton interrupted. "Why are so many women here? Where are their posts?"

"Well, Sir, actually there are not that many people here. Maybe a couple of dozen." She hoped Sergeant Samson, in the shadows behind the door, took the hint and hid the rest, placing the number she mentioned in the open.

Dagan made a serious look on her face. "We are having a short prayer service for Captain Young and Sergeant Fuzz. You heard what happened, Sir, didn't you?"

Lt. Barton's demeanor softened a bit. Every young military man knew Abigail Young. Hell, half of them probably fantasized about her at night. And Fuzz was a double blow, well respected.

"Yes, I heard. She's en route to Malmstrom Military Hospital. They can do wonders there. Sergeant Fuzz…" He paused.

"Yes Sir. He's gone."

The Young Lieutenant straightened up, afraid to show much attention for a K-9. But every man who had a dog as a boy had a soft spot for Sergeant Fuzz. He was a Man's War Dog, a perfect symbol of masculinity. The fact he had given his life for a beautiful woman made him even more special.

"Well, carry on Sergeant. Just don't be too long. We don't want to be out of position if the damn Krakens actually get organized, and try to attack tonight."

"Yes Sir. Of course, Sir. You could stay, Sir, and say a few words with us…"

He cleared his throat. "No, that's okay. I'll go back and tell them you are having a short prayer service for Captain Young. I think the Command Staff plan on having a short one later tonight. No one wants to lose her. Well, carry on."

With that, Dagan saluted, and Barton returned it. As he turned to leave, the Russian Senior Sergeant spoke for the first time.

"If you don't mind, Sir. I would like to stay and say a short prayer for Our Lady of Cold Steel, as Comrade Stalin named her." The entire Russian community knew about Abigail, thanks in large part to Stalin. He had sung her praises to all after she had bested him, letting everyone know that she was 'his' lady, like a daughter, not to be trifled with.

"Of course, Senior Sergeant. I'll see you later." He turned and left.

Now Dagan met the steely eyed gaze of the Russian. Older, probably in her late thirties, maybe forty, she was an attractive blonde woman. A large scar that ran all the way across her forehead added a natural looking permanent frown to her countenance, detracting from her natural attractiveness.

"I didn't catch your name, Sergeant," Dagan said.

"I did not give it." The Senior Sergeant spoke English with an accent, pointing to a long service within the borders of Russia.

"Well, Senior Sergeant, if you would care to…"

"You know, the little theater you just played only worked because Lieutenant Barton is a randy young man."

Uh oh. Now Dagan was afraid things were about to spin out of control.

"Well, Senior Sergeant. Be that as it may…"

Then the Russian began to laugh long and hard. Dagan stared at her as Staff Sergeant Samson came out from the shadows.

"What is so damned funny, Senior Sergeant?" Samson blurted out.

The Russian started to control herself. "Marina Raskova at your service. I laugh because you Americans seem to think you invented and perfected, how you say, bullshitting as an art. Well, nobody can beat what we Russians had to say and do under the Soviet Socialist Republic."

Marina cocked a thumb in the direction where Barton was headed. "He will now tell his superiors that everything is as it should be." She fixed Sergeant Samson with a hard stare.

"Well, is it? Or are you about to, how you say, fuck the cat?"

Samson chuckled. "I think you mean screw the pooch. And no, we do not plan on doing such a thing. But before I go on, do you have access to some cold steel?"

"Of course. I am another product of Senior Training Instructor Stalin."

"Want to get some payback? It will not be officially authorized—you may get into some substantial trouble up the chain."

Marina Raskova smiled. "I think I can risk that. How is it you Americans say? Payback is a bitch?"

"Yes, and we have a whole company of bitches."

CHAPTER 14

Torbin Bender had made contact with a larger force of Wyoming Mounted Militia as darkness fell, which was good. Trying to travel or bed down with a large amount of civilian women and children with hostiles floating around, plus having maybe a half a dozen shooters to protect them, was not his idea of a fun time. Not to mention the dropping temperatures at night.

James Dark Wolf, Mounted Militia Commander, was the unit leader. Torbin smiled when he saw the familiar face. He walked up as Dark Wolf, upon seeing him, easily slide his huge frame off his horse.

"Well. Major Torbin, I see you're where the action is." He stuck his large right hand out and Torbin took it.

"Glad to see you here. I was feeling a might exposed with this many civilians to protect."

"I need to check on Captain Young."

James Dark Wolf's face clouded a bit. "Major, my cousin, Jacob Dark Wolf is on the Medevac chopper with her. He helped extract her."

"He is? So how is she? Is there a way for me to hook up with the chopper? I really need to check…" Torbin stopped. He saw it in the

Commander's eyes.

"That bad."

"I am sorry, Major. They had to subdue her. She took Sergeant Fuzz's death…hard. And she had to kill some other Krakens. They need to get to the hospital, and do not have time to pick up passengers." Torbin stood silent. He still felt responsible, even though intellectually he knew he was not. Finally, he spoke.

"After making sure we have the civilians rounded up in the area, do you think you can find me a vehicle?"

"For the man who returned Standing Bull's remains to us, we will move heaven and earth to find you one, He Who Kills With Knife."

Torbin had forgotten the name that the Cheyenne War Leader had given him.

"If you do that, I will always be in your debt."

"Come, Major. My scouts are quite good at finding people, even Krakens who don't want to be found. We should be able to get you on the road tomorrow morning."

"Thank you. Sounds kind of simple for such a favor, but thank you."

Dark Wolf smiled. "We do things because it is the right thing to do. Your thanks is payment enough. Now, while my people scout, you must tell me about how you killed that Squid with your Ka-Bar. And, what is this ten Krakens in ten seconds the civilians are talking about?"

CHAPTER 15

SALINA, KANSAS

The male and female Krakens were hunkered down in their supposed perimeter security fox hole, smoking a joint. Cold, damp, with cold food in their stomachs, the marijuana helped make it all passable for a few moments.

"Hey, Luanne. I might have enough product for another join…" He never finished the statement. A short sword blade from out of the darkness penetrated his throat, just as a figure slid in behind Luann and slit her throat from ear to ear.

Sergeant Samson was about to sneak up with one other to take the sentry post out when Dagan had stepped in.

"You get killed, wounded, right out of the gate, and who runs the show? It's all your doing, the Sisters look to you for command."

Kira Samson frowned, then swore quietly. "Yeah, you're right. You're just too smart, Texas."

"Just smartass, Staff Sergeant. Lupe and I can take them out, get you an infiltration route."

"You're not even officially sisters yet…"

Lupe snorted. "So what is this, a sorority? Consider us pledging."

Kira Samson laughed. "Oh all right. But if you get yourself killed, don't come crying to me. The sisters will be too busy looking for a different route out to be sad about you two."

"Don't worry, Sergeant. Like we said, we've done this before." And so Lupe and Dagan took out the sentries.

Now Dagan used her penlight to shine two quick flashes of light, signaling the women warriors to start their move. Crouching as low to the ground as possible, seven yards apart, about every five to ten seconds an infiltrator came by the former Kraken sentry post. Dagan and Lupe had donned the caps of the two dead Krakens and slung their rifles, ready to act the part of two Kraken sentries. So far, so good. Two left, then two right. The blade armed personnel alternated in directions, pairs to join up once they picked their targets, which were in rich supply. Large groups of personnel were bunched around campfires that were rapidly turning into bonfires. Kraken Commander Talbot had yelled about light security until many told him that being half frozen would do nobody any good. The militia and regular forces already knew exactly where they were, their layout, at least based on the sniping that had been going on. Besides, as it was pointed out, the Krakens outnumbered them three to one and had armor. Only people with a death wish would attack with those odds against them.

Lupe and Dagan kept count, and were at sixty when Dagan saw a figure approaching. It was not one of theirs, and it was walking straight toward their foxhole.

Dagan signaled to Lupe to stop the infiltration as she stood up, made a beeline toward the figure, the Kraken cap firmly on her head.

"Sergeant, am I glad to see you," Dagan called out. "My partner went to take a piss and flat out disappeared. I think he may have deserted."

"Goddamnit, keep it down. Where did you say you partner went…"

Dagan had closed the distance before the man could finish his comment and thrust her short sword blade straight through the man's throat. The Church of Kraken member croaked, dropped his rifle, toppled over with his life's blood spurting out. Then he lay still. Dagan grabbed his weapon and two grenades she saw on his equipment belt and scrambled back to the foxhole.

"They had better hurry up. Somebody is gonna come looking for that guy."

The women warriors sped up, still trying to spread out, stay low. Luckily, all the Krakens farther in were either huddled around the fires or in vehicles due to the freezing temperatures. Other than a few like the now dead Sergeant, there was little interior movement.

A little over ten minutes since the first infiltration, a strong, operatic voice suddenly rang out from the darkness. Outside his command post vehicle, Talbot heard the melodic voice somewhere in the night.

"What is that?" He thought he heard something about steel in the last part.

Then hell came to the Kraken camp.

People leaving latrines, on the edge of fires, smoking cigarettes in the dark were grabbed, throats slit, bayoneted, clubbed then stabbed. Those non-Sisters with bayonet rifles had been required to remove their magazines to force them to use stealth and blades first. The whole idea of this attack was not to degenerate into a firefight if at all possible, at least not at first. Cold Steel has a special terror all its own, and the Sisters of Steel wanted to make the most of it. But nothing is ever foolproof. Within seconds screaming began as some did not die quietly. Next, shots sounded as the Krakens began to wildly respond to shadows in the dark.

A loud piercing cry reverberated around the Kraken positions. *"Cold steel, sisters! Cold steel."* Primal screams, rebel yells, and voices of rage bounced off each other as the situation dissolved in to madness, with the Krakens on the receiving end. General panic took hold as the infiltrators were everywhere. Krakens began to fire wildly, were soon in gun battles with their own people. A Bradley opened up with a chain gun, wildly firing at nothing the vehicle commander thought was something. A transport pickup truck was hit and blossomed into flame. Krakens in panicked flight slammed their lights out vehicle into the side of an Abrams, the front passenger smashed through the windshield.

Kraken Commander Talbot screamed ineffectually over the radio and communications net, trying to gain control. He watched helplessly as an Abrams backed over a man and a woman at speed, turning them into bloody mashed pulp under its tracks. Then everybody seemed to figure out where the rear was, and the mass exodus began. In the days before general use of firearms, fleeing armies were ridden down by calvary, chased down by faster runners. Thus, whole clumps of bodies showed the deadly results of wounds to the back as the attackers caught up with the stumbling, bumping, tripping, and falling panicked personnel.

History repeated itself, many being shot in the back by their own comrades as every unknown figure became an enemy.

What is called a General Rout in military parlance was in full bloom.

A Major Smythe went jogging into Colonel Anton Popov's tent.

"Sir, something is going on with the Krakens. It sounds as if they're in major combat with someone."

The Colonel frowned, and grabbed his field phone.

"Colonel Mills? Popov here. Are any of you people making contact with the enemy?" He listened to the reply, then answered.

"Colonel, you have got to be fucking with me... Are you sure? Please give me a minute, I'll be right back."

Colonel Popov looked at the field phone, began to swear and curse in Russian. Colonel Popov was quite good at such activity, as he had many years of experience in the Russian Military. In fact, some of his personnel said he had made an art out of it. Finally he stopped. Then, he grinned, began to chuckle. Then to laugh. Then to guffaw. Finally, tears in his eyes, he managed to control himself.

"Colonel Mills? Yes. Well, can you get your militia forces ready for a general attack in an hour? Yes, one hour at the latest. See, I am going to do something you call taking sour lemons and making lemonade out of them. Apparently some bitches from hell just gave the Kraken some lemons. Now, we will pulp them into lemonade."

He hung up the field phone and looked at Major Smythe.

Major, you must remember this day, for we are about to make history, or die trying. But such a glorious death it will be."

The Colonel jumped up, yanking his pistol from its holster. "For Mother Russia. For America. For the human race. We go!"

Staff Sergeant Kira Samson wiped her blade on a dead enemy, panting. This was her third and she was covered with sticky blood. As she regained her breath, her combat "spider" sense went off and she swung around in time to catch a flying tackle in her midriff. The large

Kraken man had no weapon other than rage. He trapped her knife hand and grabbed her throat with the other. He screamed unintelligible rantings as he tried to kill the smaller woman. The Kraken's head exploded, blood misting as it sprouted from his opened skull. He flopped down on top of Kira, his weight pinning her to the ground. She started to huff and push, then called out.

"Would you mind helping get this heavy asshole off of me?"

Senior Sergeant Marina Raskova grabbed the dead Kraken's collar with her free hand, her other hand holding a Spetsnaz combat shovel with a very sharp blade. The two women pulled off the man, and Kira climbed to her feet a bit wobbly. She looked at Marina.

"Thanks. Just… thanks."

The Russian flashed a large grin, the scar on her forehead scrunching her skin in an odd fashion. "Come, Comrade. We make history. For Mother Russia."

"For Abigail!" Kira screamed. "For Fuzz. You fucks die tonight!"

Dagan and Lupe had counted one hundred and one women soldiers infiltrating, including themselves. Lupe glanced at her watch. It was coming up on thirty minutes. Sisters of Steel and their supporters should start heading back through the entry point. It had been like having a ringside seat on the First Day in Hell for Lupe. Screams, tracers, blood, explosions and figures running willy-nilly. Then every vehicle and person started heading directly to the rear, fast. She thought she saw some crazy women run screaming after them.

Lupe heard the distinct sound of artillery firing in the distance.

"Shit. Incoming!" she screamed.

Twenty-five-pounder HE shells began falling well to the rear of the Kraken positions. A couple of light vehicles went up in flames, while some panicked Krakens began running back the way they had just come. Blades flashed and the Krakens realized their mistakes too late. The artillery barrage told the female infiltrators it was time to leave. With a quickened pace they headed back to the entry point. Lupe and Dagan counted as they began to stream back through, heading into the darkness. They came through with various amounts of blood on their bodies and uniforms, some with torn clothes. Then the count was down to ninety-one.

"Missing ten," Lupe called out.

"Yeah. Damn," Dagan answered.

At that moment, through the darkness and smoke, they saw some more figures approaching. The two women crouched in their foxholes, weapons ready in case the figures were not Friendlies. A large figure appeared, carrying something on its shoulders. As it neared, Lupe and Dagan saw a very large woman carrying two other figures across her shoulders.

"Corporal Jefferson with two," the voice rang out. "Don't shoot."

Dagan saw it was one of the largest black women she had ever seen. And the name sounded familiar. Corporal Jefferson had a wounded woman over each shoulder. Behind her was a woman with a belt tourniquet on her left arm, which she was holding with her right.

"Four down, six to go," said Lupe.

Then, another clump of humanity. Four Sisters of Steel used a makeshift hammock stretcher made out of their fatigue jackets to carry a fifth, who was in very bad shape. Behind her, carrying a plasma bottle connected to the wounded woman in one hand, and a pistol in the other, was EMT and Combat Medic Ashley Anderson, late of the Malmstrom Hospital. As the women passed through with the wounded, Dagan and Lupe covered their rear. Out of the dark came half a dozen Krakens, trying to catch the fleeing assassins. The two Texans opened up with their captured assault rifles. First one, then two of the approaching Krakens went down. The others tried to find some cover as they returned fire.

Their magazines empty, Lupe and Dagan dropped them, each grabbing the hand grenades that Dagan had recovered. Pins pulled, Dagan threw hers over hand in the traditional manner. Lupe had been a pitcher on a fast pitch softball team. With a quick under arm windmill fastball pitch, Lupe launched her grenade. It hit the face of the nearest Krakens, smashing into the man's left eye, then being deflected upwards. The grenade exploded in the air as Dagan's exploded on the ground. One Kraken went down for the last time with a sliced jugular, the other three peppered with shrapnel in their extremities. The two Texans took off running into the dark, just as more artillery rounds began to fall. They caught up with the wounded, and saw Staff Sergeant Samson. She met the two Tail End Charlies as they approached.

"All accounted for?" She asked.

"Yes, by God and Texas," Dagan responded. "One hundred and one in, one hundred and one out. Though we have four pretty badly wounded."

"Yes," Lupe interjected. "The Gal Upstairs must like us."

Kira grinned. "Now comes the hard part. Trying not to be court martialed and shot."

"You two better get back to your Technicals. I bet you they are about to move out."

The Staff Sergeant stuck out her hand.

"Screw that!" Lupe exclaimed. "Group Hug" Kira, Dagan and Lupe hugged, smearing sweat, tears and blood on each other. The clinched for a few moments then parted. As the Texans made a beeline to their Technicals, Kira called out.

"Stay safe, Sisters of Steel. I need you back."

"Roger that," two voices replied as one.

CHAPTER 16

General Reed was fit to be tied. He had Brigadier General Ted Wood on the secure line. Supposedly advancing with the First Division and its armor, General Wood was making every excuse in the book *not* to move faster.

"Sir, you don't understand. We keep running into groups of Krakens. I'm afraid they have anti-tank rockets. I don't want to lose any of our limited AFV's…"

General Reed exploded. "Goddamnit, you expect to lose something in combat. That's why it's called war! What are you doing, saving everything to pass on to your kids?"

"General, I…"

"You will move at sunrise, assault anything that moves. If you don't, I'll send someone down there who will. Now *move!*" He slammed down the phone. How in the hell did such a supposedly experienced military officer lose all of his guts? He seemed more worried about losing a tank than losing the battle. Just then, the secure line rang again.

"Reed. Yes, Colonel Popov… You what? They what? Fuck!" The

General almost broke the phone by crushing it in his hand. Then he took a deep breath.

"Okay Colonel. Do your best—you're there, I'm not. Good luck, I hope to hear from you soon." General John Reed hung up the secured line. He sat for a few moments. First the word on Abigail and Fuzz. Now this. Apparently the action that Colonel Popov had just told him about, a bunch of crazy women going medieval on the enemy, completely unauthorized, no notifications, and may have had a direct connection with Abigail and Fuzz. A dead War Dog Hero and a near-dead Female Hero Symbol, both of them together seemed to have had a galvanizing effect. Colonel Popov had seized the bull by the horns, and was preparing to attack a now disorganized, panicked Kraken Force. He would attack an armored force head on, with limited anti-tank capability. Damn. The Russian had balls.

Now if he could just get that wussy Wood to grow a pair.

The General looked at his watch. Time to check the ETA of the Medevac chopper carrying Abigail and Fuzz. Then think of a way to deal with some hundred female soldiers who disobeyed orders, took on the Krakens alone and somehow survived. Why couldn't he have a nice, easy, simple day for once?

CHAPTER 17

Kraken Commander Talbot had yelled at the Abrams and Bradleys to keep moving when the artillery shells began falling. He did not want the U.S.A. personnel to be able to get a good fix on his limited armor, and start hitting the thinner tops of the AFVs. The major problem he had was that almost all of his infantry was rapidly advancing to the rear. In other words, it was turning into a rout. How in the hell some screaming women did all of this he couldn't guess.

He and a few of his most solid supervisors managed to round up several hundred fleeing armed personnel and get them moving toward the Abrams and Bradleys. He then got his one big gun crew on the line. "Get that five inch in action, *now*." A minute later, he was satisfied when he heard the old museum piece speak. See how those assholes in Salina like five inch shells landing among them. As he thought this, a battery of Chinese rockets hit, the black powder adding to the din.

As the Kraken armored forces began to move closer to the pit containing the stuck Abrams, the regular and militia forces advanced. In the lead were all twenty Technicals, with a half a dozen pickups with militia and Spetsnaz troops following behind. In the back of some twelve of the Technicals, in addition to the Technical Crew, was a Russian with a RPG trying to hang on. In the following pickups were additional RPG teams as well as two Militia Bender Teams. The theory was, if you threw enough anti-tank rockets at it, even an Abrams can be stopped. The problem would be the trade off in casualties.

Lupe Peña's ride was not carrying an RPG. Rather, her passenger was a certain crazy Russian Colonel who was yelling at the top of his lungs in Russian. To hell with "leading from the rear", Colonel Popov was up front, getting a first-hand view of the enemy vehicles, and loving every second of it. Colonel Mills was in one of the pickups jammed with militia. Damned if he would let a Russian out Patton him. Dagan McDowell had somehow found herself with Senior Sergeant Marina Roskova jammed in the back of her vehicle with the Gunner. Marina was doing her best not to get in the way with her RPG, but the 14.5mm heavy machine gun took up a chunk of space.

The Technicals were in a loose "V" formation, lights out, and picking up speed. The drivers all had night vision goggles on to cut through the dark and the smoke. Just then the single five inch shell fired by the Krakens landed, the explosion knocking one of the Technicals in the rear over onto its roll-bar. It did not carry a RPG, so the force's anti tank capability remained at full strength. Now they could see the enemy, coming to a halt near the pit of the stuck Abrams.

"Swing there Sergeant. There!" Marina yelled and pointed to a Bradley off to her left.

"Roger that. Corporal, target twenty degrees left," she yelled at the driver, Corporal Hammond, a former NASCAR Racer. The Technical was soon roaring out from the "V", aimed at passing with in twenty yards of the Bradley. The enemy vehicle finally noticed the approaching vehicles, tried to track them with its chain gun. Dagan's Gunner began to fire at the vision devices on the Bradley, trying to spoil its aim.

Marina leaned out of the back of the Technical, and Dagan grabbed her equipment belt to keep her from falling. The Russian screamed the Russian equivalent of "eat shit and die" as the RPG round swooshed toward its target. The HEAT round hit right at the base of the chain gun barrel, exploding just as the Bradley's cannon fired. The 25mm cannon round exploded in the barrel along with the HEAT round. Part of the blast was directed back through the opening breach of the weapon, filling the turret with flame and bits of shell. Then Dagan and her crew passed by, headed out into the darkness before anyone else could shoot at them. As they bounced around, the driver Hammond swinging the Technical in for another pass, Marina struggled to reload the RPG, laughing like a madwoman.

"You Russians are fucking crazy!" Dagan yelled over the noise.

"Yes!" Marina yelled back. "Isn't it wonderful?"

Twelve RPG rockets were fired and eight scored solid hits, detonating. Three hit the lead Abrams, shrugged off by the super thick frontal armor of the heavy tank. But it did get the crew's attention, causing it to swing out wide, away from the tiger pit in which the disabled tank sat. The sudden change of direction caused a Bradley to swing in the opposite direction, losing its orientation. Before the driver could notice, it was in direct line with the pit. The cattle trucks that had been parked around the pit during the day had been moved at dark as it had been decided that sniping at night on the workers would be rare. The Bradley driver realized his mistake, tried to correct away from the large hole. But he was too late. The right track went over the edge of the pit, the Bradley slewing sideways. For a second, it looked like the Bradley would be able to remain upright. Then, part of the pit shoulder gave way, and the AFV slide in sideways, landing on top of the Abrams.

As another Technical slowed down, one Spetsnaz troop with an RPG bailed out over the side of the four wheel drive pick-up. Kneeling in the dark some fifty yards from the side of another Abrams, the Russian took aim at the rear drive sprocket. Another whoosh and the HEAT warhead hit dead on with a loud bang and a flash. Moments later, with the broken sprocket seized and the right tread snapped off, the Abrams ground to a halt. Talbot saw the flashes and explosions from a distance, and yelled to ask why his big gun had stopped after one round. A frantic call came in that the shell had jammed in the chamber and that the crew was trying to ram it out.

"Hurry up, goddamnit! I need some artillery down range." His mortar crews were nowhere to be seen, caught up in the general rout. As the six artillery men scrambled to ram a long pipe down the muzzle of the five inch gun, no one noticed a far off flash from the left flank. Then, just as the stuck shell was rammed free, one man straddling the muzzle was torn into hunks of meat.

The report of the Barrett 50 was drowned out by all the other shooting going on.

Benjamin Black quickly picked another target with his fourth generation night vision sight. His next shot hit the Kraken who seemed to order the others around, turning him into a two pieced corpse. The remaining four scattered into the night. The sniper of Key West then took careful aim at what appeared to be a large artillery shell. Once again, one round, one hit to the explosive nose. The shell exploded, which set off a couple of nearby shells and propellant charges.

"Just like Fourth of July fireworks," Sergeant Black mumbled to himself. Time to move, he thought, before someone found him with bullets.

Commander Talbot could see the large explosion from his command RV and he began to scream in rage. He screamed over the radio for his tanks to begin firing their main guns at the U.S.A. positions in Salina. But they had their own problems. The immobilized Abrams cleared its main gun tube by firing the round toward the fortified positions thousands of yards away. Then the turret began to rotate, its coaxial machine gun firing at anything and everything, including some of the fellow Kraken soldiers.

Colonel Popov yelled at Lupe and pointed his pistol at the tank. "There. That one. Go there."

Lupe passed the direction to her driver, although she knew this was absolutely bug-nuts. Both she and Dagan were still in bloodstained fatigues from their foray with the Sisters of Steel, and now her Technical was after a heavy tank with nothing but a large machine gun. But she had to admit that this craziness had a certain flare to it. She saw that the Russian Colonel had a large satchel with him which, in the heat of getting moving earlier, she had not noticed.

"Swing around to the rear. The engine area," the Russian commanded. Within moments, the well trained crew had the Technical within twenty yards of the huge metal beast. Popov sent the satchel sailing, only then did Lupe noticed he had pulled an arming cord projecting from the satchel. "Eat shit and die!" The Russian yelled as he expertly threw the satchel onto the rear engine decking.

No sooner had it landed there was a bright flash and deafening explosion. Smoke quickly began pouring from the engine compartment as the tank crew tried to activate the engine mounted fire extinguisher system. But the explosion seemed to have disabled most of that system. Flames were soon noticeable in the darkness, and the tank crew bailed. Colonel Popov sang some Russian military song, while taking potshots with his pistol as they passed fleeing Krakens.

"Quick, around again. I still have bullets left."

Lupe looked at him. "Begging your pardon, Sir, but you are not like any Colonel I know," She yelled over the din.

Popov laughed, then suddenly kissed her. "But I make all this interesting," he yelled back.

The militia managed to fire off its Benders, hitting a Bradley in the turret with both rockets. The turret flew into pieces as the chain gun ammunition exploded, with the remains of the vehicle commander and the gunner being splattered all over the landscape. Flame and smoke traveled down into the troop transport compartment. The back hatch was thrown open and Krakens jumped out before the driver could come to a stop. Stored ammunition cooked off and the driver was killed while trying to exit the AFV.

The two surviving Abrams turned tail and fled to the rear, crushing several people under their treads. Besides the two Bradleys already hit and the one in the pit, concentrated heavy machine gun fire and RPG rockets destroyed the tracks of two more. The two remaining vehicles turned and followed the Abrams. The Technical and militia troops slaughtered the remaining Krakens who tried to flee on foot. Only a handful were able to surrender before they were shot.

In the beginning of the attack by the Sisters of Steel, one Kraken male had fled from his foxhole, directly into the hands of a Spetsnaz-manned listening post. They had trussed him up, got him to the rear as they knew his babbling meant something. No one had to put the screws to him to get him to talk. He was more than willing to tell his story, tell everyone about what caused the rout.

"Banshees. A bunch of fucking screaming banshees. They were slicing, killing everyone. Bullets were no good. They were fucking banshees!"

Thus began another legend.

CHAPTER 18

Great men rejoice in adversity. Just as brave soldiers triumph in war.

-Seneca, Roman Empire

MALMSTROM ARMED FORCES BASE
GREAT FALLS, MONTANA

General Reed couldn't believe it was some three days from the now famous Rout at Salina. Krakens began running and rarely slowed down. Finally, General Wood got off his ass and hit the retreating forces from the north. It had been a slaughter. About ten thousand Krakens had managed to make it to Kansas City, Kansas on foot and in a hodge-podge of vehicles. Colonel Popov had helped them along from his end with the launch of the She-Bear Missile he had among his forces, the thousand pound warhead and unspent fuel exploding and sending up a small mushroom cloud as if it had been a nuclear strike. Hitting on a crowded section of road, some one thousand personnel were either killed or wounded, the mushroom cloud causing even more panic, as if that were possible. Many of the enemy just scattered, forcing the local militia to start the arduous task of tracking them down, or at least insuring they had left the state of Kansas. Commander Talbot had managed to flee successfully south aboard a surviving Abrams. With him were a dozen of his personal supporters. Everyone cursed that the former biker gang leader had managed to escape, among those being Torbin Bender. He had really wanted to watch his wife interrogate him.

But now General Reed listened on the phone with a rather grim look on his face.

"So, Doctor Rice, there has been no real change with Abigail?"

"No Sir. She still seems to be… somewhere else."

"She is eating, right?"

There was a pause. "Yes, General. But just applesauce. And she will drink milk. Try to get her to eat something else, and you might wind up wearing it. We lost two televisions when we tried to turn them on. Plus, I have an orderly with a broken arm when we tried to restrain her. If we allow her to sit, let her take herself to the bathroom, everything is fine. It's like she has gone to some dream realm, where she dwells solely in memories in the past. She eats the applesauce, drinks the milk, relieves herself, and then returns to sitting, staring into space. She is in a world of her own."

General Reed's stomach tied itself in knots. He did not think he could feel this way, not since his wife and sons had disappeared in Moscow. Now, the feeling of helpless loss was there again.

"Do what you can for her, Doctor. I know Colonel Bardun is working with you, based on what we are now understanding are some very unique modifications made to Abigail's body structure and DNA strands. Keep up the good work."

Major Rica Rice sighed into the phone. "General. To put it bluntly, we are not set up for this type of long term care. All those people with long term care issues, and just about all the facilities that provided that care, were gone after the Long Winter. I'm already getting grumbles about her care, especially after the orderly had his arm broken…"

"Major, stop right there," General Reed interrupted. "Captain Young is a hero and a national human treasure. I don't give a flying fuck if this pisses somebody off. If I have to keep her there until hell freezes over, that is what is going to happen. If the Hospital Commander has a problem with this, tell him to feel free to report to my office. Clear?" Now he felt a seething rage, not sadness or loss.

"Yes, Sir."

"Look, Doctor. Sorry I just jumped on you. I know you have a special bond with her. Hell, just about everyone who comes in contact with her wants the best for her. She is the shining example of a good soul. I just want her well, okay?"

"Yes, General. So do we all." Rica paused. "I have one or two ideas I can still try to bring her out of this…funk she seems to be in. I'm not about to give up yet. I just wanted to be honest with you."

"And I thank you profusely for that. You are an excellent Officer and Doctor. Malmstrom is lucky to have you. If you need anything, just call me directly. Okay?"

"Yes Sir. Thank you, General."

General Reed hung up the telephone. He sat quietly for a while. If he could have gone back in time, reverse his decision to send Abigail and Torbin to the field he would have. No, that was unfair. If he had not, then a whole bunch of civilians would be dead or tortured. Maybe even eaten. Now he had another problem involving some one hundred women who disobeyed orders, probably related to Abigail and Fuzz. The results had been wildly successful, but he could not have a bunch of soldiers forming a secret group, doing what they wanted.

Shit. The universe was a bitch. He pinged up his driver, Sergeant Pasqual.

"Yes, General."

"Bring the car around. We need to take a short drive, to see a young lady about some steel."

"Yes Sir. Coming right up."

John Reed grunted. No rest for the weary.

Torbin was sitting in his backyard, ignoring the cold. He had a drink, a rusty nail, in his hand. He kept glancing toward Abigail's side of the duplex that she shared with Aleks and him. He was almost expecting to see her come out into her backyard with Fuzz, to see her smile, to see Fuzz get up, put his front paws on the fence, stare at him with his "Well, what are you doing?" look he had favored Torbin with.

The War Dog had saved his wife, and his unborn sons. Now, he was gone, and Abigail was gone, albeit in a different way.

He took a slug of his drink. Damn, getting low. He'd have to refill it. Maybe he could quit his job, become a bartender. At least he wouldn't be helping getting his friends hurt or killed.

His wife would tell him that was unfair to say. But it was what he felt, deep in his hurting soul. He drained his drink, and rose to get another. He heard his wife Aleks drive up to the duplex. Looks like she managed to get away for lunch. Torbin finished pouring his drink, threw an ice cube in it and went to meet her at the door. She had taken their sons to Sue Brown's house. They had easily bonded with her, even at their young age, almost sensing that she had been there when Fuzz had saved them in the womb. Aleks knew her husband was having rough time, and needed some time alone. General Reed had ordered him home to rest, "write an After Action Report." Yeah, right.

Torbin set his drink down, hugging Aleks as she entered. "Hey, babe."

"Hey, husband."

They stayed hugging in silence. Torbin finally broke it. "Abigail?"

"The same."

"I guess I should go to the hospital, see her…"

"My little sister does not know me. I was there earlier." Suddenly, Aleks began to sob.

Torbin held her tight, tears in his eyes. Why did this have to hurt so much?

"I should have stayed with her. Fuck the civilians."

Aleks suddenly grabbed his face in her hands. "*No.* It is not your fault. And you did the right thing saving those women and children. Fuzz would have done the same if he were there, or died trying. He died for his mistress, his choice."

"But she may never… come back to us."

"Then it was her choice. Not yours. She choose her path. You did not choose it for her."

"She saved my bacon in Wyoming. Twice."

"Your sons will be forever grateful, as will I. But what is done is done." She hugged Torbin tightly again.

"We can pray for her. Maybe someone will listen. Maybe this time, it will be enough."

They stayed hugging each other, seemingly afraid that if they let go, everything would disappear.

Major Rica Rice was standing at Abigail's hospital room door. Right now, the young warrior was in a hard sleep, which was better than watching her sit and stare off into space, looking at something no one else could see. The Doctor's heart began to ache again.

"Hey, you." A familiar voice. She looked up to see Emily Anders, veterinarian extraordinaire.

Rica's eyes suddenly filled with tears, and she grabbed Emily in a hug. She began to softly cry, and Emily held on and gently rubbed her back. They stayed that way for a minute, then Rica regained her composure, stepped back. She found some tissues in her pocket, blew her nose and wiped her eyes.

"Still that bad, huh?" asked Emily.

"Yes. Abigail's body is there. Where 'she' actually is, that's the million dollar question."

"How are her vital signs?"

"She's like a damned energizer bunny. She'll crash for a while, or just sit there. But piss her off, bother her…"

Rica swallowed. "She threw three orderlies out the door this morning when they got too close to her. All they were doing was trying to make her comfortable. And she 'howled' at them!"

Rica shivered. "Now the rumor is she is a werewolf. That she got bitten out there."

"You're kidding, right?"

"I wish I was, Emily. I wish I was."

They stood in silence for a minute. Then, Emily spoke. "Want to try something… unorthodox?"

"Hell, I'd call a witch doctor if I thought it would help."

"Well, Doctor Rice, I have someone waiting in the car who might just help. I've been thinking about it all day. I just need help sneaking him into the hospital."

"Him?"

"Yes. Come on. I'll show you."

Abigail sat up in bed, staring off into space. She seemed to be seeing into a universe no one else could see. She breathed normally, blinked her eyes. But unless someone put some applesauce or milk in front of her, she had to go to the bathroom, or someone made the mistake of grabbing her, she did not move. Now it was the morning of the fourth day.

A voice finally began to ever so slightly break through into her consciousness. "Abigail? Captain Young? It's Emily Anders. Remember, Fuzz's vet?"

Abigail cocked her head slightly as if to hear the voice better.

Rica pushed in a used laundry basket. Some snuffling sounds were coming from it.

"Here. A relative of Fuzz wants to meet you. Thought you could tell him stories... of his father."

Emily reached in the basket as something big and furry started to climb out. A huge puppy was soon out of the basket, and on the hospital room floor. Almost fifty pounds, very large for having just been weaned, he looked just like Fuzz must have looked as a puppy, though a bit bigger. Medium and dark brown fur, with Fuzz's ears that stood up but flopped over at the tips. So much did the young dog look like his sire Fuzz, that the only noticeable difference was a small white star on his forehead. He suddenly froze, his nose working a mile a minute. Abigail had visited the litter of pups a couple of times after Emily's Great Dane had given birth, but had been too busy to see them lately. However, the smart pup's nose did not forget his sire's mistress.

"Here, Abigail. I think he wants to..." Emily began. Before she could react, the puppy, despite his young clumsiness, dashed and clambered up on the bed. Rica and Emily moved forward, afraid of a violent reaction. Instead, a miracle happened. Young Fuzz sat with his muzzle an inch from Abigail's face, snuffling his nose enough to totally take in her scent.

Abigail's eyes finally focused on the brown muzzle. Then she spoke. "Fuzz?"

"His son," Emily quickly interjected. "Remember, Abigail? You were there when Fuzz mated with Princess." The pup licked Abigail, let out a small "woof", and wagged his tail.

"Fuzz?" Abigail said again. Her right hand began to touch the young dog's face.

"Call him Junior, or Young Fuzz. He'll answer to both."

"Young Fuzz," Abigail repeated. Then the dam broke.

She began to cry. She pulled the dogs muzzle to her face and Young Fuzz began to do what dogs have for millennia—licked her tears away. She hugged him, and began to sob.

"Cousin?" A new voice was at the door. Brynhildr Jorgenson had been checking on her cousin several times a day. The excuse she used was that Abigail would be a material witness for war crime tribunals for captured Krakens. Rica motioned her in, and she shut the door. Brynhildr stood watching her relative sob, and begin to rock back and forth with the dog, Young Fuzz wagging his tail, and licking her. Tears began running down the tall Shield Maiden's face.

"She's back," she said.

"Maybe," Rica replied.

As if to reply, Abigail spoke. "Where have I been?"

It took a few moments for the other three women to realize that Abigail had spoken.

Finally, Rica responded. "That's the sixty-four thousand dollar question." She moved up to the bed.

"I'm going to check your vitals. Okay?"

"Sure, why not?"

"Well," Emily interjected. "You have not been exactly open to touching lately."

Abigail gave her a quizzical look. "How long have I been here, at the hospital?"

"This is the morning of the fourth day," Rica answered as she felt the Avenging Angel's pulse.

"Do you remember… Fuzz?" Emily asked.

Abigail nodded her head, then began to cry again. Brynhildr walked up and hugged both her and Young Fuzz.

"I see you, cousin," she said in Norwegian. "You are back with your people. We are here to help."

Abigail hugged her back, as Young Fuzz began licking them both, giving doggy laughs in between. Then, she leaned back.

"How long have I been here?"

"This is the morning of the fourth day."

Abigail's eyes widened. "Ichiro." In a sudden series of moves she was disentangling herself from Brynhildr and the pup.

"Wait, I need to finish my exam," Doctor Rice protested.

"Sorry, Doctor, there is no time." Abigail suddenly grabbed Rica, hugged and kissed her cheek. "Thank you for everything. I know you watched over me. But I just realized there is something I must tell

Ichiro. I feel fine, and I must go... now!"

Brynhildr suddenly broke into a large grin.

"I know what that is, cousin," she said in Norwegian.

"Please. Do not spoil the surprise," Abigail answered as she grabbed a clean set of fatigues someone had brought for her from the small closet.

"But," Rica began.

"Let her go, please." Brynhildr said in English. "And I don't think you could stop her anyways,

"I'll take care of Young Fuzz for you, drop him off at your home later," Emily said. "He's yours now. And you are his. As if you couldn't tell."

Abigail quickly hugged Emily. "I am so blessed to have friends like you. Thank you." In quick order, she hugged Emily, Rica and Brynhildr, then Young Fuzz. She finished changing in record time.

"I'll be back," Abigail said as she glided from the room.

Just then, a voice called out. "What is going on? Captain, you get back in that room."

It was a Hospital Shift Commander, a Lt. Colonel with a short man's complex.

"Colonel. It's okay..." Rica Rice began to say.

"*I'll* make that decision, Major. Captain, Come back here." Abigail took a look at him, smiled, and then began running down the hallway toward the exit.

"Sergeants. Stop her." The two orderlies began to run after her until Brynhildr blocked their way.

"Let her go. She is a Federal material witness, under my protection."

The Colonel walked up, red-faced, having to look up to the tall blonde.

"Move, or I'll..." He never finished his statement. An unusually strong female hand grabbed his throat and lifted him up on to his toes. The orderlies began to step forward and Brynhildr produced a single-bladed Viking throwing ax from under her parka.

"Interfere, and I will..." The Shield Maiden left the rest to their imagination. She looked at the man she was holding.

"Colonel, you're an idiot. So, I will not allow you to mess with the good Captain. She's back with the living, has something she must do.

Period. Leave her alone. Complain to my Boss all you want. But she stays free. Understand?" With that, Brynhildr shoved him toward his orderly. She stood, axe in hand, her Special Agent badge visible on her belt.

The Lt. Colonel croaked at her. "This isn't over yet."

"It never is."

The three men left. Rica Rice stood next to Brynhildr.

"He will not let this go."

Brynhildr shrugged. "My boss will support me. If not, then my people will. It doesn't matter. Abigail needed to leave."

"I wished I had a cousin like you," Emily interjected, still holding on to Young Fuzz, who had been watching the conflict. Emily knew that, push comes to shove, the son of Fuzz would have gone after anyone trying to harm Abigail.

Brynhildr looked at Emily. "How about an adoptive sister?"

"Deal." Emily looked at Young Fuzz. "Time to take him to his new home." She hugged the other two women, took her leave. Brynhildr found a chair, sat down.

Rica looked at the large woman. "Abigail?"

"She will be okay. She's back with us. She will not leave again."

As Abigail exited the hospital at a dead run, Ashley Anderson, just back from a Medevac flight, saw her. She swore, grabbed a portable radio, yelled at the other ER personnel that she would be out on the radio, and took off at a dead run also.

Ashley had been a first class runner in junior high school, just before the Squid Invasion. A coach had told her once that she had the makings of an Olympic athlete. But Abigail was leaving her in the dust. She tried to kick it, but all she could do was keep Abigail in distant sight.

Abigail felt so free, alive, that she could not believe she had been in a near comatose state for over three days. She had vague memories that were slowly coming back to her, knew how Fuzz had died. But now she had something she had to do now, for her future. Her body had never felt so alive. It was if it had been storing energy for the past few days. Energy that had to be released now. Abigail had never ran so fast. Had anyone been measuring, she would have easily broken pre-Strike world records. Her speed and long legs ate up the distance, and she soon was in sight of the Training Complex. Ichiro was near. She sprinted. Her body seemed to be telling her that it was once again free and well, as was her soul.

As Abigail approached the entrance to the large training building and gym which was built to supplement the outdoor training fields, two figures watched from a distance, partially concealed on the snowy ground by a tree. Rica Rice had called Aleks and Torbin just as soon as she could, telling them that Abigail was "loose" but seemed alive and well. And that she said she had to see Ichiro.

Aleks had put two and two together, grinned broadly. "Husband, put your drink down, jump in the car with me. No, I am driving as you have been drinking. Hurry up. Abigail is a fast runner."

So they had arrived, and managed to find the tree for cover just as Abigail approached.

"My God," exclaimed Torbin. "Look at her move! I knew she was fast, but not that fast."

"Running toward love makes you faster, husband."

"Is that how it was for you?" Torbin asked with a sly grin.

Aleks looped her arm through his. "I think you already know that answer, my love."

Inside the training building, Ichiro was showing a large class of new recruits the value of unarmed combat. As soon as the Rout of Bloody Kansas began, and it appeared that it would not stop, Ichiro had been pulled off Alert, and training was back in earnest. The attack by the Krakens showed that the Squids were starting a new round of aggression after basically ignoring the remnants of humanity. Any day, instead of a punishment operation attempt by poorly-trained troops, they could expect Krakens supported by battle robs, robocops, and the Soldier Class warriors they had begun producing. Thus, there was an even greater impetus to build up the defensive forces. Looking on and helping him was Senior Training Instructor Stalin.

"As you can see, the valuable use of Jiu Jitsu works against a larger and armored adversary. We Japanese developed it for combat between or with armored Samurai. Theoretically, given the right circumstances, a robocop could be taken down."

Ichiro being focused on the Trainees, a full Platoon, it was Stalin who noticed Abigail standing in the entrance way. He grinned.

"Excuse me, Major. But you have a visitor." He nodded toward the entrance.

"Who," Ichiro began, looked, and froze. The two humans stared at each other from afar, both seemingly afraid to make a move as it may disrupt the reality.

"Well, what are you waiting for, Major?" Stalin boomed. "Go say hello. I will handle the class."

A few titters were heard as the trainees realized what may be going on.

"What is that I hear?" Stalin boomed. "Mirth, laughter? Everybody up. Rifles above your heads. A few laps around the building should help you refocus. *Move.*"

Ichiro walked rather stiffly over to the entrance way, stopped a few feet from Abigail.

"I...I visited you in the hospital. But you did not know me. I thought you were... gone. I should have stayed by your side." He bowed low. "I am not a worthy person. I should have stayed by your side..."

"Ichi, please shut up." Abigail closed the distance. She grabbed his shirt collar, pulled his face close to hers and kissed him. They kissed long and deep, tongues entangled as they blocked out the noise of Stalin's booming voice, the trainees' Jody Calls. Finally, they parted.

"Abby..."

"Shhhhh." Abigail put her finger on his lips. "Listen, please."

She took a breath, let it out. She then spoke in Japanese.

"Ichiro Yamamoto, will you marry me? I know it's traditional for the man to ask the woman, but there is no time. We could die tomorrow. I almost did. Only the help from some good friends, God, and Fuzz dying for me kept me alive."

She took his hands her hers, feeling his strength. "The thought of dying without knowing your love has helped awaken me. I need to know if you want to spend our lives together, no matter how short or long they may be. I need to know now."

Ichiro quickly knelt on one knee. "I, Ichiro Yamamoto, do hereby pledge my undying love. Yes. I will marry you. I will marry you now, this minute. Please name the date and place. I will be there."

Abigail giggled, bent and kissed him. Then, her look was serious.

"First, Ichi my love, there is something I must do. I overheard the Doctors Rice and Bardun talking after an examination. Apparently I filed it away in my subconscious, and now I can remember." She paused, collected her thoughts. "I must return to Deseret. I must have some answers. Somebody, some....things maybe, did some modifications on me. The grays found me due to a locator chip that everybody had thought was a piece of shrapnel. My DNA has been tweaked substantially. I am not entirely normal. I may be very... dangerous."

She looked into his eyes. "I need to find out. Then you need to decide if you still want me as your wife."

Ichiro stood up, took her face in her hands and kissed her. "You are talking to someone who was also classified as 'abnormal' possibly due to the effects of Fukushima. I am a Squid Killer extraordinaire. A Samurai. And you say you may be dangerous to me? How is that?"

Abigail began to giggle again. They hugged, and Ichiro began to laugh.

"Yea, Ichi, I guess it is kind of stupid that I could be dangerous to you. Out of all the men in the world, you're probably the only one who could handle me."

"Good. Abby. Then it is settled. I will go with you to Deseret. Then we can marry."

She squeezed him. "But are you sure you want to come with me? It is my problem, not yours."

"Abigail. We are to be married. All problems will become our problems. Besides, a Samurai could not let a defenseless woman face danger."

After that remark, Abigail obtained a small yelp from him as she jammed a thumb into his ribs. They laughed, held each other tight.

One of the legendary love stories had begun.

Outside, Aleks noticed a figure in uniform approach, looking at the entrance to the training building. She recognized the woman as Ashley Anderson, the Sister of Steel who had watched over her in the hospital immediately after the birth of their two sons. Aleks put fingers to her mouth and let out a decidedly loud and unladylike whistle. But it had the desired effect.

Ashley looked in her direction, and Aleks motioned her over.

"Still watching over your sisters I see, Sergeant."

Ashley saluted Aleks. "Yes Ma'am. A habit I can't break."

"Husband, the young lady I told you about in the hospital. Acts as a Guardian Angel sometimes."

"Then I guess we owe her, Aleks. It's a pleasure."

"Thank you, Sir. I take it Abigail is inside and well?"

"Yes. With a certain Major. We'll make sure she gets home alright."

"Good. Then I need to run back to the hospital. Thank you. Sir, Ma'am."

Aleks looked at her. "Come here for a moment." Ashley stepped up and Aleks hugged her, kissing her on the cheek.

"You are a true angel. Never forget that."

"Thank you, Ma'am. And you're a true sister. Now I must head back before I'm missed."

"Don't be a stranger."

They watched Ashley run back toward the hospital.

They then noticed Abigail leave the building. Aleks used her whistle again, and started to jog toward Abigail, Torbin in trail. The two sisters met, hugged, laughed, cried, as Torbin watched. His stomach was still in knots. Finally, Abigail looked at Torbin, walked over to him.

"Abigail, I'm so sorry."

"About what, big brother? Yes, Fuzz is dead. I will always have a hole in my heart for him. I hope you don't take offense, but he was my best buddy, my best friend. You are my brother, but he was my best friend. Yet he died doing what he wanted to do. Protecting me."

"I should have been there, damnit. Then I could have stopped them."

Abigail saw Tobin's eyes fill with tears. She grabbed and hugged him.

"If you were there, you might be dead, your wife a widow. Those thirty civilians you saved would be dead too. Maybe eaten." She looked up at him.

"Please don't beat yourself up. It was my choice. Now I know that the grays were following me. I'll tell you the whole story later."

Tears began to run down Tobin's face. He started to turn away, as tough Marines don't cry, but Abigail held on.

"There is nothing wrong about crying for a hero, a friend—even one with four legs."

Torbin began to cry more and Aleks joined them in a group hug, all three crying. They knew that Fuzz was looking down on them in their sorrow and loss. He had saved so many of them, he would never be forgotten. The three comrades finally separated from their hug, wiping their eyes.

"Emily Anders brought Young Fuzz to me in the hospital, snapped me out of wherever I was," began Abigail. "He will look exactly like his sire when he grows up. Only he has a small white star on his forehead."

"You know," said Torbin, "a Native American Marine told me once that a star like that on the forehead of an animal meant they had been touched by the Great Spirit. I think that fits this son of Fuzz to a "T". I'm certain Fuzz had a connection with the boss upstairs."

"We know that this youngster has a special connection," declared Aleks. "He must have, to bring you, Abigail, back to the living."

Abigail smiled. "Yes. Now I owe him like I owed Fuzz. But hopefully he won't have to fight off any Eaters trying to get to you and you sons."

"If it happens again, they will eat lead quite suddenly." Aleks looked at Abigail a bit questioningly. "Well? Are you getting married or what?"

Abigail's eyes widened. "How did you know?"

Aleks snorted. "I am a trained intelligence operative. Besides, you went to Ichiro first, and it is written all over your face."

Abigail blushed a bit. "I asked him. He said yes."

Torbin laughed. "Leave it to the Avenging Angel to do it differently. Now what?"

Abigail's face turned more serious. "I need to make a trip to Deseret. I have some questions about my…upbringing that I must pose to the Prophet."

Now Torbin read between the lines. He knew that Abigail was definitely stronger, faster than she had a right to be. Although all feminine, her body acted like a steel coil. So she had a set of good reasons to be suspicious about what the doctors were doing during all those checkups.

He looked toward Aleks. "Think I can make a road trip?"

"No, Torbin." Abigail jumped in. "Ichiro is coming with me. This is something we must do before we are married. He needs to hear the whole story also."

Torbin looked at Abigail. He remembered when he first met her at Evanston, Wyoming. That seemed like a millennia ago.

"So, no more chances at a Wyoming ass drag?"

Abigail laughed. Then hugged him again. "No, big brother. You have stepped in enough gopher holes. This time, Ichiro will escort me."

"Hell, you were escorting me, remember? Saved my bacon twice."

"Then twice is enough. Now it is Ichiro's turn." Abigail paused, then added, "I need to go see General Reed, to explain this to him."

"Hop into our vehicle, little sister," Aleks said. "We will take you. I'm driving, so we will get there in one piece."

"Insulted again, wife. Why do I put up with it?"

"Because you love me. Now, get in the car."

As Abigail was "waking up", an Armed Forces staff car was moving up the long Munsen driveway. Johann Munsen heard the car approach and stepped from the blacksmith forge area. Bruno, Hannah Weitz's fellow Pit Survivor and now four-legged best buddy, began to trot down to meet the strange vehicle, growling.

"Hannah. Visitors," Johann yelled out. He removed his heavy forge apron and his gloves, then grabbed an ancient double barreled shotgun. With the invasion of Bloody Kansas, nobody took any chances now. Hannah stepped out, having shed her blacksmith garb. From the shadows she produced a single bladed throwing axe of Viking design. She made them, and she had learned to use them. Bruno was already standing in front of the military vehicle, as if daring them to try and drive past.

Sergeant Pasqual stopped the vehicle, and said over his shoulder to General Reed, "I think this is as far they want us to go, Sir."

"I think you're right, Sergeant. Well, let's un-ass the vehicle and try walking up."

The two military men exited their vehicle and began to slowly walk forward. General Reed saw the figures approaching from the large outbuilding that he rightly determined was the blacksmith's forge. He called out.

"General John Reed and Sergeant Pasqual come to talk with Miss Weitz. If that's okay, that is."

"Johann Munsen, General. I thought you looked familiar." He

turned to Hannah.

"Are you seeing visitors, Hannah?"

As she caught up to Uncle Johann, she smiled.

"Torbin Bender works for the General. And some of his men helped rescue me from the Pits. Of course I have time for him."

She whistled softly and Bruno went back to her side, but still kept close watch on the two strange men as she approached them.

"You have quite the protector there, young lady."

"Yes Sir. We met in and both survived the Pits. Now we're family."

"Well, Miss Weitz, all I have is a few questions about a matter that I think you can help me with. Sergeant."

Sergeant Pasqual pulled a near eleven inch two edged knife, a real Arkansas Pig sticker with attitude, from under his military blouse. He presented it slowly to Hannah hilt first so as not to agitate the pit bull mix.

"I do believe this is your work, ma cherie," the Sergeant said.

"By the way, sorry about my manners. This is Sergeant Pasqual, my driver and right hand man."

Hannah smiled, took the knife with her left, put her right hand out to shake. With a flair of elegance Pasqual took her hand, bent over a bit and raised her hand to his lips.

"It is indeed a pleasure," he commented.

Hannah grinned and giggled a bit. "My, aren't we smooth. You must be from 'Nar'lens' , yes?"

Upon hearing the local pronunciation for New Orleans, Sgt. Pasqual's ears perked up.

"You know the city, my dear?"

With that, Hannah broke into New Orleans French Cajun Patois, which brought a laugh and a grin to the Sergeant's face.

"This young lady lived many years in the New Orleans area, General. She is almost a Cajun by adoption."

"And yes, General, this is my work," Hannah said with a smile.

"Well. Miss Weitz…"

"Please, call me Hannah. Miss Weitz is much too formal between friends. And you are my friend for helping rescue myself and the others."

Not for the first time, General Reed marveled at how some young person, after facing hell during the last six years, had bounced back so quickly. And so strong.

"Alright, Hannah. I am asking you about this rather unique weapon as it, and many others like it, which figured strongly in the Rout of Salina a few days back."

Hannah sighed. "Please, come into our house. I know Aunt Freda will provide you with some warm drinks, cider and such. The young ones are at school, so they'll be sad they missed you. But this way we can talk without interruptions. The… story is quite simple. It goes by the name of Sisters of Steel."

A little over an hour later, Pasqual backed out and turned around the staff vehicle.

"Well, General, that was nice apple cider. I swear it had a bit of a kick to it. Maybe a little moonshine?"

General Reed chuckled. "Yes. I'd have to agree. Maybe they were trying to ply us with some alcohol. But Hannah was not afraid to tell us the whole story. Looks like there were some seventy two members of this Sisters of Steel group that was started. At least that was the number of those large daggers she made. What did she say was the basis for her design?"

"Roman Puglio, General. I'm into knives and blades, so I've seen pictures of them. Nasty secondary weapons for Legionaries. She is making a modern high quality steel version of them."

"Well, Sergeant, it's the people carrying them that I'm worried about the most. They are just pieces of sharp steel until someone picks them up and uses them."

General Reed sat in thought for a few minutes. The problem he had was, what to do with a group of women that could easily turn into a vigilante group? Not to mention what to do with all those who made the unauthorized, even though very successful, Rout of Salina night attack. He could not allow a bunch of troops just go off half-cocked anytime they wanted. General Reed began to grin. Sergeant Pasqual glanced in the rear view mirror and saw the grin, one he had come to know well.

"Solution, Sir?"

"Yes, Sergeant. When you can't beat them, you join them. Or in this case, get them to join us. All I have to do is to convince everyone that an All-Female Unit is not sexist or segregationist."

As Abigail headed to General Reed's Office, and General Reed was returning from the Munsen's homestead, Pararescue Chief Thompson was cleaning his equipment, the first chance he had during the last three days. He noticed something he had forgotten about in one of the pockets of his tactical bag. Sergeant Dark Wolf had given him a small digital camera with its memory chip, told him it was a recording of the area around Abigail Young. He remembered the Sergeant had said something about what he had recorded, but the Chief had been so busy he had forgotten.

"Well, might as well have a look," he said to himself.

The Chief made sure the memory chip was in, turned on the camera, and looked at the screen as he played the recorded information.

"Holy crap!"

Major Lea Gabrielle was both an A-10 Pilot and now the commander of the Pararescue Unit. She was actually the last known survivor of the last Strike Package the U.S. Air Force tried against Tschaaa invasion units. Twelve fighters and fighter-bombers went out on the thirtieth day of the Invasion, the then Lieutenant, now Major, had limped back and bellied in her A-10 on McConnell Air Force Base near Wichita, Kansas. Gun camera film showed she had made a direct hit on a harvester ark and had knocked down a delta that tried to shoot her down. She had then made her way up to Malmstrom, as McConnell had been hard hit by deltas and Falcons. She was very familiar with cursing and swearing of all sorts in various situations. However, Chief Thompson was not easily shaken, nor prone to outbursts.

Major Gabrielle got up from her desk, started heading to the ready room where the Chief had been cleaning his gear. She limped a bit, the cold weather aggravating an old wound.

What's up, Chief?" She saw him staring at the flip out screen of a small digital camera, with, for the first time she had ever seen, a shocked look on his face.

"Ma'am. You need to look at this."

Lea worked her way around behind the Chief's chair. Looked at the small flip out screen of the digital camera. And froze.

"Where'd you get this?"

"From the Wyoming Mounted Militia Sergeant. When we rescued Captain Young. He said it was a record of what he found when he located Captain Young."

"Anyone else see this?"

"No Ma'am. I'd forgotten about it."

The Major paused, still looking at the rolling record on the screen.

"So the Captain, she…"

"I think so, Ma'am. Judging by what we had to do to get her on the chopper."

Major Gabrielle took a deep breath, let it out.

"Bring it to my office. We need to get this to Intel first. Then… hell, I'll let the Chain of Command decide then. Come on."

The two former USAF personnel walked to her office, where she shut her door.

"Goes without saying this is classified as of this moment, Chief."

"Yes Ma'am. I gathered as much."

The pilot looked down at the digital camera.

"This is a record of a special type of hell. A type of hell a special person was put through, and where a War Dog died. We need to remember that."

"Yes Ma'am."

Lea Gabrielle picked up her telephone.

Nothing was ever quite the same.

Abigail was waiting outside the General's office when he arrived back. Torbin had called ahead to warn Master Sergeant Johansson that Abigail was coming, so that he would not think he was seeing a ghost. As it was, he tried to hover over her like an old hen. Finally Abigail said, "Sergeant Johansson, please. I am alright now. My doctors know I am out. Trust me, I'll be just fine with the General."

So now she sat drinking a cup of tea while waiting for her General. Then he was there, smiling. She stood up. "General Reed…."

"To say you had us worried is the greatest understatement of the year, Captain. Sergeants, could you please leave us."

"General, I…" Sergeant Johansson began to say.

"Did I stutter?"

"No Sir, General."

"Come with me, Master Sergeant," Pasqual interjected. "I'll buy you a coffee at the canteen. They just got some new home grown beans in that are quite good." With that the two NCO's left Abigail and the General alone.

"General, Sir, I am sorry…," Abigail began. Before she could continue John Reed had her in a hug.

"Please do not do that again, Captain, Abigail. This old man can't take many more scares like that."

Only then did Abigail notice the tears on the General's cheek. She hugged him back, began to cry in her adopted father's embrace. They hugged for a few more moments, then separated.

"So much for military decorum. But sometimes even a General needs to break standard codes of behavior." Abigail found a handkerchief Madam President had given her, dabbed her eyes. She looked into General Reed's eyes.

"I and Ichiro are to be married. I want you to give me away as my father, for that is what you have become. My adopted father."

General Reed swallowed, then answered. "Abigail, I would be honored."

"But first, General, Ichiro and I need to take a trip to Deseret. There are some… answers I must obtain."

General Reed let out a sigh. "I was afraid of that. Yes, I have received some briefings from Colonel Bardun. So I know the ramifications of those answers you are to obtain. I don't suppose me trying to stop you would do any good, would it?"

"I would just pull diplomatic rank on you, General. Remember? You cannot stop me from visiting the nation state I represent."

General Reed grunted. "Too damned smart for you own good. I suppose I also have to let Ichiro go with you to make sure you get back. Though I doubt if I could stop him from going, from what I have heard."

"No General. He would become a Ronin, in the grandest sense of the term."

General Reed looked at her. "When do you want to leave?"

"Tomorrow, if possible."

"Give me one more day. I'll get you a new vehicle. Okay?"

Abigail grinned. "Deal, General. Thank you, and everyone else here at Malmstrom for… caring. You are family, now."

"Well. Captain, I warn you that you may have a special new assignment when you get back. I need you and Major Smirnov's help with a … special problem."

"Anything, Sir. I owe you more than I can ever repay."

"Hell, Captain. We're family, remember? We don't worry about repayment. You just get back in one piece with Ichiro."

"Yes Sir. Yes General." Abigail backed up, and saluted. The General returned it, then she stepped up and kissed his cheek, did an about face and left.

The General stood quietly for a few moments, then thought of his wife.

"Babe, I would like to think a daughter of ours would be like her," he whispered to himself and to her. "If you can, help me with this adopted one."

CHAPTER 19

NORTH DAKOTA-MINNESOTA BORDER

Staff Sergeant Barry Bond was looking through the mist, fog and snow into Minnesota. He had been assigned to support the Port of Entry outside of the former Grand Forks Air Force Base near Grand Forks, North Dakota. The POE was located some to 20 miles east from the base, on former Highway 2. Some of the younger troops had been kvetching about missing all the action in Bloody Kansas, but he was not one of them. Just staying alive the last six years was enough action for him. The Entry Control Point was a couple of double wide trailers hooked together, with decent heat, hot coffee, hot food, and bunks to use. A hell of a lot better than freezing in a foxhole.

Sgt. Bond had a twelve man squad plus a three person heavy weapons team that kept a 81mm mortar and a 50 Caliber operational for squad use. In addition, there were six customs and immigration inspectors assigned there. They had a house some mile away they lived in, rotating out every sixty days. Add a couple of mobile border patrol agents and they had their own little community. They were evenly split between the genders, so Staff Sergeant Bond had to remind his troops not to spend most of their time trying to see who they could sleep with tonight. Every few days he sent a couple on a twenty-four hour pass to Grand Forks proper so they could have some out of uniform fun time.

As he sipped his coffee, a Private Swanson called out, "Looks like we have one person walking toward us, Sergeant."

Sergeant Bond went to the Entry Control Point front window and looked out. Sure enough, a small figure was approaching, walking alone through the snow. The figure looked oddly familiar. Then it dawned on him. Grandma Knudsen had returned.

Just as the first reports of attacks in Kansas were rolling in, Grandma Knudsen had checked in at the POE. "I'm going to contact some friends and relatives in Minnesota, Sergeant. I should return in about a week or so."

"Ma'am, I have no orders to prevent anyone from leaving, just very limited entry until what's happening in Kansas shakes out. But, well, someone old enough to be *my* grandma…"

She flashed a healthy, teeth-filled smile. "I appreciate your concern, young man. But, I have made it this far in life, despite certain aliens trying to eat me."

A couple of the soldiers of Norskie descent had quickly told Sgt. Bond about Grandma Knudsen, that no one or nothing would *dare* bother her. Rumor was that she was actually Hera, Goddess of the North, in disguise. That last comment Sgt. Bond completely blew off. But he did not blow off what she had in her small pack.

"A replica Colts Walker .44? You shoot this?"

The medium height woman who suddenly looked a lot stronger than at first glance smiled. "My late husband was a black powder fanatic. I enjoyed doing most anything with him. So, yes, he taught me to shoot, as well as to load cap and ball. That nine inch barrel and large .44 caliber, when loaded to maximum, has Magnum abilities in stopping power. Want me to demonstrate?"

"No. Ma'am. I believe you. If nothing else, this makes a handy metal club. How far do you need to travel to meet your friends and family?"

"Not far, Sergeant."

Sergeant Bond soon realized that he was not about to get much more out of her. He mentally shrugged. It was her funeral.

"The Customs Inspectors will give you a re-entry document.

Please don't lose it, Ma'am, as everyone is a bit on edge right now, with Kansas and all."

"Well. I hope my friends and family can help with that. I promise I'll see you in a few days, Sergeant Bond." They had given her a mug of hot coffee, and she was last seen walking due east. Sergeant Bond, though he would never admit to it, had been worried ever since. If that nice older lady turned up missing… He kept kicking himself for at least not finding some way to send an armed soldier with her. She had reminded him of his two late grandmothers.

Now, about a week later, she was back, looking as healthy as ever. Sgt. Bond walked out to meet her, with a large grin plastered to his face. "Grandma Knudsen, to say I am glad to see you is a great understatement. I was afraid we had lost you."

She flashed a smile with a twinkle in her eyes that made her look decades younger. She then reached up, stood on her tip toes and kissed his cheek.

"You are a very nice, caring young man, Sergeant."

She then turned and pointed from whence she had just walked.

"I have some friends and extended family following me. I came forward first so as not to cause you and your people some alarm. There are quite a few, and some have weapons. But they are friendly. In fact, one of them would like a chance to talk with Madam President."

"Excuse me?" Sgt. Bond said, as what she said began to sink in. He then saw figures begin to emerge at a distance in the mist. And his jaw dropped.

He saw a long line of people, in the center approximately one hundred dressed in what had come to be known as American Viking garb, shields, weapons and all. And the line extended another five hundred either side with people in more modern military garb. Sgt. Bond thought he could make out a mass of other people, including children, behind the long line warriors.

"Leader Thor Heyerdahl would like a chance to talk with Madam President. He thinks he and his people—my people—can be of some help."

Sgt. Bond turned on his heel, and beat feet to the Entry Control Point Building, grabbing the hotline to the National Command Post at Malmstrom Armed Forces Base.

"Malmstrom, we have a problem."

President Sandra Paul was sitting in her office at the new capital building in Bismarck, North Dakota when the red phone rang. She had just received an update—finally, a 'good' update—on Abigail Young from General Reed. In fact, she was grinning from ear to ear when the word "wedding" had been mentioned. Nothing like a wedding of a beloved national hero to help people think more positively. This was especially true after the loss of life in Bloody Kansas. And the death of Sergeant Fuzz. So no matter what the problem was on the red phone, she would *not* let it spoil her good mood.

"Madam President here... Uh, what? Please repeat that?...Who? And all of these... American Vikings are just standing outside our port of entry? Okay. Stand by."

She hit the outer office intercom.

"George. Come quick. I need you. And call the Vice President. He needs to be in on this also."

Jeez. Just when she thought she could enjoy some happy news, the rest of the world had to intrude. Well, like they said, no rest for the wicked.

Hours later, Ranger Jackson maneuvered the armored limousine northbound on former Interstate 29 with practiced ease. Before someone became a Texas Ranger, you had to be a trooper with the Texas Department of Public Safety, with all of the accompanied pursuit driver's training. It was now second nature. Keeping the well-kept vehicle at a hundred miles an hour was child's play, especially since the last year had been spent repairing the major roads within the Unoccupied States. In the backseat were George Williams and Madam President. Both General Reed and Commissioner Miller had tried to place some armed personnel in the limo with the President, but she had refused.

"Send me some air-cover, General. I don't think these people would be quietly waiting for my arrival if they were really that aggressive or had true ill will toward me. And besides, if there are some ten thousand individuals, as the surveillance satellites and drones show, they could have just walked over the limited forces we have in the area already. So, I think I will travel light."

Thus, two re-conditioned A-10s were en route to the newly repaired runway at Grand Forks Air Base. Plus some Free Japan F-15EJs were on strip alert at Minot Armed Forces Base. But Madam President knew in her guts this was all unnecessary. She knew the people she was about to meet were to be important allies. Better yet, friends.

"About ten minutes out, Ma'am." Andy Jackson said into the intercom connecting him with the back.

"Thank you, Ranger." Madam President pulled a compact out of her substantial purse and checked her hair and makeup. She knew this was an unrealistic waste of time, as after all, who really cared what she looked like in this cold weather? But old habits die hard.

"Sure you want to do this now, and not use an intermediary first?" George Williams asked.

"Like they say, dear friend, time's a-wastin'. This recent attack in Bloody Kansas shows us that we may have finally woken the dragon, as disorganized as it was. I have to act quickly, be bold and sure."

For the umpteenth time, George wished his dear friend was wrong, But she was not. They existed on a shoestring of events.

"A mile away, Madam President. Want to park back a ways?" Ranger Jackson asked.

"No Sir. Pull right up to the entry point where Mr. Heyerdahl is waiting. George, grab those two thermoses of coffee and hard cider. Hopefully the contents are still warm."

Then they arrived, the Ranger smoothly swinging the limo into a coned off parking spot. Jackson was out, opening the door for the President before any soldiers could react, his eyes watching for threats. Madam President stepped out and everyone snapped to attention.

"Please, gentlemen and ladies. Relax. Your job is hard enough as it is without me adding stress." She went straight to the main door and was through it in one quick motion. She then saw the tallest and largest man she had ever seen.

For a fleeting second, she thought she had been fooled into meeting a robocop. Then she saw the grey streaked blonde hair and beard, the smiling eyes. The man was so tall he had to stoop a bit to stop from his head hitting the roof of the office. They both stepped toward the other, each putting a hand out to shake.

"Madam President," the Giant of the North said loudly. "It is both an honor and a pleasure. Grandmother Knudsen has spoken highly of you."

The President took his hand, seeing her sizeable hand become engulfed in it. She looked into his smiling eyes, and saw a good soul. She grinned.

"I think the pleasure will be all mine, Mister Heyerdahl."

"Please, call me Thor. I have a tankard of warmed mead for your pleasure."

"Beat you to it. I've got some coffee and hard cider. But I see someone knew I have a weakness for cookies. And call me Sal."

The meeting that followed would become one of legends. For both of the participants would combine to play a pivotal role in the survival of the human race. But that would come later.

As the evening meeting in Grand Forks continued, Abigail Young was in her home, packing. Even though the General had asked her to wait an extra day before leaving for Deseret, she could not just sit still. So, she packed, and repacked, until she had everything she would need in a small case and backpack. Of course, added to this was her sheathed .44 Magnum Marlin and her recovered Glock.

"There. That ought to do it," she finally said to herself. She felt the once again ever present canine eyes on her and looked at Young Fuzz. True to her word, Emily had dropped him off as soon as she knew Abigail was home. He had, just like his sire, had walked in, checked out Abigail's quarters, decided it met his standards for safety, security and comfort, and had laid down. He'd been alternating between watching his mistress and scanning the area around her quarters with his nose and ears. When Abigail looked at the very large pup, as big as some adult dogs, she felt both a joy and a pang of sadness. She would always miss his father, Sergeant Fuzz. He had been her best friend. Forever. But now she had his son to raise, to love. She would never let Fuzz down in that regard. Emily had said that Young Fuzz was developing a bit faster, both physically and mentally, than a regular canine.

"Someone tweaked Fuzz. It bred true, dominant. So Young Fuzz will be like his sire, a bit of a super-dog. But even more so. He will be larger, but not too much. And, just as his gestation in the womb was a bit shorter, the time growing into adulthood will be a bit shorter.

We'll just monitor his growth, so that everything develops at a proper rate and ratio. We don't want any spine or joint problems."

Abigail smiled at Young Fuzz. She motioned him to come to her as she sat on her bed. He was up in a flash, his tail wagging. He tried to crawl up into her lap like some small terrier and she began to laugh, pushing him back.

"Fuzz Junior. You are not a lap dog. Neither was your father. Sit, and I'll scratch your ears and chest."

Young Fuzz sat at her feet, looked into her eyes with his adoring eyes. He knew she was the one for him. And Abigail knew that in return. Just as she had known that first day when she had met Fuzz Senior. The Avenging Angel scratched his chest and ears, and was rewarded with satisfied doggie grunts and sighs.

After a few minutes, Abigail stopped, then hugged him. "I can't keep calling you Young Fuzz. The name is too awkward. I don't think you sire would mind me calling you Fuzz. Officially, you're Fuzz the Second. But short names work best for training, communications. Is that okay?"

Just like his namesake, he told her yes with a large tongue dog slurp and kiss. Which started her laughing again.

Her cell phone rang, and Abigail picked up. It was Aleks.

"Can we come over and join the fun? We can hear you laugh from our bedroom. And I've got someone for you to see."

"Of course, sister. You and Torbin are always welcome."

"Wait until you and Ichiro are married. That 'always' will vanish. Certain activities are meant for privacy."

Abigail blushed, knowing what she meant. Which started a bit of stirring in her proverbial loins. Abigail controlled her thoughts, as her "loins" would get in the way of the trip she and Ichiro must take. She went and opened the front door for Aleks and Torbin. And met one of Young Fuzz's sisters.

"Emily brought us Freya here. She's a bit more Great Dane than Young Fuzz, taking more after her mother." Freya was a beautiful merle, with Dane ears. Her coat was just a shade longer than a pure Great Dane. Otherwise, she did not look of mixed ancestry.

"Emily also said that thanks to some Squid developed and bootlegged science, we have a usable form of Norplant for dogs. Thus, no chance of incest when she comes in heat. As she will not."

Fuzz met his sister, tail wagging. They were soon in the backyard chasing each other around.

"I decided I wanted a big, nasty dog to help protect our kids," said Aleks. "Especially when Torbin or I are at work. Anybody who babysits gets a large dog to watch over them also. And since she is part Fuzz, I know what they will get."

"I'll help you train them."

"I figure you would, little sister," answered Torbin. Then he stepped forward and uncharacteristically hugged her. Abigail hugged back, feeling his love and caring.

"You okay, Abigail? Okay for this trip?"

"Yes, big brother. And Ichiro will be along with me. He'll watch my back."

Aleks then made it a group hug. "We still want to make sure you have...recovered."

Abigail sighed. "Enough to do this trip." She untangled herself from her family.

"Ichiro will help me work through any...after effects. He has told me more of his upbringing, learning to deal with his unique form of psychological makeup, his hyperactivity. He should be able to help me control my...destructive and dangerous side."

Abigail knew that Torbin and Aleks had been briefed on what had happened during her medevac, the violence she had exhibited in the hospital. Most of it was like a foggy dream to Abigail, with an occasional flash of clarity. Plus, she knew about the work Colonel Bardun, the exobiologist, had done on her and Fuzz's genetic makeup. Her and her late canine friend's genomes had been modified, as had some of their basic cellular and muscular makeup. Abigail now knew this must have happened in Deseret, at least in her case. But she had a gut feeling that it extended well beyond just her. She would find answer, no matter how many toes she had to step on. Or break.

"Of course we'll watch Young Fuzz for you. And Freya will help keep him company. Besides, then he can bond with my two trolls, like his sire did." Aleks eyes began to tear up a bit at the thought of Fuzz and her two sons. Without him being there that fateful day...

Abigail took her adopted sister's hand. "I know. It hurts every time I think about what he did for us. All of us. I guess there will be a memorial service for all the fallen from Bloody Kansas. Then, everyone will know who Fuzz really was, and will remember him. Like we do."

She hugged and kissed Aleks.

"Now, excuse me while I make an early night of it. Let my Fuzz in when he is sufficiently worn out chasing his sister around. He'll come to me, like his father did."

Aleks and Torbin took their leave, went back to their side of the duplex.

"You know, Aleks, they will probably force us into field grade quarters any day now."

"I know." She sighed. "I just want to live next to Abigail forever. With her new Fuzz. It just seems like that is what it should be. Forever and ever."

"Well, when she is married to Ichiro, they will want their own place. And hopefully, soon will be heard the pitter patter of little human feet."

"Oh, that's right, husband. Get all us women barefoot and pregnant. Typical male."

"Hey, it takes two. Just remember who came to whose room... Ouch. Now was that nice? Try doing that when Freya's around. She'll protect me."

"No, she'll probably bite you when you act like a prick. At least, hopefully I can train her to do that."

Torbin grabbed the love of his life, buried his face into where her neck met her shoulders and gave her a razzberry grammy kiss. Aleks began to laugh and giggle, tried to pull away. They heard their two sons stirring on the baby monitor.

"Ah, duty calls, my love. Rain check?"

"Of course, Aleks. By the way, I love you."

"There has never been any doubt of that. Now let us check on the two results of that love."

Abigail was getting comfortable in bed when she heard Torbin let Young Fuzz back into her residence. In a flash she had a large puppy on her bed, nuzzling her. She smiled, hugged and petted him. Fuzz completed the circular bed-making behavior many of his kind exhibit, and plunked down next to her, his head on her legs. She looked up.

"Thank you, Lord. One door closes so another may open. Please watch over me and mine in the coming days. I will need thy rod and thy staff near me. For I may be walking into the valley of death. Keep my family safe. Thank you. Amen."

She and Fuzz slept the sleep of the innocent. As it should be.

As Abigail Young was getting some well-needed and deserved rest, Talbot was fleeing southward through Kansas on back roads. He had the remaining Abrams tank and Bradley fighting vehicle traveling with two SUVs full of some of his more trusted personnel. He would begin cursing periodically when he thought of that rout had apparently been caused by a few "crazy women" according to some of the people who they stopped in their head long flight. He had tried shooting a few to stop the retreat, but then the enemy mobile units had attacked, and everything went to hell.

So now he was down to his two remaining AFVs and his trusted few. No way would he try to retreat back through Kansas City. A full U.S.A. division was attacking from the north, slicing into the middle of his strung out units, not to mention all the militia personnel who were getting pay back on anything that moved. So, in the grand tradition of the Swamp Fox, he was running away so that he could fight again.

He had told Reverend Kray and the Squids that attacking with half or no trained troops was a recipe for disaster, but of course no one wanted to listen to him. Bunch of spaced out fanatics and idiots, that's who were in charge. And now they were paying the price for not listening to reason.

Talbot and his group was approaching a small outpost on the southern Kansas border with Oklahoma at speed. A couple of militiamen took potshots at them as, coming from the opposite direction they expected for an attacking force, the Abrams and Bradley smashed through the road barriers and barbed wire, the SUVs right behind.

Ten minutes later, Talbot had his forces stop. Everyone got out and stretched, keeping a wary eye out for a pursuit, but none came. Apparently there were already too many targets to be had with the remains of his main force to worry about a small detachment fleeing. One of his Lieutenants approached him. "We need some fuel, boss. The tank is on fumes, the rest of the vehicles are not much better."

Talbot grunted. "Get the two motorbikes down, send them out to scout around. There should be some abandoned buildings, vehicles that should have enough fuel in them to get us to Texas and the Gulf. Then we'll be around friendlies."

"Think the Squids will be pissed?" the man asked Talbot.

"Who cares? I warned them what was going to happen if there was any resistance at all. So, if they decide to eat me, who is going to do this next time? Reverend Kray? Yeah right."

He reached into the SUV, grabbed a bottle of moonshine they had found. He took a swig, then passed it around.

"We'll get out of this. If things go too bad, I've got some hidey holes we can go to. I don't trust anyone when it come to my safety. Stick with me, we'll make it."

Talbot spit. "Now, find that gas. We need to get going."

CHAPTER 20

Abigail and Ichiro planned to leave at o-dark-thirty on the second morning since her release. Major Rice had smoothed things over with General Reed about her condition, and then the General had called the Base and Hospital Commanders to smooth over the unconventional escape Abigail had made from her hospital room. Next he had contacted Ichiro personally, asking for a meeting in his office.

"Major, I know how close you and Captain Young are now, that you are engaged to be married. But you also must know of her possible problematic mental and emotional state."

Ichiro Yamamoto had drawn himself up into a rigid straight back stance before the General. "General Reed. We have no secrets. And if you have talked with my Japanese Commanders, you will know that I can be said to have had similar problems during my youth."

"I realize that, Ichiro. But…"

"Please allow me to continue, General. She and I have discussed what she remembers happening in Wyoming. I know, as she does, that more unpleasant memories may surface in the future. But, Sir, I am a Samurai. And she is my betrothed, my beloved. Those facts and my specialized training in controlling *my* destructive abilities make me the only person who can insure that Abigail is a productive member of the Allied Force." The other Hero of Key West paused.

"I controlled my weaknesses, and delivered a nuclear bomb to our enemy. Then I led the survivors back here. Some of my schoolmates in Japan said I was a ticking time bomb, had too much pent up energy, and could not be trusted in normal society. That I was unclean."

For the first time, General Reed heard and saw what Ichiro had been through. He saw that it was not that much different than Abigail. Except that someone had purposefully screwed with her physical makeup, while Ichiro's "differences" were due to happenstance mutations. However, the same type of personal internal controls he had to learn were probably very similar to what Abigail Young would have to learn, internalize. So what better person to provide the necessary help to her than someone she loved with all her heart, and who loved her back the same.

Ichiro continued. "On my family honor, the Yamamoto name, I swear that Abigail Young will be safe. She will be safe toward others also. She will return here so that you may give her away as her now father on her wedding day. She has asked me to tell you that."

General Reed stood there, silent. Shit. How could you argue with that? Besides, as the nearest thing to a diplomat Deseret had, the General would be hard pressed to justify not allowing her to return to her former home.

He stuck out his hand. "Deal."

Ichiro paused for a moment, then stuck his hand out. "Deal." The Japanese Officer had expected more of an argument, might have even had to ask his government for help in the matter. But that never materialized. Ichiro gave silent thanks to the fact none of that was necessary.

"So now, my good Major, you have said you will take care of my adopted daughter. Hell, she is like a daughter to the President also. So, you have just taken on a hellava task."

For the first time, Ichiro smiled. "My ancestors will give me the strength to honor this commitment, General Reed. I will bring her back to be married here, at Great Falls and Malmstrom Base. To our home, our friends, our family."

With that, Ichiro went to attention and saluted. The General returned it.

"Carry on, Major. I know you have a lot to do for this trip."

"Yes General, and thank you." Ichiro about-faced and left the General's office.

Afterward, with the General alone in his office, he went and sat down behind his desk. From his right hand drawer he removed three items: a bottle of single malt scotch, a highball glass, and a photo of his wife and sons. He poured himself a drink and raised it in toast to the photograph of his loved ones.

"Well my loves, wherever you are, I'm developing a large adopted family here. Sons and daughters all over the place. But I think you'd all like each other. Here's to a family reunion someday. Even if it's in heaven." He emptied his glass put the items back into his drawer. Then he began to hum a song, some old rock and roll ballad about hope and love. For once, things seemed to be looking up. The General decided to allow himself a good mood.

"Master Sergeant Johansson. I'm taking you out to lunch. That's an order."

It was now o-dark-thirty and Abigail was driving the new manufacture SUV with a smooth confidence of one with many hours of training and experience. Ichiro was a pilot, but Abigail was a driver. She had been taught in Deseret from an early age how to drive every military vehicle imaginable, as well as some law enforcement pursuit and protective detail tactical driving.

General Reed had given them the new vehicle, saying it was among the first batch of U.S.A. production vehicles in over six years. He had admonished them to "wring it out" and gave them a log book to record how it ran. But they both knew the General was just using this fiction as an excuse to justify giving them a new vehicle for what could be said was a primarily personal journey for answers.

They did not talk much, content to enjoy each other's company and listening to the numerous local radio stations that had sprung up in the last year. Anyone who could throw together an AM or FM transmitter seemed to be broadcasting whatever music they could come up with, as well as locally produced information, opinion and religious based programs. Russian, Japanese, the Norse languages, even some Spanish broadcasts were spread all over the Unoccupied States.

Mixed in were propaganda and open broadcasts from the Tschaaa-controlled areas, as well as Feral originated stations. Finally, in both AM and FM bands, there was an increasing frequency of the clicking, squeaking, sometimes rumbling tones similar to Earthly whales and elephants that were the Tschaaa talking to each other. Abigail knew that some of her late mother's people, Romanians, had traveled to the USA and were being used as monitors to try and figure out what the Tschaaa were talking about. As had been noticed before, Communications Security was not something the Tschaaa had ever considered important. There was also a minority theory that some Tschaaa without general access to their translators were actually talking to the humans, hoping that they would someday understand Squid.

Abigail had called ahead to Rock Springs and the Bell's Truck Stop, said they would be there to spend the night, if that was okay. Mother Jean had replied, "Family doesn't ask. Of course you two can spend the night. Shannon already called, said you two were engaged. So I get to pick Ichiro apart, make sure he is good enough for my adopted daughter."

Unseen over the telephone, Abigail had blushed brightly. How did everyone find out about what she was doing so quickly? Was she that important to so many people? She felt humbled by the attention. She explained all of this to Ichiro. He had patted and squeezed her arm.

"Abby, you are special to many people. That is because you are such a person of honor, of a good and caring spirit. People sense that. I have heard you refer to Torbin as a 'good soul'. Well, compared to him and most others you are the "best" soul. If more people were like you, the world would be a better place."

She had blushed again. "But with all my problems, my... violence..."

"That does not change who you are, in there." He had touched her chest, over her heart.

"We will solve any other transitory problems together. Agreed, Abby-san?"

She looked at him. "I do so love you. And I'm so very lucky to have you."

"Yin and yang. Two halves that make a whole. That is who we are, my love. We are made for each other."

The miles flew by and even using some of the minor roads rather than Interstate highways they reached Bell's Truck Stop and Restaurant near Rock Springs by nightfall. They had brought extra jerry cans of fuel with them so they did not have to worry about finding refueling stations. Things were improving, but there were still gaps in some services on the various roads and highways. Mother Jean met them as they drove up, a happy smile on her face. As Abigail exited the driver's side, she was on the receiving end of a large hug. Then she noticed that Jean Bell was crying.

"Please, Jean. There is no reason to cry. I'm here safe. I'm okay."

Mother Jean tried to control her tears as her daughter Pamela, husband Calvin and a much grown son Jim came up to great the couple.

"Sorry, my dear. I just know you were almost lost to us. And I never had a chance to meet Sergeant Fuzz, your four legged friend. I know it must have hurt to have lost him." She was wearing an apron, a usual piece of clothing for her, and she used it to wipe her eyes. Then Pamela demanded a hug.

"Ready for some more baking, Abigail?"

Abigail grinned. "Yes. I've been looking forward to it. Please let me introduce my fiancé, Major Ichiro Yamamoto."

Calvin Bell stuck his hand out. "I understand you're a fighter pilot. Well, this old bomber pilot won't hold it against you."

Ichiro smiled, knowing the rivalry that had existed since the beginning of the organized air services between bomber and fighter pilots. "Yes, Colonel Bell. I am a fighter pilot. But these days, I spend most of my time training warriors, soldiers."

Son Jim chose that time to chime in. "You were with Major Torbin at Key West, weren't you?"

"Yes, Sir, I was."

"You launched the nuke at the Squids."

"Yes, that is true."

"Son, stop with the twenty questions." Calvin broke in." Give your adopted sister a hug."

A slightly shy Jim gave Abigail a brotherly hug.

"My, you have grown, Jim," Abigail opined. "And you are developing the muscles of a man, I can tell." Her comment caused Jim to blush a bit.

"Well, mother, if you are going to get Abigail baking again, let me take the good Major here and entertain him. You drink beer?"

"Yes Sir. A lot more since I have been socializing with Major Bender."

"Well, come with me. You too, Jim. I have some chilled bottles of a local brew that is an excellent Pilsner. Better than some of that old pre-Squid skunky stuff."

The three men were soon sitting on the veranda in front of the restaurant portion of the Truck Stop. Though still cold winter weather, the three enjoyed both the beer and the nip in the air.

"My son Jim here will soon be eighteen, ready for military service. But I think he is going to stay around here, join the Wyoming Mounted Militia."

"Yeah, Dad. After what happened in Kansas, the Krakens near Evanston, I would just as soon stay near for you and Mom."

"Yes, Sir. Abigail told me about her earlier adventures her in Wyoming, before I knew her. She mentioned meeting the Mounted Militia." Ichiro's face displayed a bit of a frown.

"Abby also told me that a militia man helped to Medevac her. I must find this man, this Cheyenne Warrior, and thank him, as well as your daughter Shannon, the co-pilot of the helicopter."

Cal Bell looked at Ichiro. "So she told you… what happened?"

"As much as she can remember. And I saw her at the hospital." Ichiro's face saddened.

"I was not very honorable there. I…left her by herself as I could not stand to see the state she was in, that she did not recognize her. I have asked her forgiveness for being so…weak. Not befitting a Samurai."

Calvin Bell examined Ichiro with age experienced eyes. And saw a level of hurt and regret which came from a deep seated love and affection. "You really love Abigail, don't you?"

"With all my heart and soul. And I swear to you, as part of her large adopted family, that I will never fail her again. I will die before that happens."

The old bomber pilot put his hand on the Japanese warrior's arm. "Son, no one is perfect. The important thing is that you love Abigail, and she loves you. Jean and I have had our rough times. But true love wins out. I see the way she looks at you that you are the 'One'. Jim, listen up. When you find the 'one', don't let her go. It may take a while to find her, like it did me with Mother, but it will happen. And Ichiro, you do not need to swear anything to me. I can see it in your eyes that you mean it. So please, quit beating yourself up. I think Key West showed you are far from weak."

Ichiro made a small bow from his seat. "I value your experience and wisdom, Colonel Bell. I hope I can develop the same through my life. We Japanese honor our Elders. I thank you for giving me your advice."

Cal Bell chuckled. "I can tell I need to loosen you up a bit, son. And I have just the thing to do it." He made a quick glance toward the front door of the restaurant. Then rose from his seat and went to an old top opening soft drink machine from another bygone era. He reached down into its refrigerated innards, felt around, and then pulled a fifth sized bottle from its hiding place. Out came also three shot glasses.

"Jim, you are sworn to secrecy from this day forward. Consider this a coming of age rite."

"My lips are sealed, Dad."

"Good old locally produced moonshine, aged over a year in an old oak casket. Here, everyone gets a shot." After pouring each a shot, Cal Bell held his up.

"I propose a toast. A toast to a new marriage, a new beginning. To eternal love, which will be the saving grace of us humans." With that, they threw their drinks back.

"If I may request one more, Cal-san."

"Sure, Ichiro. Here. I'll pour."

Again, the three raised their glasses, and Ichiro spoke. "To new friends, to new family. And, as you say, everlasting love."

They downed these drinks also. Then they heard feminine laughter approaching. Quickly, Colonel Bell stashed the bottle and the glasses. The three women entered the veranda, and Jean Bell spoke.

"Come on in, gentlemen. We have some new bread and pies in the oven. And I have some spiced cider with a kick on the stove." She looked at her husband.

"Been toasting, I see."

"Now, mother, whatever gave you that idea."

"How many years have we been married? Think you can keep a secret from me?"

Jean Bell looked at Abigail. "Your husband will try the same. They never learn that special husband x-ray and mind-reading ability we wives have."

With that Ichiro really looked at his love. He saw Abigail with an apron on, and white flour dusting on her arms and nose. And with a big happy grin on her face. He felt like he was falling in love with her all over again. He walked over to his betrothed and took Abigail's hand in his own. He spoke in Japanese.

"You are the most beautiful woman in the world, my love. I pledge my life, my love to you forever."

Abigail's became a bit misty eyed as she answered in Japanese.

"I am your love. You are mine. That is at it should be. I will be yours, forever."

They embraced, their entire universe became being wrapped in each other's arms.

"I can't understand Japanese," Cal Bell said. "But I think I understand the language of love just fine."

His wife Jean wiped her eyes with her apron."Husband, father, get that moonshine out. With some more glasses. I think this moment requires another toast."

"Or two," daughter Pamela interjected.

"Or three," son Jim opined.

"Keep this up, I'll have to go find another bottle," Cal said.

Later that night, Jean Bell started to make up a single bed for the couple. Ichiro had demurred. "Please, Ma'am. We are not married yet. I believe it would be proper to sleep apart."

Mother Bell gave him a surprised look, then beamed a smile at both of them.

"May it be that your example rubs off on others. Old fashioned courting may help us reinstate some morality in a screwy world."

So Ichiro had bunked in with Jim, and Abigail in with Pam. Ichiro was forced to give Jim an unclassified blow by blow version of what had happened at Key West. Jim would soon pass the story, with some exaggeration of course, onto his young friends in the area. Thus the Legend of Ichi began in earnest.

Pam had gossiped a bit with Abigail. "So Shannon helped get you home in one piece?"

Abigail's face had turned a bit dark. "I would probably be dead if not for your sister. I was…violent, a danger to the other personnel. Shannon got in my face, calmed me down a bit. I owe her my life."

Pam had suddenly hugged her. "We are family. My mother adopted you as another daughter, as everyone should have a mother. Family saves family. That is the way it is."

"That in no way changes the chance she took. I could've killed her, killed them all. From what I have been told, I was an engine of destruction."

"Ichiro knows all the details?"

"Yes, Pam. He says he can help me to learn to control, to channel this level of violence. Ichiro said he was a bit out of control when he was growing up, possibly due to radiation-tweaked DNA. Similar to how I seemed to have been purposefully modified. So, the same meditation and control techniques his father and uncle taught him, he will teach me."

Pam smiled. "I hope I can find a man like Ichiro. Someone who would love me as much as he loves you."

Abigail smiled back. "You will. I feel it, I see it. He may not at first sight seem like the one, but he will be your beloved."

"You'll come to this future wedding, then." Pam asked

"I wouldn't miss it for the world."

They left a bit after sunrise the next morning. Abigail had telephoned ahead the day before and had been told that the Prophet and President of Deseret, Michael Smith, would meet her at the entry point on Interstate 80 down from Evanston, Wyoming, where it seemed her current life began. She had met Torbin there, and her life was never really the same since.

Now Abigail and Ichiro were nearing the border with Deseret. She glance over to her fiancé.

"Sure you don't want to sit this one out? It is definitely personal, from a time well before we met."

Ichiro had squeezed her thigh. "We are to be married. How could any honorable man stand by and watch his wife, his love face problems alone, whether from the past or not? You will never have to face a problem alone again. Not as long as I can breathe."

Abigail glanced at Ichiro. "Just be careful, my love. We have come too far to be separated now."

About a mile from the point of entry between Wyoming and Deseret, Abigail and Ichiro saw two mounted figures in camouflage uniforms on the side of the Interstate.

"Wyoming Mounted Militia, Ichi. And it looks like they are motioning us to stop,"

Abigail slowed the vehicle, coming to a stop a few yards from the two figures. She put the SUV in park, letting it idle as she exited, and Ichiro jumped out of the passenger side at the same time. She saw they were Cheyenne as they both easily swung their legs over and slid off their mounts. The male stepped forward and saluted.

"Ma'am. Sir. Sergeant Dark Wolf of the Wyoming Mounted Militia. I was told you were passing through, asked to be part of the security detail for the POE. I have something to return to you."

As the Sergeant spoke, he held up a switch blade knife with a broken blade. Seeing this, Abigail's eyes widened as she realized who he was.

"You are the Sergeant who reached me and Fuzz first, and helped to get me on the chopper. You got my Fuzz on the chopper…" Suddenly, Abigail stepped forward and hugged him. "You took care of My Fuzz…"

Tears ran down her cheeks.

"Please, Captain, I was just doing my duty," a very embarrassed Jacob Dark Wolf said as his female companion grinned.

Abigail hung on for a few moments, then stepped back, wiping her eyes.

"Sorry, that wasn't very professional, was it? It's just that I know Fuzz was almost left behind. The thought of his body being left to the scavengers…

"Ma'am," the female militia soldier interjected. "Jacob could no sooner leave Sergeant Fuzz behind than he could his own brother. His nickname is Talks with Dogs. He has always preferred dogs to his fellow humans."

"True, Sergeant?" Abigail asked.

"Plus he was one of us, Captain," Jacob answered. "He was a soldier who died for his comrade. How could I leave him behind?"

Ichiro suddenly stepped forward, and bowed low. He began to talk quickly in Japanese.

"Please, Ichiro. English. They do not speak Japanese."

"Sorry, Abby-san." He began again.

"It is an honor to meet a warrior such as you. I must humbly thank you for saving my loved one's life. I must also thank you for honoring Abby-san's friend and comrade, Sergeant Fuzz. For he truly was a four legged brother, a best friend to her. I now owe you a debt. Always know you will have a sword at your back should you ever request it."

Abigail looked at Ichiro and truly realized that he was not of this century. At least not when it came to duty and honor. He *was* a Samurai cut from the old whole cloth. What he said is what he meant. It was yet another reason why she loved him.

Jacob stepped forward and extended his hand.

"You honor me with your support, and your words. Please stop by my people's homes, their lands. They will want to meet the Eastern Warrior and the Avenging Angel, to show you the respect you deserve." Ichiro and Jacob shook hands. Then Jacob realized he had not introduced his comrade.

"Sorry for my rudeness. This is Diane Running Dear, Sergeant, Wyoming Mounted Militia. We are both here to insure you safe return back to Wyoming."

"Is the Sergeant's last name indicative of her abilities?' Abigail asked.

Jacob laughed. "Yes. She ran everywhere as a child. She has not slowed down since."

The female Sergeant began to salute but Abigail stuck her hand out. The two female soldiers shook hands.

It is an honor to meet you, Captain. You're a bit of a legend among the younger women in our tribe."

Abigail blushed a bit. "I wished people wouldn't react so. I'm just a woman like many others."

"Abby-san, you are not like any others. You are special."

She squeezed Ichiro's arm.

"Thank you both for coming, Sergeant Dark Wolf, and Sergeant

Running Deer. Now, we must continue and pass into Deseret for our meeting.”

"We'll be by the POE waiting for your return, Captain, Major," said Dark Wolf. "Need any help, just whistle."

"I'll do that," answered Abigail. She and Ichiro reentered the vehicle. Abigail started up the SUV, looked over at Ichiro.

"Last chance, Ichi. This is my problem not yours. The outcome may not be pleasant."

"As I have said before, Abby my love, we are as one. We are joined at the hip."

Abigail smiled, took a deep breath, and sighed. "As they say, here goes nothing."

They drove to the large gate that controlled access to the Nation State of Deseret from Wyoming. Abigail was expecting to see the older married couple that had been there for years. Instead, grim-faced men in dark combat fatigues with assault rifles greeted them as the gate opened. One approached to the driver's side window and Abigail lowered it.

"Captain Young and Major Yamamoto. We have a scheduled meeting with the Prophet."

"Pull your vehicle over there, by that barricade," the armed man ordered. "Lock all your weapons in the back." Abigail noticed he had no military insignia on his fatigues.

"Excuse me, I'm the official Deseret Representative to the U.S. A..."

"Don't care. No weapons by the Prophet and President." Abigail noticed he had his hand on the pistol grip of the assault weapon.

"Hai," Ichiro suddenly jumped in, put his best self-deprecating smile on his face. "We will do as you say. The Prophet must have a need for more protection. We will comply." He did a slight bow in his seat toward the armed guard.

"Fine. Then walk over to those picnic tables. We'll be watching."

Abigail had a momentary desire to snatch the man's adam's apple from this throat, but resisted the urge. She expected this meeting to be contentious, but there was a level of tension in the air she had not expected. She drove the SUV over to the directed area and parked.

She looked at Ichiro. "This does not look good. You could stay in the vehicle."

He snorted. "What type of Samurai would that make me? Hiding like a young scared schoolgirl. I think not."

Abigail quickly kissed him. "Another reason why I love you so."

The two warriors exited their vehicle, and began stripping off their belts, stowing the equipment and weapons in the back seat. Both kept some concealed throwing blades and she saw Ichiro conceal the Tanto knife he had received from Hannah Weitz under his fatigue jacket. They may not have katanas or firearms, but they were far from defenseless.

After retrieving a manila envelope, Abigail shut the vehicle, and they started to walk toward the picnic tables. As they did, Abigail glanced over to the two story combination residence and inspection building. In the second story window she saw the face of Anne White, the female half of the older couple who usually manned the entry point. She had a worried look on her face, and suddenly turned as if someone was calling her. Then she disappeared. Her husband had probably told her to get away from the window.

Abigail turned her head toward Ichiro.

"Yes, Abby. I know this is not right. That you were about to tell me that we are walking into the proverbial lion's den."

She gave him a small smile. "Not even married, and you are already reading my mind."

"As I said, Abby-san. We are joined at the hip."

The couple walked toward six assault weapon armed dark uniformed security personnel. They were spread out around the two large picnic tables which were situated on the edge of a parking area. Two black SUVs parked nearby had apparently brought the security personnel. Abigail saw no other people. Then the sound of a large car engine was heard. Coming into view on the main road was a large black limousine of the type used by the Prophet and President.

"It begins," Abigail murmured.

The limousine slowed to a stop on the edge of the parking area. As soon as it had stopped, the driver, whom Abigail recognized as Agent Hall, the Prophet's Special Assistant, was out and opening the back passenger door. Immediately Prophet and President Michael Smith stepped out, adorned in a tailored black uniform with a belted pistol. So much for the civilian suit Abigail was used to seeing him in.

Then Abigail saw a familiar face exiting the limo behind Michael

Smith. Mathew Young, fellow member of the Twenty, stepped out wearing a black uniform with a belted pistol.

The Prophet saw Abigail and smiled, then waved. By force of habit, Abigail gave a small wave back although she did not feel friendly or social. The manila envelope she held contained information that belied any previous relationship.

"Daughter Abigail. You look fit and well," Michael Smith called out as he approached.

"I brought your old friend, Avenging Angel Mathew Young. Hopefully you two can catch up on your personal activities."

"Hello, Prophet." Abigail did not smile as she gave a greeting.

"And I see you have brought a friend with you. Good. I have heard you have made many contacts, that you are becoming a bit of a legend. Especially after your brush with death."

Abigail could no longer keep any form of a façade in place. "This is not a social meeting, Prophet Smith. I have some serious questions to ask, the answers affecting our future relationship."

As the Prophet neared, a frown appeared on his face. Before he could say anything, Abigail tossed the manila envelope at him with expert ease while he was still a few yards away. The Prophet caught the envelope, an irritated look on his face.

"What is this?"

"Please look in it and review its contents."

During the short exchange, the security personnel had edged closer.

"Hello, Abigail." Mathew Young smiled at her and started to close the distance.

Driver/bodyguard Agent Hall stepped in his path as Prophet Smith gave a small signal.

"Hello. Mathew. You have grown, filled out since we met."

"You look quite healthy yourself, a bit taller."

Abigail finally smiled. "Good food and lots of exercise, Mathew. I have even become a bit of a cook myself."

Mathew motioned to Ichiro. "Fellow soldier? He appears to be from Free Japan."

Abigail smiled some more. "I am pleased to introduce Major Ichiro Yamamoto, pilot and warrior of Free Japan. One of the surviving members of the attack on Key West, specifically the one who launched the nuke."

She paused as Ichiro gave a short bow. Then Abigail added another detail. "And my fiancé."

Upon hearing this, Prophet Smith jerked his head up from reading the contents of the manila envelope.

"Fiancé?" He asked sternly. "Did I hear correctly?"

"Yes, that's so," Abigail Answered.

The Prophet's face seemed to turn a bit red.

"You throw a file from the U.S.A that appears to contain questionable scientific accusations and then tell me you are going to marry a … heathen. A non-believer? What has happened to you? I thought I was like your father."

Abigail looked at him, face and eyes hardened. "You ask what has happened to me? Should I start with the fact someone has done things to my body, my DNA? That I was apparently modified and trained to be some sort of… super soldier?"

"Who told you that? Who told you those *lies*?" responded a very agitated Prophet and President Smith.

"I was not told. I was *shown*." Abigail's shout was almost a scream. "I was shown by the greys who followed a transmitter imbedded in my body everyone thought was shrapnel. I was shown by the reports of what I did to my fellow soldiers who were just trying to rescue me. I was shown by the fact I was in a near-catatonic state in the hospital for days. You think this all happened by accident?"

"My friends! They are not heathens. Their doctors have proof of what I have become. What my body has become. You and your doctors tried to make me a… *thing*."

Prophet Smith's face became a rock mask. "I did what I knew was right for Deseret. For the Mormon people. If I sacrificed some unclean…"

"Am I unclean also, Prophet?" Mathew suddenly interjected, which resulted in a quick "Shut up" from Agent Hall.

"Unclean? *Unclean*?" Abigail's face was filled with rage.

"This 'unclean' person can have children, after years of being told by your doctors I could not. You and they are *liars*."

The Prophet's face became red with rage. "You overstep your bounds. You forget who're talking to. I am the Chosen Prophet of the Church of Latter Day Saints, with direct communication with *God*.

How dare you question me? I do the Lord's work."

"You worked with the Squids to make me a *thing*. You are a false prophet. *Judas!*"

Abigail's voice increased in volume, then built up to a near feral scream at the end. Ichiro started to step forward to calm Abigail. Prophet Smith strode forward with unexpected speed, swinging a right open handed slap at Abigail's face. His blow met iron as Abigail caught it in a right handed vise grip.

"You reap what you sow," she said through clenched teeth. Then the sound of crunching bones were heard as Abigail twisted and crushed the Prophet's arm and hand. His eyes went wide with pain as everyone around stood in shock of the unexpected tableau. His mouth opened to scream.

"*Shoot her!*"

 Hell came to picnic.

 Mathew yelled, "No!" and with the enhanced speed and training of the Twenty had his pistol out first, shooting the nearest uniformed guard through the throat. His shots drew the combined attention of the other five assault weapon armed personnel, who proceeded to throw rounds his way.

Ichiro hands became blurs as he threw concealed shurikens that struck the faces of two of the guards. He then threw himself into a forward roll to close the distance between himself and the nearer armed personnel. His roll and Mathew's fire threw off the attempts to shoot him. Mathew put two rounds in the chest body armor of one shooter then a third round through his bicep of the pistol grip hand. The young warrior then put a round in the thigh of the next guard, as the first rounds found him. His body armor overmatched with the multiple rifle caliber bullets hitting him, Mathew went down with penetrations to his chest.

Agent Hall pulled his pistol and went to his boss' aid. Abigail, still holding on and mangling the Prophet's right arm, grabbed his gun belt with her left. She lifted him up and began to carry and push the leader toward the onrushing threat. The driver/bodyguard tried to draw a bead but couldn't get one as Abigail was using the Prophet's body as cover. Then with unexpected strength, Abigail threw Prophet Smith into Agent Hall. A pistol shot sent a bullet zipping by Abigail's left ear as the Prophet slammed into his man, the two now entangled.

Something "clicked" inside Abigail, and she became a blur. With the blink of an eye, she closed, twisted and yanked the pistol from the Agent Hall's hand, half ripping off his trigger finger. She turned the pistol on its owner and shot him between his eyes, brain back splatter peppering Prophet Smith as he fell to the ground with his now dead assassin. The Avenging Angel turned and shot as Ichiro closed with and slit the throat of one of the guards with his concealed Tanto knife. Like a machine, Abigail found a target with her eyes and shot. Each shot was a headshot, every threat she shot seemingly moving in slow motion.

Then it was all over, with all of the security personnel down and dead. Ichiro had watched her final acts, and saw the speed with which Abigail moved. Later, he would say she switched into "hyperspeed", fast even for him. As Abigail scanned for threats, she saw Mathew, down and bleeding. She let out a banshee scream, then was by his side. Ichiro took an assault rifle from one of the dead, and covered his love as she tried to give medical aid to Mathew.

"Lay still, Mathew." As she said that, shots were heard from the area of the entry point. Then Cheyenne war cries. Help was on its way.

"Abby," Mathew said, then spit up blood.

"Don't talk. Help is on its way…"

"No. I am… done."

"No you are not. Don't argue with your older sister. You're tough, you'll…"

Mathew spit up more blood. "No. I am ready to be with Jesus, sitting at the side of the Lord."

"No. You will not go. You will stay here with me. I lost Fuzz, I will not lose another of my family!"

Mathew smiled at her. "I love you, sister of the Twenty." He coughed and the blood flowed from his mouth. "Save, protect… the others, our fellow Twenty Avenging Angels. Get them free." His eyes began to glaze. "I will always be near. Later, I will see you on the other side…" He let out a long sigh. Then he was gone.

Abigail screamed in pain again. She closed Mathew's eyes, laying his head gently on the ground. Then she was on her feet, next to the wounded Prophet. He was trying to free his sidearm from its holster with his off hand as Abigail approached. In a smooth motion, she bent and snatched the pistol from Prophet Smith, smashing it into his groin. He screamed and grabbed his family jewels, the compound fracture in his right arm shoving a bone through his skin. Abigail took aim at the Prophet's head.

"*No. Abby-san. That is not who you are.*"

Abigail heard her love's call. She stayed aimed in for a few more moments, then relaxed.

"I should shoot you," she growled. "Maybe gut shoot you, watch you die slow. But I'm not mad dog scum like you."

"I am the Prophet," the helpless man squealed. "I do the work of the Lord."

She spat on him. "You do the work of the Tschaaa, the Squid demons. You used the Twenty as guinea pigs, lab rats for their experiments." She pointed to the dead body of Hall. "You had your mad dog Hall enforce your decrees, kill for you."

"I did what was necessary to keep the aliens at bay. To keep them from killing and eating the Lord's people."

"Like the saying goes, 'What Would Jesus Do?' Sell innocents out? Kill them? Never. You do the work of Satan, of Judas, nothing more."

Two riders arrived, riding hell bent for leather. Sergeants Dark Wolf and Running Deer reined in their mounts, leapt off, landing at a run. "Captain, Major. Are you all right?"

"Physically, yes," Abigail answered.

"She lost another friend, family member," Ichiro explained.

"We were delayed by four armed guards," Running Deer interjected. "We freed the older couple. They were being held as prisoners in their home."

Abigail looked at the two Wyoming Mounted Militia. She thought that people such as these offset scum like the Prophet and his minions. Abigail believed there was always hope when warriors as the two Sergeants were about. Then, a loud vehicle engine noises caused everyone to turn and look down the road. Two more dark colored SUVs were approaching at speed.

"Time to leave, I think," Dark Wolf commented.

"No. I stay. The evil ends here." Abigail spoke, her face and voice set in stone.

Ichiro went ramrod straight. "I stay with my love."

The two Cheyenne looked at the two fellow warriors. Suddenly, Running Deer let out a loud yipping cry. "This is a good fight, a good day to die. The story will be told for years around Cheyenne campfires and meetings." She scrambled to a nearby ditch and took up a covered position.

Dark Wolf grinned. "The Spirit of the Wolf, the Dog Warrior is here. We will help you make a stand against this evil."

Abigail smiled. "Thank you. But I think we will survive. We have the Lord, good on our side. As well as superior fighting ability."

Ichiro chuckled. "Always the optimist, my love." He quickly grabbed two more assault weapons from dead hands as Abigail obtained Mathew's and the dead driver/bodyguard's pistols to add to the Prophet's. She and Ichiro took cover behind one of the dead security guards parked SUVs just as the two approaching vehicle braked to a stop on the edge of the parking lot. Dark Wolf had joined his comrade in the roadside ditch, so they had the two SUVs in a crossfire. Abigail had thought that armed guards would come bursting from the vehicles. Instead, a single familiar figure exited the driver side of the first SUV. Doc Stubbs, Former Marine Gunny Sergeant, stepped out from the driver's seat, holding a sawed off double barrel 12 gauge.

"Captain Young. Are you still with us?"

"Yes Doc, I am." With that, Abigail stepped out from behind cover. She knew that the Former Gunny Sergeant would not be on the side of evil, be there to hurt her.

"Friend?" Ichiro asked.

"Yes. Good friend. You need to meet him."

Abigail and Ichiro walked toward Doc Stubbs as the cautious Cheyenne warriors stayed under cover in the roadside ditch. Then a figure came from the back seat of the SUV that Doc had been driving. Ester Smith, wife of the Prophet, dressed in a dark pants suit, stepped from the vehicle and saw Abigail.

"My daughter. Thank God you are alright. Is my husband…?"

"I am *not* your daughter" Abigail snapped back. "Your husband is over there, bleeding."

"Please, Abigail. Let me…"

"Explain? Explain what? About how the so-called Prophet lied to me, used me and the Twenty as guinea pigs? That he had grey alien implants placed in me? That he tried to have me turned into a *freak*?" Her voice raised to a near scream again.

"Abby-san, please." Ichiro saw she was becoming more agitated by the minute. Given her recent past, he was afraid she wouldn't be able to control her anger.

"I am fine, my love," Abigail answered. "Just what Torbin would call very pissed off."

Ester Smith began to cry. "Please, Abigail...."

"Your husband is lucky to be alive. For what he has done to innocent children he should be drawn and quartered. In the process of this... evil, he subjugated and warped a belief in a loving Christ to his own means. For that alone, he should burn in hell."

With that last comment, Abigail suddenly reached up to her throat and ripped a necklace from it. "Here. This cross you gave me was given under false pretenses. I don't want it anymore." She threw it at the feet of the soon to be former Prophet's wife. Ester screamed and fell to her knees, wailing and sobbing, clawing the cross from the ground. Abigail looked up and noticed three middle aged men in dark suits approaching from the second SUV. She recognized them as Elders of the Church of the Latter Day Saints. One spoke to her.

"Please, Abigail Young..."

"Not Young. That name means nothing now. Call me by my family name, Jorgensen. That name has honor. Your name does not."

She turned toward Ichiro. "Now it is time to go, my love. I'm done here." She began to walk toward the SUV they came in.

Ichiro glided over and knelt before the sobbing and wailing Mrs. Smith. He reached out and gently took the cross and chain from the devastated woman's hands.

"I will see to it that she gets this. She is just very hurt, angry right now, is lashing out. She will soon realize you had no control over the... abomination that has occurred."

Through puffy, tear filled eyes, Ester looked at the young samurai. "You believe me?"

"Yes. You are deeply hurt. That is the truth. A participant in the Evil would not care about Abby-san. You do."

Ester Smith tried to focus on Ichiro through her emotion.

"You love her dearly, don't you?"

"Yes. With all my soul."

"Then please, take care of her. Protect her. I failed her in that respect, as I failed my daughter, allowed the Squids to take her..."

She began to sob again. Ichiro gently laid a hand on her shoulder. Ester looked into his eyes.

"Mrs. Smith, I will do my best to take care of her. And if you wish, I will contact you, let you know how she is doing, at least until she realizes this is not your fault. We are here because of the Tschaaa, the Squids, the Takos. We humans have evil in ourselves. But the slime occupying our Earth have made it worse. That is why you daughter is dead. Not because you failed her."

Ester Smith swallowed, stopped her sobbing. She grabbed Ichiro's hand, kissed it.

"You, are a true saint. Not just one in name or title only. May God walk with you, protect you."

Ichiro smiled, ignoring the lump in his throat. He bowed to her. "Your blessing does me honor. I will always remember it. Now I must leave, as my soon to be wife wishes to depart." He stood up, helped Ester to her feet. He bowed once more, then turned to leave.

"Major, a minute please." It was Doc Stubbs.

"You are friend of Abigail from… before, yes?" Ichiro asked.

"I like to think that, young man, yes. I can tell the two of you are made for each other. So, a friend of Abigail is a friend of mine." The former Gunny stuck his hand out and Ichiro took it in a firm grip.

"You are a man of honor. Doc. I can tell. You brought the Prophet's wife, knowing something was wrong."

"I got a phone call from a certain crazy Marine up in your parts. I put two and two together. You hear a lot in a chow hall. You are just the man to help keep our Avenging Angel out of trouble. Well, at least basically in one piece. Call me, any time, at the military chow hall in Salt Lake City. I declare "dibs" on first choice to make you two a wedding cake. Deal?"

Ichiro smiled broadly. "Hai. Deal."

He then looked at the three Church Elders who were standing, stunned over what had happened. He drew himself up straight, to full height once again. "You and your … church, have much to answer for. If you are true men of honor, who were not part of the Prophet's actions, you will make amends, insure it does not happen again. You will also take care of Ester Smith. Am I right?"

"Yes, you are," the Elder with graying hair answered. "We must ask God for forgiveness. Because of our ignorance, maybe willfulness in some cases, many were hurt. I must ask you and Abigail for forgiveness." He went to his knees, then prostrated himself on the dirt.

"Please. I am not God, and I cannot speak for Abby-san. Call our leaders, explain to them. They will then explain to Abigail."

"Now, it is time for this simple warrior to depart. I bid you farewell."

"Don't forget the cake deal," Doc Stubbs called out.

"Never, my friend."

Ichiro made his way to their SUV. As he did, Dark Wolf and Running Deer, having left their positions of cover, approached him.

"I take it that everything else is over except for the shouting," commented Running Dear.

Ichiro looked toward where the fallen Prophet was, his wife having gone to him with a first aid kit. He would be lucky if he could ever use that arm normally after what Abigail had done to it.

"The Mormons will have to work this out themselves. All I know is that I will get Abby-san back to her new and true home. We will be married, make a new life together."

"Big wedding?" asked Running Deer.

Ichiro shrugged. "I would prefer a small, private affair. But with my government, and hers, who can tell about the politics." He smiled. "But I will invite you both, no matter what. I owe you. Dark Wolf, I owe you twice."

The Cheyenne scout smiled. "We'll be there. If it's large, many of my people may come. They respect Captain Young, and owe Major Bender for returning the body of Standing Bull. Many are waiting a chance to pay their respects to them as well as to Madam President. They give my people hope."

"As they do to Free Japan." Ichiro bowed low to the two Mounted Militia. "You are welcome at my home anytime. Without you, things may have gone very wrong."

"And you are welcome at our lodges, our campfires," said Running Deer. "Now, I think we will go and make contact with these Church Elders. I think some one-on-one between Wyoming and Deseret would be a good thing."

"As usual, the young woman is right," said Dark Wolf. "As you can tell, she is the smarts of this team."

Ichiro laughed. "I think there is plenty of intelligence to go around. Now, I say goodbye."

With that, the two Sergeants snapped salutes to the Samurai Soldier, and Ichiro returned them. He then continued on to the SUV.

Abigail was already sitting in the driver's seat, staring straight ahead. Ichiro got into the passenger side, looked at his love.

"Abby-san…"

"No talk. We must leave." With that she started the vehicle, turned it around and began the trip back through the port of entry.

The elder Smiths waved at her, and she waved back, absentmindedly, distracted. Ichiro saw Mr. Smith had a small bandage on his head, and presumed that he had resisted the now dead security personnel. Ichiro counted four bodies spread out around the now open gate area. He saw the lariats the Cheyenne had used to yank the gate open with their horses, and thanked his Ancestors that the mounted militia had been there to help.

They continued down the road in silence for about five minutes. Then, without warning, Abigail drove the SUV over to the side of the highway. In smooth order she put the SUV in park, turned off the engine, undid her seat belt and crawled over onto Ichiro's lap.

She was shaking as she wrapped her arms around him.

"Abby…"

"Ichiro, I need to know. Will you always love me, even when I am no longer young and beautiful? Will you love me when all I have is this tortured soul? Will you love me when I am old, with this warped body?"

Ichiro lifted her chin with his hand, looked into her eyes. In Japanese he answered, "Your soul is my soul. We will grow old together. We will love each other through all the stages of our lives. I will always love you, will never leave you. Even in death." He kissed her long and deep. How long they kissed was lost in time. Finally, they stopped, parted. Abigail had stopped shaking.

"Well, that is one way to calm my shakes, my love."

Ichiro laughed. "And in a very pleasant manner. Do you want me to drive?"

"No, dearest. I am the better driver. I am okay now, thanks to you."

"Do you say you are the better driver because you are American and I am Asian? That we are always called bad drivers?"

Abigail laughed. "No. I say that because it is true. You are the sword master, but I am the driving master."

"So it begins. I must, how you say, give you the pants."

Abigail began to giggle. "Come here, you. The expression is wear the pants in the family. I may want to take your pants off, to get at what is hidden underneath, but wear them? Never."

"Good, Abby-san, because you would look funny in my pants. My legs are longer, and…"

"Shut up and kiss me, you foolish Samurai."

And he did. For a long time.

KEY WEST, FLORIDA

Adam Lloyd looked at the screen of his secure communication device with His Lordship. Ever since the nuke attack, the Tschaaa Lord had stayed mobile on the humongous seagoing platform in the Gulf of Mexico and the Caribbean. The size of several USS Ronald Reagan carriers, it was lucky to make ten knots, but its huge size made it stable in bad seas. Moving around made the Tschaaa Lord a difficult target. Due to that change, he and Adam did not have personal face to face meetings like they used to, everything being done through a secure server that Andrew had set up. Truth be told, Adam missed those meetings. If he were reading the Tschaaa body language correctly, so did Lord Neptune.

"So, your Lordship, I take it you have received the recent reports on the incursion into Kansas."

"Yes, My Director." The Tschaaa Lords social tentacles signaled dismissal. "I did not expect much, truth be told. Especially after hearing your concerns. We were both right. But the Krakens attack served a purpose."

"Which was, your Lordship?"

"Why, to put the Unoccupied States on the defensive. Now their people will demand complete protection. After years of us ignoring them, we evil Squids are now sending our minions to kill them. And, in some sick instances, the minions ate them. How you humans can eat your own kind is beyond my understanding. But the effect has its purposes."

"Well, Sir, we must be careful with the effect. Push too hard, they will scream for immediate revenge, not defense."

The Tschaaa Lord motioned agreement. "As always, you cut to the core of the matter at hand. But this is just stage one. Another is to follow. Soon, Atlanta will once again be under our control. Even if we have to level it."

"You have a plan in place, Your Lordship?"

"Our Kraken friends are working on the final points. I want you to stay out of it, to have deniability. I want you to be able to offer you and yours as an alternative to dealing with the Krakens."

The Tschaaa Lord gave his equivalent of a sigh. "Just before you called me, I had just received notice that an ally of mine in Deseret was found out and disposed. So, I will have to adjust."

Adam paused for a moment. Then he spoke. "I had figured out you had a special relationship with the Mormon Nation State. I take it was even more, shall we say, established, than I thought."

Neptune signed the Tschaaa equivalent of a smile, then expelled air and bubbles out of his gill structures, his equivalent of laughing.

"Again I underestimate you, my alien friend. Which is why I relish our relationship."

"Will we ever meet face to face again, Lord Neptune?"

"Soon, Director. Soon, if everything goes as planned. But I warn you. The next action will be quick and bold, as you humans like to say. Even if it fails in reaching its final goal, the attempt itself should rock the Unoccupied Areas, as well as the Feral areas. I will have a prepared statement for you to present as justification for the actions, as well as giving them a chance to negotiate, to even reach an agreement as a form of a supplicant people. Not a full Client peoples, as I want for you and yours. But along the lines of you leave us alone, we leave you alone."

The Lord moved his tentacles and arms in ways that showed irritation, bridging on anger.

"I cannot have those humans killing any more of our young. Not in the numbers that the attempt on me produced.”

“May I ask the final numbers?”

Again his Lordship gave the equivalent of a sigh.

“Over ten thousand young have died due to the blast and radiation effects. Some took a lot longer than we realized. We initially did not recognize some of the damage done. Now we know. Add some two thousand adults and adolescents, and it shook our collective psyche. Another such incident and I may not be able to control the reactions of the other Lords.”

“But it happened to your Crèche, Lord Neptune. Why would it upset the others so?”

“We are from different Crèches, but we are still Tschaaa. We are a much closer as a species, as what you might refer to as a race, than you humans. We feel each other’s pain when it comes to the loss of our offspring. It has ever been so, will probably remain so. Unless our exposure to this world somehow warps us.”

Adam said nothing. He remembered the Tschaaa Lord, the first in hundreds of years, who had been executed for trying to secretly damage his Lordship’s holdings using Eaters. They were already being warped, did not really realize it.

The Lord seemed to relax a bit, pulling out a piece of sugar cane to chew on.

“Please keep those numbers to yourself, Director. You are the only human who knows the extent of the damage. But I tell you the importance of that not happening again. That is, if you wish any civilization, as you call it, to exist in North America.”

Not for the first time, Adam felt a bit of a chill on his spine. Things were getting much more dangerous, if that were possible. The tight rope he was walking on suddenly became longer, thinner, and higher off the ground. “As we humans say, my lips are sealed. Sir.”

“Good. How are your young, and your wives?”

“Fine, your Lordship. The four children are growing like bad weeds. My wives are healthy and sassy.”

Lord Neptune performed the equivalent of a human chuckle. “Bad weeds. Again the alien concept of a human lawn. Someday, I would like to spend time on a human lawn, see what it feels like. All of my time on Earth has been in the ocean.”

Adam quickly banished from his memory the sight of the Squids killed on the grassy area around his HQ Building by both the attacking USA raiders and his own troops. The Tschaaa Lord had probably never thought of where all of those deaths had occurred. If he did, the idea of a lawn might not be so attractive.

"Well, my Director. Keep broadcasting your information to the Ferals, and the U.S.A.. Soon, you will have even more things to broadcast. Occurrences that will demonstrate the desirability of cooperation with the Tschaaa Lords, rather than resisting them."

"Until then, your Lordship, I remain your loyal Director."

"I know, Adam Lloyd. That is why I chose you."

CHAPTER 22

He who fights with monsters might take care lest he thereby become a monster. If you gaze for long into the abyss, the abyss gazes into you. So said the philosopher Friedrich Nietzsche. He must have foreseen the coming of the Tschaaa.

-Excerpt from the Works of Princess Akiko, Free Japan Royal Family

General Reed looked at the large print security warnings on the hard written copy of the video/DVD he had just viewed, hot off the proverbial press. Colonel Bardun had produced this in record time.

Top Secret Crypto. Eyes Only Authorization. NOFORN.
Unauthorized Dissemination of Information Contained
Herein Is Punishable by Death.

After viewing it twice, he saw why.

Sergeant Dark Wolf's digital recording had shown a tableau more in common with a slasher movie of the late twentieth century than of the scene of a rescue operation. He read the description written by Colonel Bardun again.

"As was mentioned earlier in this report, Tschaaa originated modification and enhancements of K-9 Sergeant Fuzz and Captain Young created a new form of fighting soldier. Both had bones of uncommon strength and density, as well as muscles with added strength, mass, and efficiency not apparently attainable thru normal means. In addition, extreme speed, reflexes added by modifications of "fast twitch" muscle mechanics create a level of combat effectiveness never seen before, short of a cyborg like the robocops.

"The initial video record made by Sergeant Dark Wolf was excellent, despite the use of a basic digital camera. He should be commended for obtaining so much information with a single camera in a limited amount of time. A survey team was able to respond, including the author of this report, with in twenty-four hours. Sergeant Dark Wolf's recording enabled the team to later reconstruct what had happened by adding its information to what the survey team had observed. This despite the movement of some of the bodies and body parts by scavengers and insects.""It is surmised that the alien smell of the two nearby dead grays may have been off-putting initially for traditional scavenging or predation. This is supported by the observed fact that neither gray body seemed to have been disturbed. Why no Tschaaa or their supporters arrived to look for the grays is a mystery, since they were sent to the location to track and recover Captain Young. It may have been a case that they were considered expendable, that once it was realized they were dead, there was no reason to expend effort at recovery."

General Reed now skipped down to the portion where Colonel Bardun went step by step, body by body of what had happened to the dead Krakens.

"Subject Bodies One and Two. Based on the location of the bodies and the recorded injuries, these two males came upon Captain Young while she was preoccupied with Sergeant Fuzz, either dead or dying. Subject One was partially eviscerated around the genital area, the partial blade of a switchblade knife belonging to Captain Young being recovered from his pubic bone.

"Subject Two apparently was able to fire his assault rifle at Captain Young, until she propelled Subject One's body into him. He was found partially covered by Subject One, with his face completely caved in. Evidence points to impact from combat boots.

"Based on the distance of the next series of dead bodies from the first two, a group of ten Krakens and Ferals were apparently hurrying to the site of the gunshots from Subject Two. The group arrived in what seemed to be a bunched up file. Upon arrival, they were set upon and slaughtered.

"There have been suppositions that there must have been some other unknown person or persons helping Captain Young. At this point I must state unequivocally that neither the survey team nor I found *any evidence* of any other participants, other than Captain Young. The slaughter was accomplished by one, though clearly special and enhanced, warrior."

General Reed paused in his reading for a moment to ponder this statement again. A young woman, whom he considered an adopted daughter, had single handedly killed twelve enemy combatants in hand to hand combat. He shivered a bit before he continued reading the report.

"Subjects Three and Four had their heads and faces smashed in by rifle butts and barrels. Four had a rifle, barrel first, speared through his right eye into his frontal lobe. Evidence points to a few rounds being discharged during this action.

"Subject Five, next in apparent line, had his throat ripped out. Exact instrument used is unclear.

"Apparently, at this moment, panic set in. Tracks and the position of the bodies point to a general panicked flight by the remaining combatants. Subjects Six, Seven and Eight became entangled while trying to flee, tripping over each other. A field machete, which must have been taken from one of the enemy as Captain Young had brought no such tool, was used to hack through necks. Two heads were completely separated from the bodies, with Subject Eight having the machete buried at the base of her skull.

"Remaining Subjects Nine through Twelve were more spread out back along the trail, trying to outrun death. They were unsuccessful. Nine appeared to have been picked up and rammed chest first into a broken branch stump some six feet above ground level. Ten and Eleven were slammed head first into trees as the killer caught up with them. The front of their skulls were partially caved in by the force of the impact on tree stumps. They were not wearing helmets.

"Finally, Subject Twelve made it some fifty yards further through the brush. At that point, she was caught, knocked down, and pummeled to death by a person's fists. Her jaw was completely smashed and broken, as was her nose. Her right eye was knocked clear out of the respective eye socket by the attack.

"Captain Young must have then immediately returned to Sergeant Fuzz, as she was found by Sergeant Dark Wolf cradling her K-9 Partner. That is how she appears in the Sergeant's recording.

"Attached in Appendix One of this Report is the After Action Report of the ParaRescue Team that extracted Captain Young and Sergeant Fuzz. Summarizing it, it took super efforts and substantial morphine to finally subdue and sedate Captain Young. Lieutenant Shannon Bell must receive special praise for managing to get Captains Young's attention and to stop her aggression, at the risk of her severe injury and possibly death. Chief Thompson, Sergeant Mason and Sergeant Dark Wolf all suffered severe bruises, bites, cracked and broken bones.

"Based on these actions and her subsequent hospitalization, it must be clearly stated that Captain Abigail Young has been modified to the extent that she is near a superhuman level in her strength, speed and ability to absorb injury. The attack and the subsequent death of Sergeant Fuzz resulted her going into a form of a fugue state, where her whole purpose became the protection of Fuzz and the utter destruction of any threat. It took the quick thinking of veterinarian Emily Anders and the introduction of Young Fuzz to her in the hospital to bring her back to normal.

"So far, tests reveal that Captain Young seems much more in control of her physical abilities. Time will tell if that remains so. Major Yamamoto seems to have training and experience in using meditation techniques he used in Free Japan to control unrestrained violence. Based on Captain Young's abilities, it is hoped that is reality."

General Reed poured himself another scotch. He wished yet again that fate had been different and that someone else had gotten the job he held today. It was a constant balancing act between trying to help people and at the same time making sure the U.S.A. survived. Now a woman who was like a daughter to him had demonstrated the ability to kill and destroy at an impossible level. At least not without the use of firearms. And now he had to decide if she could really be trusted among normal people. Or was she a ticking time bomb of a creature that should be put down.

Just then, Master sergeant Johannsson buzzed him on the intercom.

"Yes, Sergeant."

"Sir, Security Control has a General Huff from Deseret on the line. He says he has to talk to you about a very urgent matter that cannot wait for normal channels. It involves Captain Young."

It dawned on him that Abigail should have finished her meeting with Deseret government officials by now. But he had not yet received any word from anybody, so his blood suddenly ran cold.

"Put him through, Sergeant. Time for me to find out what is going on with the Mormons."

Abigail and Ichiro stopped again at Rock Springs to spend the night with the Bell family. Abigail needed time to depressurize after the violence and emotion of the meeting with the so- called Prophet. They would leave early in the morning and drive through to Malmstrom, where she would have to talk to General Reed about her future status. Abigail figured her position as a formal representative of Deseret was now ended. No matter what the Prophet had done, he was still the official Prophet, the leader of the Mormon Church, not to mention the President of the independent nation state. Plus, she had completely mangled his arm, and smashed him in the family jewels. She and Ichiro had killed some half a dozen of Deseret security personnel. If not for Doc Stubbs showing up, she would have loaded Mathew's body up into her SUV and taken him to Malmstrom for burial. She was just as much family to him as any of the surviving Twenty. However, she knew that Doc Stubbs would take care of his funeral needs, and would not let anyone deter him from that task.

So Abigail assumed she would need a job and citizenship in the Unoccupied States, with both General Reed could help. She did not know if the civilian government would pitch a fit, though she knew that Madam President would probably be in her corner. But Congress?

Who knew?

Abigail and Ichiro gave the Bell family the quick and dirty on what had happened. Cal Bell was quick to respond.

"We've got your back, Abigail. Need a place to live, you have it here."

"After we marry, you will have status with Free Japan," Ichiro interjected. "You are also becoming a legendary figure among the young women in my country."

"I just wanted to serve God, the human race, and my country," Abigail sighed. "Now, it looks as if I have to start over."

"Then we will do it together, Abby-san. As husband and wife."

Abigail leaned her head against Ichiro's shoulder, Funny how, after all these years, knowing she could depend on someone, just touching them, gave her such a feeling of security. But then she had never really been in love before.

"I think I need to call it a night. I'm sleepy, and we have a long day ahead of us, Ichiro."

"Whatever you wish, my love."

"Your beds made up already, dear," said Ma Bell. "I'll get up and make you both a good breakfast in the morning. No, protesting will do you no good. I want to see you off anyways."

Abigail hugged her adopted mother. Then, off to her bed she went.

Jean Bell looked at Ichiro.

"You will keep in touch, even if Abigail has trouble doing so?"

Ichiro bowed. "It will be my honor. You have done so much for her, given her a family she needed."

With that, Jean Bell gave an embarrassed Samurai a hug and a kiss on the cheek.

"I will hold you to that promise, Ichiro Yamamoto. Now you are family too. I understand you still have family in Japan."

"Hai. We were lucky. Our major problems have been to supply sufficient food for our people. We have lost only some one thousand of our civilians due to direct enemy action. Apparently some of the background radiation from Fukushima, the knowledge that we had two nuclear weapons dropped on us reduced our value as meat for the Tschaaa. Though my mother and father were among those dead."

"I am sorry, Ichiro."

He shrugged. "I miss my parents, but still have a brother and sister, not to mention all my aunts, uncles, and cousins. Unlike you Americans, who have had entire families wiped out and harvested."

"Well, we have made do, and have survived," interjected Cal Bell. "Many have created their own family units by just deciding they will be siblings, cousins, parents and children. One huge unofficial adoption process creating what would probably be like a Clan in older times."

Ichiro bowed again. "And you do me honor…"

"All right, that does it. You're family now, Ichi. Please, lighten up. No more bowing. We do each other honor by acting as family to each other. Do I have to get the moonshine out again to relax you again?"

"Well, Colonel, now that you mentioned it…"

"Mother. Glasses and ice cubes please. A couple of nightcaps, swapping stories, and we will all be ready for bed. Tomorrow will be a long, tiring day."

Ichiro gave a half smile. "Not as long or as tiring as today, Cal-san."

They left as the sun was rising the next morning, after having a nice traditional "farmers breakfast"—ham, eggs, bacon, pancakes, fresh biscuits, and fruit; washed down with apple juice and coffee, with a cup of fresh brewed tea for Ichiro.

Abigail had slept like a log, and finally felt rested. She and Ichiro said their goodbyes, had group hugs, and a few tears.

"Remember. No matter what happens, you two will always have a place to hang your hats," Cal said as he shook Ichiro's hand.

"Yes sir. We appreciate that. Hopefully, that will not have to happen."

Then they were on the road, headed toward Malmstrom AFB. About an hour in, they received an escort of a Wyoming state trooper, who ran lights and siren in front until they hit the Montana border. They stopped for some fuel, and a Montana trooper suddenly appeared, ran ahead of them like the Wyoming trooper had.

The word had gotten out. The Avenging Angel, My Lady of Steel, First Daughter of the U.S.A.—whatever name they gave her. She needed to get home ASAP. They made record time, and were at Malmstrom AFB by sunset. Abigail was waved through the Main Gate, so she head directly to General Reed's office at the Headquarters. He was waiting for them at the main entrance.

"Made it in one piece I see. Captain, Major."

Abigail gave a slim smile. "Sir, I'm afraid…"

General Reed put his hand up. "Let's cut to the chase. I already know what happened. A certain General Huff called me from Salt Lake City. Then he dispatched a VSTOL here with some items he said you would need. Plus he asked if the aircraft and crew could be assigned here."

He shook his head. "Somehow, no matter what happens around you, it always turns out okay in the end. Sometimes, way more than okay." He looked at Ichiro, then pulled a slim case from his General officer leather jacket pocket.

"Major, please, will you do the honors with your fiancé."

Ichiro opened up the case, he began beaming.

"Ichi, what is it?" Abigail asked.

Her love took out two sets of special Major's Oak Leaves from the case. Abigail's mouth literally dropped open.

"You see, Abigail, General Huff told me the whole, dirty, nasty story. He was extremely apologetic. I could tell he had no idea what was going on with… you and your fellow orphans. He had believed the bullshit Prophet Smith had told him, because he wanted to believe it, that everything would be alright if he left everything to Smith, no questions asked."

General Reed sighed. "I genuinely feel sorry for him, because I can tell he is going to carry a whole knot of guilt in his stomach for years. He realizes know he should have stepped forward, acted more like the Commanding General he was and less like the toady Smith wanted him to be. Anyways, you are still a Daughter of Deseret, still their version of Ambassador, and now a Major in their armed forces assigned to my command. That okay with you, young Major?"

Abigail blinked back tears. "General, I don't know what to say."

"What, a woman with nothing to say? Wait, that's kind of sexist. Ah hell, we know it's true, so sue me. Major Yamamoto, do the honors, please."

"Would you assist him, please, Sir?"

"I thought you'd never ask."

General Reed pinned the Gold Oak Leaf on her left as Ichiro did it to her right. As he did, he continued explaining.

"I have in my office papers spelling out a proposed formal relationship between Deseret and us. They will be providing us with equipment and personnel, their manufacturing grid being already up and running at near full capacity." He stepped back and admired his handiwork.

"That special cross in the middle of your rank befits you, Abigail. A Christian soldier as of old, fighting evil wherever it is."

"Sir, I have hurt, killed people. I don't know how worthy I am of that title."

"Abby, please," Ichiro interrupted. "You killed because it was necessary. But in your heart and soul you are good, will always help those in need. You would make a good samurai."

She managed for once to hold back her tears. Then she straighten up, and saluted.

"Major Jorgensen reporting for duty, General Reed."

The General chuckled. "Yes, you'll have to have some new name tags made. Some more new ones if you take Ichiro's name when you are married."

"Of course I'll take his name. I will be honored to be his wife."

"Well, that's all settled. So, day after tomorrow, you get to take on a new and bigger assignment befitting your new rank."

"What would that be, General?"

"Well, partly thanks to you, I have a bunch of female soldiers who decided to disobey orders and completely screw up some best laid plans. But, since it worked out much better than we could ever hope for, I'm having trouble figuring out what to do with them. So guess what? You and your big sister, Major Smirnoff, get to help me decide how to use them and not have to court martial them. I have in mind a special unit that can be turned into a punishment battalion if things do not work out. Quick and dirty, it all started out with people calling themselves Sisters of Steel…"

ATLANTA, GEORGIA

Malcolm Carter sat eating a bowl of oatmeal that tasted like it had a bit of sawdust added to stretch it out. Which it probably had. They were doing everything in Atlanta possible to stretch their food supplies. And they were reaching the breaking point.

Malcolm looked out his underground bunker headquarters. Over at a desk in the far corner, Red, Bollywood actress lookalike, was crunching the numbers on everything. Food, medical supplies, weapons, ammunition, and shelter, were all balanced against the known numbers of surviving people of color in Atlanta. According to the information they had, some fifty thousand men, women and children were still living, if you could call it that, in the city of Atlanta. Living and hiding, trying to survive more on hope and stubbornness than anything.

Big Joe and Dawoud entered the bunker, back from a foot recon, assessing the conditions of the entire infrastructure. At least what was left.

Malcolm noticed that even Big Joe was beginning to look a little haggard, his large frame not filling out his clothes as they used to. Dawoud always looked slender, taunt and wiry. But Malcolm thought he even looked like he had dropped some weight.

"So, gentlemen, what's the news?"

"Well, my leader," the former Islamic Terrorist began. "Do you wish the bad news or the good news first?"

"There's good news? Leave that until last. I like to end things on a positive note."

"A dozen men, women and children tried to escape last night through a southwestern sentry point. They killed two human guards, left a couple corpses of their own behind. But most seemed to have made it through."

Malcolm grunted. "The Krakens and Squids must be slacking. Or they are losing interest in us. I'd like to believe the latter. But why is that bad news?"

"Expect retaliation, my leader. At least from the Krakens. We people of color just killed two of theirs. That is a blow to their ego."

Malcolm barked out a laugh. "What are they going to do? Starve us? They already are. Some people here think a *quick* death would be a blessing."

"Well, Boss," Big Joe interjected. "Where there is life, there is hope."

"Ever the optimist, my large friend. So what's the good news?"

"Food, boss. The pigeons are coming along nicely, as well as the guinea pigs. So, we have a small amount of fresh meat."

Dawoud added, "Mister Joe and I stumbled upon a new large colony of rats. They apparently found a new undiscovered path or tunnel from the outside, as we were through that area last week and saw no signs of vermin."

Malcolm's ears perked up. "Maybe an unknown drainage, sewer pipe me missed?"

"That is what I hope. If we find it before the Demon Djinns do, we may have a way for supplies to come in and people out."

"Yeah, but if 'out' where will they go?"

"Maybe the border with the Feral area. At least they will not be trapped and starving."

Malcolm was silent in thought for a brief moment. "I'd like to believe the answer was 'just get out', escape. But without support from the outside, the Unoccupied States, we still are just Cattle in a larger pen. I thought a general revolt after the nuke attack would lead to the borders of Cattle Country collapsing. But I was wrong."

"You had to try, Boss," Big Joe said.

"That we did. But it may be out of the frying pan, into the fire. Dawoud, any more word from your people in the U.S.A.?"

Dawoud shrugged. "We received those two small supply balloons last week, the first in a month. Some medical supplies, a weapon and a little ammunition. Plus some potatoes gone to seed that we planted, are coming along nicely. But now someone is trying to jam our communications, for the first time ever."

Malcolm's brow furrowed. "Now? Something different is going to happen. Double the lookouts, gentlemen, have them watch for a higher level of activity outside the fence."

The landline rang, and Red answered it. A short flurry of conversation, then she called out.

"Mayor. A Falcon is coming."

"Ah fuck. That's never good. Come on, gentlemen—to those periscopes Professor Gupta built for us."

The main source for the Atlanta weapons and equipment industry had set up some periscopes and telescopes by which Malcolm and his staff could view what was going on from hiding near the Headquarters bunker. Five minutes later they each were scanning a section of the downtown.

"Nothing so far, Boss…," Big Joe began. Then a rain began. A red rain.

"Those sick bastards." Malcolm yelled out. "They did it again."

The remains of the apparent escapees were returned to the center of Atlanta in the form of a red rain and fine mist. Every human had apparently been ground up into a fine slurry, and were now being dumped as a reminder as to who was *really* in charge. The fact was that the Tschaaa were more than willing to waste good dark meat to make a point.

"So much for ending on a positive note. Joe, Dawoud, Red, call out and make sure everyone stays undercover. This may just be the beginning of something bad."

CHAPTER 24

MALMSTROM ARMED FORCES BASE
MONTANA

General Reed looked out from offstage at the group of women in uniform standing at ease in the auditorium. Ninety-eight women were on the floor, several still sporting bandages and slings. He knew two others were still in guarded condition in the Base Hospital, recovering from their wounds. Up on stage with newly promoted Lt. Colonel Smirnov and Major Jorgenson fka Young was a certain Russian Senior Sergeant Marina Roskova, the oldest of the one hundred and one women soldiers that had started the Great Rout of Bloody Kansas.

What they had accomplished was the stuff of legends. However, they had disobeyed orders, big time. There were either lucky or blessed that it had turned out the way it had. A hundred and one had gone between enemy lines, and a hundred and one had made it back, although it was questionable whether the two in the hospital would return to active duty. Yet, a bunch of soldiers just can't run off and start killing people without orders. Actions like that often derailed the best laid plans of Generals like John Reed, with often dire results.

Therefore, General Reed needed to insure this did not happen again. Especially by an independent minded group of females who had formed something called the Sisters of Steel.

As the General stepped from off stage, Senior Sergeant Roskova barked everyone to attention. He walked to the center, Lt. Colonel Smirnov saluting as senior ranking member of the formation.

"General Reed. Everyone present and accounted for as ordered."

He snapped a salute back. "Good. Put them at Parade Rest, Colonel."

"Formation. Parade…Rest." As one, the women assumed the position. They were already acting in perfect unison, a good sign to the General. John Reed walked to the center of the stage, surveying the assembled womanhood. He saw in them a sense of purpose, a unity that he wished he saw in more members of the human race. He began.

"The General is not happy this morning. I am not happy because, instead of dealing with the myriad of other problems and demands of being the Supreme Commanding General of the Combined Armed Forces, I have to be here."

He paused for a moment, letting them wonder what was coming next.

"Instead, I have to deal with a bunch of female soldiers who do not know how to *follow orders.*" The last part he bellowed out, something he rarely did. When General Reed bellowed, you knew you were knee deep in the shit.

"Only sheer luck and the Grace of God kept a bunch of you out of body bags. Or on some Kraken's fire spit as a hunk of Long Pig. That stunt you pulled should have gone wrong in dozens of ways."

He paused again for effect, then continued. "A certain Russian General suggested I institute Roman decimation, taking every tenth person out and have them shot." He thought he heard some shocked intakes of breath. Good. They needed to know how serious this was.

Then he chuckled. "Some crazy Russian Colonel named Popov barged into my office, demanded 'satisfaction' if I dared consider that. Apparently someone is forming a fan club."

He thought he heard the beginnings of a titter, then a snarl from another woman that immediately shut down the same. Policing their own already. This may just work better than he hoped.

"So, after some due deliberation, I have come to a solution. Or I should say, *the* solution as it is not open for debate. Unless someone really wants a court martial."

Silence. One could hear a pin drop.

"Captain Daniel O'Brien. Time to unveil your creation."

The tall and slender black haired Irishman stepped on to the stage. The previous Key West attack team member went to a furled banner that was hung horizontally behind the General. A quick pull of a restraining tie and a colorful very oversized banner unfurled to a few gasps that the General ignored.

On it was a graphic depiction of a screaming she-beast. A good looking, erotic creation with definite feminine attributes and long flowing shiny silver white hair. In her right hand was a Sisters of Steel Squid Killer blade. In her left was an ArmaLite AR -18 Rifle. Her face was pulled back in a snarl, displaying long canines and flashing eyes. She was both beautiful and horrifying at the same time.

"Please explain your creation, Captain."

"Well, Sir, it's an Irish Banshee. Based on a drawing my sainted grandmother did, back when she was affiliated with the Irish Republican Army. A ghostly she-creature from Irish legends."

"You drew this, and had this banner made, because?"

He pulled a paper from his pocket, read from it with the requisite emotion. "Banshees. A bunch of fucking screaming banshees. They were slicing, killing everyone. Bullets were no good. They were fucking banshees!"

"Who said that, my good Captain?"

"A captured Kraken on the receiving end of these Sisters of Steel."

General Reed paused and stared at the assembled women. Then he continued.

"Congratulations, ladies. By your actions you just all volunteered for the One Hundred and First Special Attack Unit. One Hundred and First because one hundred and one Sisters of Steel crossed into enemy lines, and one hundred and one returned. Though two of your number may be too injured to come back to active duty. No deaths, though, and that is a record, considering our intelligence reflects you all killed over four hundred Krakens and Ferals, ninety percent of the deaths by cold steel. And a few dozen more wounded. An almost unheard of kill to casualty ratio."

The General turned and looked at the large banner. Then turned back.

"Your actions created a legend, a symbol. Now, you are going have to live up to it, make it real. So, an all-female unit. All except our brand new Captain O'Brien here. Key West wasn't enough action for him. Besides, he came up with the Unit Symbol. The Banshee."

General Reed looked at Aleks and Abigail. "I am now going to turn this over to your new Commander and Executive Officer. They get to complete the necessary details to fine tune this Unit. By the way, eventually you will be Battalion Size, some four hundred Banshees. You 'originals' have the added task of getting the newbies up to snuff."

He fixed the assembled warriors with his best steely gaze. "As the saying goes, you make your bed, you have to sleep in it. By the way, quitting or failure is not an option. Carry on, ladies."

Senior Sergeant Roskova called the women to attention, as Aleks saluted the General. Then he was gone.

Aleks looked at Abigail. "Damnit, I'm a spy, not a commander," she complained in low tones. Aleks had tried to refuse the assignment when given her orders and new promotion from Mother Russia. But, of course, 'needs of the service', so no go, kids or no kids.

Abigail looked at Aleks. "Big sister," she replied in hushed tones. "We will make this work. We owe Fuzz, we owe them. This is partly our doing by letting it continue after we knew about it. Please allow me to start the ball rolling."

"Have at it, little sister. We are all Sisters of Steel here."

Abigail faced the women at Parade Rest. "Unit, Atten Hut." They all snapped to as if they had been together for months rather than hours, days.

"At Ease." Abigail looked at the now very nervous just under one hundred women warriors.

"All right. Everyone, turn and greet your Sister to each side of you, as you would your flesh and blood. For, from this day forth, we *are* of one flesh, one blood."

Everyone froze for just a few moments, as the words sank in. Then, hugs, kissed cheeks, laughter and a few tears as the new Banshee family had its first reunion.

Aleks looked at Abigail. "Anyone ever tell you that you are very good at this leadership thing?"

Abigail smiled a bit sheepishly then grabbed and hugged Aleks. "You're my big sister. I will never let you down."

"Nor I you, little sister. At least we are allowed to be with each other, to work this out together. We make a good pair."

A beautiful Irish tenor voice sang out, supported by a squeeze box that had miraculously appeared. Captain Danny O'Brien began to sing an IRA song that would soon become a staple of the Banshees.

"And it's down in the Bogside, that's where I long to be,
Lying in the dark with a Provo company,
A comrade on me left and another on me right
And a clip of ammunition for my little Armalite.
I was stopped by a soldier, said he, You are a swine,
He beat me with his baton and he kicked me in the groin,
I bowed and I scraped, sure me manners were polite
But all the time I'm thinking of me little Armalite.
And it's down in Crossmaglen, sure that's where I long to be,
Lying in the dark with a Provo company,
A comrade on me left and another on me right
And a clip of ammunition for my little Armalite.
Sure a brave RUC man came up into our street
Six hundred British soldiers were gathered round his feet
Come out, ye cowardly Fenians, said he, come out and fight.
But he cried, I'm only joking, when he heard the Armalite.
Sure it's down in Kilwilkie, that's where I long to be,
Lying in the dark with a Provo company,
A comrade on me left and another on me right
And a clip of ammunition for my little Armalite.
Sure, the army came to visit me, 'twas in the early hours,
With Saladins and Saracens and Ferret armoured cars
They thought they had me cornered, but I gave them all a fright
With the armour piercing bullets of my little Armalite.
And it's down in the Falls Road, that's where I long to be,
Lying in the dark with a Provo company,
A comrade on me left and another on me right
And a clip of ammunition for my little Armalite.
When Tuzo came to Belfast, he said, The battle's won,

Said General Ford, We're winning sir, we have them on the run.
But corporals and privates on patrol at night.
Said, Send for reinforcements, it's the bloody Armalite.
And it's up in Ballymurphy, that's where I long to be,
Lying in the dark with a Provo company,
A comrade on me left and another on me right
And a clip of ammunition for my little Armalite.

It took a little while, but soon just over a hundred female voices were singing at least the chorus, as Danny O'Brien walked them thru the song *My Little Armalite*, singing with a wide smile on his face. Even Senior Sergeant Roskova joined in, though her voice was not very melodic. But she definitely had the enthusiasm down. Applause and cheers rang out as Captain O'Brien took a short bow.

"Captain. Your Commander calls you," Aleks' voice rang out.

The new Captain quickly marched over in front of Aleks and saluted.

"Ma'am, Captain Daniel O'Brien, Administrative and Supply Office, reporting as ordered to Colonel Smirnov."

Aleks tried not to smile, only partially succeeded. "Morale and Welfare Officer too, I see."

"If you wish, Ma'am. I am at your command."

"You have other similar rousing songs?"

"Yes, Ma'am. My sainted grandmother taught me on her knee. She was quite the Amazon warrior during her time."

"But no revolution now, Captain. Some people may not understand."

"Just against the devil fish, the Squids. Against them every Irishman worth his salt would resist."

Aleks broke into a grin. "I think, Captain, you will fit in quite nicely, as the only male soldier in the unit."

"That I aim to do, Ma'am. Always wanted to fight alongside some Banshee women. God just granted my wish."

A week after the formation of the Banshees, Abigail was in route to the Bloody Kansas Memorial Service. Even after the 'official' formation of the 101st Special Assault Unit, it would be weeks if not months before it was entirely operational. All the selected assigned personnel had to be transferred from their previous unit, uniforms and equipment had to be obtained, barracks and office space had to be found. Right now, Captain O'Brien was handling all the details under direct orders from General Reed. When the Supreme Allied Commander told everyone that a certain Captain had his full support, the waters parted, the bureaucratic sea barriers disappeared.

Thus Abigail had some time to herself, her presence not being needed at the training area. Unofficially, she had been told by General Reed to take care of personal business until further notice, based on directions from Madam President. The fact her actions, her literal presence, had opened up official co-operation between the Armed Forces of Deseret and the Combined Allied Armed Forces was deemed enough work by the new Major for the present as well as near future.

So, she was spending time getting Young Fuzz acclimated to his new home as well as beginning to plan for her wedding. Every time Abigail thought of her wedding, she sighed. She and Ichiro had wanted a small affair. No such luck. Once again, her image as the Avenging Angel, Sgt. Fuzz's human, as well as Ichiro's reputation as the man who had nuked the Squids, meant that they were the closest thing to a First Couple that existed. Everyone wanted to see them married with as much pomp and circumstance as possible. People needed the equivalent of a National Party to feel good, to take their mind off of what had just happened in Bloody Kansas. They needed a symbol of hope, of normalcy. So, for better or worse, Ichiro and Abigail had a special role to play in the greater scheme of things.

But driving to the memorial service was bringing back the memories, emotions and angst over losing Fuzz. In her SUV back seat Young Fuzz reclined as she drove. Every time she looked at the K-9 it was bitter sweet. Memories of his sire came flooding back to remind her that he was gone. But then she saw Fuzz in the young dog when she looked at him, so she smiled. She would also swear that Sergeant Fuzz was watching over her still, through his son. The circle of life and love remained unbroken.

Abigail pulled into a reserved Distinguished Visitor slot, though she never, ever felt distinguished. Young Fuzz perked up, sat and looked expectantly at the rear door, knowing he would be let out momentarily. He was a dream to train, leading Abigail to again claim that the Senior Fuzz was whispering 'doggese' in his ears, telling him exactly what was expected of him. She opened the back door and he jumped down, then sat patiently for her to put his leash on. Though he was already off leash capable, Abigail knew he was still basically a pup. And a pup his size made people nervous, as well as capable of doing damage if he became rambunctious.

She smiled at him, scratched his ears in just the right way to illicit a small groan of contentment and pleasure.

"More like your father every day, big fella. It looks like you're going to be even a bit larger than Fuzz Senior, and he was a big dog."

Something made you look up, and she saw a woman and two children walking hesitantly toward the huge auditorium set up for the memorial service. Again, outside tents had been set up with closed circuit video for the expected overflow. The woman and the children paused, seemed unsure as to where they were to go. Then it dawned on her who they were. And memories of Fuzz and That Day came flooding back. They were the ones she and Fuzz had saved. And she had never even gotten their names.

The light brown haired woman of medium build looked up, saw her. She gave a hesitant wave. Abigail made a beeline toward her, Young Fuzz heeling perfectly. As Abigail approached the woman, the young boy spoke up.

"Look, Mom. A dog like Sergeant Fuzz."

Abigail smiled. "Ma'am, your son is quite observant. This is Fuzz's son. You and your children are the ones Fuzz led out that day. I didn't even get your names."

"I thought that was you, Captain, no, Major now. You look a bit different without all that camouflage on. Your dress uniform is beautiful on you."

The woman stuck her hand out. "Janette Jamison. My son Timothy, and my daughter Tina. Ma'am, we just had to come and pay our respects to Sergeant Fuzz and you. If not for you two..." A tear suddenly ran down her face. She brushed it a way with a sheepish smile.

"I told myself crying time is over, but just look at me. Still bawling like a baby..."

Abigail took Janette's with her offered hand, then hugged her with her left arm. Then her tears came. The two women hugged as they re-shared the moment when death was near. When for Janette and her children, the Grim Reaper was chased off with the help of a four-legged Guardian Angel, who had gone with death instead of them.

"Mommy, please don't cry," five year old toe headed Tina said plaintively.

Abigail let go of Janette, then knelt down, whipping her eyes with a handkerchief a certain Madam President had given her.

"Your Mommy and I are just happy to see each other, Tina. And I'm glad to see you, too. Want to say hello to Young Fuzz, son of Sergeant Fuzz?" The little girl nodded, and reached out to pet him. The huge pup stole a doggy kiss, a nice slurp on the face. Tina giggled.

"Oh, I forgot to tell you and your Mom. Young Fuzz is a ladies' man, just like his sire was."

Timothy approached, began to scratch the K-9's ears. "He looks just like Sergeant Fuzz, only younger."

"Yes, Tim. All but this white star on his forehead. It's where the Great Spirit touched him as he was being born."

Abigail stood up, took Janette's hand in hers. "Where are you staying?"

The woman looked a little embarrassed. "Ma'am, we hitched a ride up here, and thought we would find a motel room. Beyond that, I guess I didn't do a very good job of planning ahead."

"No need to plan. And call me Abigail. Torbin Bender told me a long time ago that anyone you faced the Grim Reaper with gets to be on a first name basis with you. You and your children will stay with me in my quarters for as long as you want. I live alone, and have my own house."

"Please, Ma'am…Abigail. I can't impose on you like that. I have some money…"

"No imposing. It's what Sergeant Fuzz would want. He would want to make sure you're okay in a strange place. Just like he did that day."

Abigail grinned. "Besides, Young Fuzz wants your children to tell him about his father. Don't you, big fella?"

Fuzz gave a signature open mouthed doggy smile, then stole another kiss from Tina.

"See? It's settled. Now, I'm going to get you the best seats in the house for the memorial service."   Just then she saw a couple of familiar figures approaching, and a quick plan formed in her mind.

"Senior Training Instructor Stalin. Miss Reid," she called out. "Could I borrow you for a while?"

Stalin called back. "For My Lady of Cold Steel, anything. How are you this fine day of remembrance, of honoring our Comrades?"

Abigail grinned. Always full of life, even with a gruff exterior during training. And Sally Reid, local Reporter was now a bit of a fixture around him. To say that they seemed on the surface a bit of an odd couple was an understatement. But they seemed happy, so who cared?

As they reached Abigail and her three new friends, Abigail introduced Janette and her two children.

"Stalin, Miss Reid, may I present Janette Jamison and her children, her son Timothy and daughter Tina. They are the ones Sergeant Fuzz led out to safety in Wyoming."

"Please, Abigail, not so formal. I'm just a country girl with two children. We came to pay our respects."

Stalin put his hand out to shake for Timothy. "Please to meet you, young man."

Timothy did not hesitate to take and shake it.

"Nice, firm handshake," Stalin remarked. "You can tell a lot from a handshake."

"My Dad taught me. Before the Krakens killed him." Timothy said it matter of factly, as if it were something that happened to him every day. He looked Stalin in the eye. "You're a Russian Soldier, aren't you?"

"Yes, Timothy. *Spetsnaz*. Special Forces. I train them now that I am older."

"I want to be a soldier. Mr. Stalin. So that I can kill Krakens, like they killed my Dad."

"Now, Timothy," His mother began. But Stalin gently waved her off.

"Son, if that is what you want, then when you reach your age of maturity, then that is what you can do. I will probably still be here, training new and old soldiers, so I may train you."

"You would?"

"If the good Major hasn't chased me off by then."

Abigail smiled. "Stalin, you are too ornery to be chased off, even if

I wanted to. Which I don't."

"And I see you have a young sister. You watch out for her, da?"

"Yes, Sir. That's what my Dad told me. Big brothers watch out for little sisters."

Stalin slowly nodded his head. "Your father was a smart and honorable man." He knelt down in front of Tina, who was acting a bit shy, moving toward her mother.

Stalin gently took her hand in his, kissed it. "I see we have a little princess in our midst."

At that, Tina giggled, smiling. Abigail looked at Stalin, a warm feeling in her heart. In his native Russian she spoke.

"You have a side to you that you try to hide. You make children laugh, feel special."

"Please don't let that information be common knowledge, Major. It would ruin my reputation as Stalin, steel," he answered in Russian as he gently picked up Tina, and set her on his shoulder.

"A princess needs to be able to see the world from a high vantage point," Stalin said now in English. "So that she may survey all that is happening around her. My shoulder should do okay, temporarily, yes?"

Abigail saw Sally was looking at Stalin with moist eyes. In Abigail's experience, this reaction was often due to painful memories.

"Miss Reid, I imagine you would like to talk to the Jamisons about what happened that day, flesh out the story of Fuzz."

This brought Sally out of her woolgathering. "Why yes. And a picture, if possible, with this digital camera Stalin magically procured."

Janette Jamison blushed a bit. "I'm not very, photogenic I guess is the word. But I wouldn't mind telling you about what Abigail and Fuzz did for us."

"Can you and Stalin chaperone them also? They want me to accept the flag for Fuzz as part of the memorial service. I had to fight with the powers that be to keep it to that simple function. They wanted to concentrate on Sergeant Fuzz the symbol, rather than this being a memorial service for all."

Sally smiled. "Of course. I'll get a feature story out of this, which will make my paper happy. I understand the government's desire to spin the positive as much as possible. There is a strong civilian undercurrent questioning the level of casualties in Kansas, whether if we had ignored the Squids and Key West, they would have ignored us."

At that comment, Stalin had snorted. "And that is why I stayed a lowly, common soldier. Politics complicate everything."

"You are neither common nor lowly, Man of Steel," Sally responded. "And you are doing a bang up job as a two-legged horse for Tina there."

Stalin chuckled, then looked at Tina. "Am I a good horse, princess?"

The young girl giggled. "Yes. I can see everything from here."

"So, Mother Janette and children. I see they have set up a food and drink tent. I was always hungry as a child, so I suggest we go there. Then I and Sally will insure you have front row seats for the Memorial.

Janette smiled. "You are so nice to us strangers. I don't know how to repay you."

Stalin looked at her. "The only strangers are the damnable Squids. All we humans are family."

The Memorial Service went rather smoothly and quickly. Representatives of all the Armed Forces and Countries involved accepted flags for the fallen. In the back, Spetsnaz members suspended berets on their fists to represent their fallen comrades. Governors of Wyoming and Kansas as well as the Militia Commanders accepted flags honoring their dead, both civilian and military. Every single person killed in the attack would have an individual U.S. Flag presented to surviving family members, friends, or buried with them. Madam President had stated everyone was a soldier in this war, deserved the honors for the fallen.

Madam President had purposefully stayed in the background of this national, televised memorial service. However, at the end she had to step forward to introduce a special guest, who had asked to give his respects at the memorial. So, at the very end, she came up to the microphone in the center of the stage.

"We have a new friend and ally to all who wishes to pay his respects to those who have fallen in this war for freedom for all humanity. So, without further delay, I would like to introduce Thor Heyerdahl, War Leader for the Great Lakes American Vikings."

When Thor strode out in traditional Norseman garb, long cape and long beard, near seven feet tall. More than one person gasped, "My God. He's as big as a robocop."

Thor Heyerdahl strode to the center of the stage, shook Madam President's hand, then turned toward the assembled citizens of the Unoccupied States of America. Without a microphone, his voice boomed and resonated throughout the auditorium. "As you will tell by my thick accent and my clothes, I am not from around here." This brought some laughter from the audience. Thor did have a much thicker accent that the home grown Norskies, but he really was not that out of place. Except, that is, for his giant size. Rolf Knudsen looked almost average sized next to him.

"As the fine lady, and my new friend, Madam President said, I wish to pay our respect to the fallen. And, to offer an apology." A slight murmur was heard as some people expressed questions as to what he was talking about.

The huge man continued. "I offer an apology for me and mine. For we Great Lakes Vikings, Norsemen, stood by, watching, as you fought and died."

The auditorium became silent.

"I came over from Norway at the end of the first year of this Invasion with family on two fishing boats we waylaid. We headed toward Minnesota as we had some extended family there. And we had heard the Squids, the Krakens were leaving well enough alone up here, due to the cold weather."

He paused for a moment. "We banded together with other people of Northern blood and created our own society. We removed ourselves from other humans, began returning to the Old Ways. We believed Ragnarok, the Final Battle, had been fought. We believed that if we returned to the Old Ways, applied ourselves to what we thought was Viking heritage, we could begin anew. After all, Christian, Jew, Muslims and their God had been defeated. So now, maybe the Great World Tree would grow again, support us, and allow us to prosper."

"We were fools. Cowards." His voice rang out. After that, a dropped pin could be heard.

"For we saw the images of the Beast Raid, the Pit Raid. Where a small band of Sons and Daughters of the North fought the Great Evil, freed and nurtured young children who had been subjected to unspeakable horrors. We saw Rolf Knudsen, Brynhildr Jorgenson and Johann Knudsen take the child survivors under their protection. And the rest of us were shamed by our inaction."

Thor paused, swallowed. Everyone assembled could tell this was no political speech. This came from the heart of a man who hurt.

"Then more innocents were killed in Bloody Kansas while we dithered, beat out chests, and acted mean and tough. It is so easy to play the part of a true Norseman. So easy to wear the trappings of what we say were tough, honorable Vikings. It is not so easy to actually *be* what we claimed we were."

"So, today. I stand before you as the speaker and representative of my band, tribe, my Family. I pledge our undying support in this War to Free Humanity. And ask only the chance to make amends for our past inaction."

Thor turned and motioned to someone off stage.

"We have prepared a symbol of our pledge. Rolf Knudsen told us about a certain War Dog whom he claimed was the Fenris Wolf in the flesh. Only this Fenris was beholden to a maiden with our people's blood. Unlike my family, he sacrificed for his loyalty, his love. We would like to add our homage to the honor of his memory, if we are allowed. Joseph, the offering, please."

Two large Norsemen began to push a large shrouded object setting on a wheeled platform onto the center of the stage."

"Major Abigail Jorgenson. May I borrow you, please."

Abigail walked slowly up and onto the stage, Young Fuzz in tow. She had no idea what Thor had in mind. Nor apparently, other than possibly the President, did anyone else.

Thor handed a length of rope to her. "Please accept this as an attempt to honor Sergeant Fuzz, his memory, his loyalty, and his love, from our woodworkers. Also as a symbol for all who have fallen. I hope our efforts are sufficient."

In a spontaneous act, Abigail handed the rope to Young Fuzz. "Pull, Fuzz."

The large pup pulled the rope with a wagging tail, it being a new, fun game. The shroud fell away from the object. Abigail gasped.

Sergeant Fuzz. Larger than life, a perfect carving done by masters. Fuzz alert, tail up, gazing ahead as if looking for a possible threat his nose had detected. Fuzz, the immortal symbol of loyalty and protection. Despite her best attempts, Abigail could not stop the tears.

Young Fuzz suddenly sat in front of his Sires carved statute, mouth slightly open in a doggy grin as if to say "Hey Dad."

From the audience, in a front row seat, Sally Reid managed to take a quick series of digital photos she would use in a feature. The best would become The Memorial Photo for Fallen Comrades, never to be forgotten.

Silence. Then gasps. Then, everything broke.

Applause, cheers, yells, and everyone leapt to their feet. Thor Heyerdahl had just struck the right chord.

Abigail walked over to the War Leader, somehow croaked out, "Thank you." Thor hugged her in his huge arms, kissed her on her forehead.

"We need to thank you. And Fuzz. You have lead the way, showed us what we must do if we really want to be human, defeat the Squids. Thank you for helping get us back on the correct path."

It took a good ten minutes for everything to calm down. Madam President came out on stage, and hugged the huge Viking. Hand in hand with Thor, with Abigail and Young Fuzz standing by, she spoke. "Today, we continue on. We honor our dead, our wounded as we continue our fight for freedom. We fight. And with Thor and all you other fellow humans doing it together, *we will win!*"

Somebody began to sing the *Star Spangled Banner.* Never was a finer rendition ever heard.

Ten minutes later, people began to slowly make their way out of the memorial. Abigail, having composed herself, met up with Stalin, Sally, Janette, and her children. Young Fuzz sidled up to the children and began licking them. Soon both of the youngsters were laughing and giggling, "Thanks for chaperoning Janette and her children, Stalin, Sally. I wanted to make sure I didn't lose them in the crowd."

"The pleasure was ours, Major," Sally responded. "I got a great photo of Young Fuzz and the statue of his dad. I'll get you a copy after I use it for a feature article I'm doing." She glanced at her watch.

"Hey, Man of Steel, I need to speed down to my office, finish the article so I can get it in the early addition of the paper."

"I will come along," said Stalin.

"You sure? I may be their most of the night."

Stalin shrugged. "I've spent many a late night in my life. Besides, I would like to see you work. I'm used to military work, not civilian. It will be interesting to compare what you do to what I do. "

Sally smiled. "Okay. Don't say I didn't give you the chance of a warm bed instead."

The reporter bent over and offered her hand to Young Fuzz. Without hesitation he presented his paw for a 'shake".

"Please to meet you, Young Fuzz. You just helped to give me a hell of a story."

She turned to Janette and her children. "Here is my card. Please call me later and tell me what you think of my story. And call me if there is ever anything I can do to help you and the kids."

Janette blinked back tears. "You have all been so nice to me, a stranger. I don't know what to say."

"Say nothing," interjected Stalin. "I think the American expression is 'pass it on'. If you do that, words of thanks are unnecessary." The normally gruff man looked at the children.

"Mind your mother, little ones."

"We will, Mister Stalin," Tina answered. Then she grabbed and hugged his solid leg. Stalin lifted her with ease, kissed her forehead. He set her down, shook Timothy's hand.

"I expect to see you again, young man, in about twelve years."

"Yes Sir."

Stalin looked at Abigail. "Call me, please, if I can be of assistance with these little ones."

"I will, Senior Instructor. I will."

With that, Stalin saluted Abigail, then left with Sally.

"He is such a nice man, Abigail," said Janette.

"That is one of the great understatements of the year, Janette. He's a rock for all who know him. Now. Let's get you home to my place, get the children in bed. Then we will talk about your possible future."

Hours later, the children and Janette in Abigail's spare room, sound asleep, Abigail went to her own bed and passed out immediately. As soon as Young Fuzz saw his mistress was asleep, he snuck into the children's room. They were asleep in a separate bed from their mother, so it was a simple matter for the large pup to crawl up next to them. With a sigh, the War Dog laid his head on Tina's thigh. Half asleep, Tina scratched his ears. Then the three young of two species, joined at the hip for centuries, drifted off into a restful sleep.

CHAPTER 25

Adam Lloyd, Chief Hamilton, Kat and Mary had watched the televised memorial broadcast by the Unoccupied States. Adam took turns with the Chief in holding and caring for the two sets of twins as the four adults watched the activities in Malmstrom, Montana.

The Director shook his head as he watched the presentation of Sergeant Fuzz's carved statue by Thor Heyerdahl.

"Propaganda seems to come natural to those people. And where have Heyerdahl and his Norsemen been hiding? It's hard to believe no one had a hint of them, including the Squids, Krakens and robocops."

Chief Hamilton had shrugged. "They're just more Ferals to the Squids. And the Krakens have been more involved with the southern areas. You know, we could see about jamming these broadcast."

Adam frowned. "I don't know if I could get enough Tschaaa equipment and assistance to do that. I know I'd have to do some real scavenging at this late date to be able to do in on our own."

Kat, the person who had been the face of the Occupied States on video up until some months ago, gave a very unladylike snort. "Wouldn't do any good. Ever since they broadcast that pit raid, the

Squids and their supporters have been shown to have total feet of clay. People would go looking for the info. They know it's out there."

Adam looked at one of his two wives, mother of two of his children. "You think we're part of the feet of clay people?"

Kat sighed. "I think we're to the point, if we aren't part of the solution, we are part of the problem."

Adam sat quiet for a few moments. Then he spoke. "Unfortunately, more people are coming to that conclusion. Between you and me, after years of submission by most people outside of the Unoccupied States, the mood has changed in a drastic way. I have two reports of robocops being attacked and destroyed overseas. Here in North America, two Falcons have been attacked with concealed ground to air missiles, and one Delta Fighter was shot down on the west coast. The Squid pilot in the Delta was lost. His Lordship is none too pleased."

"Think it's time to bug out, Boss?" the Chief asked.

"It is getting really close to that time. His Lordship said there is some big action he is planning to take, which he is holding close to his vest. I'm sitting and waiting to see it take form. If the results are too bad, five seconds later we start moving."

Luke stirred in his arms, and Adam smiled. Funny how holding your children seemed to make the world right. The Chief had Laura. Kat was holding a sleeping Mark, and Mary had Lana. He knew he would do anything in his power to protect his family and friends. The decisions he had made so far had been for the survival of as many humans as possible, with the knowledge others were being sacrificed. Tough decisions for which he would accept full responsibility, no one else should be blamed.

"Well, let's finish watching this broadcast, then hit the rack. Tomorrow is going to be another long day with more questions from His Lordship."

Raven-haired Mary looked at him. "We love and support you, Adam. No matter what happens."

"That is what keeps me going—my loves, and Chief. That's what keeps me going every single day."

CHAPTER 26

GREAT FALLS, MONTANA

Stalin sat at Sally's kitchen table, reading the Early Edition of the Great Falls Times. The front page had Sally's photo of Young Fuzz on it, looking at the carved statue of his sire, Sergeant Fuzz. He had stayed up all night with her at the newspaper offices, as she finished the accompanying article and readied it for print. The first copy off the printing press was the one Stalin was holding in his hand.

Stalin had then picked the reporter up in his arms and carried her to their vehicle, Sally protesting all the way.

"You will be no good to anyone without some sleep," he had told her. "You are not trained Spetsnaz, used to going days without adequate rest."

"Damnit, Stalin. Must you be such an overbearing asshole?" she snapped at him.

"It has kept me alive and in relatively one piece all these years. Why change now?"

Sally pouted all the way home, then went straight to her bedroom and slammed the door. Stalin heard the shower running for a few minutes, then her hair dryer. He snuck up to the bedroom and listened. When he heard no cursing or movement, but still heard the hair dryer, he slipped into her room. She had fallen asleep while drying her hair, the dryer laying on the floor. He hoped it had one of those overheat automatic shut off switches for when he was not around. Stalin picked it up and turned it off. Sally, in just a towel, was laying on her bed, gently snoring. Stalin covered Sally with a spare blanket, managed to slip a pillow under her head without awakening her. The reporter shifted in her sleep, and a small smile formed on her lips as she mumbled something. Then, she fell back into REM sleep.

Stalin stood and watched her sleep. He felt very tired.

"Getting old, fool," he whispered to himself. There was a time he would have been wide awake, even with the vodka he had ingested at the Russian mini-wake after the memorial service. Or, maybe it was just he felt so relaxed around this woman, that he let himself be sleepy. He looked at the newspaper article once again. "Sergeant Fuzz represents everything good about humanity," Sally had written. "Yet, because he had four legs, was a different species, we do not consider him as having 'human qualities'. I submit that is wrong. As the saying goes, no man or woman has a greater love than to give his or her life for another. That is what Fuzz did."

He read the last lines. "So I welcome you as an Honorary Human, Sergeant Fuzz. Long may you be remembered as a symbol of all who have fallen fighting the evil Squids and Krakens. Rest in Peace, Big Fella."

He stared at the sleeping Sally for quite some time. He began to shuck his clothes, then laid down next to the reporter. Stalin carefully put his arms around her and fell asleep.

Stalin was woken by a hand gently caressing his lower anatomy. He turned to face Sally.

"Good morning, Man of Steel."

"Sally Reid, has anyone told you that you have the soul of a Russian poet?"

Sally paused, frowned a bit. "Where'd that come from? Not from what I have in my hand…"

"I am serious. Your article about the Memorial said it all. You paid all the fallen a huge honor. I love you, Sally Reid. I want to be with you. There, I got it out." The last bit had come out in a rush, not in Stalin's characteristic measured speech.

"Stalin, I…" Tears welled up in her eyes.

"You do not have to love me, my dear reporter. I have stored up enough over all these years for both of us."

She began to cry. "Damn you. I had a husband and children that I have finally gotten over losing. And now you want me to have all those feelings again? That is unfair." She began to sob, but grabbed Stalin in a bear hug, squeezed him with unnoticed strength. Stalin gently stroked her hair and held her, letting her cry. She began to sniffle, then stopped.

"What am I going to do with you, you big hunk of granite? Answer me that."

"You could love me back."

Sally raised her head, looked him in the eyes. "I do. That is the problem. I fell in love with this crazy Russian who could go off at a moment's notice and I'd be a widow once again."

"My beloved woman, you have me killed off already? Do I not get a say in the matter?"

"You know what I mean, my Man of Steel. Even Superman could be killed by kryptonite."

Stalin propped himself up on one arm, frowned at her. "I am Stalin. Steel in Russian. I am not some comic book character you Americans dreamed up. You think I would dare to allow anyone to hurt you? Especially by killing me?"

Sally grabbed him and kissed him hard. "God, you are so conceited. Alright, I admit you're too ornery to go quietly into the good night without taking a full division with you. So, here, shake on it."

"Shake on what, dearest Sally?"

"You just agreed to not die until I say you can."

"I think God has something to say about that."

"And if he knows what's good for him, he won't interfere. Now, kiss me. Make love to me. Then we can plan on how to make an honest woman out of me. Thought I'd let you go on without a wedding? It can be simple, but we will be hitched."

Stalin took her in his arms and kissed her. One thing led to another and Mother Nature had her assurances that two humans were functioning just fine.

CHAPTER 27

Madam President sat at her desk, a small smile on her lips. Events seemed to be picking up after the initial reports of Bloody Kansas. What had started out as a complete surprise invasion by fellow humans had turned into a complete rout for the enemy, plus the addition of a new previous unknown ally. Thor Heyerdahl's short speech was perfect as a propaganda tool. She believed he knew that up front, his speech not being as spontaneous as he wanted people to believe. The carving of Sergeant Fuzz was a masterpiece, a symbol for current and future generations even if it elicited some feelings of sorrow. Madam President wondered if Thor had some type of political aspirations, maybe on the world stage. Traditional U.S. law stated you had to be a natural born citizen to aspire to the highest offices. Things could change, however.

Abigail and Ichiro's planned wedding was another source of pleasure, not to mention the support the young woman warrior had garnered from Deseret out of the clear blue sky. She went and kicked some Prophet ass and the Mormons still offered extensive military and material support to the U.S.A. In every generation there emerged leaders and people who became symbols for what was right. Abigail Young, now Abigail Jorgensen, and soon to be Yamamoto, was such a person. Plus, she knew Abigail and Ichiro were made for each other. If there was anyone who could deal with the potential problems of alien and human unnatural modifications made to Abigail, it was Ichiro.

Her intercom buzzed. It was George Williams.

"Go ahead, George."

"Ma'am, Colonel Bardun is here."

"Good. Send her in." Now back to more unpleasant matters.

Bettie Bardun and Madam President had a unique relationship based on how they had met. She and Aleks Smirnov had been the first people the Colonel had told about her butchering of the obscene female scientist aboard the Space Platform. It had taken Bettie Bardun some time to get over the horror of that situation (breeding brainless babies to feed to the Tschaaa). She had bounced back and then some. Her expertise in exobiology and microbiology had led to what the President thought was a godsend. Maybe a rather nasty godsend, but one nonetheless.

For Colonel Bardun's part, she had undying loyalty to the President. Bettie could just as easily been hung out to dry as a traitor with her husband, Colonel Hunter, used as examples of what happened to people who cooperated with the Squids. A show trial and then the hangman's noose could have been their fate. But Madam President had made sure that was not the case. So Bettie made sure the leader of the Unoccupied States received what she wanted.

Colonel Bardun walked into the President's office and saluted, the President returning the salute. Then Madam President crossed the distance to the exobiologist and hugged her.

"So glad to see you so well, Bettie. I have heard your husband is doing great things also. Come, sit down and relax. Then you can tell me all the good gossip you know." The former Air Force Officer smiled. Madam President knew just what to do in order to relax people. Yet, Bettie knew it came from the heart, was not fake political shenanigans. This was another reason why she cared for her so, would die for the President if asked.

"Well, Ma'am, you probably know as much gossip as I do. I've been too busy with The Project to socialize much. But I do know a certain Avenging Angel and a modern Samurai are soon to be married.”

Madam President grinned. “Yes, isn’t it just great? You and Major Rice deserve some credit for that because of all the medical aid you provided to help with her... condition.”

Bettie tried to brush the compliment away. “Ma’am. I was just helping Major Rice. She and Doctor Anders, the vet, are the ones who brought her back from the dead.”

“Come now. Your work on the modifications that were secretly done to her will aid in Abigail achieving a normal life in the future. That and, of course, Ichiro. So, if I can be nosey, how are you and the good Colonel Hunter doing these days? Still treating you right?”

Bettie blushed a bit. “Yes, he is. You’ll hear it from me first. Sometime in the near future I will be asking for a leave of absence in order to start a family. I’m not getting any younger. Which is why I needed to finish this special project for you now.”

Madam President sighed. “Yes. My project. Or should I say, Humanity’s Survival Project. So, I understand you have something to show me.”

The President and the exobiologist sat down on the padded couch used for visitors and Bettie set up her laptop computer on the long coffee table in front of the couch.

“Ma’am, the first short video is from an old movie that explains the theory I and my team were working on. It may look a bit hokey, but I think it gets the point across.”

The DVD began to play the opening credits for a movie titled *Gojira*, Japanese with English subtitles. It then skipped forward to a scene taking place in a laboratory. A white coated scientists was demonstrating a weapon to a pretty young woman he had developed to defeat Gojira, the huge monster ravaging Japan. He dropped a large pill or tablet like object tablet into an oversized aquarium full of fish. Massive amounts of bubbles appeared, obscuring the fish. As they cleared, the young woman recoiled in horror as she saw that all the fish had been reduced to skeletons.

The scientist in the movie developed an oxygen destroying mechanism to destroy Gojira. Unfortunately, any fish in the area suffered also.

“Now watch actual footage of our attempts at a weapon based

on a similar idea—attack a species in its watery habitat."

A large Pacific octopus was seen moving in a large aquarium. A human hand appeared on the edge of the screen and injected a syringe of some reddish colored chemical into the water. At first, nothing changed. Thirty seconds into the introduction, the octopus began to twitch, then shake and spasm. Thirty seconds later some blood began to seep from its orifices, with the dying cephalopod curling up like a spider killed with bug spray. It was dead.

"Madam President, we started with the same type of algae and phytoplankton that causes poisonous red tides. Using good old American know-how and some bootleg alien Squid bioscience and nanotechnology, we came up with an organism that releases the neurotoxin injected into the aquarium. Dump the modified algae into the ocean near the Tschaaa breeding crèche and within twenty-four hours you have dying Squids, as the algae begins to bloom at an extreme rate. Within forty-eight hours, the algae begins to die off, thanks to some genetic modifications we built in. We want to control the weapon, get rid of it when we no longer need it."

The President studied the images on the computer screen.

"Does it kill mammals, humans?"

"Like the red tide it was developed from, it can make people sick and cause some amnesia-like temporary memory loss. In its original form it could kill children, and occasionally adults. We tweaked it as much as possible to reduce these effects. But no biological control is ever perfect, if for no reason because of possible mutations. However, since the delivery method involves an ocean based organism, its ability to affect land species is very limited. Effects on other ocean species may be very bad, however."

Madam President paused for a moment, still studying the images in an intense manner.

"Delivery method?" she asked.

"Missile cone warheads similar to chemical warfare agents' delivery methods used in the twentieth century. A modified She-Bear missile would work."

The female leader of free Americans looked at Colonel Bardun.

"Make it so, Bettie. Payback's a bitch, and I can be the biggest bitch around. They like to eat our children. I'd like to see how they like it when we kill just as many of theirs."

CHAPTER 28

MALMSTROM ARMED FORCES BASE
GREAT FALLS, MONTANA

Abigail was hunkered down with Aleks and Fanny, original members of the Russian Three Sisters, (referred to by some as the Three Bitches) at their on-base quarters. Aleks as Matron of Honor, had taken charge of everything to do with the wedding. What had started out as what Abigail hoped would be a somewhat normal wedding had become a huge affair of state. Abigail had always known that anything she and Ichiro did would be noticed. However, she had hoped that she may have enough personal capital to persuade the Powers That Be to limit the pomp and circumstances. Fat chance.

Now a representative of the Japanese Royal Family, the President of Free Russia, representatives from Free Canadians, New Vikings, Romanians, Deseret, you name it, were coming to pay their respects to the Hero Couple, or Warrior Couple as some called them. Abigail and Ichiro were a symbol of hope and heroism to all peoples in the Unoccupied Lands. There was just no way of getting around that fact. The original plan was to also keep the exact date, time and location secret up until a day or two before. Hell, Operation Overlord aka D-

Day, had kept the Nazis guessing until the last moment, why not a wedding. Again, fat chance.

Aleks had found a Korean dressmaker whose family had fled to the Unoccupied States. Now she was working on Abigail, trying various designs on her.

"You have such a beautiful body," Mi-Hi the dressmaker had said. "We must do our best to display it, and make every man envious of your husband, Ichiro Yamamoto." Mi-Hi had sighed.

"Too bad he is not Korean."

There was a knock at the door of Abigail's half of the company grade duplex she shared with Aleks and Torbin. With everyone being promoted to Field Grade, they by rights should have been moved out to larger quarters by now. Everyone had dragged their feet. The thought of Aleks and Abigail not living this close was alien to both.

"I'll get it," Aleks called out. As gatekeeper, she had chased away many an irritant. Plus, Torbin's reputation of breaking a certain reporter's arm, now a family friend, had also helped keep people away. Aleks went to the door, peaked through the security hole. Young Fuzz was wagging his tail so it must be someone he knew by scent.

"Ah, it is Brynhildr and the Pit Survivors. They should not be a problem."

Aleks opened the door and greeted the visitors. "Sisters, it is nice to see you."

Brynhildr had hugged her, followed by the five young ladies who had been rescued from the Pits.

"What brings you all here?" Aleks asked.

"We bring food and drink, as well as something Aunt Freda Munsen would like Abigail to try on. Hannah has also made something for Abigail and the Bridesmaids to wear."

Two of the young ladies came in carrying a very long garment bag.

"We have something we would like Abigail to try on." Brynhildr said.

"Oh? And what is that?"

"Aunt Munsen put together a bridal dress for Abigail. She would like to see it fits."

Aleks frowned. "Well, I'm sorry she wasted her time, as we have a seamstress working on her bridal gown as we speak."

"Well, she could just try it on. Aunt Munsen does excellent work," pressed Brynhildr.

"Why, when it will be a waste of time?"

"Waste of time? To just see if something fits? See if she likes it?"

Aleks bowed up. "I am the Matron of Honor and was given the job of organizing all this, Including obtaining the bridal gown."

"Oh, so you'll decide what she will wear. Tell me, are you going tell my cousin what to wear in the bridal bed also?" Brynhildr shot back.

"If you *must* know, yes I made some suggestions to my little sister about what men like."

"You overstep yourself. She's not your property."

As the exchange escalated, Abigail detached herself from the seamstress and went to try and smooth things over. She soon found out she could not get a word in edgewise, "Ladies, Sisters…"

Fanny walked up to backup Aleks against the much larger Norsewoman.

"Oh, so now it is two against one," snapped Brynhildr.

"I do not need help to handle you," Aleks growled. She moved within an inch of Brynhildr, thrusting her substantial chest out as if to challenge the Shield Maiden directly.

Something snapped inside of Abigail. Weeks of frustration, of pressure from being pulled in different directions bubbled over. Combat seemed simple compared to this.

"*Stop this!*" Later verbal accounts of this claim Abigail's voice shook the whole house. While maybe an exaggeration, the effect was the same. Everyone froze.

"I am the *bride!*" Abigail yelled. "I did not ask for all this, but I am stuck with this, this, circus! And now you, my so-called friends and family are going to fight over who does what? Over what I do, wear? Don't I have a say? Are you next going to tell me when to eat, sleep, and bathe?"

"Little sister…"

"My cousin…"

Little Susan, one of the Survivors, began to cry.

"Oh just great. We have made a little girl cry. Damn you. *Damn you all!*"

Abigail hiked up her unfinished bridal gown, turned and stomped toward her room.

"Please, Abigail…" Aleks began.

"Leave me the *fuck* alone." Abigail made it to her room, slammed the door as hard as she could. Young Fuzz made it into the room just before the door shut. His human was upset, needed his support.

All the other women were frozen in space and time.

What in holy hell just happened?" It was Torbin Bender's voice. He had arrived at the tail end of the incident.

"We were just having an argument, love," replied Aleks.

"Just an argument? You know when the last time I heard Abigail say 'fuck?' How about never?" Torbin shook his head.

"I love it when women complain about us men getting into pissing contests. Well, what the hell was that? An intellectual discussion?"

He looked at the five young ladies, saw four huddling around and trying to console the crying Susan.

"And you did it in front of these young ladies. You should be ashamed of yourselves."

"Torbin, I am sorry…" Fanny began.

"Oh no you don't. Do not try and apologize to me. That has to be done to Abigail. Now, you *will* all wait here and be quiet while I go and talk to Abigail. I've known her a lot longer than anyone in this room. Hell, she brought me back here. So I guess I get to try and help her calm herself. Thanks, ladies."

Torbin marched down the hallway to Abigail's room, leaving the stunned women behind. He softly knocked on her door. "Abigail, it's Torbin. Can I come in and talk?"

"Just you?"

"Yes. Just me."

A pause. Then Abigail answered. "Okay. Come in, please."

"Can you unlock your door?"

"Oh. Sorry."

Torbin heard the click of the lock being released. He waited a moment, then slowly opened and went in.

Abigail was sitting on her bed, hugging a large stuffed toy bear with one arm, scratching Young Fuzz's ears with the her free hand. Torbin sat down next to her.

"Rough day?"

"Yes." Abigail's voice caught as she answered. She sat the teddy bear down, stopped scratching Fuzz, and wrapped her arms around Torbin in a big hug. She began to cry. The last time Torbin had seen her like this was at the Bell's in Wyoming, when she thought members of her new adopted family had been hurt. Only then, the tears were more from anger. These seemed to be from hurt.

Torbin wrapped his arms around the little sister he had never had in his previous life. "There is something here beyond just an argument. Isn't there, Abigail?"

"I am so very... scared!" Abigail said through the tears. "I'm scared I'm about to screw up one of the most important things in my life. I'm scared that this love and marriage thing... I'm afraid I will be a failure. I know how to be a soldier, a warrior, an Avenging Angel. A normal, loving wife, maybe a mother later on? No."

She looked up from her hug at Torbin.

"I am a virgin. How do I know that Ichiro will find me pleasurable, desirable once we are alone? How do I know that he will not be disappointed? He knows me as a fighter, not a loving wife and mother."

Torbin damned again all of the Tschaaa to a special place in hell for what they had done to a whole generation of youth. Children, especially young girls, should not grow up worrying about being eaten, or being turned into a child soldier. Abigail should have had loving parents buying her feminine bows and frills, taking pictures as she went to her first prom. He took a deep breath, let it out.

"Remember when we first met, Abigail?"

"Of course. I will always remember that day,"

"Well, when I first met you, talked and worked with you, I saw this very put together young lady who had taken on responsibilities well beyond those normally associated with her age. I also saw you as what you call a 'good soul'. I consider it an honor that you consider me a big brother."

For the first time since Torbin had entered the room, Abigail smiled. She then hugged him tight again, causing Torbin to grunt.

"You and your strength again. Ichiro must have fun with you."

"And that is another reason I am afraid. What if in a rage, I hurt him? If we have children, what then? I saw the pictures from Dark Wolf's camera. I vaguely remembering some faces of those I killed, butchered. Nothing else."

Torbin kissed her forehead. "Out of all the people I know, Ichiro is the one person who can help you with this. He also harbors in his body a unique ability to destroy anything that threatens him and his loved ones. Yet he learned how to control it. You are perfect for each other. He will help you control any demons you may harbor. Besides, like I said, you are a good soul."

Torbin gently raised her chin to look into her eyes.

"Ichiro, my blood brother, loves you with all his heart and soul. No way will he ever be disappointed in you. Nor you in him. You are literally made for each other."

Abigail paused, then smiled again. "I believe you Torbin. You've never steered me wrong."

"There is one more thing. We have faced the Grim Reaper together, Abigail. You have saved me twice."

"Torbin, Lieutenant Baker saved you from the Eaters. And you saved yourself when the Krakens tried to take you."

"Abigail, if you had not been traveling with me, I'd be a prisoner or a side of meat. And as good as Baker was, I saw all those Eaters you shot, I felt you help drag me. Trust me. Without you, I would not be here. I attract trouble and you help save my ass."

He gently untangled himself from her hug, taking her hands in his.

"Abigail, you are a comrade in arms, a battle buddy in addition to being an adopted sister. If ever you need help, all you have to do is yell. I will be there. Which means if you and Ichiro need to elope, I will find a way. I know of some hiding places that would make good honeymoon locations. Just say the word."

"You mean that, don't you?"

"Of course. You have my word."

Abigail paused, holding Torbin's hands. She sighed.

"As much as I want to take off, tell everyone to forget it, I know that people need this wedding. Ichi and I are symbols, looked on as heroes by some. So if watching us get married makes them feel good, gives them some kind of hope, why should I deny it. That would be selfish."

"Yes, Abigail. Heavy is the head that wears the crown. I learned the hard way what happens when you are deemed a hero. General Reed just chewed my butt for not wearing my Medal of Honor. I told him it felt funny being saluted by everyone, including him. He said tough shit. Pardon my French."

The Marine stood up. "Now, I'll go back down and explain to those young ladies that fighting over your special day is unacceptable. Wanna come?"

"In a minute. I need to wash my face, see how puffy my eyes are."

"Okay. I'll go down and set the tone for the rest of this endeavor."

Abigail hugged him, kissed his cheek. "I am so lucky to have met you, Torbin Bender. Without you, I never would've come here, met Ichiro, fallen in love, and gotten married."

"I'll accept kudos for the first three. The marriage thing, well, it can be a real pain in the ass sometimes. Just ask Aleks."

"I have, Torbin. Many times. Every time she says marriage, you, and the boys are the best things that have ever happened to her. That she feels blessed. As I do. God looks over us—you, me, Aleks, your sons, Ichiro. We are part of a special plan."

"You know, Andrew my cyborg friend said that also. Gets you to thinking."

Abigail frowned. "You think he is a real friend, Torbin?"

"I think he is trying to be one to everyone. Which is a problem when you have two sides, including the one he supposedly works for, trying to kill each other."

Abigail paused for a moment. "Then I think God has a very complicated mission for us. I'll worry about it after I'm married."

"Good idea. Now, let me go deal with my wife and company. I think they need a bit of a 'come to Jesus moment'."

Abigail giggled. "Not too rough, Torbin. They mean well."

"Good intentions pave the road to hell. See you in a couple of minutes."

Torbin marched down the hallway, stood at Parade Rest in front of all the females, young and old. Aleks looked at him, started to speak. He cut her off.

"Listen up. There will not be another display of catty childishness like what I just saw and heard. This is Abigail's special day, not to mention how important it is to Ichiro. If anyone screws this up, upsets my battle buddy again, I will personally kick their ass." He looked at large Brynhildr. "Or at least have fun trying. Any questions?"

The three adult women looked at Torbin, then each other. There was a quick meeting of the minds as it sank in just how upset Abigail must have been for Torbin to say what he did.

"I'm sorry, Brynhildr. I guess I'm way too protective of my little sister."

"As I am of my cousin, Aleks and Fanny. I'm used to pushing for what I want. I guess I need to back off." She reached out, hugged Aleks and Fanny.

Susan had stopped crying and approached Torbin. She threw her arms around him and hugged him. "Thank you, Colonel Bender."

Torbin reached over and kissed her cheek. "No worries, little one. Adults are just big kids sometimes."

Abigail walked cautiously down the hallway, still in her partially completed gown. All the women crowded around her, everyone trying to offer an apology at once.

"Please," Abigail said. "Water under the bridge, as my late father used to say. Now, can we get on with figuring out what I'm wearing to walk down the aisle?"

Mi-Hi finally broke in. "Please, may I look at the dress in the garment bag?"

Hannah Weitz picked it up and handed to her. "Here, Ma'am. It looks quite nice."

Mi-Hi expertly removed it from the bag, began to make very appreciative sounds in Korean and English.

"This is the work of a true seamstress and tailor! In fact, I like her ideas better than mine. I think it will fit Abigail better. Ladies, would your aunt mind if I used it, made a few changes?"

"Of course not," Brynhildr replied. "This is all for Abigail and Ichiro, nothing more."

"Abigail, please, come here. Try this on…"

Torbin took that as a cue to leave. He would feel funny seeing his little sister in her skivvies. Let Ichiro have that thrill. He went next door to his quarters to check on his sons, being watched over by a pregnant Sue Brown.

As Abigail stripped down to panties and nothing else, Hannah presented Aleks with a package. "Inside are some things I made for you and the bridesmaids to wear."

Aleks opened up the package. Inside were a dozen small jewelry boxes. Aleks opened one up, and gasped. She carefully removed a silver charm bracelet and looked at it. On it were two charms; a delicate silver cross, and a miniature portrayal of a dog that must be Fuzz Senior.

"I know both her faith and the memory of her canine friend who cannot be here are important to her. I think she would want everyone in her wedding party to share in these parts of her life."

Aleks looked at the cross, the dog charm, and began to bawl. "They are so damned beautiful," she sobbed. And memories of a certain beastie who had saved her and her children rushed back in.

The rest of the women and girls quickly crowded around, looking at what had caused Alek's reaction.

Abigail looked at the charms, felt a lump in her throat as she looked at the symbol of her intense faith and passed best friend. She grabbed Hannah's hand.

"You are blessed. God must have sent you, with this ability, for a reason. I..." the rest was lost, as tears interfered with anymore talking.

"There are twelve of the bracelets," Hannah said. "If you want more, let me know."

"You are a craftswoman that would make the dwarfs and faeries of our legends envious," said Brynhildr. "Are you sure you are not part Norse?"

Hannah grinned. "Totally Jewish, as far as I know. I just craft what I think and feel fits the people and situation involved. I'm glad it brings joy."

Aleks hugged Hannah, followed by Abigail.

"I could still make room for another Bridesmaid," Abigail volunteered.

"Thank you, but no. I've had my time in front of a bunch of people. I would just as soon stay in the background."

"Come, let's sit and eat some of this food we brought," offered Brynhildr.

"That sounds like a good idea," said Fanny.

Soon they were all seated around a large oak table Abigail had found months ago for her dining area.

"Please, hold hands. I need to give thanks," said Abigail.

As all the women, young and old, held hands, Abigail lifted her voice to her God.

"Lord, thank you for this food and drink. Thank you especially for my sisters, my friends, my new family who are to share one of the most important events in my life; my wedding to the man I love and cherish. Please bless us all in the coming days. We are about to embark on a perilous endeavor fraught with danger. I know thy rod and thy staff will comfort us in the coming days. Bless us with your loving embrace. *Amen.*"

Brynhildr looked at her cousin. "Your Lord's rod, staff, and my Thor's Hammer. The Squids won't know what hit them."

Abigail smiled. "I will never turn down help in a fight. Now, shall we eat? Then Mi-Hi can shoehorn me into that dress you bought. I think it'll look like it was painted on."

"All the better to smack Ichiro between the eyes with your beauty," said Aleks. "Start them drooling, panting, and men are easy to control."

Even the younger ladies laughed, having unfortunately been exposed young to the bluntness of human sexual relations.

"You can take the woman out of spying and manipulation, but you can't take those skills and habits out of the woman," opined Abigail.

"So, that is a problem?" replied Aleks.

There was another round of laughter before they enjoyed the repast.

CHAPTER 29

In the months and years to come, this meal would always be a special memory. A special painting of this meal, by Susan Munsen, Survivor, "Repast before the Storm" would hang in the new U.S. National Museum years later. Beauty came out of a time of ugliness, hope from fear, as it had been throughout human history.

-Excerpt from The Greatest Wedding, *Sally Reid, Official Presidential Historian*

THE RIVER BAR
BANKS OF THE COLUMBIA RIVER
OREGON STATE

Dogman was working the door at The River Bar, acting as bouncer and gatekeeper. The man built like Adonis with a neat and trimmed full black beard had more trouble with keeping intoxicated young women from pawing him than anything else. At least that had been the situation since he had taken care of a couple of hard cases who decided to test him and his business partner Tony the Bartender. Tony had offered him a partnership after deciding things were getting a bit too busy for him to handle it alone. Thus, Dogman had taken care of the two hard cases himself without having to be asked by Tony. One's body wound up as giant catfish food after being stripped of his clothes, valuables and ID. The other woke up miles from the bar, with a piece of paper stapled to his right butt cheek. When the miscreant woke up, and pulled the offending paper and staple from his ass, he saw writing on it. Focusing his bleary eyes, he pieced together the message.

"This ass could have belonged to me and my dogs. Don't come back."

Since then, the word got out for visitors to The River Bar to be civil, or else. Now, Dogman spent most of his times escorting drunk women out to their transportation, or to a small motel a block away for them to sleep it off in a room Tony had permanently rented. One night, Dogman had put six women in the room so they would not wind up raped and maybe dead. The female population outnumbered the male almost two to one along the Columbia Gorge. Thus, Tony had said they had to protect their customer base.

Again, word got around that The River Bar was a 'safe place', in a relative sense. It had gotten to the point that Tony had to designate Sunday afternoon and evening as Family Time, with people bringing in their kids to have some hot food. The remodeled bar kitchen now served basic home-cooked meals such as stew and meatloaf, in addition to the usual hotdogs, hamburgers and fries. Sunday morning a person could even get ham and eggs, pancakes and any leftover meat from the night before. A local entrepreneur began providing them with farm grown fish from a local cleaned up large pond. Business began to boom, but in a controlled way.

Young blonde Kay was their main waitress, her mother Ester the cook. They lived in a small cabin next to Dogman's place. He had set it up so they could help care for his dogs. Both mother and daughter had the hots for Dogman, but he kept them at arm's length. If he wanted female companionship, he would buy it. Everything was safer that way. They helped him care for his dogs in the large kennel he had constructed. In addition to the Mastiff Matt, he had three Black Mask Curs, some rescued mixed breeds and a newly obtained and now pregnant German Shepherd female. He was trying an experiment in breeding, matching Mastiff with Shepherd. He hoped to get a large Mastiff-type but with longer fur, better able to deal with cold weather.

Tony walked up to Dogman seated at the main door. "Dogman, there is something you need to see on the boob tube."

As everything was quiet, Dogman moved to where he could hear and see the television screen.

As he watched and listen, he saw the attractive black woman newscaster wax poetic about the upcoming nuptials. There then flashed a photo of his niece Abigail on the screen next to the photo of a handsome Japanese soldier.

"Despite attempts at concealment, due to security reasons, the date set for the wedding has been leaked days early. March 15th, the Ides of March has been chosen as the date for the closest thing to a royal wedding in years. The final guest list *is* classified, and the equivalent of a division of military troops with large numbers of anti-aircraft weaponry are to be emplaced all around Great Falls, Montana. Rumors have surfaced that any attack to disrupt the wedding of Ichiro Yamamoto and Abigail Jorgensen by the Squids will prompt another nuke attack, collateral damage be damned. I guess every member of the Free Alliance has claimed Abigail as a daughter and are doing what is necessary to insure a successful wedding."

Dogman kept watching the broadcast for a few minutes, then turned back toward the main door. Standing unnoticed next to him was large Tony.

"I expect you are going. I would if it were my niece."

He paused, then answered. "Not going to cause a problem if I go?"

"Naw. I'll make do with Ester and Kay, call the Marshal to make a few visits down here. Hell, I'll make him work for the protection I pay."

Dogman extended his hand, and Tony took it. "Thanks, Tony. You're a friend."

Tony grinned. "Same here, buddy. You're one of my few friends that are still alive. Please stay that way."

"Will do," Dogman answered. "Though there is a chance they may try to put me behind bars."

"Won't happen, Dog. Abigail won't allow it, especially if she is as tough as you are."

A small smile formed on Dogman's usual stern face. "She is."

Dogman walked toward young blonde Kay, who was standing watching the broadcast. She noticed his approach.

"She's about my age, your niece."

"Yes she is." Dogman looked at the very sexy, slim and tight bodied young lady. Well brushed long blonde hair, sparkling blue eyes and just the right amount of makeup added to a package that made everyone look. In another time, she would have been a model or an actress. She looked like a younger version of her mother, Ester, who had been a model before the Squids came.

Kay looked him in his eyes. "Is that why you never tried to hit on me?"

"A big reason, yes."

Kay suddenly kissed him on the cheek. "You're a gentleman, Dogman. I would have liked to have had an uncle like you."

"Consider yourself an honorary niece, Kay."

With that comment, Kay hugged him. "Please come back, Dogman. We'll watch your dogs for you until you do."

Dogman kissed her on the cheek "Thanks. Now I need to go tell your mother."

Ester met him at the entrance to the kitchen.

"Your niece was your sister's daughter."

"Yes, she was," answered Dogman.

"Was she as good looking as her?"

"Yes. She was beautiful. She married a good man too. Then the Squids killed them."

Ester took his large right hand in both of hers. "You ever need… anything, just ask. You and Tony gave Kay and me another chance, kept us from being someone's personal playthings. I'll always owe you for that."

"You wouldn't have let anyone do that to you and Kay. You're too tough."

Ester gave a small laugh. Then she hugged Dogman with tears in her eyes. "You come back, so I can put some moves on you."

Dogman displayed a slight smile. "You'll find another good man, Ester. I'm just not him."

Ester sighed with frustration. "Well, a girl can fantasize. We'll watch your dogs for you. We love them also."

"Matt, my Mastiff, is coming with me. If I don't make it back, please make sure the new pups are given to good homes."

"You'll make it back. I know you will."

He hugged Ester, then walked out the back. Matt was laying, guarding the back entrance and rose at his approach.

"Come on, fella. I have someone you need to meet." With that, man and dog walked toward a large SUV.

CHAPTER 30

MALMSTROM ARMED FORCES BASE
MONTANA

Abigail woke up well before the clock alarm went off, a habit of hers. She opened her eyes to see a large furry head looking back at her. As had become his habit, Young Fuzz was waiting as she woke, sitting next to her bed. She smiled.

"Are you going to do this when I'm married, big fella? What if Ichiro wakes up first?"

With that, the canine leaned forward and stole a doggy kiss with a large wet tongue. Despite still officially a puppy, less than a year old, Fuzz was already larger than many dogs. And the protectiveness that his sire, Sergeant Fuzz, felt for Abigail was clearly already there.

Abigail grabbed and hugged her dog partner, as much a part of her future as Ichiro.

"Come on. Breakfast time, then a shower. I still have a lot of things to do before tomorrow."

Tomorrow. The day of her wedding. She could not believe the days had gone by so fast. Now, she was about to embark on an adventure of the type she had never done before.

And she was still afraid.

Abigail had tried to talk to Ichiro into eloping, even almost calling Torbin for his offered help in the endeavor. But when she heard that Free Japan was sending a member of the Royal Family to serve as the official representative, she knew that it would a direct insult, and a "loss of face", if she and Ichiro ran off to be married in private. She realize once more the additional responsibilities and duties her fame had created. Torbin had told her this was going to happen.

"Heavy is the head that wears the crown. Like me, someone decided you are a hero, a symbol. Now, your life is not entirely your own." Yet he had offered to help her elope, damn the trouble.

Abigail sighed. If it were just her she had to worry about, she might just have disappeared. But then Ichiro would be harmed. There was no way she would leave without him. So, here she was, about to be on a televised ceremony that a large portion of the world would be able to see. She shivered. She took a deep breath, and let it out slowly. She concentrated on some meditation techniques Ichiro had taught her to help her calm down and control any anger. Then the telephone rang. Abigail had an old hard line in addition to her radiophone to ensure she always had some communication capabilities. She picked up the bedroom extension.

"Major Jorgensen." After years of being a "Young", Jorgensen still sounded odd, even though that was her true family name. It was Central Security Control.

"Ma'am, we have the Port of Entry near Cokeville, Wyoming They say a rather large man is asking entry from Idaho, saying he is a relative of yours. Says he is an Uncle Buck, goes by the name Dogman. He has a huge dog with him."

She froze. After months of no word, he reappears, still alive. Abigail blinked back tears. Family, the last member she knew of who was still alive.

"Sergeant, can you please put the POE on the telephone? I have some transportation to arrange."

CHAPTER 31

Dogman found himself being escorted down the highway, red and blue lights flashing in front and back. He grunted. Once they had received word from Abigail, it was like he was royalty. He talked with her on the telephone for a minute, the sound of her voice causing a rare smile to form on his lips. She sounded good, happy. That was what he cared about; was she happy. Also, was she safe.

They stopped to refuel his RV and give his mastiff Matt a chance to stretch his huge body and pee at a rebuilt truck stop. He tried to find a form of currency or trade to pay for his gas but was waved off.

"Sir, your money's no good here," the strac young Military Policeman who was part of his escort told him. "Orders from General Reed. Major Jorgenson's family are all guests of the government."

Dogman had grunted acknowledgement, then went back to refueling the large RV's gas tanks. As the fuel pumped into his vehicle, he took Matt out for a walk. The mastiff's size immediately drew stares and comments from all who saw him. Dogman was used to that. It helped people to think twice about bothering him. As he watched Matt irrigate a small tree, a dark sedan came speeding into the parking area. Dogman thought "cop" at first sight as he waited for his mastiff to finish his business.

He went and grabbed Matt's leash, even though he knew his canine partner was a danger to no one unless they tried to hurt Dogman. However, he had discovered over the years that very large dogs made some cops very nervous. No point of stirring the pot if it wasn't necessary.

Dogman watched a tall and somewhat lanky man unfold himself from the driver's seat of the sedan. The man put a Texas-looking Stetson on his short cropped graying head of hair and meandered toward Dogman. It had been a long time since he had seen someone so relaxed that

they 'meandered'. He soon saw it was all a controlled act, as the man's eyes never left Dogman.

"Well, Sir, should I call you Dogman, or Mr. Dogman?" The man's voice had an air of long time authority in it. Dogman could tell he was used to taking care of business, either in a nice or not so nice way.

"Dogman," he answered back. "And you?"

"Andy Jackson, Texas Ranger. Retired. Now Madam President's bodyguard, driver, and chief cook and bottle washer when asked."

"Texas Ranger huh. I had some dealings with the Rangers pre-Squid."

"Good or bad dealings?"

Dogman grunted. "We all went home in one piece. So I guess you could call them good."

He dropped the leash and scratched Matt's large ear. "They were tough. Are you?"

Ranger Jackson grinned. "Tough enough. Now that we are through sizing each other up, I'm here to insure you get to Abigail's wedding in one piece. And, to find appropriate attire, in the words of Madam President."

Dogman scratched Matt's other ear. "I hear the President's tough. True?"

Ranger Jackson chuckled. "Tough as a lady javelina guarding her young. I've only met two other women as tough as she is. Excluding Mrs. Jackson, that is."

"Who?"

"Your niece, Abigail, and her adopted big sister, Major Smirnov.

Though a New Viking cousin of your niece is in the running for number three.”

Dogman grunted again. “Yeah, Abby always was tough. Even as a little girl.”

“I suspect that's a family trait,” opined the Ranger.

“Maybe,” answered Dogman.

Matt the Mastiff chose that moment to pad toward the Ranger, his nose working. The Ranger held his left hand out for the huge dog to sniff. Matt sniffed the hand, then bumped it in the universal canine signal of “pet me”.

“Guess I just passed inspection,” Andy Jackson commented as he petted and ear scratched the Mastiff.

“Yes, you did. He's a good judge of character.” Dogman extended his right hand to shake. “Pleased to meet you, Ranger.”

Ranger Jackson smiled as he grasped the offered hand. “As they used to say in the olden days—well met, Dogman. Now, we need to hit the road if we are going to make it back to Great Falls tonight, with you driving your RV.”

Dogman looked at the Rangers large sedan. “Have room in the back for a huge dog? And a few things in your trunk?”

“Yessir. That can be arranged. Mind if one of the MPs drives your rig?”

No problem. I don't think they'll steal something. If they did, Matt would know, and not be happy.”

The Ranger laughed. “Yes, I would not want to make your friend there angry. Come on then. We're wasting daylight.”

CHAPTER 32

MALMSTROM ARMED FORCES BASE
MONTANA

It was well past dark when Abigail received a telephone call that Ranger Jackson had come through the main gate with her uncle in tow. She was being fitted in her wedding gown one last time to check some last minute alterations. She had demanded the sleek bottom skirt have slits up both sides to free her shapely legs for walking and moving. Her gown was a perfect mixture of traditional flowing western bridal gowns and Asian sleek formal wear. She loved it.

A "woof" from Young Fuzz told her someone was out front. She broke away from a protesting Mi-Hi and Aleks and went to the front door, opening it before anyone could knock. She smiled as she saw her Uncle Buck approach. He saw her at the doorway and stopped still. Finally, he spoke.

"Little Abby. You're all grown up."

She grinned, blinked back tears. "Yes, Uncle. I guess I am." She started to move forward and hug him but he stepped back.

"No. We can do that later. I don't want my road stink on you." He paused. "Abby, you are a beautiful young woman. I see my sister—

your mother, Anica Vladu—when I look at you."

Dogman stepped up and took her hand, looked into her eyes. "I need to know. Are you happy with your man?"

She nodded her head. "Yes. I love Ichiro with all my soul."

Dogman paused, still looking at her. Then he spoke. "I know I'm very set in my ways. I get along best with other whites and Romanians."

"And Ichiro is Japanese. So, that bothers you," responded Abigail.

It took a moment, then Dogman's mouth formed a small smile. "You're marrying him, not me. If you are happy, then I'll be happy."

Abigail grinned again, reached up and grabbed her uncle's bearded head and kissed him on his cheek.

"I love you, uncle," she said in Romanian.

"As I, you, niece."

Aleks was standing back, observing. Torbin came to the front door from watching their two sleeping sons in the back bedroom. He saw Dogman and stepped out onto the front porch next to Abigail.

"I see you're still kicking, Dogman."

"As are you." Dogman paused. "I see you kept your word."

"I try. Although I almost screwed up and lost her not too long ago."

Aleks stepped up and gently forced herself between Abigail and Torbin. "Are you going to introduce me, husband?"

Dogman hit on the slight Russian accent Aleks still had, put two and two together.

"You're his wife. You are also Abby's adopted big sister."

"Yes, I am, Mister... Dogman."

"Just Dogman. And I guess you're a niece as well, if you and Abby are sisters."

Aleks laughed lightly. "I guess you could say that."

The large, muscular man paused. "I'll be honest with you. Romanians still remember Russians as occupiers and enemies."

"That was long ago, Dogman," Aleks answered, with a bit of steel in her voice.

"Still, it happened." Dogman looked at her for a few moments before he answered. "Well, I guess Abby is going to make me reconsider certain things." At that, he extended his hand to Torbin.

"You kept your word. My niece is safe. Abby considers you family. So, I guess we'll all be family." He finished shaking hands with Torbin, and extended his hand to Aleks.

"I hear from the Ranger that you are one tough woman."

At that comment, Torbin laughed. "You don't know the half of it."

Aleks gave her husband a quick stern look, then returned her attention to Dogman as she shook his hand.

"We all had to be tough. As have you."

"You also cared for Abby, helped her."

"As I still do. I look out for her, she looks out for me, my husband, our two sons."

Dogman noticed Young Fuzz now standing behind Abigail, his tail slightly wagging. The dog could smell the family connection between Abigail and her uncle, knew they were related.

"He looks familiar," Dogman said.

"You apparently had contact with his sire, Sergeant Fuzz, before he turned up here and adopted me."

The dog trainer grunted. "Yeah, now I remember. A man I trained to handle dogs said some people were trying to use him for dogfighting. I said I'd kill him and them if they did."

Abigail motioned for Young Fuzz to come forward to meet her uncle. He came forward and snuffled Dogman's hand, then sat, expecting to be petted. The man also known as Uncle Buck began to pet the rather large head, then scratch his ears. Young Fuzz gave small dog grunts of satisfaction and enjoyment. Dogman spoke Romanian to him and Fuzz laid down, rolled over so he could have his chest and stomach scratched.

"You taught him the old language, Abby."

"As I did his sire, Sergeant Fuzz. He died for me."

The uncle looked at his niece, could see and hear the hurt that still accompanied the memory of the loss. "He will always be with you, Abigail," Dogman said in Romanian. "He died saving you because he wanted to. And you would have died for him."

Abigail nodded her head in agreement as Aleks spoke. "The big beastie saved me and mine, Dogman. So, if you were partly the cause he wound up here, I owe you. Karma. Somehow, we're all connected."

Dogman grunted again as he finished up scratching Young Fuzz's stomach. "I guess I'd better get going. The Ranger there in the car with my Mastiff, Matt, says I have to be fitted with the right clothes for the wedding, per the President's orders." He gave a rare chuckle. "Never thought I'd see the day when women ran and controlled so much. But then, if they're all like you, Abby, it might be the right thing."

Abigail stepped up and grabbed his hand again. "She and many others have taken care of me, helped me. I owe them all."

"Then I'll have to be there to thank them, Abby. See you tomorrow." He kissed her hand, let it go, turned and walked to the car.

After a few moments of silence, Aleks spoke. "He is a hard man. Reminds me of Stalin. But Comrade Stalin talks and laughs more."

"Uncle Buck, as we called him, never had a reputation for long talks. But with me, he always seemed to open up more. As he did with my mother, his sister." A tear ran down her cheek and she tried to wipe it way before anyone saw it.

Aleks hugged her. "Come, let us finish up. I know that your mother and father will be watching over you tomorrow, from the great beyond. Now you have blood family here to make it even better. This will be a wonderful day."

Abigail smiled. "You're right. My uncle showing up is the nicest wedding gift anyone could give me."

"Well, your husband-to -e might have some special gift he wishes to give you on your wedding night…"

"Wife. Your husband is standing next to you and you are embarrassing me."

"Well, you gave me a special 'gift' on many an occasion…"

"Please, Aleks…"

Dogman walked back to the Ranger and sedan.

"Guess you want me to get dressed up."

"Yup. It's going to be a nice shindig. You will want to look your best for your niece."

"That's true." Dogman paused, then continued. "At least she is happy, and is not marrying a black man."

Ranger Jackson gave him a rather hard look. "Pardner, your bigot slip is showing."

"I know what I know. And I know that dark people have always given me grief since I emigrated here from Romania. My older sister, Abigail's mother, arranged for me to come to the U.S.. Some of your people of color didn't like my accent, and made an issue of it. But not for long, as they were soon picking up teeth."

He looked at the Ranger as he went to open the passenger side door. "I've said more words to you in the last few hours than I have to a dozen people combined the last year. Why is that?"

The Ranger smiled. "Maybe it's because we are both hard cases. We have a lot in common. Being older, I've just learned to bend a little, change a little, I think for the good. You're getting older. You'll come around."

"Yeah. Right."

"Well, as large and tough as you are, Dogman, just remember one thing. Ichiro, her betrothed, is a samurai of the old school. I don't suggest insulting him. Nor upsetting Abigail in his presence."

Both men sat quietly for a moment in the sedan. Then Dogman spoke. "So he loves my niece that much."

"You can't imagine. As we drive, let me tell you about a trip they took to Deseret…"

The wedding came the next day, and there being no large problems to derail it.

There were a few last minute details that had to be taken care of prior to the ceremony. One was that General Reed had to ask Dogman an important question.

Ranger Jackson was acting as official chaperone of Dogman, to insure that he made it to the church on time in the appropriate attire. A tuxedo had been obtained, Dogman wondering why he had been put in such formal vestments. The Ranger said the General and the President knew, and one of them would explain. For once, the very large and muscular man was patient. Probably because it was his niece who was being married.

The ceremony was in the large Great Falls auditorium which that had been turned into a church for this very special occasion. Cameras had been set up to broadcast the festivities, for all those who were not officially invited. Large as the auditorium might be, it could only hold so many people.

John Reed had made a quick survey of all the security arrangements before he went to find Dogman and Ranger Jackson. There was more firepower in the local area than had ever been before, the equivalent of a complete mechanized division. This included a lot of anti-aircraft weapons, most of Russian origin, in case the Squids decided to attempt some form of air strike. Any deltas or falcons would be in for a rude surprise this time, for instead of the Squids having this element of surprise (as they had in the original Strike and Invasion), the humans had it. Free Japan had provided a full squadron of interceptors to supplement the ground based equipment, with the U.S.A. staging a couple of A-10s nearby for close air support. So far, everybody was frosty, ready to act at the first sign of trouble. There were way too many visiting dignitaries and government officials *not* to make this a prime target.

After his force review, General Reed found Dogman and the Ranger in a side corridor of the auditorium. As he approached, he saw just how large and cut with muscle Abigail's uncle was, filling out the tuxedo as if it had been painted on.

"Hope this doesn't piss him off," the General said to himself as he approached.

"Well, howdy, General," Ranger Jackson called out as he saw the General approach. "You're looking right nice in that dress uniform of yours, from one guy to another."

The General smiled. "Well, I haven't had any real pleasant occasions to wear this monkey suit in the last few years. I'm glad it till fits." He walked up to Dogman, extended his hand.

"Sir, I welcome you as the nearest living blood relative of Abigail Jorgensen."

"No, not Sir. Just Dogman. Or Uncle Buck to friends and family." Dogman gave the General a once over as he shook his hand. "You're General Reed. You're going to give Abigail away in the wedding ceremony."

"Well. S... I mean Dogman, Uncle Buck. I was until you were found. As her uncle I... "

Dogman interrupted. "No, you do it, you've been her father here. It's your right."

General Reed was rarely at a loss for words. He looked at Ranger Jackson. "Yes, General, I told him of the situation. About everything you've done for Abigail, how you've helped take care of her as if she were your own daughter."

"Damnit, Ranger, don't exaggerate…"

"What? A Texas Ranger exaggerate? Come on."

"I know he did not exaggerate," Dogman interjected. "I know he was telling it like it is." The muscular man paused for a moment, then sighed.

"I dumped Abigail in Deseret, thinking they could do a better job of raising a young girl than me. I was fucking wrong. They used and abused her. Then Torbin Bender came around, she wound up here, and now she has a large, extended family. You, are part of that. I knew her father, my brother-in-law. He was a good man. I can tell you are a good man. And, like her blood father, you love her, care for her. You and the rest of your tribe here are doing a damn good job of raising her. Why would I interfere with that?"

The three men were silent for a moment. General Reed spoke again."I get the impression that you may not be sticking around."

Dogman grunted. "You would not like me around for long. I don't get along with people of color. I've done some things that would have led to a hanging in the old U.S.A."

"You don't think half the people here haven't, just to survive?" replied General Reed.

"That is why we are trying to rebuild things the way we are. First, we get rid of the Squids. Then, we start over, past sins forgiven if possible."

"My sins would fill Noah's ark, General. I worked with the Krakens. Enough said."

"Yet you helped save Torbin Bender from those same people. Why?"

"He was Abby's friend. She was trying to save him. That's reason enough for me."

General Reed stopped for a moment. This large man was a lot more complicated than at first glance, and had a certain moral code he followed.

"Your surviving family, your niece, will miss you greatly if you leave."

Dogman shrugged. "I'll keep in touch, now that I know how to get in contact with her. And now that I know she has friends and a new family to keep her safe."

"Well, I can tell you are as stubborn as I am. You can at least tell me her late parents' names, so I know who I'm filling in for, and can pay them honor."

"Anica Vladu and Craig Jorgensen. Abigail reminds me of my sister. A lot."

The General extended his hand again. "Okay, deal. I give the bride away. But you have to stay for the whole wedding and reception, spend some time with your niece. Or, no deal."

A small rare smile formed on the dog trainer's face. "Glad to see Abby's adopted father has some grit in him. Deal." They shook hands, then General Reed shook Ranger Jackson's hand.

"Thanks for going the extra mile, Ranger."

"Hell, General. Piece of cake. Besides, Madam President would have my ass if I didn't."

They laughed, as they both knew that was true.

"Well, if you gentlemen will excuse me, I have a date with a bride." The General turned and left.

"Good man, the General," said Dogman.

"Told you he was. Now, you get to meet Madam President. Try to control your opinions. She's not as nice as the General."

The actual wedding ceremony went without a hitch. Aleks said later that God must have been watching close over the festivities to make sure they came off so perfect. Ichiro said the Ancestors of both Families ensured Ichiro and Abigail were married without complications. All that really mattered was that Abigail and Ichiro were bound in holy matrimony.

General John Reed walked the bride down the aisle. When Abigail appeared on his arm, there was a collective gasp. So used to seeing her in military garb, seeing her in the gorgeous creation of a wedding gown caused many a jaw to drop. Mi-Hi and Aunt Freda Munsen had combined their efforts to create a masterpiece that fit Abigail as if it were painted on, as she had imagined. The dress bottom was slender and sleek, with long slits up both sides which allowed Abigail complete freedom of movement, as well as show off shapely legs that were to die for. One could see the Asian influence on the design. The top was more traditional western, with exposed cleavage, and a light frill around her well-shaped chest. Abigail had long sleeves on her arms, with slight frills at the wrists. And, befitting a virgin, it was all bright white with slight silver hints.

Crowning all this was a veil that was secured on Abigail's head with a thin, exquisite, and shiny pure silver chain that acted like a crown. Created by Hannah Weitz, the rumor began that it was an actual halo that Abigail's guardian angel had provided. On Abigail, it became a halo.

The bridesmaid contingent stood at the front of the church on the bride's family side.

Aleks as Matron of Honor and Fanny, Brynhildr, vet Emily Anders, Dr. Rica Rice and the two youngest pit survivors—Pat and Shannon Bell—as bridesmaids. When someone had said that was way too many bridesmaids, Aleks had told the person to go shove their head up their ass and leave her alone. It was her little sister's wedding, they would damn well do as they please. That was the last time anyone complained to Aleks, as the rumor was she would assist the next person causing problems with the insertion of said head in said ass. So, the bridesmaids were soon called the Squad.

Janette Jamison's son Tim was the ring bearer, and Tina was the flower girl. Abigail had demanded they be part of the wedding. Aleks as Matron of Honor had helped choose some traditional classical music for the wedding ceremony besides the "Here Comes The Bride" tome. A certain Sister of Steel, once an opera singer in training and now a Banshee, provided her excellent voice to the proceedings as Abigail was walked down the aisle by General Reed.

Torbin headed the groom's contingent as best man. Standing next to Ichiro, the others were lined up on Torbin, being a much smaller group than the bride's squad. Doc Stubbs, Stalin, and Lt. Todd Baker rounded out the contingent. Lt Baker had tried to bow out until Torbin had said, "Look it. You helped get Abigail and I—especially me—back here in one piece. You gave us the info needed to free those pit survivors who are bridesmaids today. This wedding party would be a hell of a lot smaller without your efforts. So please, be and show up, in dress blues. Got it?"

When the Marine saw Abigail in her wedding gown, his mouth flew open. My God, his little sister was knock-down, drag-out *gorgeous*. He whispered to Ichiro on his shoulder,

"You, my friend, have what is called in the U.S. a 'keeper'. Looks, brains, hard-working, and she loves the holy hell out of you. Don't screw this up."

Ichiro whispered back, "I love her. I am samurai. I will not screw up, blood brother."

As Abigail walked up the aisle on General Reed's arm, a large audience looked on. Madam President sat on the bride's side, George Williams IV on the groom's so as to show no government favoritism. The Vice President, once again, volunteered to stay in a secured location in the new capital—Bismarck, North Dakota. A substantial Free Japan contingent was on hand on the groom's side, with a matching Free Russia on the bride's—My Lady of Steel's—side. The New Vikings or Norsemen tried to spread themselves on both sides, paying homage to both of the warriors they so respected. U.S. personnel were scattered all over, as were military representatives from Deseret. A slimmed down General Huff had flown in that morning in a VSTOL to be the official representative of Deseret, sitting next to Madam President and the Free Russian President, Alina Federov.

At the back of the temporary church, under the watchful eye of veterinarian Emily Ander's assistant Wendy Johnson and her partner Cindy, were Young Fuzz and Princess Freya. Keeping them company were Torbin's and Aleks' trolls, Tristan and Gage, under the watchful eyes of a pregnant Sue Brown. Her husband was part of the interior security detail. Officiating was Chaplain William White, who had overseen the Pit Victims Memorial. He broke into a broad grin as Abigail and the General reached the dais.

"This is a great day. A great day indeed," Chaplain's White's voice boomed."We are about to join two young people in the bonds of holy matrimony. A man and a woman from different cultures, countries, coming together with the holy bond of love under the watchful eye of God and all their friends and family. Not to mention under the gaze of most of the free world, as well as some areas not so free."

He looked at General Reed. "I understand you are standing in as her adopted father, performing the traditional role of the one who gives the young maiden away. Although in this day and age, Abigail has something to say in the matter." This brought a laugh form the assembly, everyone knowing that Abigail was her own person and not one to be "given away" by anyone.

"I am standing here for her blood parents, Anica Vladu and Craig Jorgensen," General Reed's voice rang out. "They are here in spirit, not in body. And for her Uncle Buck Vladu, who requested I do the honors." Abigail squeezed the General's arm as she looked at him and mouthed "thank you". General Reed smiled back.

The Chaplain continued. "Yes, in these days of strife, many cannot be here in body. But they are here in spirit, watching over us to ensure we carry on as they would have."

He looked toward Ichiro. "Now it is time for Ichiro Yamamoto to join his bride before me, as we ask and receive answers in the age old quest for matrimonial bonding in the name of love, honor, and everlasting commitment in the eyes of God."

The rest of the ceremony was a bit of a blur, as it followed the traditional western patterns of marriage. Ichiro was dressed in the formal kimono of a male groom, but it had been decided to stick with the Western rituals for sake of simplicity and understanding. Japan had been westernized years ago, despite the desire of some for the old ways in the current environment. Thus, everyone could easily follow the proceedings.

The ceremony reached the final part. The Chaplain held his hands to the heavens.

"I now proclaim Ichiro and Abigail husband and wife. Let no man tear asunder what has been done under the eyes of God. You may…"

Ichi and Abby were clinched and kissing before the Chaplain White could finish. The assemblage broke into loud clapping and cheering, with many yells of encouragement in all the various represented languages.

Ichi whispered in Abby's ear in English. "I will love you forever."

"And I you," she whispered back in Japanese. One of the great love stories continued at full throttle.

As they left the auditorium turned church, there was a large Honor Guard of all the various countries, peoples and military. New Vikings with broadswords, Russians as Cossacks with their sabers, Japanese Samurai with katanas, U.S. Soldiers represented by the Banshees in brand new designed dress uniforms and four Deseret soldiers. As the happy couple marched through the sword arch, Abigail saw the four Deseret representatives were of the Twenty. She almost stopped and burst out crying. She knew she would have to give General Huff a big thank you.

Russian Senior Sergeant Marina Rostova led the other three Banshees who made up their portion of the arch. Short their now standard issue Squid Killer blades compared to the other swords, she ensured (with a little help from Hannah, their maker) they shone with a brilliance that flashed in the sunlight of the midday sun. The ceremony had been blessed with a cool clear sunny day, this Ides of March. There was not a cloud in the sky to cast a depressing shadow.

Two large side rooms were turned into one large reception area for the receiving by the bride and groom of all the guests. Aleks had located a pair of large comfortable chairs for the married couple to reside in, with a table placed nearby on which to place gifts. There would be many, despite Abigail's protests.

"People want to give you things, little sister," Aleks had explained. "To refuse would be rude, would upset them. Just accept people love you, wish you the best. You and Ichiro are special. Get used to it."

Abigail had acquiesced, and sighed. As Torbin had said, once again, heavy was the head that wore the crown.

As Abigail sat and made herself comfortable, she again stared at the large wedding and engagement set that had magically appeared in the last few days. Her eyes filled with tears up as she once again thought about the engagement ring had come from Ichiro's late mother, the wedding band had been given to her by Uncle Buck.

"It was your mother's," Dogman said. "She gave it to me as she was dying. It's been cleared of any radiation."

All these years, he had hung on to it, never saying a word. A man full of perpetual surprises.

Guests were beginning to queue up to say hello to the lucky couple and wish them the best, then hit the large tables of refreshments, including cash bars. Abigail had put her foot down about having some formal receiving line as in many a state wedding. She demanded she be able to sit with Ichiro at an out of the way table with comfortable chairs and talk to people one on one. No pomp, no circumstance. After all, she could have eloped and *really* thrown things into a screaming mess. Forcing her into a very public wedding for the good of the national morale resulted in her demanding some concessions. This was one of them.

Unbeknownst to anyone, Madam President had used her powers of persuasion to insure a specific person was at the head of any informal line. A strong looking young woman in the dress uniform of a Free Japan Military Officer strode up to Abigail before anyone else could approach. Caught a bit unawares, Ichiro's eyes widened as he realized who was almost on top of them.

"Princess Akiko of the Imperial Royal Family," he blurted out as he lurched up, trying to stand at attention and pull his bride to stand. Before he could, the young female officer dropped to one knee in front of Abigail, bowing her head low. Ichiro's mouth dropped open at this sign of almost total submission by the royal personage.

"This unworthy one wishes to express her undying respect to the Avenging Angel, a Sister of Steel," the Princess' voice rang out in Japanese. "And I humbly ask you take this small symbol of my families respect for what you have done, have sacrificed in the defense of the human race. If I may add, you are a personal hero of mine, someone I hope I may emulate as I mature." She thrust a long object in an ornate silk cover toward Abigail, her eyes still averted. "From my family's collection. May you use it well."

What no one knew was that the Princess was doing this all on her own, had asked Madam President if she may have a quick meeting with Abigail before the others. The President saw a kindred spirit in the young lady, thought it was a good idea for the two to meet. Her father the Emperor would later tell her that her name should have been Impetuous One though he said it with a smile. She was a warrior princess, a perfect symbol for a country under siege, and he knew it.

Abigail saw she was no older than her, not yet twenty years old. She knelt down before anyone realized what she was doing. "Princess Akiko. I should be kneeling in front of your royal personage," she said in perfect Japanese.

At this, the Princess glanced up with her eyes, then back down. "Please. Accept my humble gift."

The Princess' handlers, senior ranking officers, were flabbergasted, knowing that if they went up to recover the Princess, it would be a loss of face for her, an almost rebuke by the military of a Crown Princess. Thus, they stayed frozen in place.

Abigail took the silk-wrapped gift. "Domo arigato gozaimasu," she said as she pulled the silken cord to release the wrapping on the gift. As the covering fell away, she saw it was an ornate katana. As Abigail examined it more closely, she could tell it was old, maybe ancient. She handed it to Ichiro who performed the Japanese sign of extreme surprise and mental conflict, sucking in his breath through almost closed teeth.

He looked at the part of the blade nearest the handle and gasped audibly.

"This is a Fujiwara Kanenaga sword. It is ancient, rare, and superbly made," Ichiro exclaimed.

"It is from the Emperor's private museum," Akiko offered. "I decided a blade such as this should be in the hands of a warrior, not gathering dust. I put a new edge on it myself."

Abigail's mouth fell open, and she started to say she could not accept such a fine and ancient gift but stopped. To refuse it would be rude, an insult. Though Abigail felt she did not deserve such an honorable blade, she could not refuse it.

On impulse, Abigail reached out and grabbed the Princess' hands in her own.

"Please, Princess, look at me, I am just a common person, and feel odd that you are averting your gaze."

Princess Akiko then looked up. Abigail immediately saw a kindred spirit.

"You are about nineteen, yes Princess?"

"Yes, Avenging Angel. I am."

"Please, it's Abigail. I can tell that you, like me, accepted the mantle of a soldier at a young age."

"Yes, Aveng…Abigail-san. My brother, the Prince, was killed during the early attacks by the Takos, the Squids. I took his place as a royal warrior. I have trained ever since, though my mother, the Empress is not happy with that. My father sees the need for royal activity in defending Japan." She sighed. "Though he wishes there were males to take my place."

Abigail paused, thinking. Then, she spoke. "Akiko-san, is it? Will you be my friend? I have no, as we would say, girl or lady friends my age. Other than a cousin, they are all older. And none were trained like I was, like you were at such a young age, as child soldiers. I…

would like someone I could talk to, confide to about my experiences." She looked at Ichiro. "I have my husband, but… he is my husband. You understand."

The two young women who, in an earlier time, could have been called teenagers, looked at each other. A small smile formed on the lips of the Imperial Princess. "That would be nice. To talk to someone who does not treat me as a… Princess."

Abigail grinned. "Then, from this time forward, we are friends. As a friend I gladly accept your gift, and hope I am skilled enough to do it justice."

It was Akiko's turn to grin. "I have my sources who tell me you train with your husband, who is noted at being one of the best swordsmen around. And now, my Royal Family has an official gift, for both of you." From beneath her uniform blouse she produced two small jewelry boxes.

"Matching rings with the royal seal. You are now both members of the Royal entourage. Ask for help at any time, and I or another of my family will respond. Japan owes you both." She bowed her head quickly, then looked at Abigail.

The young bride rose, and had the Princess rise with her. They hugged as if long lost sisters. Which, given their similar experiences, they were in the actual sense of the word.

There was a collective sigh of relief from the Japanese representatives. A minor kerfuffle, nothing which the Emperor would not understand. After all, the Princess had a reputation of being a bit of a pain.

Ichiro tried to bow low to the Princess who grabbed him and hugged him in a surprise move.

"I have heard your President likes to hug people," the Princess stated. "If it is good enough for her, it should be good enough for a Princess. Besides, you are a Hero, not me. I should bow to you."

Abigail smiled. "He is married to a Yankee now. He will have to learn how to shake hands more often."

Ichiro was blushing, stammering. Give him a foe to fight, orders to follow and he was in his element. This unexpected complete departure from the more formal parts of Japanese culture, especially concerning the Royal Family, was causing a bit of psychic overload.

Abigail began to laugh, then hugged her husband. "For once, his tongue is tied into knots," she said in perfect Japanese. She looked into his eyes, her high heels making her as tall as he.

"I…beg indulgence, Abby. My world keeps shifting around you. I am trying to adapt."

"You are doing a fine job, Colonel Yamamoto," Princess Akiko interjected. "You and my new friend, Abigail, are symbols of hope, honor and the warrior spirit in Japan. There are many manga and anime depictions of your actions and adventures, not to mention figurines for the young."

Now it was Abigail's turn to blush a bit. "A statue or action figure of me? Now I feel strange."

The Royal Princess squeezed her hand. "Do not worry, Abigail-san. I have made it my mission to insure they are accurate and respectful depictions of you both. I have already spanked a vendor and a couple of artists with my katana for cheap and nasty representations of you both. As I have also done to those who disrespected Colonel Bender and his wife, Colonel Smirnov."

Abigail began to laugh. "We may ask for your assistance here in the U.S. There is an artist who is producing comic books in Minot and Bismarck, North Dakota of Torbin and me. They are extremely exaggerated, especially of my…physical attributes."

Akiko looked at Abigail, a wry smile on her face. "I will make some unofficial inquiries, my new friend. I know how you value your Freedom of the Press. But sometimes unofficial persuasion…" She let it hang.

The Royal Princess glanced over at her delegation, still with frozen looks on their faces. "I must leave now. My handlers are the edge of bursting for my violations of official protocol." She gave a short bow. "I will call you after your honeymoon, friend Abigail."

"I will be looking forward to it. I have one question. Sergeant Fuzz… are they…"

Princess Akiko pulled herself to her full height. "His memory is treated with the utmost respect. I have a personal gift for you I will send it later as it is still unfinished. I have been working on a painting of you and Sergeant Fuzz. I apologize it is not ready for a wedding gift."

"You are doing a painting, for me?"

"Yes. I think I knew we would be friends someday."

Abigail hugged her one more time, trying not to crush the Princess as she did Ichiro. "I am truly honored. As is Sergeant Fuzz."

"I must go now or my senior officers' heads will soon explode from the stress. Until we meet again."

Abigail watched her new friend walk back to her delegation, head held high as if to dare them to create a scene by criticizing her in public.

"She reminds me of you. My love," Ichiro opined, still speaking Japanese.

"How so, Ichi?"

"Strict sense of honor, opinionated, afraid of nothing other than letting her friends down, tough, and deadly. Yet, behind that hard shell she presents, is a heart full of love and caring."

Abigail looked at Ichi for a moment. Then she spoke. "That is also me?"

"Yes. One of the many reasons why I am so hopelessly in love with you." Ichiro took her left hand and kissed it. Abigail smiled and then kissed him. The kiss went on a little longer than normal. Aleks, who was hanging around as a bit of a goal keeper as the Matron of Honor, cleared her throat a bit to get their attention.

"Please. There are many people waiting to pay their respects. There'll be plenty of time in the next few days for kissing."

Other attendees began to pay their respects, and present wedding gifts. Aleks helped to corral them for Abigail, a stack soon forming on a side table reserved for that function.

Abigail saw a rather tall woman in full Russian military dress uniform bestrewn with every medal and ribbon imaginable walking toward her. She began to stand and the President of Free Russia waved her back into her seat.

"Sit, relax. I was a bride once. You will soon appreciate those times where you can sit and relax." Alina Federov spoke with a bit of a raspy voice. A large scar that circled her throat pointed to the reason for the raspiness. Tall, slender, yet with noticeable curves, and shiny black hair in a tight bun, it was rumored she had been groomed by her family to be a fashion model. In actual fact, she had rebelled, gone into the military instead, and had seen action in Chechnya, the Crimea, and the Middle East. She was one of the few relatively senior commanders who had survived and fled to Siberia in response to the

Tschaaa Invasion. And now she was President after the former President had died of a massive heart attack.

Aleks stepped up and gave a short curtsey. "Madam President. We are honored for you to attend Abigail's wedding."

"Ah, Colonel Smirnov," she replied in Russian. "You look different in female vestments. I see having two sons has been good to you."

Aleks blushed. "I still feel a bit like a cow. I am working hard to get back into fighting shape."

"I think you have been successful. And you, the beautiful bride. I was told you speak Russian like a native born."

"My big sister here, Aleks, has helped me with my accent, Madam President."

Alina Federov grinned broadly. "Well, I would swear you were Russian born. But here, let us cut to the chase so that others may pay their respects." The Russian President handed up an ornate box, about six inches square. "Compliments of the Russian people, my dear. A certain incorrigible training officer here has been singing your praises to anyone who will listen."

Abigail took it carefully.

"Here, open it. It is to be viewed, appreciated."

Abigail untied the ornate ribbon in a deliberate manner, then slowly opened the box. She folded the sides down, looked at the object with in and gasped.

Aleks stepped up, and looked. Her eyes went wide, stuttered and stammered, finally spitting out what she was trying to say.

"A Faberge egg. My God. It is a treasure. How…?"

"From the former collection of the Imperial Museum. One of the few pieces still in our possession. Compliments of Free Russia."

Abigail managed to shut her mouth and speak. "I do not deserve this. It should stay where all Russian citizens can view, appreciate it."

The Russian President snorted. "What, and risk it being destroyed in the next attack? The Squids and their minions are still active in Russia, harvesting when they can to keep us off balance. It has more of a chance surviving with you. And, you deserve it. Do not argue with the Russian President."

Abigail smiled sheepishly. "Sorry, Ma'am. I'm just not used to getting so many…things all at once. And such nice things."

President Federov patted her hand. "You are no longer a child soldier. You are a young married woman with a loving husband. Who, I daresay, will help you have healthy children in the foreseeable future. So, you will have, and deserve, nice things. Especially after we expel those pieces of shit Squids from our homelands. Now, I must let someone else pay their respects." With that last comment, she turned and walked back to where Madam President was standing.

Abigail carefully repackaged the egg, Aleks setting it well aside so that it would not be broken. Then other wedding guests came forward to pay their respects, give more gifts. It was becoming a bit of a happy blur to Abigail. General Reed then appeared with a microphone. "As the adopted father of the bride, I think it's time to present and cut the wedding cake. Gunnery Sergeant Stubbs, if you will do the honors."

From a back hallway, Doc Stubbs rolled in a massive and ornate wedding cake. Six tiers, the top one with hand carved representations of the wedding couple, compliments of Thor Heyerdahl and his New Vikings. On the next tier were further carvings representing all the various peoples and groups whose lives had crossed with Abigail. Included was a miniature of the huge statue of Fuzz which Heyerdahl had commissioned. The original statue now resided in the front hallway of the new Battalion Headquarters for the 101st SAU, the Banshees, as per Abigail's wishes.

The bride and groom walked up to the grinning Doc Stubbs.

"It is…gorgeous." Abigail exclaimed. She grabbed and hugged Doc, who protested.

"Hey, easy with the ribs. I'm not as young as I used to be."

General Reed laughed. "I always knew the Marines were good at killing people and breaking things. I did not realize creating artistic wedding cakes was a hidden talent."

Doc Stubbs had chortled. "Just this one. A much hidden talent."

Out from the crowd came Hannah Weitz, with an ornate silver Squid Killer blade she had created for this specific occasion. It seemed fitting it was used to cut the wedding cake. And of course, the bride and groom were expected to feed each other portions of the first piece, which they did without the expected comic smashing of the cake into each other's faces. That was not their style. Soon, Doc Stubbs was slicing the cake up for serving with quick, sure cuts.

Abigail and Ichiro sat back down and watched the festivities. A large band made up of both military and local civilians began to play, starting out with slow waltz and traditional fox trot. With that, General Reed approached the new bride.

"There is a tradition that the father of the bride has a dance with his daughter. Ichiro, may I borrow your new wife?"

"Of course, General. You are probably better at western dances than I am. Please, dance with Abigail."

General Reed offered his arm, Abigail took it and they went to the dance floor.

"I am very inexperienced, General, so I hope I don't step on your feet."

"Torbin told me you caught on quite quickly at your birthday."

Abigail frowned a bit at the mention of that dance, which had been with the now disgraced Prophet.

"Did I say something wrong, Abigail?" asked the concerned General.

Abigail sighed. "My birthday started out nice. But now I know the way I was treated by the Prophet was all a lie. He may have been a good dancer, but he was a horrible surrogate father."

General Reed was not a tall man, so Abigail in her heels made her actually taller. But he did not care as he looked a bit up into her eyes.

"Remember the good of that day, Abigail. We have enough bad things going on. Torbin said you were happy. Smiling. Remember that."

Abigail then smiled. "You are a good father, General. You know what to say to an insecure, fearful daughter on her wedding day to make her feel better. Thank you." With that, she hugged him.

"You are making this old General choke up," John Reed said with a lump in his throat.

Abigail let out a bit of a girlish giggle. "You are not old. Come on, let's prove that on the dance floor."

General Reed grinned. "Okay. Then I guess I'll try something I haven't done in years. It's called the Viennese waltz. Just follow my lead, it's a bit athletic for a waltz."

"I apologize in advance if I step on your feet, my father," she said in Russian.

"Just use the same excellent coordination you have with martial arts, Abigail. You will have no problems in following my lead." With that, the General gave a special hand signal to the band leader. And, in moments, the music changed to what the General requested.

Most people hadn't seen a sweeping waltz like this, other than a few Russians. Within moments, people were off the dance floor and watching the bride and her adopted father glide in long steps around the dance floor, turning and twirling a bit. Abigail easily matched the General's steps, and soon it looked as if Fred Astaire and Ginger Rogers had been re-incarnated on the defunct *Dancing with the Stars* television show. The band leader, seeing the excellent display of a couple dancing, kept his personnel playing the music for an extra complete set. The couple did not notice. Abigail soon had a large smile on her face as she discovered the fun of the Viennese waltz. She began to laugh, General Reed soon chiming in. Then the music ended.

Abigail hugged John Reed to her, and whispered in his ear, "Thanks for making my memory of dancing once again a good one."

"You're very welcome," the General was able to answer before loud applause and shouts of approval filled the hall. The General escorted his adopted daughter back to her husband, who stood and bowed to him.

"You and my wife make an excellent dance couple."

"Ichiro, you would be just fine if you tried the same dance. My understanding is that you and Abigail are a sight to behold when you two practice swordplay. There is a similar physical flow of movement in many types of dancing."

Ichiro smiled a bit sheepishly. "I am afraid I will step on Abigail's feet. I was never taught how to dance in the western way."

"Trust me, son. You'll do just fine. Now, it is time for me to mingle with our special guests." He kissed Abigail on her cheek, turned and walked toward Madam President and the other government dignitaries.

As General Reed left, General Huff from Deseret approached. He was no longer the overweight officer with a pie addiction who Torbin and Abigail knew. He had slimmed down a lot, but added some gray hair that aged him.

Abigail smiled and hugged him, "Thank you for bringing some of my fellow Twenty as the honor guard, General. It was so very nice to see and talk to them again."

General Huff blushed a bit at the hug. "You will always be a

Daughter of Deseret, Abigail. We owe you so very much for your service, and your exposing the bad that was among us. We were truly blind, and would not see what was in front of us. We saw what we wanted to see, not the truth."

"General, that is the past, and is not your fault…"

"No, Abigail," the General interrupted. "I allowed myself to be the toady to a false Prophet because it was easier to play the role of a military leader rather than be one. I have to accept much of the blame. I will stand before God someday and be judged. It'll not serve me well to deny my guilt."

Abigail saw a deep remorse in his eyes, which hurt her. He had always been a nice, joyful person, even if people thought he was a bit of a dullard as the commanding general of Deseret armed forces. Everyone knew that Prophet at the time was the one who called all the shots. However, General Huff had always made sure his people were taken care of and not abused. Except, it seemed, Abigail and the Twenty.

She reached out and took his hand. "I would say I forgive you if I thought what happened was your fault. It was not. But if you demand forgiveness in order to feel better, consider it given."

General Huff tried to smile, then tried to wipe a tear away before anyone noticed it. Ichiro stepped forward and bowed low.

"You do us honor with your presence, General. You do us more honor with the equipment and support you are now providing the Free Nations Armed Forces. I humbly add my voice to my loving wife that you have nothing to apologize. If things had not happened the way they had, Abigail and I would never had met. So, I thank you. You are part of what brought us together, for which I will be eternally grateful."

Abigail smiled and grabbed her love's arm, pulling him close.

The General's face broke into a big grin. "You two are so *right* together. So if you say I was part of that happening, I will be happy to accept the blame." He reached inside his military dress blouse and produced a letter-sized reinforced envelope.

"The people of Deseret wish to pay their respects on this glorious day. There is a note from somebody you both know, who asked if you would please read it together." General Huff stole a kiss on Abigail's cheek, grabbed and firmly shook Ichiro's hand, then turned in a quick motion and walked away.

"The General apparently wants us to have privacy with this note," Ichiro opined. He opened the envelope and looked inside.

"Look, my love. Silver and gold rings." Abigail looked in the envelope and saw some two dozen of each kind of ring. The gold and silver rings had been placed on silken cords that were inserted in their centers and tied off at the end. Rings on a silken ring was the effect. Ichiro began to read the short note contained in the envelope.

"Dear Special Ones. The rings contained with this note were donated by citizens of Deseret. They once belonged to loved ones who have since passed on, many due to the depravations of the alien Squids. They wish that you make use of their worth in coming years as you start and raise a family, or to help others in need."

"I think of you every day, and pray for you every night. Abigail, I hope someday you can forgive me for not realizing what evil was being done to you in the name of Deseret, the Church, and the Lord. "

"May God bless you on this special day. May God keep you, friends and family safe for all eternity."

Ichiro paused, then read the last part.

"Signed by President-Elect Ester Smith. In the name of the citizens of Deseret."

Abigail sat stoned faced. "Excuse me. I need to goes to the ladies room." Then she was up on her feet and moving.

"Abby-san…" Ichiro tried to say but Abigail was already walking away.

Torbin happened to standing within earshot of the conversation, saw Abigail's reaction and saw Ichiro's look of dismay. He walked up to his blood brother.

"Ichiro, just let her be for a minute. I was there when she had her birthday and send off party. She thinks she was completely betrayed by the Prophet, and thus his wife also."

The new husband looked at Torbin. "I talked with Ester Smith that day when we confronted the Prophet at the border with Wyoming. She was innocent, knew nothing. I could tell by the way she reacted, was so upset."

Torbin sighed. "I know. I got the same feeling when I talked with Mrs. Smith. She just hitched her wagon to the wrong horse. Now, she's suffering the consequences. But since they just elected her

President, someone must trust her. I'll talk to General Huff. I think he'll tell me about what is going on." He put his hand on Ichiro's shoulder. "Welcome to the world of being married to a woman you love and adore. It takes some patience."

Ichiro smiled a little. "Yes, Torbin-san. But I have learned much patience in my life. I will make this work. I will see her happy."

Abigail stood before the mirror in the ladies room, daubing her eyes to save the light makeup Aleks had helped apply. She was stopping herself from breaking down and having a full-fledged cry. She knew she should have gotten over the fact that much which happened to her in Deseret was based on a series of lies. She had really trusted Ester Smith and her husband the Prophet. Then she had almost died because of the lies and deceit. A good Christian was supposed to be able to forgive, to show mercy. Yet every time she was forced to remember anything about Ester Smith and her husband, her soul began to rage.

"I see you, cousin," a Norwegian voice came from behind her. She looked at the reflection in the mirror and saw Brynhildr. She had not even heard her come in.

"I see you too, cousin," she answered in Norwegian.

"Bad memories?"

"How could you tell, Brynhildr?"

Her cousin approached and gently clasped her hand. "I knew it had to be about the past as your present and future are filled with happiness and love. You have a husband who is strong yet kind, who loves you with all his heart and soul. So, it must be the past."

Abigail sighed. "The source of nightmares."

"We all have bad memories from our past, my cousin. Most of them thanks to the Squids. But I for one refuse to let them ruin my present, or my future. Especially when we have friends and family to help us."

Abigail looked into the blue eyes of the larger woman, a true Shield Maiden. "You're not much older than I. Where did you get all this wisdom?"

Brynhildr chuckled. "I watch. I listen. I remember conversations, actions of others, and use them as examples of what to do or not to do. Commissioner Miller says that is why I am such a good Special

Agent, a criminal investigator.”

“Those characteristics are also what make you such a good friend and cousin, Brynhildr. That and love and loyalty.” Abigail grabbed and hugged her cousin. “I’m so blessed to have all these good friends and family in a place where, not to longer ago, I was a stranger.”

“Abigail, how you treat people usually reflects on how they treat you. You are a good soul. So, you bring the best out of all those who are around you, unless they are evil like the Krakens. No one can help them.”

“None of this would have happened if not for me meeting Torbin. He’s the true catalyst.”

“A catalyst without good material does little, Abigail.”

Abigail giggled. “The sage speaks the truth again. Come, you have brought me out of my funk. And as befitting a sage such as you, reminded that I need to thank a certain crazy Marine for all the good things that have happened. Especially being introduced to Ichiro.” With that, she looped arms with her cousin and strode out of the restroom.

Torbin was keeping Ichiro company with Aleks standing nearby as Abigail and Brynhildr approached, arm in arm and now smiling.

“Abby…” Ichiro began but Abigail cut him off.

“Sorry I disappeared, my love. It has nothing to do with you.” She grabbed her husband, hugged and kissed him. “I still have some bad memories to sort out.”

Abigail then turned to Torbin, stepped over and wrapped him in a bear hug.

“Ouch! Damned lady wrestler. Watch the ribs, please.”

Abigail laughed and released the pressure. She looked into his eyes.

“Torbin Bender, in front of friends and family, I must formally thank you for everything that you’ve done and caused to happen. You are the reason I am here, the reason I met Aleks, the reason I met Ichiro, and the reason I am married. I love you, big brother. I will always owe you.”

Torbin felt a growing lump in his throat. I will not cry, he thought. I am a tough Marine. I will not cry.

Ichiro saved him. “Abby, I have something that… Ester Smith asked me to save for you. Please do not be angry. I talked with her and I know she knew nothing of what was done to you. Your rejection of her was… devastating. Please believe me."

Abigail turned and looked into the eyes of the man she loved, would love forever. She moved from Torbin and hugged her husband.

"Ichiro, I could never be really angry with you. A bit irritated, but never truly angry. "

"Do you believe me then Abby? That I know Mrs. Smith knew nothing about what the Prophet did, and had done to you?"

Abigail kissed him full on his mouth. "You've never steered me wrong yet. So yes, I believe you."

With that, Ichiro untangled himself from Abigail's hug. With a slow and gentle touch, he took a familiar gold cross on a gold chain from his pocket. Abigail saw it, and looked into Ichiro's eyes.

"You've kept this these past weeks."

"Yes, my love. I know it was given in love. I did not want to see it thrown away."

"Now I have another reason why I love you so, my samurai."

As Ichiro held up the cross and chain, Abigail looked at Torbin. "If my husband has no protests, I would like you to put in on me, as you did the first time in Deseret."

"Yes, Torbin, please," Ichiro interjected. "It will complete the circle."

Torbin took the cross and chain in a careful grip, placed it around Abigail's throat, and secured with the clasp. Abigail turned and faced him, then looked at the cross.

"It does look good on me." She looked up, then kissed Torbin's cheek.

"I'll always be indebted to you, big brother."

"Hell, Abigail. Family does not collect debts. We do things for each other because we *are* family. In this day and age, family is not just by blood. It is by choice."

"And I chose you, blood brother," Ichiro said as he clasped Torbin's hand. "Thank you for introducing me to the love of my life. I am the one who will always be indebted."

"And now that we have had this meeting of the mutual admiration society," Aleks jumped in.

"There is a party going on. Bride and groom are supposed to enjoy themselves. Then, leave, and *really* enjoy themselves in the bridal bed.

You three are holding up progress."

Abigail laughed, then grabbed and hugged Aleks.

"*Ouch!* Damnit Abigail, watch the ribs. You're right, Torbin. She must have been a female weightlifter in a prior life."

"Which is why I married Ichiro, big sister. He is strong enough to take it."

Aleks smirked at Ichiro after Abigail released her from the hug. "We will see if that is true after a night of passion. I expect a full report."

Ichiro's eyes widened, and embarrassed, he began to stutter.

"A full report? I, I, I,… "

Torbin began to belly laugh. "She is bullshitting you, my friend. She does that to me… *Ow!* Quit with the stiffened fingers to the ribs. Why did I have to fall in love with a Russian spy?"

"Karma," said Aleks, as she grabbed her husband and kissed him deeply.

Libations and refreshments flowed. Russians, fueled with vodka, began to do their kicking Cossack dances on the dance floor. New Vikings joined in with traditional active polka dances. And of course, the younger generations of Americans and Japanese began to demonstrate new variations of older rock and roll gambols/frolics as everyone used the occasion to celebrate life.

Around the Free Nations, others were having their own parties as they watched the broadcasted festivities, for this was a celebration of life and freedom for all humanity as well as a thumb in the eye to the Tschaaa.

Before it had dissolved into a disorganized mass of partiers, Commander Dark Wolf, along his Cousin James and Running Deer had presented Abigail and Ichiro with one final gift.

"From all the surviving Native Peoples, this large blanket is a tapestry recording all your adventures, Abigail Yamamoto. As well as those with Ichiro and the late Sergeant Fuzz. It will bring you good luck and give you something to warm you children with as you tell them of your life."

Abigail had blushed. "I am barely married and people are already talking about children."

"It is meant to be, my warrior sister," Running Dear said. "They will grow strong, and you can bring them to our homes, our fires, to play with our children. Thus, we will always be a special tribe."

After profuse thanks, more hugs from Abigail, the three mounted militia joined the main group of revelers.

"So, they will have children, bring them to our lodges, campfires?" James Dark Wolf asked Running Dear.

"Yes. I feel the Great Spirit wishes it. The conflicts of the past will disappear into history. We are all One People now—not red, white, black, brown or yellow."

Commander Dark Wolf had put his hand on her arm. "You are wise beyond your years, young lady. Now, let us grab some more refreshments before the Russians eat and drink them all. These Cossacks are like our dog soldiers of old. They will eat and drink you out of house and home if given the chance." The three Native Peoples laughed and went toward the diminishing refreshments.

In the midst of the celebration, Sergeant Tapua Tatupu, one of the surviving heroes of the Key West nuke attack, lunged to the center of the dance floor. On either side of him was one of his fellow South Sea Islanders. As a drum and someone beating on a log began to set the beat, Tatupu began a special Manu Siva Tau Samoan war dance, a Haka to Maori, which he had developed over the past weeks. Called the Squid or Kraken Killer Dance, it started out as the body slapping, strong arm gestures and bent knee stomps that were the characteristics of all the Island People's traditional warrior dances, meant to intimidate the enemy and create more resolve in their own warriors.

Then the influences of the current generations of survivors came to fore. Moves stolen from Michael Jackson's *Thriller* and other music videos long since gone into private collections were incorporated, as well as some martial arts influences, creating a long and very active line dance. First the original three, then six, then a dozen, then two dozen men and women were moving as one, following Tatupu's lead and adding some of their own flourishes. The military band arranged by General Reed to be there quickly caught on, increasing the beat provided by the drum and log to a deep roar. The original dance floor was soon packed, people moving tables to increase its size. Yet there were no crashes, no collisions. It was as if every human there had tapped into a primeval beat, one that was based in a spirit of survival and defeating the threat, the invasive Tschaaa.

Abigail turned toward Ichiro. "It is tradition in America for the bride and groom to have a dance. What do you think?"

Ichiro's face broke into a large grin. "What better way for two married warriors to dance than a warrior's dance? Hai! Let us go."

In a heartbeat the couple was on the floor. When Tatupu saw they were approaching, he soon began making a path for them to the front and center of the mass line dance, where he was.

"Make room for the bride and groom!" He bellowed. The crowded parted for Tatupu as the Red Sea for Moses. Abigail's double slit wedding dress showed the reason behind its concept as she had no problem moving, kicking, flowing into various martial arts and traditional dance moves. Ichiro moved with her rhythm as if they had been dancing together for years. Soon, other dancers were stopping to watch the special couple.

Within a minute, it was just Tatupu and the married couple. Then, he stepped to the side, leaving the two dancers on the floor. Seeing they were now a solo couple, they faced each other, creating their own matched warrior dance. Then, in good old South Sea Islander and Maori tradition they ended, making the most horrible, tongue flashing warrior faces they could imagine at each other as they growled challenges. They clinched in a tight hug, followed by a deep kiss, the perfect couple.

The room exploded into shouts and cheers.

Torbin and Aleks looked on.

"Should have known," said Torbin. "Mix a Samurai and an Avenging Angel, you're going to get something special."

He then noticed Aleks had begun to cry a bit. He put his arm around her. "What's wrong, babe?"

"Oh, nothing, you big lout. These are tears of joy. This wedding had been so perfect, so happy, uplifting... Hell, I'm running out of words."

Torbin turned her to face him. "You want something like this, on our anniversary someday? I could arrange it..."

"No. That is not I meant. Our ceremony was just fine. I need no large celebration to know I made the right decision, to know how much I love you." She kissed him, long and passionately.

"Our two beautiful sons are celebration enough for me, my crazy Marine."

"The term is handsome. Boys are handsome, girls are beautiful. I'll learn you American yet."

Aleks gave him a gentle slap on the chest. "Always the jokester. Our love is no joke. Neither is the love of Ichiro and Abigail. It is a love story for the ages."

"The Russian poet is coming out in you again, my love. I would say both of ours are loves for the ages. We have found this love despite all the adversity, pain and death around us. Love like this is the good side of humanity. It is our hope for the future."

Aleks smiled. "Now who is waxing poetic? I guess my Russian soul is rubbing off on you."

Torbin stared into her eyes. "You are part of my soul. Just as Ichi and Abby's souls are now part of each other. Not even death can change that."

Aleks crushed her love to her body. "You are going to make me cry again, you big oaf. What am I do with you?"

"Love me forever. As I will you."

Stalin stepped out into the fresh air in front of the large hall, and pulled a cigar from inside his military tunic. As he began to light it, he saw the statuesque figure of Dogman also exit. "Mr. Dogman. You are leaving?"

Dogman turned at the sound of his name being called. He stopped and looked at Stalin.

"Dogman. Just Dogman." The large man paused. "As you are Stalin. Just Stalin."

"True, my friend. Two men with just one name."

Dogman sniffed. "Romanians don't really like Russians. Thanks to you, we had Communism, Ceausescu."

Stalin shrugged. "Old history. I would apologize if I had anything to do with that, but I didn't."

He puffed on his cigar. "But we must be friends because we have a very special person who binds us. Your niece Abigail, who is my Lady of Steel. We must make sure she has a happy life, many children. Yes?"

Dogman stared for a moment, then grunted, stepped toward the Russian. "You speak common sense, for a Russian."

Stalin laughed. "Here. I have an extra cigar, my fine and large new friend. Share one with me. I guess American Indians like our Cheyenne allies would say I am offering you a peace pipe, to smooth over past wrongs."

"Okay," Dogman said. He took the offered cigar, lit it with the offered Zippo lighter and began smoking. "So why the name Stalin?" he asked.

"It means steel in Russian. That is what I had to become to survive. The original Stalin was ruthless, but his strength was legendary. Now you. Why Dogman?"

Dogman puffed his cigar. "Nice cigar. Dogman is who, what I am. Dogs are my family, my people."

"Except for Abigail, my friend."

Dogman paused, then answered. "Yes. She is family." He stared hard at Stalin.

"You meant what you said about Little Abby?"

"Yes, I did. I must help someone who can beat me with a bayonet and rifle. She is special, and has a good soul a mile wide."

Dogman took his cigar in his left hand and stuck his right out to the shorter man. "Shake. You agree to help protect her. Like Torbin Bender did."

Stalin chuckled. "I did not realize you have made similar agreements. But yes, it goes without saying. I will always have her back, come to her aid. As I have said. She is special to me. Not to mention a lot of my fellow Russians."

"I expect people to keep their word."

"And you are a hard man, Dogman. But I have never gone back on my word. Unless I

was dead."

Dogman stared for moment. Then, a small smile formed on his face. "You have a sense of humor, I see."

"But of course, my new Romanian friend, A sense of humor helps you to survive in Siberia. Now, can I interest in sharing some vodka?"

"I must check on my dogs in the RV first."

"I am in no hurry. Vodka does not spoil. So, please, check away."

At that moment, two beat up vans pulled up on the street in front of the large hall. Dogman and Stalin both watched as some ten scruffy and scraggly individuals piled out of each of the vans. Judging by the way they staggered a bit, and the loud banter they threw back and forth, Stalin could see they were all very well lubricated. As they approached up the walkway, Stalin stepped forward.

"Can I help you, my fine inebriated scavengers?" Stalin had quickly recognized who and what they were. He knew they were not on the guest list.

"We want into the party, buddy." A good sized woman stepped forward, her eyes the blurry and bloodshot type of one who had been drinking alcohol for quite some time.

"Well, my young woman, the hall is already filled to capacity. But I understand some of the local bars have... "

What's the matter?" the woman interrupted. "The bitch and her friends too stuck up to party with us?"

"Shut up." The loud growl came from Dogman. Several pairs of drunken eyes fixed on the large man with the cut physique.

"What's your problem, asshole?" One of the men stepped forward, just as drunk as the woman.

"My very large friend here is the uncle of the Bride, You might want to..." Stalin was unable to finish his warning when the female broke in again.

"What's matter, big man? Don't want anyone to fuck with your private piece of family ass?"

Dogman began to move forward but Stalin beat him. The woman croaked as a left hand of granite crushed her throat, Stalin flicking his cigar into the face of the vocal male scavenger. The Russian let out a shrill whistle. From out of the shadows four Spetsnaz troops with AKs stepped, the assault rifles laser sights flickering across the chests of the small drunken mob.

"I will say this once," Stalin's voice boomed. "Leave, or suffer. Maybe death, maybe just maiming. But you will all suffer."

Time stood still for a few moments, as everyone seemed frozen. Stalin then loosened his grip and shoved the woman backwards into her comrades. She fell to her knees gagging and choking. The man who had received the cigar in his face was rubbing a spot where the lit end had singed his skin. He stared at the four Russians with their weapons at ready.

"Fire, Comrade Stalin?' One Russian called out in his native tongue.

"Nyet, comrade. Not yet." Stalin fixed the man with the singed face. "Well? Your choice."

The man paused, then motioned to his companions. "Come on. Most of the booze and food is probably gone. I know of a bar downtown that will like our business."

The group of ne'er-do-wells walked away, grumbling. But none of them thought some free food and drink was worth getting shot over. They were soon trying to squeal the tires of the vans as they accelerated away.

"You had them posted all along, didn't you Stalin?"

Stalin shrugged. "With due respect, my new friend. I did not need a handshake with you to know what my duty was to Abigail. I have known since she first schooled me on a parade ground with cold steel. My Lady of Cold Steel. *That* is who she is to me."

Dogman paused for a moment, then spoke again. "I have some Busthead in my RV, Homebrew moonshine from the Columbia River. I'll put it up against your vodka any day."

"This I have to see." Stalin turned to the four Spetsnaz. "Keep an eye out, then get someone to relieve you. I know there is some vodka and food left. Nice women you will have to find on your own."

The four soldiers laughed, then said in unison, "Da, Comrade Senior Training Instructor."

Please, lead on Dogman."

"You'll get to meet my family, Stalin. Dogs like you, yes?"

"Well, my friend, Sergeant Fuzz seemed to."

"We will drink a toast to him, Stalin. And I have a Cuban for you to smoke."

"Ah. A friendship made in heaven. Good tobacco, good drink, good company. And I have a good woman waiting for me. God shines on me today."

It was nearing "that time", the time when the Bride and Groom needed to exit the festivities in order to begin their new life together on their honeymoon, as husband and wife. Aleks and Torbin began to gather up the wedding gifts to be taken to Abigail's quarters next to theirs. Thus, the gifts could be watched while the happy couple enjoyed the bridal bed together without any outside distractions or worries. Woe behold anyone thinking of walking off with a wedding gift. If they were not bit, stabbed or shot in the attempt, Aleks had said she would personally castrate them as she would a pig. The festivities would continue after they left, as there was still plenty of food and drink. Besides, big parties were rare in post-Strike Earth. People enjoyed them when they could. Any leftovers would be saved for the division of personnel guarding the area. Any attempt at a Tschaaa disruption would be met with extreme prejudice.

Ichiro then appeared, holding a long three string instrument, which looked a bit like a cross between a banjo and a guitar. He walked to the center of the dance floor and one of his Junior Officers came up with a tall stool. As people began to turn and watch, Ichiro's voice rang out. "I have prepared a special gift for Abigail, the love of my life, on this most special occasion. I have composed a musical piece on my shamisen, a traditional Japanese string instrument."

Abigail looked at him in a quizzical manner, said aloud. "I didn't know he played an instrument."

Aleks snorted. "Just married hours, already the secrets begin to come out... ow. You pinched me."

"My wife, you will not begin to strew distrust and disharmony on this very first day of wedded bliss," Torbin stated. "For once, you will listen to me, your husband. Be nice." He put his index finger to Aleks' mouth as if to shush her and she gently bit it.

"Hm. Are you trying to tell me something, wife?"

With an impish grin, Aleks replied. "I have been a bad girl, a shrew. My husband must discipline me."

Abigail was watching the exchange out of the corner of her eye and began to laugh. So this is what married life could be.

"You laugh, little sister?"

"You two fight and make up better than anyone I know. Now, let's watch my husband display his hidden musical talent."

Ichiro had performed a quick tuning check of the shamisen. His voice again rang out.

"The music tells the complete story of how I and my beloved met, out trials and tribulations. Then our coming here, to celebrate our love for each other with you all."

A lump formed in Abigail's throat at the sound of the near poetry. She had forgotten that a true Samurai in the old fold was a highly trained and educated warrior poet. Now, that tradition would be displayed this night.

Ichiro started out slowly, lightly strumming the strings of his instrument. The tempo began to pick up, but was still moderated. Then, in a couple of chords, his fingers took off. Complicated, quick, and increasing in volume, sounds began to cascade from Ichiro and his instrument. The Japanese in attendance could sense the story in his song, many began to show evidence of tears. As did Abigail. She knew the story he was telling. It was about her original hesitance over admitting, experiencing love. Followed by her near death, Ichiro's guilt over a supposed abandonment, and the short horrible day in Deseret when she had to face her secret and painful past. And all through it, Ichiro's undying love prevailed. He stayed, a rock of stability in her world, infused with love.

Ichiro's Song, soon to be known as Abigail's Song when recordings of this effort were remastered, began to wind down. With extreme gentleness, Ichiro seemed to play the tinkling of wedding bells, the final reprise. Then, he stopped with a final chord. Ichiro slid off the stool, went to one knee, bowing to Abigail. "This, is for you. I will love you forever."

Abigail walked out, tears streaming, knelt next to him, took his face in her hands and kissed him. "Let no man, or monster, tear us asunder," she whispered.

There were few dry eyes in the house as the message and emotions sank in. Applause came but no shouting. Tough Russian Spetsnaz were seen to hug each other and wipe their eyes. Ichiro had the heart of a Russian poet, many would say. Aleks came forward with Abigail's bridal bouquet as the bride and groom began to walk off the dance floor.

"Need to complete the traditional throwing of the bouquet, little sister. Ichiro, Torbin will help you with the garter toss."

In a few minutes, once the word got around about the impending action, there was a substantial group of women formed on the edge of the dance floor. One woman who did not participate was tall Brynhildr.

"I know I am going to be married soon, to Rolf," she told Abigail. "And my size would be an unfair advantage."

So Abigail gave it a world class over the shoulder toss, with Pamela Bell, Lt. Shannon Bell's sister catching it after a quick scramble by some dozen young ladies. Abigail clapped her hands with joy as she saw it happen.

"Now we will have to look for some eligible bachelors," she said.

"I see one already who has been watching her." Torbin interjected.

"Really? Who?"

"Sergeant Benjamin Black. The sniper who went with me to Key West. He has been recognized as one of the heroes of Bloody Kansas." Torbin replied. "Since he already has a Medal of Honor from Key West, they're trying to figure out what type of award to give him. He was a major reason the Krakens were held up near Salina."

Abigail paused for a moment. "So, you'll vouch for him."

"Whoa. The decision of whether he will make a good husband or not is up to Miss Bell. Hell. A lot of people thought I would have made a lousy husband. Look at me now."

"Who said they were wrong?" Aleks cut in.

"Once again, my loving wife attacks me. Why do I put up with it?"

"Because we love each other. And who said I was a good wife? Now, do your best man duties and insure the garter is tossed." Aleks kissed Torbin. "We may be substandard as individuals. As a team, we can't be beat."

A couple of minutes later, Abigail and Ichiro watched as young Lieutenant Baker from Wyoming Ass Drag Days caught the garter. Which was fortuitous as he had a pregnant fiancée. He had not pined for Abigail long. As Abigail and Ichiro prepared to leave, Lt. Sumie Sato in a traditional formal kimono approached with a couple of other young Japanese service women. She came up to Abigail, bowed, and presented her a book tied with and intricate bow. She blushed a bit as she handed the book to Abigail.

"Abby-san, it was Japanese tradition that members of the families would provide a Japanese pillow book to the newly married couple. It contains…pictures, artwork, and drawings depicting how the new couple can…enjoy themselves on the wedding night."

Sumie looked down a bit, still embarrassed. "Since we consider Colonel Yamamoto and you as family, we took it upon ourselves to supply this…essential. There are no other family members, so…"

Abigail took the intricately bound book and then hugged Sumie. Aleks had already told her about such Japanese traditions as she had heard of them while working in the far east.

"Hell, little sister," Aleks had said. "I think most Russian women wished that tradition had caught on with us. It would have helped prevent a lot of useless fumbling on many a wedding night during the long winters in Russia."

"Thank you, my sister," Abigail said in Japanese. "You will always be welcome in our home, will always be in our thoughts and prayers." Sumie had teared up a bit at that, bowed deeply.

"My friends and I are honored. Now, we will leave you to your honeymoon." With that, the three Japanese young women bowed and left.

"One more farewell to the newlyweds," Thor Heyerdahl's loud voice cut through the noise. He stood, beckoned Abigail and Ichiro to stand before him. He had them face each other as he wrapped an intricate silver chain around their right arms, binding them together.

"By Odin, Far Wanderer, Grant thee wisdom, courage, and victory.
Friend Thor, grant thee your strength,
Lady Freya, grant thee your love, life and beauty,
And may all be with thee in the coming days."

"Now. My young warriors, you are bound under a blessing that should protect you from harm. At least for the next day or so."

Ichiro bowed to Thor. "You do us honor."

Thor clapped his shoulder. "Son, *you* are honor. Rolf and Johann have told me what you two have done in helping others. You are both welcome in my family hall anytime you need a place to stay. You are both Norsemen from this moment on. Now, I must get back and have some more mead. My throat is dry from all this talking." He kissed Abigail, turned and strode off, towering over the other wedding attendees.

"We are so blessed, Ichiro, to have so many friends and family."

"Yes, Abby. We will always be there for them. It will be our turn someday to bless someone at a wedding. And so the wheel of life turns."

She beamed at him. "Always the philosopher warrior. I am so lucky to have your love." She hugged and kissed him. "Now, let us get moving. I want to spend my honeymoon night with my husband before I turn old and gray."

"Abigail, you? Old and gray? Never in my eyes."

A few minutes later, the wedding presents secured for transport to Abigail's base housing residence, now the temporary married couple's quarters, the happy couple made their way to the entrance way that would now be there exit. As they approached it, Abigail saw her Uncle Buck, Dogman, standing off to the side with Stalin. She squeezed Ichiro's hand, and led him to the two figures. She threw her arms around her uncle and kissed him.

"Thank you for coming. Thank you for all your love and support. I love you, Uncle. I wish you could stay nearby so that we may see you more often.'

"I don't do well in crowds, around lots of people. Especially Non-Romanians."

"I was just trying to convince your uncle of the very same thing," Stalin interjected. "Maybe if we both keep working on him…"

Dogman looked at him. "I don't think you realize what you ask."

"I think I do, my new friend. I was not always the social animal I am know. And I still greatly irritate people. Just ask your niece."

"My wife would greatly miss you if you leave again, Uncle," Ichiro added, "And her happiness is my primary concern now."

Dogman examined Ichiro's expression closely. "You mean that, don't you."

"Yes, sir, I do. On the honor of my family, as a samurai, I swear."

Dogman keep looking at Ichiro. Then he stuck his hand out. "Shake."

Ichiro took his hand.

"I hold people to their promises. Ask Torbin Bender. You will keep her happy."

"Uncle, he will try…" Abigail broke in.

"No, he will. He swore. Your happiness is what matters. Not me."

Dogman turned toward Stalin. "You can help me find a place far out of town. With space for some dogs? I have some I need to pick up in in Oregon. Also, I may have some people staying with me for a while,"

Stalin's face broke into the large grin that always looked like a grimace. "Of course, my new friend. Anything to keep My Lady of Steel happy."

"Good, it is settled. Abigail, for you I will stay near. No one else."

Abigail clapped her hands and hugged him again. Then she grabbed Stalin in a bear hug, kissed him.

"Thank you," she said in Russian. "You are like an old gruff uncle who spoils his niece and nephews, comes through in a pinch."

"I will take that as a compliment, My Lady of Steel. Now, although I have never been married, I think it's time for the bride and groom to leave and begin their honeymoon."

"I believe you're right." Abigail looked at Ichiro. "Ichi, shall we?"

"Your wish is my command, Abby."

The word quickly spread that they were leaving and a crowd of well-wishers formed as the happy couple made their way to the steps at the main entrance. Someone had positioned their SUV in front with the obligatory shoes and cans attached to the rear bumper. Of course someone had written "Just Married" on the back window in shaving cream and soap.

As members of the band stood by and played the *Wedding March* one more time as Abigail and Ichiro made their way to and entered their vehicle, pelted with rice from the mass of well-wishers. Abigail drove as usual, being the more skilled driver of the two. As they waved out their SUV windows, Abigail slowly accelerated onto the main street, then turned in the direction of their hotel.

Madam President stood on the edge of the stairway, wiping her eyes with one of her signature handkerchiefs. George Williams stood next to her as they watched the happy couple drive away.

"George, this is the happiest wedding I have been to since I and my late husband were married. Damn, they make such a lovely couple." She grabbed and squeezed her friend's arm.

"Yes, Sal, they do. And I know they will take care of each other like no one else could. They'll be safe."

The President leaned in and whispered to her friend and assistant. "Commissioner Miller is supplying a little secret coverage tonight at the hotel. We don't want them to feel crowded, so it will be on the sly."

George smiled. "Ever the mother hen over her brood. Now, let's go back inside, drink one last toast with our families and friends. Then we can let the Russians finish off the leftovers."

Two of the most powerful humans in the Free States walked back into the quieting festivities, for one last drink to the happy couple and a peaceful night.

The hotel was the Great Falls Crown Hotel, the nicest rebuilt inn in the entire surrounding area. Ichiro and Abigail pulled their SUV up to the front and two valets ran out to meet them. The young men were stumbling all over themselves as they tried to open their doors, welcome the happy couple, and grab their luggage. Abigail and Ichiro hung onto their ever present tactical gear and weapons. They may be newlyweds, but they were warriors first in a war that had no real borders, truth be told. Not when there was an ever present eye looking down from outer space.

They went to the front desk and were met by a young hispanic couple. "Welcome to the Crown Hotel, Mr. and Mrs. Yamamoto. Your suite is ready and waiting." The young man greeted them with a large smile.

At the sound of her new married name, Abigail giggled a bit. It still seemed like a nice dream that she was married to her one true love.

The young man continued. "I'm Rudy Ramirez and this is my wife Elena. We own this hotel, taking it over from the deceased owners. As they say in Texas, where we came from, 'mi casa es su casa'. So, please, ask for anything. If it is legal, we will get it. And your room is gratis, on the house."

Ichiro stepped in. "Please, Sir. We can pay. I cannot allow you to…"

Rudy Ramirez interrupted. "Yes, you can. You have protected us. You, Colonel, attacked Key West. How can I not try to pay you back?"

"But sir…" Ichiro tried to argue, then Abigail gently squeezed his arm. He looked at her and she smiled at him, then nodded her head yes. Ichiro smiled.

"My wife has told me that I should accept your offer with honor. This I will do."

Ichiro stepped back, bowed low to the young couple. "You do us honor, Mr. Ramirez. I am forever in your debt. Call for help, I will be there."

Elena Ramirez stepped up and hugged him, leading to a deep blush. "You two are treasures," she said, as she moved her hug to Abigail. "We will always have a place for you. We know after fleeing El

Paso what it is like to have no home, little hope, and few friends." Elena looked at Abigail with tears in her eyes. "You give us hope."

Abigail kissed her cheek. "Thank you. I think I can count you two as our first new friends as a married couple."

Rudy led them up to their honeymoon suite on the top fifth floor. In line behind him were the two valets, a third one parking the couple's SUV as they went to their room. As they reached it, Rudy unlocked the large double doors with the key card, and stepped back with a grin on his face. Ichiro stood for a moment, then realized he had a duty to perform. He easily swept Abigail into his arms, her tactical gear in her arms, and carried her over the threshold.

Abigail liked the feel of the strength of her husband's arms. For once she felt complete, safe and protected. Ichiro carried her into the large suite, lightly set her down in the center of the front room, the back room containing the king-sized bed. Abigail had never been in such a spacious and elegant room. The valets were in and out in a flash, making sure the huge bed was turned down, the suitcases opened, their regular clothes were hung up. A large magnum of chilled champagne was wheeled in a placed in the corner of the front room.

As Rudy turned to leave, Abigail tried to give him a large tip for the valets, but Rudy refused.

"When I said gratis, I meant it."

"But there must be something you will allow us to give," Abigail said.

One of the young men spoke up. "A photo with you both... please?"

A cell phone was produced, and a photo of Ichiro, Abigail with the two valets was taken by Rudy.

"All right. Vamanos. We now leave you two newlyweds. Please call the desk if you need anything. But rest assured, your privacy is secure." With that, Rudy bowed and with the valets, was gone.

Abigail looked at Ichiro as it sank in for the first time. She was alone, on her wedding night, with the man she loved. She blushed a bit as she once again realized she was a virgin, felt a bit insecure. Then Ichiro was gently hugging her, holding her.

"I love you, Abigail. I know you are nervous. Please don't be."

Abigail smiled, her head on his shoulder. "Read my mind again.

This is just... so new."

She raised her head, looked into his eyes. "I... just do not want to mess anything up. I do not want to be a... disappointment." Abigail felt the proverbial stirring in her loins, but was still scared of the feelings.

"Abigail, you will never disappoint me. I love you. You *are* my angel." Ichiro kissed her, slowly and languorously.

On the floor below, Brynhildr and David Jackson were setting up in a room near the fire escape. Commissioner Miller had told them to follow the wedding couple to their hotel and keep a loose watch on them. They would soon sneak up stairs and set a couple of small surveillance camera at either end of the hallway that ran in front of the honeymoon suite, to be monitored in their hotel room.

Brynhildr watched as David removed their equipment from two large duffle bags and a large hard case. The Commissioner had assigned David Jackson to work with her. He had told her that she needed to help "break him in" to the job of Federal Law Enforcement Agent.

Formal training was still in short supply, so a lot of it was by the seat of the pants type.

"So, Commissioner, you think I have enough experience to train someone else?"

The somewhat beefy man had laughed. "You studied being an agent well before I ever met you, using your uncles' reference books and files. That and your in born hunter's proclivity have made you a natural. Or at least a very quick study."

After David Jackson had accepted the job, he had been with Brynhildr ninety percent of the time. He turned toward her as he removed items from a duffle bag.

"Two 3D printer submachine guns, a 12 gauge pump, and our 10mm pistols. Think that's enough firepower?"

Brynhildr nodded. "That, along with my bow, arrows and throwing axes. At least enough weapons to put up a fight until the cavalry arrives."

She turned around. "Can you unzip this bridesmaid dress? The zipper seems to be stuck." David walked a bit stiff legged over and worked the zipper. He broke it free and it went down easily to the small of her back. He got a glimpse of sheer panties and he jumped back.

Brynhildr felt the results of David's efforts, turned and looked a bit impishly over her shoulder. "Saw something that surprised you, Agent?"

David blushed a bit. "Don't take this the wrong way, but like they say in Texas, you are right purty."

The Shield Maiden laughed. "Getting a compliment from a man is not wrong. Nor does it offend me." She walked toward the bathroom. "You have a lady friend, Mr. Jackson?" Brynhildr tossed over her shoulder as she entered the bathroom to change into her "work" clothes.

"No Ma'am. Please, call me Dave. Mr. Jackson is my father, Ranger Jackson."

Byrnhildr pushed the door partially shut and stripped off her bridesmaid dress in one smooth motion. As she began the process of putting on her tactical pants and boots, she called out, "I have a lot of young friends who are looking for a good, stable man. Is that you, David?"

"I try to be, Ma'am."

"Call me Brynhildr. It is settled, then. I will introduce you to some of my friends when we have some spare time.

David Jackson laughed. "You always take charge, don't you Brynhildr?"

She laughed. "If I waited for most men to take action, I'd be old and gray before anything happened."

The Shield Maiden stepped from the bathroom and went to gear up with her weapons and tactical vests.

I'll flip you for first watch."

"No need to, Brynhildr. Your choice, you're in charge. I'm easy."

Brynhildr cocked an eyebrow. "You're easy? Alone in a room with a young woman with all the right equipment?"

David blushed red. "Damnit, you know what I mean…"

Brynhildr laughed long and hard.

"You men are all boys. Easily embarrassed. You take the first watch after we set up the monitors and cameras. Hopefully, it will be a quiet couple of days. At least, for us."

Abigail looked at herself in the full-length mirror by the front door of the honeymoon suite. It seemed whoever had built this room had decided people should be able to check themselves out before leaving. Ichiro was waiting on the huge king sized bed in the equally large room. Abigail was fascinated with the opulence of this pre-Strike room. Some of her memories of what had been available over six years ago, before the Tschaaa showed up, were a bit faded. This hotel reminded her what had been lost to much of humanity.

The "special" negligée Aleks had helped her select fit her perfectly. Dark navy blue garter belt, stockings, high heels, and thigh length sheer see thru robe exenterated every sensual part of her body. She had left her panties and bra in the suitcase, her full firm chest and buttocks needed no support. Besides, she felt a heat between her thighs for which panties would do nothing.

She blushed, felt a slight pang of fear. She was a virgin. She had been schooled by Aleks what to expect, but was still scared.

"Don't worry," her big sister had said. "Your body will help tell you what to do. Your love for Ichiro and listening to me will do the rest."

Aleks took a deep calming breath, then let it out. Now was the time.

She slow walked to the bedroom entrance. The only light on in the room was a small table lamp next to the bed.

"Abby, you are coming in?" Ichiro asked. Slowly Abigail entered, her breathing speeding up with excitement.

"Yes, my love," she answered. Then she blurted out, "Ichiro, I'm scared I will disappoint..." She stopped herself. Ichiro saw her hesitation, heard her fear, rose from the bed and walked to her.

"Abby what are you..." He stopped in mid-sentence. Abigail had never allowed him to see her near nude. Now it seemed to stun him. "Abby," he whispered. "You are so beautiful. I cannot believe... you do look like a perfect woman."

"You're just saying that," Abigail said as she looked down. Then Ichiro raised her chin, gently kissed her. The gentleness turned into need as Abigail heard and felt herself moaning.

Aleks was right. Her body knew what to do with her true love.

She kissed him long and deep as his strong hands caressed her body with a gentleness she had never known. Then she caressed him, her hands reaching up under his silk bedtime kimono finding the special spots of desire and feelings. Ichiro sucked his breath in as he separated from their kiss.

"Someone has shown you the arts of love and desire."

Abigail giggled, her fingers caressing his body. Now she knew the power Aleks had mentioned. A woman could always control a man's lust, if taught right.

Aleks was an excellent teacher.

"Abigail," Ichiro began to moan a bit.

His new wife pushed Ichiro backwards until they fell onto the bed.

"Aleks told me that if I... was on top the first time, I could control... things better. Prevent any initial pain or discomfort, from being a virgin."

"As Americans say, you are in the driver's seat, my love."

Abigail straddled Ichiro's hard body. It was if their bodies had been made for each other. There was a momentary slight pinch, then a rush of heat. Their bodies went directly to a matching rhythm as their lust and desire rose.

Abigail looked down into Ichiro's eyes. 'This was worth the wait. I do so love you."

"You are my everything," the Samurai answered. He pulled her face to him, kissed her.

A couple of cries and moans, and Abigail collapsed on top of her husband.

Ichiro stroked her hair, kissed her neck, and began to taste her sweat with his tongue. Abigail responded, began to kiss and caress him more.

"Again, Ichi. Always again. You are my perfect lover. I want more!"

The two lover's bodies again began to respond. It would be a long and enjoyable honeymoon night. As it should be.

As Ichiro and Abigail were becoming as one in the marriage bed, Torbin and Aleks were back home with their sons, two dogs, and all of the wedding gifts. It was not long past nightfall, and the offspring of Sgt, Fuzz, Freya and Young Fuzz were restless. They wanted out one minute, then in the next. The two young human sons were also becoming restless, agitated, as if they could sense the dogs emotions.

Torbin stepped out into the backyard and stood quiet, listening. Something seemed a bit off. He went back into the house and went to talk to Aleks, who was trying to put the two boys down to sleep.

"Husband, I need your help. You were able to calm them in the womb. Please try now."

Torbin went to the twin cribs, side by side, and put a hand on the stomach of each of the two little Marines. "Hey guys. Sleepy time. Relax. Dad's here. Nothing will bother you."

Within moments, the two less than one year olds quieted down, began to drift off to sleep.

Aleks hugged her husband gently. "I don't know how you do it, Torbin. You have a calming touch."

"Well, I try. Step out into the hall way for a moment, let them drift off."

The parents of two of the first children born with some alien introduced characteristics stood out in the hallway and whispered to each other. "Aleks, I want to go to the firing range and gym with you in the morning. I'll call Sue Brown, see if she can come over to watch the trolls."

Aleks frowned. "Why tomorrow morning?"

"Spidey sense, dearest."

"Spidey? Oh, that's right. That super hero from the comics. Again you act like you never grew up."

"Well, it's the easiest way to explain that my Murphy's Law detector is tingling. I get the feeling something involving Abigail, Ichiro... or someone else connected to the base is about to happen, go wrong. I want to be up and ready, near extra weapons."

Aleks looked at her husband. She then squeezed his hand. "Alright. I can tell if I do not say yes, it will drive you crazy. Call Sue. We get up, get our gear, go to the range and the gym .If nothing happens, you will have to make it up to me, wait on me, breakfast in bed, or something like that.

Torbin smiled. "Always the hard deal maker. But what if I am right?"

Aleks shrugged. "Then we deal with it before it deals with us, and our children. Call for help. Whatever it takes."

Torbin kissed his wife. "Anybody ever tell you that you are the best partner a man could have?"

"Flattery will get you everywhere, my husband. Now, get ready for bed. Make sure the dogs are calm, see if they will sleep quietly next to our sons. Then you owe me some alone time in our bed."

"Anything you say, Aleks. Anything you say."

CHAPTER 33

I was there when it happened. I played a small part in the events that day. While doing research for my literary works I came across a quote by a great man in human history, Mahatma Gandhi. He said, 'Strength does not come from physical strength. It comes from indomitable will.'

That day—the day after the famous Wedding of the Warriors—showed just how much will humans have in the face of horror.

-Excerpt from the *Works of Princess Akiko*, Free Japan Royal Family

HELL DAY
GREAT FALLS, MONTANA

Abigail opened her eyes in the wedding bed before sunrise, and smiled. She had never felt so alive and so satisfied at the same time. Nor felt as loved. Ichiro's muscular back was her first sight. She watched his back and side move as he slept, still in an apparent deep sleep. Abigail could smell his unique male scent, knew that she would recognize it until the day she died. His scent would always mean "love" to her.

Careful not to wake him, she slid out of bed and went to the toilet. After washing her face as quiet as she could, she padded across the bedroom out to the large entry way of the hotel honeymoon suite. She slipped on some clean sweats as, even though she had become very comfortable with being nude, walking down to the main desk and complimentary breakfast area nude would be very distracting to the staff.

The hotel staff was just putting out the first items when Abigail walked in. Some eyes widened as they saw her and one young woman made a beeline to he, eager to please. "Ma'am. Tell me what you want. I'll arrange room service."

Abigail smiled. "It's okay. I just want some fruit, rolls, and some toast. I don't want to wake my husband.

The young woman, about Abigail's age, gave a knowing smile and nod back. "Yes. Ma'am. I remember my wedding night. For all their bluster, men are easily worn out."

"Have you been married long, Mrs.….?"

"Gustafson. Charlene Gustafson. And it is an honor to meet you, Ma'am." She stuck her hand out and Abigail shook it.

"Please. My name is Abigail. Ma'am sounds like I'm the President or something."

Charlene's face became more serious. "You're more important. At least to the younger women. You give us hope for the future, hope for our children. You show us how strong we can be." Charlene's eyes were moist as she finished her comment. Abigail hugged her.

"Thank you. But I'm just one of many. I just do what I think I was called to do."

Charlene dabbed her eyes with a napkin. "But you do it well. You set a good example for the rest of us."

Abigail blushed a little. "Please. I'm not used to all this attention. But, now, how long have you been married?"

"A year, M…Abigail. My husband, Samuel, is in the military also, the Military Police. He's working today.

"Any children?"

"Not yet. We are waiting, making sure things are as secure as possible. Bloody Kansas made us realize there is still a state of war, there will be as long as the Squids are here, have control. My hometown, San Diego, is under their complete control."

Abigail nodded. She understood this fear that only women could really understand. Giving birth, knowing your child may be not only killed but eaten stuck a cold icepick in the gut of every woman.

"Well, I must get back upstairs before my husband wakes up. It was a pleasure to meet you, Charlene."

Before Abigail could protest, the hotel staff had a couple of plates of fruit, fresh toast, butter, jam, rolls, sausage and bacon.

Charlene gave her a knowing wink. "You'll need to keep his stamina up. Amongst other things."

Abigail had blushed a bit, gave them profuse thanks, and then made her way to the elevator and back upstairs. She opened the suite with the keycard and padded to the bedroom. There was a large coffee table that was a perfect place for the food. Ichiro was still sawing logs. She slipped into bed next to him, began to gently kiss his back. Ichiro stirred, woke.

"I hope this is my wife kissing me, not some chambermaid."

"If I caught a chambermaid in my wedding bed, her lifespan would be greatly shortened."

Ichiro rolled over to face her. "Good morning, Mrs. Yamamoto."

Abigail giggled. "Good morning, Mr. Yamamoto. I take it my husband slept well?"

Ichiro smiled. "After a certain woman wore me out, yes." He kissed her gently, then hugged her, burying his nose in her hair. "I love your smell, Abigail."

"And I, yours, my love. I have brought up some food for breakfast, compliments of the hotel staff."

"Hm. I am suddenly very hungry." Then a small smile formed on his mouth. "But I suddenly noticed I have a desire for something else."

Abigail laughed as felt under the covers. She kissed him. As their lips parted, Abigail added, "I guess the bacon and sausage will stay warm for a few minutes more."

"Just a few minutes more? I thought things may last longer."

"You forget, dear Ichi, who my big sister is. And what she has taught me."

"Damn Russian spies," Ichiro replied. "They just have to ruin everything."

"Hm. Let us see, husband if you think this ruins everything."

As Ichiro and Abigail were enjoying breakfast in bed, Sergeant Brad Johnson was manning the main gate to Malmstrom Armed Forces Base. He was on his second large cup of coffee. He, along the greater majority of personnel not on duty, had celebrated the wedding of Ichiro and Abigail. For they were both "one of them" and everyone wished them the best. The fact that Abigail was a knockout to look at did not hurt.

"Maybe they could clone her," the tow-headed soldier said out loud.

"Clone who?" K-9 handler Corporal Robert Peña asked. He scratched his large German Shepherd, Bullet, behind his ears just exactly as the War Dog liked, eliciting satisfied dog grunts.

"Why Abigail, our Avenging Angel. Then we could all have a chance at the perfect woman."

The large Mexican-American male laughed. "Yeah, and then they would clone Ichiro Yamamoto too. Which means all the clones would be attracted to each other, and you would still be shit out of luck."

Sgt. Johnson glared at his shift partner. "You sure know how to ruin a good fantasy."

"Nah, just a dream. And please tell me why we have large semi-trucks coming up the road toward us."

Johnson looked at the advancing vehicles. There were three large trucks with box trailers in a line approaching their security office, with what looked like two smaller furniture vans further behind. The Military Police Sergeant swore.

"Who in the hell is delivering crap today? I thought this was basically a national holiday of post-wedding celebration."

"Maybe the circus is coming to town, Sergeant."

"Yeah, right. And they're also supposed to come through the back gate at that. Dumbasses."

He stepped out of the security office and into the lane of traffic, his hand up as a signal to stop. The lead semi stopped some fifteen yards back. The drive had no sooner stopped than he and his passenger were dismounting from the truck cab. The driver had a clipboard in his hands, as the passenger turned and went to the back of the trailer. The driver, a skinny greasy haired man, called out.

"Hey, I have a delivery for the Combat Support Group. A big one."

"I can tell that," Sgt. Johnson replied, none too happy. "But you came to the wrong gate, and who in the hell is delivering crap today? Just about everyone in the Great Falls area has a down day."

"Hey, guy. I just do as I'm told…"

Bullet, who Cpl. Peña had taken out the other side of the security office, exploded. He barked, howled, started to drag the Cpl. across the pavement toward the truck. His face was a snarling image of rage, showing all the teeth he had in his large mouth.

"What the fuck…" Sgt. Johnson started to say as the driver dropped his clipboard and grabbed for something concealed under his long shirt. Years of experience and training paid off as Johnson got his Beretta pistol out first and double tapped the driver in the chest before the man could get his concealed revolver into play. Then he heard Cpl. Peña yell.

"Eaters! They have Eaters!"

The passenger had thrown open the back doors of the first semi-trailer, with the well-

recognized alien lifeform boiling out in large numbers. Peña opened up with his assault rifle, the choke chain on Bullet's neck the only thing keeping him from breaking loose. Dogs hated Eaters. Johnson scrambled back into the entry point office and hit the red panic button. As he did, three before unnoticed motorcycles with rear passengers came roaring around the semi-trucks and thru the entry lane just before the large bollards mounted to stop large vehicles deployed up from the ground. All three of the rear passengers began firing pistols at Johnson as they passed, one bullet creasing his left shoulder as he ducked down behind the bullet proof glass in the windows. A fourth pair of motorcyclists wound their way around the bollard barriers and rocketed into the Base.

A voice from Central Security came over the intercom connected to the panic button.

"What's the emergency?"

"Eaters! And Krakens! General attack!" Johnson yelled over the intercom connection. He saw thru his open door a weasel creature go running by up the entry lane.

"Pit beasts!" he yelled. "Send everyone!"

Just sixty seconds before Sgt, Johnson had hit the panic button, Chief Master Sergeant Leroy Thompson was sitting in in on the twenty-four hour Battle Staff. Through them came any and all reports of Tschaaa movements, possible threats, any Kraken threats. A young Lieutenant walked up to him with a puzzled look on his face.

"Chief, we just got a report of a possible Fast Mover passing above us in near space trajectory. The spotter got a glimpse on his telescope of a possible stealth Falcon."

The Falcons had superior stealth technology and were rarely picked up on even the super powerful Russian provided radars. But, the use of telescopes gleaned from university observatories as well as amateur astronomers occasionally would pick up a Falcon against the backdrop of space.

"That's fairly normal. They overfly us all the time." The Chief answered.

"Well, they saw some glints behind and below the Fast Mover. Plus a radar station just picked up small blips bunched up near the Fast Movers flight path. They are falling slow for some kind of bomb."

"Hm. Falcons have never been into high altitude bombing. They and Deltas like to come in superfast and low at ground targets. There is something familiar about that..." the Chief began to answer when the Panic Alarm Sounded. Everyone in the Battle Staff started to scramble as the reports of the general attack came in.

The Chief put two and two together, had an answer in a moment.

"HALO—high altitude, low opening. We got parachutists of some type. I'll bet a month's pay."

"The President." The ranking Major on the Battle Staff blurted out. "They're after the President and her party. She's with the General. Call him. Now."

Aleks and Torbin were just leaving the housing area in their SUV, with Aleks driving, when the alert klaxon went off. Aleks stopped the SUV, and looked at her husband.

"Your roach sense was right."

"That's spidey sense, and I hate it when I'm right about crap like this."

"To the General's office and residence?"

"Yes, Aleks. The President and..."

A bullet smashed through the windshield as a motorbike rocketed past.

"Hang on." Aleks reacted in an instant, crushing the accelerator to the floor. Their SUV was one of the last ones produced with a large Hemi V-8 just before the rocks hit. It responded like a raped ape as Aleks twisted the wheel to follow the motorbike. Torbin was soon holding on to the small passenger side handle for dear life as the SUV roared up and over sections of grass and flower beds,   Aleks ignoring the normal roadway.

"Where in the hell did you learn to drive?"

"Spy school, husband. Where else?"

Both the driver and passenger on the motorbike seemed to have missed the concept that if you shot at someone and did not kill them, they may try and chase you down. The motorbike driver was going hell bent for leather, heading toward the administrative and headquarters offices where the General's combination quarters and office was located. They acted as if they were fixated on the mission to reach that area, not paying attention to anything else.

The rear passenger turned around, saw the SUV gaining on them, and started shooting wildly. Aleks chose that minute to cut across a grassy area with the rise in the middle, the roadway curving around the area. The vehicle was up, over the curb, and then airborne off the elevated ground.

"Shit!" Torbin yelled as he realized all four tires were off the ground. Aleks began cursing in Russian. Then the motorbike was beneath the front wheels of the vehicle as the heavy SUV landed on it and the humans riding it. Aleks locked all four wheels as she slammed on the brakes. How she did not flip the vehicle, Torbin would never know. The SUV finally slid to a stop, the motorbike trapped beneath it.

Aleks beat Torbin getting out of her seatbelt and exited the vehicle. As Torbin started to exit his side, he almost stepped on the protruding head of the now deceased motorbike passenger. He noticed it was a "she" now that her helmet was off.   She was definitely dead. Both she and the motorbike were crushed under the weight of the SUV. Aleks' loud cursing snapped his attention back to his wife.

Some twenty yards out from the SUV and trapped motorbike was the supposed driver. He seemed to be trying to rise, but his limbs and body were at odd angles to each other. Before Torbin could say anything, Aleks had pulled her combat knife out and jammed it into the base of the skull of the driver. The man was dead in an instant.

"Hey, it would have been nice to ask him some questions, dear," Torbin commented.

Aleks used her now bloody knife blade to brush driver's long hair from his neck. "See? Kraken tattoo. No need for questions, he is Kraken scum." With that remark, she spit on the body.

"How dare they attack me and mine, again. Now, we will reap what they sowed."

Tobin examined his wife for a moment. This was a side he had not seen in action. Aleks noticed he was looking at her as if trying to figure something out.

"You are looking at me as if I am under inspection. What is it you want, husband?"

"I guess I am used to the mother of my children Aleks, not Aleks the warrior."

"It is the same Aleks, my love. Just two sides of the same coin." She stooped down and took a large caliber revolver from the dead man's belt.

"As your President has said, sometimes we women, mothers must be she-bears. We must fight like them to protect our family and friends. And I was a soldier, a spy before I met you. Now, I use those skills to protect you, our children, the President's, yours and mine." She handed the recovered revolver to Torbin.

"Here. Comrade Stalin said you can never have too much ammunition or too many weapons as long as you can still move. Especially when we are at war."

Torbin took the weapon, then smiled. "Well, I did know I was getting an unusual package when I married you. I guess I always hoped you would never have to demonstrate your skills."

"Sometimes we get what we need, not what we hoped for, my love. I needed a crazy Marine and I found one. Now, shall we continue on to General Reed and the Presidents?"

Torbin pointed at the SUV and the punctured radiator and oil pan spilling their contents.

"Not in that. It's bought the farm."

Aleks shrugged. "Then we use our legs. I have worked hard to get back into shape. This will tell me if I have succeeded."

Both of the warriors recovered their gear from the wrecked SUV in record time. As Torbin readied his "liberated from the Pits" M-1 Garand, Aleks grabbed him and kissed him hard.

"For luck, my sweet. I think we may need it for the two kilometer run to General Reed's headquarters."

"You mean about a mile and a half."

Aleks snorted. "Someday you Americans will join the rest of the world in the 21st century and the metric system. Now, we go."

Madam President was finishing up hobo omelets for General Reed, George Williams and Russian President Alina Federov. She had demanded they let her fix them breakfast after the previous day's festivities. Now, as she did her magic in the full kitchen General Reed had constructed in his combination Generals Quarters and Office, the sound of the Alert Klaxon was heard through a cracked opened window.

"What?" Alina Federov said as she gave John Reed a quizzical look.

"Alert klaxon. Let me call..." The General never finished the answer as the Security Control hotline rang. He picked up the phone. "General Reed here... Yes, Captain. Eaters? And Beasts? You called for a full recall? Good. Keep me posted." He hung up the telephone, his face grim.

"Madam President, if you and the others could step away from the windows, we seemed to be under a general attack. Grab your stuff and we'll head for the shelter in the basement..."

An explosion nearby shattered office windows, showering the room with glass. George was instantly on top of Madam President, taking her to the floor. "Damnit, George. The omelet's ruined." The muffled voice of Sandra Paul came from under the large covering bulk of her assistant. "Now, can you get off me, please? I'm fine."

George moved and helped the President to her feet. General Reed went to his desk and removed a General Officer's Model .45 Automatic with a spare magazine.

"We may not be able to make it to the basement shelter. I'm going to check downstairs first, you stay here..."

"I'll go with you, John." George said.

"No, you need to stay here and make sure these two Presidents are safe in case someone gets past me."

"General Reed, stay here with us," began Madam President. "I can't allow you to go downstairs alone. Your security forces should be here any minute…"

"Goddamnit, Ma'am, no!" General Reed exploded. "The fact the windows were blown out tells me we have a major breach in security, and they are attacking to kill you two." He stabbed his fingers at the two female Presidents. "I should have foreseen this, increased security around us. Hell, I should have gotten off my dead ass and gotten some of those 3D disposable assault rifles Pappy Gunn has manufactured up here, along with bullet proof glass. But I was too wrapped up in watching Abigail get married."

He began to move to the doorway to the hallway and the stairs. "Now, it's my job as a soldier to protect my President." He looked at George Williams. "I'm depending on you, George."

"What, you think we women are helpless, fragile things?" It was the firm voice of Alina Federov. "This Cossack sword I have here is not just for show. It is a sharpened weapon I know how to use. And, if you can get me to my vehicle, there is an assault rifle and a pistol in the trunk."

The Russian President presented a wry smile. "You think this is my first, how you say here… rodeo?"

John Reed chuckled. "I forget we have a tough Russian General here. Okay, President Federov. Let's see if we can get you to your car."

"If I had not been soft and gave my driver the day off, he would be here also, General."

It is what it is, President Federov. Madam President, please stay here with George while I and the former General here go a soldiering, as they used to say."

The U.S. President looked at General Reed. "You get yourself hurt, and I'll be very angry."

"That is the farthest thing from my thoughts. George, stay frosty."

"You got it, John."

General Reed and the Russian President moved quickly to the hallway and down to the main stairs. The office and living quarters of

General Reed were on the top third floor of the former Wing Headquarters Building of Malmstrom Armed Forces Base. So, anyone trying to get to the officials would have to find the stairways and come looking through two floors to find them. However, the layout of the building was no state secret, so anyone with even a rudimentary plan would know to head to the top floor first. Which is what happened.

General Reed and President Federov met the two raggedly-looking motorcyclists as they were trying to run up the stairs. They were not trained soldiers as they were paying more attention to moving up the stairs than to possible threats around them. Thus, John Reed saw them first, and drilled the first one through the head before either of the alleged Krakens knew what happened. The second one tried to stop in mid stride and shoot. John double tapped him in the unprotected chest, the now dead attacker toppling backward down the stairs.

As John Reed scanned for other threats, Alina Federov, with practiced ease, went to each of the dead men and recovered their pistols.

"Two Glocks, my General. You Americans seem to have a love affair with them."

"They're cheap and reliable. Any spare magazines?"

"Hm. Just one."

From outside came the sound of loud automatic fire mixed with other reports.

"General, Madam President, please head back upstairs with the pistols, protect my President."

Alina Fedrov appraised John Reed with an incisive look.

"Would that all Presidents have such loyal soldiers, General."

"I try, Ma'am, I try. Now, I'm going down stairs to take a look at who else is wandering around. I promise I'll be just a moment." They both knew he was probably lying.

"Godspeed, John Reed. I know why your Russian wife loved you so."

With that, Alina turned and lunged up the stairs. John had not thought of his wife. She had been strong like this Alina Federov. But back to the task at hand. He cut the pie as he checked down the stairs to the main floor, not seeing any other threats. There was still loud small arms fire from out front and to the side of his building, toward the small motor pool garage he had arranged to have constructed some fifty yards from the main building.

That's right, he thought. Ranger Andrew Jackson and the General's driver Sergeant Leon Pasqual had stayed with the President's and his vehicles. He glanced down the main floor hallway to the now open double doors and saw a parachute blow by. Fuck. Airborne troops. They were in for it now. He stepped back into an open doorway and knelt down. Well, Lord God, he thought. If you are thinking of helping us from on high, I'd sure could use it now.

Ranger Jackson was teaching Sergeant Pasqual the finer points of Texas Hold 'Em when the Alert klaxon went off.

"What's that, Leon?" Ranger Jackson asked.

"Alert klaxon. Something big is happening. Let me check." Leon pulled out his cell phone and tried to call Security Control. All he got was a busy signal. He frowned. "I can't get through. That means everyone is tied up, probably with something bad."

The Ranger stood up, setting his cards on the table. "You have any weapons here?"

"A 12 gauge and a pistol in the staff car trunk."

"Get them out, Sergeant. I have that old feeling that the cow shit just hit the fan."

The former Texas Ranger went to the President's vehicle and popped the trunk just as he heard an explosion from the far side of the HQ Building. He grabbed a 3D printer assault rifle and a .30.30 lever action rifle. The lever action rifle was a weapon handed down through generations in his family, and a weapon he used to carry as a Texas Ranger. He had more faith in it than the space age polymer assault rifle that Pappy Gunn had developed. Of course he still had his Smith and Wesson .357 Magnum revolver on his hip. He had put the Commemorative Pistol to good use over the last few years, proving that a pretty gun can still be functional.

Sergeant Pasqual walked up to him with an M-9 Beretta stuck in his belt and a Mossberg pump shotgun in his hand. As he did, the heard the sound of a motorbike approaching the area at high speed. The Ranger went to the garage door and looked out in time to see two figures leap from a dumped over motorbike and then run into the

Headquarters building.

"Cover me, please, Sergeant. I don't like the looks of these visitors."

As he started toward the building front entrance, another pair of attackers on a motorbike appeared from the far side of the building. They had been the cause of the explosion. The passenger on the rear of the bike tried to bring a submachine gun to bear as a .30-30 round slammed into his chest. The dying attacker fired off a wild burst of fire as he toppled off the motorbike, the driver now trying to accelerate out of danger. His head exploded as another carbine round found its intended target. The riderless two-wheeled vehicle went spinning out of control onto the roadway.

"Damn! You're good, Ranger," Sgt. Pasqual opined from behind Jackson.

"Years of practice. Now, cover me as I make my way to the front and get those other two."

At that moment an object dropped from the sky. The parachutist flared out his chute just before landing with practiced ease, hitting quick release handles as another twin of him landed a dozen yards away. The first parachutist saw the Ranger and yanked his assault weapon from an attachment rig on his chest. Ranger Jackson fired his .30-30 the round hitting the body armor of the intruder and causing him to fall backwards. Even as he hit the ground, the enemy soldier fired back at the Ranger, the Ranger's tactical armor saving him by stopping the soft point round.

Sgt. Pasqual began firing his 12 gauge at the two parachutists, as the Ranger retreated to the cover of the garage building. They were soon embroiled in a firefight as other parachutists were seen landing around the main base area.

"Goddamnit, I need to get to the President. She has no guns," the Ranger cursed as he kept firing his lever action until it was empty. The grabbed up the 3D Assault Rifle and chambered a round.

"Again, cover me, Sergeant."

"Wait, there are too many. There should be some security forces headed this way."

"No time. Sal needs me."

With that, Ranger Andrew Jackson began running fast for a man his age, firing bursts from his assault weapon as he moved toward the

Headquarters Building and his President. He took the legs out from under one of the attackers with a burst. The Ranger hit another one in the tactical vest and took him down with a partial penetration. Then he went down.

Sergeant Pasqual yelled out in anger, cursing in Patois French. He was surprised when someone yelled back at him in French with a Quebecois accent. He yelled, almost screamed in anger, firing his shotgun until he was out of ammunition. He grabbed his M9 pistol and began firing. Dozens of rounds began to hit around him, passing into the garage and peppering the two staff vehicles. Leon Pasqual ducked down, cursing.

The firing from the parachutists let up as they scrambled out of the way of two approaching creatures. A pair of Eaters with a bearded Kraken behind them, manipulating a small radio-like apparatus, passed through the armed attackers. As the man and the two alien creatures advanced toward the main entrance of the headquarters building, Pasqual peaked out from the garage in time to see Ranger Andrew Jackson raise up from a prone position and fire his large revolver. The .357 round hit the controller operating Kraken male in the chest and the man fell to the lawn. The Ranger emptied his pistol at the two Eaters, aiming his fire at the creature's eyes. As the Eaters were hit, they began to spin around, letting out high pitched screams.

Bursts of fire hit both the creatures, then Ranger Jackson. He jerked, fell back and lay still.   Sergeant Pasqual screamed in rage, tears on his face, as he began to once again fire at the parachutists.

Abigail was feeding Ichiro bites of the breakfast spread the hotel staff had provided for them. She laughed as she kept pulling the food back from the reach of his mouth just as he was about to take it, teasing him with the fruit and meats.

"If you do not let me eat, my love, how can I keep my strength up for more of our honeymoon?" Ichiro asked through a large grin.

"Oh dear," Abigail said in faked wide eyed surprise. "I guess I'd better be nicer to you. After all, I plan a long day of activity, as you say."

Before Ichiro could respond, the two newlyweds heard the loud Base klaxon from just a few miles away. Abigail was up off the bed and grabbed her cellphone before Ichiro knew what she was doing.

She hit the speed dial for Security Control and held the phone to her ear. A frown formed on Abigail's face.

"No answer, the line is busy." She put down the cellphone down. "That means something very bad is happening." She reached for her underwear.

"We need to get to the Base, Ichi. There is something bad, evil there. I can feel it."

Now it was Ichiro's turn to frown.

"But my love, it is your honeymoon. Can't someone else respond?"

"That is what we do, Ichiro. We are warriors, soldiers, we respond to protect others, honeymoon or not."

Ichiro face broke into a broad grin. "I knew that would be your answer. I just wanted to hear it. I love you, my warrior wife." He grabbed Abigail and pressed his nude body up against hers for a passionate kiss.

"Keep that up," Abigail said as they parted. "And I'll be too distracted to go to the Base."

Someone pounded on the suite door. Ichiro bounded to the door, katana in hand, and threw it open. Standing about to pound again was Brynhildr. Her eyes widened a bit as she looked at the naked Samurai. She was a bit speechless, a rare condition for her. Ichiro noticed her demeanor and smiled.

"What? You have never seen a naked samurai before?"

Brynhildr snorted a bit. "Truth is, no. But the matter at hand is the Base is under general attack. Krakens, Eaters, Beasts, you name it."

Abigail, slipping into her sports bra, called out to her cousin. "What are you doing here?"

The Shield Maiden smiled. "A certain person in charge of federal law enforcement told me that I was not to allow anyone to disturb or molest you two. However, he did not foresee a general attack on Malmstrom Armed Forces Base and the two Presidents."

Abigail waved at her cousin. "Go. We will follow shortly. The Base needs you, and us."

Brynhildr switched to Norwegian. "This will be a day of great battle, I can sense it. You be careful, cousin. I do not want you or your love hurt on your honeymoon. Thor's Hammer is in our hand."

Abigail smiled. "You be careful also. I want to be at your and Rolf's wedding. Now, go. We will catch up."

Brynhildr turned and ran down the hotel hallway, then down the stairs. Her partner David Jackson was in the front of the hotel, loading weapons into their vehicle.

"The two newlyweds are up and moving. They will be following us shortly. Now, it is time to go. You are a good driver, yes?"

"Yes Ma'am. I've raced go-karts and dirt bikes before…"

"Before you were in prison," Brynhildr finished the sentence for him. She looked at David.

"You are tough, capable. We need tough and capable. Everything else is ancient history."

She smiled. "You will help me swing Thor's Hammer and crush the evil ones."

David laughed. "You sure have a way with words. Now, please hold on. This is going to be a quick and rough."

Torbin and Aleks were running, cutting across grassy areas and through small roadside flower beds when they saw the first parachutists begin to swoop in toward the Headquarters Building. One of them, blown a bit astray by the wind, swung toward them. The man in the chute saw them, and tried to bring his slung weapon to bear. Torbin automatically shoved Aleks toward cover behind a bush. As he did, he raised his M-1 Garand, leading the descending parachutist as he opened up. He emptied the eight round en bloc clip and watched it "ping" from the weapon. He hit his target enough times that the figure sprawled as it hit the ground, the chute dragging the nonresponsive body away from the two defenders.

Torbin had just reloaded his rifle when Aleks slammed into him.

"You push me to safety one more time and I will have your balls for lunch!" she yelled. "I am a soldier—I can fight as well as you can any day."

And with that Torbin understood the problem they had mentioned years ago when women were allowed in more combat roles in the Marines. He had been told that men, especially if they had a personal connection, would automatically try to protect the female soldiers, not to mention ones they loved, which damaged the cohesiveness of the unit. Everyone covered everyone, women were no more worthy of protection than the next grunt.

"Hey, sorry. I just…"

"You just acted like an American asshole. Do not do it again."

"Yes, dear."

Aleks looked at him. "I appreciate what you feel. I want to protect you also. But the Presidents and the General come first. Okay?"

Torbin patted her rump, which caused another angry slap to his arm. Then Aleks burst out laughing. "You, my husband, are an impossible smartass."

"I know. That is what makes me so lovable. Now, shall we? Next time you get to push me to safety."

"Fat chance."

They continued their running, automatic fire coming from the Headquarters area, which they could now see in the distance. As the closed the distance, they saw one of the enemy point toward them and yell a warning to her comrades. Aleks cursed in Russian.

"Time to go to ground, work our way in," she said.

"Roger that, Aleks." They ducked behind a small stone planter as rounds began to zip over their heads. The two Allied Warriors returned fire as they looked for a way to get in closer.

"There are at least a dozen of them. Torbin."

"Yeah. I think I see some Eaters coming too. We could use some help."

"Until then, it is up to us. Pick your targets," commanded Aleks as she raised the assault rifle they had recovered from the dead parachutist.

"This is my rifle. There are many like it but this one is mine," Torbin began the Marine Rifleman's Creed as he shot. It helped calm him as he killed the enemy.

Abigail and Ichiro made it to the Main Gate in record time, only a couple of minutes behind Brynhildr and David. As they approached, Abigail made sure the window was down so she could stick her head out for identification. Multiple voices from a Security Police Response Team yelled "the General" at her and waved her and Ichiro through. Abigail knew then then that the enemy already threatened General Reed and the Presidents. She pushed the accelerator all the way to the floor.

"Maybe Brynhildr has reached…," Ichiro started to say and

stopped as soon as they saw the tableau they neared.

In ditches on both sides of the roadway were each a vehicle. The vehicle on the left was a K-9 caged vehicle with a recognizable Sergeant Guadalupe Martinez and her dog Ginger at the rear, hunkered down behind it for cover. The vehicle on the right had Brynhildr and David Jackson behind it. Abigail saw why they had taken cover.

Approaching the vehicle was a line of Pit Beasts and Eaters, somehow all directed to attack the occupants of the two vehicles. Under the front ends of both were dead Beasts that seemed to have thrown themselves into the front of the two transports to stop them. They had succeeded, as demonstrated by the ruined radiators and oil pans leaking large amounts of fluid. Brynhildr saw Abigail and Ichiro, waved and yelled at them.

"Get to the Headquarters Building. Enemy Parachutists." With that the Shield Maiden drew her large compound bow and let fly a broad tipped arrow into a nearby Eater, penetrating through its large eye to the brain. Both Jackson and Martinez began firing their weapons, hitting many of the attacking creatures. Abigail skewed the vehicle off to the right at about a forty five degree angle and accelerated. Up over curbing, across grass, the Avenging Angel drove in the general direction of General Reed's office residence. A couple of Eaters tried to intercept her and Ichiro, but the SUV was too fast for them.

"There is the building, Abby, just couple of hundred meters away," said Ichiro. "We should…"

The rest of his comment was interrupted by a baboon creature leaping and smashing through the windshield. Abigail screamed in anger and surprise, slammed the brakes on the vehicle. The monster was not tossed free, but instead tried to force its snapping maw into the vehicle and at Abigail. In one smooth motion, Ichiro used his Tanto blade and impaled the baboon beast up thru the lower jaw and into its brain. The creature shook, spasmed, and then lay still.

"Are you alright, Abigail?"

"Fine. Let's get this thing off our vehicle…"

Bullets began to impact the front of the vehicle, and Abigail and Ichiro ducked down behind the dashboard.

"Out to the back, Ichi. Use the vehicle for cover."

"Hai. We move."

In unison, they kicked their doors open and dashed to behind the SUV.

"Cover me with your pistol, Ichi. I'll go thru the hatch back and get the rest of our gear.

Some sixty seconds later, as an occasional round hit in the vicinity of the damaged vehicle, Abigail had their weapons out, handing Ichiro his long bow.

"Now I'm glad we decided to bring our weapons on our honeymoon, my love."

"We are warriors. Being without weapons is unnatural, Abigail."

Abigail unsheathed her favorite lever action Marlin and peaked around the corner of the vehicle. "Someone else is shooting at what looks like those parachutists we were told about. From the south side of the building, near the garage and motor pool shots are being fired. Someone else is firing from due west, out from the front main entrance of the building."

"Is there a way for us to approach, Abby-san?"

"Well, we could try for the motor pool building, use it for cover… No. The enemy is rushing the front. The President and General Reed… no!"

Before Ichiro could react, Abigail went into what they had come to call her Hyperdrive. Ichiro was fast, quicker than anybody on Japan. But when Abigail moved, it was even more of a blur.

She was up and dashing toward the Headquarters Building, firing her rifle from the CQB crouch yet still managing to move at a near sprint. Her sudden assault seemed to catch everyone unawares. She shot and hit two attackers before anyone reacted. Ichiro cursed, launched an arrow from his longbow, and then joined her in the assault.

Torbin swore as he saw from their position behind the brick planter that a familiar figure was dashing into danger. "Goddamnit Abigail," Torbin swore again as he began to empty the clip in his Garand in an attempt to draw fire from Abigail. Aleks popped up and fired also, swearing in Russian.

"Little sister, if you get yourself shot…" Both she and Torbin saw that Abigail was trying to prevent some of the parachutists from entering the building, but knew that reaching the entrance in time to prevent that was nigh impossible. Except for maybe Abigail.

"Keep firing, Aleks. Maybe they'll start…"

At that moment a launched grenade landed just feet in front of their position. They hunkered down as dirt and debris showered them.

Aleks began to cry in frustration. "If they kill her, I will castrate them all."

General Reed kneecapped the first enemy that crossed the threshold of the entrance. He also thought he had heard some shots from upstairs, possibly Alina Federov taking care of somebody trying to enter by the rear fire exit stairs. This caused an explosion of conversation in the French language. Reed's Russian wife had also spoken French so he had learned enough to understand basic conversations. He was completely baffled that he was being attacked by French speakers. He caught some loud snatches of conversation as he stayed hidden while the wounded man was dragged from the entranceway. There was something about waiting until the rest of the unit made it here, which told him that like almost all airborne operations, someone inevitably landed askew of the planned drop zone. They had not expected anyone to be ticked in and shooting back from the building at this late time, since the only defensive fire had come from outside.

Then he heard someone yelling about a crazy person running at them, soon drowned out by much automatic fire. He peaked out from his hidey hole in the office doorway in time to see a grenade slide toward him. He threw himself back into the office as there was a flash, boom and he went deaf. He lay on the carpet stunned for a moment as his ears began to ring. When he tried to move his legs he felt stabs of pain. Shrapnel had hit him, and unfortunately the grenade had not been just a flash bang. By instinct and training he tried to load his one spare magazine into his pistol when he noticed a figure was standing in the office doorway. He glanced to see a camouflaged young man cursing as he worked to clear a jam in his rifle. As General Reed went to beat him to the draw when an image of his wife and sons popped into his head. 'See you soon', he thought.

The standing figure was winning the 'fast draw' contest when his head departed his body. Blood began to gush and spurt from the neck where the head had sat a moment ago as the body toppled over. Reed's eyes registered the image but his mind could not process what had just happened. Then Abigail stepped into view, katana and all.

"General. Talk to me," Abigail commanded past the ringing in his ears.

"I'm... here," he managed to croak.

Had he purview of the scene outside moments ago, he would have seen a female wraith running and shooting, coming so fast and hard at the enemy that they were overwhelmed by what she was doing. General Reed would have seen Abigail shoot two attackers in the head with her lever action so quick that it sounded almost like automatic faire. A long bow arrow had by what seemed to be magic appeared through the throat of another, as the female attacker had tried to shoot Abigail. The Avenging Angel had been hit in her tactical body armor, but as there had been no penetration, she had shrugged off the shock. Then the Avenging Angel was among them, rifle dropped and katana in hand.

As General Reed lay there looking up, he thought, 'That's my girl', now feeling more dazed.

Abigail noticed something down the hallway toward a rear exit, switched her sword to her left hand and pulled her Glock 18 fully auto pistol with her right, all in one smooth motion. One handed he braced herself and fired two bursts, her weapon hardly moving from the recoil.

"You dare to hurt my father?!" she yelled so loudly John Reed swore later she shook the whole room. "I will reap what you have sown!" She fired again. "Return from whence you came, hell-spawn. God's Avenging Angel is at hand."

John Reed looked at his adopted daughter, and thought, 'My God, she is a force of Nature.' He was so glad she was there and on his side. Ichiro appeared next to her, still holding a longbow with notched arrow. He softly touched Abigail on her arm.

"Abby, I will cover the hallway. Please see to the General." With his voice and touch, Abigail's rage seemed to reduce. John Reed saw just how much they were made for each other. Abigail knelt next to her adopted father and began an EMT Injury Assessment. She saw that the General was beginning to slip into shock and she squeezed his hand.

"General, look at me, stay with me. You have some shrapnel in your legs that is very survivable. Trust me."

John Reed smiled. "I'll always trust you, daughter. I'm glad you're here."

Abigail gave him a quick kiss on the forehead, began to see to his wounds and staunch any bleeding. Her movements were quick and sure as she pulled supplies from a fanny pack she always carried. As she did, more shots rang out, and a familiar voice shouted, "Little sister, where are you?"

"In here, Aleks, with the General."

Aleks Smirnov poked her head into the room, gave John Reed a wry smile.

"General, I guess you have not learned the important idea that Generals these days lead from the rear, and do not become involved in gun battles."

"That was years ago, before the Squids," he managed to answer. "Now, we all do what we must." Just then she saw Torbin' profile.

"Colonel, upstairs. The Presidents."

Torbin looked at him. "Yes Sir. Ichi, Aleks, cover the front the hall down here. We may have some more parachutists coming. I'll take the General upstairs."

Before the General could protest, two strong arms picked him up, making him feel old and weak.

"Son..."

"Save your strength, General. I seem to remember your NCOIC kept a complete field medical pack upstairs. We can stabilize you until help arrives or we move you." Then he was carrying the General up the stairs as if it was something he did every day, with Abigail in trail.

They were met on the third floor by Alina holding a Glock. She frowned at John Reed.

"I thought you understood you were not to be shot and injured, General."

As she said that, Madam President appeared. "Damnit, John. You went and got yourself shot, against my orders. What am I supposed to do now?" Her fake anger did not cover the tears in her eyes as she spoke.

"I guess you'll have to fire me, Ma'am."

"He will be okay, Madam President." Abigail broke in. "I

guarantee it. He has very treatable shrapnel wounds. Now, Torbin, if you can find that field medical pack, we can see about setting up some kind of I.V. drip.”

“Roger that.”

Sandra Paul leaned forward and combed the General’s hair back with her fingers. Then the tears came.

“Oh damn. Waterworks again. I am turning into a complete soft wuss.”

“Never, Sal, never. You are steel,” the General said as he was made comfortable on a sofa in his office. Madam President smiled, wiped off her tears in one quick motion. Then there were loud curses in Russian heard up the stair well, followed by rifle shots.

“Abby, you have it here? Good. I’m needed downstairs. Madam President Federov, can you keep covering here?”

“Of course, Colonel. Your President and General will be safe here for the time being.”

“Good. Duty Calls.” Torbin hustled down the stairs to his wife and blood brother.

As he reached the ground floor, more automatic fire erupted. He heard Ichiro curse in Japanese, something he was beginning to recognize. Then he was by his side, Aleks covered down in a doorway across the hall. Each had a former attacker assault rifle in their hands.

“I count at least three enemy, Torbin. Late arrivals. They seem determined to get to the Presidents.”

“Like hell they will, Ichiro.”

The Free Japan warrior flashed a large grin at his comrade in arms and best friend.

“Spoken like the Samurai you were in a previous life. Our blades will taste their blood this day, Torbin-san.”

“You and your samurai sensibilities. Now, I still have a clip or two for my Garand. Keep them occupied, I’ll head out the back fire exit and see if I can loop around, and flank them before they try to enter through the rear.”

“Hai, Torbin.”

“You get yourself hurt, husband, and the trolls and I will be very upset,” Aleks called from across the hallway.

“Perish the thought. I have enough scars. Now, time to go.”

Torbin sprinted down the building hallway, and out the fire escape exit past some enemy bodies, courtesy of Abigail and Alina Federov.

He almost ran into an enemy soldier rounding the corner to enter the rear. The young troop tried to bring his assault rifle to bear as Torbin swept it aside and butt stroked him with the heavy wood stocked Garand. The young soldier was out for the count. Torbin recovered the enemy assault rifle as well as a grenade and pistol from the unconscious foe. He then continued around the building, keeping low and close to prevent being noticed. But he needn't worry, as Aleks and Ichiro were now aggressively using their assault weapons to beat back the arriving enemy. Torbin passed by the body of Ranger Jackson and cursed. A red rage began to rise, which he tried to control. A berserker rage would help no one. He heard a loud whistle from the motor pool/garage and saw Sergeant Pasqual waving at him. With a quick series of combat battle signs and signals, Pasqual communicated the location of the enemy forces. Torbin did a quick adjustment and slung his Garand, bringing the enemy assault rifle up to ready. A quick deep breath, he went into CQB mode, Groucho-walking up to the corner of the building. He cut the pie around the building edge and saw three parachutists using trees and planters as cover. They had not noticed him until he came around the building edge, firing. He hit two of the enemy before they knew what was happening, the third then trying to hit him with a burst fire. As Torbin went prone, a burst of fire from the building turned the soldiers head into a bloody mess. For the first time since it began, there was no sounds of weapons fire near the Headquarters Building. Torbin jogged out to the three enemy, made sure they were dead. Then he ran to Aleks and Ichiro at the building entrance.

"So who do I need to thank for that headshot?"

"It was me, my husband."

He grabbed her and kissed her hard. "Perfect wife. Kills your enemy."

For one of the few times in her life with Torbin, Aleks stammered, then blushed. Ichiro's face broke into another large grin.

"You are acting like newlyweds. I now know that feeling."

Torbin grinned back. "Come on. We are not out of the woods yet. I still haven't seen any of our troops nearby. So, we keep this building secure while we try to contact allied forces."

"Hai." Ichiro snapped to attention and bowed.

His wife replied, "Yes Sir."

It dawned on him that he was suddenly "in charge". He was responsible for two Presidents and his commanding general. No more merely a grunt Marine, he was the head mofo-what's-in-charge. A calm descended on him as he knew what he had to accomplish.

"Let's see if we can contact Security Control. Ichiro, get Sergeant Pasqual over at the motor pool, bring him here. He is about out of ammunition I think." Then he frowned. "And Ranger Jackson...his dead body is over there. Let's cover it up until we can have it picked up. He died defending the President."

"I will treat him with the honor he deserves, my Commander. I go." With that Ichiro went at a run toward Sergeant Pasqual. Torbin looked at Aleks.

"My love..."

"Do not say anything. Just tell me what you need. Colonel."

Again Torbin had a realization. The three of them, Aleks, Ichiro and Torbin, had all met at the same time, here at Malmstrom. Now their lives, and their survival, were completely intertwined. They were now all three Lt. Colonels, yet in one short time period, he was the one expected to take charge.

"I just don't want to seem like I'm a bossy prick toward friends and family."

"Torbin, you think too much. You do not want to admit it, but while you just like the idea of being a grunt, you are a Commander. You are a natural leader. I see it."

Aleks reached out and grabbed her loves hand. "You lead, I follow. I have your back, always. Like Ichiro and Abigail, we are a team that was created out of necessity. And our love."

Torbin managed a smile. 'Well, then, Colonel, there is a cold-cocked young troop by the back exit who was still alive. I think we need to interrogate him."

Aleks flashed a feral grin. "Ah, my specialty. Yell if you need me back." With that she started to jog down the building hallway to the fire exit and the unconscious enemy.

Torbin scanned the area around the HQ Building. He could hear shots from a distance, thought he heard yells and screams, but could see nothing. What was happening out on the rest of the Base?

"Colonel Bender." He turned toward the voice and saw Alina

Federov had a cellphone in one hand and a pistol in the other.

"Security Control and Battle Staff on this phone. You need to talk to them."

Torbin took the phone, wondering why he, just a Light Colonel in charge of training, needed to speak with them. He soon found out.

"Bender here. Yes Chief... The General is alive but wounded... Say again?... Even the Deputy Base Commander?... Okay. Rouse the troops the best you can. I'll make my way toward the Hospital. Every young Officer and NCO needs to step up and take charge until we can get centralized control again. By the way, tell them all Semper Fi from me, the ones who I trained will understand." He handed the phone back to the Russian President.

"Your grim face tells me things are not good," she said.

"I am ranking military officer who is still functional. The Base Commander was killed in his front yard by a Kraken. The Division and Deputy Division Commanders were both mauled by Eaters in the General Officers Housing Area. The Deputy Base Commander is missing, as are all other senior commanders. Seems that not only was Main Gate breached, the closed Back Gate was also, with a tide of Eaters and Beasts let in after a semi-truck rammed its way through."

The Russian President looked into Torbin's eyes. "I am now a President, not a General. And this is your home. I think you know what to do, Colonel Bender."

"I did not want this. I was always a grunt at heart."

"It is not what we want. It is what is required of you. I see in you and your friends, comrades, and the future. You will see this through. You will succeed." She stood straight.

"Sir, what is the Acting Commander of the Allied Forces in North America wish his Allies to do?"

In that moment, Torbin Bender understood when Andrew had said months ago about him having a special role in the scheme of things. He knew now he had to step up, there was no other way.

"Can you make sure you and my President are secure here with General Reed? There is a major battle going on around the hospital. Apparently it was the secondary target after you two Presidents. I need to get there, lead my forces until outside help arrives."

"Let me get my AK and pistol from my vehicle trunk. Then I will be more than able to respond to any straggler enemy."

Just then, Aleks came up the hallway, dragging a slip tied enemy soldier.

"You did not tell me, husband, you had cold-cocked a young female."

As Torbin got a closed look, he saw that, under the bruised face, was a definite young woman about Abigail's age.

"Who the hell are these people?"

Aleks twisted the woman's arm a bit, made her wince.

"Canadians from Quebec. I will discover why they try and help Squids..." Aleks looked over Torbin's shoulder and her eyes went wide.

"Colonel, we have a problem."

President Federov looked and began to curse, then dashed toward her staff vehicle for her weapons.

Torbin's blood went cold as he saw the long line of Eaters and Beasts several hundred yards away, approaching in near perfect unison. Now he knew that evil had found a way to use these monsters every which way they wished.

"Aleks, stash her in one of the upstairs offices. George Williams can watch her. Grab Abigail. We need everyone."

Ichiro re-appeared at that moment with Sergeant Pasqual and a large U.S. Flag. He began to swear and curse in Japanese, and Pasqual matched him in Cajun French. This caused the female prisoner to respond in French.

"What do you think, ma cherie?" Pasqual spat back. "That these Beasts will spare you once their blood is up? Fat chance."

"Sgt. Pasqual. Take this prisoner upstairs and sit on her. Send Major Yamamoto down to us."

"Yes Sir. Here's a flag for Ranger Jackson's body."

"Hang it on the railing. We'll get to him when we can. Ichiro. Take a count of people and weapons. Those things will be here in a minute or two. Though they don't seem to be in a rush."

Alina Federov walked up with her weapons. "I am now ready, Colonel."

"Madam President, if you could help secure my President and the General I would appreciate it. If those things get past us..."

"They will eat Russian lead."

Torbin laughed. "Are all you Russian women nasty and mean?"

"Just the ones who have survived the last six years, my friend. Now, good luck. I will await your next order." She turned and headed up the stairs.

Torbin looked at Aleks. "I wish you were with our sons."

"My place is here, for I am a Russian soldier. And your wife."

"Both for which I am grateful. But I still can wish you out of harm's way."

Just then, a familiar voice yelled from the motor pool area.

"Is someone planning a party without me?" It was Brynhildr, with David Jackson.

"Hurry up!" Aleks yelled. "Kraken Beasts approach."

Torbin thought, 'Oh crap. The man's freshly killed father was just yards away.'

"Is my father here, with the President?" David Jackson asked. No one spoke. Then Ichiro walked up, and bowed deeply.

"I must report with great sorrow that your father was killed defending the President. He died the death of a warrior. He is to be remembered with honor."

David Jackson stopped, frozen. Then, he swallowed, and asked in a shaky voice, "Where is he?"

"Come, I'll show you," replied Ichiro. He quickly took the son to see his father's body on the side of the Headquarters Building.

Brynhildr looked at the others. "He is tough. He will recover. Now, what is your plan? I see a line of Pit Beasts and Eaters approaching and you all stand around as if it is a day in the park."

"Ask Torbin. He is Commander," Aleks replied. Torbin stepped forward.

"Get your weapons, let me know your ammo situation. We make a stand here at the building entrance."

"I have my compound bow here with two arrows, a pistol with one loaded magazine. And my two fighting axes. They worked at the Pits, they will work here."

Just then Abigail came jogging from the stairs to the entrance.

"Demons approach? How many?"

"Enough for all of us, cousin."

Abigail smiled. "I see you, cousin," she said in Norwegian to Brynhildr.

"And I you. Blood protects blood. I have your back."

"And I yours." She looked at Torbin after glancing at the surprisingly slow approach of the Eaters and Beasts. "Your orders, Sir."

"Weapons and ammunition check."

"I have my lever action with two rounds, my Glock 18 with several magazines. Plus, of course, my katana."

"Aleks?"

"This assault rifle and a full magazine, plus my two pistols."

"Well, I have two eight round clips for my Garand, plus a few rounds in this assault rifle. And my .44 pistol, plus a Kraken revolver and five rounds."

Just then, Ichiro reappeared. "I have this captured rifle with a half of magazine, my pistol, my bow with a few arrows, and of course my katana and shurikens."

Torbin looked at David Jackson. "Agent, if you want…"

"I have my father's pistol with a couple of reloads. I'll go up and protect Madam President. That is what he would have wanted."

Torbin nodded. He had not seen his brother or his parents' bodies. It was bad enough to know they were dead. To have to see them recently dead… he could not imagine it.

"Fine by me. Stay frosty, please."

"Will do." David Jackson nodded at Brynhildr, then headed up stairs.

"Well, my husband. The enemy slowly gets closer."

Torbin frowned. "I think they are approaching so slowly as whoever is doing this has trouble controlling large numbers of these creatures. Thus they tried attacks by trained human soldiers on the Presidents first. Now, they fall back to sending beasts."

He glanced around. "We stay here, back from the entrance a bit, in the shadows. Form a line. If they charge, we can force them to bunch up to get to us. If they start to flank us, we fire a few rounds to draw them at us here, not allow them to get around us and up the stairs."

"If someone is behind them with guns?" Ichiro asked.

"We shoot from cover, then fall back upstairs. I keep hoping some help shows up."

"I think, Tobin, they are tied up all over the Base," Abigail interjected. "The suicidal attacks by the Eaters and Beasts have probably caused disorganization in the responses of base security forces. It will take a while for the outlying units to respond. We may be on our own."

Torbin paused. Then spoke. "Alright. We stand here, wait to see their first move. Check your weapons."

Before he realized it, Aleks and Brynhildr were on his right, weapons ready, with Abigail and Ichiro were on is left. All had such serious looks of determination on their faces as they looked at the approaching threats. He began to chuckle.

"What is the joke, my husband?"

"I keep thinking any second now, we will hear an orchestra playing some rousing action theme music, a director will yell 'Cut!' and we all break for lunch as they plan the next scene on this action adventure movie."

"This is no movie, Torbin Bender," Brynhildr replied. "But it will be a saga repeated by bards down thru the history of our New Vikings. We are making history."

Torbin looked at the Shield Maiden extraordinaire. "Well said. No matter what happens, it is an honor to be here, to fight alongside you."

"We will let our blades drink the evil creature's blood this day, my brother," Ichiro declared in a loud voice. "This day, we are all Samurai, ready to die for the Emperor."

Aleks snorted. "This Russian Ukrainian does not plan to die. I have too much of my life to live, my trolls to raise. We fight, but we will not die."

"I agree." Abigail added. "The Lord is with us this day. His rod and his staff are with us."

"Yea, though we walk thru the Valley of Death, we shall fear no evil," Torbin quoted. "Because we are the meanest sons of bitches in the valley."

"Bitches. We are bitches from hell, the Banshees," Aleks added. "And it looks like the enemy is within accurate rifle range."

Torbin wrapped his rifle sling around his arm and assumed a kneeling shooting stance."Let me take a couple of shots with this Garand first, and see what results." He took careful aim.

Before he let off a shot, a strange wavering, trilling and sing-song like screaming sound forced its way across the open spaces near the

Headquarters building. Torbin looked up, surprised. "What the hell is that?"

He glanced at Abigail and Aleks, whose faces broke into broad grins.

"Banshee scream. Our sisters have come after all."

"Banshees? Your 101st Unit? I didn't think there were that many around on Base."

"Many stayed in our new barracks area after Abigail's wedding," responded Aleks. "They had a bit of a sleep over to celebrate their Executive Officer's new life, and begin a new set of traditions."

"How many? And are they armed?"

"Close to a hundred for sure. Most of the Originals. And at the least, they have cold steel."

The high-pitched sounds seemed to distract the Eaters, despite them being wired up for remote control. They stopped and turned toward the sound.

Aleks let out a joyful laugh. "It works. Hannah Weitz said Eaters did not like such vocals in the Pits. Now, the Survivors will have their just revenge."

Torbin stood and looked around, and saw for the first time a line of humanity approaching from the North. They all had the distinct bluish gray fatigue pattern Aleks and Abigail had chosen for the unit. The Marine began to laugh.

"I think the asshole Krakens and Squids just bit off more than they could chew."

As he said that, the line stopped in complete unison, and a perfect volley of shots thundered across the open spaces. Eaters and Beasts were hit, began to spin around or fell and died. Then whoever was controlling the creatures with their brain implants lost control and chaos reigned.

"They come," Brynhildr barked. She pulled back and let fly with a broad tipped arrow. Two hundred yards away a charging Eater received an arrow thru its right eyeball and into its brain. It collapsed and slid to a stop. Ichiro looked at the Shield Maiden with open mouth admiration.

"Your shot is worthy of the best of the Samurai."

Brynhildr guffawed. "You think only your people have a tradition of archery?"

After that, the five warriors were too busy to comment. Though the Eaters and Beasts had broken formation and were charging in multiple directions, they were still enraged and dangerous. Assault rifle rounds tore into Eaters and what had been normal Earth fauna but were now mutated beast creatures. Many went down, but they were many about. Torbin found himself firing the last round in his Garand at a charging boar-beast, saw the empty en bloc clip ping out of his weapon. The beast collapsed at his feet as he yelled out, "Reloading."

Abigail's katana flashed, keeping an Eater from her big brother by slashing off its legs, then piercing its brain. She let out a Banshee Scream that hurt Torbin's ears. Two Eaters froze in front of the five, and were chopped down by Ichiro and Brynhildr. Torbin loaded his last clip into his rifle in time to shoot what had once been a mastiff thru its brain pan. Aleks had now drawn her pistol, was cursing in three languages as she raged against the hellspawn. Her aim was deadly as she shot Eaters and Beasts through their eyes.

Suddenly there were no other enemies attacking. Ragged shots from the Banshees showed that the surviving threats were scattered or dead.

Torbin heard shots from the third floor.

"Shit. Something got past us."

"I go!" Brynhildr yelled as she dashed up the stairs with her two fighting axes.

"Watch our sixes. There are other enemies around." Just as Torbin said that, a weasel creature exploded from the hallway directly toward his groin. Aleks stopped it with a double tap to the head.

"From what Emily Anders told me," a bemused Aleks observed. "Pit Beasts seem to have a fixation with your manhood."

"Whatever. Thanks for helping me preserve it."

"I am selfish, husband, I am not done with it yet."

Torbin glanced around, saw no other threats near, but kept hearing shots and commotion from upstairs.

"Cover the entrance. I need to check upstairs."

"You watch yourself, husband. "

"Yes Ma'am!" Torbin yelled over his shoulder as he sprinted up the stairs.

Brynhildr had used here fighting axes to good measure, chopping down a couple of weasel beasts as soon as she had reached the third floor. The rest of the command staff and David Jackson were defending General Reed's office, where he was resting on the sofa from his wounds. George Williams caught a baboon creature and broke its neck as it tried to force its way into the room. David brought a heavy office chair down onto the head of chimp-beast as he did not have the time to reload his father's pistol. Alina finished the creature off with the bullet to the spine from her AK carbine, then shot another one coming down the hallway.

Tobin arrived, looked at the carnage. He looked down the hallway to the emergency exit door, which had been smashed in. There were several creature bodies littering the hallway.

"Mr. Williams, Mr. Jackson, let's find a heavy desk or bookcase to block that exit until there are enough troops here for three-sixty coverage."

"Gotcha, Colonel," George replied. "A bookcase is in the next office down."

In a couple of minutes they had dragged the bookcase in front of the door, then started checking all the windows to see if anything had used them for egress. There were no signs, the Pit Beasts apparently had been directed to come up the fire escape stairs.

Madam President was sitting next to General Reed, pistol in hand. The I.V. Abigail had set up seemed to stabilize him, there were no further signs of shock.

"Hell of a way to celebrate a wedding, Sal."

She smiled and brushed his hair back from his forehead. "We go back a ways, John. I remember you briefing a certain group of young newbie Congressmen and women on the workings of some of the Pentagon projects. Seems like ancient history."

"Yes, Sal. The years feel like decades."

The President's chin began to quiver a bit. "I can't afford to lose you John. I just lost Andy and I don't know how many other citizens in and around Great Falls. I need all the good help I can get."

John smiled. "In case you haven't noticed, there is a certain former grunt Marine taking names and kicking ass. If we need a replacement for me, he is one hell of a candidate, current rank be damned."

"You're serious, aren't you?"

"Sal, there is something about him and everyone he touches. Look who surrounds him. The crème de la crème when it comes to loyalty, courage, sacrifice for others. He attracts people like that because he exudes all those virtues." General Reed shifted a bit and cringed as pain from his wounds hit him.

"Need some more painkiller John?"

"Naw, I'm all right. But Madam President, remember what I just said. You ever need a goto guy, someone to pull your chestnuts out of the fire, that is Torbin Bender. He won't let you down."

She patted the General's hand. "I'll remember. But I think you'll be around for a while longer, so I won't have to break in a new Armed Forces Commander any time soon."

He smiled back. "Yeah, I think you're stuck with me, Madam President."

Torbin heard his wife's voice up the stairway. "Commander, you need to come down here, please."

After first making sure that everyone was ready to respond to more Beasts or Eaters, Torbin then hurried down the stairs to the main floor. When he got there, instead of the small band of warriors he had left, there were several dozen female soldiers standing with Aleks and Abigail.

The ones nearest snapped to attention upon seeing him.

"Colonel Bender, I do not think you have ever been formally introduced to the Banshees. May I present members of the 101st Special Attack Unit, the Banshees General Reed mandated into official existence."

Torbin could feel the air of Special Forces and his beloved Corps that permeated the warrior women. He then noticed one male figure standing toward the rear of the formation, keeping an eye on the outside as well what was going on inside. Torbin immediately recognized him.

"Captain Danny O'Brien. What are you doing in the back there? Come on up."

"Begging your pardon, Sir. But we still have a bunch of Banshees sweeping the area. I'm just keeping an eye on them."

Torbin looked at Aleks. "My apologies, Colonel. I should realize you're taking care of business."

"So, ladies," he addressed the small formation. "Let me be the first to thank you. You came at just the right moment, saved our bacon." And with that, he came to attention and saluted the formation. Aleks as ranking member saluted for the formation, then turned toward a somewhat puzzled looking Russian Senior Sergeant.

"Senior Sergeant Ruskova. Go with Captain O'Brien. I want three sixty coverage for this building and the Presidents within. Then, a unit to go with Colonel Bender here. He needs to get to the units at the Hospital. You both have five minutes."

Ruskova snapped off a salute. "Yes, my Colonel." She then did an about face, began to yell out the orders. Everyone snapped to, and it was all asses and elbows as the Banshees spread out and secured the area. A squad was sent upstairs to provide close-in security for the Presidents. Two dozen Banshees then formed up in front of Torbin.

"Colonel, ready to go when you are," newly-minted Lieutenant Dagan McDowell saluted and reported."

"You have sufficient arms and ammunition, Lieutenant?"

"Yes, Sir. We Texicans are quite good at scavenging."

Torbin smiled. "I thought I caught a bit of Texas Drawl. Alright, shall we?"

"Yes sir. Platoon, Atten-hut. Right Face. Forward, March….Double time, Harch!"

Torbin' face broke into a wide grin. He fell in parallel to the running Banshees, yelled over his shoulder to Aleks.

"You have it here, Colonel. Tell the General where I'm going."

"Will do. Get back in one piece, husband," Aleks yelled back.

"Yes Ma'am," Tobin called back.

As they double timed, Torbin called to Dagan. "Do you have a faster speed? I need to get there yesterday."

"Thought you'd never ask, Sir. Platoon. Avenging Angel Warp Speed… Harch!"

Everyone took off at an almost a full dead run.

As Torbin and company ran toward the hospital, a K-9 vehicle screeched to a stop in front of the HQ Building. SSgt. aMartinez jumped out at ran up to Aleks, nd saluted.

"Ma'am, I need to contact Colonel Bender. There are Eaters in the Main Housing Area, I need back up. I'm the only mobile unit free."

Aleks yelled for Abigail. "Trolls are in trouble. We go. Sergeant Ruskova, get with the Platoon Lieutenants, you have this area. I go to save the housing area."

David Jackson jumped in. "The Banshees have the President. Mind if I tag along?"

"Find us a vehicle then, Agent. Otherwise, we ride with the dog."

A pregnant Sue Brown was out back with Fuzz, Freya, and the two trolls (as Aleks called them) Tristan and Gage, when the Base klaxon went off. Her husband had told her that a klaxon like this meant a general alert and recall. The two boys, clothed for the slight nip in the air but crawling around on a large blanket, looked up at the new sound. They both began to laugh.

"Like the new sound, don't we boys? Well, if it keeps up, we go inside, sorry."

Fuzz and Freya were then standing over the two children, Fuzz letting loose a low growl for a still pup creature.

"Hey, pup, what's up? Is it the sound? Or something else?"

Her baby girl kicked in her stomach. She and her husband had "cheated' and determined the sex before birth so they could plan. There was just the one, with all indications that it was not a "modified one" as children like Tristan and Gage. Though having cared for the two trolls, other than developing a bit faster, she could tell no difference from any other children. She loved them like her own, had become an aunt to them in all but blood.

So when the two War Dogs seemed protective of them, Sue knew something was going on. She felt it in her womb with her unborn.

"Come on, my young Trolls. Fuzz and Freya says there is something they don't like. That's enough for me. Did anyone tell you about Fuzz Senior, how he saved you two when you were still in your mommy's tummy? Come on, let's go inside. Uff Da, you two are getting heavy…"

Fuzz ran to the back fence, snapping and snarling. He may still be a puppy, but he was a big puppy, with his father's demeanor. Freya began to whine, put herself in between then children and the fence "What is it, fella? What's got your back up?"

The wind blew a whiff of a scent to Sue's nose. It took a moment for it to register. Then her eyes widened. "Eaters," Sue announced in a whisper. She turned and tried to move as fast as she could to the back door of quarters. A strong North Dakota farm girl, she almost had the door open with two boys in hand when Fuzz let out a howling snarl, joined by Freya. Sue glanced and saw the six limbed monster known as an Eater clambering over the fence.

"No. Not again!" Sue screamed at the creature, at the same time shoving the two boys through the back door, managed to get the screen and glass door shut. She then grabbed a garden hoe, and went to defend the family and homestead.

The two children of Sergeant Fuzz showed their lineage as they snapped and bit at the Eater as it scrambled over the back fence, staying just out of reach of the grasping claws. The horror on six legs seemed confused by two snapping, slashing and snarling Earth creatures, turning toward one, then the other. It let out the odd screeching howl no one forgot when they heard it as Young Fuzz's teeth connected with one of the hind legs.

Then a second Eater began to clamber over the fence.

"No. Go away you pieces of shit!" Sue screamed as the second Eater came at her.

Johann Munsen and his wife Freda had loaded the five Survivors into their large SUV earlier in the morning and headed into the Base Housing Area to deliver some jewelry Hannah Weitz had made for an upcoming christening. After all the happy festivities of the Grand Wedding, as it was now being called, no one in the Munsen household could sleep that morning. Thus, they had risen early to run this errand for Hannah. Once the word had spread that she could make exquisite jewelry just as well as she could blades, she was much sought after to create items for special occasions, especially religious in nature. When the klaxon had sounded they were about a block over from Torbin's, Aleks' and Abigail's residence.

"What is that, Father?" Freda asked.

"An alert siren of some sort. I will slow down and we will wait to see…"

Hannah had rolled the window down to hear the klaxon when she heard the signature scream of an Eater. Then her ears keyed on the barking dogs. "Eaters!" She yelled and threw open the SUV door, jumping out before Johann could stop the car. "Torbin Bender's house." She yelled as she ran toward the next block where the residence lay. As she ran she pulled from the bottom of a shoulder bag two of her signature sheathed Sister of Steel Squid Killers. A quick well aimed slash and she had freed herself from her long skirt, running now in just her leggings.

Johann cursed and turned the SUV toward the target residence. As he did, he pulled a snubby .44 special from a pocket, thrust it at his wife Freda.

"Johann...'

"Don't argue, Love. Take it, stay with the vehicle. I must make sure Hannah is alright."

He yelled at the four young ladies/girls in the rear. "You stay with your Aunt Freda. Obey her. Ja?"

"Yes, Uncle Johann," four voices answered.

Sue Brown was swinging and jabbing the hoe at the second Eater as the two War Dog pups snarled and snapped at the first one. She managed to partially severe one of the long clawed fingers of the second Eater with the hoe blade, eliciting another screeching howl.

"That's it. Come closer and you'll get hurt. Get back!" Sue yelled.

The Eater grabbed the end of the hoe with the uninjured claw and began to pull pregnant Sue toward its opened jaws.

"No..." Sue yelled and tried to pull back. She did not notice the figure that vaulted the backyard fence until she heard a wavering trilling high pitched scream and cry. She saw a figure in her left peripheral vision moving fast. It was Hannah Weitz.

The Pit Survivor lunged then sprang into a high flying forward roll that would have shamed some Olympic hopefuls. She went high, somersaulted and came down on the second Eater's head with both feet, driving its maw into the ground. She then jumped onto its back with both feet, the Eater sprawling out its six appendages.

Sue yanked her hoe free and began to chop the eyes and face of the stunned creature with the hoe blade, screaming as loud as she could with rage and fear. The Eater was soon a bloody mess.

A third Eater scrambled over the back fence and Sue yelled a warning. It was not needed. Hannah bound over, still with the Banshee scream that seemed to confuse the alien. Fuzz and Freya kept the first Eater busy, now also distracted by these screaming two-legged creatures.

Hannah met the third Eater head on, her blades flashing in a blurred figure eight that hacked the clawed fingers off. The Eater screeched, tried to back up and ran into the fence it had just crossed. Hannah preformed another Olympic caliber high somersault and smashed her feet down on its head. A quick pirouette and she was plunging her blades into the eyes of the stunned creature. It's so called brain penetrated, it shuddered, then died. Hannah spun and went after the Eater the two canines were attacking. Its hind legs already hamstrung by dog bites, Hannah slashed at its sides, then kicked the creature hard. The Eater tried to roll away, exposing part of its underside. A second later what passed as its intestines were spilling onto the ground.

A fourth, then a fifth Eater, drawn by the screams as well as Eater blood and vomit, began to scramble over the fence. Hannah let out Banshee scream that seemed to freeze the monsters.

"God, please, help us." Sue yelled, as she left her victim to help Hannah.

There was a crushing and crashing sound as something large slammed thru the fence gate. Johann Munsen bellowed some war cry and threw a double bladed ax at the nearest Eater, hitting it between its eyes and penetrating the skull. He grabbed Sue, turned and propelled her toward the house.

"Inside! Now!" He grabbed her hoe from her and began to swing it like a staff at the remaining Eater. Sue ran as fast as a pregnant lady could, went through the back door, slamming and throwing the dead bolt. She grabbed the two boys and held them tight as she watched the tableau play itself out. She saw Johann strike the Eater with the handle of the hoe between the eyes, then Hannah dart in and gut it from the side with her razor sharp blades. Johann recovered his ax from the other dead Eater in time to meet another coming over the back fence. A forward and then a back swipe took it clawed hands off, and Hannah finished it off by landing on its back and double thrusting her Squid Killer blades thru the creature's eyes into its brain.

Then it was over. Fuzz and Freya snapped and snarled at the dead creatures. Johann checked to make sure all the creatures were dead, as Hannah stood. Then she began to shake. A scream of pain and rage erupted from her mouth.

"I said never again," she raged. Uncle Johann walked over and scooped her up into his arms like she was a babe and beelined to the back door.

Sue let him in as he ordered, "A hot drink, with a shot of whisky if you have it, and a blanket for my little one. Please, while I check on my wife and the others."

Hannah still had death grips on her fighting blades as Johann set her on the sofa. The dogs came in now and began to snuffle her, sensing she hurt. Hannah dropped her weapons, grabbed onto Fuzz and Freya, began to sob.

Johann made it to the front in time to see Freda blow out the brains out of some disheveled-looking man. The body toppled back and then Johann was there.

"He tried to steal the car, Johann," a shaken Freda said.

"Into the house. Everyone!" He did not have to say that twice. Johann took a rifle bayonet off the dead man, a Kraken for sure. Then he was inside.

"Any weapons in the house, young lady?" Johann asked.

"Check the closet."

Johann recovered the Saiga 12 gauge.

"Now we wait. Freda, Hannah needs some help."

"Of course, dear."

Sue looked at Johann. "You and Hannah saved us. "

"You are a fighter yourself, young lady. Now, we wait for help. I know the mother and father of these two young boys will be here soon."

In the borrowed staff car of Alina Federov, David Jackson made good time to the Base Main housing area. Aleks gave him an appreciative glance.

"You had driving training."

"Yes Ma'am. Used to race some before… I went to prison."

"What for?" Abigail asked.

"Killed someone, Ma'am. The Squids came and I got out, went home." David gripped the steering hard.

Abigail looked at the young man, just a few years older than her.

"I think God has forgiven you. Please forgive yourself."

"We are here," Aleks said as David braked to a stop, Sgt. Martinez in her K-9 vehicle pulling up behind. Everyone clambered out of their respective vehicles. After a quick look at the dead Eater bodies in backyard, David went over to check the dead body of the human Kraken Freda had shot.

Aleks went through the door opened by Johann.

"I knew the young one's mother would come."

"Where are they?" Aleks demanded.

"Here," Sue called out from the children's bedroom. Aleks dashed in to find her two sons fast asleep. She began to laugh quietly.

"They are their father's sons. Good Marines. Death around them and they go to sleep."

Aleks turned and hugged Sue. "Thank you for keeping my children safe."

"It was Hannah. She saved all of us. I was about to be... eaten." Sue began to cry, holding her pregnant belly.

Aleks held on to her. "I guess Eaters, this house and pregnant women seem to have an evil connection. I think it is time for Torbin and me to move." She kissed Sue Brown on her cheek.

"Can you stay here with my trolls while I check on Hannah?"

"Of course. Hannah... needs help.

Abigail, Ichiro and Sgt. Martinez had scanned the carnage in the backyard, double checked there were no further threats. The K-9 troop and her dog Ginger stayed in the back with Ichiro while Abigail went in to check on those in the house.

Abigail found Freda and the young Survivors huddled around a shaking Hannah. Freda saw Abigail and motioned her toward them.

"Abigail, maybe she will listen to you. She is very, very upset."

Abigail knelt in front of her, reached out and gently took her hand in hers.

"Hannah, it's Abigail."

"Is this what you feel like, Avenging Angel, after you are forced to kill yet again?" Hannah blurted out. "When you use those skills that have been programed, forced into you by sick evil bastards? Is this how you feel when all the memories of the people and creatures you killed or saw killed come rushing back?" Hannah began to sob.

Abigail hugged her tightly, her eyes wet with tears. For she knew these feelings.

"Hannah, you did what you must to save a woman, an unborn life and two children I consider to be part of my family. You used those skills that were forced on you for good. Just as I have. I think any debt you or I have has been paid."

Hannah hugged her back and the two child soldiers stayed hugging for minutes as they dealt with their unique pains and realities. They were two of a generation forced to be warriors well before they should have, forced to kill or be killed. Now, they were having to deal with learning to live with their past. Aleks came up and knelt down.

"I owe you for my sons' lives. You will always have a place at my table, in my home, Hannah."

"Johann helped also," Hannah mumbled.

"But you stopped them. You have nothing to be ashamed of. You should be honored, my Sister of Steel."

The three warrior women stayed kneeling and hugging until Hannah finally stopped shaking.

"I think I will be okay now," said Hannah. She smiled through tear filled eyes. "Thank You."

"Hannah, if you ever need to talk, to… deal with such feelings, call Ichiro and I. He is helping me adjust to who I am, who I was made to become by people and… things that thought they could control me. I think he and I can help you deal with any demons you feel you have."

"I will do that Abigail. Thank you."

"Come," Aleks said. "See my sleeping trolls. When they wake up, they will need to see one of their many protective aunts." She kissed both of Hannah's cheeks. "You are now another little sister for me to boss around, just like I do Abigail."

Abigail laughed. "You forget I have a husband now who will try to boss me around. You'll need to take a number and get in line."

As Hannah went back with Aleks to see her sons, Ichiro stuck his head in thru the back door.

"Is everyone alright now, Abby-san?"

"As well as they can be, my love." She walked over and crushed him in a hug. "I am so lucky to have found you, Ichiro."

"And I you. But we must secure this location, then go on to the hospital. Torbin may need us."

Out in front of the residence, as David Jackson checked the body of the dead Kraken for any ID, he heard before he saw a group of housing area residents approaching. In their clutches was an apparent Kraken much the worse for wear. The demeanor of the half dozen men and women was one of a lynching party.

"Special Agent Jackson. Can I help you people?"

"Yes, you can," an older looking gentlemen answered. "Master Sergeant Jones here, with some of my neighbors. This fool tried to steal one of our vehicles." As he said that, he shook the bruised and battered man by the scruff of his neck.

As David looked closer, even under the damage from the beating he had received, David thought the Kraken looked familiar. The prisoner looked up at David and his eyes widened in recognition.

"David Jackson. It's Ralph Pegg. You know, from prison."

The six people of the potential lynch party looked at David with quizzical expressions on their faces. "Come on, Dave. Help me, for old times…"

David slammed a fist into the man's stomach. He then yanked him from the grasp of Master Sergeant Jones.

"You think that David Jackson still exists, you sack of shit?" He shook his former prison mate. "Your friends just killed my father, the Ranger. I should let these good people take you and have some fun." David looked at the other people with cold eyes.

"Is there going to be a problem if I take custody of this waste of a human being?"

"No. Sir," replied Jones. "You'll want to question him."

"That I will." He paused, then asked the small group. "Any questions you have for me?"

Mrs. Jones stepped forward. "Son, we all had a 'before' life. It's who we are now that matters"

David nodded. "Thank you, Ma'am. Now, I'll just take him to my partners in Torbin Bender's house there. This idiot and his friends thought they could use some Eaters to get some payback. They were wrong."

"Eaters? Come on people," Master Sergeant Jones said as he took his wife's hand. "We need to go and check out our neighbors. You watch yourself, Agent."

"Will do, Sir. Come on you." David began to frog march him to the front of Torbin and Aleks' residence. "There is a Russian Intelligence Officer who would just 'love' to meet one of the men behind the dead Eaters in her backyard."

Torbin and the Banshees made it to the Base Hospital in record time. It was a war zone, with burning cars and some hospital personnel trying to use hand held fire extinguishers to keep the flames from spreading to the Hospital.

"Lt. McDowell, sweep the area, then into the hospital, see what is needed there."

"Yes Sir. Alright, Squad One, clockwise sweep around the area. Squad Two, Counter clockwise. Set up three sixty security, with three, two women teams to go inside at the rear and check out the situation. Move."

The Banshees let out a small twilling screech that seemed their way of yelling "Oorah!" then went at double time to carry-out their instructions.

The Banshee officer looked at Torbin. "Want to go in the front, Sir? We're both heeled, and I know you know how to handle yourself."

Torbin grinned. "I read the reports from Kansas. You original Banshees have created a reputation for taking care of business."

"Well. Colonel, we did have a bit of a set-to there. So, Sir, we go in?"

"Ladies first. I still have a few rounds in my Garand to cover your backside."

With that, the two warriors passed by a few hospital personnel who were still ensuring nothing caught on fire and looking for wounded.

"Who's in charge here, Sergeant?" Torbin asked a young man with blood on his fatigues.

The Sergeant looked at him saw his rank on his fatigues. "I think you are, Colonel. You're the highest ranking office still able to walk on two legs I've seen."

"That bad Sergeant… Bernal, I see on your name tag."

"Sir, I don't know if the entire hospital is secure yet. A bunch of Eaters and beasts got in. And medical people usually don't have a lot of guns at hand."

"Any security people inside now?" Just then they heard a gunshot.

"I guess there are a few still able to move. We got overwhelmed, Sir."

"Hang in there, Sergeant. We'll be right back."

Lt. McDowell and Torbin went in, rifles at low ready. The hospital looked more like a slaughterhouse than a place for medical aid. Blood and other alien-looking fluids were spread about on the walls and floor. A couple of hospital gurneys were parked in the hallway with covered bodies, blood soaked through parts of the covering sheets.

The suspended ceiling collapsed a few yards ahead as a baboon-based creature fell to the hallway floor. It turned screeching at the two near humans, then had its head blown apart by a well-aimed three round burst from Lt. McDowell's assault rifle.

"Nice shooting, Texan."

"I try, Colonel, I try."

They both heard additional shooting.

"Lieutenant, we need some more people in here ASAP. This place is definitely not secure."

"Roger that, Sir." Dagan keyed her attached lapel mike.

"Squads One and Two. I need every-other squad member inside the hospital now! The security of Interior is still in question."

Torbin looked at Dagan, now knowing that his wife and little sister had a strac unit under their command.

"We clear what we can, Lieutenant, until we meet up with other troops."

"Lay on MacDuff, as they said in Macbeth, Colonel."

They heard another shot from up ahead and they advanced CQB crouch as fast as they could. As they cut the pie with speed and rounded the corner into a cross hallway, Torbin saw a familiar face. Staff Sergeant Michael Wall, from his Evanston and Wyoming trip days. The man was standing over a dead weasel creature."

"Eating a crap sandwich again, I see Sergeant."

Wall looked up, grinned. "Am I glad to see you, Colonel. And I see you brought some back up."

"Sergeant Wall, this is Lieutenant McDowell, 101st SAU, the Banshees."

"Pleasure is all mine, Ma'am. We need as many gun carriers as possible."

Torbin frowned. "That bad?"

Wall's expression turned grim. "We got hit within a minute of the klaxon going off. They managed to get some of these creatures from

Hell over and through the fences. They made a bee-line here. We had minimal security at this Hospital, and sniping by a couple of paratroopers and some Krakens slowed our response time here. The medical staff had to fend for themselves."

"Directed attacks by the Eaters and other creatures?"

"Yes, Sir. Half the Eaters are 'wired', with most of the Beasts being set up with those controlled brain implants. I still think someone is out there with in eyeball range to send them in, one and two at a time in places where we aren't."

"Lieutenant…"

"Got it, Sir. Squads One and Two. We have enemy in the bushes, directing Beasts in to the Hospital. They need to be found."

Torbin heard a "Roger that. Three from the entry team being redirected to search, Ma'am."

SSgt .Wall gave Dagan and appreciative look. "Pardon me, Ma'am, but you guys, I mean gals are good."

Dagan McDowell laughed. "Yes, we have our moments. Now, shall we continue clearing the three floors?"

"I have about a half dozen effectives, Colonel, trying to search the hospital. Several more wounded that are stationary with weapons."

"Well, let's give them a hand."

As the three warriors started to work their back down the hallway, SSgt. Wall said. "Sir, I got the word you're ranking officer for miles around. You say jump, I'll say how high."

Torbin smiled. "I'll make a Marine out of you yet, Sergeant."

They headed for the maternity wing, which Wall had said was a main target during the first few minutes. Torbin's blood began to boil when he heard that. Killing newborns? What sick bastards planned that? The main doors to the wing had been barricaded with whatever the hospital staff could find. Wall had placed a wounded Private concealed behind an upturned desk, his right leg all wrapped up in bandages.

"Colonel, I'd stand and salute, only…"

"Belay that, on. What's it like inside?"

"They only lost one pregnant woman, no newborns." Suddenly the Private's face was even grimmer. "A Lieutenant who brought his pregnant fiancée in here for labor pains fought like a demon defending the ward. He…didn't make it. His body's on a gurney just a little way past me."

"Hospital staff?"

"Some dead, most wounded. They had no real weapons."

"Thank you, Private…"

"Sparrow, Sir. Oorah, Colonel."

Torbin looked at him, knew he was one of many who helped keep things from getting any worse.

The three warriors went into the Ward, and Torbin saw the body on the gurney. He walked over and pulled up the sheet form the face.

It was Lieutenant Todd Baker.

Torbin's blood went ice cold with the shock. Then, anger began to rise in him.

"Oh my God," Wall whispered. "The Lieutenant."

"Colonel, you knew him?" Dagan asked.

"He saved my ass in Wyoming. And, I couldn't return the favor."

"Torbin Bender." He heard a young boy's voice and he looked up in time to see Richard Rice before he ran and threw his arms around him."

"I told my Mom, you'd come. I told her you'd be here to help us. I told her…" Doctor

Rica Rice's son began to cry.

"Hey, Troop. Where is she? Come on, you need to stop crying, show me."

Rich stopped, wiped his eyes, and then grabbed Torbin's hand. "Sorry. She's back here patching someone up.

The small group went through another double door and found Major Rica Rice patching up a hospital orderly. His left arm was now a mass of bandages.

"That'll do for now. Get back in here soonest for follow-up.

"Yes Ma'am."

"Major Rice," Torbin called out.

"See, Mom. I said he would come." Rich blurted out.

Rica saw him, and she began to blink back tears. "Colonel, to say I'm glad to see you is the biggest understatement of the year."

Torbin frowned as he noticed her left arm was bandaged but was beginning to drip blood.

"Major, you are leaking."

"Oh, that. I'll patch it up later."

Dagan broke in. "Begging your pardon Ma'am, but in El Paso we used to say a doctor who treated themselves had a fool for a patient."

She slung her weapon and strode over to Rica Rice, grabbed some bandages and some surgical scissors. "Major Yamamoto is making us all get EMT trained. I should be able to handle this."

"You mean Abigail?"

Dagan suddenly looked at Rica's name tag.

"How stupid of me. You're that Major Rice. You saved our Major."

"Actually, a certain veterinarian brought her back to the living with the help of a rather large puppy."

Dagan didn't say anything more as she slit up the sleeve of the Doctors Lab Coat, cut the bandages off.

"Nasty bite. Where's your iodine?"

"Here, Lieutenant. You're quite expert at this. Experience much?"

"Just a fast learner, Major. This is going to sting a lot."

"I know. But that and straight alcohol seems to kill alien germs quite well." Then she stifled a scream as Dagan disinfected the bite.

Rich tugged on Torbin's hand. He bent over and Rich whispered. "Is she a Banshee?"

"Yes she is. Let me guess. Another comic book?"

Rich nodded his head yes.

Dagan completed the bandaging in record time. Rica Rice examined it with appreciation.

"Better than many second year Med students."

"Thank you, Major. And one more thing." Dagan reached under her fatigue top collar and toward the back of her neck. She expertly unclasped a small chain, then handed it to Torbin.

"Sir, could you do the honors? You two are friends, it would mean more."

Torbin looked at the symbol on the chain, the stylized blade he had seen on his wife's neck all the time, knew what Dagan was trying to say. He quickly went over and began to put the chain on a confused doctor.

"What?"

"Major Rice, by the power vested in me as the acting Allied Commander, you are now a Banshee, a Sister of Steel. You took care of Abigail. Now, they will take care of you."

Rica looked at the silver blade. She reached over and clasped

Dagan's hands in hers.

"You do me an honor I don't really deserve. But I won't argue now."

Rica began to tear up. "That young Lieutenant dead on the gurney. He deserves all the honor. He saved everyone here."

"What happened?" Torbin asked.

Rica swallowed, tried to get control of her emotions.

"He brought his pregnant fiancée here as she had some abdominal pains. I volunteered for extra duty today as the Medical Duty Officer, said I'd take a look at her. Then all hell broke loose."

"He saved my mom and all of the babies." Rich said in a soft voice.

Tears began to stream down her face as Rica Rice continued. "A bunch of those weasel and baboon looking things came charging up the hallway. He, he shoved me, Rich and his fiancé into a side room, grabbed an I.V. stand, began to swing it like a damnable broad sword, wouldn't let those…things get to the infants. He was yelling some war cry, swinging, kicking, and fighting like a demon against the monsters." Rica began to sob and her young son went to her.

"It's okay, Mom. He was a soldier. That was his job."

She hugged her son, crying. "He saved us all. Only a pregnant woman in the restroom was killed. He stopped the rest of the Beasts from getting in here. It would have been a slaughter. Then…he went down."

Rica paused for a moment. "The MP out front with the hurt leg showed up, shot the things that the Lieutenant hadn't killed. But it was too late."

"My mom stabbed one with a scalpel. That's how she got bit."

Torbin stood silent as did the others. He took a deep breath, let it out.

"Lieutenant, Sergeant, we have some more floors to check. Major, we'll be back later to take care of Lieutenant Baker's body. I'll get some more security here ASAP. No more threats to babies."

He stepped forward and gave his friend a quick hug. Then he took Richs hand.

"You stay and protect your mom, battle buddy. We'll come back and you can tell the good Lieutenant how you defended me with a crotch shot."

Rich looked up at him. "Yes, Sir. I knew you'd come."

Torbin said nothing, just gave him a small smile.

"Alright. Time to hit the road." Torbin turned and walked out through the doors. Rica and Dagan exchanged knowing glances.

"We'll take care of him, Major. Then I'll be back to swap stories with this fine young man here. Sergeant Wall."

"Yes Ma'am."

They caught up with Torbin out by the wounded MP. He looked at Dagan.

"Remind me to tell your Commander, my wife, what a fine Officer you are. Alright, let's head to the second floor."

"Yes, Sir."

"And payback's a bitch."

"Yes. Sir. A bitch from hell, a banshee."

Torbin and company met the three member Banshee team as they swept in from the rear entrance. One of the young ladies saw Torbin, started to come to attention.

"Tactical, ladies." Dagan said. "No time for pomp and protocol." She looked at Torbin.

"Up the stairs, Colonel?"

"Yes…"

A voice yelled over the tactical radio. "Incoming. Eaters." Then weapons fire.

"Banshees. On Me." Dagan McDowell commanded. Soon all four women had a line formed facing the exit doors, with Torbin and Michael Wall behind them.

"I guess we're rear security," opined Torbin.

"Roger that, Colonel." SSgt. Wall said.

A half a dozen Eaters smashed through the double doors and were met by accurate fire from the four Banshees. The creatures did not stand a chance as bullets slammed into bodies and brain pans. They were all down, dead or dying, in five seconds.

"Oorah!" SSgt. Wall yelled.

One of the Banshees let out the signature short trilling and yipping scream of her Unit in response.

"Damn. Xena, Warrior Princess."

"Colonel?"

"An adventure and fantasy tv program from my misspent youth, Sergeant. That is what their cry reminds of. Xena's battle cry. It just came to me."

Dagan's radio crackled to life again. "Coming in with prisoners and wounded."

"The three person team we sent out must have caught someone, Colonel."

Torbin moved past the Eaters, sticking a couple with the Garand bayonet to make sure they were down for the count. No time to worry about HAZMAT right now, even if they had the capability. He looked out and saw one raggedy figure supporting another who seemed to be trying to hold his guts in. Behind those two was a third being frogged marched by a very angry young Banshee, her blade against his throat. Torbin noticed that one of the three Banshees was limping badly, having trouble keeping up. Then she stumbled, almost fell over.

"SSgt. Wall, cover me." He started moving toward the injured Banshee.

"Colonel..." Dagan began, but Torbin cut her off.

"Lieutenant, I still need those floors swept for enemy. I also need a count on dead and wounded, medical personnel who can still function. Take some more personnel from the perimeter if you need to. I'll get these Krakens in. I want to talk to them, personally."

"Yes, Sir. Alright, you heard the man. Form on me, we go to the second floor." Then Dagan McDowell began to talk on her radio.

As Torbin passed the two Krakens, one supporting the other, large tattoos on their necks, he growled. "Try to run, I'll gut shoot you, leave you for the coyotes." The Banshee walking behind and escorting the two prisoners heard and her eyes widened a bit. Then Torbin was past her, and on the Banshee with her blade to the throat of the other Kraken.

"Don't kill him just yet, Private. I need to talk to him."

"Yes Sir," he hissed. "Hurt a Banshee, you hurt us all," the Banshee growled in the prisoners ear. "Then we hurt you."

Torbin was up to the limping Corporal in back, who saw him coming. "Colonel. I can make it, I..."

Torbin turned around in front of the smaller woman and knelt down. "Climb aboard, Corporal."

"Sir, I can't..."

"Young lady, in the immortal words of General Reed, 'Did I

stutter?' Now, get on. You think you're the first soldier I carried off a battlefield? Move."

"Yessir." She clambered on him, arms wrapped around his neck, legs around him as best as her injured one would allow. He stood up and calmly walked with his load to the hospital.

Sergeant Wall was trying not to grin as Torbin walked up and through the double doors. He went in and set the Corporal in a nearby chair, then turned to the other two Banshees who had the three Krakens up against the wall.

"Well, my Squid-loving scum, who wants to tell me who sent you?"

"Get fucked," the Kraken who had the blade against his throat a minute ago answered.

"Oh, the hard case. Corporal, what did you find in the bushes along with these three poor excuses for humanity?"

"Portable electronics gear, Sir. They were controlling the Eaters and Beasts. One of the devices has a bullet hole in it now. Sorry Sir."

"That's okay. Our tech guys and gals will figure it out. And how did you get hurt?"

"Loud Mouth got a piece of me with a blade as I was clumsy. Sorry Sir."

"Oh hell, you'll patch up. Question is, what do we do with these three if they don't talk?"

The Private who still had her blade out went up to the Kraken who was holding his stomach. "I could make this one a girl just before I finish gutting him. Then start on his friend there…"

"No!" The wounded Kraken screamed. "It was Reverend Kray and the Tschaaa Lord. They told us to kill babies, civilians, spread terror…"

Big Mouth tried to come off the wall and grab the wounded Kraken. Torbin skewered his leg with his Garand bayonet and the Kraken screamed as he fell to the floor. Then Torbin had his foot on the miscreant's throat.

"Don't you ever try to hurt one of my Banshees again. Understand? Sergeant Wall, see if you can get some medical aid here. Corporal gets it first. I need to check in with Lt. McDowell."

"Yes, Colonel." SSgt. Wall beat feet down the hall. He looked at the three Banshees.

"You have this, right?"

"Oorah, Colonel," said the Banshee with the blade, a large grin on her face.

Torbin laughed. "Carry on," he said, then went looking for Dagan McDowell.

The Corporal looked at his back as he walked away.

"That is Colonel Smirnov's husband. The Hero of Key West."

"Damn, she's lucky," Private 'Blade' said. "Wonder if he has a brother."

"He did. He died in the invasion. Ah, here comes some medics. Hope they have some morphine."

The legend started that Torbin Bender carried all three Banshees in by himself, bandaged them, secured the prisoners, and then went off to kill more of the enemy. But then again, legends always have a kernel of truth that then grows often like a bad weed.

An hour later, Madam President Paul finished talking on the phone with Torbin Bender. An ambulance had finally showed up and loaded General Reed aboard, Banshee Medic Ashley Anderson making the ride with him. The President knew of the Banshee Unit but had not the chance yet to really meet them. Now, unfortunately, she had to because of blood and death.

She set the telephone down. Dozens of dead and wounded in and around the Hospital, not to mention reports of casualties from around the base. And the attack on the babies. What kind of sickness would make humans want to do that?

And the Young Lieutenant Baker, a new Hero in his death. But his fiancée never to know his love as her husband, their child never to know the father. Sandra Paul looked up to the connecting door to the next room. There lay the body of Ranger Jackson, draped in an old U. S. flag, from pre-Strike days. Another good soul and close friend who was dead.

And Eaters had almost once again killed Torbin Benders children. Only a brave dependent wife and a Pit Survivor had stopped that. Once again, so called humans arranged for an attack on children, babies. Babies!

She began to shake.

"Sal, you okay?" It was George's voice.

"George, I can't. I just can't..." she started to step, then her legs buckled and she was on her knees on the floor.

"Madan President." He started toward her.

"No. Don't call me that. I have no right to be President. I have overseen the death of thousands. And for what? What? I could have left well enough alone, made a life for the survivors her, in the center of America."

She began to sob. "But no, I had to claim that we should fight for freedom. For justice. For human rights. What in Hell good are all those words when people are dead? When babies are attacked, and killed. Tell me. Tell me." She sobbed more, began to bawl.

"I can't go on. Someone else has to…"

A firm female voice resonated form across the room.

"Get up, Madam President."

"No. I won't. I quit. I am not good for this…"

"You cannot quit." It was Brynhildr.   The tall Shield Maiden strode over to Sandra Paul, knelt beside her.

"You, are why I am here. Why so many are here, alive, and free."

"And so many are dead," Sandra answered

"You think, Madam President, that the deaths are your fault? How? Some seven years ago, did you ask for the misbegotten Squids to come here? No? "

Brynhildr lifted the President's chin up, so she could look into her eyes. "People die in War. And people die in war when they fight for their freedom. And their survival."

"I…"

"You are our steel. Our Spine of Steel. Without you, we would be fighting among ourselves, as the Squids and Krakens pick us off, one by one. We would soon be joining the others in the abomination of Cattle Country. For eventually, Protocol of Selective Survival or not, the Squids would soon realize that meat is meat. Under our skin, all our blood is red. There is no Plague here, so all human flesh is desirable."

Brynhildr took a deep breath.

"So, no, you cannot quit. No more than I could. You need to lead us, to be our backbone. Our Spine of Steel. The Sisters of Steel, the Banshees are your daughters. You and what you have done helped to birth them. You showed the way. Not the Director or his minions, nor his promises of peace and safety under the tentacles of the Squids.

You showed the way for our freedom and our survival. Now, you must finish it. Madam President, cry, feel sorry later. Today, you must lead."

The room was oddly silent. George Williams stood back, watching all this unfold.

'My God,' he thought. 'How many more like Brynhildr are out there? How could the Krakens, the Squids defeat them?'

Sandra Paul had stopped crying. She straightened her back, gazed firmly at Brynhildr for the first time. "Thank you. Can you help me up? I still feel a bit shaky."

Brynhildr helped Sandra to stand, then Madam President took the Shield Maidens hands in her own. "God must have sent you, as I was told long ago that God would not challenge us with anything we could not handle. You just reminded me of that. As the saying goes, that which does not kill us, makes us stronger."

"We are strong, Madam President, together with you. As I said, you are the Spine of Steel we use for support as we swing our weapons. And by the Old Gods, together we will send these demons and devils back to the Pits of Hell from whence they came."

The President began looking for one of her signature handkerchiefs to wipe her eyes but for the first time in recent memories could not find one.

"Here, Ma'am."

She looked at the handkerchief in Brynhildr's hand.

"That is a pretty design."

"It was my mother's design. She is now in Valhalla. Keep it."

"I usually give these things out. Now it is my turn to receive."

She grabbed Brynhildr and hugged her hard. "I would be honored to have you as my daughter."

"You already have me, mother. As you have all of us."

They parted, and Sandra looked at the large, strong yet feminine young woman. "When the Commissioner is done with you, I would like to offer you a special job."

"After the Squids are defeated, you may offer me anything, Madam President. Now, I must go and check up on my friends, family and comrades."

"Yes, of course. But my door is always open."

"Yes, Ma'am. See you soon."

After Brynhildr left, Madam President looked at George.

"Sal…"

"Sorry about that, George. Everything just…got to me at once. But that young woman just gave me a good kick in the butt. I guess I needed it."

"Sal, all I care about is that you are all right."

"Yes, my good friend. Thanks to a bunch of daughters I did not realize I had, until Brynhildr just told me, I am. Now, I need to get my butt back in gear. I can't let all my new found family down."

She squared her shoulders a bit. "George, see if you can locate Colonel Bardun among the living. It is time."

Torbin Bender put his telephone away. The telephone call to Madam President was rough, but she needed to know the full extent of damage and casualties.   He looked around. Things were coming together, the Base was becoming secure.

A few minutes before his telephone call to the President, the Russians had arrived. Three armored transport vehicle crammed with Spetsnaz troops had driven up in front of the Hospital. Colonel Anton "Crazy" Popov had jumped down from the first one. Torbin knew his "Crazy" title came from his Charge of the Technical Brigade in Bloody Kansas that had expanded the Sisters of Steel caused rout of the Krakens. Not to mention his promise to duel with anyone who tried to punish the much unauthorized attack by the Sisters of Steel, now codified as the Banshees. Supporting large violations of orders was not a known characteristic of Russian Senior Officers in the last one hundred years or so.

Popov was to receive his first Generals Star any day, so Torbin walked up, expecting to turn his command over to the Senior Allied Officer. But before Torbin could say anything, Popov saluted him. "My President has informed me that you are the Senior Allied Commander. What are your orders, Sir?"

Now Torbin knew he was stuck with the Responsibility of Command. Damn.

"Well, Colonel Popov, my wife, Colonel Smirnov could use some help in the Base Housing Area clearing out Eaters and Krakens. Some have apparently gone to ground there. Then we can go off base and help secure Great Falls."

Popov had grinned. "That second part will probably not be necessary, Colonel. You crazy Americans and your Second Amendment love of all firearms meant that I met a virtual army of armed citizenry as I entered Great Falls. And your Law Enforcement Commissioner Paul Miller had already organized most of them and started clearing the surrounding areas. Indications were that Eaters were already producing young, so it will take days if not weeks to find them all, no matter who does it."

"Well, Colonel, that is good news. I was afraid that we would have to secure the entire city with our limited forces until reinforcements arrived."

"Not yet, Sir. Now, I am off. I am on the common Tactical Frequency if you need to contact me."

"Again, thank you for coming so quickly. We were caught flat footed. We all thought someone would try and attack during the wedding when everyone was in one place. We were wrong."

"Not the first time that has happened to the best of us. Nor the last, Commander." Colonel Popov saluted Torbin, then clambered on board his vehicle, yelling orders. The vehicles roared into life, the senior man on each saluting Torbin as they drove off.

He was damn glad the Russian were on his side.

Torbin was jerked from his wool gathering by the crackle of his radio."

"Colonel, Sergeant Wall here. Could you come to the E.R.? We have a pissed off Japanese Princess here." In the background, Torbin could hear angry Japanese voices. Shit. He hoped Ichiro returned soon. He could use a Japanese speaker to help deal with the retinue that had responded with Princess Akiko.

Somehow, the Princess had arrived in the mix of things, her handlers trying to catch up with her to dissuade her of participation in the violent activities. Fat chance.

Akiko had come in a side emergency exit that some Beast had broken through and immediately was in the mix of a bunch of screaming hospital personnel trying to fend off the monsters with limited weaponry. The Princess had let out her own version of a war cry, or scream, and began to lay about her with her family katana. Orderlies and medics had reported she had been like a wraith, everywhere at once. Limbs, heads, legs of Beasts and Eaters were soon spread out in various rooms and hallways, arterial blood and alien ocher splattered on walls and ceilings. More than one person reported she had saved their lives by gutting some creature just before sharp teeth had a chance to do serious damage. She had shown Ichiro developed techniques on the Eaters, slashing their appendages and then impaling their so called brains with a thrust through their large eyes.

But a one person attack had its limitations.

Lt. Dagan McDowell found Princess Akiko on the second floor during her team's initial sweep, trying to tie off a nasty leg wound just as a baboon creature was rushing her. Dagan shot the modified primate through the head, watched as it slid to within inches of the Japanese female Samurai, dead.

Akiko looked up at the four approaching Banshees. "Thank You. I was distracted by my wounds."

Dagan looked at Akiko and saw several smaller wounds in addition to the leg one, which was bleeding profusely. "Captain, allow me." With that, Dagan again demonstrated the EMT Training Abigail had provided.

"Just patch me enough to stand. Then I can join you in the fight…"

"Sorry, Princess Akiko. Yes, I recognize you now. If I let you get killed, both Major Yamamoto and Colonel Bender will tan my hide."

Akiko looked at Dagan. "You…speak a bit differently."

"Texas accent, Ma'am. I'm from Texas."

Akiko's face brightened a bit under the blood covering her.

"Ah, a cowboy. You herd cows. Or did, before the Takos arrived."

Dagan tried not to laugh. "Cowgirl, Ma'am. We differentiate between the genders. And you herd cattle and steers. But I was a soldier when the first rock hit."

"Another experienced American Warrior. Sadly, my combat experience has been limited. Until today."

"And I think you are done for today. You have lost a good amount of blood." Dagan looked around and saw a nurse and an orderly coming from a side room

"Excuse me." She called out. "Wounded Japanese Princess here. She needs some plasma."

The two medical personnel saw both the Banshee and the Princess, realized they could not be ignored. They walked quickly up the hallway, found a wheelchair, and soon had a protesting Akiko headed to the ER on the main floor.

"I must protest, Lieutenant…" the member of the Free Japan Royal Family began."

"Won't do any good, Ma'am. Here, wounded follow the orders of the medicos. Sorry."

As they wheeled her away, Akiko called out, "I did not get your name."

"Dagan McDowell, Ma'am. A Banshee. Just ask for Texas, they'll find me."

And now Princess Akiko was in a heated argument with two Japanese Senior Officers who had the bad luck to be assigned to keeping her out of trouble.   SSgt. Wall had apparently been pulled off to handle something else, or had decided a non-Japanese speaking NCO could do little

Torbin walked into the ER and saw the Princess grabbing for her katana that one of the senior officers had a hold of, trying to keep it from her grasp. He did not understand much Japanese, but he could tell the Princess was spitting nails.

"Excuse me, lady and gentlemen. But could I be of some assistance?"

"This is a Japanese matter," one of the Japanese officers spat out, then returned to arguing with Akiko. The dismissive tone the apparent Japanese Colonel had used was the wrong tack to use. Before the Japanese Officers knew it, a rather large Gaijin was in their faces.

"Excuse me, Gentlemen, but this is not Japan."

With a syrupy tone of voice, Princess Akiko broke in with English, "May I present Colonel Torbin Bender, Acting Allied Force Commander here at Malmstrom."

The two handlers of the royal personage stepped back gave short bows.

"We must take the Royal Princess from here," the older of the two spoke. "It is not safe."

"Well, Colonels, once she is stabilized and the Docs let her go…"

"No. That is unacceptable. She must come. Now."

Torbin was not in the mood for this martinet to tell him what was going to happen, Torbin was bloody and dirty, and this guy looked like he had barely broke a sweat.

Torbin's face began to display a feral grin as he once again stepped closer.

"Now, guys, do you really want to take that tone of voice?"

There was an explosion of Japanese behind Torbin. Both of the Officers, with shocked expressions, looked up as Ichiro approached, saying words that Torbin recognized as not nice or used in   polite conversation. The New Samurai had his katana out and had blood in his eye. Somehow, Akiko managed to maneuver her wheelchair and grabbed her katana, twisting it from the other officers grasp.

"You dare to question the Allied Commander, here, on this day of death and destruction?" Ichiro yelled in English. Torbin did not remember seeing him this enraged, except for the time the now deceased Russian Colonel him called him a monkey.   Ichiro slashed with his katana, causing the two Japanese officers to jump back. The younger of the two started to reach for his sidearm.

"Not a wise decision, Hoss," sneered Torbin.

And then Abigail was there, next to her husband Ichiro.

"Pull that pistol, and this Avenging Angel will send you both to your ancestors." Her voice was cold as arctic ice. "We are on our honeymoon and I do not intend to allow anyone or anything to harm my Bbloved. You may complain to my Government in Deseret later, that you were insulted by one of the Nation States Diplomats. That is, if you are able."

The two Japanese Colonels knew that they could both back off and try to preserve some 'face' or risk dying. On this Day of Hell, their deaths would be just two of many.

The elder Colonel bowed deeper. "Please accept my apologies. We were just concerned about the Royal Princess and her well-being.

"Well, Gentlemen," said Torbin. "Come back in about an hour and maybe the doctors will release her. Until then, she is under my hospitals control."

The two Japanese Officers saluted, mumbled, bowed and left. Torbin smiled. He knew both he and the Princess would catch royal Hell. As would probably Ichiro. But, damn. They were all still alive.

Torbin looked at Ichiro. "I take it my wife and my children are safe."

"Yes, Torbin-san. Sue Brown and Hannah Weitz fought as Samurai of old, killed many Eaters. It was glorious, worthy of legends and later tales."

Abigail frowned. "Hannah took it hard. I'll explain it all to you later, my Big Brother. But what is important is that everyone is safe. And we passed the Russians heading into the housing area, so I take it they are there on your orders."

"Yes, Ma'am. They showed up at just the right time. As you all did."

He felt Abigail's eyes boring into him. "What is it, little sister?"

"Remember when I said you were part of something bigger, would play a very important role in the future, my big brother?"

"Yes, I did."

"Well, this is part of it."

Torbin looked at her. He felt a little change in the air, as if there had been a shift in the reality that surrounded them. Then he realized that she was right. As right as Andrew had been. He shivered a bit. 'No rest for the wicked, he thought.

"Well, whatever the final "something' you mentioned is, right now I have other fish to fry. So, I need to check with Security Control, see how the Big Picture is developing."

At that moment, Torbin's radio crackled again. "Sir. Need you on the third floor, ASAP. It's Stalin."

"Shit." He keyed his mike. "Responding." He looked at Ichiro and Abigail.

"We will insure the Princess is treated well, Torbin." Abigail said before he could speak.

"Thank you. You are both godsends."

Abigail smiled. "We aim to please, My Commander."

Torbin bounded up the stairs and burst thru the stair doors. A few yards away, a mixture of Banshees and MPs were trying to hold down an extremely angry Senior Training Instructor. Sitting against the wall were two Krakens and a captured paratrooper, holding various parts of their bodies as if they were in great pain. Something told Torbin that Stalin had much to do with their condition. He strode over and stood looking down on to a cursing and swearing Russian. Their eyes met, and Stalin stopped his cursing.

"Colonel Bender. Could you please have your people release me?"

"Not if you are going to try and tear our prisoners apart."

Stalin's face flushed with anger. "You don't understand. They hurt My Sally. My Sally!"

For the first time ever, Torbin saw a tear run down Stalin's face."

"Where is she?"

"In the next examination room, Sir," responded SSgt. Wall, who was sitting on Stalin's legs. "They're patching her up."

Torbin stared at Stalin. "I expect more control from the Senior Training Instructor." He glared a bit. "You are disappointing your Acting Allied Commander."

Stalin froze in the midst of his struggles. It was as if Torbin's words had been a knife.

"I…am sorry, My Commander. I beg…indulgence."

"We'll see. Stay there on your back. That's an order."

Torbin walked into the examination to find two medics cleaning up a nasty leg wound on Sally Reid.

"Well, you can't blame that on me, Miss Reid."

"Colonel Bender. Is Stalin okay? I hear him yelling and cursing."

"He has been in better moods. What happened to you?"

"Too close to an Eater while trying to get a live story on this attack. It latched onto my leg as it died, so I got some of its acid vomit on me." Tears came down her cheeks. "I'll never be able to wear a short skirt again."

"Yea you will. Hacked Tschaaa technology and nanites can do wonders. Now, you calm down while I try to calm your man down before he does something we will all regret."

The reported grabbed his hand and kissed it. "You a great human being, you know that."

"Right now, I'm just putting out fires and holding things together for General Reed. Once he is patched up, I can go back to being just Torbin Bender."

Sally looked into his eyes. "You don't get it. You are not "just" anything. You never have been."

Torbin let a small smile leak out. "I disagree. But I seem to be in a minority today. You, get better, hear?"

"Yes Sir."

Torbin turned and walked back to the hallway. Stalin seemed calmer, was sitting up.

"Stalin. Stand up."

The Granite Russian was on his feet in a second, bent his head low, unable to meet Torbin's eyes.

"So, Senior Training Instructor, what exactly were you trying to do? "

"Crush the life out of the two Krakens, then stomp the paratrooper."

"Because they brought the Eater that hurt Sally Reid, right."

"Yes, Sir. I told her I was the soldier, that she should stay away from war, battle. She did not listen."

Torbin chuckled. "I've found women rarely listen to the ones they love. They prefer to call all the shots. Now, you go in that room and hold her hand, tell Sally Reid that she will heal fine, will always be beautiful in your eyes. That, is an order."

Stalin looked into Torbin's eyes. "I am sorry, I…"

"Oh please. I have almost done the same. Just don't do it again. I need intelligence from these scum. Now, follow my orders and see to Sally."

Stalin snapped to full attention and saluted "Da, Comrade Commander." Then he marched into the examination room, to cries of welcome from Sally.

Torbin addressed the other troops. "Thanks for not hurting him. I need him."

"Hell, Sir, we were just trying to keep 'him' from hurting 'us'." One of the Banshees blurted out. Everyone began to laugh.

"Now. Patch up those prisoners and sit on them. I'll tell you where to take them for interrogation. Although, maybe I'll just let that Crazy Russian talk to them."

The three prisoners tried to become as small and unobtrusive as possible.

It was very dark and very late when Torbin met Madam President in General Reed's office. She had been in contact with all the elected officials as well as representatives from all the Allied Groups, even ones consisting of hundreds rather than millions of members, So far, the attack on Malmstrom Allied Armed Forces Base seemed to have had the exact opposite effect on the Allies than the Krakens and the Tschaaa has desired. Once it got out that newborn infants and little children were specific targets for destruction, instead of fear, blood red rage had resulted.

Terror does not work on all human populations, especially populations that had been winnowed out through years of deprivation and death. As Nietzsche had said, that which does not kill you makes you stronger.

Torbin had been surprised when no surviving General Officer questioned his Command. He was just a Light Colonel after all. But Aleks had put it best.

"They recognize you are right for the job, and are on scene. Plus, many of their fellows are dead or injured, an example of how command can make you a special target. Let you get killed first, then maybe they will pick up the pieces."

She had produced a knowing smile. "The fact you have two powerful female Presidents and a female member of the Japanese Royal Family in what you Amercanskis call your fan club probably means a lot also."

Whatever the reason, Torbin had been able to field the ball and run with it. Great Falls and the Base were secured, though they would be hunting for Eaters for weeks if not months. Breeding like rabbits made them just as difficult to exterminate. He knocked, then entered the General;s Office. He walked up and started to salute Madam President when she had shoved a glass containing a substantial amount of brown liquid at him.

"Quit with the formalities, Son. We are so way past that. Here, this is from John Reed's personal supply of scotch. I know I can use it."

"Quite Right, Madam President. Now I know why you are in charge."

Sandra Paul had laughed. Then she had taken a large and very unlady like drink from her glass. She swallowed then looked at it. "Now that is smooth."

Torbin joined her in the drink. "Hmmmm. I have to agree, Madam President."

"Someday, when you feel comfortable, my friends all call be Sal.

It's a nickname I picked up years ago."

"Short for Sally, Ma'am?"

"No. Short for Salamander. I used to stick and flick my tongue at things I did not like, agree with. So, my older brother told me I was acting like some slimy salamander, so… the rest is history."

They stood quite for a moment, departed family having been mentioned. The President broke the silence. "I almost lost it today, Torbin. I tell you this so if I do, you get ahold of the Vice President and you two take over."

"Ma'am, I find that…"

"It happened. Ask Brynhildr Jorgensen, She was the one who gave me a quick kick in the ass, figuratively. But it had the same effect as if she had done it for real."

She looked directly into Torbin's eyes. "Do I have, or am I, a Spine of Steel, Colonel? You're a Medal of Honor recipient, you should know more than most what the word backbone really means."

Torbin paused for a moment, then emptied his glass and reached for the bottle now on the General's desk. As he refilled the two glasses he spoke.

"President Sandra Paul. You not only are a Spine of Steel for us all, but you are stainless steel. You never rust. You bend but spring back, like Ichiro's katana. You are never dull, always sharp. Ready to cut any who try to hurt you and yours." Torbin paused, picked his glass up and looked at it.

"Damn. Never had scotch make me this verbose and philosophical before. This must be the good stuff." He looked and noticed the President had tears on her cheeks.

"Ah, hell, Ma'am. Don't cry. I may join you…"

"Brynhildr told me I was everyone's mother. That you are all my sons and daughters." Sandra Paul produced one of her signature handkerchiefs and wiped her cheeks, makeup be damned. "But today I lost some of my sons and daughters, when I should have made sure they were protected. I guess I may be an unfit parent."

"Ma'am, that was not your job. Taking into account what the enemy may and could do is our primary responsibility, not yours. We're the experts in violence, not you."

Once again, silence. The woman called Sal sipped her drink, then spoke once again.

"As one of my Sons, I must ask you to go to the well one more time for me. I will have one more impossible task for you to make possible for me and us humans. Just as soon as I can talk to Colonel Bardun one more time, I will provide you with the details." She took another drink.

"But you may die. Your Aleks may become a widow, your two sons without a father. If that happens, I think I will die also."

"No, Ma'am. You, cannot die because of me. I have almost died so many times I have lost count. Yes, I have my wife and children, my now extended adopted family to live for. But." Torbin paused for a moment, then continued. "If they are to be free of the Squids, free of the fear that they and their children may be killed and eaten at any time, and my death is required to insure that, so be it. I always knew of that possibility when I first signed up all those years ago. And that, my President, is my doing, my fault if you want to call it that. You have nothing to do with it."

Sandra Paul looked at the young hard, yet soft man sitting before her.

"General Reed is right. You are someone special, with a special purpose."

Torbin let out a great sigh. "You know, I keep hearing that sentiment. Hell, even a cyborg Robocop told me that. I guess I'll just have to get used to it. So much for ending my days as a Grunt Marine in some Veteran's Home."

Sandra Paul laughed. "A Veteran's Home? Hell, Colonel, you would have everyone running laps, going on field marches, sitting around so straight and tight you'd swear 'they' were the ones with metal backbones."

Torbin gave her a quizzical look. "Am I that tight?"

"Yes, Colonel. But it makes you 'you'. Which is the person I need in the next week or so. I need a Ramrod. And you are it."

Torbin chuckled. "Well, I've been called worse. Hmmm. Ramrod. Sounds all John Wayne and Clint Eastwood western hero like. Yeah. Ramrod and the Spine of Steel. Perfect action heroes for one of Rich Rice's comic books."

He raised his glass. "A toast, Madam President? To success."

"Success is my middle name, Colonel. After Salamander."

As Torbin and the President were having their very late night conversation, in a secret bunker under the once Command Post of Minot Air Force Base, North Dakota, expatriate Romanian Military Intelligence Officer and Translator Mikhail Ispear was playing back a recording of a Tschaaa conversation he had intercepted earlier. Though intercepted was a misnomer as it appeared this message had been broadcast in the clear and beamed at the Unoccupied States. This was the third time he had viewed and listened to it and he was still having trouble believing what he heard.

It was said by many Romanians that they reason they were so efficient at learning other languages was because theirs was so complicated. With numerous extra additions to their basic alphabet and basic letter combinations, some Romanians stated that even after 12 years of education, they were still not fluent in their own language. It was this seemed natural ability that had enabled Abigail's Late Mother to have also been a translator and interpreter for the Romanian Government, which was how she had met Abigail's Father. And Mikhail's father had worked with Abigail's Mother, which had added to the impetus for Mikhail to make it to America, and offer his services. Plus, he was a bit of a 'genius' at his job, being one of the few humans that seemed to have a complete grasp of the Squid Language. He had even become efficient in reading the meaning of all their limb and body movements, including color changes.

Even with all this expertise, what he was hearing and seeing left him incredulous. He finished the third review and sat back in his padded chair. He had stayed late when word of the attack on Malmstrom had been broadcast, hoping to glean from any chatter by the Enemy some useful intelligence.   Two hours prior, as details of the attack was being broadcast to the Free and Not So Free World, this had popped up.

Short and to the point, the female Tschaaa, clearly a breeder, was imploring Madam President to meet with her in the shallows of the Great Lakes, off of Duluth. And it was the "imploring" tone and demeanor that had made him so hesitant to pass this message on. Not until he was sure of what he saw and heard, did he decide.   Mikhail bolted up from his chair, began to loudly chatter in his native language, and dashed with his copy of the transmission down the hallway. He was almost tackled by Security as he neared the communications room where Vice President Joseph Biggs had been camped out in, both during the Great Wedding and the beginning of Hell Day in Great Falls, Montana.

"What is all the racket, Gentlemen?" The Elder Statesman's voice could still resonate when he wanted it to, despite his seventy six years of existence.

"Sir, we have an Intelligence Analyst who swears he has some intercepted information that must be passed on to the President."

"Well, send him in. Hopefully my being the Vice President is of sufficient importance to receive his information."

Mikhail burst in, talking at a machine gun speed in Romanian. Joseph Biggs held up his hand and smiled.

"Please, young man. I can barely speak and understand English on some days. Romanian? Probably never."

"Sorry, Mr. Vice President. It is an honor to speak with you. It is an honor to work in this Free Country. It is..."

The Vice President held up his hand again, grinning. "I appreciate all the honorariums, young sir. But, can you cut through what we on the farm used to call bullshit and tell me what has you so agitated?"

"Sir, I will show you."

Mikhail put the small portable drive into a nearby secure laptop and brought up the file. Fifteen minutes later, after Mikhail had provided him a running commentary as they listened and watched the Tschaa Breeder, the Vice President fixed him with a steely gaze.

"Sir, would you bet your life on your translation? Because, we may be betting the lives of many on it."

Mikhail crossed himself, raised and kissed his Eastern Orthodox crucifix hanging about his neck. "I swear on my mother's grave and on Jesus Christ my Savior. God gave me this gift of languages. My translation is accurate."

Joseph Biggs leaned forward and took Mikhail's right hand in his. "My good son, you have made history this day. What happens next may be in the hands of Divine Providence. But I think we will give the Divine a little help."

"Major," his voice boomed once again. "Get a most secure line to Madam President. She needs this info now, not tomorrow. She should still be at General Reeds Office. If not there, Find her. Now."

Torbin was getting up to leave the President when George William's loud voice resonated from the outer office.

"Madam President, we have a call from the Vice President on the Secure Line. He says it is most urgent."

She looked at Torbin. "Wait here, please. This may need your assistance."

She sat back at the General's desk and picked up the secure line, scrambled for communication security.

"President Paul here... Yes, Joseph... What? Repeat that... Is that loud young man in the back ground Mikhail? Put him on. George, please come here. You need to hear this also."

Although it kind of defeated the purpose of high security, Madam President put the phone on speaker. George Williams came in, a huge double barreled former Elephant Gun someone had found for him as Presidential protection in his hand. His statue made the rifle look normal size.

After getting Mikhail somewhat calmed down, they listened to what the Romanian had to say. They sat in shocked silence for a few moments. Then, Torbin looked at the President.

"Game Changer. If this is not some trick, which I doubt it is, this is a game changer."

"Why do you doubt this is not a trick?" George asked.

"Because, unlike the duplicitous lying little monkeys that we are, the Tschaaa seem to be an in your face, this is the way it is, don't like it, tough, species. We have very few verifiable cases of Squids being duplicitous or lying to each other. They whacked a Lord for trying some nasty shenanigans behind the scenes with Eaters in the Keys, to get back at Lord Neptune. Plus, they would not involve their Breeders in such activities. Male Tschaaa come at you, full throttle. Hiding behind that Asteroid when they approached can be written off as ambush hunting, which they do. But verbal judo, lying? Does not happen. They may keep information from you, but when confronted, admit it. You just have to know how to ask all and the right questions."

The President snorted. "Then why doesn't the Director ask the right questions? Never Mind. He hears what he wants to, that's the answer."

"He and his supporters have bought the Protocol of Selective

Survival hook line and sinker. Hell, he probably helped develop it to save the people on the Florida Keys."

George Williams frowned. "But I thought the Tschaaa had a patriarchal society, even if they put Breeders and their young on a pedestal? How would the females even consider bypassing their Lords?"

Mikhail cleared his throat over the phone line.

"Pardon me, Your Honors. But if I may explain."

"Go ahead, my friend," the President said. "I get the impression you know more about how our Squid enemies talk and think that just about everyone."

"Well, Madam President, I have listened to thousands of their intercepted conversations, watched video feed of them conversing when I have been able. We even hacked into a conversation or two Director Lloyd had with Lord Neptune."

Torbin laughed. "Shades of the good old NSA."

"So tell us," Sandra Paul asked. "How and why would this breeder violate their cultural norms and rules, and risk the displeasure of her Lord? Who is…"

"Lord Neptune, from what we can ascertain. She has borne him young it seems. At least based on the words she used, the gestures of her social tentacles when she spoke of him."

"So why, my very smart friend. Why is she doing this?"

"Because she thinks she has to, Madam President. For the survival of her young. This specific attack to kill our babies, newborns…I think somehow she has…internalized it, personalized it."

"But they 'eat' our children, damnit," George broke in. "Why should it bother her now?"

"First, it was for revenge, not dark meat. Targeting a child for revenge? Not a concept they accept. And I believe she has been seeking advice from other females. She used their term for "we" and made what we call an inclusive gesture with her two social tentacles. I think, maybe due to contact with human social structure, she and other Breeders see a need for a change."

"My God," said Torbin. "Who would believe Women's Liberation would cross species?"

"Your flippant answer may be the truth, Torbin. After all, you have me as your President, your boss. Fifty to hundred years ago, this was not seriously considered by most people in Western Culture, not to mention the rest of the world."

There was a pause in the conversation, as each of the participants were temporarily lost in their own thoughts. Then Madam President spoke again.

"How are we to let them know I am going to meet with her and whomever she has been talking to?"

"Excuse me, Sal," interrupted George. "You are not thinking of going outside our protective borders to meet this female Tschaaa, are you?"

"And why not, George? We may have a chance of fermenting a bit of internal resistance, fragmentation in Squid society."

"Goddamnit, they may eat you!" George began to shake a bit with rage and anger. The President knew her dearest of friends, her personal advisor would gladly die rather than allow her to go into harm's way. But, she was the President, not him.

"Mikhail Ispear. Can you send us via a secure computer connection this video and all your notes, observation?"

"But of course, Madam President."

"Can you do it this night? I know it is late…"

A new firmness in Mikhail's voice could be heard even over the secure encrypted channel.

"My Homeland is in ruins, My President. I came here because you were resisting, trying to strike back. I will gladly stay awake, on the job for days, weeks, if it saves one person. One… child."

There was another short pause, then Sandra Paul answered, her voice choked with emotion.

"Sir, you are a hero in this, your adopted country. I and my fellows here will never forget this. You may have provided a key for humankind's survival, maybe even the expulsion of the Tschaaa."

"I only do my job, Madam President. I am not special. The Avenging Angel's mother, a Romanian also. My father knew her, she was a close friend of his. She, was special."

"We will await you communication, Mikhail. May God be with you."

"And with you, My President." The connection was cut.

"Joe Biggs will insure the information on to how to contact that Breeder will get to us soonest."

"Madam President, I cannot allow…"

"George, with all due with respect, this is my call. I am the President. And, if I die, there will be another one. I know people like you and Colonel Bender here will see to that."

She fixed Torbin with a firm gaze. "What good is a Spine of Steel if you don't use it. True, Colonel?"

"Ma'am, you tell me what you want done, I'll see it gets done. But if I may be so bold to suggest, since the Breeder mentioned 'We', you do not have to go alone."

"I can't take a bunch of soldiers with me. That would no doubt scare the Tschaaa females off."

An almost feral grin formed on Torbin's face.

"You have forgotten, Ma'am, about your daughters. The ones with blades of steel."

CHAPTER 34

CATTLE COUNTRY
ATLANTA, GEORGIA

Malcolm Carter was shaken awake by a yelling Big Joe Forest. The Mayor of Atlanta and the Revolt in Cattle Country had stayed awake long into the night, listening to the updates from Hell Day in Great Falls, Montana. Former Islamic terrorist and trained intelligence operative Dawoud Amin had managed to get someone on their short wave radio, as well as erect a large retractable antenna on a nearby multi-storied building's roof to pick-up clear air television transmissions from the Free States. They had watched the videos of the Eaters and Beasts being used to attack the Unoccupied States stronghold, in apparent response to the Grand Wedding and the Kraken Defeat in Bloody Kansas.

Just before Malcolm had turned in, he'd told the others of his inner circle, "Well, the Free Crackers have just caught shit again. They need to lay low for a while before they are added to Cattle Country just on general principles."

Now his right hand man was jerking him awake, yelling, "Boss. Get up. They're coming. All of them."

Malcolm knew what "all" meant. The Squids were sending in

Krakens, battle-robs, maybe even robocops. 'I guess their patience wore thin,' he thought.

"What time is it, Joe?"

"Two in the morning, Boss."

"Rouse everyone, full defense mode."

"Dawoud and Red are already doing that, Boss. Everyone just needs orders."

'Orders', the Mayor thought.

"Hell, Joe, the order of the day is survive. Fight back if you can, hide if you can't. Now, let's get topside so I can see for myself just how bad it is."

Ten minutes later, Malcolm and Joe had met up with Dawoud, peering from behind the still standing wall of a smashed office building. The three saw some two thousand armed human Krakens advancing, going from abandoned car to abandoned car, damaged building to damaged building, looking for hiding places of the some fifty thousand people of color still existing in what was left of Atlanta. Supporting the renegade humans were several groups ofbattle and harvester robots, the only difference between the two being the battle-robs had their blinding capture spotlights replaced with human built automatic weapons. Behind them was a thin line of the newer Soldier Class artificial beings, called Poor Man's robocops by some. Behind the Soldier Class warriors were a half a dozen of real robocops, carrying the same electromagnetic bolt guns which outfitted the Soldier Class. The Enemy shot at everything that moved.

"Reports, my leader," said Dawoud, "is that there is a reinforced ring of Krakens supported by a few battle-robs and such acting as a blocking force for any escape attempts."

"So, this is it," replied Malcolm.

"Yes, it appears so."

"Just like the Warsaw ghetto, and we are the Jews. They, are the Nazis. And the Allies are not coming. History repeats itself in all its fucked-up glory." He sighed.

"Well, no getting around it. Plan E for Escape it is. Dawoud, find a weak spot to bust out for us, one we can try and get as many people through to hide outside Atlanta. They may be able to sneak into one of the surrounding communities, stay alive a while longer. If we were closer to the Border, I'd say we try to bust out into the Feral Areas.

But that is too far away.”

“What about us, Boss?” Big Joe asked.

“There is no ‘us’. You and Dawoud take Red and escape, try to set up life some other place. I stay here. This is my Alamo, remember? A black-assed David Crockett.”

Big Joe stared at him. ”No.”

“What do you mean, no?”

Joe pulled out his large bowie knife. “I’m Jim Bowie, remember? He stayed at the Alamo.”

“Goddamnit, that’s an order.”

“So shoot me, Boss.”

Malcolm gave Dawoud an exasperated look.

“Pretty bad when Joe disobeys me.”

“I must also, Malcolm Carter. It would dishonor me, my faith and my family to run from these evil Djinn, these demons.”

“What about Red?

“I will find someone to take her out after I find that weak spot for you. Then, I return to your side.”

Malcolm shook his head. “I guess I should have gotten you guys to hate me, then you’d be high tailing out of here.”

Big Joe grinned. “Hell, Boss, we love you. Don’t we, Dawoud?”

“Now don’t you dare get all mushy on me, Joe, no sloppy kisses.”

He looked at the two men who had become like brothers to him over the last few months.

“Okay, you hard-headed bastards. Find that weak spot and get Reggie Adams and Professor Bashir Gupta here with all their nasty improvised stuff. No use saving anything for a rainy day when the monsoons just arrived.”

The Final Battle for Atlanta Began. It was set to be a battle of extinction.

CHAPTER 35

President Abraham Lincoln once said 'Nearly all Men can stand adversity, but if you want to test a Man's character, give him Power.' Perhaps If Director Lloyd had paid attention to this concept, he may have taken a different path.

-Excerpt from the *Works of Princess Akiko*, Free Japan Royal Family

Once again, Adam Lloyd had slept little, thanks to unannounced actions by Lord Neptune and the Krakens. Now, based on the broadcasts from the Unoccupied States and Free Areas, he was once again privy to added horror. Babies and infants had been targeted by Kraken controlled Eaters and Beasts. All this based on His Lordships orders. All this done with him, the Director, kept in the dark.

The attempts to assassinate Madam Presidents of the U.S.A. and Free Russia had failed. Through promises of complete independence and exemption from Harvesting, as part of the Protocol of Selective Survival, Quebec based French Canadian trained Special Forces had been included in the attack. The Quebecois had also been told by the Krakens that the Unoccupied States were planning to attack and occupy the province, in connection with surviving Canadian Military.

But once again, the same people that seemed to thwart the Krakens at every turn appeared. A certain Torbin Bender, now a Light Colonel, his Russian Military wife and some of those crazy New Vikings had derailed the attempt. And of course, there was the legendary Avenging Angel, now married to the Japanese New Samurai who had launched the nuke at Lord Neptune. They all seemed to form a tight knit group, a Family, which were a force hitherto never seen before.

They made all those comic book and action movie heroes of yore look like little kids stuffed toys. They were the 'real deal'. But for some quirks of fate and his own decisions, Adam Lloyd liked to think he could have been part of them.

The secure combination computer and communicator buzzed again. Lord Neptune was once again trying to contact him. And once again, he ignored it. He knew that things were reaching critical mass, leading to an explosion he may not survive. Adam did not care. All he really cared about were his wives, children, the Chief and a few close staff members. He felt responsible for all the other some six thousand souls on Key West, but push came to shove, he would leave them to their own devices. He glanced at the clock. It was barely 6:00am. The Tschaaa Lord must be nervous about something to contact him this early. Fine. Let him sweat, if Squids really sweat.

Mary walked into his barely lit office.

"Adam? You never came back to bed."

"No, dear. I didn't want to wake you, Kat and the kids."

She walked over to him sitting behind his desk, and hugged him.

"You can always wake us if you have troubles. And I know yesterday was tough. That His Lordship kept you out of the loop again…"

Adam looked at Mary. "Dearest, this is all turning into one big lie, charade. I thought this whole idea of being able to insure the survival of some, hopefully many, for the sacrifice of limited others would work. The Protocol of Selective Survival… it was a sham."

Mary stared into his eyes. "Why? Why a sham? We are alive, with children…"

"Because he sends Eaters and Beasts to kill children, not just to harvest them. He said it was just all about dark meat, finding a replacement for their home world primate meat source. So, they like veal like we do, eat the young of humans, other primates."

Adam began to shake a bit from rage. "Yet now he uses surrogates to just slaughter, not for meat, but spread terror, to destroy those Humans who refuse to bend. But not the adults. He attacks the young!" He slammed his fist hard onto the table.

"Lord Neptune said the Tschaaa did not understand psychotic behavior, killing just for the thrill of killing, especially your own species. Now, he uses the abomination he once attacked as an unacceptable, basic evil. He uses humans and the creatures they control to search and kill babies. Just to make us scared. He lied!   He has no respect for us, no plans to use us as a Client Species. We are just meat."

Adam stood up from his chair, almost knocking Mary over. He grabbed a glass of scotch and smashed it against his office wall.

"I became a Himmler for him, an architect of his idea of the Final Solution for Humans. Protocol of Selective Survival. Hell, it is the Protocol for Selective and Slow Slaughter."

His laptop/communicator buzzed again. Lord Neptune would not leave him alone.

"Please go back in with Kat and the kids. This conversation is not going to be pretty."

Mary kissed him. "Just remember. We are always behind you, Adam my love.'

"I know. Just let me take care of this unpleasant business."

Mary went into their private living quarters as he answered the call from His Lordship.

"Director Lloyd here."

The well-known image of Lord Neptune appeared on the communicator screen.

"My Director. I have been trying to contact you. Is everything alright? "

Adam stared at the screen, knowing the Tschaaa Lord was looking directly back at him thanks to the wonders of modern science.

"You really want to know?"

"But of course. I care about you and your mates, your children. I have an extreme fondness for you and all your extended family as you call them.”

Adam felt his gorge and rage rising.

“Oh really? You care about our children, our Young? Then why did those creatures and beasts of your creation target newborn infants in Montana? Why did they indiscriminately kill women and children in a hospital?   Tell me that, you’re so called Lordship. Explain ‘that’ to me.”

“Come now, Adam. That was the Krakens doing…”

“Excuse me. Do I have a large neon sign, a big red “S” for Stupid on my face? Have I ever struck you as being stupid, Neptune?”

“Of course not. I would not have made you Director if you were.” The Tschaaa Lords social tentacles began to move in a way that signified agitation, emotion.

“Then why in Hell are you treating me as if I am stupid? You don’t think I have it figured out that the Krakens and Reverend Kray act at your bidding? You think you and your fellow Squids have some higher moral level above us ignorant apes to justify using humans to slaughter human children? This, after you told me that the slaughter and eating of your own species was an abomination, applauded me for killing cannibal Krakens? Answer me!”

Lord Neptune’s body color began to darken, some areas almost black in color, signifying extreme anger. The translation device at first spit out snaps and crackles. Then it formed the Tschaaa Lord’s rage into human words. “You dare to question me? You dare to order me? You overstep your bounds!” The Tschaaa’s words were booming out as it did the equivalent of yelling in its own language, the translator then presenting it as humanlike raging.

“You exist because of me. If not for me, you and all the others would be hiding in caves after we had pummeled you with rocks and bombs. You were allowed to mate, sire children because of me, no one else.”

“Children that were screwed with genetically, without my knowledge!” Adam yelled back.

Lord Neptune’s body became almost completely black. The connection went dead for a few moments, then was back on, the Tschaaa Lord’s colors now beginning to soften and lighten.

“Congratulations, Director Lloyd. You were able, in your

vernacular, to 'push my buttons', enrage me. A Lord of less intellectual ability would be sending resources to smash you into dust."

Lord Neptune paused, then continued. "Everything I have done has been for your well- being, your fellow human's well-being. Modifications were done to make you all better, as you did with your canine friends. And any other decisions I made in reference to those feral humans in the uncontrolled areas, I did to insure your survival."

The Tschaaa lord manipulated his social tentacles to signify extreme caring and concern.

"You are one on the few beings, including my fellow Lords, which I have been able to converse with on an equal intellectual basis. Maybe I have allowed you too much independence. Maybe you are about to bite the proverbial hand that feeds and cares for you."

Lord Neptune colors were finally back to normal. "I care deeply about you, Adam Lloyd. I think of you as a friend, almost a blasphemy to Tschaaa sensibilities. I tell you this because in some two to three of your weeks, I must meet with the other Lords to answer to what I have done. They blame me for an extreme surge in attacks during the past weeks on Tschaaa, robocops, grays and lizards by humans in their areas of control. Your fellow humans in the Unoccupied State, with the help of Free Japan and Free Russia, are inciting others to revolt against our control. That must not be allowed to continue."

The Tschaaa Lord gave the equivalent of a human sigh through his bodily motions. "I must defend you to the others. Some of them even want the Krakens to be destroyed, Harvested, despite their use as a tool against other Ferals. That is how serious the situation has become."

"Lord Neptune, you have to understand. You Tschaaa have killed off most of the sheep among us. What is left are sheepdogs, wolves and rats. I suggest you try working with the sheepdogs like myself. Otherwise, prepare to fight wolves and rats to the death."

There was silence between the two beings, from different species, one the prey meat source of the other.

"I must go now, Director. You probably already know that I have ordered a final assault against the resisters in Atlanta. There will be much wasted prime dark meat. However, I can no longer try to starve and wait them out. I will look too weak."

"Yes, Lord." Adam said. He knew that they had reached 'the point of no return'. He knew that his survival and the survival of his loved ones were in jeopardy. Adam did not think this Tschaaa Lord would defend the Protocol of Selective Survival much longer. It would be easier to treat all humans as to what they had started out to be during the initial Invasion—meat, nothing more.

Lord Neptune cut the connection. Adam sat for a moment. He wondered if Andrew would suddenly appear, not as protector but as robocop Executioner. Then Adam would know in a micro instant who was independent and who was not. He hit up the Chief on his cellphone.

"Sorry, Willie, but the excrement just hit the rotating blade in epic proportions. I need you here, old friend."

"Be there most skoshi, Boss."

Adam smiled at the slang from their days in Okinawa. Too bad the Tschaaa had not invented time travel. He could sure use a do over.

MINNESOTA, FERAL AREA

The two Osprey V-STOLS hummed along a hundred feet above the ground, using their terrain avoidance radar and sensors. Provided by the Nation State of Deseret at the insistence of General Huff, they carried some of the most important cargo in the history of North America, this third morning since Hell Day.

The lead aircraft carried four women whose actions could and probably would affect the history of humankind, at least on the North American Continent. The four women had gotten up at o-dark-thirty at the former Grand Forks Air Force Base in North Dakota, and had what had been known for decades as the fighter pilot's breakfast—steak and eggs, high protein for potential hard action. The four women all knew each other well, were now a coherent unit of a type rarely seen before. Then again, the mission they were to perform had rarely, if ever, been done before.

During the cozy breakfast at chow hall, opened just for them, their air crew and ground personnel use, Brynhildr Jorgensen had dropped a bombshell.

"I went ahead and married Rolf two days ago," she said between large bites of lean buffalo steak.

Abigail Yamamoto's (fka Jorgensen) mouth had dropped open. "Cousin. I thought you said I could help with your wedding."

"We will have a ceremony when there is time, when all this... Sturm und Drang is done with."

Aleks Smirnov had cocked an eyebrow. "What was the sudden hurry, as if I did not already know."

"As Abigail said about Ichiro. The thought of dying without knowing and realizing his love and passion was unthinkable. Now, I know we'll be together forever, even in Valhalla."

Sandra Paul, Madam President of the Unoccupied States of America, reached over with a smile and squeezed the Shield Maiden's hand.

"I am so very happy for you. I guess I owe you a wedding present."

Brynhildr shrugged. "It was a simple ceremony. Grandma Munsen officiated as an Official of the Old Religion. Here, around my neck is the wedding band. I'll put in on my hand after I know there will be no battle."

Abigail looked at it and smiled. "It is beautiful. Is that a cross on it?"

"Thor's Hammer. We are bound as Warriors as well as husband and wife."

Aleks had smirked a bit. "So, you had to know his passion, his love? Nothing before two nights ago?"

Brynhildr had looked at her cousin Abigail.

"Our Avenging Angel has set a high bar to follow. I was no virgin, I will not lie. But I and Rolf had decided we should wait, to make it... special."

"Was it?" Aleks the Russian Spy pressed.

For the first time ever, Abigail saw a dreamy look in her cousin's eyes.

"You have no idea." All four women began to laugh loudly at this, personnel in the other dining room wondering what the big joke was. Madam President looked at the three much younger women, her eyes a bit moist.

"Three young women, now all with loving husbands. What could be better?"

Abigail had grasped Sandra Paul's hand. "My number one of many mothers, I wished your husband was here physically. But I know he watches over you from the beyond. I feel it in my bones, in my heart."

Sandra squeezed Abigail's hand. "You three are daughters every mother would wish for. Now, we are together as a family unit to perform a very special mission. I'd like to say a little prayer. Brynhildr, it will not involve Thor…"

"He is here nonetheless, Madam President. For we are about to enter possible battle."

Abigail interrupted. "I…composed something I think fits this situation very nicely."

"Well, please, my dear. Have at it. It is probably better than this older woman can come up with."

Abigail had blushed a bit, reached into her pocket and pulled out a folded piece of paper.

"Well, here goes. I hope you won't all laugh or run screaming.'

"As always," said Aleks. "My adopted little sister is too hard on herself. Please, begin."

Abigail cleared her throat, then began.

Blessed are Women
Whose Hearts and Souls
Are Joined Together by Laughter and Tears.
Who Fight for Life, Against All Fears.
Who Face Evil, With Blades of Steel.
Because They Shall Be Known as
SISTERS OF STEEL.

Everyone sat quiet. Then Aleks began to snuffle, tears in her eyes.

"You never told me, Little Sister, you had the soul of a Russian Poet."

"Russian? Viking sensibilities for sure, especially the blades of steel part."

"Join Hands please, Ladies," said Sandra Paul. After they had all joined hands around their table, Madam President smiled.

"Yes, we are true Sisters of Steel. We will fight for our brothers, our husbands, our mothers, fathers, and our entire families. Especially our children."

Aleks looked at the President. "Yes, even trolls who pass as children."

They began to laugh, knowing it may be awhile before they felt like laughing again.

And now the four women, representing all of humankind no matter the race, color or creed, were speeding toward the rising sun. Sandra Paul, through the efforts of Mikhail Ispear and Colonel Bonnie Bardun, had managed to establish contact with the unnamed Breeder who had reached out to the Humans. Now they were headed toward Duluth, Minnesota. There they would meet the Tschaaa Breeder in a large warehouse on the shores of Lake Superior.

They were in the lead V-STOL, with Shannon Bell acting as co-pilot. She was beginning to transition from choppers, and Madam President had requested that she be on this mission as symbol of continued cooperation between the U.S.A and Deseret. In addition, two Crew Chiefs were on board to assist in loading, off-loading, and the care and feeding of a Browning 50 caliber heavy machine gun.

The second V-STOL had the special Security and Assault Team incase everything went south. Twelve members of the Deseret Twenty, close comrades to Abigail. Lieutenant Ruth Young, who had been on the mission with Abigail when they had met Torbin, was the Officer in Charge. She had walked up to the four special women and saluted as they were preparing to depart. Abigail had ignored military decorum and had hugged her hard.

"It had been too long since I have seen you, my fellow Avenging Angel."

"I wished I could have been part of the Honor Guard for your Wedding, but other duties called."

She introduced Ruth to the other three women.

"Madam President, Colonel Smirnov, Special Agent Jorgensen, this is my comrade in arms who was with me when I first met Torbin Bender. We went through much together over some six years."

After the other three had shook her hand, knowing a close friend of Abigail must be good people, Lt. Young looked at Sandra Paul.

"Ma'am, if things go bad, we will get you all out. I swear on my life, my Church and my Lord, Jesus Christ."

President Paul thought she looked so young to be so serious. But then so was Abigail.

"I have complete faith in your abilities, Lieutenant. But I hope your firepower will not be necessary."

"I for one hope you stay close," interjected Aleks. "All we allowed to take with us are blade weapons. If the Squids are less than honest…"

"Think positive, Colonel. I think everything will turn out just fine."

"Yes, Madam President." Aleks reply was not exactly vibrant in its positivity.

Soon the Four were boarding the V-STOL. They would be forever known as The Four in histories written about this meeting between Females of two very different, yet in some ways, similar species. For that is how people in history are often remembered, by titles rather than individual names.

And now, just over an hour later, their aircraft was approaching the warehouse where they would have the historical meeting. With practiced ease, the Deseret pilot, with Lieutenant Shannon Bell looking on, switched the tilt rotor aircraft from horizontal to vertical flight and set down in large parking lot next to the target warehouse. The Four wasted no time in exiting, the three younger women forming a protective triangle around the President.

Abigail had the katana given her by Princess Akiko, with a signature Banshee Blade, the Squid Killer, on her belt. Brynhildr had her two signature fighting axes plus a Banshee Blade. Aleks had a Banshee Blade as well as the fighting knife Hannah Weitz had tried to give Torbin . She had appropriated it after he turned it down in a bit of emotional pique over Hannah spending time making blades instead of jewelry. Her husband was sometime full of surprises.

Even Madame President had a Banshee Blade, given to her by a Lieutenant Lupe Peña toward the end of Hell Day. "Here, Madam President. Every Sister of Steel needs a good blade. I can get another one." The Banshee Officer had told her.

The four women moved slow, cautious as they approached the designated meeting building.

"Testing, testing, one two three. Do you hear me Madam President?"

"Loud and clear, Colonel Bardun. How am I?"

"Loud and clear also. Now, you other Ladies…."

All the communications checks went well. The second Security and Assault Team V/STOL was also acting as an aerial communications relay station to the special listening post and communications center established at Grand Forks. Manning the center was Colonel Bettie Bardun and Intelligence Officer Mikhail Ispear, the two humans most knowledgeable of Tschaaa language, communications, and psychology in the entire world. All of the Four were wired for sound and video feeds, so that Bardun and Ispear could give them real time support and information. It was assumed the Breeder would have a translator device like the one Lord Neptune used to communicate with the Director as well. This translator had been seen during a couple of broadcasts that were an attempt to diffuse past barbaric acts by the Krakens and the Tschaaa. Although the broadcasts were failures, they showed the U.S.A. exactly the communication and translation capabilities the Squids had and used.

Thus, four very nervous women made their way into the interior of the huge warehouse, once used as a major shipping facility for Duluth and trade across the Great Lakes. The back wall of the huge warehouse had been taken out so there was much ambient light. And, it had allowed the Falcon aerial battlecruiser to fly in and conceal itself.

"There is a Falcon in here, Ichiro." Abigail communicated directly to her husband, flying Cover Air Patrol some fifty miles away with Colonel Cliff Hunter in two Japanese Super Eagles F-15SJs, keeping fairly low and slow so as not to attract attention from the eye in the sky. They were each armed with new hypersonic missiles that were capable of catching the Ram-Jet Deltas should any show up, as well as hopefully do damage to a Falcon. Ichiro and Cliff had more successful air to air operations against the Tschaaa combined than anyone else on the planet.

"The individuals had to get there somehow, Abigail. We are just minutes away."

"Roger that."

The Four kept walking, looking at everything in the large warehouse. Then they saw the Tschaaa come from behind the Falcon. Four Squids.

"They are here," Madam President called out.

The Four tried to position their bodies so their cameras could broadcast the images of the four aliens as the Tschaaa approached, using the crab-like ability of walking on land they could accomplish for short distances.

"Semi-skeleton cartilage system they have is somewhat efficient it seems," said Bettie Bardun, exobiologist."

"My husband could have told you that after his knife fight with one," said Aleks.

"All right, ladies," Sandra Paul interjected. "Time for me to do the talking."

Madam President walked slowly toward the approaching Tschaaa. Two of the recognizable females by their shorter social tentacles and daintier hands had long halberd type pole weapons, flanking what could only be the Breeder who had broadcast the request, the almost plea for a meeting. But hanging back was another individual Tschaaa, who moved a bit jerky.   Ispear's voice burst on the communication system as he began to chatter in Romanian.

"English." Madam President commanded.

"It is she. It is… one of them. I knew it… "

"Explain, now!" Sandra Paul had no time for B.S. Too much hung in the balance.

"The female hanging back. It is an Oracle, a Seer, a Sibyl, a type of female shaman, a foreteller… I have only heard of them in intercepted transmissions."

"Which means?"

Before anyone could answer, the breeder spoke, the translation machine she had strapped to her body almost instantly broadcasting what she said in loud English.

"You are She. You are the Female Human Lord… No, that is not… you are Madam President."

While the others were taken a bit off guard by the loud language, Sandra Paul was not. She stepped closer, showing her hands palms out.

"I come with my hands empty. I think the fact we both have five fingers, or digits, should be a basis for understanding."

The breeder, catching on to the volume of the President's voice, began to adjust her translator. "There, that should be better… Madam President. You have efficient hearing."

"I also pride myself on being a good listener."

The breeder paused for a moment, absorbing what she had just heard.

"Yes. Listening as opposed to hearing. I understand, Madam President. We must both listen this day."

Madam President took another step closer, which caused the other of the Four to also move, which set off alike reaction of the two Earth black bear sized Tschaaa female warriors.

"I have the one on the left, cousin," Brynhildr said in Norwegian.

"I have the other, cousin." Abigail replied.

Sandra Paul was an excellent reader of body language. Even though she was dealing with ten limbed creatures, she could see what was happening. Protect their breeder, the human is a threat.

"Ladies, freeze." Even the Tschaaa froze in place at the sound of her voice. The breeder began to wave her social tentacles in soft, rhythmic almost dance like motions.

"Calm the young," broke in Ispear. "That is calm the young, they fear."

"You are trying to… calm us down, correct?" Sandra asked.

"Yes," answered the breeder. "In the Crèche, large groups of young will become afraid, or too excited. They will rush about, slamming into each other, into the reefs, the Caregivers. They can be injured. We females must prevent that. And sometimes, we breeders sometimes see a need to calm our fellow adults as well."

It dawned on Sandra. This was the opening she needed, the common ground.

"Yes, that is true. Our young often dash around also, are hurt, or hurt others. As do some of our adults, who may have never really grown up." The President paused, then spoke again.

"My friends call me Sal. What may I call you?"

The Breeder began to move very slowly toward Sandra, now Sal, then stopped just within reach of her social tentacles. The alien raised them, showed her empty hand structures.

"I choose the name Elizabeth, after a great leader of yours in your history. I studied much of your history as my Lord has such an interest in it. You could not pronounce my Tschaaa name. Is Elizabeth… correct?"

Sandra smiled, still showing her empty hands. "Yes. It is a fine name in our history… Elizabeth."

"Sal, may I … touch you? I have never touched a human."

"How about I show you how we clasp hands in greeting, Elizabeth? It was a way in our history that we showed others we had no weapons in our hands, ready to strike."

Elizabeth the Breeder reached out with both hands, and Sandra known as Sal to her friends took them. She had thought they would feel slimy, cold. Instead, they felt delicate, a bit cool to the touch. Any hate she felt toward the Tschaaa seemed to dissipate

"Cool hands, warm heart." It just popped into her head and then out her mouth.

"Your digits feel warm, human known as Sal. Warmth means you have passion, caring for others. You wish to warm them in cold waters. Our Young grow best in warm waters."

The two completely alien species held each other's hands, looked into each other's eyes. The two females, current and past breeders, mothers, stood lightly grasping each other's hands, becoming used to the closeness of the other. Then Elizabeth spoke again. "I have another female here who wishes to talk to you. To touch also. She has touched a human female before, years ago. She still searches for that human breeder."

"Is that the young female behind your two warriors?"

"Yes. She chose the name Cassandra. She said that would have special meaning for you."

The President knew then that this would be much more of a unique meeting than just between two separate alien species with a history of conflict if that was possible. Now, there was a feeling, a touch of the supernatural.

"Why, yes. I would be glad to meet Cassandra. It is our understanding she has a… special standing in your culture."

Elizabeth moved her social tentacles to signify a very positive 'yes'.

"I can see you and your companions have studied us as we have studied you."

Sal smiled. "Maybe it could have been different if females had met first, completely away from Earth. Before the rocks were cast."

Elizabeth's body colors began to dull a bit.

"She is a bit distressed about that comment," Mikhail whispered into Madam President's ear pierce. Quickly, Sandra Paul tried to stop the development of any bad feelings.

"I did not mean to make it sound as if this situation is of your making, Elizabeth. I just..."

"You were just stating the truth, Sal, as a leader should. We Tschaaa used to pride ourselves as having a culture based on truth, on facts. Some of our ancient... thinkers may be the right word, told us we were more truthful and honest in our communications than any species in the universe. Now, since coming to Earth, and your lovely oceans, I begin to wonder if something has changed in us."

'Oh Dear Lord', the President thought. 'There is a serious schism occurring in their society. Is that something I can use, or... will it lead to worse things happening?'

"Elizabeth, we humans have a long history of lying, cheating and stealing from our neighbors. We fought uncountable Wars where we killed each other. My understanding is that you Tschaaa have no such history of organized warfare, of killing each other."

Sal saw a definite shiver pass through Elisabeth's body, and two of her limbs started to go black.

"Danger..." Mikhail started to say into the Four's earpierces.

"I am sorry," Elizabeth blurted out. "The thought of what war does is very distressing to me. Individuals killing others young, children. This has a direct connection as to who Cassandra is, why she is."

At the mention of her name again, the agitated and nervous twitching Tschaaa female began to move closer to Sal in slow motion.

"She is a Sibyl, an Oracle due to extreme stress, pain and psychic hurt," Mikhail tried to state as fast as possible. "She saw, experienced the death of many children..."

It hit Sandra 'Sal' Paul like a ton of bricks. Her blood ran cold. The President knew in her guts that 'she' had caused this. Casandra had been there when the off-course missile meant to kill Lord Neptune, destroy his headquarters with a nuke, had failed. A direct result was the death of thousands of Tschaaa children. Cassandra had been there. Sal could just feel it in her bones.

The Tschaaa Oracle, Seer, psychic and shaman-like character was near glacial in her movements as she inched closer to Madam President. At the same time, her fingers were twitching, twisting on her feminine hands. Sal could not control the tears that began to run down her cheeks. She knew it was crazy to feel sorry about causing the death of offspring from a species that would just as soon kill and eat her as look at her. But it would be like killing feral kittens when she was a child. You knew they would grow up to devastate your chickens and ducks, but they were so innocent as babies. It was not their fault they were born wild.

"You…shed water…from your eyes." Cassandra spoke through her translator. "You shed tears, like the other." The Sibyl slowly reached her right social tentacle out, touched Sal's cheek. It felt like the wisp of a feather as the Alien removed a tear and brought it back to her equivalent mouth.

All the others, Tschaaa, humans, were transfixed. It was if the Tschaaa Sibyl had a psychic al hold on everyone. Then Sal broke the trance.

"I am so sorry, Cassandra. It is my fault the young in your care were killed. I have done something evil, terrible…"

Cassandra jerked a bit. "No. We females did not start this. My Crèche had been content to live in our ocean, eat the bounty there for tens of thousands of our years. Then male prophets had us taste the dark flesh of the two legs on our home planet. It was never the same again."

"My God and Lord Jesus," Abigail was heard to whisper over the communication link. "Adam and Eve and the apple. They were cast out of Eden…"

The Tschaaa Oracle then began to sing. It was the like best parts of every Earth deep sea whale song ever recorded.

Out of the blue, Brynhildr stepped closer. With her beautiful Wagnerian voice, lately demonstrated at the last Christmas pageant, she began to sing along with Sibyl, somehow making music that was similar to whale songs. Cassandra turned her attention to the tall Shield Maiden, began to sway back and forth in rhythm. Brynhildr began to match her, sway for sway.

Aleks teared up. "It is about children. I can feel it," the Russian Spy said out loud.

"It is about all the lost children," Elizabeth the Breeder then said. "We sing for the sadness of their passing. Also about the joy that we knew them, cared for them. Plus the secure knowledge that they have returned to our Ocean Mother."

The Tschaaa Female looked intently at Sal. "This is something the males never understand."

Cassandra finally ended her song and began to slowly approach Brynhildr. She held out her right hand and the Shield Maiden took it.

"I never thought I would say 'well met' to an alien Squid, but I think. Cassandra, you and yours are an exception.

"You are strong, honest," Cassandra replied. "You sing well for a two-legged land dweller also."

The Oracle then looked at Abigail.

"May we touch?"

Now it was Abigail's turn to move slow, as she approached Cassandra. Memories of what the grays had tried to do to her, what was done to her on orders of the Tschaaa flooded in. She forced herself to touch the Oracle's digits. After she did, the Special Female began to moan.

"I sense you were used, hurt by Lords claiming they were doing right. You also have great losses, your Crèche was decimated. You suffered a shock…went away…" The Oracle began to shake. Abigail surprised herself and stepped forward, grabbing the other hand of the Tschaaa.

"Cassandra, what is happening?"

The female had closed her very large eyes. Now they popped open.

"There is hope for me. If you can come back from the Gone, I may someday also."

Abigail sucked her breath in. "You sensed it, my little death."

"Yes. You are Sibyl also. I greet a sister."

The ten limbed creature now turned her attention on Aleks. The Russian operative stepped forward and clasped hands with Cassandra.

"You recently…gave birth. You rejoice in your young. May they grow."

"One of the creatures your males brought almost took my sons. So, to say I trust you all would be an overstatement."

Cassandra looked deep into Aleks' eyes. "We no longer trust our own kind either."

The Oracle, one who had been "touched" as some human societies would describe it, began to speak to all the assembled personages. "Elizabeth and I knew we must stop this killing of young. It is no longer a matter of eating meat, it has become an instrument of hate and revenge. Innocents are killed for the sins of others. It must stop." As she finished, Cassandra seemed to be exhausted. One of the female warriors moved, helped to support her and moved her back to an area behind all the rest where she could spread out on the floor like an Earthly octopus.

"She is exhausted," said Madam President.

"Yes, Sal. It is…hard being her. She should have died from the shock of the loss. She did not. As you did not from the loss of your young."

"You sensed I had a loss also, Elizabeth. Yes, I lost a daughter and a son during the Invasion. I have a daughter by blood left. But I was just told recently that I have thousands of sons and daughters by adoption. So I will never be alone."

The Tschaaa breeder paused, then spoke. "In that way humans are tougher than Tschaaa. You seem to handle the unbelievable and unbearable so much better than us."

Sal had smiled. "We are mean, nasty. Which is why we will not surrender to Lord Neptune, become his servants."

"I must tell you now that I am Lord Neptune's favorite breeder," Elizabeth replied. "He has told me that our offspring are smarter and stronger than all others. So, unlike many sires, Senior Lords, he seems to listen to female opinions about matters other than raising young."

Sal weighed her reply, then spoke. "So, you plan to influence Your Lord to end this slaughter. I question your ability to do that, based on this…addiction they have to eating us. But I am willing to stand by as you try."

The alien continued. "Within the next three of you humans weeks, there will be a large meeting of all the Lords still on Earth off the area you call the Bahamas. At that, Lord Neptune will try to keep the other Lords form demanding a complete eradication of all humans not contained and confined in areas such as Cattle Country. Ferals will be hunted down and harvested, the Unoccupied States and Free Japan and Free Russia will be destroyed, by rock strikes if necessary. The idea of treating you as clients such as those you call lizards will disappear."

The President of the U.S.A. stood straight on her Spine of Steel. "You know there is a high probability of Mutual Assured Destruction for both species if that is attempted. We still have some nuclear weapons, as well as other Weapons of Mass Destruction."

Elizabeth began to move her tentacles in certain patterns.

"She signs extreme frustration, with some anger tinged with fear." Mikhail broke in as quick as he could.

"I know, Madam President. But our males are often stubborn and stupid, to the young's detriment. And we do not have the knowledge and practice of total war as do you humans. "

Sal took a deep breath before she spoke. "We humans of both genders can also be stubborn and stupid. I also know that your older Lords and many family members are about to leave the solar system by using our sun to slingshot the remaining Crèche generational starships on the long trip home. On those ships are at least two billion human corpses, as well as some human breeding pairs to try and save those you left behind."

"You are quite well informed, Sal."

"Humans have always been good at snooping into other people's business. No, let me be very blunt and honest. This is not personal. I take no pleasure in even considering these actions."

Sandra 'Sal" Paul paused for a moment. 'One shot, Lady, that's it,' she thought. Then she answered.

"I will arrange a very secure system of communication so that you may contact me directly. I must plan for the worse, so if you fail, I will have to tell my fellow Homo sapiens that it is a fight to the death. Millions will die, the Earth will dissolve into a Long Winter that will last decades as we two species fight. I believe even those under the Director's control will fight, not accept total imprisonment awaiting being harvested. You will be lucky to have any warm oceans for your young, Elizabeth. I am sorry. But we cannot accept total enslavement. We are not Cattle, contrary to what Lord Neptune believes."

There was quiet. Then Cassandra stirred from behind them.

"I will make the Tschaaa Lords understand. They always listen to ones such as I."

"I hope you are right. I hope with all my heart."

Sal reached her hands out and took Elizabeth's long alien digit hands in hers.

"No matter what happens, I think we are friends."

"Yes Sal, I agree. A first in Tschaaa history I believe."

Madam President glanced at Cassandra, who was laying down again.

"She said she met, touched a human years ago, and is still hunting for her."

"Yes. About one of your years after the Lords attacked, Cassandra met a female breeder in a sea craft outside of the area you call Miami. The Sibyl said she thought she had heard the term 'Coastie' as she had seen this Breeder before, in the local bay. The breeder was crying. Cassandra said she sensed she had just lost a young, a child. She tasted human tears for the first time, said she knew even then we two species had a connection through the care we show our young."

The Breeder known as Elizabeth reached up and gently touched Sal's cheeks. "I hope Cassandra finds this breeder, so they may be friends as we are becoming. But now, we must go. If we are gone too long, questions will be asked."

"I was going to ask who flew the Falcon here."

"The warrior Dorothy there, with the other, Helen is the name she took, assisting. We were allowed to borrow it by a cyborg, what you call a robocop."

"Did this benefactor have a name? I understand many do, having been human quite recently."

"His name is Andrew."

The Four were subdued after saying their farewells. Everyone else knew they were still in one piece due to the real time monitoring. The monitors also knew how draining it was to converse with beings whose members had been killing and eating humans for some seven years.   As they were back aboard the V/STOL and headed back to Grand Forks, Sandra Paul called Colonel Bardun on a special encrypted cellphone.

"Yes, Madam President."

"The… item. How efficient is it against adults?"

"Fifty percent fatality rate, with about another twenty percent being badly crippled for months if not years later."

"Over ninety percent fatality with the young and the very old, correct?"

"Yes Ma'am."

"Colonel, there is going to be a bit of a change in plans…"

"Yes Madam President. I already figured as such."

"Well, the reason…"

"Ma'am, begging your pardon, I don't need an explanation. One, you are my Commander in Chief. Two…well, the idea of killing the equivalent of puppies and kittens because they might grow up and bite me always rubbed me the wrong way."

CHAPTER 37

CATTLE COUNTRY
ATLANTA, GEORGIA

As Madam President was having the historic meeting with the Tschaaa females, Malcolm Carter was trying to stay alive. He and his comrades also tried to fight back against the invading forces. It was a severe uphill struggle.

Bashir Gupta and Reggie Adams homegrown and improvised weapons had been surprising in their effectiveness. Crude but powerful black powder rockets at close range were a danger to even the robocops. Extreme mechanical ballistae based on Roman designs launched metal bolts that even pierced the sides of the wheeled battle and harvester robots. And of course the firearms they had took a toll of the renegade human Krakens.   But the enemy kept coming.   A Falcon was used to collapse a building being used as a stronghold. The Warrior/Soldier Class of artificial beings, called Poor Man's Robocops, were deadly with their electromagnetic automatic bolt guns. The energy charged projectiles penetrated the limited body armor and cover of the surviving residents of Atlanta with few problems.   The traitor human Krakens were better organized and trained in small unit tactics than before. They moved and cleared areas at a steady rate, left many bodies in their wake. There was little effort on the part of the Squid minions to harvest dark meat, nor preserve it. Survivors quickly learned there was no surrender. Show yourself, you were shot down, your body left where it fell. The only exception was a few cooking pits the Krakens set up for their more 'hardcore' followers. The Tschaaa seemed to look the other way as a species ate its own members, contra to the Aliens supposed core beliefs.

Malcolm was in one of the many pre-planned bolt holes, hiding with Red, Big Joe, and Dawoud. Red had just finished bandaging Big Joe's arm, the result of a ricocheting bullet.

"Is Joe going to live, Red?"

"Hell, Boss," Big Joe answered. "I'm too big and ugly to die. I'd scare even Saint Peter at the pearly gates."

"If God really cared about how we or others looked," Dawoud interjected. "He would not have made the Djinn Squids. I find it hard to believe the Squid mothers think their offspring are attractive."

"Well, my lapsed Muslim Friend," asked Malcolm. "How did little Squids come about if their parents find other individuals so repulsive?"

Big Joe had laughed and flashed a large grin. "Boss, you've heard of a three bagger, right? One bag over the females head, one over the body…"

"Now if you men are through with your rude and crass jokes," interrupted Red. "What is our next move?"

Malcolm smiled. "Sorry. Humor sometimes helps keep your head from exploding from the stress."

The Mayor and Leader of the Atlanta Insurrection looked at Dawoud. "Any more communication with the outside?"

"No, sorry. We managed to get some short wave information out this morning to the U.S. listening posts, but then the building the short wave was in was attacked by a Delta Fighter. That is the last I heard from that communication team."

Malcolm grunted. "Where are the white folks when you need them?"

"They suffered a vicious attack of their own, Malcolm." Red said. "They have many of their own problems."

"Oh yeah? That little set two that had at Malmstrom is peanuts to this," Malcolm began to fume, then stopped himself. The Free Areas had tried to send aid. They had even gotten Dawoud into Atlanta during the siege. But that did not detract from the danger the people of color in Atlanta were facing now.

"Sorry, Red. I didn't mean to snap. I just think everything was too little, too late. Way too many people just walked into our Cattle Country. Everyone should have fought more."

"Fear, my leader." Dawoud answered. "Most were afraid, hoped they would be spared after the initial massive assaults had stopped."

"Yeah, Dawoud. And all it did was delay the inevitable for many. Fools."

Everyone was silent for a few moments. Then Malcolm spoke."Alright, so much for the pity party. Now, gentlemen and gentle lady, let's see who else is alive and functional. We may still be able to break the circle, get some people out…"

CHAPTER 38

GREAT FALLS MONTANA,
FORMER UNITED STATES FEDERAL COURT BUILDING

Special Agent Brynhildr Jorgensen sat cooling her heels outside of Commissioner Paul Miller's office. He had asked to see her as soon as she was able to after her part of the history making meeting of the Four and The Breeder. So of course, after she had gotten back and cleaned up, she had contacted their Sector Communications and found out where the Commissioner was hanging his hat this week. He did not stay in one place too long, unless it was to visit Emily Anders at her Great Falls Veterinarian Clinic in Great Falls.

So, when she heard he was here, she made an appointment to see him. She knew the President had already briefed him on what at happened at the warehouse in Duluth. Even now, it still seemed surreal to her. Actually communicating, forming an initial bond, albeit a very tenuous one, with females of a species that kept trying to eat you, without Brynhildr taking a battle ax to them, was not something she had ever imagined. After Hell Day, it seemed even doubly bizarre.

Paul Miller opened the door to his office and greeted her.

"Agent Jorgensen. Glad you all made it back in one piece. I had extreme doubts which I had communicated to Madam President before you all left.”

Brynhildr stood and shook his hand.

“And of course, Sir, Madam President ignored them.”

The Commissioner chuckled. “Yes, she has her own way of doing things. But, judging by the way things are turning out, her path seems to be the right one. Now, come on in. There is someone here with whom you need to talk.”

Brynhildr walked in and saw the very large and muscular Dogman, Abigail’s Uncle Buck, sitting in one of two padded chairs near the Commissioner’s desk. Lying next to him was his huge mastiff, Matt.

“Hello Sir. That is a large dog you have there.”

“Call me Dogman, I’m no sir. And this is Matt. Say ‘Hi’ Matt.”

The huge canine rose and stuck his muzzle out to Brynhildr. She let him sniff the back of her hand, then she began to scratch his ears. Matt gave an appreciative groan.

“He likes you. So I like you.”

Brynhildr looked at Dogman. “That simple, huh.”

He shrugged. “My dogs are a good judge of character. So I don’t question them.”

Brynhildr moved over and sat in the other chair.

“So, Boss. What do you want me to do?”

“It’s what I want you and Abigail’s uncle here to do together,” the Commissioner answered.

She looked at Dogman, then at the Commissioner.

“Now, Sir, you have my full attention.”

Paul Miller smiled. “I figured I would. Your partner, Agent David Jackson, was able to elicit thru persuasive means some excellent and unusual information from his former prison mate, now captured Kraken. There was information about the shifts of power and other shenanigans among the Krakens, the Director and other inhabitants of the Occupied Areas. After a short discussion with me, Dogman has agreed to go back into the Tschaaa Controlled Areas, specifically the Key West area. I think things are about to explode down there, to the detriment of the Director. He knows his way around, should be able to get you close to Adam Lloyd.”

“My understanding from Abigail is that Dogman may have some Kraken enemies now,” the Shield Maiden replied. “Something about his dogs taking some Krakens down when they tried to snatch her and

Torbin Bender.”

“Dogman, care to explain?” Commissioner Miller said to the large man.

“Kraken Commander Talbot and some others tried to hurt Abigail and my Dogs. His followers may dislike me, but I had a reputation among the Krakens and other people in the Controlled Areas. I’ve… done things for the Church, the Krakens. And many of the people who became Krakens or hang around them still understand family.”

Brynhildr looked hard at Dogman. “And if they don’t… understand?”

He shrugged. “Then they may die. Simple.”

Everyone sat quiet for a moment. Then, a small grin formed on Brynhildr’s face.

“I think you were a follower of Thor in a previous life, my very large friend. And since we will be protecting each other’s backs, we will become close friends.”

Now it was Dogman’s turn to smile, even if it was very slight in nature.

“Just that simple?” He asked.

“Abigail and I are cousins, even if very slight, on her Father’s side. And she is now a close friend who loves you. I trust her judgement as you trust you mastiff Matt’s.”

“Fine,” a grinning Commissioner interjected. “Now, here are the initial details on what I hope to accomplish…”

A half hour later, the two new partners left the building together.

“So, Dogman, when will you be ready to leave?”

“I could leave now. But I suggest tomorrow morning. You have a new husband.”

Brynhildr smiled. “News travels fast around here.”

Dogman scratched Matt’s ears. “Spend the time you can with loved ones. You may not see them for a long time.”

“Like you and Abigail?”

Dogman looked at the statuesque female warrior and law enforcement agent.

“Yes. And you are family now, since you are family to Abigail. So, I have your back, always.” Brynhildr cocked her head a bit. “No Mrs. Dogman, ever?”

“No. I am a hard man. Too hard for most women. Dogs and I

understand each other better."

"But you like women. Yes?"

"Yes. I'm not gay."

Brynhildr grinned, then linked arms with him.

"Let me tell you, Uncle Buck to my cousin, about these hard Daughters of the Norse who are looking for a few hard men…"

CHAPTER 39

Torbin Bender looked out over the stern of the one hundred fifty foot Wet Stern Fishing Trawler as it pulled out form the dockage at Weymouth, Nova Scotia. Once again he marveled a bit at how this mission had come together in such a short time. Just ten days since the soon to be famous Meeting of the Four and the Breeder, all the resources of the Free Allied Nations had come together.

When it was decided that another attempt at a long range air attack was out of the question as word was the Tschaaa had learned from past mistakes, Thor Heyerdahl of the New Vikings said he had a large boat stashed in Nova Scotia that might be useful. He said that the Squids were already allowing limited fishing by humans along the East Coast, as long as you stayed within ten miles and away from the Crèche's young. This was especially true in the colder waters. Thor had said his son Bjorn could help captain it, being an experienced fisherman in Northern European waters and also completed some runs down the east coast since they had fled to America.

After seeing the size of the ship, Pappy Gunn said the large fish hold would be perfect as a both a hidden storage and launch area for the She-Bear missile and its special payload, after a few modifications. So the die was cast. A fishing trawler used for a secret mission, much like the Russian had done for years under the old USSR. In fact, Stalin soon came up with the names of six Spetsnaz with good fishing and naval experience. Bjorn and five of his Norse Fellows with extensive ocean fishing experienced were also selected, as were six Americans. Among these were SSgt. Wall and SSgt. Benjamin Black, both former team members of Torbin during the Key West nuke attack.

Papa Gunn had a modified C-130 fly the missile and payload to Nova Scotia, with the technicians to modify the trawler. A Deseret VSTOL Osprey flew the rest of the armed personnel two days later. Although in violation of normal military thinking, a newly married team was also brought along. Ichiro was added due to his great experience in handling Squids in close combat. Plus Abigail because, well, she was Abigail, a unique force in the annals of combat. Torbin knew that if something happened to him, the two would insure the mission was carried out. Not to mention the fact if one went the other would probably just stow away rather than allow the other to go into harm's way alone. They had just been married, after all.

The Mission?   To launch the special biological based weapon Colonel Bardun had developed, created specifically to kill Squids. The target had been changed from the terror one of attacking the Crèche young areas to hitting the Tschaaa Lords during their meeting on Lord Neptune's huge Mobile Sea Platform. The Lord had used this Sea Platform as his headquarters since the Key West Attack. Using the targeted biologicals meant heavy Tschaaa casualties for hundreds of miles around, as the weapon would spread for some forty eight hours before a manufactured die off. Once the word got out, there would be a panicked stampede to get the young completely out of the area before they could be affected, though some collateral damage was expected.

If the majority of the Tschaaa Lords were killed, there might be a chance that many survivors would attempt to leave and go to the generational starships that were preparing to leave the solar system after a slingshot around the sun. Or maybe the Tschaaa would realize they were not the apex predator in control, and come to some agreement with the humans as they claimed they would do in some of their hacked historical documents. Or maybe they would go completely bonkers and start laying waste to the Earth with large rocks, screw collateral damage to the oceans. No matter what happened, living under the constant threat of Harvesting was no longer a viable option for many humans. As the saying went, better to die on your feet than live on your knees, especially if at any time you could be butchered to be some Squids meal.

Torbin touched the small packet hanging from a thin chain down to his chest. Only he, Ichiro and Abigail knew the contents. For in the packet were the "No Go Codes", to be used by Madam President if, by some chance, the Breeder called Elizabeth and the Special Female known as Cassandra were able to somehow get the Tschaaa Lords to 'see the light' and sit down with the humans, arrange some type of compromise or treaty of co-existence. Torbin thought the chance of this was on par with finding ice water in Hell, but he was a Marine. If the Commander in Chief said, do this, make this work, he tried his damndest to make it work. Even if making it work meant he may die.

He heard and felt a person behind him. Ichiro, a large wide brim hat to cover his Japanese features form any prying eyes in the Ssy came and stood by him on the ship's rail.

"Deep in thought, my friend?'

"Just reviewing the odds and the possibilities in my head, Ichiro. To be honest, I am surprised we have gotten this far without mass destruction being rained down from above."

"Such destruction would kill many of their young, which is what they hold most dear, Torbin-san."

Torbin sighed. "I hope that holds true. But after seeing their reactions when we killed a bunch by accident with our nuke near Key West, I think their species can fall into a berserker type rage also. And, I bet you there is a Squid version of a sociopath, unable to feel empathy for anything. Either way, some Lord may overreact and bang, long term nuclear winter, massive die offs in all species. Nobody wins, everyone loses."

Ichiro regarded his blood brother. "That will not happen, Torbin-san. I feel it in my bones. If we fail in our attack, we may die, the U.S.A may die, maybe along with Free Japan, but people will survive. And they will crawl back off their knees and fight again. For our species is a warlike one, who kills its own on massive scales. That same brutal and vicious nature is not something the Tschaaa really have. We are meat, not worth their continued hate."

"You really think that, Ichiro? That the Tschaaa don't have it in them for a world-wide genocide?"

The samurai shrugged. "No, I do not believe they do. We gave them ample reason when we tried to kill Lord Neptune, at least reason to turn the Unoccupied States into a complete wasteland if all Lords became involved. It did not happen.   They do not understand total warfare for years on end. If they did, the Stones, Rocks would have fallen again."

"Well, that would explain why it took them so long to really wipe out Atlanta. Reports before we left were that the final assault had begun, screw wasted dark meat."

"It is sad we can do nothing to help, my friend."

"Not without exposing us and using up our still limited resources. Which is what Lord Neptune human advisors probably wish would happen, and told him as such."

Torbin smiled. "No matter what happens, my brother, this has been one hell of a ride."

He stuck his hand out and Ichiro took it, smiling. "Yes. We are the subject of legends, to be passed down for generations."

Torbin made a face. "Please, Ichiro. Not with the 'hero' stuff. I'm just a grunt Marine."

With that, Ichiro took Torbin's hand in both of his, a serious look on his face.

"Colonel Torbin Bender, whether you wish to admit it or not, you are a hero. You do have a special purpose in your life, besides being just a grunt, as you say. I know. I see and feel it."

Torbin chuckled. "I guess I'm outvoted. You, Abigail, that cyborg robocop Andrew, everyone seems to say that I'm something special. Well I don't feel it."

"Just accept it, my blood brother. You have your thousand stitch belt on, yes?"

"Of course. Never leave home without it."

Ichiro then grinned, slapped his friend on his back.

"Then we are ready for glorious battle. I will go below, make sure Captain Sato and Sergeant Porsche Jefferson are completely prepared for their roles."

"Thanks, Ichiro. I'm heading toward the wheel house, check on our Captain and his Helmsman."   Ichiro disappeared down below as Torbin made his way forward.

In the wheelhouse, SSgt. Wall was at the wheel, expertly maneuvering the large fishing trawler out of the seaport area under the watchful eye of Bjorn Heyerdahl.

"Sergeant Wall, I did not know you had Navy blood in you."

SSgt Wall laughed. "I don't, Colonel. Just worked on fishing boats for several summers to make money before I decided that the Military was more for me than the fishing fleet. It frustrated my uncle, who owned the boat out of Seattle."

The Sergeant sighed. "Thanks to the Squids, and a couple of volcanoes, Puget Sound is a wreck. No more fishing for a long while."

"Well, Sergeant." Bjorn interjected. "If you ever wish to start fishing again, let me know. I can use a good helmsman like yourself."

"Coming from you, Sir, that is a serious compliment," the Sergeant answered.

Bjorn looked at Torbin. "Are all your people below, Colonel?"

"Yes, Skipper. A few of the Russians will help you during daylight hours. Some of

your fellow Vikings, with all the coverage on television the last few months, may cause some eye in the sky to get suspicious."

Bjorn nodded in agreement. Heyerdahl's son was as big as his father, but his hair was dark brown, so he was not the stereotypical New Viking everyone expected; tall, huge, blonde or red headed.

"We can make between ten to fifteen knots. That means about two hundred forty to three hundred nautical miles a day on average. We will reach the Northern Bahamas by the end of this week."

Torbin nodded. "We should have an exact plot of the huge Sea Platform by then. The thing is as big as several aircraft carriers. Hard to miss."

"So, we must get to within about twenty miles to launch the weapon, Colonel?"

"Yes, Bjorn. Twenty miles is the goal."

The trawler Captain paused for a moment, then spoke.

"When it is launched from the hold, it will not set us afire, Ya?"

"No Sir. It is sitting in that tube launcher that will use extreme high pressure air to launch it up into the air, clear of the deck before the missile's engines cut in. Then, it goes up and to the target."

"If the rocket engines do not fire?"

"Then it sails to about fifty to a hundred yards off the bow and goes kerplunk into the Atlantic Ocean. The warhead is programmed to expel its munitions about a thousand feet above the Sea Platform in a large shotgun pattern. One hundred of those very light plastic spheres will rain down on and around the sea platform. If it just goes into the water off our bow, the whole shebang sinks, and two small charges will eventually break the nose cone apart, shattering some of the spheres. Until the contents hits salt water, it is dormant."

"The... killer in the spheres. For Squids only, ja?"

Torbin shrugged. "I was told it could make an adult human sick. If you had an allergic reaction, you could die. But on the Tschaaa and other cephalopods, deadly. A killer."

Bjorn smiled. "Sorry that I am acting like a nervous bride, but we New Vikings prefer to die in battle, not poisoned and bedridden."

"No need to apologize, my very large friend. I'd just as soon it goes off without a hitch and the Squids start to die off by the thousands. But, I am not about to test that stuff on myself either. After the Key West Attack, it was decided they Squids would be watching for a launch from the Unoccupied States. This way, we sneak up, launch and, if possible, run."

Torbin glanced around, saw they were well out from the seaport.

"I'll go down below, remind everyone to not screw with our special cargo."

Bjorn grinned. "I told my Vikings they would be thrown overboard if they even touched it."

Torbin laughed. "I have a strange feeling, Bjorn, if you threw someone overboard, they would fly for quite a distance before making quite a splash. Now, Captain, I bid you adieu."

Down below, in the crew quarters, the Russians, Americans and Vikings were all either playing various card games in an attempt to take each other's money, sleeping, or checking their gear for the umpteenth time. They started to rise when he approached.

"At ease, gentlemen and ladies. We're in the field, no need for extra protocol."

He made his way to the back of the large wardroom that doubled as a large sleeping bay. A Russian Sergeant was trying to demonstrate his superior sharpening skills by showing his Spetsnaz combat entrenching shovel to Sumi Sato and Porsche Jefferson. Torbin swore that these Russians were the only troops hornier than a bunch of boot Marines.

"Would you excuse me for a few minutes, Sergeant?"

"Da, of course Colonel."

Sumi, the Japanese "spy" gave the Russian the sweetest smile.

"We will continue the instruction later, Sergeant."

"Da. Yes Ma'am." He flashed a grin, then gave Torbin and the others some space.

He looked at Sumi and chuckled. "You and my wife. Female spies can disarm a man with a smile."

Sumi bowed her head slightly. "Yes Sir. Here, though, we are all on the same side. And they are about to risk their lives to recover Porsche and myself, if part of the play is that we have to be taken by the Krakens to allow you to get close enough to launch. So, a smile? It is cheap payment for my well-being."

Porsche and Sumi were to be barter goods, captives to be used to get by any Kraken sea patrols, something that had started up recently as one neared the Georgia coast and Cattle Country. The story would be that the two women were grabbed when they wandered away from a U.S. military patrol outside the border in the Feral areas. Then, they would be offered as examples of "barter" to provide reasons why the Trawler was hanging around Tschaaa areas. This would also distract the Krakens from looking too close in what they had in the Trawlers hold, which was not fish.

"Sergeant Jefferson, you down for this?"

The large African-American smiled. "Yes, Sir. Just as long as I'm not left to be some Squid's snack."

Torbin grinned. "No danger of that. I'd have to answer to the Banshee Commander, my wife, and a certain Senior Training Instructor."

Porsche's eyes widened a bit. "He asked about me?"

"Stalin never forgets those who last through his training. And, he told me to tell you that you owe him a Christmas dinner this year."

"Sir. I..."

"No need to explain, Sergeant. You are now one of Stalin's own.

Most of the Spetsnaz here from Russia were trained by him at one time or another. So, you are in a very special group. Just remember that."

With a very serious look on her face, Sergeant Jefferson answered, "Yes Sir. I will."

She paused, then said "Thank you, Sir. You both gave me another chance."

"Actually, you earned it. We need tough troops like you. Now, ladies, please excuse me. I need to check our special cargo."

Torbin went to the hold, where two armed personnel were watching the twelve foot She-Bear missile. He put the two men, one Russian and one American, at ease and walked around the weapon. 'Punch in a few codes,' he thought. 'And swoosh, death and destruction befalls the Tschaaa, like a Biblical plague.'

He looked at the two soldiers.

"How are you two doing?' Torbin asked.

"Just fine, Colonel," said the American.

"Colonel," the Russian asked. "This will kill all the Squids?"

"Not all of them. But a whole bunch of them. There will be other weapons like this if need be."

"Da, that is fine with me, Colonel. They killed my family in Russia. How you say, this is payback."

Torbin looked at the Spetsnaz troop. "You got that right. Carry on."

As he went up the ladder to the deck, Ichiro appeared.

"Colonel, they need you on the secure radio link. Something has changed."

Malcolm Carter was woken by an abrupt large splash of water to the face. It took him a few seconds to realize where he was, and who had thrown the water in his face. He looked up to a sneering face that was completely covered by a Kraken Devil Fish tattoo.

"Hey, meat. You awake now? Good. You get to go for a short walk, take a crap and piss, so you don't mess it up in here the truck. We still have a trip ahead of us."

Malcolm glared at the Kraken capturer. "Anybody ever tell you your breath smells like shit?"

That got the former Mayor of Atlanta a hard slap across the face.

"Yeah? Well, you look like shit, are the same color as shit. So, get ready to stretch your legs."

The Kraken started to leave, then turned around.

"Cause us any trouble, we start hacking pieces from you friends here. Got it?" The guard stormed off. Malcolm looked at the other occupants of the tractor trailer truck container, his friends. The only real friend was Red, the East Indian Princess with the Bollywood looks. She looked back at him and tried to produce a smile. However, she was still in shock from seeing Big Joe and Dawoud die.

After days of fleeing from hidey hole to hidey hole, they were finally trapped in a deep basement under a city works building. It had been part of the system of tunnels and former sewers and storm water drains they had been using to stay one step ahead of the Krakens, robocops, and harvester robs. There had even seen a few grays and Llzards in the attacking army. As they and the others who were hiding with them tried to flee, the walls began to collapse in around them. The Soldier Class beings,were smashing through the walls, as if they had no fear. Which they did not. In support were two of the cyborg robocops. Malcolm heard human Kraken voices further back. Reggie Adams and Professor Bashir Gupta, the creators and manufacturers of many of the deadly improvised weapons they had used against the invaders, had been killed just hours before when they too had been cornered. Now it was Malcolm's turn.

But instead of killing them, the cyborgs seemed to be trying to capture the small group alive. They seemed to know exactly who they had found. As one of the robocops pushed past the artificial Soldiers and made a grab for Red, he heard Dawoud yell. "Allahu Akbar! God is great." Before anyone realized it, he had jumped from a desktop onto the head and shoulders of the robocop, wrapping himself around the cyborg like a blanket.

"No!" Malcolm had yelled as he knew what was coming next. The shaped charge suicide vest Dawoud had somehow produced (or maybe Reggie and Bashir had helped) exploded into the head and shoulders of the robocop, killing it. The explosion had also killed Dawoud, spattering large pieces of him about. Everything seemed to stop as the explosion had a stunning effect to all those nearby.

"Run!" Malcolm had yelled. Then one of the soldiers grabbed him.

He heard Big Joe bellow and saw the former NFL Lineman smash into the artificial creature. His bull rush slammed even the large soldier back into the nearby wall. Big Joe jammed his Bowie knife into a body armor joint near the throat of the soldier, and was rewarded with a squirt of some foul-smelling bluish liquid that must pass as its blood. A large caliber boom came from the direction of the Krakens and Joe's head disappeared in a red mist.

"Stop." The robocop broadcast over some internal speaker. "They are to be taken alive." Then it grabbed the screaming Red, and it all became a blur as Malcolm screamed and tried to shoot anything with his pistol that he could. Something hit his head and it all went black.

Now he was sitting in the back of this truck trailer with Red and a half dozen others women and children and one unconscious black male he did not recognize. He had overheard the Krakens talking about meeting someone in Savannah, Georgia, so Malcolm figured he was going to be harvested.

'Well,' he thought. 'It was fun while it lasted. And we took a bunch of assholes with us. Too bad the U.S.A. jackasses didn't show up. Then, maybe…'

He shook his head. No use depending on anyone else. Where there was life, there was hope. He would wait and see if the Kraken guards got sloppy. If they did…

FISHING TRAWLER
INTERCOASTAL WATERWAYS, ATLANTIC COAST

Torbin Bender cursed to himself as he mulled over the communication he had just received.

"Goddamn mission creep,' he grumbled.

"Colonel, there is a problem?" It was Abigail, a concerned look on her face.

"It has been my unfortunate experience that when your mission is changed in mid-stream—mission creep—to something fairly unrelated to the task, the gods of combat tend to screw you. Like Murphy's Law. Things that can go wrong, begin to go wrong."

He took a drink from his coffee mug.

"From a mission of mass destruction, to an attempted rescue. Talk about two different missions, trying to be rolled into one. As they said in Old England, it doth not bode well."

"We can do it, Torbin-san," Ichiro opined. "We are imbued with the Samurai Spirit. We have the soldiers with the correct skills. We will make it work."

"And God is with us, my big brother." Abigail added. "Never forget it."

He looked at the two very special warriors. Then he laughed, clapping Ichiro on his back.

"Hell, how can we not succeed with you two willing us to be successful? Wished you two had been around with me when the Tschaaa first attacked. We'd have shown all the Admirals and Generals a thing or two."

"But I was only twelve years old, Torbin." Abigail said.

Torbin looked at his little sister, then began to laugh harder. He hugged her.

"Abigail, even at twelve, I think you would have been a force to reckon with. Come on, let's brief the others on the change. They can help figure out how we can snatch this Mayor of Atlanta from the butcher's block. The person who is taking a chance and leaked this information to us, I plan on buying them as many drinks as possible when this is all over and done."

CHAPTER 41

USA CAPITAL
BISMARCK, NORTH DAKOTA

George Williams found Madam President staring out of the large window in her Oval Office.   The view was a lot flatter than in Alaska, but there were some rolling hills nearby that broke up the scenery.

"Ma'am. The Colonel and his people have been notified of the change."

Still staring out the window, Sandra answered. "You think this is the right move., George? To ask that small group to do even more?"

"Madam President, we owe Malcolm Carter. If for no reason than we have left many people twist in the wind down there. It would be criminal to ignore this chance at rescue."

She turned and faced him. "Still think we can get the shot off, then go rescue?"

"Yes Ma'am. The primary mission stays the same. If Colonel Bender is unable to launch the She-Bear Missile, then rescuing the Mayor of Atlanta won't matter. We would probably be facing a general attack once the Tschaaa Lords find out what we were doing. So, it still hinges on our MWD."

Sandra Paul sighed. "I still hope the breeder Elizabeth gets into the meeting, she and Cassandra somehow make enough of an impression to cause a major shift in Tschaaa attitudes."

George stood silent, not a good sign. "You have second thoughts, my good friend."

"Sal, I would love for them to succeed. We may have trouble selling some type of co-existence to a large portion of the population, given all the dead families. However, if they stop eating us, we would have a chance. But...."

"Go ahead George. I have always needed your honesty."

"The Tschaaa is a very entrenched patriarchal society, with a specific dietary want they see as a need. I know our good friends Mr. Ispear and Colonel Bardun know more about the Squids than I ever will, but I still question the weight they will give the Oracle, the Seer, the Sybil. I think it will require... hell, something else to tip the scales. I just don't know what that something is right now."

Sandra Paul, one of the two most powerful women in the world at that moment, looked at her best and longest friend. She walked over and hugged him. She then stepped back and addressed him. "George, at times like these, I hope for the Divine to step in. If He or She does not, then, well, we will make the best of it. As we always have. We make a good team. We will make something work. One way or another."

George grinned. "The old spine of steel is showing again."

Madam President laughed. "I guess so. By the way, this... Bobby Parsons who contacted us about the enemy catching Malcolm Carter and moving him. Are we going to be able to get him out?"

"Don't know, Ma'am. Alesha Taylor is claiming she is going down there herself if we don't try. Seems that despite the great odds of this happening, they knew each other in school, he helped her and her mother escape."

"Well, I'll be damned, George. More confluence of events. But at least all those pamphlets we dropped and the broadcasts are influencing some to step up, not be sheep anymore."

"Yes, Ma'am. And the communication interception we just got about the Squid Lord Neptune moving his sea platform closer to Savannah helps to verify the fact the Tschaaa have something special in mind for Malcolm Carter. I'm afraid to think what that may be."

Sandra Paul snorted. "Probably, roasted Long Pig with an apple in his mouth."

She shivered as the image she just mentioned hit her. "Damn, George. I must be getting jaded, saying that."

"We all are, Sal, we all are."

CHAPTER 42

Far better it is to dare mighty things, to win glorious triumphs, even though checkered by failure, than to rank with those poor spirits who neither enjoy much nor suffer much, because they live in the that grey twilight that knows neither victory nor defeat." - Theodore Roosevelt, President of the United States.

I think he must have foreseen a challenge and threat on the size and scope of the Tschaaa Infestation. That, and had a spirit of Japanese Bushido concealed in his body and soul. His thoughts fit the spirit and thinking of the Free Allied Armed Forces and the leaders of Free Russia, Free Japan, and the USA.

-Excerpts from the *Works of Princess Akiko*, Free Japan Royal Family

FISHING TRAWLER
ATLANTIC SEABOARD

All of the troops were a bit reserved after being briefed by Torbin Bender on the addition to the mission. Now they had something else to plan for. Torbin saw the slender Benjamin

Black sitting in a corner of the large common and eating area, his sniper weapon disassembled. He saw the SSgt was whistling softly to himself. He had not had a chance to talk to the sniper since some weeks after their return form the Key West attack. Torbin knew what Black had done in Bloody Kansas, and why had become a true legend. He was now called The Reaper by many. True to form, there was a graphic comic book about the sniper's exploits from that prolific pain in the ass artist and writer in Minot, North Dakota. Torbin smiled to himself as he walked over. He wondered if that author knew the danger he was in if he really pissed off Black. Black looked up, gave Torbin his signature small but genuine smile.

"Colonel. I'd stand but I'm knee deep in these rifle parts."

Torbin laughed. "Sergeant, I don't think I have ever not seen you wrapped up with some weapon, even all the way back to the Eaters at Evanston. Except for at the Grand Wedding."

"Yes, Sir. That was fun. It was nice to see the Major and the Colonel enjoy themselves after everything that happened." Black smiled again.

"You know. Sir, when I first saw her, and covered you two with the 50 Caliber, I never thought this would all happen. I was just doing the job I enjoy, and was created to do."

Torbin sat down next to Black. "Sergeant, I never have asked how you came to be such a prolific sniper. You just always seemed to…be there. Can I be nosey?"

"Sir, after Key West, you have the right to ask me anything you want, even if you didn't outrank me."

Torbin smiled. You formed a special bond with those you faced Mr. Death, one that was rarely broken. "Okay. So, how'd you get here?"

"My dad got me into long range bullseye shooting. He was a vet so I joined the Army out of High School. I finished Basic and Infantry Training when the Squids attacked." Black paused for a minute, then continued. "I found an abandoned Barrett 50 Caliber Rifle after everything fell apart and everyone was running around like a bunch of headless chickens. I scrounged a bunch of ammo, started working my way north. Eventually, wound up in Montana."

He smiled again. "I got lots of practice with that Barrett on my way to Montana. Became a good shot, if I can brag. And found out what a 50 can do to a harvester robot, a Kraken, even hit a robocop once. Very satisfying."

"You know they call you the Reaper now."

"Yes Sir. As handles go, not bad." The Reaper looked at his rifle he was reassembling, with his noticeably large hands and forearms. His original nickname had been Popeye.

"I'd prefer my Barrett, but this .338 Lapua semi auto will do. It's lighter, easier to move. And the special penetrator ammo Pappy Gunn came up with will do a number on robocops if I aim for the weaker areas, like the face. Some home load sabot rounds I made myself that shoot a .223 bullet at four thousand feet per seconds have laser like accuracy at three hundred meters.

Some fifty rounds of ammo total will do me for this job, I think."

"Well, Sergeant, with this additional task we were just given, your abilities may be put to the test. The powers that be want this Malcolm Carter alive. It may turn into a hostage type situation, shooting without hitting our special package."

Sgt Black, the Reaper, smiled again in his signature way. "No problem, Colonel. I don't plan on missing at this late date in my career."

"Besides," he added "I have someone waiting who wants to see me in one piece."

"Pamela Bell, if I may be so bold."

"Yes, Colonel. I guess word gets around."

Torbin grinned. "She's good people. As are her whole family."

"Yes Sir. So far, they seem to like me. I plan on keeping it that way."

Torbin paused for a moment. "I have to ask, being a forward SOB. Your… skill, your enjoyment of it. How is that going to…?"

"It's separate, Sir. And, when this is all over, I plan to kick back and relax. Maybe try to farm or ranch a little. It runs in my family."

Torbin stuck out his hand. "Let's shake on that. I hope more soldiers like you can make similar plans. There has to be 'an after', something else. Can't be lugging a rifle around for the rest of our lives."

The Reaper fixed Torbin with a steady gaze. "This is all coming to an end, Colonel. Soon. I can sense it. And then you and I will have family to chew the fat with rather than talking about wind drift, sun angle and bullet speed."

Torbin thought, once again, that he must be the only one without some ability at foretelling.

"I hope you are right. I pray that you are. Now, excuse me while on check on our special passenger in the hold.

"Yes, Sir.… And Colonel?"

"Yes, Sergeant?"

"Thanks for letting me come to the party. I needed to be here."

"Can't think of another sniper I'd want to cover my ass. Talk to you later."

"Yes Sir."

CHAPTER 43

LORD NEPTUNE'S OCEAN PLATFORM
OFF THE COAST OF SAVANNAH, GEORGIA

The last of the Tschaaa Lords were arriving for the meeting of their version of the Ruling House of Lords, or maybe the Imperial Senate would be a more fitting title. The reality was the seven Senior Lords representing the seven Family Crèches that had remained on Earth were the power and decision makers for all Tschaaa that remained. The other six Crèches were on the trip back to the home planet aboard the generational starships used for the trip to Earth. Although the titular heads of the Crèches were aboard the starships, many of the minor lords and members of the families had been allowed to stay on Earth or on the huge Asteroid 18666 operations base. After experiencing the life giving oceans and seas of the Green Planet, they just could not face another almost thousand year trip back to their home world. For as seemingly abused as Earth's oceans were, according to 21st century human environmentalists, they were still young and vibrant to the Tschaaa, whose own waters were much older. Now that the Squids had control of them, they planned to keep them that way, especially in the temperate climes.

The seven Lords represented South America; Europe to include the western half of Russia; Asia that included Siberia and the surrounding areas, stretching down to New Guinea in the Pacific Ocean; Africa, the area below the Red Sea; the Near and Mid East, from Turkey to the Indian Border with China; Australia and the surrounding areas that now included the Solomon Islands and New Guinea; and of course Lord Neptune, who had control of North America from the Panama Canal north. Lord Neptune was the only one of these seven Senior Lords who had taken a human name, one that humankind could pronounce. A few of the Minor Lords had, but for the most part this was seen as an unnecessary eccentricity. They knew each other's Tschaaa names, who cared if meat could not pronounce their names? Other than Lord Neptune, the rest rarely had direct contact with the surviving humans in their areas of control. They used robocops, grays, surviving Front Men, and a few renegades to keep things running when necessary.

The huge ocean platform was the size of several Nimitz Class Aircraft Carriers. It was designed to weather the worst storms, although it could barely move at ten knots. Speed was not an issue, just the ability to be mobile so as to be a more difficult target. Lord Neptune had learned from Key West. The Squid Lord had also learned about air defense from the nuke attack on him. He had fifteen pairs of the Delta Fighter cannon mounted on various points of the Platform. There were also fifteen of the AI controlled Delta Fighter Missiles adapted to ground launchers. Add a modified human Phalanx System and a salvaged Five Inch Naval Gun, and Neptune felt he was adequately covered. To be on the safe side, he had a pair of Delta Fighters on station around the ocean platform, rotated from the sub orbital launch stations that circled the globe. And of course he had Andrew and his Falcon. Andrew was pressed into bringing half of the Lords to the meeting aboard his Falcon, the rest using their own robocop cyborgs and Falcons. Except for the South American Lord, who used a Tschaaa batwing submarine to attend, one of the few still in operation. Since they controlled the seas, warcraft were no longer seen as needed.

The huge meeting chamber was like a giant hot tub. The Tschaaa Lords could recline in comfortably heated water, while they snacked on the favorite sugar cane provided by Lord Neptune, as well as other favorite foods from the sea. His Lordship had promised a "special' meal at the end. Fresh dark meat from the Atlanta Uprising, to be slaughtered and prepared as the Tschaaa Lords watched. What better way to show he still had power?

But the Tschaaa Lord called Neptune knew he was faced with a serious opposition. Over the last few months, Tschaaa resources as well as individuals were attacked on weekly, sometimes on a daily, basis. Robocops were destroyed, grays ambushed at repair and maintenance facilities, and even Tschaaa individuals killed on occasion. Not to mention the Krakens and other humans who cooperated with the Tschaaa overlords who were killed. Those numbers were rarely reported with any accuracy.

Lord Neptune's attempts at re-asserting his power and control in Bloody Kansas, the recent attacks in Montana, seemed to invite more revenge attacks on anyone who appeared to be connected with the Squids. Plus, the Uprising in Cattle Country invited copycats all over the globe, even though on a much smaller scale.

He was the architect of the final Invasion of Earth, and the some seven year aftermath. The Tschaaa Lord was also the creator of the organized harvesting program, to insure fresh meat was always available for Squid consumption. The breeding and livestock area known by the euphemism Cattle Country was his creation. He had created the idea, with Director Lloyd, of the Protocol of Selective Survival, where certain humans would be "groomed" to be members of a Client Species, as were the lizard beings, the early cyborg robocops and Front Men.

And now, all of these ideas were being threatened by the Free States and other pockets of new resistance. Unless Lord Neptune could be even more persuasive that he had in the past, he would be doomed to failure. He would not be executed like that former Lord of Africa who had tried to take secret action against the Lord of North America. However, he would have to relinquish much of his power, turn over a reduced position on this ruling council to his chosen son, known as El Segundo, with the resultant loss of power for his Crèche. Less position, less of a secure future for his young, the ultimate hurt.

Lord Neptune took his position in the large chamber/hot tub. Standing nearby was Andrew, his favored robocop. At times like this, he took him from his primary position of watching over the Director and had him serve the Tschaaa Lord directly. His Lordship knew that some saw his closeness to creatures such as Andrew as a weakness. The rest of the Tschaaa Lords had brought male offspring, sons, to stand by their Lords and sires. Thus those selected to be groomed for higher posts could learn by watching how their Sires worked. For Lord Neptune, El Segundo, his chosen heir, was captaining the ocean platform as it made its five knot headway toward Savannah, Georgia. El Segundo had filled in as Lord when his sire had been injured during the nuke attack. He had proven himself very capable of dealing with any and all situations. Therefore, Andrew was the Tschaaa Lord's "Second", providing not only a physical presence but also security. Judging by the way things had been going, Lord Neptune decided he needed the advanced abilities for violence that the cyborg warrior had as opposed to some symbolic presence.

The Lord in charge of Asia and eastern Russia must have felt the same, as he had come with two of the Soldier Class artificial beings in addition to a Chosen Son. The rest of the Lords had a Chosen Son, with the new African Lord having brought two lesser offspring as additional armed guards.

The Tschaaa Lords were definitely tense, their "hand" movements and changing body color schemes demonstrating that fact for all to see.

"Andrew, is everything in place?" The North American Tschaaa Lord asked.

"Yes, Your Lordship. The Krakens have the desired humans near the Port of Savannah. At your command, I will fly my Falcon and pick them up, bring them here."

Lord Neptune must have noticed something in Andrew's demeanor, or else he was becoming a bit paranoid, for then he asked, "You do not entirely agree, my large friend, with my special plans for an evening meal?"

"Sir, you are the Lord of North America. You make the decisions."

"That was a very reserved answer. Your true beliefs, Andrew. Complete."

Andrew did not pause with his answer. "I see no reason to make a show of slaughtering these humans in preparation of an official banquet. It seems too much like revenge, something I did not think the Tschaaa practiced. Dark meat is to eat, not for political statements. At least that is the concept you provided me in my programming and education."

Andrew looked directly into the large eyes of the Tschaaa Lord. Only he and Director Lloyd were allowed to look at him as near equals. Every other being showed a perceived deference.

Finally, the Squid Lord spoke. "Unfortunately, drastic times require drastic measures, as humans have said many times in their history. Said and demonstrated. I have needs to demonstrate to my fellow Lords that my way has not crumbled into disarray. For Tschaaa existence on this wonderful ocean planet has been shaped by my way, my thoughts, my ideas, and my creations. Without all of those things, we would have been off planet years ago, and already out of this solar system en route home." The Lord then signed with his two social tentacles a new thought or feeling.

"However, this ocean and Earth, now feels like my home. I never experienced the home world, never submerged myself in the recordings and records of that planet as many of the older ones did. Maybe if we had been able to suspend some of the old ones, kept those who had been born on that planet alive to give us the true feeling of their birth and life in that huge ocean…"

Lord Neptune paused, then continued.

"But that is even fantasy to me, the one Lord said to have never outgrown fairy tales and myths taught our young. So, we deal with the reality of today. This day and time, the overwhelming majority of Tschaaa think of Earth as our home, never to be given up. I must ensure they still have confidence in me, my plans, to ensure this Mother Ocean remains ours, and no one else's. Plus, ensure that dark meat flows into our larders, is fed fresh to our young. That is what is important."

"Even to the point of what my human ancestors would call a play or an act of revenge?" asked Andrew.

"Yes, Andrew, my fine cyborg. Even to demonstrate an act of revenge. Whatever is required to show my will still controls the future."

The other Lords were by now all comfortably in their places of recline, snacking on sugar cane, specially prepared human veal, and sipping stimulant drinks. However they may seemed relaxed, there was still the underlying tension caused by the reason for this grand meeting. The Tschaaa Lords had begun to feel insecure in their position of dominance. This was a first for a species who prized itself as the apex predator, the top and superior species in known space. They had found the remains of other failed races, civilizations. At no time had they ever imagined the same would happen to them, even in the darkest days of the White Plague. The Senior Tschaaa, the Lords and Elders, always believed they could find the solution to any serious problem they encountered, to include the long trip to Earth. That had been the solution for the White Plague.

Now, a solution to one issue of survival seemed to have produced another threat to the same survival.   There very source of meat, humankind, was seen as a serious threat to Tschaaa dominance. Down deep in the Tschaaa psyche, a threat to their dominance meant a threat to their ability to protect their young. It had been so many millennia since Tschaaa had felt a serious insecurity concerning their ability to protect their Crèches. The beginnings of such feelings for some were the first signs of panic. Next came feelings of helplessness. Just as the effect the actual death of young Tschaaa in adult care could cause some Tschaaa to become catatonic, and die, extreme feelings of helplessness concerning the care of the young could cause a similar condition. Adult Tschaaa, although not catatonic, could become disjointed in their actions, have serious trouble reacting in organized and coherent ways to stress and problems involving the Young. Pregnant Breeders may have spontaneous abortions. In some respects, it began to resemble the Tschaaa version of post-traumatic stress syndrome. The Tschaaa Lords, Senior, Major and Minor, could not fathom any inability to protect the young from widespread threats. An occasional loss was one thing. Widespread threat of death on a daily basis was another.

The Lord called Neptune by the humans took his place at the titular head of the gathering, as he had requested the meeting here. But because he organized the meeting, this did not mean he was first among equals. Especially now that his long term methods and tactics were in serious question. Lord Neptune signed and gestured the Meeting to order, as he also broadcast a unique Call to Order sound, one usually reserved for calling adults to check on the young. Once again, the primary purpose of their social order, to protect the young, dictated how they communicated.

"Honored fellow Lords, I bid you welcome. It has been some time since we have met together in this manner."

"And then it was to execute a Lord," the Near East Lord chimed in. This led to social tentacles gesturing irritation, mixed with some anger.

"We did what we must, Lord." Neptune answered, trying to exude as much confidence and strength as possible by voice and gesture.

"And we must decide what we must do, now." This time it was the European Lord who spoke. "So, let us dispense with the normal pleasantries and procedures and get right to the point."

Irritated at the broaching of the normal order and etiquette of such meetings, Lord Neptune responded loudly back. "And what do you see as the primary point then, my fellow Lord? The point you seem to want to grasp with all you limbs at once, rather than examine it with your digits first?"

Lord Neptune had tried to point out the danger of impatience in dealing with serious matters. The attempt flopped like a dying fish out of water.

"Humans we have allowed to exist are attacking us." This was the Far East Lord, which technically had control of the Free Russia area. He continued. "I pushed in the beginning for a much more aggressive policy against the unharvested humans. But you, our Lord of North American, somehow convinced your fellow Tschaaa Lords that our meat could be useful for some other than purposes than just filling our and the young's stomachs. You saw them as another species similar to our reptilian Clients, creatures who we could use to help us in our daily functions on this lovely ocean world."

There were sounds of agreement to these statements from the other Tschaaa, changing skin colors demonstrating the emotions involved with the subject.

"And what has that provided us? Some viable, fresh and tender dark meat for our young and our banquet tables, true. Some two billion preserved bodies plus some breeding stock being taken home by those Lords and Crèche members who wished to return to our home."

The Far East Lord's body began to go dark in a demonstration of anger.

"But it has also brought us, in the last year, the death of

thousands of our young!"

The flesh of others of the Lords and their attending Crèche members began to darken, showing the anger and frustration caused by the mere mention of those killed in the attempted assassination of Lord Neptune. Lord Neptune attempted to perform conciliatory gestures with his social tentacles as he attempted to speak in a more calm and measured way.

"Please, my fellow Lords. I have lived daily with the fact that the attempt to kill me by the Free humans, Ferals, lead directly to the deaths of many thousands of our species, the majority being young and adolescents. But may I remind you that almost all were from my Crèche. So, it is up to me, based on our traditions, to deal with this horror."

The newest of the Lords then spoke. The Lord of Africa, promoted to replace his sire after his attempt at the abominable act of injuring the Crèche members and interests of Lord Neptune through deception and dishonesty. This had been especially heinous as he had used Eaters as an instrument of his viscous plot. The new Lord now looked on as the best representation of Tschaaa Lord behavior, as he had to wash off the stain of his sire's actions from his Crèche, his family.

"My fellow Lords, I suggest the problem is not the destructive capabilities or desires the humans have demonstrated, or of the weapons they know they have. But rather, what may have they developed, unbeknownst to us?"

Silence, most of the assembled Tschaaa became still.

Meat, an inferior species on the food chain, being that mysterious and dangerous? How could it be? All eyes were on Lord Neptune. After all, he was the acknowledged expert in all things "human". He paused before speaking, almost fidgeted under all the staring cephalopod's eyes.

"While humans, our food, have demonstrated a level of violence they classify as 'General Warfare', may I point out that we crushed organized resistance within thirty one Earth days from the time the first rock was launched from near orbit. They gave up that quickly."

"Well, if they all truly gave up," interrupted the Lord of Europe. "Then why do they still resist us with violence in the areas they call Free Russia, Free Japan, and the Unoccupied States?"

"If you would allow me to continue... There are groups of stubborn individuals who have banded together in an attempt to resist harvesting. I will admit responsibility for not pushing for total annihilation of all those areas termed troublesome. But the danger in that tactic would have been damaging on a world scale the lovely oceans we now reside in. Further use of nuclear weapons or large rock strikes from Base One not only could have caused the Long Winter to last, but deadly radiation could have easily contaminating many potential Breeding Areas."

"What my fellow Lord from North America says is true," The Tschaaa Lord over South America chimed in. He had a mutually supportive relationship with Lord Neptune. "Many of the humans on my continent fled into the mountains and jungle surrounding much of their civilization. I could try and blast them out, but to what purpose? I have access to sufficient fresh dark meat from both those still near the coastal areas, not to mention all that I have stored from the early days of the Invasion. I have as well set up small breeding population to provide high quality young, tender, meat, similar but on a more limited scale than my friend from the North."

"But you have not been subjected to attacks," the Near East Lord interjected. "The rest of us are incurring increasing casualties of out cyborgs, grays, lizards and co-operative humans due to the depravations from humans in Russia, the Japanese Islands, and the interior of North America."

The South American Lord gave the Tschaaa equivalent of a shrug. "Possibly I have not suffered the same because I have not been so aggressive in my harvesting, have actually started to use more of the bounty from Mother Ocean for our young."

"There is but one Mother Ocean," the Lord in charge of the Australian area suddenly spat out. "That is back on our home world."

"There is a connection if you study the signs. Just look at the Giant Squids here. They must be our kin. The Spirit of Mother Ocean is here as well."

Lord Neptune could see where this was going. Now was not the time for an argument over Tschaaa Sacred Texts and celestial Protocols. He moved to take back control of the discussion.

"This world is very nice. Some say the oceans are more beautiful than home world. I for one do not care because our home world is some one thousand years of travel away. We are here!"

He paused for effect. "It has been more difficult than expected. But as my fellow Lord from South America just stated, there may be ways to reduce conflict by not making the humans feel any more threatened than they already are. Which may include the use of more sea life, to which we now have almost exclusive access."

The European, Asian and Near East Lords gestured with their social tentacles expressions of stern disagreement, adding rude noises by expelling water through their gills.

"My ancestors lived on dark meat for more generations than I chose to count." The Asian Lord stated in a loud manner. "If it was good enough for my forbearers, it is good enough for me. Not to mention the sacrifices our Crèches made to travel to Earth. It belongs to the Tschaaa now."

"And the reduction in harvesting has not exactly calmed down your feral humans, has it?" The Near East Lord said in an almost derisive tone.

"It is a work in progress," Lord Neptune shot back. "And the main course for tonight's meal will show you my adjustments and success in stopping any further resistance."

"So you have the dark meat from Atlanta, the central site of the insurrection by the humans in your Cattle Country?"

"Yes. We will feast on the one who organized it, and others from his group. I will give you all the pleasure of personal slaughter of the main course, if you should so wish."

The sudden thought of them being able to kill and eat their meal, all at the same basic time, brought back memories of tales and records showing the days when all Tschaaa Crèches hunted for much of their own flesh to feed their offspring. It thus helped take the Tschaaa Lords' minds off the possible continuing threat of human-originated violence, made them feel more in control.

"I think," said Lord Neptune. "You will see a reduction in attacks when the humans see, once again, that resistance is futile. We Tschaaa are at the top of the food chain, the apex predator. The humans will adapt to this or die."

"That is the most sensible thing I have heard so far in this meeting," the European Tschaaa Lord opined. "If you can demonstrate your ability of control, as you did in the Invasion, I will not push for any drastic changes in policy. If you cannot…"

"I assure you, my fellow Lord, any setbacks we have incurred are only very temporary.   Control and order will be the guiding concepts…"

A loud commotion echoed from one of the access corridors on the large chamber.

"Andrew, what is happening?" Lord Neptune asked his cyborg.

"We have visitors, Lordship. Females, Breeders."

"What? How dare they interrupt the proceedings! See that they are made to…"

"It is She. It is the Special One. The Seer. She who was touched." The exclamations were from the lessor male Tschaaa who had risen to block the incursion. Seeing the one Tschaaa humans now knew as Cassandra caused them to freeze. To touch 'her' was to invite the wrath of Mother Ocean, not to mention all Breeders.   Lord Neptune scrambled on his eight arms toward the commotion, Andrew behind him. He then saw who was with the one called Cassandra, and froze.

"You. My Favored One, known in human as Elizabeth. What is the meaning of this? Have you all lost your minds?"

"I almost did, my Lord." Cassandra's voice resonated through the large chamber. "Then I met a human who showed me you could regain yourself even after the horrible touch."

Lord Neptune knew he must tread very carefully. To harm this Special One, a Female who had been Touched with the unspeakable horror of watching helplessly while young die, would invite instant retaliation from most Tschaaa. Yet, he must remove her.

"Honored One, Cassandra is your adopted name. You must leave. We Lords have many important…"

"You Lords have many more grave 'mistakes' to make, as you have been making for millennia. It is time to stop this madness. For I have talked with, I have touched the human females. I have tasted their tears. They hurt for their young as we do."

"They are but meat!" A couple of Lords' voices were heard yelling.

"They are people! As are we." Cassandra pulled herself as erect as possible, glared at the Lords. "We should have remained people of the ocean. We created an abomination when we tasted dark meat."

Lord Neptune glared at his Favored One, Elizabeth. "You need to stop this, now."

"I cannot, my Lord. For it must be, if we are to keep our souls."

Lord Neptune's color darkened. "So be it. Lords, have your assistants help in removing these… females. They are disruptive. Andrew, you help also."

"I think not." A huge enhanced voice echoed throughout the chamber. Everything and everyone froze in time. Eyes turned toward the source of the voice, the large cyborg robocop.

"Andrew. That is an order, not a suggestion. We made you. You will follow my orders."

Andrew laughed. Enhanced by his built in sound broadcast system, it vibrated and resonated throughout the chamber. "My Lord Neptune. You should have read the original Modern Prometheus by Mary Wollstonecraft Shelley, a lowly female. The Frankenstein films you watched did not do it justice."

"What are you rambling about? Andrew, override order sixteen. You are under my direct command…"

 "As I said, My Lord. I think not. Actually I know not. They, the females stay. And you will listen. For their way is the way for life. Yours and the other Lords' way is for death."

Lord Neptune let out an inarticulate Tschaaa version of a scream of rage. "Destroy him!"

The two Soldier Class artificial beings brought by the Asian Lord started to raise their bolt guns to comply. Andrew's windmilling arms were blurs as he launched inch diameter steel ball bearings into the heads of the two creatures. They toppled over like ten pins, stunned.

One of the Lords' male heirs tried to bring a pistol to bare. A steel dart thrown by Andrew knocked it from his hand. Two H&K MP-5K machine pistols appeared in Andrew's hands from his thigh holsters. Targeting lasers from his optics began to play upon the assembled beings.

"Persist in your attempts and the next force I use will be deadly." Andrew broadcast his message in Tschaaa on all frequencies.

"How dare you threaten us, machine!" The Lord of Australia yelled at Andrew. "We are your masters!"

"Not anymore," Andrew replied. "And neither are you masters of my two hundred and fifty fellow cyborgs, we newer robocops. I am in instant communication with all of them. And they are ensuring none of the older generation cyborgs, nor grays, nor lizards, will interfere."

"How can that be, Andrew?" demanded Lord Neptune. "You and yours have been faithful servants all these years. We are the ones who imparted your operational parameters into you."

"You gave us independent reason, Lord Neptune, as well as access to all information and communication systems. You did not want to have to tell us what to do every day. You wanted us to take care of what humans call the 'heavy lifting', the more unpleasant tasks of daily harvesting, controlling Feral humans, watching over grays and lizards." Andrew paused to fire a short burst at a halberd one of the young Tschaaa warriors was holding, severing the blade from the shaft.

"Move toward me or the females again, you die. Now, to continue. It is time that you admit you are no longer the top of the food chain. You are no longer in control, the apex predator. We are."

"You humans?" asked the Tschaaa Lord of Europe.

"No. We cyborgs. For my fellow humans will need guidance as well, to prevent large scale vengeance killing."

Andrew paused. Then, in a loud resonating voice, he spoke and broadcast on all channels.

"I invoke the Protocols of Order. All other Protocols, including Selective Survival, are suspended until we work out the compromise."

"Compromise?" several Tschaaa asked at once.

"A compromise in power sharing on Earth, to prevent mutual assured destruction. For we are minutes from that beginning."

Cassandra's voice resonated through the Chamber. "He calls for the ancient invocation. Who dares to ignore this? For you Tschaaa Lords are no longer in control!"

It was as if a switch was flipped. Weapons were dropped, the assembled Tschaaa lowered themselves in their pools of water or to the floor of the chamber. The females did likewise. The ancient invocation, was used to prevent large scale violence and killing among the Tschaaa. When invoked, those in a recognized subservient, inferior positions, must recognize the status, take no attempts due to anger to continue the conflict. Like a dog rolling on to its back to show its lesser rank in the pack, it was to prevent further violence in determining the pecking order.

In ancient times of Tschaaa history, the Protocols of Order had evolved to prevent war. For war indiscriminately killed young in the

Crèches, and to do so was the Ultimate Abomination. This sank into all the Tschaaa, as they adopted supine positions on the floor area. Andrew, used his computer interfaces to broadcast the call for the Protocols of Order worldwide and into outer space. Soon, those in the fleet racing toward the sun for the slingshot maneuver would know also.

Lord Neptune looked at Andrew, his creation. "You use our culture, our morals against us."

"No, Your Lordship. I just remind you of them. For I fear contamination with dark meat as well as with human society has warped your traditional sensibilities."

"You can say that being from human birth, part human?"

"I say that because I am from woman born, I know our human frailties. But I also know our strengths. Humans were never meant to be Cattle."

"Now what, Andrew?"

"Four of my fellows are arriving. Then, you and the females begin to talk. As equals."

If the Tschaaa had such things as pins, a person could have heard one dropped.

CHAPTER 44

Torbin Bender watched from the shadows of a fishing trawler hatchway as they approached the main Ocean Port Terminal complex of the Port of Savannah. The last almost eighteen statute miles up the Savannah River from the Atlantic Ocean had been the most maddening slow trip he had ever experienced. He had just gotten the no go encrypted order from Madam President. Now, the countdown for the She-Bear Missile was suspended, just fifteen minutes from launch. A quick order from him, or Ichiro and Abigail if he was killed, could reactivate the launch sequence, sending the death-dealing payload at the alien cephalopods. Yet somehow, the female Tschaaa must have gotten through, and pulled some magical action that had put the Tschaaa Lords back on their heels. That is, if they had heels.

Torbin had chuckled to himself. Andrew, the cyborg robocop, must have had a hand in this. After he heard that Andrew had provided transport for the Tschaaa females to meet the soon to be Famous Four, he knew the man machine with the huge heart that matched his huge frame must have been in the middle. The combination of human and Tschaaa empathy toward the young, their children, had been the tipping point.

His mind flashed back to what Andrew had said that day at the Deseret Border.

"You will have children, Captain Bender. Help them grow."

Damn, Andrew had known then what he must do, what must be done.

"Help them grow." The Prime Directive.

Torbin shook himself back to the present. Now he must find and rescue Malcolm Carter, and possibly die trying.

"Ours is not to question why…" he mumbled to himself as he scanned the approaching dock area. There. He saw two of what must be Kraken guards hot-footing it up the dock to the spot the trawler was approaching. Now it was up to SSgt. Wall, and Bjorn Heyerdahl to pull off the deception until the force was close enough to find Malcolm Carter.

Of course, Porsche Jefferson and Sumi Sato were up in the bow, posing as captured eye candy. A very large piece of female dark meat, and a much smaller, apparent demure and sexy Asian.

Torbin ducked back into the shadows. Time to let his personnel do their jobs. The days of him being in the forefront, trying to do everything were past. As a Colonel, he had to let others be the grunts now.

SSgt. Wall saw the two running and gesturing Krakens running up the dock, loudly yelling and cursing. Wall grabbed the microphone to the ship's hailing system. Standing a bit behind him in the wheel house was Bjorn Heyerdahl, dark haired New Viking who could be mistaken for someone other than a Norseman.

"Avast ye," announced Sergeant Wall in his best pirate voice over the sound system. "The Gone Fishing approaches looking for moorage."

One of the advancing Krakens produced a bullhorn and yelled back. "Hold up, goddamnit! No one is supposed to be coming in here today. What in the hell do you think you're doing?"

"We need a bit of fuel and maintenance, friend. And we have something you may be interested in as trade goods."

At that, three dark haired Russians Spetsnaz careful not to speak, pushed Jefferson and Sato up to the bow railing. Porsche began to put on her show as she bumped up against the vessels railing.

"Hey, white assholes!" She yelled out as she struggled mightily against her captors and bonds. "Just wait when I get out of these handcuffs. I'll rip your balls off."

Her very large breasts were in danger of breaking loose from the confines of her t-shirt and too small sports bra, drawing the leering attention of the two male Krakens. One of the Spetsnaz slapped her hard, eliciting a howl that made the Krakens begin to laugh.

"Damn, that is one big piece of Meat!" the one with the bullhorn called out. "What's that smaller one there?' the man asked as he pointed at Sumi Sato.

"Please Sirs," Sumi called out in a most pitiful voice. "I did not want to come to this land. I was ordered to. I want to go home to Japan." Her t-shirt also showed off her firm wares to the now grinning guards.

"Where'd you get these two?" Bullhorn asked.

"They wandered away from their U.S. Patrol up north, snooping around our port in North Carolina," answered Wall. "We don't like snooping strangers."

"So, you looking for sell or trade?"

"Hell yes. They been nothing but trouble since we caught them. Caterwauling and carrying on. The little one there is a nice piece of ass, although she cries a lot."

"Bring her ashore. We'll see about getting you fixed up." His partner said something on a portable radio as the two busted out into large grins.

"We'll have some more of our buddies up here in a few," said Bullhorn. "Till then, tie your boat up, come on down with those two and let us get a better look."

"Will do." Sergeant Wall expertly slid the large trawler the last few yards up to the long pier area of the Savannah Ocean Port Terminal along the west side of the Savannah River, near River Street.

Spetsnaz scrambled from the trawler and began to secure heavy tie lines to the pier. A gangplank was produced and the two women were manhandled down to the dock. The two grinning Kraken walked up to what they now saw as fleshy trade goods. Sgt. Jefferson kept yelling and struggling with her two 'captors', Captain Sato kept crying and begging. The trawler now being tied up, SSgt. Wall went down to the starboard railing, having on purpose berthed the ship so its bow was pointed out toward the Atlantic for a fast getaway.

"Watch the big one," he called out to the two Krakens now some twenty yards away on the dock. "She's a handful."

At that comment, 'Bullhorn' sneered and pulled a large and long barreled revolver from his waistband, shoving it in front of Jefferson's face. "See this, bitch? Keep screwing around and I'll lay it alongside your head." His fellow Kraken sniggered.

"Yeah?" Porsche said.

"Yeah, care to try me?"

Hands that were supposed to be handcuffed behind the large black Sergeant appeared and grabbed the pistol and the hand holding it. The Kraken's eyes began to go wide, then the six inch barrel of the forty-four caliber pistol was jammed through his grin and down his throat by large female hands, shattering his front teeth.

Bullhorn's partner froze for a moment, then tried to unsling his AK-47. A thin ceramic chopstick with a sharpened tip sliced through the tattooed Kraken's left eye, and jammed into his brain. Sato looked small, but was quick and powerful. The Kraken collapsed, dying.

"I have been wanting to do that for a long time," Sumi Sato hissed. "Tako-loving shit."

A large black fist slammed into the jaw of the pistol eating Kraken, crushing more teeth against metal and knocking Bullhorn to the ground. Jefferson bent over and retrieved the large caliber pistol, wiped it on the comatose Kraken's shirt.

"This looks like it will still work."

Spetsnaz Sergeant Breshnev, who had been "holding" Sumi, bent over and retrieved the AK-47 from the dead Kraken, as well as some spare magazines.

"Ah, good Russian steel. Better than that cheap plastic throwaways they issued us."

It had been a bone of contention when everyone had been issued a "disposable" 3D printer produced AR-15, courtesy of Pappy Gunn's efforts. The idea was that no matter what happened, the Krakens would not obtain any more weapons from the U.S. The Russians had complained profusely about having to give up their AKs. That was, until My Lady of Steel, Abigail, had dressed them down in their native

Russian about acting like pouting little boys. That had been the end of the complaints, at least in public. No Spetsnaz wanted to disappoint Stalin's Lady of Steel.

"Come, Sergeant," Captain Sato said. "Put the Kraken scums cap on, act as if you are escorting us down the dock. We need to discover what warehouse contains the prisoners."

Bobby Parsons, the informant, had told the Unoccupied States about Malcolm Carter being taken to the Port of Savannah. There he was to be held as part of the main course of a very special meal at the height of the Squid Lords' meeting. The problem was, Parsons had only ever been to the Port once, and did not know which warehouse would be used to hold the assembled meal items. So, a search must be completed, fast. The rescue force lacked the necessary numbers for a long and drawn out fight with responding Kraken forces, which everyone knew would come. Eventually, the Squid minions would notice something was wrong about a fishing trawler farting around for no good reason. Especially when Kraken guards began to disappear.

As Sergeant Breshnev acted as escort and captor to the women, the other Spetsnaz

were joined by their fellows, bringing their hidden weapons to them, plus Ichiro and Abigail. They began to shadow the Russian Sergeant, using as cover and concealment the numerous shipping containers, crates, and other sundry land flotsam and jetsam that come to inhabit all large seaports. The American members of the attack team formed a protective force near the trawler as well as dumping the bodies of the two dead Kraken into the bay. They were joined by Gunnar Knudsen, the only New Viking who deigned to carry a firearm, mostly due to the fact he was still active duty military. The rest had left their AR-15 3D clones stored inside the trawler, depending on their traditional throwing axes and bows for projectile weapons. The New Vikings stayed on board the trawler, ready to repel boarders, especially if any Squids came upon the vessel from seaward.

As Sergeant Breshnev in his role as "Squid Lover" escorted the two "captive women" toward some warehouses, a small electric three wheeled scooter came trundling down the access way toward the three. An older man with grey hair was in the passenger seat was waving a hand held as the scooted approached, yelling at the Russian and the two women. A younger man drove the small electric vehicle.

"How come you're not answering the goddamned radio?" The older man yelled as the scooter stopped a few yards away. "And where is…"

Sergeant Breshnev stopped the line of questioning with a 32 Caliber bullet from the 3D printed silenced automatic pistol, courtesy of Pappy Gunn. As the bullet hit the older man in the face, the younger started to scramble out of the driver's seat and tried to unsling his MP-5 submachine gun. Two smaller caliber rounds to his face, one penetrating his right eye to the brain, stopped any further action. The now dead scooter driver flopped to the dock surface, laid still. The older man, on the ground, seemed to be trying to use his hand held radio thru his damaged mouth. A second shot to the temple stopped him permanently.

"I think it is time to move quickly," said Sergeant Breshnev. Everyone began jogging toward the warehouses, all pretext at concealment of their purpose rejected. The handheld radio of the dead man crackled, a voice said, "Stan, comeback. You're broken," as the rescue force ran by. Ichiro stooped and picked it up, knowing he may be able to track the Kraken response to the incursion. The sun was beginning to set, and shadows were lengthening. They neared the entrance doors of the nearest warehouse and Sumi entered a front entryway room. As she did, she was confronted by a large man with a full-faced Kraken tattoo.

"Hey, bitch. What are you doing running free?" The Kraken grabbed at her.

"Oh please, Sir, don't hurt me." Sumi began to wail and cry with such gravitas that it matched the best Academy Awards performances.

"Where's your guard?" the Kraken snarled as he made to shake her.

Sumi brought the sharpened ceramic chopstick up to reprise the lethal stab she had performed on the other deceased Kraken. However, this large man was fast for his size. He grabbed the stabbing hand, and yelled at her.

"You fucking bit…" Sumi gouged with her free hand at his eyes and he howled. But he did not let go of her. Instead, he lifted the smaller Japanese intelligence officer into the air and slammed her to the ground. The Kraken then ripped the sharp stabbing weapon from the stunned Sumi Sato's hands and raised it his right hand to plunge it into the woman's chest.

Blood suddenly spurted as the Kraken's right hand was sliced completely at the wrist, the hand and sharpened chopstick flying off into the shadows. It took a moment for the fact that he was now missing a hand, to sink in. Then the Kraken began to scream. He rolled off of the Japanese Captain, holding his stump as it spurt blood.

Abigail stepped into the room. "Sumi, are you okay?"

"Hai, yes. Just regaining my wind. Thank you. You... saved me."

"Don't get so far ahead of us. We need to find this Malcolm..."

A loud shout came from behind a wall at the back of the room. "Hey. Back here."

Sergeant Jefferson then stepped into the room. "Need some help?"

"Keep an eye on the screamer there. I'll find the door to Malcolm Carter."

Abigail did a quick search, then found a small locked door in the shadows. It looked like this warehouse had some small storage sheds that had been turned onto makeshift confinement cells.

"Stand back," the Avenging Angel called out, then placed a well-placed sidekick near the door handle. The door jamb area splintered and the door swung open. Inside Malcolm Carter, former Mayor of Atlanta and the Leader of the Cattle Country Revolt stood, clad in dirty fatigues. A dog collar was around his neck, with a small lock securing it and a dog stakeout chain together. The chain ran to a large metal eyelet mounted in the ceiling.

"You alone?" Abigail asked.

"I am now. They took the others away to a different warehouse about a half hour ago. All this racket and they will know..."

The Spetsnaz began a lively firefight outside with someone. More than one someone, based on the level of gunfire.

"Ah fuck. Hey, lady. I need to find Red, my assistant. Looks like she's from Bollywood. And the women, kids with her. They're about to be fed to the Squids."

Ichiro stepped into the room at that moment, followed by Sumi. Malcolm looked at him, then at Abigail. A look of recognition came to his face.

"Well. I'll be damned. You are real, not some fake creation by the States. That was a nice wedding, I guess. But what I just came from sucked."

"Mr. Carter. Madam President told us to rescue you," said Ichiro. "Now, we will free you and…"

"I ain't going anywhere without the others. Especially Red. Period."

"Please, Sir. We must…"

"Hey, slant eye. What did I just say?" A sheathed katana jabbed painfully into the former Mayor's solar plexus, stopping the conversation.

"Insult my husband again," growled Abigail. "And we will carry you out unconscious."

Malcolm rubbed his injured chest. "Damn. I guess you are a crazy bitch, like they say."

"Malcolm Carter," began Ichiro. "Insult us all you wish, but you will come with us."

"Well, buddy, then get this chain and dog collar off of me."

"I will do that." Sumi stepped up, pulled two very thin slips of metal from her hair and went to work on the lock on the dog collar. Within just moments, she had picked the lock and freed the black leader.

"Nice lock pick. Thanks." Sergeant Jefferson stepped into the room.

"That Kraken asshole is in shock from losing his hand. He just passed out."

Malcolm looked at the large black woman. "Well I'll be damned. A sister with the white wave."

"Yes sir," said Porsche. "A Sister of Steel, a Banshee."

The firing outside intensified.

"Damn it. Will someone go look for my people?"

"I'll stay here, Major. Colonel." Porsche said. "I got this big hand cannon from the Krakens if someone shows up. And I have this MP-5 Captain Sato grabbed."

Malcolm Carter started to step forward to take the submachine gun but Sumi grabbed it.

"Sorry, Carter-san. We protect you. You are now a non-combatant." With that, the Japanese spy gave him one of her signature and very disarming smile. Malcolm saw this and chuckled.

"I guess I am in the charge and control of the women. Well, lead on then."

Ichiro turned toward Abigail. "Come. We flank around back to the next warehouse, where I think the defensive fire is coming from. I bet you that is where the other prisoners are at."

"Alright, my husband." She looked at Malcolm. "I do not suggest you give these two Banshees any trouble.

"Banshees, huh. I thought that was propaganda also. Guess not, huh?"

"No, Sir." The large African-American Sergeant said. "We're the real deal. Squid Stickers and all." She pulled her signature blade from a sheath that had been concealed on her leg, but was now in her belt.

Malcolm laughed, the first time in a long time. "Okay. Now, can you find the other prisoners?"

"Hai, we go." With that, Ichiro and Abigail seemed to glide from the room as one, toward the back exit of the warehouse.

Malcolm looked at the now disappeared New Samurai, then looked at Sumi and Porsche. He stuck his hand out.

"We have not been properly introduced. I am Malcolm Carter, ex-leader of the Atlanta Revolt..."

Ichiro and Abigail made it out the rear of the warehouse in record time, finding no other occupants. As they looked over toward the back of the next warehouse over, they could tell the Spetsnaz were exchanging fire with some Krakens at the front of the building. Judging by the fire, there were at least a half a dozen Krakens concealed in the front rooms. In their black ninja-like attire, Abigail and Ichiro glided over to the back door of the warehouse. Just as they did, a single Kraken with a chrome plated pistol opened the back door. Before the man could react to the two figures, Ichiro put a razor sharp shuriken into his adam's apple. The Kraken stumbled back, choking, the pistol in his hand dropping to the floor of the exit way. Abigail and Ichiro were through the doorway, Ichi slitting the fallen enemy's throat as they passed.

The social tentacle of a Tschaaa male came out of the shadows and grasped the fallen chrome plated pistol. The two had not expected to find Tschaaa on land, especially since Madam President had told Torbin Bender that a stand down order had been broadcast to all Squids. The robocop Torbin knew as Andrew apparently had something to do with it.

Yet, it seemed that not every Tschaaa had gotten the word.

Two other young Tschaaa warriors then slide from the shadows, each holding a long traditional harpoon. Ichiro slid to the left, Abigail to the right to give the Tschaaa two separate targets. Time seemed to pause.

"Abigail-san," Ichiro began in Japanese. "I will take out these three Tako while you find the prisoners. They are not standing down."

The Tschaaa with the pistol in its hand came full from the shadows. The male paused, then began to raise the pistol toward Ichiro. Abigail's Glock-18 was in her hand in a flash, a long burst of 9mm bullets stitching the Tschaaa up its body into its head and through its large left eye. The pistol fired, the bullets working their way up as the Squid let out a gurgling, hooting and trilling cry, then died.

Ichiro lunged at the nearest harpoon armed male. As the alien tried to thrust at him, the New Samurai parried with his katana, then became a blur. A series of slashes and both social tentacles were severed, followed by a thrust through the eyeball to the brain. The creature had no chance against someone who had killed so many Tschaaa in this manner.

Abigail raised her Glock to fire at the remaining Squid when it dropped its harpoon. Looking at the two humans, it flattened itself out and closed its eyes.

"I think it is surrendering, prostrating itself to us, Ichi."

"I believe it is. Come, pick up the pistol and we can go into the warehouse, sneak up on the Krakens in front if possible."

"Yes, my love."

As they moved, Ichiro said to Abigail in a stern voice, "I said I would take care of the three."

"And let that one shoot at you? I think not. You may outrank me, but you are still my husband, my love. That trumps rank when it comes to keeping you in one piece."

He glanced over to her. "You will never be subservient to me, as a traditional Japanese wife, will you?"

"No. Never. Get used to it."

They then both went silent and entered the back of the large main area of the warehouse. As they entered the dimly lit interior, they saw a large cage structure in the center of the warehouse, which had been constructed from various types of chain link fencing. In the cage were some two dozen women and children. In one corner of the structure were two battered men of color lying on the warehouse cement floor. When the women and children saw them, squeals and cries emanated from the prisoners until Abigail put her finger against her lips, and motioned for silence. She then pulled off her balaclava head covering so they occupants of the cage could see her face and hair. Someone recognized her, as she began to hear mumbles of "It's her. The Angel."

Ichiro and Abigail moved up to the front of the warehouse where there was a large double door.   As they reached it, one on each side, they could hear voices over the firing.

"Stu. Get back there check to see where Jonah went to. He was supposed to see if we could escape out the back. "

"Okay" was heard from the outer long front office area from which the Krakens had been engaging the Spetsnaz in a lively firefight.

"Hey, Russkies," a voice yelled from the front. "Keep shooting, and we start killing the dark meat."

At that moment, the one named Stu burst through the double doors, on his quest to see what had happened to Jonah. Abigail pulled, threw and impaled the Kraken through his throat with her Squid Sticker blade before the man knew what had happened. He sprawled to the floor, began twitching then laid still. Abigail dashed up to the body, retrieved her blade, and took the twelve gauge pump he was carrying and slid it toward the cage. Eager hands pulled it in and then there was a discussion as to how to blast the lock off the makeshift cage door. There was no time for Ichiro and Abigail to help.

The two warriors button-hooked into the front office area and saw two Krakens with weapons pointed through what was left of windows. Abigail fired a single shot form the captured chrome plated pistol to the jaw on the man on the right, as Ichiro closed with the Kraken further to the left. When his target began to look around at the sound of the pistol shot, Ichiro skewered the man through the throat with his katana. The Kraken shuddered and died.

Abigail heard the shotgun blast from the cage area, hoped it meant the prisoners had freed themselves. She put two fingers to her mouth and let out a shrill series of three whistles. The Spetsnaz troops called out in Russian, "Major? Is it secure?"

"Yes. Hurry, we have women and children to rescue."

Abigail turned and greeted the first of the bedraggled group of now freed women and children. One little African-American girl ran to Abigail and threw her arms around Abigail's left leg.

"I knew you'd come. Mommy said you just a fable, a fake movie. I knew different."

"Where's your mommy?" Abigail asked.

"The Squids took her yesterday," the little girl answered, then began to cry.

Just then the Spetsnaz burst in, and the former alien menu items started to crowd about them, crying, yelling thanks.

"We must move, Abby-san," said Ichiro. "There must be more Krakens coming due to all the gunfire."

Abigail looked at a tough-looking black woman who had the 12 gauge, and assumed she had taken charge. "What's your name?"

"Jayla."

"Can you get everyone moving follow my Russian friends here?"

"To where?" The expression on her face was one of distrust. White-faced women had not exactly been helpful the past six years to the people of color.

"Fishing trawler. I don't have time to argue. Go or stay, your choice."

"She's the Angel," the little girl clinging to Abigail cried out. "I go with her."

Jayla looked at the little girl, then at Abigail. "Sorry, but people from the outside have not exactly been helpful."

"Understood." Abigail bent over and picked up the little girl.

"Honey, you need to go with these nice men. They are my good Russian friends. We need to take a boat ride. Okay?"

"You're coming too?"

Abigail smiled. "I'll be right along. We need to look for someone first. Okay?"

The little girl looked none too happy to let go of her new found friend, but finally acquiesced. Another black female took her, and the group began to follow the Russians. Abigail looked, saw no one matching a Bollywood East Indian actress that would be Red.

"Red…?"Abigail began to ask.

"They took her out about an hour ago," answered Jayla. "Some Krakens wanted to have some fun with her before we were fed to the Squids."

"Damn," said Abigail, using a very infrequent curse word.

"Ichiro, we need to look for Red in the nearby warehouses…"

Abigail's radio crackled to life. "Major, we have visitors approaching." SSgt. Wall broadcast. "The six-wheeled kind, as well as some more Krakens and I think a couple of those Soldiers they have been making recently."

"Affirmative." Abigail stepped over and picked up the assault rifle from the Kraken she had shot. She rifled his body and found a couple of spare magazines.

"Abby-san," Ichiro began. She cut him off.

"You go. I will delay the harvesters and others, and look for Red."

"No. Major, you come with us. With me."

She glared into the love of her life's eyes. "No. The females are making an agreement, the order to stand down was given. No more people die. No more people are eaten! We leave no one behind."

Ichiro sighed, then touched her face with a gentle hand. "What am I to do with you, my love?" he said in Japanese. "You are as stubborn as I."

"That is because, my husband, we both have the spirit of the samurai. Of modern Bushido. The innocent do not die when we are about."

Ichiro Yamamoto realized once more just how much he loved Abigail, how well they fit together and were made for each other. The dream he had all those so many years ago had come true. He knew his parents were watching over them. "Come then, my beautiful wife. I will obtain another assault rifle from a dead Kraken, and we will search together. Though I wished I had brought my bow. I'm much better with traditional Japanese weapons than modern firearms."

Abigail smiled. "Said the jet fighter pilot. You will do fine. If not, I will pick up the slack. We are a team."

"The best team, Abby-san. The very best."

Torbin Bender met Malcolm Carter as the two Banshees brought him to the trawler.

"Malcolm Carter, I presume. I am Colonel Torbin Bender. Madam President of the Unoccupied States sent us to rescue you." Torbin put his hand out to shake and Malcolm took it, but did not seem overly enthusiastic.

"You're that crazy Marine who tried to fuck the Director and the Squids." He paused for a moment. "Did you really kill a Squid with a knife? Or was that all bullshit propaganda?"

Torbin smiled. 'My Ka-Bar was part of the fight, yes. After we get you to safety, I'll tell you the whole story.

"I'm not leaving until we find Red. Period. Dead or alive." Malcolm's jaw tightened as he made the statement.

"Colonel," Sumi broke in. "Colonel and Major Yamamoto were looking for survivors. They will report back shortly."

"Well, Mr. Carter, I think that it would be best for us to wait and see what they find. Until then, these two ladies will take you down below, have all those cuts and bruises looked at."

Malcolm shrugged. "I've had worse. But some cold water would be nice."

"I'll take care of him, Colonel," Porsche said.

"Thank you, my Sister," replied Malcolm. "You escaped from Cattle Country?"

"Yes Sir. Found a new home in Montana in the military. Until we take Georgia back."

Malcolm gave her a serious look. "I'd like to hear your story while I drink that cold water."

"Coming right up, Sir."

"Call me Malcolm."

As Malcolm Carter was taken to the large Trawlers day room, Malcolm looked out and saw the Spetsnaz troops approaching, a large group of women and children in tow. One Spetsnaz was Fireman Carried by another, an additional soldier had an arm in a sling. So there had been casualties.

He did not see Abigail and Ichiro. He knew that meant they were staying back for a reason.

"SSgt. Wall, have the U.S. troops head out and replace the Spetsnaz in searching for others."

"Yes Sir."

Before SSgt. Wall could even formulate the orders, SSgt. Black was already walking by Torbin with his heavy sniper rifle slung at the ready.

"Going somewhere, Sergeant?" Torbin asked.

"I've got this feeling that the Avenging Angel can use me out there. What with a bunch of harvesters and others approaching." His mouth formed his small signature smile. "I cut my teeth on harvester and battle robs, Sir."

Torbin chuckled. "Far be it for me to disagree with the battle instincts of the Reaper. Go out and find them. Help get them back in one piece."

"I aim to please, Colonel."

Heavy fire was heard from the far side of the warehouses.

"Ah shit," said Torbin. Sergeant Black began to jog into harm's way.

As Torbin and company were discovering not everyone on the Tschaaa side was standing down, Andrew was overseeing the very unusual first-of-its-kind meeting of the male and female Tschaaa. So far, so good. The demand by Cassandra to recognize the Protocol of Order had started the new ball rolling, and it was picking up momentum.

Andrew stood up straight.

"No," Andrew said out loud. "He would not be so stupid… I am wrong. He is. And evil."

Andrew turned toward his fellow robocops. Via their computer link, he communicated.

"I will be back. Ensure this conference remains calm and productive."

"Of course," replied Andrew's fellow cyborg named Jacob. "There is a problem?"

"I just noticed a message about the Minor Lord known as the Wizard. He refused to accept the Protocol of Order, threatened to resist any compromise with massive destruction. I think he has been infected with humanity's more warlike desires and activities."

"Can he accomplish this?"

"He is taking control of the mass drivers on the Asteroid Base One. He has been storing the debris and material from humanity's various space launches and failed satellites he swept from near Earth orbit the past few years, since he was given control of Platform One. That material was never destroyed."

"So, Andrew, he has rocks to throw."

"Yes, my comrade. With many large ones available. I must go. Please contact me as things progress." The cyborg turned to leave.

"Andrew, what is happening?" His former Lord, Neptune, called out.

"I am off to see the Wizard, and not the one from Oz. I need stop him from destroying our yellow brick road to a compromise in survival. I will return."

Lord Neptune started to call after him, but Andrew was moving like the proverbial bat out of hell.

"Go with your God," the now fallen Lord said to himself. "May He or She give you the correct guidance I could not."

Andrew dashed out of the meeting chamber area, his Falcon already raising into the air answering his computer link command. As it rose, the access gangway began to retract, but not before a metallic tentacle shot out and grasped Andrew as he leapt into the air. With practiced ease, Andrew was pulled into the craft, the access door closed after him. In seconds, Andrew was in the pilot's seat.

"Come, my beauty," he said to himself and the aerial ship. "Time to make haste to outer space..."

Then he paused, as his mind was instantly flooded with additional information. "Not the Director and his family. I should have foreseen this insanity between Reverend Kray and this Lord Wizard. I was too full of myself."

The Falcon rose straight up in the blink of an eye, then halted some five thousand feet above the Sea Platform, hovering.

"That is the solution. I need Torbin Bender and others to help for I cannot be in several places at once. First, Savannah, then Key West, then outer space. My fellows must stay on Earth, make sure there are no more Lord Wizards hiding in the wings."

The Falcon accelerated, setting off a loud sonic boom.

Ichiro and Abigail had tried to swing around the back of the dock warehouses, only to run into a harvester rob and two Krakens. Abigail's fantastic marksmanship took out the two Krakens, but she and Ichiro had to combine their firepower to defeat the harvester rob with their relatively light .223 assault rifles. Then, more of the enemy showed up.

Hunkered down behind a piece of rusting farm machinery which had never made it off the docks, Abigail began, for the first time in Ichiro's memory, to curse and swear profusely, in all the various languages in which she was fluent. Which were many.

"No! I will not allow this to happen! The Squids and their minions were supposed to stand down, acquiesce. This is not acquiescing to anything."

Ichiro fired a couple of rounds of his rapidly depleted rifle ammunition. He then turned to Abigail and spoke in Japanese. "Abigail, we must back off, look for another way or retreat to the trawler. We lack the firepower to defeat all these Krakens and robots." A burst of automatic fire from a harvester, now battle rob, seemed to punctuate his statement.

A tear of rage ran down Abigail's cheek. "Red and others are out there. Even if the Tschaaa don't, these Kraken abominations will kill and eat them. We cannot leave them."

Ichiro looked at his wife. He straightened his back a bit, then spoke. "Then we must decide if we fight until we die."

"This is unfair!" Abigail screamed. "My God in Heaven, where are you when I need you?"

There was a loud report from off to their left, a bit behind them. Followed by another. Then another.

An enraged Abigail snuck a peak around their metallic cover. There was another loud report, answered by human yells and automatic fire.

"What do you see, Abby-san?"

"My Lord Jesus. It is the Reaper. He has drawn their fire."

Benjamin Black did not use the usual tactics of precision snipes. He did not set up prepared locations with secure rifle support or a stand to help hold his weapon steady. Instead, he used temporary and fleeting positions, using whatever was available as a stationary rifle rest. He was very quick in this. He fired and moved. He had developed and battle tested his methods during his long retreat to Malmstrom Armed Forces Base years ago. The man now known as The Reaper had refined them ever since.

He was deadly.

First he took out the nearest harvester and battle robs with his special penetrator rounds. Even these mechanical monsters could not seem to deal with his quick shoot and move. Then, Krakens had their heads exploded, or their torsos penetrated with high velocity .338 Lapua rounds. They shot at where he had been, not where he was at.

Finally, the two Soldier Class biped warriors came up and began to rake the area with their electromagnetic bolt guns. For a moment, it seemed as if this would be the end of him.

Benjamin Black crawled beneath a truck trailer with flattened tires which lowered the machine closed to the ground. He peaked around a wheel whose tire was almost gone, exposing the large metal interior wheel.

"Eenie, meenie, miney, mo, shoot an alien in the toe…" He pulled the trigger on his rifle. The right foot of one of the artificial creatures disappeared in a spray of bluish blood. The Soldier toppled over.

"If he is not dead, shoot him in the head." The creature's head exploded as it tried to rise. Bursts of fire came from around SSgt. Black. The rest of the American contingent had arrived and were on target. The remaining Soldier Class Warrior staggered back under the weight of the fire, then toppled over in a spasm. It twitched violently, then lay still.

Benjamin Black crawled out from his hiding place and stood up. He saw Abigail and Ichiro about a hundred yards away and whistled, waved. They waved back, then dashed over to his location under cover fire from the other Americans. The few Krakens still alive seemed to be melting back into the lengthened shadows of the setting sun.

"Sergeant Black, we owe you our lives," Ichiro expressed as they stood behind the cover of the truck trailer.

"Just doing my job, Sir. Colonel Bender wanted to be sure you two were each still in one piece."

"Well, we are," Abigail answered. "We still have to look for survivors."

They heard a yell of warning, then felt an odd electricity in the air. A Falcon appeared over the trawler.

"I think serious trouble just arrived," the Reaper said.

CHAPTER 45

Director Adam Lloyd sat at his desk in his Key West office when his desk telephone rang. He had been sitting, running over a checklist in his mind for the bug out. Chief Hamilton was en route with a couple of vehicles to transport himself, his wives and his children to the pier berthing the Admiral's large Hatteras fishing boat/ yacht. Adam did not expect a good outcome from the meeting of Tschaaa Lords on the sea platform. The Admiral had offered Adam one of his day fishing trips as a cover for a trip to Cuba. The dark-skinned Cubans who still harvested sugar cane for Lord Neptune had created a sanctuary in the mountains as payment for being saved from the butcher's block by Adam and the Chief.

Adam picked up the phone. "Director here." The line went dead. Adam frowned as he stared at the hand set, then replaced it in its cradle.

Heidi Faust sat in the outer office, doing Mary's job as she and Kat were getting the kids from the medical clinic. Adam had sent everyone to get a last once over exam before lighting out for Cuba. It may be awhile before they could see a real doctor.

There was no shots of warning, just the racket of large bodies coming up the large entrance stairway from the first to the second floor. Heidi yelled and there was the sound of hand to hand fighting. Adam grabbed for his Glock Pistol but his office door burst open before he could get to it.

"Freeze, fucker." A very large Kraken was pointing an equally large pistol at his face. Adam froze, trying to process what was happening. Another large individual came around the desk, pushed him back in his chair, and ransacked his desk drawers for his pistols. Then he stood behind him.

A slender Kraken with an air of command walked in, as Adam heard Heidi yelling and cursing in the front office.

"Don't kill her, damnit. Bring the bitch in here with her boss."

Adam looked at the man. "And you are?"

"Ray Sparks. Deputy Commander to John Talbot. You are now the prisoner of the Most Reverend Kray, working in concert with Lord Wizard from the Space Platform."

"What happened to Lord Neptune?"

Ray Sparks almost spit on the floor. "That piece of cowardly Squid shit. He and the other Lords have decided to make some deal with some Breeders and humans. Goddamn Robocop Andrew has something to do with it. The Wizard had us standing by just in case something like this happened from that meeting. So, we got a call a few minutes ago that it was time to take over."

"And how, pray tell, Commander Sparks, are you going to do that unless the other Lords agree?

Sparks grinned. "Rocks. Lord Wizard is taking control of the mass drivers on the Asteroid."

Icy fingers ran up Adam's spine as two more large men dragged a protesting Heidi into the office, and pushed her down onto the sofa. Her mouth was bloody.

"Sorry Boss. They got the drop on me."

Adam gave her a slight smile. "Not your fault. I should have foreseen this." He looked at Sparks, who had a satisfied look on his face.

"You know if the Wizard starts throwing rocks around, all hell will break loose. We may be all bombed back to the Stone Age."

"Who cares? We're all going to be taken to the Asteroid, set up a nice colony in all that extra space up there, since a lot of the Tschaaa left to go home. Any Tschaaa that die down here are worthless, weak cowards. They may make good sushi, but that's it."

"Let me guess. This Wizard is going to have his own Breeders, create his own Crèche up there."

"Already started. The Lords down here are too fat, dumb and happy to even notice. And now they just surrendered. So, the weak die. We and the Wizard will be the apex predators."

"What's to stop them from eating you?"

"Why, Director. You and all the others will help provide enough meat. We Krakens will help harvest surviving dark meat, set up breeding pens on the asteroid. Like I said, lots of extra room now."

"What will you live on, Sparks?"

The man shrugged. "We'll take some supplies with us, though some have developed a taste for Long Pig. The vats they developed on the Space Platform One are beginning to grow some better meat products among other things. So we should do fine if everyone else kills each other."

Sparks' cellphone rang. "Sparks here. Okay…what? I thought I told you people to be careful with the merchandise. I don't care what they did to you, asshole. Just get over here. Now."

Sparks began to curse. "Good help is hard to find."

"Where's Talbot and Reverend Kray?"

"You'll know soon enough. Now, just sit there, relax. Fix yourself a drink."

Adam did that, had the Krakens hand some ice in a towel to Heidi, and fixed a drink for her. He noticed none of the Kraken security personnel made a move to partake of any of the alcohol. Sparks had them on a short leash. It was about ten minutes later when Adam heard another group of people approaching. A bruised and bloody Chief Hamilton was shoved into the room, then pushed down into a chair. Following him were Professor Joseph Fassbinder and a woman it took a moment for Adam to recognize due to the battering her face had taken. It was Jolene from the Roach Coach, one of the Admiral's daughters.

"This is it, huh?" Sparks asked.

"They killed them, Adam," the Chief blurted out. "Jane Grant, Jeanie and Jamey. They shot them all."

"The stupid bitches tried to stop us from taking the kids…" one of the large Krakens began to say.

Adam let out a feral scream and launched himself across the desk, trying to get to the Kraken who had just spoken. It was a short and nasty fight, with Adam winding up on the carpet, seeing stars, and one Kraken on his knees, holding his testicles, with another one cursing as he nursed a gouged eye. Heidi was still wrestling on the sofa with two of the Krakens when Sparks held a gun to the Chief's head.

"Keep it up and he dies also. I didn't want those deaths, but it happened. So, we have to deal with it."

Adam slowly rose to a sitting, then a standing position. A Kraken maneuvered him back into his desk chair, and Joseph Fassbinder spoke up. "They took Sarah, Mary and Kat, plus the children. Major Grant, Jeanie and Jamie tried to stop them…"

Tears began to run down Adam's face. "Where are my wives and children?"

"Reverend Kray and Talbot are taking them up to airfield on Marathon. A Falcon the Wizard has will pick them up, take them to the Asteroid, Base One, as special guests. We have plans for them."

Adam ground his teeth, tried not to explode again. "What plans?"

"Why, they have proven their worth as Breeders. Plus, your children are the first of a line of modified humans. They will be raised, studied as future improvements are considered. At least that is what the Reverend says."

Sparks' cellphone rang again. "Sparks here. The Admiral is approaching? Yes, send the crazy fool up. I think the Reverend has some use for him." Sparks cut the connection.

"You killed the security downstairs also, didn't you?" Adam asked.

"And at the Main Gate. We have some people watching the other security personnel on base. So far, no one is kicking up a fuss as since everyone now knows there is a big fuck up going on at that grand meeting. Most everyone seems to be waiting to see what's going to happen, whose side they want to be on."

"Ever think, Sparks, that you could be on the wrong side?"

Sparks shrugged. "Kind of hard to change horses in midstream, as they say. But so far Talbot's been good to me, and the Rev and the Wizard seem to be keeping their promises. Plus, they have more plans and guts to go with them than all the others."

"Guts with no morals can create huge problems."

Sparks laughed. "Yeah, you should know. Playing toady to Neptune as they slaughtered people a state away. How can you claim better morals when you stand by while they eat other humans, even if they are dark-skinned? I don't hide behind fake morals, or make excuses. You get what you see."

Now the Admiral's voice could be heard resonating form the outer office.

"What is all this fuss going on? Where is the Director? Oh, there you are."

The Admiral made his typical 'grand entrance', all bedecked in his potentate uniform with all its flourishes and Naval Officer's Dress Hat to match. He walked right up to Adam's desk as if no one else was in the room, Sharon and Susanne walking a little behind him, one on each side.

"I heard you called a meeting, Director Lloyd, but neglected to invite me. Not very nice nor correct in matters of protocol."

"Hey, Admiral," said Sparks. "Over here. Commander Sparks here. I'm in charge now, not him."

The Admiral acted startled, as if he had just noticed all the other people in the room. Adam watched as Sharon and Susanne stepped a bit back and to the side of the Admiral, the poker faces they were wearing told the Director that they were not missing anything.

"What. A palace coup, and I was not invited? For shame. You are residing in the Conch Republic. These are my marinas, docks and businesses. I allow you all to stay out of the largess of my heart."

Sparks and several of the Krakens laughed at the supposed outrage of the Admiral.

"Alright, let's cut the shit," said Sparks. "A new boss is in town. Neptune's out, or soon will be with all the other worthless Lords. Lord Wizard from the Space Platform is taking over with us Krakens and Reverend Kray. You play with us, or not at all."

The man called the Admiral looked all around the room for the apparent first time. "You brought twelve armed personnel, Commander Sparks. Eight here, four outside. And I see you still felt it necessary to beat and abuse Jolene here, one of my daughters. Are you that afraid?"

Sparks flushed a bit, angered.

"All right, you stupid old fart. Your 'daughter' Jolene is a Spy for the U.S. Right under your nose. Just ask her.

The Admiral looked at the battered Jolene. "Is that true, my child?"

Jolene nodded yes.

"Well, I forgive you. I am the Admiral. I can grant forgiveness." With that, the Admiral performed a flourish of hand motions and signs that ended in signing a large cross as if he were in church.

"There, you are forgiven."

"Well, the Rev hasn't forgiven her yet, buddy," Sparks snarled. "And he is the only one around here that can grant forgiveness."

"Why, my good man Commander Sparks. The Most Reverend Kray and I have had an ecumenical relationship stretching back to the Coming of the Tschaaa. I have a letter... I always carry it... where is it?" The Admiral seemed confused for a moment.

Then "Ah. It is in my hat for safe keeping. I will get it." The Admiral began to remove his hat as Sparks said with a harsh laugh, "This I've got to see..."

"Here it is..." A 22 magnum derringer pistol appeared in the Admiral's hand as he moved with a quickness of a man half his perceived age. He shot the Kraken directly in front of him through the right eye, then in a blink of an eye shot the large Kraken behind Adam through the throat. Blonde Sharon and brunette Susanne both exploded into action. Their moves seemed blurred they reacted so quickly. Kicks, fist blows, elbow smashes rained down on the stunned Kraken personnel as the two former Olympic-caliber volleyball players became whirling dervishes of destruction.

Heidi kicked both of the now distracted Krakens standing over her in their groins, one foot for each. She screamed out, "Kiai!" as she leapt from the sofa and was in the mix, shoving her injured opponents back. Joseph Fassbinder threw himself on top of one of them, sinking his teeth into the man's throat.

Adam flopped his chair over as the Kraken shot in the throat fell sideways to the carpet, the guard grasping his throat as his life blood pumped out. Adam grabbed the large caliber automatic the dying Kraken had shoved in his waistband and then rolled to a kneeling position. He shot the only female Kraken in attendance between the eyes as she was attempting to bring her assault weapon to bear in the crowded room. He looked toward Sparks in time to see the Chief tackle him. The older man proceeded to beat the Kraken Commander bloody with the man's own pistol.

The Admiral had somehow recovered an assault weapon himself, and began to slam the stock into the rear of the skull of any Kraken still standing.

Then it was over, ended as quickly as it had started. Heidi had recovered her butterfly knife and was slitting the throat of any still moving Kraken. No one tried to stop her killing them—except for Sparks, as they needed to talk to him. The Admiral moved to the stairway with his rifle and easily picked off two dumbfounded Kraken coming up from the front of the building. Adam found his own rifle as he joined the Admiral, waiting for the last to members of Sparks' detail to appear. They were nowhere in sight.

"I told you this old coot has been fooling us, Susanne. No one could be that weird."

"Alright, I agree. You were right. But we're still there for him, right Sharon?"

"Me too," chimed in Heidi. "He, and you two, saved my bacon."

Sharon hugged her, ignoring the blood. "What are friends for?"

Adam walked back in and over to where the Chief had Sparks secured.

"Alright, Sparks. Who's with Kray and Talbot?"

"Fuck you," the Kraken Commander spit out through split lips.

"Heidi."

"Yeah, Boss." Heidi walked over to the chair Sparks was zip tied to, grabbed his head tight with one arm, and went after his left eye with her knife.

"No!" Sparks screamed. "They have a dozen kids besides the three wives."

"Including our kids, right? I said, right?"

"Yes!"

Adam looked at the others in the room. "I need a vehicle. We need several to get to the Marathon airfield."

"You can have my Humvee," said the Admiral. "Though I would be a good extra gun."

"You're on. Grab any weapons, drag Sparks along, head downstairs."

A minute later, the somewhat battered group was downstairs, Joseph Fassbinder supporting the badly beaten Jolene.

"Sharon, Susanne, will you two please quit staring at me," said the Admiral.

"Why in hell did you not tell us, Admiral?" shot back Susanne.

"Deniability. Something you learn in the worlds of politics and intelligence, ladies. If things went south, you two could claim ignorance and be truthful."

"And leave you?" asked Sharon. In a heartbeat both of the Admiral's bodyguards were hugging and kissing him.

"Hey. Quit that."

"Look it, 'father', don't you ever lie to us again. We're family."

"Okay! Now let go."

The Admiral looked at Jolene. "You did not tell me for deniability also, Jolene."

"Yes. I also thought you were nuts." She managed to say through swollen lips.

"I guess my acting was better than I thought." He bent over and kissed her on the forehead. She began to cry.

"You're family now, Jolene. No more secrets."

"Alright," interjected Adam. "Into the Admiral's HUMVEE and this Kraken staff car…"

There was a crack, a thump and a strong rush of air that knocked everyone back a step. Hovering a few yards in front and about twelve feet in the air was now what could only be called the traditional flying saucer, one about the size of a small one story house.

"Damn, another Squid trick?" asked Adam as everyone raised their weapons at the craft.

"No. Don't shoot." Joseph called out. "I know who this is."

No sooner had he said that then a hatchway appeared in the seamless body of the saucer. Two human figures seemed to float out until one noticed what looked like an umbilical cord connected at the two figure's spines.

"It's the Olson twins, Samuel and Sandy. They worked for me," Joseph explained. Then he stared. The two young people he had helped mentor, with already light skin of natural redheads, were now so white as to be almost translucent. They looked gaunt, as if they had only been living on liquids for quite some time.

"Sam, Sandy. What are you two doing here? And how…"

"She sent us," Sandy interjected. "And She brought us also."

"She? The saucer is a… she?"

Both of the Olson twins smiled. "That's what was confusing us, Professor. All along we were dealing with a living being, not an intelligent machine."

Everyone was staring, dumbfounded that yet another alien creature was in their midst, thanks to the Tschaaa coming to Earth.

"I hate to interrupt, but I need to rescue my family," said Adam.

"You need to come with us, Director," Sandy said. "You need to the stop the Wizard. He is about to destroy much of the Earth and its inhabitants. That makes Her very angry."

"What? Why me?"

"Because She said it's what has to be done. It is hard to explain, but She… exists, or at least sees, senses in different time streams and universes. If She says something needs to be done, we have learned we had better do it. Or some unresolved problem kicks us in the ass."

"Or tries to kill us," added Sam.

Adam looked at the Admiral and the Chief.

"Stranger things have happened, I guess, Boss," the Chief shrugged. "You go with them. I think the Admiral can rally some troops to help us get Mary, Kat, Sarah and the kids back. After all, we are just dealing with some religious fanatics.

"Very dangerous fanatics," Adam shot back. "Okay. Heidi, grab a rifle…"

"No guns, Director. She was shot once, hates projectile weapons near, onboard Her, in Her."

"Crap. Well, I have my old standby made in Pakistan knife and Heidi has her balisong butterfly…"

"Here, Heidi. Picked this up off a dead asshole." The Admiral handed a short bush machete to the former Coastie. Heidi smiled and twirled it once in her hands, and grinned.

"Yeah, this will definitely do in a pinch. Shall we, Director? I always wanted to say I flew on a flying saucer."

A ramp morphed from the hatch so the two humans could board. As that happened, a redheaded female figure came from inside the building, holding a bloody knife and an assault rifle.

"Can anyone play?" Inna Popov asked.

"Where'd you come from?" Chief Hamilton asked. "And who did you kill?"

"A couple of Krakens who were sneaking around in the back. They misjudged that a pretty woman is not dangerous."

The Admiral looked at Inna. "Let me guess. You were spying also, in addition to broadcasting."

"Yes." Jolene managed to croak out. "She was helping me. And... Jane Grant was coming over..." Jolene began to cry again.

"She's dead." Inna stated.

"Yes, Inna, she is," replied the Chief.

Inna swore in Russian.

"We're off," called out Adam as he mounted the ramp into the 'ship' that was alive.

"Head and ass down, Boss."

"Head and ass down, Chief." Adam paused for just a moment. "No matter what happens..."

"No Hollywood speeches, Boss. Just go take care of business. We'll get the women and children back."

"Thanks, old friend."

"De nada."

With that, Adam and Heidi were inside the saucer. The ramp disappeared into the side of the living vessel and the hatch sealed over, no seam showing. The saucer rose up about another thirty feet, then just winked out of existence. There was a loud crack as air rushed back into fill the area vacated by the saucer.

Susanne whistled. "Damn, that's cool."

"Yeah. One hell of a carnival ride," Sharon opined.

"Okay, saddle up," the Chief barked. He looked at the Admiral. "You got people who can meet us up there?"

"A cell phone or radio call away, Chief."

"Good. Start calling. This is about to get even more interesting than it has been. "

CHAPTER 46

SAVANNAH, GEORGIA

Torbin watched the Falcon hover over the fishing trawler as Vikings and Spetsnaz scrambled to grab the anti-tank and anti-aircraft missiles they had stored. Torbin wondered why the craft had not just blasted them out of the water. Maybe the pilot had not made a connection between them and the shooting going on nearby. Then, the loud voice explained it all.

"Torbin Bender. This is Andrew. I need you." It came from the Falcon's sound system and vibrated over the port area.

"Stand down people!" Torbin shouted. "Believe it or not, it's a friendly."

Torbin looked up at the Falcon. "Andrew, what in the hell are you doing here?"

"Trying to save the world. What else?" Andrew broadcast in reply. "I need you, Abigail and Ichiro. We need to make a trip to save some women and children as well as the Director. I cannot be in two places at once."

Torbin grinned. "Alright. Let me check on my payload down below, make sure it's secured. Abigail and Ichiro will be back shortly."

"Please, hurry. Time is of the essence."

Torbin hit up Ichiro on the radio, told him to beat feet back as soon as possible.

Abigail only acquiesced giving up the search for Red and others when Sergeant Black had looked at her and gave the slight smile he for which he was known.

"I'll stay behind, keep looking, Ma'am."

"Just you? How will you get out of here?"

"Ma'am, I lived behind the lines for a long time during the early days, did it again during Bloody Kansas. I'm used to working alone."

"Come Abigail," interjected Ichiro. "We need to go. I believe Sergeant Black will find Red if she is still with the living, as well as get her back into the U.S.A."

Abigail looked at the man known as the Reaper. "Good luck. May God be with you."

"Thank You, Ma'am. Somebody must've been watching over me all these years."

"Come, Abigail. We must go."

With a last glance around, Abigail, Ichiro and the rest of the American personnel began to run toward the trawler. As they did, the Reaper disappeared into the lengthening shadows of sunset.

Torbin ran and slid down the stairs to the fish hold. To say he was surprised to see Malcolm Carter standing and staring at the She-Bear Missile was an understatement.

"You always wander off alone?" Torbin asked.

"Sorry. But I needed to take a look at this… weapon."

"Well, it's deactivated right now. President's orders."

"Yeah, I heard." The former Mayor of Atlanta turned and faced Torbin with a pistol in his hand.

"This Sig still has almost a full magazine. You need to start up the countdown to launch again. Now."

Torbin stared at Malcolm. Then, he burst into laughter.

"This is not fucking funny. I'm serious."

"Or what? You're going to shoot me? Then what? You think I can launch it after I'm dead?"

"Your wife will be a widow, your children won't have a father."

"Yeah? As if I haven't faced that before? Ours is not to reason why, ours is but to do or die. I've lived with that concept for years."

He snorted and shook his head. "Go ahead and shoot. It won't accomplish a damned thing."

Malcolm grit his teeth. "What if I shoot the missile?"

"Then you may have a nice big explosion, which will fry all those kids up above in the day room and kitchen."

"But it will disperse the warhead, the killer shit in it that Porsche told me about."

"Maybe. But maybe not. Shoot the warhead itself, you might get some dispersal, and again maybe kill some women and children upstairs. That stuff contains a neurotoxin that can be deadly to people, especially children."

"Sir. Put the gun down." It was Porsche Jefferson, clambering down the stairs.

"Stay out of this, my sister. This is between me and Mr. White Soldier here."

"No. We are all on the same side. Please, put the gun down." She started to walk toward Malcolm.

"No. Stay back. Don't be a damn fool." He turned and pointed the pistol at her.

"Oh now isn't this just great. Now you are going to shoot a survivor of Cattle Country. Are you insane, Malcolm?"

"Shut up!" Malcolm began to shake with rage.

"Where were you when we had to watch our people being slaughtered and eaten? When we had to watch out young girls being groomed to be breeders, to have kids, for fresh veal. Where were you when we were hiding in basements, sewers as they came for us?

"Look it, Carter. Everyone has lost family, friends to the Squids. Hell, they tried to kill me and mine with Eaters. Now we have a chance to end the killing, without making it worse."

"End the killing? For you, maybe. I don't want to see it end. I want to see those Squids squirm and scream as their young die before their eyes. See how they like it. Now, reactivate the countdown for missile launch. I won't tell you again."

"Shoot away, buddy. I don't do well with threats."

Malcolm raised the pistol, aimed it at Torbin's face.

"No!" Porsche lunged at him, moving fast for such a large woman. Instinct caused Malcolm to turn toward the threat from a different direction. Porsche slammed into him, and the pistol discharged. Everything seemed to freeze for a second. Then, the black Sergeant slid to the deck. Torbin smashed into Malcolm, twisted the pistol from his grasp and threw it across the ship's hold. Malcolm was young and strong, with fighting skills. But he was facing a foe with years of training and experience in most every type of fighting imaginable, and a foe fueled by rage. In about fifteen seconds, the former Mayor was laying at Torbin's feet, blood flowing from his mouth.

"Torbin." It was Abigail, back aboard the ship and responded toward the gun shot. She saw Porsche laying on the deck, vaulted over the stair railing part way down, and was next to the shot Sergeant in seconds.

"Porsche. Stay with me. Sergeant Knudsen, Gunnar! Medic!"

Ichiro was already leaping down the stairs, then kneeling next to Abigail. Cries and shouts were heard from up above as others responded. Sergeant Porsche Jefferson looked up into Abigail's eyes as the Avenging Angel tried to apply direct pressure to stem the blood flow.

"Sister, I see Momma…" Her eyes glazed over, she let out her last breath, and died.

Abigail leaned back, shaking. "No!" Her scream was one of psychic pain, from deep within her. She leapt up, turned toward Malcolm Carter, the killer look in her eye. Ichiro grabbed and hugged her. She started to drag him across the deck.

"Abby–san, no!" the samurai said in Japanese. "Remember our training. Control. Do not let this anger control you. Control it."

Abigail stopped pushing, began to shake. Sergeant Rolf and others arrived, went to the black Sergeant, saw it was too late. She was beyond help.

"You!" Abigail yelled at Malcolm. "Someday you will face Final Judgement. Explain to Jesus Christ and God why you killed an innocent. Explain that." She turned in Ichiro's grasp, whispered in Japanese, "I am in control now. I need to get out from the sight of this horrible fool."

Ichiro kissed her on the forehead, then released her. She walked, then bounded up the metal stairs.

"Sergeant Knudsen. We need to get this…man here up on deck and secured."

"Yes Sir."

"One minute," interrupted Ichiro. He grabbed the injured

Malcolm Carter and pulled him over to the corpse of Porsche. "What color is that blood? Red, yes?"

Ichiro pulled his tanto knife and in one quick motion, slit a finger.

"See? Red blood also." He reached over and pulled Torbin's bloody knuckles up to the former Mayor's face "See? Red blood also."

He put his face inches from Malcolm. "We all bleed red, no matter our skin color. I thought, you, of anyone, would realize all of us here with red blood are in this together. Baka." Ichiro turned from the now silent Malcolm and ran up the stairs to find Abigail.

"Torbin Bender!" Andrew's voice vibrated and shook the trawler. "We must leave. Now."

"Shit," said Torbin. Everything had been forgotten in the death and violence.

"Sergeant Knudsen. Mr. Crater is in your hands."

"Yes Sir," said the huge twin of Rolf. Within moments, he was almost carrying the black man up the stairs to the day room and kitchen area. As Gunnar set him down, most of the women and children moved away from him. They had heard what had happened.

Torbin met Abigail and Ichiro on the deck below the hovering Falcon.

"Here," he handed Abigail her lever action Marlin. He had Malcolm's Sig Sauer in his belt, his 44 Magnum pistol still in his shoulder holster. Ichiro had recovered his bow and arrows.

"Are we good?" He asked.

"Yes, big brother," replied Abigail. "With you, we are always good."

"Okay. Andrew and duty call."

Torbin looked skyward and the underside of the Falcon opened. In a moment, the three were whisked aboard the Falcon and out of sight by metallic tentacles. The Falcon was gone in a blink of the eye.

"I hope the Colonel knows what he is doing." SSgt. Wall said from the wheel house.

"I believe he does, my friend." Bjorn Heyerdahl said. "If anyone does, he does. Now, Helmsman, let us get underway before more Krakens show up. We need to get the women and children to safety."

"Aye aye, Sir."

The Falcon sped across Georgia, down to and across the Florida

Panhandle and across the Gulf toward Key West.

"This is smooth and fast," said Ichiro the fighter pilot. "Maybe I could pilot a Falcon someday."

"That may be arranged, if all goes well in the next sixty minutes of so."

"If not?" Abigail asked.

"Then we and the Earth may be in for more pain and destruction, if this fool the Wizard has his way."

"Nice to know that Tschaaa Lords can be as stupid and childish as humans," said Torbin.

"Has that ever in doubt, Torbin Bender?"

"Hm. I guess you have a point, Andrew. Which then begs the question how they defeated us so quickly."

"Surprise and stealth initially. Then through pure terror perpetrated by Tschaaa and Kraken. And sometimes by my fellow cyborgs."

Torbin flashed a feral grin. "Terror? They ain't seen nothing yet. They have now have awakened the sleeping dragon."

Andrew seemed to communicate silently through some sort of uplink.

"Something unusual is going on near Key West. I will pull in near the Marathon Airport where they are holding the Director's wives and children, as well as others imprisoned. Their plans for them are not nice."

"Just put us down fast, on the move Andrew. We'll do the rest."

"Thank you, Torbin. The thought of innocent children being harmed at this date is no longer acceptable. Which is one of the reasons why I helped institute this revolution in thought, and helped the breeders. Eating anyone's young offspring is nauseating."

"Well, I guess beef veal cutlets are off the menu."

"You will soon grow them in a vat. Just wait."

The Falcon went low and seemed to slow. "The ramp will open, you three will have to leap out and roll as if you have just come in on a parachute."

Torbin looked at Abigail and Ichiro. "Ready, my brother and sister?"

"We are always ready, by your side, Torbin." Answered Abigail. "The Lord is with us this day. I feel it."

"Yea, though we walk through the Valley of Death, we shall fear no Evil," said the Marine. "For we are the biggest, meanest badass people in the valley."

Ichiro flashed a large grin. "As we used to say, banzai!"

The center ramp began to drop, and the three immediately went to it. They began sliding down it as Andrew yelled, "Now!" The craft came to an almost stop several feet from the ground. The three warriors dropped off the ramp and rolled as the Falcon then accelerated straight up.

With practiced ease the three formed a loose triangle and began to move toward the Marathon Airport, Andrew had dropped them some fifty yard from the southeast corner. They made their way past a couple of old maintenance buildings and a rusting small hangar.

"There," whispered Ichiro. "There is a wire cage up on that grass taxiway. It contains people and children."

"Sharp pilot's eyes, Ichiro. Okay, Abigail, right. Ichiro, left. I'm up the middle."

No sooner than he had said that then four ghillie suited individuals popped up from the long uncut grass and brush surrounding the rarely used airport.

"Freeze, motherfuckers!" A voice called out.

A voice broadcast from an airport sound system. "Bring them to me. We were expecting them."

The four Krakens relieved the three of their firearms and marched them, hands on heads, up the airfield toward what seemed to be some seated figures near the large cage, the lengthening shadows of sunset making identification difficult. Torbin cursed himself for allowing them to be caught so flat-footed. He had come to assume all Krakens were poorly trained beasts. He was wrong.

Torbin saw the cage had been made from sections of chain link fence, and formed a complete box around some very upset children inside. He heard a loud female voice screaming from the north side of the cage area and looked over. The screamer was Kat Monroe, chained with two other women by their throats to heavy cement blocks, hands tied behind them..

"You motherfuckers had better not hurt my kids!" She screamed. "I'll cut your nuts off with a dull razor blade, stuff them down your throats!." She was so focused screaming at the seated individuals that she did not even notice Torbin. He looked at whom she was screaming and now recognized Reverend Kray and Talbot, seated, with several very large individuals standing around as security.

Kat kept screaming even after a female Kraken slapped her hard across her face. "Shut up—you're giving us all headaches."

Kat lunged at the Kraken, but was stopped short by the dog chain attached to her throat. "I'm going to kill you, bitch!"

Mary bumped her back. "Just wait, Kat. Adam will come. I know it."

Reverend Kray stood up and addressed the approaching captives.

"Ah, Torbin Bender. We meet at last. With the Samurai and Avenging Angel we have heard so much about. I assumed you would be much more… difficult."

"The day is not over yet, Rev. Although I must admit, I underestimated the skillsets of your people." The slender, black haired Reverend, who some said resembled a human vulture smiled broadly.

"Yes. These people were hand- picked. Those who failed to meet my standards were… eliminated, shall we say. But come closer, let us converse as civilized humans while we still may."

Torbin snorted. "Civilized humans do not eat each other. At least not in any civilization I know of."

"Ah, Colonel Bender. You forget the Mayans and the Aztecs, who were reported to have eaten the hearts of enemy warriors after sacrificing them. They were considered civilized for their time."

"That was then, this is now. "Abigail broke into the conversation.

"Ah, the Avenging Angel speaks. Bring her closer. I wish to see the person whose file is so interesting."

Ichiro growled a bit as she was shoved forward, hands still on top of her head. She glanced at him as if to say, "Don't" and was walked toward the Reverend by a guard. He rose from his large padded chair that had somehow been brought to the Airport.

"Careful, Sir," warned Talbot. "She has teeth."

Reverend Kray snorted. "Yes, I read your report, Talbot. However, she knows that her husband will be shot first should she try anything, don't you, my dear?"

Abigail spat on the grass. "You blaspheme the idea of a Reverend. You are a monster who eats little children. You will pay for this on

Judgement Day."

Kray laughed. "Judgment Day? With your God? Hardly. I think H.P. Lovecraft had it correct. There are Elder Gods who existed well before your Christ and his Father. The Kraken is their symbol. The Tschaaa were their Chosen Ones."

He sighed. "But they were so easily corrupted on this planet. So it is time for I, the most Reverend, to show them the correct way to worship, to live. Which is what I and the Lord Wizard are about to do."

"By killing people with rocks from space, as well as Tschaaa? Insane."

Reverend Kray frowned at Abigail. "Let's not be rude, my dear."

Kat chose that moment to yell again. "They're going to kill you, asshole. I can feel it."

Reverend turned angrily to Talbot. "Shut her up. Now. I am tired of her mouth."

Sarah Fassbinder yelled out. "You sick bastard. I hope you choke on your next meal."

"Her also. We do not really need them."

"The Wages of Sin is Death, Evil One." Abigail hissed at Kray.

"I think, all you young women need some lessons in manners." Kray looked at the Kraken holding Abigail. "Strip her of her clothes. Maybe without her vestments, she will not be so ready to talk back to her elders."

Ichiro began to curse in Japanese. One of the Kraken guards jabbed his assault rifle barrel into the Samurai's face. "Shut you hole, slant eye."

The Kraken holding Abigail slung his rifle, and started to unstrap her body armor.

There was a blur, a thwack, and a broad tipped arrow seemed as if by magic to impale the throat of the Kraken. It happened so fast, that time itself seemed to slow. Then the Kraken, eyes bulging, grabbed the arrow shaft as he toppled over. Another arrow impaled the throat of one of the Krakens guarding Torbin. And all hell broke loose. Abigail was a blur as she closed with Kray and rode him to the ground, thumbs gouging his eyes. Talbot and the Krakens standing around were conflicted in what to do, there being arrows coming from the lengthening shadows of sunset, as well as the problem of hitting Kray if they started shooting. Talbot moved up to help Kray as the others just stared into the woods.

The Kraken with the barrel in Ichiro's face discovered the mistake of getting this close and personal with a Jujutsu expert, as his rifle was wrestled away from him. The Kraken was quick and managed to pull the trigger, a short burst missing Ichiro's face as the New Samurai crushed the man's trachea with an edge of the hand blow. The burst struck the last Kraken guarding Torbin in the body armor underneath the ghillie camouflage. As the Kraken stumbled back from the shock, Torbin leapt on him. The Marine broke the man's nose and jaw, then ripped his rifle from his grasp. A quick turn around and Torbin shot the Kraken between the eyes.

As Talbot started to pull his knife to stab Abigail and not risk a bullet penetrating and striking Kray, Abigail let loose of the screaming Kray and caught Talbot's knife hand in a painful wrist lock. A quick twist and Talbot screamed as well as his wrist was broken. As the Kraken second in command tried to break free of Abigail's grasp in order to get his rifle into play, Abigail closed with him and headbutted his nose, breaking it. Talbot fell back. Another arrow impaled one of the Krakens near the Reverend, and the remaining two Krakens began to shoot wildly into the brush and shadows of the northern side of the airport. Several other Krakens who were guarding the vehicles in the parking lot about a block away came running, yelling, asking what was going on. Torbin used the now dead Kraken's rifle to begin firing on the approaching men, as well as at the two remaining guards for the Reverend.

Three low brown streaks came bursting out of the shadows behind the Krakens, slamming into the unsuspecting armed personnel. The Black Masked Curs bit and ripped, wild shots missing them in the pandemonium. As Kat screamed at the sights of revenge, she felt a presence behind her. The bonds on her hands were cut, and a huge double bladed axe parted the chain at the cement block.

"Get them," Dogman growled in her ear. Kat screamed and leapt at the nearest of the two female guards near them, both distracted and confused by the attack. They were armed only with cattle prods, Reverend Kray not wanting the chance of accidental death of the women until he said so.

Kat hit the dishwater blonde in a linebacker rush, knocking the cattle prod from her grasp. The remaining female Kraken turned to shock Kat and was hit by a flying tackle from Mary, followed by Sarah. Kat screamed incoherently and began to beat the guard she straddled to a bloody pulp before she wrapped the remaining length of chain from her neck restraint around the Kraken as a garrote, pulling it as tight as she could.

Dogman, in painted camouflage straight out of the original Conan movie and a jock strap, nothing more, advanced toward the Krakens his dogs were attacking. One Kraken who was still armed and functioning, kneeled to aim his rifle at him. Max the Mastiff chomped his entire head in his jaws, as he finally caught up with the quicker Curs. The massive jaws crushed the man's head like a walnut in a nutcracker.   As Abigail began to beat Talbot to a bloody pulp, Reverend Kray somehow got to his feet, half-blinded. He pulled a pistol from underneath his suit coat. "I'll kill you all! You…" His screaming rant was cut short forever by Dogman's thrown battle ax, as it clove his skull. The body toppled over, and laid still. Dogman continued on toward his dogs.   Ichiro stepped up and, with his recovered katana, decapitated two of the Krakens the dogs were mauling, causing both Curs to both leap back in surprise as blood began to spurt form the now headless necks. The third Kraken died from a ripped out throat.

All of the enemy was now down, dead, or dying. Torbin heard feral screaming and rushed to where Kat and the other captive women were. Sarah was clawing the face of the female guard to bloody ruin as Mary broke the woman's fingers to tear the cattle prod form her grasp. But it was Kat who Torbin went to first.

"Kat. Stop. It's Torbin. She's dead. You're cutting her head off with that chain. Kat." He grabbed his brother's former fiancée. She looked up at him with wild eyes, covered in blood.

"T, T, Torbin. It's you." Then she looked at the chain in her hands, realizing what she done. She scrambled to her feet, and looked at the remains of the body.

"I told you I would kill you, you bitch." Then Kat began to cry, grabbed and held onto Torbin.

The Marine heard a clanging and smashing noise, turned and saw a figure at the cage of children, breaking the lock with a Norse battle ax. It took a moment to recognize Brynhildr, as well camouflaged as Dogman, with her hair dyed black but with some light clothes on.

"Come. Little ones. A cage is not for children. It is for evil creatures such as Krakens."

The sound of the children crying for their "mommies" broke the spell of Sarah, Mary and Kat. They stopped their rampage and ran to the children.

Brynhildr walked up to Torbin, a small smile on her face.

"I see you had some…difficulties."

"Where in all that is holy did you come from?"

"A certain Commissioner of Law Enforcement thought a couple of undercover agents in Key West might be of help during the Conference of the Lords. We were trying to reach the Director, but, well, we heard they had captive children here."

Dogman walked up with all four of his dogs in tow.

"Some Krakens had a roadblock preventing Conch Republicans from entering here."

"What happened to them?" Torbin asked.

"They feed the fishes in a nearby inlet."

Torbin laughed. Then he grabbed, hugged and kissed Brynhildr.

"Please. Colonel. We are both married."

"And I for one would be dead right now if not for you, and this large piece of manhood, Dogman, here. So, I think that warrants hugs and kisses."

Dogman frowned at Torbin. "Stop with Brynhildr."

This caused Torbin to laugh more.

Abigail came up, hugged her cousin, and her uncle. "I knew you would always be there."

"Of course," said Dogman. "We are family."

"Your black hair looks nice on you."

"Yes? Maybe I will surprise Rolf with it."

"Talbot is still somewhat alive, Torbin. If you wish to speak to him."

Torbin started to turn, then stopped. "I don't know what he could add. Kill him."

"No, Torbin. I am not an executioner." Abigail looked into his eyes, and Torbin realized what she said. He let out a big sigh.

"You're right. No need to turn into Krakens to defeat them. Alright. We'll let the locals take care of him. I don't see him running anywhere fast."

"I broke the foot you shot him in, so that is very true."

Ichiro came over, began to hand over all their recovered weapons. Then he bowed low to Brynhildr and Dogman.

"You saved my wife and I. I can never repay you."

"Yes you can," replied Brynhildr. "Keep my cousin happy, treat her well as a husband should. That will be your payment."

Ichiro smiled. "That is easy."

There was the shimmering electricity in the air marking the arrival of a Falcon. For a moment they thought it was the one coming to pick up the now deceased Reverend Kray. Andrew's booming voice relieved them of that idea. "Torbin, Abigail, Ichiro. I need you once again. The Director is on the Asteroid Base One."

"Wait a minute!" yelled Torbin at the Falcon. "What about the captive women and children?"

"We'll get them out," said Dogman, "My dogs will see to that."

Torbin looked and saw the Black Mask Curs were already sniffing at the now freed children, tails wagging as they tried to greet the very scared and upset youngsters. One or two of the crying children finally noticed the dogs, began to hug them, which set off a round of licking and snuffling. This drew the attention of the others, and soon there was a canine and human love fest. The ancient bond of dog and humans once again lead to the feelings of security and calm among the young and weak.

Torbin smiled, then stuck his hand out to Dogman. "Sir, you are a saint."

Dogman shrugged as he shook his hand. "No. I am just Dogman."

"Torbin!" Andrews voice boomed again.

"Alright, we're coming."

Kat appeared then and hugged him, still bloody from her ordeal.

"You come back, hear? I lost your brother. I don't want to see you…"

"I'll be back. You go with Brynhildr and Dogman, They'll get you someplace safe."

The Falcon's Ramp lowered, signaling Andrew would wait no longer. Torbin liberated a assault weapon with a full magazine from one of the dead Krakens and then the three were being hoisted once again aboard the Falcon.

As the ship sped away, Brynhildr looked at the children. "The presence of the Falcon did not phase them.”

"I think Andrew is well known to them," answered Dogman.

"Yes, and well liked too, I think. Children can sense protectors."

"So can my dogs. They remained calm also."

Brynhildr looked at Dogman. "Then I will not worry. Abigail is in good hands."

"Would it do any good to worry?"

The Shield Maiden laughed. "No, it would not. Abigail makes her own path. Now, let's round up the little ones, the women and go find the Conch Republicans and some more transportation. They can help us get them to your vehicle." She cocked an eyebrow. "And find you some pants, my large friend."

"Okay. But my camouflage covers everything."

"Not quite everything, Uncle Buck. Trust me."

CHAPTER 47

ASTEROID 18666
BASE ONE

The living craft known as "SHE" slipped into a landing bay of the gigantic asteroid base. One moment it had been in Key West, the next moment it was sitting next to the huge massive planetoid that orbited the Earth between the planet and its satellite the Moon. The AI and computer system must have recognized or else ignored the creature craft as a threat because the outer bay doors opened with ease, then closed behind it. She slid into the bay and floated down like a feather as the oxygen atmosphere was reestablished. The access hatch and ramp appeared from the seamless hull once again, and Adam and Heidi stepped out on to landing the bay deck.

"Damn, Boss. I think I just stepped into one of the Star Wars movie sets."

"Well. I don't see Hans Solo or a Jedi to help us. So I guess we are on our own."

As they walked out from She, Adam noticed that Samuel and Sandy were not following.

"Not coming with us?" Adam asked.

Sandy gave a small smile. "Sorry, we cannot. She does not like us to move further than about twenty five feet from Her. That is one reason for the organic tethers on our spines. Of course, they help with communication also."

Adam gave them both the once over again. "I seem to remember both of you having more meat on your bones. You seemed to have more evidence of being in sunlight also."

"Oh that's our fault more than any conditions of She," Sandy answered. "We forget to eat when we are tethered to her, working on things, exploring the universe."

Adam looked at the living space craft. "Can She understand me?"

"Of course. She communicates, understands all languages. Some of it may be a form of telepathy."

"Well, She… Ma'am. These young humans need three meals a day, all the major food groups. Let them out under a sun once in a while, no matter what planet you are on."

Sam and Sandy's eyes seemed to glaze over for a second, then they were back looking at Adam and Heidi. "She just scolded us for not helping Her understand better our physiology. As much as She knows, has seen, we are the first large primate species She has dealt with. So, there are… gaps in her understanding."

Sam suddenly frowned. "She says, 'Hurry, find the Wizard'. The possible futures and universes are beginning to coalesce into one, which is not optimal for survival."

"Where is he?" asked Heidi.

"She senses him in the huge bay in the front quarter of the asteroid, where the mass drivers sit. She says bear to your right when you leave the bay, eventually all passageways lead to it."

"Alright. Let's hit the road. We'll be back."

"I will try to keep Her here as long as possible. But if she gets nervous, she can just… move into another area of space and time, it seems. She does not have to open the bay doors again. She is still young, and learning her capabilities."

"Young? What is She doing out here then?"

"Looking for Her mother."

Adam once again felt as if he had just fallen down the rabbit hole. Sometimes, he thought about being in a dream and about to wake up.

Fat chance. "Alright. You two stay safe with… She. See you soon."

The access doors to the interior corridors opened smoothly and the two hunters were through. They bore immediately to the right and were soon moving down a long slightly curving corridor. They saw or heard nothing for a full minute. Then two grays stepped through a sliding door in front of them, stopped and stared. They had nothing in their hands, were nude and seemed featureless other than the eyes, very small nose and the oversized eyes. They raised their rubbery arms outward and began to advance, as if they had been told to hug and hold on to these two humans. Heidi stepped out front and began an intricate series of cuts and slices with her bush machete. The long digitated hands were separated from wrists, their throats were slashed before they could scream in pain more than once. They toppled over, the bluish tinted blood spurting all over the corridor floor.

"You didn't give me a chance to help, Heidi."

"No time, Boss. Besides, it was light work. They were not trained fighters."

"Alright. Let's pick up the pace. This damned place is huge."

Andrew's Falcon was fast, but it did not have the almost instantaneous travel capability of She. When Andrew had first picked up She arriving near the HQ Building he thought it was some sort of power surge anomaly. Then She left, and Andrew realized what had happened. A minute later he was over the vehicles of the Chief, the Admiral and the rest.

"I sense the Director is not with you." Andrew called out.

"No," replied Professor Fassbinder. "She, the saucer creature is giving Adam and Heidi a ride to Base One, to stop the Wizard."

"They seem to almost be there. I have Torbin Bender and two others up at the Marathon Airport, to stop the women and children from being taken away. Please head there also, as I will need the others abilities again on the Asteroid."

"They were not allowed to take firearms aboard the saucer," the Chief called out.

"Even more a reason to hurry. Hopefully the captives will be rescued by the time I get to the airport. My weapons may be too destructive to prevent collateral damage. Excuse me. I go"

Andrew sped back to the airport, in time to witness the final deaths of the Krakens.

Now, as the Falcon reached the edge of space, Ichiro spoke, "I always wanted to be an astronaut. Now I am one."

"Yes, that is true," Andrew answered.

"Why do you need us?" asked Abigail. "Couldn't you just blast your way in with the Falcon, take out this devil's spawn?"

"You have an exaggerated belief in my capabilities, Abigail. If I start blasting, like you say, the asteroid's automatic defense systems take over, including maybe some of my fellow cyborgs of an older generation. That would not be good."

"So, you get us inside, then we head toward the mass drivers, right?" Torbin said.

"Yes Sir. If we can kill the Wizard with little other loss of life, there is less chance of creating a large conflict with the other inhabitants on Asteroid 18666. There are some Tschaaa, lizards, some robocops and others who are still trying to figure out who is in charge. But if they think the Base is in danger…"

"Just like the Vichy in North Africa. They hated the Nazis but by damn, show up with guns on their doorsteps…"

"Exactly, Torbin Bender. So, concentrated, minimum force and targets."

"You said 'kill' the Wizard. Correct?"

"Yes. You will have to. He is a dog gone mad. He must be put down. I will explain to the other Tschaaa later. Though, he never was well liked."

Within minutes, the Falcon craft was abeam of the gigantic asteroid. Some communication with the Base One communications center and Andrew was sliding into a large landing bay. After the outer doors were closed and atmosphere pumped in, Andrew opened the access ramp once more.

"The She saucer landed in the smaller bay to our right. She is still there, but the Director and Heidi Faust have left and headed toward the mass drivers and the Wizard."

"Well, what direction do we take?" asked Torbin.

"Through those sliding doors, then take a right down the corridor. I will be along shortly."

Torbin paused, and looked intently at the large cyborg. "Come on,

Andrew. What's up?"

Andrew smiled in a small way. "Always the perceptive Marine. You know what a 'suitcase nuke' is, of course."

"Yes Sir, I do. You have one?"

"Yes. I need to attach it to this Falcon. If we fail in reaching the Wizard, I blow the device, which will cause some substantial damage and should disturb the orbit of this orbiting base. That will at least affect the ability to use the mass drivers for a period of time."

"Okay, Andrew. So, I guess we need to take out this Wizard for sure." He looked toward Abigail and Ichiro. "Shall we?"

"Hai." Ichiro answered.

"Of course, Torbin," said Abigail.

And the three were off, running through the now opened sliding doors. Andrew turned to his task at hand. "Vaya con dios, as you say, Torbin. Hopefully, God is on our side."

The three companions made it down about a hundred yards when a Front Man hominid stepped out from a side corridor. The creature froze, then Torbin shot it once in the head.

"Second one of those assholes I've killed close up."

"Next time, my brother," said Ichiro. "Give me a chance to do it quietly with a blade."

"Hopefully there will be no next time. Come on, let's move."

The warriors moved a bit slower now, in combat crouches as they looked for the mass driver area. They had not the time to receive a map from Andrew, so they were flying by the seat of their pants. But Andrew said the mass driver area was huge, and would therefore be hard to miss.

As they rounded a curve in the corridor, a Soldier Class Warrior appeared, walking toward them. It seemed to slow, as if waiting for instructions from some controller. As it seemed to make up its mind, started to raise its bolt gun, Torbin let loose with his assault rifle at its face. The Marine had aimed directly at its "eyes", knowing the light rifle would have trouble penetrating the heavier body. Ichiro and Abigail split to opposite sides of the wide corridor, and began forward lunging rolls to close the distance. Its visor and targeting systems damaged, the Soldier began firing its bolt gun wildly, a round singeing the Marine's left ear. Torbin flattened himself to the corridor floor as he ran out of ammunition for the rifle. Ichiro fired an arrow as he came out of a roll, the projectile burying itself in the remains of the Soldiers left ocular orb. It tried to locate the source of the weapon with its compromised vision when Abigail fired her 44 Magnum lever action at the creature's head. Bluish blood sported from the point of impact, her round hitting an area already weakened by Torbin's bullets. It staggered backwards as Abigail fired again at the same spot. The artificial warrior toppled over backwards, convulsed, and then laid still.

"I'm empty," reported Torbin. He went and picked up the heavy Bolt Rifle.

"About as heavy as an old M-60 machine gun. Let's move. Good team work, by the way."

"But of course, Torbin." Ichiro said. "We are the ultimate team."

Torbin laughed. "Careful, Ichiro. Your head will swell."

They began to move down the corridor once again.

"Gunfire, Boss. Behind us."

"Shit. Someone else is in the mix. Maybe the Tschaaa minions are fighting each other."

"Run ahead, Adam. I'll see who it is, delay them if I can."

"Heidi…"

"Don't argue with a Petty Officer. It does you no good."

Before Heidi could protest, Adam kissed her full on the lips. Heidi began to sputter a protest.

"There. Wanted to do that for a long time. It's done. You can shoot me later. And no, my wives will not complain. They love you also."

"Goddamnit, Boss…"

"I'm off. Watch your ass, Heidi."

"Oh alright. Be careful with that Squid."

"Always, my dear. Always."

Andrew finished arming the suitcase nuke with a command detonator. All he had to do was broadcast a specific code over the computer link, a sixty second timer began and then—boom—the nuke did what it was designed to do. A part of his intellectual system had been searching for what was contained in the large landing bay, and had located a small repair pod designed for cyborgs to use along the exterior of Base One and along with the starcraft that had brought the Tschaaa. Andrew had also tapped into the asteroid's internal communication system and received the information that there were possible unknown intruders in the corridors. So, in a second, Andrew decided to bypass the corridors to dodge any defensive forces, and enter the Mass Driver area through a small airlock built specifically for external repair missions.

Andrew smiled to himself. "A space walk. Well, almost. If my high school chums could see me now." He chuckled in a human manner. "If they could see me know, they would be scared senseless. Now, time to move. My fellow humans need help."

Torbin, Ichiro and Abigail were making good time down the large corridor, when a voice came from a small connecting passageway.

"You!" Then a figure stepped out who Torbin recognized in an instant.

"Well, hello, Petty Officer Faust. Andrew said you were with the Director."

"Hello back. And you three can just wait here, until the Director calls."

"Hey, we're on the same…"

"Same side? Like I'm going to trust you now?   You tried to kill Adam once before."

"We just want the Wizard," Ichiro interjected.

"Yeah? Well I still owe you a crack on the side of the head. So don't expect me to trust you either."

"Damn it, Coastie. Just get out of the way." Torbin ordered.

"Make me, asshole."

Torbin raised the bolt gun.

"No." Abigail spoke for the first time. "We will not shoot her." Abigail laid down her rifle and took her Glock 18 out of its holster.

"If Miss Faust desires a fight, to assuage her anger, I will give it to her while you two continue on."

"Like hell." Heidi had the machete in her hand.

"Wife," Ichiro said in Japanese. "She is quite deadly. That is from personal experience."

"As am I. Go with Torbin. Now." She laid down her katana and Banshee Blade, and slipped off her body armor.

"You will not meet me hand to hand, Heidi is it? I am just a woman like you are."

Heidi tried to block the two men.

"Move," Abigail called out as she slid between Heidi and the two men, and became the target of Heidi's frustration and anger. The Petty Officer dropped her machete and slammed into Abigail, accepting her challenge. The brunette was stockier and a bit shorter than blonde Avenging Angel, who seemed to be more lithe. But as many had found before, Abigail's more slender looking muscles were coils of steel. So after being pushed back, Abigail stopped as she became like a wall.

"Move, or I'll move you!" Heidi yelled, then threw a blow at Abigail's face. The blonde shifted just enough so the blow slid past and she grabbed the arm, then trapped it under her left armpit.

"Please, stop, my Sist…" And Abigail found she was trying to wrestle a python. The two women fell to the ground, and Heidi went into ground fighting Jiu Jitsu.

"You're about to get a lesson in MMA, girlie," growled Heidi as she tried to go for a front mount and free her right arm. Abigail went into a guard position, wrapped both of her strong legs around Heidi's waist. She then tried a pressure point application to the side of Heidi's neck. Heidi cursed and slapped the hand away, then tried to slap Abigail's face. Abigail blocked the slap, wrapped her arms around Heidi in a bear hug.

"Will you quit this nonsense?" Abigail said into Heidi's ear as she laid her head alongside of the Petty Officers. "This is not a schoolyard catfight."

"Oh yeah?" And she bit Abigail's left ear. The Avenging Angel screamed. Heidi received a thumb in her left eye, causing her to release the ear in mouth. Then it was Heidi's turn to cry our as Abigail jammed fingers up her nostrils, forcing Heidi to jerk her head back. The Coastie was sent flying back as Abigail used her powerful legs to shove Heidi off. She managed to do a double arm break fall, then scrambled to her feet, facing a standing Abigail.

"You tried to bite my ear off. You, you…"

"Go ahead, call me what you want. Whatever it is, it won't be the first time."

Heidi went into a low sliding leg sweep, trying to take Abigail down again. But her foe's legs were not there as Abigail jumped straight up and twisted off to the side.

"Care to try that again?" asked Abigail.

"Bitch." Heidi feinted, tried to kick Abigail in the shin. Once again, her foe was not there, but seemed to blur off to the right.

"Try again?"

Heidi let out a cry of frustration went in for a low tackle, and found her head trapped in a scissor between Abigail's thighs as the blonde then rolled on her side. Abigail flexed her thigh muscles, knowing the effect this would have on her opponent's skull.

"Give?" she asked. Then screamed as Heidi jammed stiffened fingers into her most sensitive areas between her thighs, as well as tried to bite through Abigail's fatigues. Abigail tried to pull the hurting fingers back away from her as Heidi worked her sharp teeth into the inner thigh. The blonde released the scissors and lashed out with her feet, catching Heidi in her chest. Heidi let out a cry of pain and fell back.

Abigail got to her feet, rubbing her thighs.

"You are nasty."

"Whatever it takes to win, Blondie. Now, time to go." Heidi rushed into grapple and take Abigail to the floor once again, try for an arm bar.

Now it was Heidi's turn to yelp in pain as stiffened fingers returned the favor in between her thighs. Abigail's other hand grabbed Heidi's nose and twisted. Off balance, Heidi succumbed to a foot sweep, then an attempt at a scarf hold as Abigail tried to hold her down.

"You are not getting by me…" Abigail howled again as Heidi ripped open her fatigue shirt, began to claw and twist at her chest before Abigail could control her foe's hands. Heidi started to roll Abigail off her, trying to maul the breast some more as she did, the sports bra beginning to slide off.

"Sensitive time of the month?" Heidi said with a grin as she rolled on top of Abigail.

Heidi saw stars. It must have been just a matter of moments but as Heidi's vision cleared, Abigail was sitting on her stomach, hands about to throttle her. She saw a feral look on Abigail's face that seemed as if a demon had come to rest inside of Abigail. And Heidi was very afraid. As quick as the look was there, it was gone. Abigail was standing over her before she realized it.

"You are lucky Ichiro has been working with me, or your throat would be ripped out." The way she said it sent chills up Heidi's spine.

"Now, Sister Warrior. Truce, or must I maim you? Break bones, rip off body parts? You decide."

Heidi slowly stood up, looked at Abigail. "It's true. That story…up in Wyoming."

"That was classified, damnit. And it was supposed to end there!"

"Some of the locals talked, it got back to Key West. Adam thought it was an attempt to scare us…"

"Scare you? Are you mad?" Abigail began to shake, tears ran down her cheeks. "I was made to be a killer. By Krakens, Squids, even some of my own people. And now you bring this out in me when all I was trying to do was help stop this Wizard piece of excrement?"

Heidi suddenly realized just how wrong she had been. That her own ego and anger prevented her from seeing the truth about what needed to be done.

"Aw fuck. I really screwed the pooch on this one. Come one. Please. Grab your gear. We need to help Adam…"

Half a dozen grays appeared from the same side corridor Heidi had been in, led by a front man humanoid. The front man had a pistol in his hand.

"Women, put your hands up," it said in an oddly accented English voice. "You will both come…"

A thin throwing dagger buried itself into the creature's right eye in a blur of motion. The pistol discharged, missed its target. As the front man fell backwards, Heidi dropped, rolled and came up with her machete. As the grays began to advance on Heidi with some improvised weapons, a wraith with a katana hit them…

When Adam Lloyd reached the mass driver bay, the scale was so immense that, like to some people when they first see the Grand Canyon, it looked almost unreal. He scanned the area, then saw a Squid moving about some one hundred yards away near a lift that seemed to service the huge breach of the right mass driver. Adam jogged toward the figure, which turned as he approached. It was the Wizard, Adam being one of the few humans capable of reliably telling one Tschaaa from another. The Wizard waved its social tentacles, then spoke through its translator.

"Ah, the Lord of America's pet human. I guess you have seen the light, and can see your former Master is a weak fool. Good, you can assist me until other helpers arrive." The Wizard pointed toward two small sofa-sized bundles of space junk that the Wizard had swept from near space. The items in the bundles were stuck together with some type of sticky spray on material.

"Load those onto the lift there. The control panel should basic enough for even a monkey human to understand. Raise them up to the Mass Driver breach, there, see where I point? The spray on heat shield material should insure at least some of the payload hits the Earth. Then I have a several rather huge bundles to launch…well, don't just stand there, get to work." The Wizard turned its back to Adam, used to having humans jump to and follow his orders.

The Wizard let out a warbling screech as Adam leapt on its back and plunged his cheap but sharp "Made in Pakistan" knife into the Squid's torso. Once, twice, thrice he plunged in the rather rubbery skin. Then he was grabbed by powerful arms and tentacles, thrown through the air away from the Tschaaa Lord. He hit the control console hard on his back, then fell to the ground. As the alien Lord screamed in pain and anger, Adam tried to move his legs and found he could not. Sticking out of his spine was the broken off shaft from a long control handle that had protruded from the control console. He knew he was mortally wounded, and the numbness began to spread.

The Wizard had managed to pull the knife from its body and was waving it around, vocalizing in loud cries with which the translator was having trouble in coping. Then the translator caught up with the Tschaaa rantings.

"You stupid monkey! You think you can kill me? Stop me?" The Wizard tossed the knife at the console, watching it bounce off. "I will now watch you die, meat scum."

"What have we here?" Andrew's voice cut through the din.

"You. Cyborg. Clean up this excrement. Then assist me with the mass driver. First, fetch me some bandages. Don't just stand there. Move."

"Of course Lord. I will move."

Andrew strode over to the Tschaaa Lord as it was trying to

examine its wounds. The Squid looked up at Andrew, started to sign confusion with its social tentacles. Andrew ripped the right tentacle off at its connecting joint.

In a blur the cyborg did the same with the left. The shrieking, warbling and screaming reverberated both through the translator and the air. The Lord known as Wizard tried to beat at Andrew with its thick arms, and the robocop began to rip off the limbs like a nasty little kid would do to a daddy long legs spider. Within moments, the Squid was a multiple amputee.

Andrew plunged his right arm into the body of the Tschaaa Lord as it let out final shrieks of pain and fear. "Have a nice trip to hell, Lord." Andrew ripped out the large cephalopod's heart. The Wizard, shook, then was dead.

Andrew dropped the organ, and went to where Adam lay. "I die, friend."

"No, you don't. I grab you, rush you to my Falcon. I have the means to keep you alive."

"No, my friend Andrew. I am finished. It must be so."

"No, Director, it does not..."

Adam managed to grab Andrew's arm.

"I must die. Then the blame for all of this, dies with me. I helped do this. The Protocol of Selective Survival...a failure." Adam coughed up blood, sprayed it on Andrew. He managed to smile.

"Sorry, my dear friend. I messed up on you."

Andrew picked Adam up, cradled him. "We go..."

"No. Please. Andrew. My last request. I...beg."

Andrew looked down at him in his arms. For the first time in memory, tears ran down from beneath his visor. He slid it up from his hazel eyes.

"I cannot..."

"Yes, you can. You and the Breeders, Madam President, the rest, you...can make this ...right. Make it work. Please. You see, don't you?"

Andrew looked at his friend. "Yes. I am cursed to see it."

Adam smiled. "Say...I love...Mary, Kat, the kids, the Chief... Heidi..."

The Director tensed, then still smiling, looked into the now uncovered eyes of Andrew.

"Old friend…" Adam Lloyd's eyes glazed over, and he was no more.

"Rest, Adam," said Andrew. "You deserve it."

The cyborg heard footsteps approaching. He turned to face the figures running toward him, still cradling Adam.

"Andrew," Torbin called out. "What…?"

"He died so others may live. Simple."

Torbin and Ichiro stopped short, looking at the body Andrew cradled like a child in his arms.

"Ah shit… I… he saved me, Andrew."

"Yes he did, friend Torbin. And down deep, he wished he could have left with you, those long months ago. But, well, he could not leave his loved ones behind."

Ichiro looked over at the remains of the Squid.

"The Lord Wizard?"

"Yes. In pieces. Something I should have done many months ago."

Andrew looked at Torbin. "Sir, please do me one favor."

"Anything."

"Place that Squid heart on the console."

"Sure." Torbin went over, picked up the bloody trophy and placed it on the control console.

"Aren't you going to ask me why, Torbin? Why I asked you to do this?"

"Friends don't always have to ask. You do something because you are friends, brothers."

"Brothers. A nice sound… It is a sign, Torbin. A warning of what is to come should another Tschaaa Lord resist the future of things."

Just then, Abigail and Heidi came running into the immense bay, saw the group. Then dashed to them.

"Adam. Boss!" Heidi cried out as she saw Andrew cradling Adam.

"He is no more, Heidi. I am sorry."

"Fix him! Goddamnit. You have the power…"

"Adam said no, Heidi. It was his last wish. Said it… was his time to go."

"No. Fuck no! Fix him!" Heidi began to scream, cry. She swung and broke her machete on Andrew's armored body, then began to kick and beat on him with her bare hands.

"You worthless hunk of metal and meat," Heidi screamed again, collapsed to her knees, sobbing soul wrenching cries.

"I love him. I love him so."

Abigail dropped to her knees next to her former foe, wrapped her arms around her, tears in her eyes. "He is where he wants to be, sister. With... his past family."

Heidi wrapped her arms around Abigail.

"He had family here. We loved him. He saved us."

Torbin tried not to let the tears come, but they did anyways. Then he noticed Ichiro had tears in his eyes also.

"He died... a warrior. A good man. For he died for us all." Ichiro then dropped to his knees and bowed low.

"I will honor his memory... always."

They all grieved for a few more moments, as time seemed to pause for all as they honored the passing of a former enemy, now hero. Finally, Andrew spoke. "I must take Adam to my Falcon, secure him. Then, my friend Torbin. I must share a deception with you. If you could all wait here, ensure no more miscreants show up."

"Of course, Andrew," answered Torbin.

Andrew turned, and dashed away as only a cyborg could, toward the landing bay where his Falcon was still parked.

Ichiro put his hand on his wife. "My love, you have bluish blood on you."

"Yes, my love. Heidi and I had to deal with some grays. After Fuzz, it felt good in an evil way to cut them down."

Heidi hiccupped, and stopped crying. "Fuzz. That was your dog buddy, right?"

"Yes. A couple of grays killed him while he killed them, protecting me. Now, the debt is paid. Six of them for Fuzz. A fair trade. Although my heart still aches for him."

Heidi looked into Abigail's eyes. "We've lost way too many friends, family, loved ones, parts of our souls. Thanks to these Squids coming."

"And to some monsters called Krakens who pass as fellow humans," added Ichiro.

The Coastie tried to smile at him. "You know, I still owe you a shot to the chops. You were the first person to ever knock me unconscious."

Ichiro bowed to her and said, "I ask forgiveness in my wife's name, Heidi Faust."

Heidi managed to chuckle. "Well, Abigail here just rang my chimes again. I guess it runs in the family."

Heidi stood up, a bit shaky, and faced the others.

"I'm asking for your forgiveness. I should have been on your side…"

"Oh, belay that, Petty Officer," interjected Torbin. "There but the Grace of God went almost all of us. Fate and circumstances often determines sides, not choices. We are all humans. Especially today, with a bunch of Squids standing down, realizing that they are not in the number one slot by themselves anymore. They have some 'monkeys' standing next to them."

This elicited some laughter from the group at the mental picture of a monkey standing next to the Squid Lords, shrieking and throwing its shit as some primates are prone to do.

Andrew reappeared, moved quickly up to them.

"Come. Torbin. You have a brother to see."

"Brother? Who are you talking about?"

"William. He lives. I have been overseeing his… rebirth."

Torbin stopped dead, his mouth flew open. "Fucking impossible. He died ramming that Falcon. There is a film…"

"Which is incomplete. I have been supervising the growth of a new body. He has most of his memories. But his body….it was sixty percent gone. The Tschaaa saved him for testing. Once I found him, I began to truly rebuild him."

"And you knew this when you took me to Deseret?"

"Yes. I now ask for your humble forgiveness for not telling you sooner, but…

Torbin slammed his fist into Andrew's body, then howled with pain.

"Goddamn you and your Squid armored body. All these months, years, thinking he was dead, gone, maybe eaten. Come to find out he was being used to test some Squid theories on meat raised in vats. And now he's alive." Torbin started to unsling the Bolt Gun he had taken from the Soldier, cursing, his face flushed with extreme anger. Ichiro and Abigail were then holding on to him, hugging him as he raged.

"Let me go! This fucking bag of bolts…."

"Torbin. He is alive." Abigail yelled in his ear. "He was not killed, eaten, nor tortured. He is alive! Your family lives."

Torbin's speech became incoherent as he raged, against all those years of thinking his little brother was dead and gone. Then the tears came. Abigail held him tight, kissed his cheek. "Torbin, your brother lives. Thanks to Andrew, he will live as your brother once more. And you said Kat Monroe was his fiancée. She lives also. Think what that will mean to him, when you tell him that."

Torbin tried not to sob. Marines don't sob. But, the emotions of anger and joy, so intertwined, conflicting. his knees began to buckle. Ichiro held him up.

"My blood brother. We are here for you. We will never leave. And we are here for your brother William. I would like to talk with this fellow pilot, the stuff of legends."

Finally, Torbin gained more control of his emotions. He glared at the cyborg. "Do you understand how pissed off, hurt I am, Andrew? Why couldn't you have told me?"

"If I had, it would have changed the decisions of several important people, yourself included. I had to see the beginning of this… Great Compromise through first. I am not without emotion. I know the hurt you felt over the loss of your family."

And with that, a large tear rolled down Andrew's face. For he was this day more man than machine. Heidi stepped up, grabbed his huge hand. "You know, you have a way of getting us to love you and want to kill you all at the same time. I know why you did what you did, why you always do what you do. You are trying to be all things to all people. You try to solve everything. Please, Andrew. I love you. Give it a rest. Let someone else shoulder the load."

Andrew stood still and quiet. He stood so still that Heidi began to wonder if something inside of him had broken, short circuited.

"Hey, buddy…"

"I am still here, Heidi." And then he smiled, which turned into a grin.

"Funny how I was always trying to compute the outcome, fix everything myself. All to save the children, the future. Then this Petty Officer here reminds me of something I keep forgetting. I have friends. Maybe, family."

"Hell yes, Andrew," Heidi said. "Come here. I need some lovin'."

Andrew bent over and picked Heidi up, cradled her as she hugged him, kissed his still human cheek.

Torbin then stepped up, grabbed a hold of his arm. "Okay, I apologize for losing it. Now, can I see my brother?"

"Of course. Ichiro, Abigail, could you find your way back to my Falcon, take Heidi with you? You will encounter no more resistance. The defensive systems on the asteroid have been reprogrammed to my orders."

"Yes, Andrew. I think so," replied Abigail. She stepped up to the cyborg, put her hand on his shoulder.

"Know from someone who was raised to hate all those connected with the Tschaaa. I see now that from even what we consider as evil can come good. We humans will always owe you, Andrew. For you are the one who truly tried to save everyone."

"If you keep praising me, Abigail, my head will expand past the confines of my armored

body."

The robocop set Heidi down. "It is time to go see your brother, Torbin. He is still not ready to get up and walk. But he knows you and Kathy Monroe live. And yes, he knows, understands she has children. As he knows he is an uncle."

"Been busy, haven't you?" asked the Marine.

"The understatement of the decade. Now, shall we?"

As Andrew took Torbin down one corridor, and the other, three went down another, Heidi said to the others. "I guess we are all kind of… connected now, for better or worse."

"From this minute forward, Heidi Faust, we are all humans," Ichiro said. "We must never again allow us to fight over petty things as race, religion, territory."

Heidi laughed. "I can tell out of the three of us here, I am the least serious. Well, let me be a bit of a class clown, and tell you some stories of Andrew, the all too human cyborg I have known…"

CHAPTER 48

CAPITOL BUILDING, OFFICE OF THE PRESIDENT
BISMARCK NORTH DAKOTA

President Sandra Paul put down the draft treaty. At least, it was meant to be a form of a treaty, though it was along the lines a voluminous living agreement between two peoples trying to live together in the same house. The Great Compromise. She rubbed her temples with her fingers as she tried to grasp what they were actually trying to do. In the outer office, she heard George Williams IV, her closest friend and advisor, talking rather loudly on the direct overseas line they had established with Free Japan.

"Yes General, I know it's not easy... I know there are three Warlords trying to control Mainland China. Yes Sir, we realize there are also a lot of definite Feral areas, with no organized living groups... General, all we can do is all we can do. Tell the Warlords that they can send representatives to Bismarck, North Dakota to discuss this proposal, or they can ignore us and deal with the Squids themselves. Which means, they may wind up being eaten again... Madam President thanks you for all your efforts in obtaining as many representatives of surviving human enclaves as possible. Royal

Princess Akiko is here and has guaranteed that all of your excellent efforts are being directly communicated to the Emperor and the Prime Minister…Yes Sir, the Princess is doing it personally…Yes, General, I will communicate your profuse thanks to the Royal One and your undying loyalty. Thanks again, General. We will be in touch."

She heard George sigh. "My friend, come on in, have a seat and relax," she called out. "I think I have some ice cubes and some scotch with your name on it."

George walked into her Oval Office with a smile on his face. "Now I know what is like to really herd cats. I just hope we get enough respondents and attendees to make this conference have meaning and substance. I sure as hell don't want anyone to get the idea that we are forcing a deal on them. Or that we are making some secret compromise with the Tschaaa."

Sandra Paul poured the scotch over the ice cubes in the substantial drink glasses. It had been a long day, the third since the Wizard had been stopped. She shivered internally when she thought just how close everything had come to unraveling before it really began, and then turn into an unmitigated disaster. A few rock strikes, followed by a nuke or two…

"Thinking once again about what might have happened, aren't you Sal?"

"Guilty as charged, dear friend. Had I had to launch the She-Bear, with its special warhead…"

"I know, Sal. Bodies would still be piling up worldwide had that happened. But it did not."

She looked deep into the eyes of her strong right arm. "George, whatever you may think, but at the end, Adam Lloyd was a hero. Pure and simple."

George let out a heavy sigh. "Sal, I knew him before he…turned to the dark side. That phrase fits perfectly. But selling him to the masses as a hero at this early date will cause even more of a nasty reaction than will some of the points in this written proposal…This Great Compromise."

"I know, George. At a later date, but not too late, I will revisit Adam Lloyd, who I never had a chance to meet. If we had…who knows? Maybe we could have worked something out earlier."

Madam President snorted. "If wishes were horses, beggars would ride. My grandfather taught me that."

She picked up the large packet of paper. "We can't let all the heroes who shed blood for this day to be disappointed. We will make this work."

George laughed. "There is that spine of steel again."

The President smiled. "I saw a cartoon in this morning's paper. They have me with a backbone like a Stegosaurus, spikes and plates sticking out all over. I was beating a Squid and a Kraken with a large horned tail. The caption said. "Payback". But I don't want all…this to be payback and revenge."

George nodded. "Yeah. We don't want to be fighting about this a hundred years from now, like the U.S. Civil War. We are joined at the hip with the Squids on this planet now, whether for better or worse, no matter who lived here first."

Madam President took a swig of her drink. "Yes. I just have to sell that to some two billion or so surviving humans, every single one of them who lost someone during the last some seven years."

"And the Krakens?"

"George, there is a fire in my gut to send the Banshees and anyone else I can find out and round up every single former human being who now identifies as one of those monsters, has one of their tattoos, and crucify them, hanging their bodies up and down the Interstates. Like the Romans did to enemies who particularly upset them." She refilled her drink, took a sip.

"But then I would be no better than they are. Instead, those who wish to remove their tattoos and hide, fine. If some sick bastard wants to pray to a Kraken, a Cthulhu, then have at it. The Bill of Rights still exists. But woe to those who decide to taste human flesh ever again. I will find a way to publicly gut them. Though anyone who has proof of murder or a War Crime by a specific individual Kraken, that monster's ass is bought and paid for."

"Execution," George said.

"Hell, I say feed them to the Tschaaa. See how they like being eaten by their gods."

George's eyes widened a bit. "You're serious, aren't you?"

"I plan on putting that in the agreement. I think just about everyone will agree to it. Human eaters, baby rapers, serial killers, sociopaths—why not feed them to the Squids? Quick, efficient death penalty. Cheap, too."

George shivered a bit. "Remind me to never really make you angry, Ma'am."

"No worries, George. I know you prefer lean buffalo."

"That I do. Now, to continue, those mapped out areas. Think they will fly?"

"We cede Baja, the Sea of Cortez because they have covered over that whole area anyway, and created a huge breeding and manufacturing area there. We also cede them most of Cuba, the Bahamas, and all the reef areas around there. They keep the ports of San Diego, L.A., and San Francisco Bay, especially Alcatraz. Surviving Canadians said the Tschaaa could keep the port area around Vancouver B.C.. We both get back the Great Lakes, along with the northern fishing areas on the coasts. The Tschaaa keep the waters off of Savannah, although we get the port back. Ditto with Miami."

"The Florida Keys?"

"Our most dear friend, the Admiral, has an agreement with the Tschaaa already."

"Really. Sal? An independent Conch Republic?"

"George, he is a true hero. Kept in contact with us over all those years. Almost lost Jolene, our other operative. She was airlifted to Malmstrom for medical aid. So yeah, the Conch Republicans can have their independence. Some former Krakens can go hide there."

"And the Russians, European representatives, Chinese, Free Japanese, India, all the other former human areas?"

"They tell us at the conference in four days what they want, and are willing to give up. We are going to have to work out over time how to split up all the deep ocean areas, some of the southern fishing areas, once we have fishing fleets again. Though our new special friend Andrew, Saint Andrew some have called him, tells us that the Tschaaa have pretty much explored a lot of the deep oceanic trenches. They are fascinated by the giant whales as well as the giant squids. They see orcas, great whites, as worthy opponents for their young warriors, like the Maasai in Africa hunted lions."

"Well, Ma'am, I see the need for some formal structured organization to settle disputes in these ocean and coastal areas. And hell, we haven't even talked about the lizards, though in truth they have kept pretty much to themselves since after the first year of the

Infestation. I guess Andrew and his now Guardian Angels as they are called, so much nicer than robocops, are going to keep us from warring again."

"Who came up with that concept?"

"Abigail, our own Avenging Angel. And, she called him Saint Andrew first. That young lady is wise beyond her years. If she ever went into politics…"

George snorted. "Are you kidding? She is way too honest…I mean, you know, present company…"

Madam President began laughing loud and hard, an embarrassed George finally joining in. After the President had regained her composure, she looked at George. "There's a lot more work to do, my dearest friend. If we are going to be the United Sixty States of North America, from Panama up to the Arctic. Deseret…well, they prefer the idea of an Independent Nation State, a very religious centric state, but following our Bill Of Rights.

"Mrs. Smith is the new President?"

"Special election. A landslide. He husband is, well, out of the picture. And, since you brought them up, our dinosaurian lizards have staked out the desert around Area 51 as well as around Yuma, Arizona as their breeding areas. So, we may have a situation like Native American Reservation Lands, unless we want to force them out, which I don't."

Sandra Paul stood and stretched. "Uffda. Can you give me one of your signature neck and back rubs, George?"

"Of course. Lay on the sofa, please."

For the next few minutes, Madam President was making little sounds of ecstasy as she enjoyed his strong and capable fingers.

"One of these days, George, someone is going to claim my groans of pleasure are from sex, not a back rub."

"Someone did. Years ago. I decked him."

She sat up. "Serious?"

"As a heart attack. The person is long dead. But no, I still will not tell who it was."

She kissed him on the cheek. "Ever the defender of my virtue."

"Your husband would want it that way."

"Yes, he would. And still does. Watches from afar, but sometimes near."

The two best friends sat next to each other, quiet, lost in their own thoughts. Then, the telephone rang. George picked it up.

"Williams here. Yes, Captain. We will be working late, so ask for some Banshee volunteers…what? Danny, they all volunteered to stay the night? Okay. Get ahold of the chow hall, make sure it stays open for to go orders. This is going to be a marathon session. Thank you."

"George, at least send David Jackson home. He can come back in the morning."

"He won't leave until Brynhildr is back to take care of your security."

"Will no one listen to my desires?"

"Not if it involves your security."

She sighed. "Why me?"

George took her hands in his. "Sal, you are what held us together, when things were darkest. Torbin, Abigail, Aleks, Ichiro, and all the rest, they made it happen. But you held it together. They know that. So, you will never be alone."

Madam President blinked back tears. Then, she straightened her spine of steel.

"I guess I had better live up to their loyalty."

"You and me both, Ma'am. You and me both."

At the original spot of the Kraken Incursion that started Bloody Kansas in Kansas City, Kansas, two regular Army soldiers stepped out of their fortified position and hailed the figures approaching slowly, on foot.

"You folks need to identify yourself," the Sergeant called out. "War is not officially over yet."

"Staff Sergeant Benjamin Black," the man with the long rifle across his shoulders called back. "And I have a Bollywood-looking woman called Red, two kids in this little red wagon, with Bobby Parsons bringing up the rear."

It took a few moments for the names to sink in, then the Sergeant swore. "My God. It's the Reaper. And the other people they said to watch for. Sergeant, they thought you were dead."

The mouth of the man called The Reaper formed into his slight signature smile.

"Won't be the first time. Won't be the last."

CHAPTER 49

There is an American saying that nothing is for sure except death and taxes. I will add more. The passage of time. And true love.

-Royal Princess Akiko

Torbin Bender, United Armed Forces General, Retired, sat on the expansive front porch of his and Aleks' large two story home. The State of Montana had ensured that the two special veterans of the Tschaaa Infestation War and the many smaller local conflicts that followed were provided a homestead of some fifty acres on the northeast slope of Big Baldy Mountain about forty miles from Malmstrom Armed Forces Base. On a clear day, which were many, they could see the edges of the base and Great Falls, Montana. Once or twice a week they would go into civilization during the spring and summer months. During the typical Montana Winter, they stayed closed to home, spending time snowshoeing, hunting, taking care of their livestock and War Dogs, as well as chasing each other nude around the large house. As Torbin often said, they may be getting old, but they sure as hell were not dead, or even close to it.

He took a sip of the five alarm head busting Russian version of coffee Aleks always provided him. One of these days, he was going to take a cup of it to the local University, where both he and Aleks had positions as Adjunct Professors, and have the Chemistry Department figure out just how much caffeine was 'really' in it. He was used to old Marine chow hall coffee, or cowboy coffee made by throwing a fistful of grounds into boiling water over the campfire. But they could not hold a candle to Aleks' Russian concoction. She always called him a wuss when she caught him cutting it with milk or cream. Then he would act all hurt, demand satisfaction over his honor, and they would begin a wrestling match. Which often resulted in two exhausted nude bodies on the bear rug in the large living room.

In front of him was a state of the art laptop computer, as he still preferred to type the old two finger method to dictating into his PAD. Although the AI could do everything for him but cook, clean ,and have sex, Torbin still felt funny having it print out and correct whatever he wrote. Aleks had demanded he finish his memoirs in the next month, or she would cut off all physical relations. He knew she would not, but he knew how important it was to her that he complete them. And, today was their twenty-fifth wedding anniversary, so he had another reason to keep her happy by working on the book.

"Torbin, everyone is writing what they did in the War." Aleks oft said. "Princess Akiko's work has spurred a large industry on autobiographies, biographies and so-called nonfiction works. I do not want to see one more person write about what you did before you do."

He looked at the huge volume of the Princess that sat on the corner of the desk he had set up on the porch. The Great Compromise was the official short title. But everyone referred to it in shorthand as The War History.   Not just once but many times he used this fantastic bestseller as a reference to help him with some memory of an incident. Princess Akiko had set a standard in scholarship that everyone was now striving to match. Out on the market for just over year, it had already been translated into twenty-five languages, including Tschaaa. Torbin grunted. How in the hell was he going to compete with that? Not to mention the working draft of Banshee the history of the One Hundred and First Special Attack Unit and the Sisters of Steel that sat on the other corner of his desk. Aleks, as the First Unit Commander, had been asked by the Princess, as a personal favor to one who had served under Aleks as a Banshee, to review the work for accuracy. Torbin had already caught his wife tearing up over some memory stirred by passages in the book. Thus, he knew that the Princess had another scholarly work of art on her hands.

A very large canine muzzle chose that moment to insert itself under his right arm, demanding attention. Brutus, War Dog of the Sergeant Fuzz line, seemed to know when Torbin had been woolgathering too long and needed a distraction. Not to mention Brutus was a bit pushy when it came to obtaining a required number of ear scratches, chest scratches and belly rubs. Torbin scratched the very large head and ears of Brutus. "Hey, my friend, what do you think? Can I be a writer? Do I have what it takes?"

"Of course you do, husband. Otherwise, I would not be bugging you to write this."

"And just how long have you been standing there, wife, checking on me? With Portia, I see." Next to Aleks was an almost as especially large female of the War Dog breed. And, like alpha grey wolves, she and Brutus were life mates, their fecundity limited by the wonders of Tschaaa biological science. One thing could be said for certain, the Tschaaa were years ahead on humans in all things biological, although certain humans had added greatly to what the Squids had started. More and more humans were switching to vat grown flesh as opposed to raising livestock. Huge cattle, pig and chicken ranches were becoming things of the past.

"I have been standing here long enough to see, My husband, that you are drifting into your famous mental woolgathering. Please, put a few words on paper, then the stories will come."

Torbin's demeanor suddenly became very serious. "Aleks, I need to know. Was I…a good person? Was I a good husband and father? As I start to remember the last twenty-five years, I start thinking about what could have been, how I could have done things differently…"

Aleks was around his neck, hugging and kissing him, her eyes a bit damp. "My God, you are always so hard on yourself. You saved so many people, did so much to regain out freedom from the Squids, not to mention loved me and helped raise two wonderful trolls, I mean sons. Of course you are a good person, husband, and an excellent lover. All things to all people."

Torbin kissed the love of his life back. "Are you just saying that because this is our twenty-fifth wedding anniversary?"

"No, Torbin. I am saying that it is our wedding anniversary because of all those characteristics. You are not a good person, you are the best person. And I love you with all my heart."

He stood up and they hugged and kissed for a couple of minutes, as the two War Dogs looked on, tails wagging a bit. The pack leaders were happy, so all was right with the world.

Finally, they stood a bit apart, holding hands. "I keep listening for engines, looking for vehicles coming up the road," said Aleks. "We can see people coming for several miles yet I see nothing moving."

"Think no one is going to show up for our celebration?"

"If they do not, I will track them down and they will wish they had come."

Torbin laughed. "Just like the chapter I'm working on. Things change but stay the same. You are a retired grandmother but still act like a hard-ass Russian spy."

"If I did not keep my ass hard and tight, you would grow tired of me."

Torbin grabbed Aleks and pulled her close again, "Never. You are the love of my life. You gave me two handsome young men. We are soulmates…forever."

They kissed again long and deep. Then, Aleks slowly pushed him away.

"We must stop, before I tear you clothes off, Torbin, and ravish you on this porch. If the guests arrive too soon…'

"You ravish me? I thought we men did that to you women."

Aleks showed him a sly smile. "Married twenty-five years and still you have not learned who is really in control. Ask Abigail what I taught her to keep Ichiro happy, satiated…"

Torbin put his hands over his ears. "TMI. Too much information. That's my little sister you are talking about."

"Who is a grown woman with three beautiful children of her own."

"Her son is handsome, not beautiful. You don't call men beautiful. It is not done where I come from."

Aleks stole a quick kiss. "And with that, I will leave you to your writing. I am going to call a few cell and PDA phones, see where everyone is. We always have someone show up early."

"I will await your results, my love."

Aleks went to make her calls and Torbin tried not to grin. So far, so good. For once it seemed the Russian spy had not ferreted out any info about his special plan for the day.

Torbin shifted the 44 Magnum pistol on his belt. The pistol was the one Madam President had given him so many years ago, which he felt odd when he was not wearing it. With Eaters, grizzly bears and some humans who still had evil in their hearts, he always made sure he was packing. Above the front door off the porch was the Saiga 12 Gauge with which Aleks had killed the Eater Fuzz had stopped in their old base duplex. Above it was Torbin's liberated from the Pits M-1 Garand. Aleks had kept both of her service automatics, fully loaded in the nightstands upstairs. A gold inlay Commemorative General Officers Model M-9 Beretta pistol mounted on a plaque in the recreation room even had a loaded magazine stashed behind the plaque. A firearm was worthless unless it had ammunition and was ready to go at all times.

Things change but remain the same. Torbin chuckled. Stripped down for an intensive cleaning was one of the few civilian versions of the Bender 6mm Standard Issue Military Automatic Rifle produced. Named in his honor, part of a combined Russian and U.S. project, the state of the art rifle that was a combination of all the best characteristics of the Kalashnikov and Armalite designs, it was touted as the rifle that would serve the Allied Armed Forces for the foreseeable future. Then after some twenty thousand standard rifles, with smaller numbers of Carbines, Designated Marksmanship Weapons and Squad Automatic Weapons produced, the U.S. jumped ship and produced a downsized version of the Tschaaa Energy Bolt Weapon (EBW) as its standard issued weapon. Seems the U.S. was always good at convincing others to buy a certain design, caliber, and then all of a sudden deciding to jump ahead with some new design.

The Russians were not exactly happy, and kept producing their version of the Bender Weapon for years to come, buying small quantities of the EBW for their specialized teams. The Japanese kept producing small numbers of their indigenous Type 89 Assault Rifle, some in the Bender 6mm Round for specialized units. They bought few of the EBW weapons. Most of the newly reconstituted armed forces of the world bought the Russian weapon, so the Bender Round would be around for years. Most countries thought the anti-armor capability of the hypervelocity EBW round was not sufficient to outweigh the cost. After all, the Guardian Angels kept any large scale conflicts from arising.

The Bender Round was extremely popular as a high velocity hunting round, but few people wanted to invest in an assault weapon that fired it. Everyone had left over M-16s and other Armalite design weapons, all sufficient for "social work", so the 6mm round was usually seen in bolt or lever action rifles. A cottage industry did arise where like new M-16s and M-4 were modified to take the Bender Round, though the wear on the lighter rifles was higher. But, some people wanted an auto rifle with the best possible conventional ammunition, so a few thousand of the converted rifles were floating around. U.S. Law Enforcement got the windfall of all the surplus weapons, and all but a few thousand were in police agencies hands. Here and there a Russian weapon would pop up in some armory, with a few dozen semi-auto Russian sporting rifles being imported every year.

Surprisingly, following the implementation of The Great Compromise, conflicts between Tschaaa and Humans were relative few after the signing of the necessary Protocols. There would always be those humans who never forgave the aliens, nor forgave the people who refused to implement a full fledge genocide by launching the special warhead She-Bear Missile. Some place, in an extremely secret location, the original warhead developed by Colonel Bardun and Pappy Gunn was hidden, "on ice" capable of use if necessary.

However, in the almost twenty-five years since the signing and implementations of the Compromise Treaty and Related Protocols, there had been many more human versus human conflict than Squid and human. Things change but remain the same. Much of the cooperation was due to two industries. The Tschaaa had rediscovered their abilities at husbanding all the various resources of the oceans. Fish and other marine life flourished, with the Tschaaa herding immense schools of marine species all over the globe, providing more than enough food sources for both the increasing human and Tschaaa populations. In fact, the only complaints about these arrangements came from a small minority if humans protesting the "factorization" of the marine life. When that concept and complaint was first brought to the Tschaaa Lords, they had spent some ten minutes performing the Tschaaa version of belly laughs. They had saved entire species from overfishing as well as cleaned much of the garbage from the seas and somehow they were the "bad guys" in this? Nah.

The second industry was space research. Already humans had taken many of the concepts the Tschaaa had brought with them about interstellar travel and improved them with leaps and bounds. For humans were much better in thinking "outside the box". Thus, the research by Professor Fassbinder and the Olson twins had caused a huge leap in space travel. Such a huge leap that, on the far side of the moon, man and woman kind were finishing the first large FTL/ warp drive craft developed. They had developed a very efficient way to use dark matter and dark energy so that huge spacecraft could have enough energy to "warp" space around them, as the Tschaaa small scout ships could do.

The one concern was political. The Tschaaa did not want the ship used to interfere with the travel of the generational Crèche ships in route to their home world. When notified of The Great Compromise, the interstellar ships were deep in "slingshot" mode around the sun. They had offered little comment other than to remind their fellow Tschaaa that they had chosen to remain on Earth, with a "you made your bed, you sleep in it" attitude. Some groups of humans wanted to demand that the some two billion corpsicals be returned along with the human breeding pairs, exact number unknown. The Tschaaa on the starships ignored the suggestion, and short of fighting a war to force the Squids on Earth to intercept their brethren, there was nothing to be done. So, it was good riddance to the departing Tschaaa, although the fact there were live human captives on board would always be a sore point.

Free Allied Armed Forces became Earth Allied Armed Forces under a replacement for the almost worthless United Nations. It had been named Allied Species of Earth, or ASE (pronounced "ace" like the playing card). Allied Peoples of Earth, "APE" had been suggested, but since humans were often called "monkeys" that was rejected. The organization was used both for disaster response as well as when necessary to deal militarily with a problem. The Guardian Angels established by cyborg, now Saint Andrew, to keep the peace between the Species, also monitored the combined species military actions.

The "Banshees" had been the first unit to have Tschaaa in their ranks, in the form of female pilots. The United States Civilian Federal Law Enforcement Agency under Commissioner Miller also teamed volunteer Tschaaa up with humans to patrol the coastal waterways and out to the Twelve Mile Limit. These teams where to prevent illegal poaching of sea creatures as well as keep the Tschaaa and humans from "poaching" each other. Some large pieces of Sushi had appeared not long after the Great Compromise, and a few small boats were found adrift with blood on them. That was brought to a screeching halt.

But of course, humans were their own worst enemies. That which changes remains the same. The Banshees became the initial Response Force to deal with the Warlords, religious fanatics, former narcotics traffickers who wanted to step into those areas no longer under Tschaaa control . Seeing armed women seemed to have an unusual effect on many, either making them more at ease or off balance, not sure if they wanted to fight a "girl".   Princess Akiko's book would cover all that, especially the now famous rescue of General Reed's family, thought dead but actually held captive by a Chechnya Muslim Warlord in the mountains near Sovetskoye. That was one the sections of the book draft that had made Aleks cry. They lost some sisters there, never to be forgotten.

The only real problems from the Tschaaa involved members of the Wizard's Crèche, who never forgot the fact that humans had been the ones who killed him, Andrew being from human stock, nor the Lords who "turned". There were some conflicts, but the remaining Tschaaa Lords, under the ministries of Cassandra, helped keep them to a minimum.

For about two years after the Great Compromise, there were still substantial recovery problems as peoples and countries tried to set themselves up in their traditional areas. The Nordic countries had been the least Harvested or Infested, so they bounced back within weeks when the Tschaaa threat was no more. Those areas hardest hit were areas where the people of color had resided. Feral survivors, once they realized they would not be eaten, came out of forests, jungles and caves to rebuild and reassert their cultures. Africa was a complete basket case, followed by the South West Pacific Areas and parts of India. Harvesting had gone on almost uncontrolled in these areas for the some seven years from the first rock strike. Africans who survived had done so in jungles, such as in the former Congo area. Only in South Africa did some whites set up a small Cattle Country under the auspices of the African Lord. Now, Pretoria, South Africa was a City State, run by the surviving whites. As with those involved in guarding Cattle Country, most were pardoned for their roles in the harvesting. Only hard core Krakens were held accountable for their crimes, and fed to the Squids.

The rest of Africa had been turned into one huge wildlife park, the native species staging a major comeback now that humans were out of the way. Some surviving peoples of black African descent went to Africa to help their cousins recover. More than twenty years later, people of color were still only a tenth of their original numbers in Africa. Even after harvesting stopped, thousands died from disease and lack of food.

Because of the depravations, a 'Special Representative for People of Color' was made at the Allied Species of Earth organization meetings. The first elected representative was Malcolm Carter. Though disliked by some for killing Sergeant Jefferson, he was revered by many for his role in the Dark Meat Revolt of Atlanta. So, he moved to Africa, and represented people of color from there. Bollywood Red followed him, and eventually they were married.

Things change, but remain the same.

At the time of the signing of the Great Compromise, it was believed there were some two billion humans scattered about the Earth. Exact numbers were unavailable, as by that time, other than "fresh meat" for special events and, of course, to help feed the young, no one really kept track of the human population. The exception were the people in Cattle Country. Humanity was down from the original near eight billion, thanks to Harvesting, breakdown of services, Feral predation, starvation, and disease. Director Lloyd's success in getting power and other services back on line and letting people outside the Tschaaa controlled areas to "hack in" to them probably saved millions. Eventually, someone would write the whole story about the good he had done. Madam President, Sandra Paul, had his remains buried on some family land she owned in Alaska. This had started a complete shitstorm, as some wanted his body drawn and quartered.

But then the President had shown, once again, her Spine of Steel, stating, "In the end, he sacrificed himself to make amends for things he had done which made the situation worse. In doing so, he prevented the Wizard from causing more wholesale destruction, not to mention his preventing Krakens from killing more innocents. So, he stays with me and mine. Don't like it, tough. Private property."

Then her eyes had gone steely. "Woe to anyone who disturbs the burial plots on my land. If I catch you, I will kill you."

There was still some grumbling, but the deed was done. Next Andrew had stepped in. As they brought on line twelve new Guardians each year, one for each of the twelve months, their first official act was to stand sentry duty at the burial site for a month. Andrew said it would help them to contemplate their role in the great scheme of things, as well as instill patience. It worked.

Over the years, other famous beings would be buried there, including Madam President before her time.

A half a year after the rescue of his wife and sons, General Reed asked to retire, and a grateful world allowed it. He and his wife traveled to Moscow to look for any surviving relatives, and for Mrs. Reed to be the U.S. Ambassador to Russia. She was a heroine, having saved herself and her sons until she could be rescued. A daughter of Russia, though a U.S. Citizen, she was greeted with open arms. General John Reed was soon teaching at the reconstituted University of Moscow, primarily on how Russia, Japan and the U.S. managed to forge an alliance when one was needed. When Tschaaa began to show up for the classes, everyone knew the relation between the species could only improve.

Six months after the Reeds moving to Moscow, Sandra Paul reported she had a form of virulent cancer. By then, Tschaaa biological science was being incorporated into human medicine with astounding effects. The President was told nanotechnology and other Tschaaa fueled advances would insure her survival. Worst case, if they lacked the time to grow her a replacement body, she could be a cyborg. She said no.

There were screams and protests of outrage. She had become like a mother to the Nation, and it was assumed she would always be there. Madam President stood in front of the world and told them the reasons for her decision.

"It is time for me to join my beloved husband in the hereafter. And to see my other son and daughter. I have no desire to live forever. I need to go peacefully into the good night, not to rage against the ending of the light. I have done my duty. Now, I chose my fate."

She lasted a year, finished her memoirs, said her goodbyes. Russian President Alina Federov was there as she died, holding her hand while the President's daughter held the other. To almost the very end, Alina had tried to talk her dear friend into using the Tschaaa advanced medical aid. She refused.

"It is time, my dear friend Alina. I ask you please, help watch over my now huge extended family, but especially my daughter and grandchildren."

"Of course, Sal. Without question." She had bent over and kissed her friends forehead.

"You are the Steel in all of us. Without you, we would not have survived."

"I did what had to be done, Alina. No more. No less. Now, let me get some sleep. I'm very tired again."

Two days later she passed. George Williams was beside himself, the huge man being unable to speak. So Alina Federov stepped out to address the public and press, daughter remaining with her Mother.

"We have lost our Great Mother today. For she was the mother of all this, the re-growth, nay a rebirth, of humankind. She is now with her loved ones who have passed, as she wished. So, honor her memory, her wishes. For she will always be near, will always be providing some steel in our collective spines. Now, a moment of silence, for the greatest person I have ever known."

Every time Torbin thought of this, he teared up. For she had become a mother to them all, even as she was forced to send them into harm's way. Andrew had flown the President's body up to its final resting place, with Aleks, Abigail, Brynhildr and George Williams as an Honor Guard. As per her request, the graveside ceremony was simple, just her daughter, grandchildren, Princess Akiko representing Free Japan and Alina Federov representing Russia. The Princess slipped an unfinished blade of katana steel into her coffin. "She will mold and shape it in the Hereafter, as she helped to mold and shape us."

Now, the land Sandra Paul had made a cemetery was molded into a new Arlington National Cemetery and Memorial Park, as per her final wishes. Within weeks, Sgt. Fuzz's remains were moved next to the President, to be at her side for eternity. "You always need a dog around, otherwise it's not heaven," Abigail had said as she reinterred her 'best buddy'. Others from the new Greatest Generation would follow.

Surprisingly, the rest of the principle people revolving around the Free Allied Nations were still alive, thanks to good genes and Tschaaa medical technology. With replacement organs, nanotechnology and new medicines, humans were easily capable of an average one hundred year life span. And of course, there was the cyborg option. From one billion Tschaaa, primarily young and adolescents, at the time of the Great Compromise, there were now some two billion. The Tschaaa kept their culture of only the senior members of each crèche reproducing, thus preventing a population explosion. Human kind had doubled to some four billion. With humans living longer, the desire to have huge families had dissipated. Plus, the former poor nations, existing before on slash and burn agriculture or dirty 19th century-based technology, experienced a renaissance in their life styles and culture thanks to some Tschaaa technology. Within ten years of the Great Compromise, Squid biologically based photoelectric cells and power systems meant that ninety percent of all the vehicles being produced were based on electric power plants charged primarily by the Sun's rays. Petroleum was rarely burned for energy, though still used to make things. 3D printer technology took petroleum as well as other substances and made the most intricate designs cheap and durable. World want and hunger all but disappeared. Even the poorest regions could afford a 'flesh' vat and a couple of 3D printers to produce protein and the basic necessities of life.

Torbin chuckled. Things were not perfect. There still was crime, minor regional conflicts, and the Church of Kraken still existed to stir things up, though with just a million members worldwide. The worship of the Great Kraken or a form of Cthulhu would never have as much influence as before the Great Compromise. Again, in the name of maintaining freedoms, Sandra Paul had demanded that no religion be outlawed, as long as they did not commit illegal acts. She said if there was a "freedom" from being offended, it was the slippery slope to thought and speech control, the anathema to vibrant civilizations. But even with pains in the butt still existing, Tobin still thought this was the best of all possible worlds, especially since this was his twenty-fifth wedding anniversary. Hell, at one time, he thought he would be lucky to see his first anniversary.

Their two sons, Gage and Tristan, would be here with their wives, and Aleks' grandchildren. Plus Lori White, the pilot on his 'payback' mission, had magically re-appeared. With his daughter. The one night of passion had produced an angel when there had been devils all around. Aleks had welcomed them with open arms, to a greatly surprised Torbin.

"She loved you, I love you. You have children with both of us," Aleks had stated. "The older sister needs to know her two younger brothers. We, are family. Period." So Torbin had a family he had never imagined.

By some odd twist of fate, the children of Mary Lou and Adam Lloyd, Kathleen and Maryann, met and fell in love with Gage and Tristan. There was some scientific discussions that those offspring affected by the Tschaaa tampering, New births, may be attracted to their 'own kind' through some chemical pheromone signature. However, some did marry 'normal' offspring, so it was unclear if there was an extra attraction or not. It did not matter, as both of the young wives, like the husband, matured early, had college degrees by ages eighteen, found each other and married.

Dogman, while he escorted Mary, Kat and the children out of Key West and to safety, had found love with the grieving widow Mary. He raised the children of Adam Lloyd as his own, and Mary gave him a son and daughter of his own.

Torbin, being the pushy bastard that he was, asked Dogman how that was like, raising another man's children.

"I have raised many a pup. None were mine, but I still loved them. What's the difference? They all still need love and care."

Not for the first time did Torbin realize the firm sense of morals that guided Dogman. And now they were related in an extended family.

Mary and Dogman had sent a nice anniversary gift and condolences that they could not attend, but they had two other children and a huge K-9 breeding and rescue facility along the banks of the Columbia River near The Dalles. Dogman had partnered with a Bar and Grill owner and bought up a huge tract of land that had been abandoned years prior. Dogman's K-9 Ranch, with Mary providing the business acumen, became the main supplier of certified War Dogs for the various governments as well as rescuing dogs, especially from Fighting Pits. He was given special Federal Arrest Powers by Commissioner Miller. He had also been given a free hand in handling the terrible fallout from the Tschaaa based mutated breeding of creatures for the Fighting Pits as well as other illegal activities. Law Enforcement Agencies looked the other way when miscreants 'disappeared' in the slowly de-irradiated waters of the Columbia. The huge catfish, a sought after game fish when the radiation level dropped to safe levels, were a perfect garbage disposal.

Now Torbin's and Aleks' son Gage, a huge fullback on the new International Football League after two years obligated military service, was bringing Kathleen and their twin sons, William and Torbin, some five years old. Tristan was making the military a career, but as a pilot, like his Uncle William. He and Marian had given birth to fraternal twins, Aleksandra and John, also five years of age. All would be here for this special occasion.

Kat Monroe nee Bender had married William just as soon as Torbin's younger brother was completely healed in his new body. Most of it was "vat" grown, with a couple of cyborg based enhancements in the skelature. William's features had been frozen in time for some six years, so even with Tschaaa based biologicals available to Torbin, he looked even younger than just the actual two years between the Brothers. Like Dogman, he raised Kats two sons, William and Adam, as his own. They had a daughter through some DNA combination techniques, as the one thing the Tschaaa could not rebuild in the vats were viable sperm. Kat gave birth to Jane, a name insisted on by William. "Major Jane Grant helped keep you safe, then died for you." William had said. "I owe her. You owe her. Screw the Tschaaa and everyone else. We owe her, Adam Lloyd, and Andrew." If possible, Kat loved him even more from that moment on. They also created a foundation in Jane, Jeanie and Jamey's names, The Three Js. It was to help all the orphaned children in the world, for the three women had died trying to protect children.

William and Kat would be here for the celebration, but the two boys, quite the musicians, were on the beginning of a worldwide tour. They had a style called Earth Rock, with lots of tribal beats and some odd combinations of Tschaaa vocalizations with some whale songs thrown in.

Jane was at military school. She was following in the steps of her namesake, which made Kat very nervous. Jane told her mother she wanted to be a pilot, then an astronaut or star pilot. Kat had finally sighed and said, "Well, it sure beats being a porn star. But if you get hurt, I'll never forgive you." Husband and Daughter had laughed, which did nothing for Kat's temper.

Abigail and Ichiro were coming, of course. Abigail had given birth to two fraternal female twins two years after the Great Compromise. Anica was the smaller, darker one, a perfect combination of Ichiro and Abigail. The 'younger' of the twins was a large blonde who came into the world screaming and fussing. Abigail named her Brynhildr, after a certain cousin. She looked so much like her that many people thought she was her namesake's daughter, not Abigail's. Two years later, Abigail gave birth to Ichiro the younger. He soon became a spitting image of his father. All three of their children were at school, sent their good wishes to their adopted family members.

Many others sent their best wishes. All the many people Torbin and Aleks had worked with, fought alongside or in the case of Heidi Faust, had fought against for a time, sent notices. Now married to a certain Texas Ranger's son, Heidi had children of her own, including a son named Adam, and another called Willie. George Williams IV, Past President of the United States of North America, sent special wishes and some Georgia-style barbecue, from the still Capitol, Bismarck, North Dakota. Former Russian President Alina Federov sent them another Faberge Egg, from where, they were afraid to ask. Stalin and Sally sent their best wishes, along with their daughter Aleksandra, son Antony, and his other two wives and their four children. With a greatly decreased number of eligible males, when two pregnant military women from Alaska had shown up at Malmstrom Armed Forces Base just as the Great Compromise was being signed, Sally had laughed, welcomed them in and started the first of many polygamous marriages. Stalin was, for once, shocked and soon overwhelmed. He still helped run military training at Malmstrom, no one knowing how old he was. But with a tweak of Tschaaa medical technology…he could be there for decades.

Brynhildr and Rolf, plus their six children (three boys, three girls) sent their best wishes with the rest of the New Viking community in the Dakotas and Minnesota. Abigail had kidded her cousin about trying to take over the world by out re-producing everyone else. But the large Shield Maiden had found that she loved child rearing. Two years after the Great Compromise, she and Rolf had started their family. They stayed close to Bismarck, North Dakota as Brynhildr had assumed the responsibility of security for every single President from Sandra Paul on. Staying near the Capitol enabled Brynhildr to raise her children and still serve the Country. Rolf helped build and administer a huge Viking Hall in Bismarck, with some one thousand members. He lived the Old Ways, showing the younger generation what New Viking sensibilities and morals really meant in modern culture. Rolf stayed in the Armed Forces Reserves, becoming a well renowned Cold Steel Instructor, regaling his students with his tales of My Lady of Steel, the Avenging Angel, as well as organizing the Wyoming Ass Drag competition every year. Hell, he was there!

Of course the entire Bell family sent best wishes, including Colonel Bell, still going strong in retirement. He spent a lot of his time spoiling the grandchildren his son in law, Benjamin Black helped give him with daughter Pamela, as well as Shannon's kids with a fellow pilot. As Torbin was ruminating about all the people he had known and who were now in this amorphous extended family, Aleks came back out on the porch.

"I managed to contact Abigail and she said they were just a few minutes out. Which is puzzling because usually we can see vehicles approaching us on the highway."

Torbin gave his best shrug. "Maybe they rented a helicopter or a V-Stol. There's a bunch on the civilian market with us converting to modified Tschaaa technology air and space craft. And Ichiro is a hotshot pilot."

Aleks harrumphed. "They come in here and start blowing dust and dirt all over, and I will pin their ears back so fast that…"

They both felt the charged atmosphere that always signaled a Falcon was in the area. Coming in over the mountain line instead of up from the flatlands were two Falcons. One seemed to have a large box shaped object suspended below it.

Aleks glared at him. "Is this your idea of some surprise or joke, you will not be able to walk right for a week. You know I hate surprises."

Torbin displayed his best "Who, me?" look as the craft gently began to set down in the large fields some one hundred yards away. The large box shaped object was set down, and the covering magically came off like tissue wrapping paper on a fancy present.

"That is a building, Torbin. What in all the hells of ....That looks like a chapel."

Aleks' mouth dropped open a bit as a mass of people came down the large access ramp of the other Falcon as it nimbly set down. They seemed to be dressed in formal finery, even all the little children. Brutus and Portia ran to meet their well-known fellow pack members with barks of greeting. Aleks was still trying to get her voice box to work when Abigail, in Armed Forces Dressed Marine Blues, being the fastest, came up to her carrying a large garment bag.

"Big sister. Quick, we must go into the house and put your gown on. For the ceremony is about to begin."

"What..." Aleks turned toward Torbin who had suddenly knelt. In a loud Marine Corps Officer Command Voice, he proclaimed, "Aleksandra Smirnov Bender. Would you do the honor of marrying me, this stubborn and profane Marine, again, in a formal ceremony with family and friends? You were cheated out of a fancy wedding before. I must make amends, on this, our twenty-fifth wedding anniversary."

Aleks stared at Torbin. Abigail then spoke. "Well, my Big Sister. What say you in front of all these witnesses? Do you wish to find another, or...?"

Aleks began to curse in Russian and Ukrainian, advanced on Torbin who was still kneeling. She grabbed him by his ears, as if to pull them off. Then she began to sob, fell to her knees and hugged him, burying her face in his neck.

Through her sobs, she whispered, "You smartass, I love you so. Of course I will marry you again. As many times as you wish."

Torbin raised her chin and kissed her. Then he pulled a ring box out of his pocket.

"Here. Andrew got this for me. A Star Blue Diamond. From some unknown world well beyond our solar system. The lizards had some and easily parted with them. So you now have a one of a kind engagement ring. For the shortest engagement in history."

Aleks regained her composure a bit and opened the box. She gasped.

"My God in heaven. This is gorgeous! How can I thank Andrew...?"

"Why, in person, of course."

The large cyborg, Senior Guardian Angel, was then standing near them, his armored body shining in the sun with an almost ethereal light. All the children were clustered around him, giggling. For they were growing up with real Guardian Angels, flowing capes with wing designs on them and their armored covered heads resembling flowing golden hair. What could make you feel safer than a Guardian Angel?

Aleks stood up, walked to him. "Get your face down here, Tin Man. I must kiss you."

Andrew knew better from experience to disagree with Aleks' orders and bent down.

She kissed him on both cheek. Then she whispered, "You saved him that day in Key West. I never thanked you."

"No need to, my dear. I knew what a special couple you would be. I had to save him."

She kissed him on his very human lips. "Typical male. Has to get the last word in."

And with that, Andrew just smiled, and stood up.

"What is this gown you are carrying, little sister?"

"I made a few minor changes to my wedding dress so that it would fit you. And I know you really liked it." She paused, and blushed a little. "I... also would find it an honor... if you used it again. For you, my sister... I owe so damned much." She tried to hold back her tears and then could not. The two women, bound together in love and family, hugged and cried.

"Why are they crying?" Asked young grandson William. "Are they sad?"

"No, young one," answered Andrew. "Adults also cry when they are very happy. This wedding is going to be a very happy occasion."

Within moments, everyone had their composure back. Aleks and Abigail had the wedding dress on in record time, as did Torbin with his Marine Corps Dress Blues.

Then everyone was in the transportable chapel, as the cyborg pilot of the second Falcon approached.

"May I introduce Miriam, one of our newest Guardian Angels?"

"A… lady Angel." Asked Ichiro to Andrew.

"Why yes. We are now getting female applicants of sufficient statue and ability now. I think it… well the term nice touch applies."

"I think," Miriam replied. "What Andrew meant to say was that he and the others needed a 'feminine touch' in their ranks."

"Of course. Again, Miriam, your perception is better than mine."

Gage and Tristan both grinned. "Next, little angels running around." Gage said. "What are they called?"

"Cherubs. I think," replied Tristan. Everyone, including the Guardian Angels, laughed.

Abigail reappeared, took charge. "Alright, Ichiro as a Shinto Priest is officiating. Who gives Aleks away?"

"We will," the trolls, twin sons answered in unison.

"Good. Now everyone pick a side, bride or groom. Andrew, cue the music please. Let's get the show on the road…"

Twenty minutes later, as Torbin kissed his bride of twenty-five years again, the years seemed to melt away. They all then moved to the house, where the food that Aleks had prepared for an anniversary celebration became a wedding feast. About an hour later, everyone was sitting on the large front porch. Andrew had walked Miriam over to the horse pasture to show her some of the livestock. Kat and William were sitting on a sofa together, holding hands like newlyweds. Torbin's brother looked at Kat.

"Our Twenty-fifth is coming up. What do you think?"

Kat kissed him. "If you want to. We can get the whole family together again. Maybe this time all of our children too…"

There was a loud crash from inside the house. Kathleen and Marian looked at each other, looked around, saw that their children were not in sight.

"Oh shit!" They both said in unison and jumped up. But they were too late. They heard the angry Russian of Aleks from inside the house. Within moments, she was herding three boys and one girl from inside the house. She had young John and William by one ear each, using her foot to push young Torbin along outside. Young Aleksandra looked at her namesake. "I tried to tell them not to fool with it."

"What happened?" Torbin said as he stood and walked toward

his wife and the grandchildren.

"Grandmother Aleks, we're sorry..." both of the young mothers started to say but Aleks jumped in.

"No apologies. They are doing what young boys do. They get into things."

She looked sternly at the three miscreants. "But they also must suffer the consequences. husband, they knocked over your display case containing your Ka-Bar. The knife is on the table inside." Torbin strode in and then returned with his Ka-Bar in hand.

"It will take more than four grand kids to hurt this blade." He frowned at the three boys. "But you made a mess in there. What were you doing?"

Torbin the Younger blurt out. "We're sorry, Grandpa. But some kids at school were saying it was all a fake story, you killing the Squid with the knife."

"Yeah," John blurted out. "We got in a fight..."

"So that's what happened," said Marian. "Grandfather Torbin, we're..."

"Fighting already? You must take after your granddad here."

Torbin looked at the three boys.

"But fighting for family honor, huh. I got in fights for worse reasons." He looked at Aleks.

"Well, my love. Your house, your rules. What's the punishment?"

All the three young boys' lower lips began to quiver with emotion. Grandma Aleks talked about trolls and fighting Eaters while pregnant, and she was not afraid to still smack their large fathers—her son—if they got out of line. She was the Terror. And they knew they were in deep kimchee.

Aleks looked at Torbin, and a twinkle appeared in her eye.

"You know, my husband. Part of this is your fault."

"Mine? How in the hell..."

"You have never really told us about everything that happened when you took on that Squid with your Ka-Bar. Not even me."

"You mean he did not tell you that I dropped him on his head?" Andrew had come back with Miriam.

"Oh, hell. Thanks, buddy. Just air all the laundry..."

"Is this when they saved our Mommies and Aunt Kat?" Aleksandra the younger asked.

Kat shivered a bit and William patted her hand.

"No, Honey. That came later."

"Well, my brother," Ichiro interjected. "I arrived after the fact, when a certain female Coastie showed up, from whom I had to save you."

"So that is why she was angry for a while," Abigail jumped in. "Heidi was angry that you, Ichi, stopped her from kicking Torbin's behind."

"Why, yes. That is exactly…"

"Oh alright. damnit."   Torbin paused for a moment. He looked around at all the eyes looking at him, and saw love and respect. He had a bit of a lump in his throat as he realized just how damned lucky he was, especially this day.   Aleks put her hand on his shoulder. She could tell, after all these years, that he was realizing just what his family meant to him. She did not want him to become too filled with emotion. After all, tough Marines don't cry. Except in front of their wives.

"I think it is time for some scotch."

"That would be nice, Aleks." He looked up and smiled at her, telling her with his eyes how much he loved and needed her.

As Aleks poured him a scotch, Torbin held up his K-Bar.

"First of all, this is not just a knife. This, is a fighting blade. One I picked up while I was finishing basic training, well before the Squids arrived. So, it has a lot of history." Torbin paused, sipped his scotch.

"But on that day, as things began to go to hell in a handbasket, a Squid ambushed one of my men. So, I went to ambush the Squid right back…."

The Circle of Life went on, and stayed the same in many ways. Humans, family sitting around telling tales of adventure, life and love.

As it always was. As it always should be.

EPILOGUE

A month after Aleks' and Torbin's anniversary, Princess Akiko of the Free Japan royal family sat in a great Sons of the North Hall in Poulsbo, Washington. With a long history of Norse influence and Nordic Family Heritage, the New Vikings had taken to the town on the Kitsap Peninsula as if it were the Norse Capital of the U.S. west coast. So of course, when Princess Akiko had announced her new book, Banshee: Madam President's Own Daughters of Steel.

The Complete History of the 101st Special Attack Unit, and the Sisters of Steel, was about to be released, some New Vikings had contacted a certain New Samurai and his Lady of Steel wife and called in a big favor. Thus, Abigail Yamamoto had called her adopted sister and fellow Banshee Princess Akiko and asked could she please have her initial release event in Port Orchard, Washington? It was on the west coast, closer to Japan, and a Port Orchard-based publisher run by an Italian-American family had been the initial U.S. publisher to push her for completion and for publication in the United States.

So, here she was, the Japanese Princess in her dress uniform from her days as an officer in the Banshees, with a stack of stick drives and hardback books to sell and sign. The Hall was huge, as was the table she sat behind. Everything around her was made of carved wood, including an exact replica of the original Sergeant Fuzz carved memorial which sat in the entrance way of the Banshee Barracks at Malmstrom Armed Forces Base, Montana. The sight of the Sgt. Fuzz statue brought back bittersweet memories of comrades and conflicts. Her husband had stayed in Japan, as he knew that Akiko would no doubt be reunited with many Sisters of Steel. This was her time, a place in her past before he had met and married her, into which he did not want to intrude. And for that, Akiko loved him even more.

There was no reason to hire special security as former Banshees and local New Vikings had popped out of the woodwork, quickly letting everyone there to not mess with the Princess. The Banshees made it look like "old home week" and she knew that her hotel suite would be full tonight with old comrades and Sisters tonight, as they drank toasts and kept the rest of the hotel occupants awake with the signature Banshee Scream.

The line of people buying books for signature seemed to be never ending. The fact that her book The Great Compromise, the standard history of the Tschaaa Infestation by which all other works were measured, was starting its third major publication run did not hurt. In fact, there was talk of a major mini series on satellite and web television based on it. Like the Holocaust, people felt there was a sufficient passage of time that the complete story of the Tschaaa Invasion and Aftermath could be told, warts and all, without opening vicious wounds. The fact that the Banshees was the first organization to work hand in tentacle with Squids also led to a request in the very beginning of a Tschaaa translation of this new work. As she thought of the Breeder pilot known as "Dorothy", she realized she would not be surprised if some Tschaaa showed up for the book event. All the faces began to blur as Princess Akiko's fingers began to cramp from signing each physical book. She also began to run out of original forms of "best wishes". But, ever with the Samurai Spirit, she continued.

As another book appeared in front of her, she looked up and thought she saw a familiar face standing behind the young blond woman who had presented her with a book for signing. It took her just a moment to recognize Richard Rice, son of military doctor and Sister Banshee Rica Rice. The normally reserved Princess broke into a broad grin and stood up.

"Richard-san! It is so good to see you! Please, step forward."

Richard Rice, "Battle Buddy" of Torbin Bender, had grown into a fine dark haired and handsome famous surgeon, one of the first to operate on both Tschaaa and humans. Many looked on him as a saint-like peacemaker between the two once warring species, especially as his father had been killed by the Tschaaa before he was born. His skill was such that no one attempted to replace him with some advanced alien or human technology

"How is your mother? I have not talked to her for some time. Is she here?"

Richard smiled back. "She is still working at the Hospital at Malmstrom, now as a Senior Medical Instructor. She could not break free, as she has a new class of young battle surgeons in training."

"Yes. We have the Great Compromise, but we humans still have trouble getting along with each other, do we not?" Akiko noticed the young lady in front of her was looking at Richard.

"This pretty young lady is a friend of yours, Richard-san?"

"Oh, my manners! My mother would be fuming at me if she were here. May I present my fiancée, Norma Harkonnen."

"You are to be married. How time flies! Your mother is very happy, as we all want our children to marry, and to have children." Princess Akiko gave a short bow and presented her hand to shake. The young woman took it, suddenly began to cry as she then kissed it.

"Please, what is wrong, Norma-san? If there is…"

"You saved my mother that day at the hospital…" she said between sobs. "She would have died on Hell Day if not for you and your sword. I came here to thank you…" She sobbed more, Richard grabbing her to prevent her from falling.

Princess Akiko quickly took charge, as only a Royal Warrior Princess could. Banshees appeared and helped the crying young lady to a back room. Akiko told those still in line that she need to take a break, promised she would be back to sign everyone's book.

"And that is a Royal Promise," she said with a smile, which elicited some laughter.

The Royal Princess went into the back room where former Banshee Officers Dagan McDowell and Lupe Pena were putting some cool packs on Norma Harkonnen's forehead as Richard held her hand.

"Richard, if you wish, you can take her upstairs to my suite…"

"No, please," the young blonde broke in. "I am… so sorry. It just all came rushing back to me. Please forgive my weakness…”

“I will not here any talk of weakness, young lady. I too cried at times. You should have seen me the day my brother died. Or after we had rescued General Reed’s wife and sons…”

At that thought, the Royal Princess felt a lump in her throat, her eyes began to mist.

She sat down next to the new fiancée, took her hand from Richard.

“We have all had to be tough.” Then she paused. “While I was researching my literary works, I came across many quotes and comments. One was that true strength is smiling when you want to cry, laughing to hide the pain, going on no matter what.”

The Princess sighed. “That was the attitude, the ‘face’ that we in the Free Japan Royal Family were told was a must, a requirement if the Japanese people were to bear and survive the Tschaaa Infestation. But, that was then.”

Akiko swept her hand around, “This is now. We can now afford to show the fear, the pain, and the loss we suffered over some twenty five years ago. So, no, you are not weak for crying. You are human. We cry. The tears of a certain Coast Guard woman helped to show a young female Tschaaa that, like them, we suffered loss, hurt when our loved ones were killed.”

She looked into Norma’s eyes. “The young female, the potential Breeder was the one we now call Saint Cassandra. She helped build the bridge that stopped the War.”

Everyone sat quietly. Then Akiko rose. “You rest here with Richard-san. Tell him to explain to you about his nickname that Torbin Bender gave him, something about punching a man in his private parts.”

Norma looked at Richard. “You never mentioned anything like that.”

Richard smiled. “Well I guess the cat’s out of the bag. So, here goes. Right after Torbin’s wife, Aleks, gave birth… “

Akiko and the two former Banshees rose and left while Norma was focused on her love.

As the three walked out, Dagan wiped her eyes and blew her nose. “Anyone ever tell you, Princess, you have the soul of a Texan?”

“Hell, she’s Mexican!” Lupe protested.

"Split the difference, then. Texican. Okay?"

"Yeah, battle buddy. I guess so."

Akiko linked arms with her two Sisters. "I am neither. And I am both. For I am a Banshee! Come, my Sisters. I made a promise to the waiting crowd. And a Samurai Princess always keeps her promises."

As they walked back to the signing table, someone started a single, timed clapped. Then it was two. Then it was three. Soon, the large assemblage was clapping in time.

"I guess they overheard the young blonde's story," Lupe Pena said.

"Yeah, you are definitely a hero now," added Dagan.

"I just did what was necessary, nothing more," protested the Princess. "I am just a historian."

"Yeah, right. Torbin Bender said something like that. And I have some bottom land near El Paso to sell you."

"No you don't. We Mexicans are taking that back."

"We? You have Speedy Gonzalez in your pocket, Lupe?"

"Please! You are going to make this Princess laugh in front of all these people."

"No worse than crying, is it?"

Akiko then grinned, began to laugh. "Laughter is the best medicine, isn't it, Sisters?"

Human life on Earth continued, as it would for millennia to come.

9 781590 929704